The Sil Chronicles

By

Stephanie Keller de Nuñez

S Keller de Nuñez

...I hope you enjoy the story!

Thank you!

ISBN: 1-4140-2984-5 (e-book)
ISBN: 1-4140-2983-7 (Paperback)

Library of Congress Control Number: 2003099149

This book is printed on acid-free paper.

Printed in the United States of America
Bloomington, IN

1st Books – rev. 02/25/04

This book is dedicated to Missi Chapman Whigham,
a truly courageous young woman, a warrior in her own right,
fallen in the battle against cancer.
An inspiration to all whose lives she touched,
she strove to be her best as an athlete, a friend, a loyal wife and mother,
a hard worker, and a woman of faith.
We will not forget her.

Grateful acknowledgement to all advisors and supporters of this book's creation:

Sue Brown Morgan
Sheila Hanson
Dr. Sandy Keller
TKD Master Phil Peplinski
The Howell family
RVHS staff and Foreign Language Department
All my Keller, Chapman, and Nuñez relatives
My extended family
and
My ever-inspirational students

The Solar Systems of the United Galaxy:

(Planets listed in order from closest to farthest from the helion's sun. Inhabited planets are underlined.)

1. The Firoba Helion:
   Planets: Helium1, Helium2, <u>Palat, Diro</u>, Helium3.
2. The Soren Helion: (Contains artificially spawned planetary atmospheres from the Torreon-Firoba Sister Planet Project)
   Planets: Sor1, <u>Sor2, Sor3, Sor4</u>, Sor5
3. The Lapas Helion: (Sil's home)
   Planets: Bahn, <u>Gird, Liricos, Tambuo, Lapa</u>, Yan
4. The Gold Wind Helion:
   Planets: Zar, <u>Rybalazar, Xiantalix</u>
5. The Thrader Helion:
   Planets: <u>Nitrogen1, Fitmalo, Jawlcheen</u>, Nitrogen2
6. The Keres Helion:
   Planets: Mercury1, <u>Mercury2, Mercury3, Jain, Karnesh, Godel</u>
7. The Sant Helion:
   Planets: Argon1, Argon2, Argon3, <u>Argon4, Santer</u>, Argon5, Argon6, Argon7, Argon8
8. The Takash Helion:
   Planets: Hydrogen1, Hydrogen2, <u>Hydrogen3, Venitus, Taka, Platt</u>

Locations of inhabited helions within the galaxy:

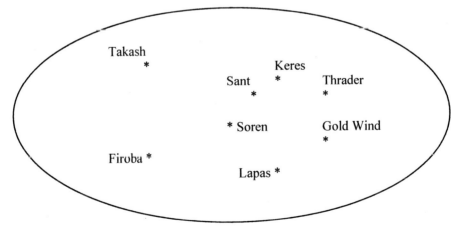

Part 1: INNOCENCE

Chapter 1: Arrival

A rolling mass thundered toward me just beyond my future's horizon. It grew. It swelled. It leapt skyward in streaks. Its crystalline pinnacles froze into fang-like weapons, clattering, shrieking. I pulled together the full material of my being as if tugging the cord of a parasail to lift myself out of the tsunami's path. The crashing shards of ice lurched forward, threatening to slice through me, their slick surfaces reflecting images I did not wish to see.

A familiar presence pressed himself behind me, imbibing my being with his own. His dark hands offered to steal me away from this nightmare, but I pushed him away, reluctant to accept his power. I wrestled with the elements around me, desperate to soar above the roaring shards, but the surging mass stretched higher, like an approaching mouth ready to sink fangs into the flesh of its conquered prey. I panicked, feeling myself slip into its crushing wake.

Then the tumultuous vision suddenly halted. The tempest and its entire vast ocean jerked backward into darkness, its density swallowed up by the vacuum of my fears. My body expanded with a breath. I exhaled the dream. I inhaled the quiet air of consciousness.

I awoke to the dull, electronic song of stats monitors. The ordinary ship's interior foiled the churning sea of my subconscious. I knew the source of my nightmare: fear of my final examination. I had to stay centered, stay calm. Misinterpretation of my sixth sense now would get us nowhere. I stuffed my worries aside as I shifted to sit straight. Reason stepped in to bolster my confidence. They'd never seen talent like mine in a trainee. I had to impress them.

Still three thousand kilometers from the atmosphere of Sor3, Yalat dozed. Her blue and silver skin lay smoothly over her calm Lizard face. No disconcerting nightmares plagued her mind. Her eyes: closed, silver spheres, were a picture of serenity. How I envied and admired her. I always knew she had more patience than any being I'd met, always remaining hopeful for me despite my multiple failures. I knew she listened to my thoughts now as she snoozed contentedly, her scaled lips hinting at a smile.

The green planet loomed before us on the helm screen. I briefly checked the monitors around the main deck. I would miss this little ship. I'd spent the last two years of my life shuttling around in it. I glanced again at my professor, now with slick, onyx eyes open. I would miss her, too. Apart from the placidity in her face, I noted a sense of pride in her. She believed she had finally found success with me.

"Calm, child," she crooned. "Everything will turn out as it is meant to be."

"Yes, ma'am," I affirmed, folding my hands onto my lap.

I closed my eyes to envision the solar system we traveled. Its orange sun blazed quietly in its center. Its three inhabited planets turned lazily as they nurtured their biospheres of teaming life. The other two uninhabited planets spun carelessly along their orbiting paths. I vaguely envisioned our ship and dozens of others traveling within the helion. I also glimpsed an unexpected object floating nearby.

An observer microship followed us too closely, just behind our right wing. It crept beside us, either to detect our communications or to use our ship as cover in order to observe something on the planet. I mentioned this to Yalat. She moved the rear sensors to show the microship on one of the screens before us. The mushroom-shaped flying object was a recent model, less than two square meters in diameter.

"Hmm. It's proximity to our ship goes against aerospace law. We could capture it and turn it in when we arrive on the planet, but it may have a self-defense device. An explosion in our cargo hold would not be agreeable to our purpose. Let's leave it there. We have nothing to hide. If someone wishes to see what we do, let him see. Perhaps whoever it is will learn something about how well you can handle this old ship." Yalat gave me a mischievous look. She winked at me.

I smiled. "May I?"

In a serious voice, she said, "Yes, but when we arrive at the atmosphere you must return it to autopilot." She waved her claws at me with consent.

I disengaged autopilot and gave the ship a quick turn eighty degrees to the left. The microship disappeared from the screen for a moment, but soon returned to our side. I shot us toward the planet. The microship lagged behind in the distance. Our velocity monitor blinked an alert, reminding me I was breaking the speed limit at such close range to a planet. As our sensors detected atmosphere, I slowed fiercely using the reserve oxygen tanks at the front of the ship.

Yalat jiggled with laughter. Then she began to sing, as she sometimes did when things were going well.

"*How looong will I staaay by your si-ide? A million tomorrooows have come and gone, and stiiill you sing ooon. How looong will I staaay by your si-ide?*" she trilled. She lifted her protruding, wrinkled snout to me. "I'm singing to you, Sil, dear. I'm sure I'll be with you only a few days more. I know they will accept you."

I smiled with gratitude and thanked her.

Yalat growled contentedly. "Good child," she thought aloud.

Yalat communicated with the descent tower about our identities and purpose. She gave ground control the code for our autopilot program. Once linked, the ground personnel guided our ship remotely.

I shut down diffusal shields as the ship slowed to local shuttle speed. This cleared the distortion from our external cameras, giving us a better view of the landscape. A mountain chain perforated the clouds before us. Its tallest peaks resembled the posts of a hammock. Between them hovered a bed of cloud that glowed with city lights. Beneath the cloud huddled the most populace city on this planet: the Public Valley. We did not approach the city, but continued down the mountainside and through the blanket of cloud. Tall, succulent evergreens covered the slopes of the mountains. Below them stretched a vast, green landscape. I admired its scattered lakes and ponds. Their sheen surfaces mirrored the hazy sky, causing the land to resemble a thin, floating crust, eroded through with pockmarks of blue.

We headed for a small Organization center about thirty kilometers from the Public Valley. This was the Center for Advanced Training and Testing of United Galaxy warriors, both intelligence trainees and military hopefuls. Additionally, it was used as a safe meeting place for interstellar officials.

· The completion of my test, if successful, would usher me into intelligence work. My parents feared I would be sent into action too soon as a military recruit. To appease them, I chose the less blatantly risky career. Still, I would be expected to aid interstellar law enforcement in any way my contact general saw fit, including anything from simple computer research to target capture or even assassination. I hoped, of course, to never have to kill another living being, but I would carry out such drastic orders if faced with no other choice.

The architectural symbol of the United Galaxy's integrity clarified before us. The C.A.T.T. consisted of three broad cylinders. Milky half-spheres of solar energy collectors topped their roofs. Several smaller rectangular structures stood nearby, most of which were hidden by the thick matte of trees. An amphitheater graced the front courtyard, which connected to a wide, glassy lake. An upturned U-shaped building flanked the lake along with a broad, tree-lined landing field.

The tower personnel landed us close to the trees. The Vermilion man on the screen welcomed us with disinterest, but expressed enough civility to send a guide cart to help us with our luggage.

We went through standard shutdown and air pressure balancing procedures. Yalat checked the safety hazard scanner for parasitic or viral threats in the immediate biosphere and found none. We then stepped into the omnicorporal scan unit. The air tower medical personnel remote checked us for contagions. Once we cleared med checks, we entered the cargo hold to unstrap the travel boxes from their holding nets. I served my tutor by carrying the boxes out of the ship.

The grass felt lumpy under my boots. I hadn't walked on vegetated ground for over a month. Yalat scuffed off the ramp with me and sealed the main door.

The guide cart idled at the nose of the ship. From the front end of the cart protruded a tall, rectangular post with arms. It appeared to have a personality. The rest of the cart provided a seat and space for light cargo. We left our boxes in the back of the cart and sat together. As we rode to the tower, the post turned its sensor to face us. It welcomed us to the Center in much the same manner as the air tower attendant.

"Would you like information about the Center?" it asked.

Yalat asked it where we would be housed during our stay.

The post read Yalat's title pin and scanned through the Center's accommodations list on its computer link for a second. Then it projected an image into its metal hand, which showed a cylindrical building. It highlighted the fifteenth floor in blue, then a specific room in purple. "Building Three, level fifteen, room one-five-nine."

"And where," asked Yalat, "may we find food and drink?"

The post projected the same building again, highlighted the fifteenth floor in blue and the same large room in purple. "Building Three, level fifteen, room one-five-nine," it hacked.

"Apparently we'll be having some sort of room service," beamed Yalat. "Where may we find Professor Banjil?"

"Classified information," the post retorted. It turned its sensor away from us and fell silent.

We ignored its curt reply, as we found the man standing in one of the tower lobby doorways awaiting our arrival. He was a Grey, almost like a human, but with long arms and a short nose nearly connecting with his mouth. The gray skin on Banjil's face grew yellow in its thickest folds, showing his age. He approached our cart in a meandering gait. He bowed and welcomed us by name.

"Allow me to show you to your room," he then offered in a polite, gravelly voice.

Yalat made small talk with Banjil as we followed him to the building the post had shown us. We entered to find a gleaming white, L-shaped hallway. An interior glass wall to our left revealed a central garden filled with palms and tropical plant life. Rounding the corner of the L, we found an elevator. I felt a chilling premonition about this elevator. Something foreboding would come from it. When Banjil opened it,

6

however, I relaxed to find it clean and empty. Yalat noticed my feeling. She patted my arm reassuringly.

At the fifteenth floor, Banjil showed us to a doorway at the end of the hall. We entered a small, dark hallway that doubled up on itself, first left, then right. This opened into a broad floor space, which tiered downward onto two other floor levels. This room was bigger than most full dwellings I'd seen. I surveyed the place with awe.

The top floor area where we stood consisted of a dining area to our left and living area to the right. Long, cushioned benches protruded from the wall in the living area. The dining area contained a table and chairs, kitchen amenities, a computer with wall screen, and a mini-elevator for food delivery. A half-wall covered with local decorative plants bordered this floor level. Stairs descended to a small gallery area and another half-wall. Finally, a much larger gallery protruded from the bottom level. The outer curved window of the building served as the main wall of the room.

"How impressive," Yalat croaked.

"Oh, yes. This room and a few others on this level were designed especially to impress our trainees and to accommodate testing preparations. You won't find any individual helion's intelligence agencies with this level of luxury for their recruits." Banjil's throat puffed with pride.

I set the luggage boxes down in the living area. "Where do we sleep, sir?" I asked.

"Ah. Come with me." Banjil stepped down the set of stairs in the center of the half-wall into the first small gallery. It lay empty, but behind us on either side were doors leading to bedrooms beneath the dining and living room areas.

"The two dormitories are the same," he explained as he guided us to the room on the left.

The motion sensitive lights flashed on as he entered. We followed him down three steps into the room, which was equipped with a bed, desk computer, and bath. Yalat poked the computer's keyboard to wake it. Three bubbles puffed out slightly from the computer's projection string on the wall, one bubble on top of the other, each showing a slightly different view of the Center, giving it a three-dimensional effect. Banjil explained the computer's common features as well as a pathway for local information and U.G. connections.

I glanced to my left, at a reflection of the three of us in the full-length bathroom mirror. I shied away from my own image, tall and awkward compared to my two elders. I cast a critical eye at my straight, flyaway hair. My cinnamon hands smoothed the dark locks, but static still affected them. I frowned, turning my attention again to our host. He indicated a small wardrobe at one corner next to the computer desk.

Yalat looked it over and surveyed the quarters with satisfaction. Then she pressed on the bed with a pudgy hand. "This will be my room. Sil, bring my things, please."

I nearly responded, but Banjil interrupted. "Ah, but you haven't seen the best of this place yet. Please come and see. You will be impressed." We followed his lively gait down the stairs.

"This gallery is for levitation and personal defense practice," he proclaimed.

A mat of long grass covered the floor of this gallery. At one end rested a cluster of levitation stones of various shapes and sizes. The wall at the other end displayed a mural of history. The half-wall we had seen in the previous gallery was actually a larger wall as seen from this standpoint. It served as a blank screen for a projection system. Finally, we admired the view from the huge window. From here, we saw Building Two, the amphitheater, the tree-lined lake beyond it, and the foothills of the mountains, which disappeared into low-lying, misty clouds.

Banjil spoke proudly of the Center and its surroundings for several minutes. Then we thanked him for the tour, retracing our steps to the top level. He bade us goodnight and reminded us of our preliminary interview scheduled for ten o'clock the next morning. We bowed as he disappeared through the dark corridor.

After he left, Yalat explored the automated kitchen facilities. She clapped her paws and rubbed them together with a smile. She enjoyed room service. She selected the foods on the kitchen computer and waited impatiently for them to arrive in the mini delivery elevator. She ordered two full plates of her favorite noodles with steamed blue beetles. I ate fruits from the local forest. I did not want to fill my stomach, since I still needed to practice tonight. I drank plenty of water, however, since Yalat always nagged me about the fact that my species needed more water than hers. After our meal, I returned the dishes to the mini-elevator. They descended to the kitchen automatically.

"Bring the boxes downstairs now. I want to bathe and sleep early. Practice for a while if you want, but don't spend too much time on it tonight. Sleep early to wake early," Yalat ordered.

I obeyed my teacher, practicing only one hour. I changed the pattern of the levitation stones a few times but did not read the mural of history. With profound tiredness I went to my new bed and covered myself with the fleecy sheets.

I perceived Yalat's matronly presence. I knew I was ready to leave her side, but I would miss her as though she were my own parent. I recalled with affection the day we said goodbye to my parents and sisters ten weeks ago. I had left them many times before to travel with Yalat and other

8

trainers, but never this long. Presuming my testing would go according to plan, I would not see my family again for more than a year. I felt proud to finally honor them by presenting my test. Still, homesickness feathered my heart.

I thought of the haven my parents and teachers had created at our school: its stone architecture, its gardens, its practice fields; all nestled among the rolling hills and forests of Liricos. They had created an atmosphere of privilege, safety and nurturing that most children never dreamed existed. They had almost made our lives too peaceful, too perfect. Leaving my family to visit other places and cultures had been a shock at first. I was grateful for the company of my trainers on these journeys. They were always strict and protective of me. Now I felt apprehensive about taking on a new life on my own. I prayed my commanding officer and coworkers would prove to be as trustworthy and well intentioned as my professors. But I felt unsure of it. I felt I would meet a darkness in the upcoming year, one I could only face with bravery, for I would face it alone. As I closed my eyes as the wave of future dilemmas rolled through the undercurrent of my mind.

Chapter 2: Alaban

Sunrise filled the gallery with a desert-like atmosphere. The levitation stones became giant chunks of sponge in its light. I decided to levitate them and practice defense at the same time. I stood in the center of the gallery floor and turned to a ready stance to begin form one of the personal defense moves. While in this stance, I levitated four stones to float over my body in a straight line.

The stones followed me above my head while I performed the movements of the first form. These were slow, flowing moves for stealth. Every five steps ended with a series of rapid punches. The second form contained movements only slightly faster than those in form one, but with a different combination of punches. Form three combined punches from the previous forms, adding low kicks and two spinning jumps. The fourth form contained more jumps, punches, and medium kicks. I did not begin the fifth form since Yalat ordered me upstairs to serve breakfast.

I carried the food to the table where my professor sat. We shared the meal with anxious optimism. I drank three glasses of water to appease her. When Yalat chomped open her last green fruit, she found it contained a writhing worm.

"Aha! I've won the green worm prize! This means I'll be enjoying a good day, ha, ha." She swallowed it with a slurp and click of the tongue.

I glanced at the clock on the computer again. It was nine twenty.

"Don't worry, girl. We have half an hour," Yalat advised. Then she spoke with a chirpy voice. "I want to watch you practice with those rocks once more."

She eyed me if she were planning something sneaky. She smiled and finished her live meal. After breakfast, we descended together to the training gallery, where I learned why she had given me that look.

This time during practice, Yalat, not I, moved the stones. She jumbled them around until they formed what looked like a man standing before me.

"Now, begin form one," she ordered with a smirk.

I tensed momentarily, somewhat intimidated by the life-sized puppet. I shook off the feeling to begin the first movement. Yalat moved the stone man into a stance that mirrored mine. This was to be a practice of concentration and distraction, a practice I was used to, but this model was different. We had worked before with distractions of noise, flying objects, people, but never an invincible man of rock.

I moved my own body in the correct manner, following my training despite the distraction of the stones. When the moment came for the series of punches, the stone man advanced towards me. Yalat moved the stone torso backwards, leaving space for my fists to swing freely. My instincts told me to counterattack my enemy, but I had to continue with the indicated form. Yalat expected me to work around him, not fight him.

When I turned at the tenth movement, the stones followed. They recompiled themselves in front of me, standing sternly akimbo. I would have to hit a stone or move it myself. I struck forward. My first punch pushed the center stone backwards. It returned to its place in the imaginary body as quickly as I had moved it. I then hit it with the ten quick punches that followed. I felt a throbbing pain in my fists from this encounter, but did not stop the practice.

I turned again for the twenty-fourth movement. This time the stone man expanded with outstretched arms to encompass me. I rejected all squeamishness and continued the steps. I pushed heavily against the

10

surrounding stones in order to keep up with the required moves. At the final series of punches, the stone man leaned against me as a wall. I struggled against the power of my teacher to move the stones and send my fists into the air in the right place. Now the stones bunched around my arms as if to crush them. I used my full ability to part them. I succeeded, but scratched my wrist badly against one of the rocks to complete the last punch. My wrist bled slowly.

Yalat arranged the stones to bow as in the conclusion of a match. I returned the bow to my not-so-imaginary opponent. The rocks glided back to their place on the floor and rested.

"Well?" asked the professor, reclining over her tail.

"That was hard," I admitted. "I wanted to fight against the stones. Actually, I think I did," I said, viewing my hands and wrist.

"Why did you not alter your form?" Yalat pressed.

"You asked me to practice the form, not to spar."

"True. What lesson did you learn?" she asked patiently.

I gathered my thoughts. I asked myself what Yalat had tried to communicate to me by using these new props at this time. It had to be allegorical.

"I couldn't treat him as an enemy, even though he got in my way. I think you meant I have to stay focused and not be distracted by new people I'll be assigned to work with."

"Yes. You did well." She nodded, grinning slyly. "You stay focused. You keep your integrity. As our credo says about integrity…"

I accepted this cue to repeat the passage to her. "I will pursue integrity despite my expectations of others and despite others' expectations of me. I maintain integrity through my own high expectations of myself."

"Hmm. You will encounter many challenges to that credo in the upcoming year. May inner peace and faith see you through." She pushed herself up with her tail to stand again on two feet as I bowed to her in reverence. "Now let's get ready for that meeting."

I bathed and brushed my hair quickly. I dressed in my gray uniform; the one used for official meetings: a long tunic split at the sides, long pants underneath, and black boots. Yalat yanked my hair into a large twisted butterfly clasp, fitting it across the crown of my head. She pulled the hair too tightly. It hurt especially on one side, but it looked pretty and we lacked time to correct the problem.

At the second floor, Banjil showed us to a small meeting room, containing only a square table and three chairs. The glass wall overlooking the garden was the only source of light. The soothing daylight calmed my nerves only a little, however. This was a mild beginning to a harrowing drill of examinations.

11

Banjil folded his wrinkled, discolored hands onto the table. He smiled formally. "First it is my duty to ask you a few basic questions. If all goes well, we will go, your teacher and I that is, directly to the first committee interview in another part of the building."

"Do you mean to say they are already prepared for our interview?" Yalat asked him in surprise.

"Yes. This is not the only testing we have this week. Several professors are already assembled in conjunction with another pupil's testing."

"Ah. I understand, sir. Proceed, please," Yalat said contentedly.

Banjil asked Yalat the usual questions: how long she'd known me, how my performance in her areas of expertise compared with that of other students, and so on. He asked her for the reports on my academic grades and my year at basic training, and for proof of completion of the U.G. procedural preparations courses. Finally, he asked for her signature as sponsoring tutor on my recommendations list. I glimpsed the list on the flat screen that lay on the tabletop before us. My father's name headed the list, with ten other professors' endorsements after it. Yalat gladly signed the space by her name with the stylus.

"Ooh, how time flies," she chuckled. "I've been her levitation and personal defense tutor since she was a little girl. Now she is testing to enter the work force. Where does the time go?"

Banjil grinned affably at this, but then curved his lip into a thoughtful frown. He removed the screen from Yalat's grasp and turned it to flip through the information once more. His old eyebrows lifted, tugging the skin on his eyelids to form wavy gray curtains over his dark eyes. He produced a short noise I did not know how to interpret. Then he spoke.

"How old are you now, Sil?"

"I am twenty-three, sir," I answered honestly.

Banjil puffed his throat slightly. "Yalat, why did you not bring her for testing three years ago? Human warriors normally test at twenty years of age."

"Each person is different in personal development. Sil was born with advancement in the spiritual and psychic talents. However, her mastery of manual skills progressed at a fairly slow pace. So," she explained plainly with open hands, "we lagged behind in completing her requirements. She only mastered weapons assembly this year."

"I see." Banjil paused to think for several moments. He rubbed his yellowed chin as he gazed out the window. I wanted to perceive what he was thinking, but could not. He blocked me from reading his mind.

He questioned me on several aspects of my education from mathematics to combat skills. He asked me about the other professors who had helped to teach me as well. I named them and told him in which areas of study they had instructed me.

"How many of these professors were of your own species?" he asked.

This question offended Yalat, but I was obliged to answer. When he heard there were five, he seemed satisfied. Banjil finished the meeting with an air of optimism.

The two elders then escorted me to the elevator. They sent me on my way back to our room while they headed for their interview with the committee. I bowed to them as the elevator doors closed. I selected the fifteenth floor on the building map and then leaned against the wall. I released a sigh of relief mixed with worry. I hoped Yalat's next meeting would go as smoothly as our meeting with Banjil.

The elevator quickly stopped, not at the fifteenth floor, but the fifth. The doors opened to reveal a person of tenacious presence. He was human, slightly younger than me, dressed in a dark blue combat uniform. He wore his folding sword strapped to the outside of his left thigh. His other three weapons lay concealed in a pouch at his right. His body quivered from exertion. Sweat seeped through his uniform. His breathing and pulse strained. Short black hair stood in hundreds of matted points on his head. His dark brown skin glistened with sweat. His dark, slanted eyes, besides showing exhaustion, also gleamed with pride. He carried himself with satisfaction from his performance. My pulse quickened to see him again.

It was Alaban, a former classmate. Secretly, as students, he had fascinated me. I had always enjoyed his company. And his spirit intrigued me. I felt drawn to him.

I greeted him joyfully. "Alaban. You must have just finished your testing. Congratulations. Do you remember me?"

He regarded me at first in a way that made me feel that I had bothered him at this moment, but when he realized whom I was, he beamed.

"Sil! Of course I remember you...ma'am."

I laughed. "Don't call me that. I don't have my title yet. I haven't even tested."

His manner softened to mild surprise. "How is that possible?"

I explained it was a long story, but that I'd love to tell him about it and hear about his life, too. At the fifteenth floor we both left the elevator. I asked if he was staying on this level.

"Yes. We're at the end of this hall." He pointed to the left. He stared glowingly into my eyes.

"I'm at the other end," I said, explaining briefly that I was waiting for Yalat and why. "What about you?"

"My professor is out. Could I visit you in a while?" he asked.

"Yes. I'd like that. I'll leave the door open for you."

"That's great. I'll see you in twenty, or fifteen, um, twelve minutes," he spoke, walking backwards. He turned and advanced to his room. I watched him eagerly. Despite his exhaustion, he nearly sprinted.

I smiled after him and waved, impressed with his friendly demeanor and new height.

I had first met Alaban when I was fifteen. He had come to my father's school for exceptional students on a four-year Organization scholarship. He was advanced in every subject and area of training for his age. We called him the gifted one. He was especially good with levitation, math, and the manipulation of tools. Before leaving Liricos, he'd made a little robot for each of us. Mine danced and played a few notes of music. I always prized the gift as a treasured memento. He left just before my twentieth birthday to go who knew where with his sponsoring tutor, Professor Trau, also a human. Professor Trau had always seemed angry to me. I could tell Alaban didn't feel comfortable around him.

Alaban had said just now that his professor was out. This seemed strange. Professors never left their students during testing. Besides this, the test he had just finished was the most important. I wondered what had happened to him.

Chapter 3: Competition

When Alaban came to my room, he found me meditating on a bench in the living area. He woke me with a perturbed grin. I apologized for my sleepy appearance. He assured me not to worry about it. I drilled him briefly about his exam. He warned me of trick questions the panel might spring on me. By coincidence, Banjil was one of his levitation committee members. He had given him a trick question about levitative fall factors. I vowed to keep that in mind. After a few minutes, Alaban suggested we go out to the amphitheater for some fresh air. Since Yalat was out and wouldn't be back for at least another hour, I agreed with him heartily.

On our way down to the first floor, he eyed me sternly. "You're going to need my help soon," he said.

I blinked at him.

He elaborated. "I'm not sure with what, but it's going to be on the first floor and it's going to be ugly. I have this weird premonition."

I raised my eyebrows. "It's something to do with this elevator. I had a premonition, too. Can you see any more about it?"

"No. It's not time yet." The elevator doors opened. "Let's get out of here."

We hurried outside to the empty amphitheater and to the water's edge. He leapt up to a platform and spread his arms wide to the sky. He threw back his head, breathing in deeply. I stood a few meters from him, admiring the lake.

"Ah. I like this planet. Plenty of unsettled space." He jumped down from the platform. "Did you know the planet Godel has allowed so much pollution that most people buy their drinking water from its neighboring ice planet? I hated that place. I never want to have to go back there, but you never know where they'll send us."

"So you've been on Godel for the last three years?" I guessed.

"No. I was only there for three months, but it seemed like years; I hated it so much. After that we went to Fitmalo. Actually, I'm not sure which was more dangerous. For the last month we've been in this solar system."

"We've been traveling this helion lately, too. I've been analyzing satellite corrosion for my final comsystems project."

"Satellite corrosion. Dull," he complained, turning to look at the lake. "How well can you swim?"

I looked at him questioningly. "As well as our species is expected to. Why?"

"Could you swim the entire length of this lake?"

I gazed across the tranquil water. The lake was only about two hundred meters wide at our end but extended to a length of about one kilometer. I could barely see the other end through the hazy air.

"If I had to, but…"

"How about a challenge?" he interrupted. "A contest. I dare you to swim it with me. Whoever gets to the other side first wins." He turned toward the lake. He folded his arms and placed a hand on his chin, tapping his face with his fingers. "Let's see, what should the prize be?"

I frowned at the idea. I tried to dissuade him with another kind of game. "Alaban, if you want to get across quickly, why not run?"

He twisted around to see me. "Are you saying we should run across the water? Levitation the whole way? That would be more exhausting than the swim. We'd fall in and drown three quarters of the way over."

"No. That's not what I meant. I was talking about running around the shore. Use a little power, maybe..."

Now Alaban grimaced in my direction. "Well, that's no fun."

He strode to the edge of the amphitheater floor and then hopped off to the rocky shore of the lake. I stood at the edge watching him. He was stronger, taller, more agile than when I'd seen him last. I was sure his maturity had grown along with his physique, but at the moment, he chose to ignore it. He was on vacation now, celebrating the end of his exams, enjoying one last lark of youthful freedom before beginning his new job.

He picked up a rock and threw it at an angle to the lake. It sped seven meters away, and then skipped off the surface of the water, bouncing another meter before it disappeared.

"Hey, here's an idea," he said as he grabbed another rock. "Let's see who can skip them the farthest. No rules. Use levitation or whatever you like."

This seemed only slightly more intriguing than his previous idea, but I joined him at the shore, persuaded by his good humor. I picked up a few rocks and shot them across the water. They disappeared near the spot where his rock had sunk.

"Oh, that was good, but can you beat this?" He threw the fist-sized rock with a strength I hadn't recognized in him before. His rock passed the middle of the lake easily. He picked up another about half a size larger and did the same throw again. His playful sense of competition was something I had forgotten, but I kept up with him.

We each took turns throwing the rocks for several minutes. Each time I threw and levitated, my rocks barely passed his. His tenacity increased with each effort he made.

"Oh, you're playing seriously now," he teased.

"I'll give you one to get serious about," I said to humor him. I threw one the size of my head with more force than before. It passed the point where his rock had dropped. I puffed from effort.

"So you're the competitive type, then. You just *have* to win, don't you? Didn't you learn your lesson about winning and losing games? Don't you know that inner peace and satisfaction come from knowing you've played to the best of your ability?" He paused to throw one much farther than mine. "And not whether you've won or lost?"

"Of course I know it. That's why I'm playing my best right now." I threw the next one and gave it a heavy burst of levitative power half way across the lake. This one sped off into the distance so far I could not see it fall into the water. I looked at him in triumph, sweat beading from my brow.

"Ah, but I'm not finished yet," he said. He picked up a small rock. He rubbed the stone in his hands, concentrating energy on it, and then shot it forward with explosive force. It skittered over the water like a bullet and then glinted in the sunlight as it passed the point at which my last stone had disappeared.

"I win," he said simply. He jutted his fists into the air to show his victory.

"What about the rule you just recited?" I asked him with a grin.

"I know the rule. That doesn't mean I believe in it." He noticed the suspicious look I gave him, so I glanced back at the lake.

The water frothed and rippled in the middle.

Alaban continued. "Don't tell me you believe every rule in the Organization handbook. Granted, most of them are logical, but some are senseless."

Waters from the middle of the lake fanned and waved. A large gray fin showed itself, and then receded again.

"What's that?" I asked.

"Like that rule about calculating and keeping certain hours of sleep. Why can't a person trust his own body and sleep when he feels tired? That's ridiculous. It's juvenile, like a rule they teach to little kids or non-exceptional students."

A large aquatic face and dorsal fin appeared in the water. Short waves began to lick the shore where we stood. I reached for Alaban's sleeve.

"I would love to argue with you about that, but I think we'd better move. Look," I said, pointing.

When he turned, the face was gone. Water rippled around where it had been. The waves lapped at the shoreline.

"I think we bothered someone with those rocks we threw." I backed away to the edge of the amphitheater floor. Alaban remained at the shore, scanning the lake for a glimpse of what I'd seen.

Suddenly, three immense figures rose from the water just a few meters from us. The water-dwelling creatures shouted at us in a low frequency followed by a high-pitched scream. I couldn't understand their language, but I knew their message. We scrambled back up to the amphitheater floor. They splashed and spewed water, sand, and mud at us as they shouted, showering us with foul-smelling filth. As we scampered up the stairs, they returned to their watery home.

I was appalled, embarrassed, and furious. Fishy-smelling, oily sand blotched our clothes. It was sure to stain permanently. What would Yalat say about this? We didn't have much money to spend on new uniforms at this time. I was expected to appear before the committee in official gray. How would I get another uniform this week?

Alaban sat on one of the amphitheater stairs, contorting with peals of laughter.

"Why are you laughing? How are we going to explain this to our professors? Oh, how nasty! You're laughing because your teacher isn't here." When he only laughed harder, I chided him further. "You're acting like an absolute brat! How did they let you test already? You obviously don't know when to take things seriously." I flung globs of muck from my arms.

He stopped laughing and stood on the terraced step, towering over me. He pretended a defensive mood. "Don't tell me I shouldn't be testing. You're just jealous that I'm testing early and you're testing late."

I stopped myself. He was right. I had forgotten my temper. I had made myself vulnerable to fleeting emotions.

He sat down cross-legged on the step. He faced me with anticipation, eagerly awaiting the apology he knew I'd give. I gave him the apology with demonstrated humility. Alaban sat back, still staring at me. He placed his hands together over his mouth and tapped his forefingers in thought, scheming.

"You still owe me something," he said after a moment.

"What do you mean?"

"I won the rock skipping contest. You owe me something."

I softened my manner. "Alaban, all my worldly possessions are women's clothing and basic weapons. The only gift I'm willing to give you is my blessing of happiness and long life."

"No. I will not accept it. I want a promise from you," he said, matter-of-factly.

"A promise? All right. I promise not to mention this to your professor," I allowed.

"I don't care about my professor. I want you to promise that after I'm awarded my title you will spar with me for half an hour." He moved his finger to point to his left. "In that sparring room. No weapons, just hand-to-hand combat."

I glanced at the building he indicated. It was one of the small rectangular buildings near the cylinders of the Center. This one displayed an ornately decorated main door, but no other doors or windows. I looked back at Alaban. His eyes demanded compliance.

"I want to see this place before I agree to spar in it," I deferred.

"Let's go," he said, bounding up from the step.

As we neared the doorway, a red light came on at the side. It needed an access code to open. Somehow, I wasn't surprised that he knew the code. He pressed the numbers into the panel under the red light, which turned off when he finished. The door slid open to reveal a room bright with sunlight.

Alaban stayed at the door as I stepped inside to look around. The roof was a clear convex curve. The walls were bare and white except for the gray concrete posts and foundation blocks. A woven mat covered the floor. No weapons decorated the wall, no paintings, and no wall designs of any kind. It was a place for a match without distractions.

"We'll need a referee. If you can find someone to judge us impartially, I'll promise to spar with you here," I granted.

He bowed and gave me a sly look. "How about a practice round? Five minutes. I promise not to mess up your hair," he smiled.

Despite the recent frustration and splotched clothing, this proposal rekindled my sense of competition.

I arched an eyebrow at him, but then turned and paced to the center of the room. He approached me at a leisurely gait, stopping just a meter before me.

He nodded. "Ready?"

"Ready."

Alaban attacked with a levitative spinning kick, which I dodged easily. As he landed, I threw a punch to his ribs, but he swiveled to avoid it. I hopped away. He bounded towards me and jumped high, aiming a palm strike down toward my collarbone. I did a back flip, missing his hand and knee as he kicked. I landed, immediately hurling both legs at him, using the momentum of the flip. He blocked and caught my leg, but I wrenched free from his grip, faking a couple of punches to the face to distract his blocking arms. He twisted to give me a double roundhouse kick: one at the hip, the other high to the face. I blocked, meaning to catch his ankle as he had done with me and kick him at the waist, but he jerked away too quickly.

I burst at him with a triple windmill kick, and then jutted both fists forward, causing him to block high at my leg when I was aiming low for the punch. I hit him with both fists at the inner thigh, and then cart wheeled away to the right. He recoiled from the blow, but came back at me with a smart combination of punches and kicks powered by flowing turns. I deflected his attacks, learning from his moves. Finally he opened my blocking cover at the torso. He caught me in the ribs on my left side. This would have been a powerful punch, but its angle was such that it glanced off the ribs and caused little damage. Encouraged by the touch, he threw several punches, but I deflected each one. Soon, we both kicked low with opposite legs, bruising each other's shins. We leapt backward.

19

"I can tell you've improved these last few years," I admitted, mentally working out the pain in my leg.

"I wish I could say the same for you," he taunted.

He charged at me with a bizarre combination of strikes, but I dodged him every time, leaving him swinging at the air.

I struck him under the arm as I dodged his last punch. I tried to trip him, but he came back with an elbow that barely missed my face. I back flipped again to put more distance between us, but he followed closely.

I saw him drive a punch at me that I tried to block with arms and knee, but he angled his punch so it threaded between my hip and elbow, successfully impacting my abdomen. This punch bowled me over to one side. He relentlessly came at me with an axe kick while I was down. I moved to catch his foot in its momentum, pressing it to the floor as I catapulted both heels upward into his chest. I sent him teetering to one side while I flipped back up onto my feet.

I attacked with a tornado kick. He ducked it and caught me at the knee with both hands. He flipped me upside down so that my head hit the floor with a crack. At the same moment, he straddled my other leg and stood on my arm, pinning me. My back arched and strained. My free arm flailed uselessly. All my weight concentrated on my neck.

I felt a release of tension from my scalp. I thought quickly. I pulsed a wave of levitative power at him. He careened backward, skidding away from me in a seated position.

"Stop," I heaved.

I slowly stood, caressing the back of my neck. My hair fell around my ears. Alaban remained seated with a look of appall.

"You broke your promise," I said, taking the broken pieces of butterfly broach from my hair, holding them up for him to see. "You said you wouldn't mess up my hair."

He shouted with laughter as he lay back on the floor. He sat up quickly again with a grin. "Oh. For a minute there, I thought you were afraid I'd complete that move."

"Maybe I was," I admitted, returning his gaze.

"Oh, come on. If I'd completed that move, you'd be dead or paralyzed. Then what would I do? I'd have to lug your dead body around with me. That wouldn't look suspicious at all," he spoke sarcastically. "What would the guards say? 'What's that you're carrying there, young man?' 'What, this? It's just some fresh meat for the kitchen. I'm doing some community service here.' 'Oh, good. Carry on.' Ha."

My face conveyed my continuing doubt. He hopped up lightly. His manner turned more serious. He walked to me.

"No, really. I wouldn't have completed that move. Believe me. I guess I played it too realistically, huh? You are okay, aren't you?" His hand crept beneath my hair to rub the back of my neck brusquely.

"Yes, I'm fine. It's alright," I said, gesturing to him to leave it alone. I turned toward the door to leave.

He followed closely. "You gave me a good scrape on the chest with all that sand on your shoes." I glanced at the neckline of his tunic. A bright welt with scratches shone just below his throat.

"I'm sorry," I told him.

"It's nothing. Hey, why don't you cut off all your hair so we can fight fairly next time?" he asked.

"I'll consider it," I said truthfully.

"I'm just kidding, Sil. You've got to lighten up a little." He stopped me abruptly at the doorway. "I am sorry. Don't be mad at me. Why would I cause serious injury to my good friend, Sil? We are friends, right?" He offered a handshake. I reluctantly shook the hand, which he squeezed too tightly.

"Yes, friends." Despite my acceptance, I regarded him warily.

"Good," he spoke warmly. He let go of my hand and guided me out the door by the shoulder. "Well, my friend, let's go stink up Building Three."

Chapter 4: Preparation

Back in my room, I felt foolish as well as relieved. I'd had no reason to worry about a ruined uniform. It came clean in the bathtub with a little soap. Still, I felt guilty for allowing myself to adapt to Alaban's childish attitude. I enjoyed his company, but his behavior disappointed me. He had always been mischievous and competitive. However, I hadn't remembered him being so flippant about regulations or so dangerously careless during sparring. I couldn't imagine what trials he'd lived through in the three years we'd been apart, but whatever he'd experienced had implanted a disturbing seed of negative aggression in him.

I rubbed my shoulder and the back of my neck. These would be sore for the next couple of days. After today's practice, I felt apprehensive about our next match. I wasn't sure if his realistic technique of attack was admirable or flawed. I hadn't sparred with such a rough opponent since basic training.

Obviously, Professor Trau had not been his only teacher of personal defense these last few years. Alaban's skill was now highly advanced, apparently more than mine. I could tell he had held back on speed during our bout, either to allow for the unequal physical strength between the sexes, or to analyze my moves. In any case, he had won the practice round easily.

In a way, I considered his abilities might be a disadvantage to him. Usually the warriors with the highest level of skill were sent to the most dangerous areas to work. Alaban hated Godel, but that's exactly the sort of place where he would be most useful to the Organization.

Tomorrow he and his professor would be called before his examination committee to hear their decisions and to receive his title. Then he would have a three-day period of preparation and rest before the announcement of his first year assignment.

I'd found out from Alaban that Professor Trau was absent from his final test because he had been called to bodyguard a Fitmalo representative in the Public Valley. Alaban wouldn't say what the meeting was about. Perhaps he didn't know, but he admitted it was unusual. Also unusual was the fact that he'd had his personal defense test in the morning. It had been postponed from the previous day because Trau had to leave the afternoon before. But he hadn't even returned in time today to see the rescheduled event, so the committee had asked Alaban to proceed without him.

My own professor's arrival interrupted my thoughts. I heard the door open and close. I heard her soft steps as she entered the dining area. I listened to the blips of the kitchen computer as she ordered something to eat. She did not call me, although I knew she felt my presence in the room. I hesitated, hoping to hear her voice. After moments of silence, I took the initiative and climbed the stairs to meet her.

She opened the mini-elevator to retrieve a meat roll and a tiny fig branch. She brought the plate to the table herself, sitting quietly without looking up at me. She munched the fig branch solemnly. I sat next to her, poised to hear the news.

"You will test," she said in a defeated voice. "You will test in two days."

She stared across the room, lost in thought. Her message relieved me, but I wondered about her manner.

"They've assembled the most odious group of traditionalists and strict methodologists for your panel. There are only two young professors who will see your performances, and only three females in the whole group." She reached out to cover my hand with hers. "You will have to do better than your best to impress this crowd, Sil. You must do nothing but study and train for the next two days."

This was grave news. I fixed a firm visage of determination. "I'll do it. Give me a mock test on anything. I'll be ready."

This statement lifted the cloud of disappointment from Yalat's eyes.

She quizzed me on information from each academic category. I answered every question on espionage communications and psychological profiling correctly. I answered nearly every question correctly on interstellar law and history. Aerospace engineering questions took longer to answer, but I got most of them right. Mechanical and systems engineering left me floundering. I only guessed half the answers on this topic. She gave me the answers with a sigh. I couldn't possibly make up for years of advanced engineering study in the next few hours. I could only attempt to memorize a few rules and standards. At a late hour, we abandoned the academics to practice personal defense.

Forms one through twelve flowed perfectly. Form thirteen proved painful because of its shoulder stands used for upward kicks and counter pinning. Form fourteen contained three sets of windmills, which, after aggravating my neck injury, gave me a throbbing headache.

I hadn't told Yalat of my encounter with Alaban, nor of my neck injury. I was sure she would scold me for it. I had hoped the injury would not inhibit my practice. Unfortunately, forms fifteen and sixteen with their crouched side flips and tornado kicks turned my headache into a migraine. Form seventeen incorporated back flips, for which I lost my sense of balance. At the landing of my first flip, I rolled backwards, smacking my head against the floor.

Every muscle in my face and neck clenched. The room sloshed. Yalat swayed above me. Then she disappeared. I closed my eyes and tried to relax, but my skull throbbed. Soon Yalat returned with a hot compress. She lifted my head, set the compress at the nape of my neck, and then wrapped it around my head.

"This won't happen tomorrow. I promise," I faltered.

"How did this happen? You've never done this before," she implored.

As the pain subsided, I recounted the sparring practice. I apologized for my recklessness.

"You are fortunate the personal defense test is last instead of first. You shouldn't have sparred without supervision. Any judge would have called him off for illegal force of battery to the back of the neck. Why did you agree to simulate real combat? It may have been fine for him. He's already finished with his testing. You're lucky you don't have to present your test with a more serious injury. Now go sleep it off. I'll be waking you extra early in the morning."

As I stood holding my head, the room spun a little less. I reluctantly apologized, wary of another barrage of criticism. This time, however, Yalat held her tongue. Grateful, I stamped up the stairs and into my room.

During the night, my mind warped my injury and recent events into nightmares. I dreamed of being paralyzed during the fight. Then I dreamed the lake creatures attacked us. I tried to calm my mind, but to no avail. The most disturbing dream played itself over and over. It stayed with me throughout the next day as a shadowy daydream.

I dreamed I was lying in this same bed, only in travel clothes. I lay frozen on my back; my hands limp at my sides. I couldn't move, but my eyes saw everything. Alaban appeared beside me. He wore a dark red uniform. He sat with me on my bed holding a tiny brown box, which resembled a miniature coffin. He smiled at me with that mischievous smile of his, knowing I couldn't move.

He opened the box and reached inside. He pulled out a long acupuncture pin. I watched in discomfort as his arm slowly craned above my torso, pin in hand. He smiled again as he lowered the hand to press the pin through my uniform, puncturing my skin. I felt the uncomfortable pinprick, but could not retreat from it. My body lay as a mound of clay on the bed. He left the pin standing in my flesh and reached for another. I tried to stop him with levitative power, but this ability had left me as well.

He repeated the frustrating action of inserting pins into my abdomen until he had made an X-shaped pattern with them. When all the pins were gone from the box, he set it on the floor. He leaned forward and peered into my eyes one at a time. He held my face in his hands. I fought to resist him in some way, but remained powerless. His eyes gleamed with secret intentions.

Then he glanced furtively at the door. He turned back to me anxiously.

"No. Don't see. Stay blind," he said to me. "Stay blind," he repeated.

With this he surveyed the pins he'd placed and plucked one out. He leaned to my face, holding the pin in his fingers. He moved it towards me until it was ready to pierce my eye. I pleaded with my body to move but I lay paralyzed, impotent to stop him.

24

As the horrible pressure of metal penetrated my eye, I woke up. I writhed in my bed, flailing at the air where he had sat. I stumbled to the bathroom mirror to check for pins. Of course there were none.

I shook off the creepy feeling. I still needed to sleep. Yalat would come to wake me in two hours. I returned to bed hoping to dream nothing, but the same nightmare returned to me at least three more times. Sometimes he pierced both my eyes. Sometimes he only pierced one. I flopped restlessly in bed, longing for peace and rest.

Amid the last tormenting dream, Alaban vanished. Yalat sat where he had been. This time it wasn't a dream. She was here to wake me for our last day of training.

Chapter 5: A Disappointing Celebration

"Make me a stairway, Sil, to the top of the wall. I should be able to climb it without using my own levitative abilities." Yalat tapped her claws impatiently.

I did as she requested. The stones that had formed my rock opponent now swirled into a stairway pattern. I watched her climb the stairs to the top without wobbling. She then turned and descended them again.

"Good. Good. That will be all for the levitation practice. You are better at levitation than anyone who'll be observing you anyway. Tomorrow you have academics at 0900 and levitation at 1400."

"Yes, ma'am," I said. I had known this before. They would always test mental abilities in the morning and physical abilities in the afternoon to give the trainee a healthy rest between each. However, if the judges on the committees were as tough as she implied, there wouldn't be much advantage to that plan.

"Now, continue practicing your personal defense forms. You have not finished an entire set of thirty since we were on Sor4."

"Yes, ma'am. I'll go change." I moved toward my room, but she held out a hand to pause me.

"In a moment." She stared out the window with intent suspicion. "That microship looks familiar," she spoke, pointing a blue claw toward the air just beyond Building Two.

I turned to glimpse the tiny observer ship. It hovered where she pointed, at the same elevation as our own floor, apparently recording activity in Building Two. It stirred gently as in a breeze. A policing monitor zoomed after it.

The policing monitor looked like a robotic snail that skimmed the building's surface. It blinked red lights at the hovering ship. A manned police hovercraft soon arrived, flashing bright white warning signals. The microship remained for a few seconds before rising into the clouds. Other policing monitors began to patrol around the building.

Suddenly one of the snail monitors appeared on the window of our own building. It glided up the glass like a metallic sea creature. Hundreds of suction cups smacked the glass wall and popped off in an undulating motion as it propelled itself upward. It viewed activities inside as well as outside the building. This seemed more like a search than a show of defense.

"I think it was the same one as before. I wonder what it was doing here," I said. I watched our policing monitor slide upward until it rose out of sight, now observing the floor above us.

"Unless it's classified, there should be news of it later today," she said. "We'll be sure to investigate it."

Now that the show was over, I changed into my dark blue uniform with full armor. I stretched for several minutes before beginning. My neck and shoulders seemed fine now. All signs of headache were gone.

"Let's start with form one today. I'd like to see the complete performance as you'll be presenting it to the committee."

"Yes, ma'am," I replied.

It took well over an hour and a half to complete forms one through sixteen, since these were the slower forms. Forms twenty though twenty-five were the sword forms. I felt confident with these, even with the unsheathing and unfolding of the weapon at the beginning of each form and the folding and resheathing of it at the end. This movement tended to appear clumsy, but I tried my best to imitate Yalat's grace. The sword was rarely used in confrontations these days, but it was a revered traditional weapon, symbolic to the warriors of the U.G. as an historical means of liberation. I expected the only practical purpose for this skill nowadays would be to chop away thick vines and undergrowth. Practical or not, I enjoyed the challenge of handling the weapon.

Next came forms twenty-six through twenty-eight. These were partially free forms, since only a few moves were standard in each. The rest demonstrated weapons of my own choice. In number twenty-six, I used my laser cutter. A weapon as well as a tool, it fit snugly over my right fist. It was black with straight horns at either side. When activated by a pulse reader at the thumb, it sent a tiny red laser beam between the two horns. It sang like a bee's wings. The beam could cut through most porous materials. Since nearly all living creatures feared amputation, this was a good weapon to flash at unruly people who would think twice before challenging me.

In form twenty-seven, I demonstrated my hand bow technique. I didn't actually shoot the explosive arrows during this practice. The acid spray would corrode the walls and leave harmful gases in the air circulation. I only mimicked the actions for it. The hand bow fit over my left hand and could be used on a target five to ten meters away. On impact, the dual capsules within the arrowhead would mix together to react in an acid explosion of half a meter in diameter. Depending on the type of creature I shot, my enemy would either die from the arrow's impact or burn to death from the acid explosion.

For the twenty-eighth form, I pretended to use my fan blaster. This was a simple handgun with a wide, rectangular barrel. It sent out a rippling band of atomic energy: a glowing, golden wave that expanded horizontally as it traveled forward, executing the highest level of damage at between ten to twenty meters away. After twenty-one meters, the ripple fanned out to become a harmless sound wave. This could be used on vehicles or buildings for defense destruction.

Forms twenty-nine and thirty involved no weapons, but required a demanding combination of physical and levitative abilities. The twenty-ninth form contained eighty-four different moves. This was the most elegant of all personal defense forms. Horizontal levitative whirls blended with evasive and offensive power moves. Backward and forward flips sprung into soaring levitative glides. It was a martial dance.

Number thirty was the form most dangerous to the performer. It required a vertical seven-meter jump, somersault, and a straight fall face down. I stopped just centimeters from the ground, whirling upside-down with limbs outstretched. Finally the form ended in a flip and returned to the first stance of form one.

Once I completed the thirtieth form, I held the stance, waiting for Yalat's order to at ease. My heightened breath aggravated my lungs, but I kept my muscle tension under control. Without moving from her place by the stairs, Yalat asked to see the last two forms again.

"Yes, ma'am," I puffed.

I performed them both again. At the end of this second performance, my jugular vein pulsed so that it leapt from my neck like a frog. Still, she did not allow me to stop.

27

"Now show me the movements I call out to you. Form seven, moves eighteen and nineteen."

"Form seven, moves eighteen and nineteen, ma'am," I repeated, as required. I twisted right, punching downward with a back fist, and blocking high with the left. I followed with a right upper cut.

"Form twenty, moves six through twelve."

I repeated the order. I unsheathed the sword, opened it, and made two wide swipes above my head. I whirled right, jammed the sword backward, and pulled it forward again. I then jumped high, somersaulting in the air. I landed swiping left, then right in a figure eight motion.

She tested me this way for more than half an hour, just as the judges would during the real test. When finally she gave the order to stand at ease, I imagined I looked worse than Alaban had the day before. She gave the order to retire. I bowed and stepped lightly to the stairs.

"You realize, of course, that you'll have combat and disarmament immediately after your general forms performance," I heard her call to me as I entered my room.

Short of breath, I managed to answer. "Yes, ma'am."

The combat and disarmament of two opponents would be a true test of endurance after a long performance of physical ability, but it would give the panel an idea of how I might perform on the job with real assailants. I was sure to be ready.

About half an hour later I joined Yalat in our meal. This time she insisted on serving me. I felt confused at her offer, but obeyed her command to sit at the table as she brought the food to me. She also placed five glasses of water before me.

"Your performance was fine, Sil. The only comment I have is to widen your stance on landings." She allowed me to thank her before continuing. "Listen, Sil, dear. I don't want you to wait on me anymore. Apart from necessary formalities during testing, I want you to act as if you were already on your own. I'd feel better if you would not call me by my title anymore except in formal situations. Call me Yalat."

I looked up in surprise. "Already? But I haven't begun the testing yet. What if they don't pass me?"

"No," she proclaimed, holding up her hand to silence me. "No. If they refuse to pass you, I refuse to continue as your sponsor. It's time for me to retire from teaching."

I blinked. An awkward silence filled the room. So ensued a change of seasons in both our lives. Yalat moved into her winter. I was stepping into summer. I couldn't find words worth saying, although I wanted to talk with her more about this.

"I am certain you will pass. There is not a doubt in my old heart. I foresee a great career ahead of you."

"That's very kind of you." I refrained from calling her ma'am, though it felt wrong.

After another prolonged and difficult silence, she said, "Your friend must be finished hearing the final statements from his committee now. I'm sure he'll be wearing his title badge with pride. Will you go to congratulate him?"

"Yes. I would like to, with your permission."

"You don't need my permission anymore, Sil. You are your own girl now—your own woman, in fact." She reached out to pat my hand. She grinned and blinked her huge eyes compassionately. "And I am proud of you."

I took her rough hand in both of mine. "I can never thank you enough for..."

"Don't bother, dear. I know your heart. It gives me all the thanks I'll need for a lifetime," she crooned. She withdrew her own plate and returned it to its place. I did the same with mine, downing my last glass of water.

"What will you do this afternoon, Yalat?" I asked, finally using her name. This made her grin even wider.

"I'm going to do some snooping about that microship. Take care, my dear," she spoke, patting my arm. "I'll see you later tonight." She waved and disappeared through the door.

How extraordinary, I thought, to be given my freedom just like that. I was now my own woman, as Yalat had said. As terrifying or gratifying as this truth might have been, it was now my burden to carry.

After a brief meditation and several hours of cramming for my test, I decided to forgo my studies to congratulate Alaban. There was no answer at his room, so I went downstairs to search for him. Earlier, I had noticed a terrace on the third floor, which appeared to be a public dining area. Perhaps I would find him there with his professor, or now former professor.

At the third floor, a plethora of lights and colors competed for my attention. This was a commercial floor. I found a wide variety of public facilities: shopping, a grooming salon, a wellness center, and a large open area offering interstellar foods. A strange medley of melodramatic music played softly around the food area as I meandered through. I counted more than one hundred beings lounging or feeding here. I did not, however, find Alaban or Professor Trau.

Determined to look for Alaban outside, I reentered the elevator, followed by a group of hairy, apelike Arbormen. They chuckled to each other about one man's children, who had recently learned to swing by their tails. As the elevator doors opened on the first floor, the Arbormen trudged out before me. One of them nearly collided with a human rounding the corner of the hallway. Finally I'd found Alaban, but in an unusual state.

He walked in a slow, staggering gait, dragging his hand across the wall as he advanced toward the elevator. A spatter of blue stained the chest of his traveling uniform. He did not wear the expression of someone who was happy to have received his title. He sauntered dejectedly towards me. When he noticed me before him, he immediately molded his clayed face into a smile. He tripped into the elevator and leaned heavily on the wall.

"Floor fifteen, please, scholar," he ordered with a slur.

The doors closed. I selected floor fifteen, keeping an eye on him.

"You've been drinking alcohol, haven't you? You've even spilled it all over your uniform," I said in disgust.

"I'll have you know I never spilled my drink. Someone threw hers at me." He blinked at the stain groggily. Then he stood straight and hung an arm around my shoulder. He swallowed his grin along with a hiccup. "Trau took me to the Public Valley. Did you know they have eighty-one drinking bars in one building?" he spoke into my face.

I grimaced. I wrenched his arm from my shoulder and held it firmly to keep him from swaying. "Ugh. You reek of it. Why would your own professor take you to a drinking bar?"

"He's not my professor anymore. Besides, he only took me there and left me. And it wasn't one bar, it was three." He put his arm back on my shoulder again, this time to keep his balance.

The elevator opened at the fifteenth floor. I reluctantly helped my soused schoolmate towards his room. He grew heavier with each step. We stopped once in the middle of the hallway so he could find his feet again. He leaned on me, breathing with a terrible stench. I looked away in disdain.

"Thanks for the lift, Sil," he said. His nose pressed into my cheek. "Did you ever notice that you're beautiful?"

Then he punctuated the statement with a sloppy, wet kiss to my jaw.

I pushed him away. He backed into the sand-covered wall, scratching his hands on it. He blinked his bloodshot eyes several times, and then eased himself back up to stand. He shook his head. A feeling of nausea came to my stomach as I wiped my cheek. He teetered near me once more.

"Don't do that again," I warned, half-carrying him to his room.

"Do what again?" he slurred, resting his face on my shoulder.

The door opened automatically for us. I heaved his dragging body into the living room area and sat him on a cushioned bench. I was surprised he didn't fall over and sleep right away. He grabbed my hand and pulled me toward an empty space on the cushion beside him, but I resisted.

"Sit and talk with me a while, Sil. Come on. You can cheer me up." He sat back, thumping his head on the wall. The alcohol delayed his wincing reaction. He blinked his eyes slowly. The grin gone from his face, he actually looked grave.

I marched to his kitchen to order a concoction for this kind of predicament. Apparently, it was popular stuff, since it appeared in the service elevator within seconds. I held the putrid liquid to Alaban's face, imploring him to take it, even though it smelled like a sweaty Furman. He scowled at the glass.

"If you want me to stay here and talk with you, you'll have to sober up. Drink this," I commanded.

He gingerly grasped the vessel and then downed the whole thing, gasping and coughing afterwards. I took the glass from him and returned it to the kitchen. I brought him a plain glass of water to wash away the taste. He swished it repeatedly with a strained face before swallowing.

"What happened with Professor Trau?" I asked, hoping he would be coherent enough to understand.

"Ugh. He said he had a meeting in the Public Valley. He said he was going to take me out to celebrate. I should have known he wasn't going to celebrate *with* me." Alaban's face succumbed to gravity. He sighed dejectedly.

I sat as far away from him as the seat would allow. I asked him to elaborate. I listened intently.

"He said he'd buy me a drink downtown. So I said, 'Thank you, sir. That's great'." Alaban grinned a little, mocking himself and nodding his head loosely. "He just gave me some money and left me at the bar tower. He said he'd come back for me in an hour." Alaban's voice trailed off. He swallowed hard. He rubbed his face with his hands and looked away, as if unwilling to continue his story.

"He didn't come back for you?" I asked tentatively.

Alaban shook his head somberly. "He sent a driver for me about four hours after I'd been there. It's a good thing he did, since they'd already thrown me out." He began to giggle and stretch his arms.

I looked at him with compassion more than disappointment.

"Where is Trau?" I asked. "Are you sure he's not in danger?"

"Ha. He's not in any danger. No, he's in very good hands. He won't be back until tomorrow. Don't look so surprised. He pulls this kind of trick all the time. It's the first time he gave me money, though. Too bad it didn't last long. That's why they kicked me out." He wrinkled his nose. A sleepy half-grin appeared on his face.

"I'm sorry to hear about all this, Alaban. I was hoping to find you happy and sober."

He looked at me through the slits of his eyes. They wanted to close, but he determined to stay awake to talk to me.

"I'm sorry you had to see me like this. Don't think this is how I turned out. It's all Trau's fault. He's such a…" He shook his head.

"Yes, well, he didn't force you to drink so much, did he? It's your own fault, too," I told him sternly.

"Oh, let me blame it on him. He gets away with too much. Let's change the subject. Let's talk about you. "He gazed at me fondly. He seemed to focus a little better.

"You know, I feel…" He opened his hand and made a patting motion near his heart. "…strongly when I'm around you. I missed you, but…" He opened the hand as if trying to grasp his next words. "I don't know how to explain it. It's like…you're always with me." He closed the hand into a fist. "Is that crazy? Do you know what I mean?" he asked awkwardly.

I did feel something similar. He seemed to have materialized before me yesterday when I was already carrying him around with me in my mind. I felt inexplicably close to him. I mentioned that Yalat once said we have compatibility with certain people and not with others. He said he believed we were compatible.

I quickly abandoned this uncomfortable topic to talk about life with our professors during the last three years. We spoke to each other over glasses of plain water. I learned that Trau was ten times stricter than Yalat. He demanded all kinds of difficult exercises from Alaban: trailing imaginary suspects for days at a time, writing reports on them, search and seizure of objects which he later had to return without alerting anyone, hours of physical training with different instructors, highly advanced math, economics, and aerospace courses, corporal punishment for imperfect scores. No wonder he was glad to be out of his care. After several minutes, Alaban set the water glasses down. He looked into my eyes intently.

"Sil, you're a seer, aren't you? I want to ask you a question," he spoke. "I've been dreaming about this weird thing…" He sighed hoarsely.

"What is it?" I asked quietly.

"Do you think I could ever be…evil? The bad guy?" He kept his head down, waiting for my answer. He was serious about this.

I tried not to scoff at him. I gave him an honest answer. "No. I don't think you'll ever be evil. I think you're just feeling anxiety about starting your first job. That's what's giving you bad dreams. Once you start your job and get used to it, the dreams will get better." I waited a moment, not noticing any reaction from him. I thought of the irony in my statement.

Here I was explaining away nightmares of his when I suffered the same thing.

He caressed his head in his hands then sat straight and gave a sleepy grin as he thanked me. "Oh, yeah, I almost forgot. You were going to congratulate me on my title." He sat straight. He pulled the golden title pin forward, slightly ripping a hole in his uniform. He covered it with one hand and patted it.

"Congratulations," I said.

He nudged my shoulder. "At least I get to celebrate it with someone I know. And you're much better company than the old man, believe me," he mused. He rubbed his hand heavily up and down my back.

"I guess so." I grinned half-heartedly. I gazed at his dark face. He gazed back with interest, still rubbing my back.

"Why are you doing that?" I asked.

"Because I'm still a little drunk," he said placidly. "And I find you *very* attractive."

He slid close to me, moving one arm around my back and one hand to my chin. I wanted to back away from him, but his eyes warned me to stay. He kissed my mouth. I wrestled free from him and stood wiping my face. He sat blinking with one arm extended to me as if he expected me to return to his side. Flustered, I did not hide my anger.

"I'm not a temporary concubine. If you want one of those, go back to the city," I stated roughly.

Shock covered his face. Then he assumed his old mischievous tone of voice. "Oh, one of those? I already had one while I was there—a Vermilion. The four hands were a real turn-on, but I prefer humans. Less limbs to get in the way, you kn…"

"What? You could be infected with one of the 84G viruses!" I shouted. "Haven't you heard the latest health advisory for this helion? I'm taking you down to the infirmary right now." I knew he was sometimes foolhardy, but I didn't know he could be so stupid. I stepped to him, but he rocked forward and cackled.

He almost rolled off his seat. "I'm joking! It's a joke." He cackled again. When he finally caught his breath, he panted, "See, that's what's wrong with you, Sil, you're too serious about everything. You're such a weird girl." He stopped laughing, but stared up at me with a bright grin, hands clasped before him.

I moved a little closer to the door. He read the sad distrust in my eyes and realized he had offended me.

"Don't go yet. Come on. I wasn't trying to make fun of you. I'm sorry," he begged.

Despite my scorn, I still felt sympathy for him. "Alaban, I like you as a friend, but right now I can't trust you. I have to go. I'm not staying here with you."

His face turned worrisome. He stood adamantly. "No. Please don't leave. Forgive me. I'll keep my distance. I won't make any more jokes. Just stay and talk with me a while longer."

"I forgive you, Alaban, but you have to understand I only like you as a friend. We should wait to talk tomorrow when you're completely sober."

He nodded gratefully despite his disappointment.

We stared at each other tensely. Finally, I said a quick good night, turning to pace out of the room. His anxious face quavered in my mind. In my heart, I regretted having to leave him there alone.

As I walked back to my room, I wiped my lip again, more disturbed by his amorous gesture than his behavior. Although his spirit enticed me, I felt no physical attraction for him. I wondered again about the strong closeness I felt to him. It seemed almost unnatural, and yet his spirit filled my mind.

Chapter 6: Testing

Yalat entered the room late in the evening, but spoke with me a few minutes about what she'd found out about the microship. It was in fact one that had been tracked since our descent to the planet. She believed it had been sent to spy on one of the meetings in Building Two. The fifteenth floor meeting consisted of a Fitmalo military chief and a cabinet of local representatives. This meeting most likely dealt with some kind of arms agreement. Another meeting also took place on floor fourteen. This meeting had begun when the microship was spotted. It was a convention of military scientists from four planets.

"It would be in the interest of many to steal information from a meeting of that kind. What I find most disturbing is the fact that the microship was tracked since we entered the atmosphere, yet it was allowed to get close enough to Building Two to require the notification of police monitors," Yalat professed.

I agreed it was strange.

"I sense Fitmalos in the mix. Several warriors have been called for emergency bodyguard duty at the Public Valley recently, mostly in private homes of Fitmalo expatriates," she said.

I opened my eyes wide. "They could be Fitmalo rebels. The rebel movements have threatened the Fitmalo government lately. They could be here to organize some kind of attack."

Yalat agreed to the possibility. However, she sensed a more complex situation. She assured me that she would get more information tomorrow. I mentioned to her that Alaban's professor had been one of the men called to bodyguard at the Public Valley. She seemed surprised. Offhandedly, she questioned me about my evening with Alaban. I explained to her openly about Alaban's state and his account of how Trau had left him at a drinking bar.

Yalat balked. "What kind of professor is this Trau? I've heard sideways remarks about him before, but nothing like this. What else do you know?"

As I told her what I knew about him, Yalat paced and scratched her claws together fervently.

"I can only say for your friend that it good he passed his test, just to be rid of that man. If my sixth sense is right, he had something to do with the spy vessel, too. Please don't look for your friend tomorrow. You may run into his professor instead," she stated. "We don't want him sensing our suspicion of him."

I couldn't imagine why a trainee's sponsoring professor would have anything to do with a spy microship or Fitmalo rebels, but I was not about to disagree with an elder. I asked Yalat what she thought we should do about it. She implored me to do nothing but focus on my testing and that she would handle the research. I conceded, but my curiosity about the situation distracted me. In a way, I welcomed the distraction to keep my mind off my nervousness. Tomorrow would be my day to stand before the strictest judges. I studied hard before bed, gleaning through the academics one last time.

The next morning, at ten minutes before nine, a human escort came to our door to usher us to my first exam. Yalat followed him first. I followed after her. All was silent. Even the ominous elevator seemed to hum a little quieter this morning. As we entered it, I glanced in the direction of Alaban's room, hoping he still slept peacefully there. At floor six, the escort guided us to a closed door. He entered the correct code on the panel and then stood aside to let us through.

The room was wide and dim with a holographic projection stand in the center. Behind this stretched a long table of committee members. One seat was reserved for Yalat to my left at the wall. The five judges whispered amongst themselves as we entered, but soon fell silent. The glow from the holographic projector obscured my view of the committee at first. My eyes adjusted to the strange lighting slowly.

A Torreon spokesman stood at the table, revealing his height of nearly four meters. He bowed, welcomed us to this first stage of testing, and then introduced himself as Professor Sub General Marced. He added that he had been with the Organization now for fifty-two years and had overseen trainee testing on this planet for the last ten years. He stretched out a long arm to introduce the next person on the panel.

The second judge was a Vermilion: Professor Parsh of Jawlcheen. She had been with the warriors thirty-eight years. Parsh stood to bow briefly. Her reddish-orange skin and silver hair and eyes shimmered in the low light.

The next professor was a fat, pale green Lizard, a warrior of forty-three years called Cinder. The fourth judge was Professor Pauber of the Jain planet, a veteran of forty-nine years. Pauber was a human with golden brown skin, bald, but with a long white beard. The fifth judge was Professor Sart, from the Gold Wind helion and a veteran of fifty years. Sart was a Lizard, like Yalat, only with purple, scales, which hung loosely in folds of wrinkles around his collar.

I understood now why Yalat had called the group old. Not one of these professors was young enough to fairly represent the age groups in the Organization. If they refused to pass me, I could easily present an argument on this technicality to the testing board officials. Yet the panel's years were to be respected. I bowed humbly to them.

They questioned me, one by one, increasing the level of difficulty each time. One question Marced asked took at least six minutes to answer. He asked me to explain the complete process of accessing information in a specific language selection from a prerecorded tape coil on an Organization-issue lap computer.

I took a deep breath. I explained to the committee the computer's use of photonic and inverse mineral pulses, the recorded bands of the tape coil, and the laser pins that penetrated the coil frame. I detailed how the laser pins sent beams to the tape coil bands, which reflected the light to the sensors within the pins. I went on about the subterfuge processor, the paraprocessor, the main processor, and the language-filtering program. I explained how the filter program redirected the characters and meaning to the imaging processor. Finally, I ended with details about the viewer symbols and the selected language codes for display.

I hoped for some facial confirmation of my explanation, but the judges merely glanced down expressionlessly to their notepads.

The female, Parsh, spoke next. She asked me to explain the Organization's official procedure for researching a vehicle in an intelligence investigation. I mentioned research from major vehicle distribution and regulation databases, Organization-recorded data on the vehicle's legal status holder, his financial records, personal history, and recorded movements and habits, and requests for additional information on all the vehicle's recorded passengers. Again, I received no indication of response from the panelists.

The professors asked questions from the full array of topics, each more challenging than the next, sometimes without allowing me a breath between answers. For some questions, the holographic projector was used. Its sharp light left me blind after each use. My legs grew stiff from standing in the same place for so long, even when we were only half-finished.

Professor Pauber asked, "In the history of your own planet of Liricos, in what year did the interregional government first meet with representatives of the planet Rybalazar for intergalactic unity talks, and what was the outcome of this meeting?" This was a trick question.

"There has been no such agreement between the planets in either of the solar systems you mentioned, sir. The only peaceful contact Liricos has had with Rybalazar has been in war-prevention negotiations," I replied.

Still I received no response.

Marced lifted a pulsing gray hand toward the holographic projector, which lit up with a three-dimensional model of a solar system. The light flickered, and then swooped into a close-up image of one of the helion's planets. This planet had four visible moons, one of which rotated in the opposite direction from the other three. A spaceship appeared at the top of the diagram. Marced asked for orbit and landing procedures.

I was stumped. I wasn't sure of the make or model of the spacecraft. He hadn't indicated specifically where to land or what distance or area of orbit he wanted. I was not allowed to ask about it. I stayed blinking at the model for a few moments. I had to begin my answer within a minute or it would be discounted from my score. I gave the best answer I could manage, making up his missing information myself, and wishing he would show me some kind of reaction to it. He did not.

The questions and cross-questions became more difficult. Professor Cinder questioned me on engineering and mathematics. He gave several engineering questions, some of which I guessed at and some I could not answer at all.

For one question, he projected a stratospheric tank with a highlighted cooling system and several foreign tools hanging in the air above it. He asked which of the tools and replacement parts would be needed to repair the cooling system. He frowned when I forfeited the question and then plucked the image from the holograph with a grunt.

In the final round of questioning, each professor cross-questioned me at least twice. Then the professors fidgeted with their notes. A few whispered to each other. When Parsh leaned over and whispered something to Marced, he nodded and stood, towering above us all.

"The time allowed for this test has ended. Your grades will be announced at final statements in two days. You may consider this portion finished and passed." He smiled.

I bowed profusely.

The panel stood, bowing all at once, but made no more statements. I turned to Yalat, who clapped her paws and smiled. We marched out of the room together. Once out the door, Yalat jumped to hug my neck. I laughed and hugged her back.

"You passed wonderfully, my dear. I told you," she said, releasing me. "Let's go have some flavored ice downstairs." She waddled quickly to the elevator.

I smiled as I watched her waddle double-time to the shiny doors, but then an image, a premonition, came to me. As the elevator doors parted, I saw the broken image of a mouth and spiny legs of a creature. Yalat trudged through the apparition happily. The image dissipated when she turned to see me, mouth agape.

She did a double take. "Sil. Come here. Tell me what you saw."

I hurried to her side and explained. I also mentioned Alaban's premonition about the first floor.

"I'll tell you what, Sil. I'll buy you the flavored ice if you want, but I have to do some investigating. This vision of yours has given me an idea."

"I'd rather go back to our room. I want to research this creature on the information log," I told her.

We both agreed. Yalat went to the first floor. I raced to my dormitory and scrolled through life form information until I found arachnid-type beings. I filtered through these until finally I found a picture and information about the same creature I'd envisioned. I scanned through the information aloud.

"Grows to three point six meters in height. Weighs between seventy and eighty kilos adult weight. Carnivorous. Defense: spikes on legs, spits acid. Can shoot leg spikes at enemies or prey, shoots acid to three meters. Planet of origin...Karnesh? Why is it all the way out here?" I leaned back in my chair.

On a hunch, I brought up information on Building Three to see its general layout. Much of the information was classified. I selected the building's blueprint. Floors one through seven were public areas. Floors eight through twelve were listed as classified. Thirteen through seventeen were hotel-like accommodations. Floors eighteen and nineteen were classified. Floors twenty-one and twenty-two were classified. Floor twenty-three was cleaning service and maintenance. Floor twenty-four was solar collection and energy production.

Where was floor twenty? It appeared on the blueprint as an empty space. I tried selecting it to see its level of classification, but I wasn't even allowed to select it.

The spider was on the twentieth floor. It had to be. I wondered what else might be there. Perhaps it was a science lab. The meeting of military scientists came to mind. I pondered the mystery with only suppositions to guide me, but I knew very little. I would need Yalat's information to help piece things together. However, when Yalat returned, she deferred my interest, promising to compare notes later. Right now we had a levitation test to attend.

We followed our escort, confidently this time, to a fourth floor gymnasium-sized room. At one end, I saw six piles of stacked objects of various shapes, sizes, and weights. As in my first test, five judges sat at a table awaiting us, this time accompanied by two Vermilion translators. I took my place in the center of the room. Yalat took her seat at the side.

The levitation testing committee consisted of Professor Teffin, a Grey like Banjil who acted as spokesman for the group; Lido, an albino Arborman; Eswalk, a female Mantis, Jiao, a young human male; and Kite, a Beetle. The only significant differences between this group and the last was that Jiao had only been with the Organization for seven years and that the two Sectoids, Lido and Kite, needed translators, since their language consisted of buzzes and clicks instead of words. Their translators were of the Vermilion species. The Vermilions were the only Torreonoids who could imitate Sectoid language, since the palettes of their mouths were split and flexible, and they were equipped with a second set of vocal chords in the nasal sinuses. The translators stood behind them complacently, with eyes closed.

I bowed to them all with respect.

Teffin spoke. He said I would be called upon to move several objects and also to answer questions about levitation.

"Let's start with personal flight. Imagine you want to spy on this group seated here today. Show us what you would do."

"Yes, sir," I affirmed. I rose high above them to a corner of the beamed ceiling. I cloaked a blind spot in front of me, watching the group all the while. Yalat chuckled as the members of the group exchanged looks of amazement. They hadn't expected me to levitate at such distance.

"Yes, yes. That's enough. Please come down now," Teffin sputtered. "Floating above us would have been sufficient."

I returned to the spot on the floor where I'd been. Lido the albino questioned me next. "Tell us. What is the probability of fall for a non-levitated object resting atop a levitating object?"

I smiled a little, remembering the trick question Alaban had warned me about. "Any object resting atop a levitating object is, by technical definition, also a levitating object. Also there would be no fall factor unless the levitator wished it to fall, sir."

The Mantis, Eswalk, gave a different kind of command. She hummed and squawked to her translator, who said, "Use that pile of plastic bars to make an orbiting circle around you."

"Yes, ma'am," I said. I did as she ordered.

Through the translator, she told me this was a dual-action task. I was to lift at least one other pile of objects and rotate them in orbit around me at a different axis.

I lifted a pile of pebbles and rotated them at a forty-five degree angle using my head as the axis point. I lifted a pile of glass spheres. I rotated them at an opposite angle. I lifted four large lead bars and rotated them horizontally in a wider orbit.

Eswalk squawked an order. The translator quickly told me to return the objects to their place. I bowed slightly and obeyed. Eswalk continued to screech, but waved the translator away. The rest of the panel seemed shaken as well. Yalat had been right. My levitation skills surpassed theirs.

Jiao spoke next. "I was going to give you an order having to do with weight, but now that you've lifted the lead blocks, I'd like to see you lift even more. Can you lift all of the objects at once?"

I thought for a moment that this might be a trick question, but I realized my reaction should be the same whether it was a trick or not. I concentrated my vision on Jiao's eyes, pridefully defying humility. I replied, "Yes, sir."

He waited a few moments. "Well, please do so," he spoke impatiently.

"But, sir, I already am," I said directly.

He looked around him in awe at the objects that had been on the floor, at himself, the table, and the other beings on the panel, Yalat, and me, all ascending slowly from the floor.

He and the others gawked and exclaimed together as they rose into the air. My strength held on evenly. I flexed my telekinetic power as if it were a muscle lifting a barbell. The exercise did not wear me out, but rather warmed me up for the next challenge.

"I've never seen…please, put us all back down now," he said.

"Yes, sir," I replied, returning all to its original place.

I gazed out the window as the judges chattered together. My calm manner changed to apprehension and anger. Just a few meters away from our window floated that same microship. There was no doubt about what it observed this time. It was observing us. I wondered with aggravation who would want to spy on my examination and why.

Professor Kite used his translator to tell me that he was supposed to give me a test of distance, but since I had already moved everything in the room, he had no further requests.

"If you will permit me, professor, I know something distant to move for you." I pointed with a glare at the microship. The whole group turned awkwardly in their seats to see it. The panel argued about it for a minute.

Finally the albino spoke. "Yes, bring it close to the window if you can."

I drew it towards us slowly, pausing to glance at Yalat. I gave her a questioning look, which she didn't seem to understand.

"Should I bring it in, Professor Yalat?" I asked her aloud, this time straining to keep my concentration. She looked a bit nervous.

Teffin asked, "What do you mean 'bring it in'?"

Yalat hopped off her chair. "Yes. This is the right time to use your power; not for the test, but because that thing needs to be captured."

As the microship came in contact with the window, the panel members ducked and ran in the opposite direction, thinking the window would shatter upon impact. Instead, I let the ship slide through it, commanding cooperation between the molecules of the glass and the ship. I accommodated every molecule to a new position, keeping everything intact after they had passed each other. I brought the microship to the floor, working against its engines to keep it on the ground. It whined loudly, and then shut itself off. I panted from effort.

The committee members made an uproar of astonishment. Yalat moved near me, keeping an eye on the ship. Suddenly I realized my mistake. It was my turn to step back in fear. When the ship turned itself off, a red light blinked on one side, indicating its auto defense mechanism.

Professor Jiao leapt over the table to rush towards it. He clutched a wide metal plate near the top of the mushroom-shaped object and yanked at it fiercely. "Help me tear off this containment facing!" he shouted. The rest of the group ran for their lives towards the door, but Yalat stood by me.

41

Yalat and I both helped to wrench the containment facing away with a levitative pulse. Jiao dove into the opening of the machine, fought with some latches within it, and pulled out an egg-shaped bomb the size of both his fists. He twisted the top and bottom sections of the bomb in the right configuration to separate them. Then he pulled apart the two halves of the egg and frantically peeled away the soft explosive from within a tangled mesh of webbed plastic. He dumped the egg halves to the floor and gingerly cupped the plastic in his hand.

"Be thankful I'm a weapons specialist," he breathed. "Otherwise we'd all be dead now."

Teffin realized the danger was over. He stomped back into the room. "I've never seen abilities like that before, but an irresponsible use of power is as dangerous as that time bomb. I don't know how you developed that kind of skill, but I do know you weren't thinking when you brought a live explosive into our training center! Your examination is suspended." He glared at me, and then stormed out of the room, calling for security on his clip phone.

I stared abashedly at Professor Teffin, and then at the machine. How could I have done something so stupid? I'd endangered the lives of the people I respected. I had ruined my examination in my best subject. I knelt next to Yalat. She held my shoulder as I stared woefully at the menacing microship.

"Don't worry, dear. I'll talk with the testing officials. I told you to bring it in. I'll take full responsibility for it," she resolved, moving towards the silent hunk of metal.

Suddenly, Alaban burst through the door with his singe gun in hand. He rushed to my side. "Are you hurt? Are you all right?" he asked breathlessly.

"Yes, I'm all right. What are you doing here? This was my levitation test," I said with embarrassment.

"I had a vision. You were in fear for your life. What happened?"

I stayed kneeling on the floor, staring at the machine. "It had a live bomb. I didn't think," I admitted. "I almost got us killed."

Alaban examined the scene, attempting to comprehend it. Professor Jiao sealed the two sides of the bomb and the soft explosive in separate white plastic bags. Security personnel soon arrived in pairs to dismantle the object and carry it up to investigations at Building One.

"How did a microship get in here?" Alaban asked.

"Through the window," Yalat said simply.

Alaban quickly pointed out that this window didn't open.

I lifted myself to stand. I sighed. "Let's just say you're not the only gifted one." I glanced at his puzzled face. "I brought it in *through* the window."

He returned my gaze with what I read to be shock and jealousy.

"Show me. Teach me how," he spoke anxiously.

I stood shaking my head. "I..." Three staunch investigators interrupted me.

"Sil Gretath? You are required to meet with security in Building One immediately. Professor Yalat Regal? Your presence is also requested," one man said flatly.

Chapter 7: The Spider

After an hour of explaining and re-explaining to a few committee members and to C.A.T.T. security, we were escorted back to our room, this time by an armed military guard. Whether our story was believed or not remained to be seen. Yalat assured me they would lift the suspension and let me continue with the testing on schedule. However, I worried that perhaps they hadn't believed Yalat when she claimed responsibility for the incident. They might have thought she was covering for the foolish mistake of her pupil to avoid a scandal.

Yalat urged me to put worries out of my mind. She reminded me that she had friends on the board who would vouch for her if necessary. She distracted my anxiety by detailing what she'd learned about our mystery.

She had somehow found out that a military scientist worked and lived on the twentieth floor. Also, the two meetings the microship could have spied on in Building Two were linked in some way. However, she had no explanation as to why it had appeared at my levitation test. She was anxious to find out more before Center officials classified related information to a higher level of clearance. She suggested I rest and practice in the room while she continued her investigation. Of course I obeyed, although my worry hindered my concentration.

The next morning, at ten minutes before nine o'clock, an escort arrived at the door for my third test. I sighed a prayer of thanks. He led us to a small room on the second floor, much like the one where we had sat during my preliminary interview, with a view of the interior garden. The committee this time sat, not at a table, but in individual seats in a half-circle at one end of the room. Yalat again had a seat at the back. I stood in the center of the room facing the group of professors with great humility. There would be no showing off in this test.

The creature at the far left stood first. He was a Furman: brown and otter-like, obese and furry with a heavy throat. "I am Ongeram," he said in a resonating voice. He smiled kindly. "Tell us, please, who you are, what position you are seeking with the Organization, and why."

"Yes, sir. My name is Sil Gretath of Liricos. I am testing to enter the civil intelligence program because I believe my skills will best serve this position, and I would like to be part of a team that helps stop high-level crime."

Ongeram nodded with smiling eyes. "Good to have you with us. This is Professor Fahn," Ongeram said, turning to the man on his left. A Torreon like Marced, Fahn was also a kindly old man. His knees jutted out far in front of him. He bowed slightly.

Fahn asked, "Imagine you are in a ship above a warring country. Your ship is confused with an enemy vessel and is fired upon. You are on weapons detail. What is your procedure for handling the situation?"

"I reinforce shields and flash a counter charge to deflect the shot. Then I sound the alert. I do not establish communications with the shooter without orders from my commander, sir." He nodded satisfactorily.

"This is Yin," Ongeram said, indicating the six-limbed black Lizard sitting in the middle of the group. Yin clasped all his feet together in a peaceful position. He nodded to me.

"Name for us two forms of common espionage recording devices," Yin said.

I felt uneasy about his question. It had so many possible answers.

"Audio-visual sensor worn on the body and a tracking satellite, sir. If you mean a model or brand of device, I can be more specific," I ventured.

"No. That will be fine," he stated calmly.

Now I felt apprehensive. These first three examiners had shown a reaction to my answers, whereas the panel from my first test had made an effort to show none. Something was amiss.

Ongeram introduced the next being in the room, Professor Omeh, a large white Furman, lightly furred, with exceptionally wide arms.

"Answer this question cautiously," he warned. "Imagine you are in a position in which you must decide whether to go to battle or retreat. You have been asked as a U.G. warrior to participate in battle. However, you are pregnant. What do you do?"

This question caught me completely by surprise. I'd never thought of myself in such a predicament. I knew the Organization afforded expectant mothers the right to inactive duty, but it did not demand that they assume inactive duty. There was no official rule governing this type of situation. I did not know which choice the panel would prefer. If I answered that I would join the battle, would they think I did not sufficiently value the life of a child? If I answered that I would retreat, would they consider me an untrustworthy coward? He had said to answer cautiously.

I thought deeply for a few moments, and then spoke. "I'm sorry, sir. I need more information about the problem before I can give an answer. I can only say that I would do what I believe to be right for all those involved."

Omeh accepted my deferral with raised eyebrows and a nod.

Ongeram introduced the last judge, named Professor Krabach, a human of late middle age.

"Imagine you are witness to a murder. The murderer is still armed and ready to take your life next. What will you do?" he asked.

"I disarm and capture, knock out if necessary, and then turn him in. I would not kill...without orders, sir." Krabach nodded solemnly.

Ongeram stood again. "Well," he boomed, "I believe that's all from us. Your third test is complete. You may go in peace." Ongeram bowed, as did the rest of the committee.

I stood astonished. They had only asked me one easy question each. I wanted to ask about this, but I was not allowed to question the decision of the group. I only bowed in return and thanked them all. Yalat reacted with uncertainty as well. The panel held wise stares, but added nothing more. Gingerly, Yalat and I walked out together. As we rounded the hall, I asked her what she thought it meant.

"It seems this particular committee was willing to pass you no matter what you said. Apparently they heard about our incident at levitation yesterday and they support you. By requirement, they only needed to ask you one question each to make this test valid. That's exactly what they did."

"But is that fair?" I asked.

"Fair or not, it's done. Now we have a little extra time to investigate and be ready to face that spider."

I followed her, duly impressed, but feeling like a simpleton. The committee hadn't really tested me at all. They had only fulfilled their requirement and passed me on like an errand girl.

As we returned to our floor, I heard Alaban calling after us and asking what happened.

Yalat spoke to him. "Come with us, young man, if you wish to help us. We must prepare for battle."

"Yes, ma'am," he replied heartily.

We went directly to the computer in Yalat's dormitory. She brought up the blueprint of our building on the screen, explaining to Alaban what we knew so far. He ogled the blue print with us.

"Look. The opening of the doorway to the main elevator at each floor is smaller than the elevator door itself, except at the first floor," he mentioned.

"Oh. An excellent observation, young man," grinned Yalat.

"That's why the spider won't be getting off at any other floor. It's too big to fit through, except at the first floor..." I paused to indicate the empty space on the blueprint. "...And the twentieth floor."

"I wonder what else lives on that floor," Alaban mused.

"Military science experiments, apparently," grumbled Yalat.

"What can we use against it?" I asked.

Yalat turned off the computer and swished the calloused tip of her tail across the floor in thought. Alaban leaned against the wall, but not as he'd done the night I carried him home. This time he was sober and thinking.

"My weapons are no good," I said. "The fan blaster would cause structural damage to the building. My hand bow only shoots acid explosives, which probably would do little damage to a creature like this."

Yalat nodded. She owned a sonic scythe, but it would only cut off one of its legs and make it angry. Her needle gun wouldn't hurt it at all. Alaban's singe gun and flame curl thrower would have no affect on the spider's exoskeleton.

Alaban suddenly turned to me and smiled, not with his normal mischievous smile, but with a smile that indicated he'd got an idea. "I have the perfect weapon. I don't have it now, but I can get it. I *will* get it," he vowed. "Trust me. I'm your weapons man for this project. In fact, I'd better go see about that right now." He glanced at the clock. "I'll meet you both later. Professor. Sil." He retreated out the door, bowing as he walked backwards. We heard him bound up the stairs and leave the room.

Yalat commented, "That boy is a bit hyper."

I grinned.

46

At ten minutes before two p.m., the official escort came again to our door. He took us to the fifth floor, probably to the same room where Alaban had tested. Despite the terrible episode in the levitation room, this morning's mockery of a test gave me confidence that the group would pass me without indecision. I could perform my final personal defense test with peace of mind.

I followed Yalat to the center of the room. Then she turned to the left and walked to her seat at the wall. This was a dimly lit maroon-colored room. The only light gleamed against a curtain that separated the committee of judges from the performance arena. They had a clear view of me, but I could not see any of them. I stood still, waiting for a command to begin forms one through thirty.

A female voice, much like Yalat's, gave me the order to begin. I gave my best performance ever: graceful, strong, and well timed. I even corrected my landing stance as Yalat had said. When I finished all thirty forms, my balance was so well tuned that I was not even out of breath. I stood at ready stance, head bowed.

I waited, breathing deeply and evenly, for instructions. I heard the door to the room open. Two sets of footsteps resonated behind me.

The female on the committee who had spoken to me first informed me of the rules for the combat and disarmament demonstration. "On my mark, you will demonstrate defense on the first opponent and offense on the second opponent. Each opponent carries more than one simulation weapon. You will be judged on your overall skill. Points will be taken away for any paint shots you receive. You will be timed by the committee."

"Yes, ma'am," I replied in the calmest voice possible.

The presence of the two men behind me made me jumpy. I meditated to sense their stature and weaponry. One man was a short, stocky, blue Fitmalo. The other was a tall, muscular Vermilion. The Vermilion moved a few meters to my right. The Fitmalo moved to my left.

"Begin," the woman said.

I tightened my fists. I sensed the Vermilion back away from me. The Fitmalo advanced. I was only allowed to move defensively against him, so I waited for him to approach. He drew a mock singe gun and held it to my back. I immediately twisted away and dropped below his line of fire. In one motion, I snatched the weapon from him and flipped him onto the floor. I jerked his second weapon from its holster. The Vermilion approached, gun drawn. I spun to shoot him twice with the paint gun as I cloaked a blind spot. Before he could shoot back, I became invisible to him. I flew above them, sending the Fitmalo's weapons floating in the air high above us. I charged down, burying my elbow into the side of the Vermilion's neck. He instantly knelt to one side. I wrenched his gun from

47

his hand and moved like a streak. He still held a laser pistol at his waist. He reached for it, but I slapped away his arms and slipped it out from his belt before he completely grasped it. He swiped at me, but I sailed away from him. I levitated all four weapons above us.

The Fitmalo I had floored earlier rose to his feet again. He reached for a third weapon at his shin. I jumped behind the Vermilion, shoving his massive body towards the Fitmalo. They did not collide, but this served as a distraction to allow me to zip past the blue man. I simultaneously grabbed his head, jammed my knuckles to the side of his neck, and whisked my heel between his feet to kick near the Achilles tendon, the combination of which rendered him unconscious. The Fitmalo crumpled to the floor. I collected the knife from his shin and sent it skyward with the rest of the weapons before the Vermilion could grab me.

I skirted his grasping digits, evading him once again with a cloak. I had learned years ago that a man's overdeveloped brawn represented the bulk of his power and that although such sinewy musculature was impressive, it could also slow him down. The trick was to keep out of his grasp, because once caught, a woman would need all her psychic ability to keep from being crushed. My physical ability was no match for his. But my psychic power made him the lesser opponent.

Sensing my position, he pounced at me, swinging all four fists. I fought back, using all my limbs to counterattack his strikes. Finally, I leapt over him and arced my body around his as fast as I could. I delivered a punch to the backs of both his knees at once. He fell backwards as I shot myself between his feet. His body thudded again to the floor. I scanned him quickly for weapons. He had none.

"Stop," the female ordered.

I returned to attention, allowing the weapons to rest at my feet. I bowed my head again, avoiding looking directly at either of my felled opponents.

The Vermilion staggered to his feet with a grunt. He stepped to his Fitmalo companion. He slung the blue man over one shoulder. He levitated the weapons to return them to their holsters. Bright red paint dripped from his uniform. He puffed in aggravation as he marched out of the room. The door opened and shut behind him. A moment of silence chilled the room.

The female voice informed me that the committee members would now double-check my forms movements. She commanded me once more. "Form eight, moves twenty and twenty-one."

I repeated the order and performed the movements.

An elderly male voice said, "Form sixteen, moves twelve through nineteen."

I repeated the moves and performed them. Two other elderly males gave orders. I complied with each command. My breathing heightened. My heart rate rose. The four panel members who had already spoken continued to give me a variety of orders. I performed all these in my now sweat-soaked uniform. I wondered, chest heaving, if the fifth panel member would ever ask me to perform something. The first four panel members remained silent for a few moments.

Finally the fifth panel member spoke. "Form twenty-nine," he said.

I waited for him to specify which moves, but he did not. He must have meant for me to perform the entire form anew.

"Form twenty-nine, sir," I replied.

I performed the whirls and jumps as gracefully as I could despite my fatigue. I ended the form with the beginning stance. I now breathed heavily, my pulse barely under control.

I heard the committee members lean back and forth in their seats. They whispered to each other.

The female spoke. "This section of the test is ended. You may now meet your committee members," announced the female.

The curtain retracted slowly, revealing the table of judges.

I turned to see the spokeswoman. She was a Lizard like Yalat, only with lighter blue skin. She introduced herself as Professor Sub General Redet. I bowed to her.

The curtain continued its progress to reveal the second judge.

Redet said, "This is Professor Sub General Channol. You will recognize him as the brother of Sub General Wilbaht, the former chair of the Organization's educational board."

I did recognize him. He was almost identical to Wilbaht. He was a Torreon with dark gray skin, curly gray hair and a light beard. I bowed to him as the curtain slid away from the third judge's seat.

"This is Professor Stennet. He is the father of Professor Jiao, whom you met yesterday." Although Stennet's complexion was much lighter than Jiao's, and although his chin was hidden by a short beard, I recognized the family resemblance. I bowed solemnly to him, remembering how Jiao had saved our lives by disarming the bomb.

"Next we have Professor Terah from Sor4." He was a large blue-green Kangaroo Lizard. I bowed to him. The curtain finished its passage along its track.

"Finally we have a human from your own planet of Liricos. This is Sub Professor Ocelot."

I looked up at him. Terror slammed my thoughts to a halt.

I only saw his face for a split second. Then it burst like a pane of shattering glass. The shards expanded, swarmed after me. They became a whirlwind of jagged visions that sailed at me from another dimension, scattering around me, through me. They were so overpowering I could hardly see my true surroundings. I fruitlessly shielded my face with my arms. The images were unrelenting. The whirling pieces flickered with scene after scene of terror: explosions, battles, bloody Fitmalo soldiers, firing military ships. Broken images of slick-bodied monsters, spattering red and yellow blood, and smoking wreckage zipped around me. I saw gory carnage, a Mantis wielding a sword, warriors running. I saw Alaban rolling on the ground from a wound to the leg. I saw a group of frightened children, crumbling walls, a fleet of attack ships. Image upon image of terror careened through me. My heart throbbed madly in my chest. I averted my eyes, but the images did not stop. Instead they attacked me all the more, swarming into my mind. I saw Fitmalo soldiers shooting at me. I saw repeated motions of violent death, assassination, struggle, stabbings, suffering, and mourning. Sharp fragments of visionary debris sliced through my being. I cringed. I staggered backward. I felt the terrible pieces collect within my heart as an anchor of lead. I squeezed my eyes shut. I cried out.

I scarcely felt Yalat pull at my sleeve as I fell backward into unconsciousness, spinning darkness, cradled discomfort.

I awoke to find myself in my bed. Yalat patted my face with a cool, soggy cloth. I sat up immediately, startling her and nearly knocking her over.

"Well! You gave us a scare. Well, mostly you scared them, not me. I recognized the signs."

"You saw it too?" I asked her hopefully.

"I saw nothing but you falling down. I only recognized that you'd received an incredible vision. What was it?"

"There was too much. I couldn't stand to see anymore. It was horrible," I said, covering my face. I was surprised to hear myself panic. My own reaction frightened me. I shook with emotion.

Yalat jumped up on the bed behind me and covered my shoulders with her hands.

"Oh, no, dear. It was only a vision. It can't hurt you unless you allow it to. Relax. Rest. Here," she gestured to me to lie down again. I did as she indicated. She hopped off the bed and held her hand to my head to try to calm me. "If it causes you suffering, put it out of your mind. Let it flow out of you with your exhalation."

I apologized for my unusual behavior. I hoped it wouldn't happen again.

"Don't apologize, dear. It was beyond your control. Things happen that way every now and then. Visions are not always to our benefit. Unless it's something we can prevent, you should let your conscience rest for now.

Remember, your friend Alaban will probably return soon with whatever weapon he was looking for."

"Yes. Of course, you're right," I said, confused and angered.

I couldn't believe this. This was supposed to be the time in my life when I was given the chance to show my future employers what I had learned in training. I was supposed to shine like a good prospect for them. They were supposed to be impressed by my performance. I was supposed to make them think of possibility, not liability. The professors must have thought I was a complete lunatic; performing fantastic feats one moment and succumbing to fits of mental illness the next. Why should they hire someone so unpredictable? They would sooner slip me into a straight jacket than give me an important task to manage. I shook and pouted with frustration and embarrassment.

Yalat understood. With a sigh, she recommended that I work it off. I ran up and down the stairs until my legs burned and my steps slowed to a trot. I then bathed away my ill content along with my sweat in the bathtub. Finally, I sat resigned to any fate. I watched the water swirl away, imagining it as the anxiety leaving my body. This worked for the most part. I gathered my strength of spirit to plod on. I had to give this examination one more try. My final statements meeting would convene tomorrow. If they did not pass me, I would have to think of some way to appeal to them for a retest.

In the dining area, I found Yalat reviewing the information we'd found. As I approached, she swiveled her head towards the window. Then she closed her eyes and stirred the air with her snout as if to smell her surroundings. Something was happening. She slipped to the floor, ready for action.

"The spider is out. Let's get to the first floor now."

I redirected my frustration to concentrate on the challenge at hand. I jogged with Yalat past the elevator and entered a door to its left, which led to the stairwell. We both hopped over the railing of the winding stairs and levitated through its center all the way to the first floor. As we floated down, we heard a thumping noise and a scrape from the elevator shaft.

"There it is," I said as we passed the noise.

"At the eighth floor now," she agreed.

We reached the bottom of the stairs and dashed through the door, glancing back at the elevator, which remained shut, with no evidence of anything out of the ordinary.

"Alaban is nearby," Yalat said, tugging at my arm.

We rounded the corner of the hallway, nearly colliding with two human maintenance men heading our way. They stopped to stare at us in surprise.

"Did you just come from the elevator?" one of them asked.

"No, sir. We took the stairs," I said. "Why?"

"That elevator's been going up and down without opening. We've had complaints about it. We're going to try and repair it now. It should be running fine in a few minutes."

I stopped him. "I wouldn't go near it right now, sir. You could be risking your life." I didn't want to give more details. He would never believe me.

"No, there's no danger. We've dealt with this kind of problem before," he said, waving me away proudly. He continued toward the elevator, but his partner regarded us doubtfully.

We paused there at the corner, anticipating the worst, but without proof. The first repairman walked up to the doors of the elevator and entered a maintenance code. The doors slid open slowly. We only saw a dark, empty shaft with a grooved shaft pole at the back of it. The elevator box itself still ascended several floors above us. The shaft pole rotated to move the elevator box upward, then downward, and then up again.

The spider, if it was the one I'd read about, was of the seventh intelligence. It couldn't read, speak, or use tools. It could only strategize enough to protect and feed itself. The spider must have been hitting the control panel with its leg spikes as it moved around looking for a way out.

As the shaft pole rotated downward again, Yalat and I retreated to the protective corner wall of the hallway with the high glass window behind us. The repairman lifted a panel casing from the side of the elevator. The shaft pole continued to rotate downward.

Yalat unsheathed her sonic scythe. I did the same with my sword.

"Stand back, gentlemen," she warned.

The repairman next to us saw our intentions and sidled closer to us. The man at the elevator didn't move away. He turned slowly to eye us inquisitively. We watched with morose fascination as the elevator box appeared. It contained four pairs of bone-yellow spiked legs, which continued for at least two meters.

The repairman at the door saw the look of shock on his partner's face. He turned his head to see the monstrosity behind him. Duly shaken, he staggered away slowly.

Next the spherical abdomen came into view. The spider shuffled around, looking at the back of the elevator with most of its eyes. When the elevator came to rest, the repairman closest to us bolted down the hallway and toward the exit. The other man still backed away slowly, thinking he wouldn't distract the beast. Unfortunately, the spider wobbled around to face the man.

Yalat and I stayed partially hidden at the corner. We had to fight it whether we had the best tools or not. Yalat could get at least one good shot at it with the scythe. Then we could disappear around the corner and levitate up the wall when it came after us. Our best bet was to play tag with it this way until it lost all its legs. Then it could be destroyed by a strike through the head.

The remaining repairman turned to run, but the spider hissed and spat, pegging him in the back of the neck with a sticky glob of acid mucus. The man screamed, but was quickly paralyzed. The bones and tissues of the nape of his neck deteriorated into a puddle of foaming blood. The spider pounced at him. It dropped its spiked body onto its victim's ribs and chomped at his shoulder with protruding sets of fangs and pincers. The spider began to feed, but its attack was mostly defensive. It was not interested in food. We had little time before the monster would leave its victim to explore its new surroundings in search of a hiding place.

Yalat pulled me back behind the corner. "Let's stay away as long as possible," she said. "Seeing how that thing jumped makes me think it will not be so easy to engage it."

I looked down the hall to the main door of the building. The other repairman had successfully escaped to find help.

"There's a niche in the hallway at either side of the door. We might stand a better chance hiding there," Yalat said.

We hurried as quietly as possible to the end of the hall and into a niche at the left. The motion sensors caused the door to open as we stepped near it. Before the doors could close, the spider turned the corner, either to pursue us or to explore the hallway. At the same moment, Alaban rushed in with a small orb in one hand and something else tucked under one arm. He skidded to a halt. The spider and Alaban stared each other down from opposite ends of the hall as if acknowledging one another as opponents. They both stayed frozen this way for several unnerving seconds.

"Psst!" we hissed at him. He glanced at us and then backed into the niche on the opposite side of the door.

We heard the clacking percussion of the spider's approaching feet. Yalat pointed a thumb upward, telling us to levitate. Alaban and I nodded. The three of us elevated to the ceiling. We passed silently above the spider as it went to the door.

The door opened automatically as the spider drew close to it. Outside, the repairman had gathered a couple of security officers. They opened fire when they saw the atrocious beast. Their singe guns did no damage to the creature, but they did at least deter it from leaving the building. The spider spat acid at them before retreating again through the hallway, warbling and hacking in anger. We stayed above and at the corner of the hall to watch it. It traveled back and forth inside the hallway, finding itself trapped again.

Each time it neared the main door, the door opened, the guards shot, it spat, and then it retreated as before. After three tries, it slowed its pace, stumbling toward the exit, but did not get close enough for the automatic doors to open. It had learned finally not to approach too closely. It stood motionless, waiting.

Alaban pointed to us to drop down to the floor behind the corner wall out of the spider's line of vision. We ducked near the body of the unfortunate maintenance worker. Alaban grimaced at it, and then handed the orb to Yalat.

"This is a shield orb. You'll both need it if you're going to act as bait," he said.

We looked at each other. "You have the weapon, then?" asked Yalat.

He held out the item he'd had tucked under his arm. It was the egg-shaped explosive device that Jiao had pulled from the microship. Only Jiao had dismantled it. Now it was back in one piece with a green light blinking, indicating it was ready to program.

I gasped, "How did you get that?"

Alaban gasped, imitating me. "I stole it. Isn't it great?"

"I think I understand your plan," said Yalat, ignoring his clownish response. "You want to set the bomb to explode under the creature while we lure it to the right spot."

"Yes, ma'am," he said as he twisted the bomb to program. "When I press this, we'll have seven seconds. I'll stay behind the wall to arm it if you'll stand by the window."

"What kind of blast capacity does that thing have?" I asked him.

"Don't worry. I took out some of the explosive putty. It won't do any structural damage to the building," Alaban reassured us.

Yalat eyed him cautiously, wondering whether to trust him or not. She then turned on the shield orb, which we each held together. The shield orb sang as it formed a gelatinous energy seal all around us.

We moved toward the window. The spider didn't seem to notice us at first. Yalat made a loud clucking sound. The spider turned. It took a few steps forward, then stopped. I tensed, petrified to see the hideous yellow beast in our direct path. Yalat clucked again. This time it raced forward on its spiny, clacking legs. Alarm gripped my nerves, but I had to stay still.

Alaban set and threw the bomb. The spider should have just reached it as it exploded, but the creature was so fast that it passed the bomb and was almost ready to pounce on us when it blew. Since the explosive force was behind the creature, the explosion popped and splattered its abdomen and broke away its six hind legs, but sent the head and remaining legs toward the window and us. We ducked. The flying remains of the spider barely missed our shield. The head smashed into the window, and then landed behind us. The thick glass thudded and vibrated violently. Then it cracked apart, creaking like thin ice. Finally, the lower half of the window collapsed, shattering as it fell, covering the entire corner of the hallway in snowy flecks. Metal throughout the building hummed from the low boom of the explosion. Our ears rang.

Yalat and I turned within our protective seal to see the remains of the spider. The head and most of two legs still writhed beneath a thick pile of broken glass and dust. Yalat poked her weapon out of the shield to cut the legs off just as the spider shot its spikes at us. The spikes glanced off the shield. The head of the spider gurgled. It was still alive.

I readied my sword. I advanced towards the wiggling head, prodding and turning it with the blade so the mouth pointed up toward us. With both hands, I thrust the tip of the sword through the spider's brain by way of its open mouth. The gurgling stopped. I left the sword in the beast, knowing if it were withdrawn too soon, it would splash us with acid. The impaled head lobbed over to one side, guided by the weight of the sword.

We looked around at the awful mess. Sticky globs of organs and yellow blood clung, spattered, all over the walls. Glass chunks and dust covered the floor and part of the interior garden. The dead man's body oozed blood into an expanding puddle. Debris lay scattered everywhere.

"I hope we don't have to clean up this mess," said Alaban from the elevator doorway, squinting and covering his nose and mouth to avoid breathing in the glass particles.

Yalat motioned me towards him. She wasn't through with her mission. She levitated us both to the elevator, where she turned off the shield orb.

"Let's see if this will take us to the twentieth floor now," Yalat said.

Thanks to the work of the repairman before his demise, we were able to access any floor we wanted, classified or not. At the twentieth floor, we stayed in the elevator box a few moments, adjusting our eyes to the room's darkness. A light flickered close by. Another sparked. Directly in front of us on the floor lay the body of another victim of the spider.

We stepped over him cautiously. A light from the back of the room came on automatically. I stiffened; mortified to find that this floor held more carnage than the one we'd just left. We counted five bodies in the open office area, three of which were Fitmalos. One was a Furman armed guard: the man we had to step over to enter the room. The other body had been human. He wore the uniform of a Center official. He had not been a victim of the spider. A lightning-shaped sword protruded from his chest: a Fitmalo burial sword. His assassination had been a message to someone.

Yalat moved towards the body to examine it. Alaban observed the other men.

I edged away from the slaughter and to a double door marked "Life Storage Lab". A pool of red and yellow blood coagulated at the base of this door. I shuddered to remember this scene from one of my visionary shards. I sensed no life in this area, so I entered, levitating to avoid the puddles of blood.

Rows of open cages lined the walls of the lab. Whoever killed the official had also ordered the destruction of all beings kept here. Each cage contained a dripping carcass. At the far end of the lab, a large door lay open. This must have been the spider's cage. Next to the cage door, I found two computer consoles and a mainframe casing that had been blasted apart and partially melted. Someone had destroyed research evidence.

I guessed this had all been the result of a combination blackmail and assassination gone wrong. The Fitmalos must have asked the official for some kind of information. The official refused. As punishment, the Fitmalos ransacked his lab. In the process of destroying his lab animals, the thugs must have opened the spider's door to shoot it, but were chased out when their shots did it no harm. Then the spider probably wrecked havoc on the group of men. At some point one of the Fitmalos managed to kill the official before dying by spider attack. The Furman at the elevator must have tried to escape, opening the elevator too late and allowing the spider to leave the floor. I retreated from the sickening massacre to find my comrades.

We investigated other areas of the floor. Many rooms were either ransacked or locked. We found no other beings here, living or dead. We didn't know the exact motives of these Fitmalos, who they represented, or whether anyone else had been present at the scene before the spider attacked. Being careful not to disturb the crime scene, we returned to the elevator with more questions than answers.

Chapter 8: Interrogation

We followed Yalat to the smaller, safer, elevator of Building One, which unloaded another group of security officers to our battle site as we got on.

This time, Yalat informed us, we were not going to the security office. We were going straight to the on-site military investigations office.

Alaban and I stood straight. This was a time to behave as formally as possible. The military investigations board always intimidated the rest of the Organization. These were people who invisibly controlled lives of other warriors, altered or invented recorded information for a secret purpose, and played a significant hand in the direction of economy and politics. Yalat was a shrewd professor to face them head-on.

At the nineteenth floor, Yalat marched up to the clerk's counter and demanded to see the nearest available military investigations official about the assassination of a military scientist here in the C.A.T.T. Center just minutes ago. The Lizard clerk jerked out of her seat and told us to wait just a moment. She scurried off down a corridor, disappeared for a moment and then returned in the same hurried manner. She ushered us toward the General's office.

We found General Lam fastening the top button of his uniform. He looked disheveled, as if he'd just woken up. He stood at attention, however, to greet us as we entered. The General was a human from Xiantalix, the sister planet of Rybalazar, my own planet's sworn enemy. He had a Xiantalix shield and a picture of the Gold Wind helion on his wall. It may have been only this first impression that made me distrust him. Or it could have been something else. I felt we would receive little cooperation from him.

Yalat, being the senior member of our group, immediately became our spokeswoman. She talked so quickly about all that had happened that the General only blinked the first few minutes with a frown. She explained first about the microship, then about our visions of the spider. When she told him about how we had defeated it, the General interjected a few words I'd never used before and never hoped to. Yalat didn't pause to react to this, but continued about the assassination on the twentieth floor.

When the General heard this information, he immediately pressed a button on the wall and called in the clerk. She slid into the office.

"Get General Samson. Tell him there's a level one security breach and he needs to see me first," Lam ordered.

The clerk winced as if struck by a flying object, then breathed, "Yes, sir!" She disappeared again.

Yalat was about to continue her story, but Professor General Lam stopped her. "I advise you not to say another word, Professor. Wait until our interrogation aides get here. We need this information recorded officially." He became very stern. "You'll each give a separate statement. Say nothing until the aides question you."

Yalat folded her arms and said no more. The General eyed us carefully. He stared longest at Alaban. I wondered how many hours ago he had stolen the bomb. Maybe Lam glared at him because he had been aware of the theft before we arrived at his office.

Only a few moments passed before the clerk arrived with General Samson, a Vermilion man. Lam told him only that we needed to be voluntarily interrogated at a top clearance level. Samson beckoned his aides to secure a recording room for each of us. His aides were of his same race. They almost looked like triplets. Yalat followed one down the corridor and to the left. I followed another to the right. I glanced back at Alaban. He followed another aide. Lam and Samson stared after Alaban. Lam pointed to him and muttered something.

My interrogation aide led me to an empty recording room. Two stair-like ledges on either side served as seats. The interrogation aide held a recording control in his lower hands. His upper right hand rubbed his forehead. His upper left hand pressed a mechanism behind his ear to receive instructions. He spoke to his general aloud.

"Yes, sir. Understood. Beginning now, sir." He looked up at me. "We'll begin recording now. Tell us everything you can remember."

Since this was a voluntary interrogation, the aide felt at ease and did not pressure me. From time to time during my story he asked me to wait because he was receiving information from his general. Then I continued speaking. My statement was very long. I wanted to be sure it was complete. I even told him about my suspicions of Professor Trau. After I'd finished details about our battle with the spider, the aide stared spellbound with interest. Then he jerked his head to one side.

"Hold on a moment," he told me, listening to the General speak in his ear. "Yes, sir. Yes, sir."

"Do you know how and when Alaban retrieved the explosive?" he asked me.

"I don't know, sir. He never told us. He said only that he could get the perfect weapon for the job. He left our room at about 1300 hours to see about it. The next we knew of it was when he showed it to us just before he used it on the spider. He said he'd stolen it, but he didn't give any details," I said. I hoped they wouldn't reprimand him too badly for it in these extreme circumstances.

58

"You identified the explosive as the same one Professor Jiao had deactivated from the microship you captured. How do you know it was the same one?"

"I don't know that, sir. It's only that this particular bomb was a kind I'd never seen before and it's unlikely that there would be two of them in the same place at the same time."

He paused a moment, listening to his earpiece. "Do you or Professor Yalat communicate often with anyone of the Fitmalo race?"

"No, sir."

He listened to his earpiece once more.

"How long have you had such vivid premonitions?"

"All my life, sir. Actually, they've become much stronger recently, probably from emotional stress from my testing."

"Did Professor Yalat teach you how to move objects through each other in levitation?"

"No, sir. No one taught me. I was just experimenting with things one day and found I could."

After the interrogator had no more questions, I dared to ask him one.

"Sir, if anyone knows why the microship was filming my levitation test, I'd appreciate the information."

"The microship is still under investigation. If you are allowed to know anything about that investigation, you will be told," he said coldly.

I frowned.

He stopped to listen again. "Normally, a trainee's final statements meeting is held one day after the personal defense test, but yours will be delayed due to the emergency investigation of Building Three. You and your professor will be accommodated here in Building One this evening. No one is allowed to enter or leave Building Three except on special clearance, which you don't have. You are not to mention any of today's events to anyone upon penalty of temporary suspension."

"Yes, sir. I understand."

He guided me out of the recording room to a waiting area where Yalat already sat. She stood when she saw me. There was no sign of Alaban.

A guard escorted us to a floor with narrow corridors. At the end of one corridor, the guard opened a door. The room was extremely small, only as large as the interrogation room. Where the stair-like seats had been in the interrogation room, here were bench cots covered with a thin layer of padded fabric. A doorless bathroom interrupted the bunk, with only a tiny sink in the middle of the wall and a small toilet at the floor. The guard bowed to us and said good night. He turned to march back down the corridor.

Yalat observed this closet of a room. "Well, there's nothing to do here. Let's go find something to eat," she spoke, trudging down the corridor after the guard.

The food service area in this building consisted of a wide dining hall connected to a single kitchen counter. Dozens of military and security personnel sat in clusters, talking excitedly about the problems in Building Three.

A Kangaroo Lizard took our order and processed it. While we waited, I asked Yalat if she'd seen Alaban after her interrogation. She hadn't. She suspected he would be held for some time. Judging from the kinds of questions we were asked regarding him, she was sure General Lam would cross-examine Alaban himself.

The Kangaroo Lizard gave us our food on trays, which we carried to an empty end of a table. At the other end several military servicemen discussed today's events. They were clearly concerned about their jobs here, and in fact, their lives, since such danger had invaded their place of work. They laid blame on the Fitmalos. One even said the U.G. should put the planet Fitmalo on economic restriction until their government changed hands.

"General said don't discuss that," I heard one man dressed in a military uniform say.

Yalat heard him, too. We exchanged a furtive glance before finishing the rest of our meal in silence. I hoped to catch another part of their conversation, but after this comment, things grew quieter at their end of the table. Soon the men left.

"You were right about something funny going on around here," I said.

Yalat didn't answer. She only gazed around the room with deep thought on her face.

As we left, we walked between the tables of gossiping workers. I noticed the repairman that had been with us: the one the spider had spared. He caught my gaze and nudged the man next to him. He pointed at us. I couldn't hear what he said, but I nodded to him solemnly and kept walking. Soon we heard louder voices from the dining room. They were talking about us, pointing, staring. We both quickened our pace. No one stopped us, but we both jittered until we successfully left that floor of the building.

We were so exhausted with all of the day's trials that even the thinly covered cots were a welcome sight. We both lay in our beds fully clothed and slept.

During this night, the dream of Alaban and the pins returned to me. This time the dream started almost where it had left off. Alaban sat next to me. I lay on my back in the dormitory at Building Three. An X-shaped pattern of pins stood out from my abdomen. He held a pin in his fingers and drew close to me as if to puncture my eye as in the last nightmare, but this time he leaned over toward the floor, picked up the box, and put the pin back in it. He looked into my eyes hesitantly. He said nothing, but seemed sad. I saw him reach for another pin from my stomach. He pulled it out quickly and returned it to the box. He did the same with another and another pin. While he did this, I heard a knock at the door.

The door didn't open automatically, as it would have in reality. It stayed shut. Alaban viewed the door with apprehension, and then with resentment. Another knock sounded from the door. Alaban shrugged his shoulders and continued about his work, plucking the pins from my body and returning them to the box.

When yet another knock resounded, Alaban pointed his finger at the door in anger and growled, "Let them wait."

He returned to take the last of the pins away, enclosing them all inside the box. The knocking continued. This time Alaban threw the box of pins fiercely at the wall, where it smashed loudly, spilling pins and splintered wood all over the floor.

"I know!" he shouted. "I know! Shut up already! I know!" He looked around the room nervously.

He then regarded me with baleful eyes. He lifted me up by the neck and arm, cradling my head against his shoulder.

"Hold on," he whispered to me. "I'm sorry. Just hold on to me. Promise me you'll hold on." He stroked my face and ear with his hand.

I awoke still feeling his hand's gentle touch on my face. What did it mean? This was not such a nightmare like the other had been, but it disturbed me more. I only hoped Alaban was not in danger.

Chapter 9: The Sparring Match

In the morning, Yalat proposed we find Alaban. I sensed him nearby, but couldn't be sure of his location. We returned to the nineteenth floor to ask about him. The clerk stood as we approached. She answered our question before we asked it.

"Your friend is at the meeting for the announcement of his first assignment," she said quickly.

We retracted from the office uneasily.

"I hope they don't send Alaban to the Keres helion. He hates that place," I told Yalat.

"Keres is the least of his worries now. I see a rough life ahead for him," Yalat spoke.

"You had a premonition?" I asked.

She nodded introspectively. "I saw him working among his own enemies. He's destined for deep espionage. That life is a lonely one."

I wondered about my dream. Did it have something to do with his assignment? Were the people behind the door from his testing committee? I considered telling Yalat about my dream, but I felt it was for me alone.

We went to see if Building Three was open yet. A few security guards gathered at the door. A containment truck full of debris idled near the entrance. A general stood speaking to a guard nearby.

As we approached, Professors Stennet and Jiao, father and son, left the building accompanied by two military guards. They passed us, moving toward Building One. The young Professor Jiao glanced at me and nodded as he walked by. I did the same. They appeared disconcerted. They didn't speak to each other as they walked. They had probably been called in for questioning regarding the stolen bomb.

Yalat asked the general by the truck if we could enter. He made a call to someone before allowing us in. He told Yalat to use the stairs.

The hallway was perfectly clean now. Some men on a motorized scaffold supervised its repainting. The rest of the window had been extracted, allowing the hallway to open into the central garden. The elevator was blocked off, but the door to the stairway stayed open.

Yalat scampered up the stairs on all fours. I followed on two feet. Once in our room, we consulted my dormitory computer. Yalat said she suspected the deceased Fitmalo blackmailers on floor twenty were actually Fitmalo secret military soldiers. She asked me to access information about Fitmalo military and government to learn more background information. We scanned the data together.

The current Fitmalo executive military director and political leader was Prime Minister Lock Steelbrey. We found a picture of him and a brief description of how he came to power. His cabinet members included twenty-seven people from the various regions of his planet. Each prime minister and cabinet member held a six-year term. Lock had two years left in office.

Yalat pinpointed the Fitmalo cabinet members and military generals who controlled weapons research and acquisition. She then looked up Fitmalo government budgeting allocations. On a hunch, she also looked up fundraiser banquets that these leaders had attended in the last few years. A certain portion of several fundraisers had gone to an internal peacekeeping fund, which Yalat explained was another name for a special military account. Additionally, a certain percentage of Fitmalo planetary taxing went to the peacekeeping fund. She suspected they were stockpiling this money for a specific defense objective, like the purchase and implementation of new weapons, or a new, well-equipped military base, or both. According to her calculations, the Fitmalo military would certainly have enough money by now to arm themselves better than any planet in their quadrant of the galaxy.

With this in mind, and applying the clues we'd found on the twentieth floor, she expected they had offered to buy some sort of biological weapon from the now assassinated official but were turned down, and if there had been other Fitmalo agents present besides the bodies we'd found, they most likely had either succeeded in stealing the weapon from the lab after the official died or they were still nearby, regrouping and planning an alternative way to get it. The Fitmalos were known for their perseverance.

"I've considered something else as well," Yalat added. "Lock only has two more years in office. A move for this type of weapon could mean he's planning on staying in office much longer. He may be trying to form an illegal dictatorship. One does not buy weapons of biological terror without long-term purpose. Unless the weapon is meant to be kept a complete secret for silent bargaining, in which case we should fear whomever winds up with it. I want to know who those Fitmalos were on the twentieth floor and for whom they were working."

However, she was not allowed access to the twentieth floor case information and was afraid she'd discovered all she would be allowed to. Also, she had searched and found no trace of information regarding our microship. It had either been erased or so highly classified as to be unlisted on normal Organization research probes. She decided that one of two things had to be true. Either the microship and the twentieth floor had nothing to do with each other, the fact of which would leave us with fewer problems to consider, or they were related in some way, the fact of which would mean that some extremely dangerous people had taken an interest in my abilities and that I could be in danger. Regardless of the truth, Yalat encouraged me to be cautious and to use my sixth sense liberally. Frustrated and tired, we decided to go down to the third floor for the flavored ice we'd meant to buy before.

As we left our room, we were relieved to see Alaban exiting the stairwell. I waved to him and smiled. My smile soon faded, however, when I saw Professor Trau following him. They both wore official uniforms and expressions of antipathy. Alaban waited for us to approach. Professor Trau reluctantly did the same.

Trau stood only slightly taller than Alaban. His graying hair and beard were short and well groomed. His dull green eyes criticized our presence. We all greeted each other with frigid formality.

I told Alaban quickly where we were going and that perhaps we could get together later in the day. We parted company as stiffly as we had met.

At the third floor café, I asked Yalat, "Do you think Trau suspects we said something about him to the General?"

"I'm sure he does," she said, munching her ice. "However, his opinion of our honesty shouldn't matter. I suspect he will soon be interrogated as well. The generals are sure to keep an eye on him."

"May I join you for a moment, ladies?" I heard an elderly male voice say. I turned to see Professor Banjil bowing and smiling.

"Certainly, Professor," answered Yalat.

Banjil sat close to her. He smiled a bit nervously. "Everyone heard rumors of what happened yesterday. It was you, then?" he asked.

Yalat held up a hand to me, letting me know that I should not speak this time. "Yes, we were in the group that destroyed the spider, if that's what you mean."

"I only was curious, as everyone else, as to where it came from and why it was here." Banjil beamed at her, eyes filled with coy curiosity.

Yalat told him she thought perhaps it had escaped during a feeding. She claimed it must have come from a private zoo collection on the twentieth floor.

Banjil raised his white eyebrows. "Really?" he said. Then he transferred his gaze to me. "And will the Fitmalos keep the zoo, or will they have it moved out?"

Yalat and I exchanged glances of suspicion.

"I saw the body bags. I sensed Fitmalo bodies in some of them. I would be willing to fight against the establishment of a Fitmalo rebel outpost in our Center, if there is to be one. Do you know anything?"

64

"Banjil. You can rest assured there will be no such outpost established here. Have the rumors really pointed to that? I'd hoped people would be more sensible than to think such things. The Organization would never openly condone a coup party. They certainly would not house one in hiding at a testing center," Yalat said calmly, still crunching the ice.

"Well, we sometimes let our imaginations run away with us," he said apologetically. "I'm glad to hear all is well. I wish you the best of luck." He bowed twice.

I stood to bow in return, but Yalat merely nodded at him. I watched him gimp off to a table full of Greys and Lizards. They all leaned in to hear him when he sat.

"I can't imagine people would believe the idea of a rebel outpost here, but I hope they believe what you said about the zoo," I said.

"I'm sure most intelligent people will not. It will only serve as a temporary distraction. Hopefully, by the time people start asking about it again, we'll be off this planet," she said. Then she blinked heavily as she peered across the room. "Well, I'll be. It's Sub General Wilbaht himself."

I turned to see him shaking hands and embracing his brother, Channol, the one who had been on my committee for personal defense testing. I recognized him from his picture. Every academic text from the last three years displayed a photo of him on the opening page. Before becoming chairman of academic education, he had been a war hero. He had helped squelch the Mercury3 uprising in the Keres helion many years ago.

"I wonder why he's here," Yalat thought aloud.

We noticed some people at Banjil's table leaning out to speak with people from other tables as well. We left quietly, avoiding eye contact with them. I felt some staring and pointing as the people had in Building One. I felt as if we'd suddenly become famous, or perhaps infamous.

Two hours after we'd seen Alaban and Professor Trau, we found ourselves back in our room. Yalat went to her dormitory to read. I stayed in the living room to meditate, waiting for Alaban.

I didn't have to wait long for him. He arrived with a mischievous smile that brightened his dark face. He grabbed me by the shoulders and spoke quickly.

"I found a man to judge our sparring. He'll meet us at the sparring room in ten minutes. Hurry and get ready. I'll meet you there," he said excitedly. Then he rushed out.

I didn't stay thinking long, but went to tell Yalat where I'd be. She was surprised, but accepted this. I changed into my combat uniform and pulled my hair back with a band that wouldn't break this time.

I left my weapons in their box, since Alaban had proposed to spar without them. I realized suddenly that someone must have picked up my sword from yesterday's spider mess, because I hadn't retrieved it. I hoped to get it back. It had taken me several tries to put it together properly and I wasn't looking forward to assembling a new one.

I hurried to the sparring building. The door was open. I entered to find a man sitting on a foundation block with his back to the wall. He was a human with a long beard. He held a black square atomic clock with white glowing numbers. As I moved closer, I realized I recognized this man. He had been one of the judges from my academic test committee.

"Professor Pauber?" I asked.

He stood and bowed. "I was asked to judge a sparring match here. Are you the young man's opponent?"

Just then, Alaban entered in his combat uniform, without weapons, just as we had agreed. "I'm sorry I'm late. A professor held me up. Shall we take a few moments to stretch?" he asked.

"I only have half an hour to spare, so it would be best if you kept it short," Pauber rasped.

"Yes, sir," he replied.

I only stretched a little, but Alaban showed off. He did a slow back flip ending in the splits. From this position, he did a handstand on both hands, then on one hand. He turned himself ninety degrees, then leapt into an attention stance. He rolled his head and shoulders. He flexed his chest and arms like a gorilla. I got the point. He was bigger, stronger and just as agile as me. I shook my head.

Finally, he stood at attention. "I'm ready. How about you?"

"At your command, sir," I said.

Professor Pauber changed the atomic clock to timer, with thirty minutes on, ready to count down.

"This match will last thirty minutes or until one of you stays down for more than ten seconds. Self-levitation is allowed. Levitation of one's opponent or objects is not. Any blows to the eyes, throat, or spinal column will disqualify your points. Points are gained only by knocking your opponent completely to the floor. Please take a ready stance." We did.

"Begin," he said, starting the countdown of the clock.

Alaban shouted loudly and jumped toward me, and then hopped back, playing. He hopped up and down, swinging his fists in all directions. I took two tentative steps forward, pretending to be wary of his power. Then I shot myself forward on a full-body levitative pulse with my right leg extended in an extreme power move. At this speed, he could not dodge or block. My foot hit him directly over the heart. He sailed backwards several meters before falling to the floor with a "whop," losing his breath from the impact.

"One point for Sil," Pauber announced emotionlessly.

I returned to my ready stance, regathering my power. I might have been wrong to expend so much energy at the beginning of a match, but it was worth it to keep Alaban's ego from leading him to overconfidence. Alaban got up as quickly as he could. He wasn't hurt, but his playful attitude was gone. He was ready to fight. He gritted his teeth with determination.

I walked backward in a semicircle. He came after me in a flying windmill kick. I strafed away, and then hook-kicked him on the underside of his thigh. He plummeted both fists toward my ribs. I dodged and bounded away from him.

He retreated a few steps, but I pounced at him with a sideways levitative scissor kick. He did a handstand to dodge me. He whisked his body around in the air and hooked my neck with the back of his ankle to flip me. He meant to bring me to the floor, but I rolled with the momentum and landed on my feet. We whirled to face each other.

I attacked again, passing him and pivoting. He punched repeatedly at my face, but I parried his arms with quick slaps. I stepped in close to position my foot and then yanked myself backwards, hooking the underside of his knee and swiping his foot out from under him. He dove into a pushup position, but didn't hit the floor all the way, so I didn't gain a point. He flipped three times sideways just above the floor while I axe-kicked at his whirling torso. At the last axe kick, he levitated upward, crashing into my leg and knocking me off balance. He came at me with a heavy tricep to my chest. I hit the floor, winded.

"One point for Alaban," Pauber spoke.

We returned to ready stance. He charged at me with a levitating punch, trying to imitate my power side kick I'd used at the onset of the match. I dodged, barely feeling the skin on his fist as it grazed my cheek. He gave a triple kick. I dodged. He flipped above me, and then spun to kick me in the face, but I ducked. He landed facing me in ready position again.

I stepped in toward him. I pretended to prepare to punch, but then leapt diagonally to give a kick that caught him on the arm. He tried to grab my leg and slam me like he had the other day, but I whisked myself backwards. He followed me closely.

He turned an outside block into a shoulder clamp, using my shoulder as a support to flip himself upward. Then he let his full weight fall on my back. He knocked me forward, but I didn't fall. I dipped my head

67

and shoulders toward the ground and rotated, flipping my body into a double scissor.

Several minutes passed in which we were able to dodge each other's moves every time. Soon fifteen minutes remained on the clock.

Alaban sailed up behind me to my right. I turned to block to the left, assuming he'd made a half-circle, but he had faked it. When I turned back around, he bludgeoned me with a fist to the stomach, which sent me plunging to the floor. This blow was painful. I rolled for a few seconds, and then forced myself back on my feet before the ten-second limit.

"One point for Alaban," Pauber spoke.

I held a ready stance, but stood slightly doubled over in pain. A wave of nausea came over me. I kept my eye on Alaban, remembering how he'd kicked at me when I was down the last time we'd sparred. This time he kept his distance. He stayed at a hunched ready stance, waiting for me to approach, or so I thought. He suddenly did a flip, hurling his legs at me. I rolled to the side, and then stood with difficulty. Pain and nausea attacked the pit of my stomach. Sweat trickled down my face in streams. He punched forward in a rapid combination of fists and knife-hands. I deflected these, but took a real beating to the arms. Then he ducked and hooked his arm around my thigh. He lifted me upside-down in the air. He tried to slam me to the floor, but I levitated us both toward the ceiling. Since technically I was only lifting myself, this move was not disqualified. He was simply holding onto me as I flew up.

He let go of my leg, and then turned to embrace me around the arms, squeezing tightly and restricting my breathing. We flipped right side up. I tried to hit him with the back of my head as we floated downward again, but he kept his chin pressed into my shoulder.

As I struggled momentarily in this position, Alaban whispered to me, "So tell me, Sil. Do you like acupuncture?"

I gasped. The image of my nightmare returned to my mind. Did he read my dreams? Did he cause them? I couldn't speak. I had to counteract fast.

I spun frantically and crushed him into the floor in a blast of fury. He released his grip on me just enough for me to fly up away from him. He groaned for a moment, rubbing the back of his head. My own head ached as well, since I had hit it on his chin.

"One point for Sil," Pauber said. Ten minutes remained on the clock.

I returned to the floor several paces away from him. He stood, wavering and shaking his head. He blinked and squinted. He held up one hand toward Pauber.

"Stop the clock," he said. "Time out for head injury." He leaned forward. He placed his palms on his knees. He continued blinking, shaking his head, and stretching his neck.

Pauber stopped the clock.

I didn't wait for him to shake off his dizziness. I approached him to whisper at him angrily. "Why did you say that about acupuncture?" I asked.

"I know you dreamed about it," he said with eyes squinted shut.

"How? How did you know it?"

"I planted the idea while you slept. Psychic suggestion." He panted and blinked innocently.

"Don't ever do that to me again," I hissed, pushing his shoulder. "You know I'm psychically sensitive." I walked away from him, and then turned to assume the ready stance. "Stay out of my head," I commanded.

He looked offended, then angered. He took a ready stance. "Ready!" he yelled.

Pauber started the clock again.

Alaban shot forward. He acted as though he would kick me in the stomach, but he was faking again. Somehow I knew he was actually going to try and pass me to backward scissor kick at my legs and cause a fall. I jumped up, flipped behind him, and slapped him on the back of the head with both hands as I turned. I floated away from him. He tried to distract me with repeated roundhouse kicks and then threw an upper cut at me. I dodged. I continued to constantly dodge and counterattack with ease. Less than three minutes remained. Alaban was perturbed for not succeeding in any of his strikes against me for the last few minutes. He breathed hard now from his wasted exertion.

Then Alaban hurled himself at me, throwing a right jab and then a left palm strike towards my chin, but I blocked and kicked his instep, pulling his arm at the same time to throw him off to the side. He pushed away just as I threw and uppercut to his cheekbone. He flinched, and then caught my wrist. He yanked it, flipping me toward the ground into a crab position. I zoomed away from him to avoid his elbow and knee to my abdomen.

I feigned an attack to his left. I whirled into the air above him and back to his right with a powerful kick to the torso. I hit him with my greatest force, over-extending my muscles, causing a tunneling pain in my own ribs. I recoiled from the sprain as he bounced away and rolled to the side. He only stayed down for a moment. He got up and staggered, slightly bent over in pain.

"One point for Sil," Pauber announced. We had one minute left.

I moved to ready stance. We both breathed sharply. Our uniforms showed dark sweat marks. Our faces were flushed and drenched. Sweat stung my eyes. Alaban turned his left side towards me, protecting his right.

69

He still bent forward and grimaced. I might have cracked one of his lower ribs with my last kick. He didn't usually attack from a left stance. Or was he preparing for a different kind of attack? I was winning by one point. He was sure to try and bring me down with his most powerful move in the last few seconds.

All of a sudden, he bounded into the air and disappeared. I believed he would fly back down toward me at bullet speed. I rose cautiously into the air, searching for him. He cloaked well. I closed my eyes. I sensed him near me. Where was he? I felt a tap on my head. I punched toward the ceiling. If he was there, I didn't touch him. I felt another tap on my shoulder, but when I spun to catch him, I missed entirely. He could have been below me. He didn't seem to be there.

Suddenly the floor came hurtling toward me. Alaban was riding on my back upside down, hugging my waist. He used the speed drop from form thirty to plummet us downward. As the floor came to meet us, I used all my energy to lean backward.

Alaban let go of my waist but couldn't get out of the way in time. We hit the ground in an awkward position. He landed on his back with knees bent and feet flat on the floor. His arms spread to his sides. The back of his head received yet another heavy impact. His eyes squeezed shut. His teeth clenched. The air was forced out of his lungs in a bursting howl.

I landed seated on his chest. My heels hit the floor just above his shoulders. A bolt of pain ripped through them. I yelped. Not only did my heels shriek with pain, but my head and my side also ached.

"One point for Sil," said Pauber. "Your time is now finished. Your scores are: Sil four, Alaban two."

I leaned forward to clutch my heels, which throbbed relentlessly. I crouched face to face with Alaban, who grunted and panted.

He opened one eye at me and asked, "Are you all right?"

"I'll be okay," I panted. "You?"

"I'm fine," he lied, equally out of breath.

He lifted me off him by the hips. I turned to give him a hand, but he rolled to one side and lifted himself to his feet on his own. We both stood at attention as best we could. We bowed to each other, then to Professor Pauber, who now stood with the clock. He returned our bow and then ambled out of the sparring room stoically.

As soon as he left, we both collapsed again to the floor. I pulled off my boots to caress my ankles and heels. Alaban stayed on his knees and hugged his head and the back of his neck with his arms. Veins stood out on his forehead. As I massaged my heels, he sank to his elbows and knees, still covering the sides of his head with his hands. Perhaps his double injury had been more serious than I thought.

70

I crawled to him and knelt. I felt the back of his neck with my fingertips, hoping not to aggravate his headache even more. The neck muscles were taut. His pulse was strained. His breathing was still swift. His own tense reaction to his pain was making it worse.

"You've got to relax or you're going to pass out," I said. "Here. Lie down." I gently pushed him forward. He leaned down, but still wouldn't press his stomach to the floor. He folded his arms under his face. He slowed his breathing a little.

I carefully ran my fingers from the crown of his skull to the base of his neck. "Let the pain drain away from your head," I told him.

I touched his forehead and dragged my hands lightly up his face, over his head, and down along the nape of his neck. The muscles in his neck and shoulders began to relax. His pulse slowed. His breathing regulated. I waited a few minutes at his side, knowing he would be fine. The aching in my own head seemed to evaporate as well. I stroked his head, neck, and shoulders. Then I rubbed the underside of his ribs, especially on the right side where I'd kicked him the hardest. My side ceased to ache. He seemed to return to normal as well. I patted his back to let him know he'd be all right. I stood gingerly on my toes and went back to where I'd left my boots.

Alaban rolled up. He sat wiping sweat from his face. He peered at me with uncertainty. Without anger, without a vengeful tone or disappointment, Alaban said, "You're incredible. Your psychic power is twice as good as mine."

I regarded him dubiously. "I think I just got a lucky start."

"You threw me four times," he said in disbelief, lifting himself to stand. "That's more than luck. You're good."

I thanked him modestly. I fastened my boots and levitated myself with only my toes touching the floor. I tiptoed toward the door. We moved to sit in the stairs of the amphitheater closest to the lake to rest. He sat one step below me and to my right. We watched the glassy surface of the water for a few calming moments.

"Are you sure you're all right?" he asked me. He touched my ankle.

"Nothing's broken. How about you?"

"You cured me. Did Yalat teach you that?" he asked.

"No. My mother taught me. It's just a normal relaxation technique," I said.

Alaban narrowed his eyes at me. "Relaxation techniques don't heal broken ribs. I felt at least two of them crack when you kicked me. They hurt like hell, especially when you sat on them at the end. That's why I wanted to get you off of me so fast," he said with a grin. He arched an eyebrow at me.

"Are you sure they were broken?" I asked.

"Yeah." He looked into my eyes. "Wow. You're a healer and you didn't even know it."

I was taken aback. "Well, everyone has some healing ability. Besides, if I'm a healer, how come my feet still hurt so much? I could heal you, but I can't heal myself? I don't know how that works."

"Let me try, then," he said. He reached over and pulled my boots off my feet. "What did you do exactly?"

I told him I simply directed the pain away from its concentrated area.

He held my calf in one hand while he gently ran his fingers from the bottom of my foot, over my heel and up the back of my ankle. As he brought his hands together in the middle of my calf, the pain subsided. I looked at him in fascination.

"It worked," I said with an attentive grin.

He went through the same motions with my other foot. I stood up without any pain at all. I turned to Alaban in disbelief. I sat down again leaning forward on my feet. They were fine.

"Either we're both healers," he paused, "or you and I may have some sort of connection that not everyone has." He gazed at me from the corner of his slanted eye.

"I don't know," I said, still amazed. "Maybe we do have some kind of connection. You said you influenced my dreams. What did you do?"

He seemed flustered. "Not much, really. I was thinking of acupuncture the other day. I don't know why, but I thought it would be a cool experiment to send someone an image while they slept and then see if they'd remember it. I sent the image of acupuncture pins to you. I envisioned you sleeping and I willed a suggestion to your mind. I guess your brain took the idea and warped it into some kind of weird nightmare, but that wasn't my intention. What did you dream?"

I told him with detail exactly what I dreamed both times. When I described the second episode of the dream, he seemed transfigured. He looked worried. He paused for a minute, clenching his hands together.

"That's really gross. I don't know how you imagined something like that." He smirked.

I smiled a little. I asked what he thought the dreams meant.

"Maybe you dreamed of me putting pins in your eye because I was being mean to you the other day. Then I took them away because I was sorry for it. I acted like a jerk the other night. I'm sorry."

I patted him on the back. "Consider it forgotten."

He hooked his arm around my knee and leaned his head on it, looking away from me and out into the landscape. "I have to leave tomorrow morning, Sil, so I need to tell you everything tonight."

He let go of my knee and pulled himself up one step so that he sat shoulder to shoulder with me. He glanced at me and then stared into the distance. He seemed much older now. His manner was grave. He held my full attention.

"They're sending me to Jawlcheen. I'll be crewed with a Grey named Zank and a Furman named Ongeram. I haven't met them yet. All I know is our basic mission. I'm not supposed to tell anyone, but this information might help you. The Fitmalo government has bigger problems than we thought. There are five different major groups rebelling against the Prime Minister and his cabinet. If two or more of these groups were to consolidate, they would be powerful enough to overthrow him. It's unlikely that they would ever put their differences aside long enough to work together by their own choice. They need some outside influence."

"The Organization?" I asked. "Why would it be in our interest to overthrow the Fitmalo government?"

"They only gave me vague information about that, but it looks like the Fitmalos are planning to combine some of their government systems with Jawlcheen. Those two planets have been at a stalemate for centuries. I don't see Jawlcheen accepting a proposal like that. The Fitmalos would have to muscle their way in."

"It's illegal to force any kind of intergovernmental consolidation. Fitmalo's government would be seized and audited by the U.G.," I said. I thought of the biological weapon Yalat had guessed about from the twentieth floor. If she was right about Lock, he might want the weapon to blackmail his political opponents into consolidation agreements. If this were true, and if the Organization knew it, then it would make sense to support the rebelling Fitmalo parties to undermine him. This explanation seemed too simple, however.

Alaban thought about this for a moment. "You're right. I don't understand it all, but I'll learn more about what's going on when I'm on assignment. I'm on covert espionage and research. I guess you'll be given the same thing, just not in the same place. I wish we could work together. We'd make a good team."

I grinned. I took his hand in mine and squeezed. He seemed surprised. He took my hand in both of his for a moment. An awkward silence ensued. I pulled my hand from his.

"So what happened in your interrogation?" I asked finally.

"They kept me a long time because of the bomb. They didn't believe I walked right into Jiao's office and got it. That shield orb was his, too. It's a good thing he had that orb. Otherwise you and Yalat would have been covered with spider guts."

I wrinkled my nose at the idea. "How did you get into Jiao's office in the first place? He's a weapons specialist. His office has to be locked with a lot of different codes. What did you do?"

"I see numbers. I know the code for any lock just by looking at it. Computer encoding is a little tougher, but I can do that, too. It just comes to me. Did you ever wonder how I knew the code for the sparring room? I didn't know it before I saw the lock. I couldn't even tell you what the code is now. But if we walk back over there, I'll open it. I've always been able to see numbers and codes. That's what got me into this business."

I shook my head at him. "You just get more and more talented by the minute. I'm sorry you have to leave tomorrow. I'll miss you. You've been a good friend these past few days."

He viewed me with obvious skepticism. A hint of a flattered smile invaded his face.

Chapter 10: The Decoded Dream

"Yalat, if you don't mind, I'd like to speak with you alone for a few minutes," Alaban said seriously.

"All right. Sil, why don't you go bathe and change while we chat?" she suggested. She shut down her palm computer and left it on the table to listen to him.

I obeyed my tutor and changed quickly into my traveling uniform. I felt more and more melancholy as I dressed. The idea of being separated from Alaban so soon began to affect me. It would have been wonderful to work with him, as he had suggested, but no two rookies were ever placed on the same job together. It went against Organization policy. I knew he felt guilty for his behavior the other night. I wanted to make sure he knew I'd forgiven him. The incident was forgotten as far as I was concerned. Apart from his drunken foolishness the other night, he had been my close friend, one I could rely on to cheer me up during the long journey that awaited us. I wished sadly that he didn't have to leave in the morning.

After my bath, I found Yalat alone at the table. She wore the same melancholic expression on her face as I'd seen on myself in the mirror just moments before. Alaban was gone. I asked about him.

"He'll return soon," she said. "He told me about his assignment. Don't worry. I know not to mention it to anyone. He also told me about the healing. I knew about that before, but had never used it. We all have healing ability, but you must know that the more you use it, the more energy and life you expend from yourself. That is why the skill is never taught to students."

"I had no idea," I said.

"It's not a standard practice of ours. The species that are best at healing are the Torreons. Since they have such a very long life cycle and an abundant source of rejuvenating energy, the healings don't seem to affect them as much. Now that you know about it, I'm sure you'll be careful with it."

"Yes, of course," I said. I sat down next to her. Our mood lightened a bit.

Soon Alaban returned clean and well groomed. He wore his travel uniform like us. He was beginning to look like a real soldier. His face was serious. His jaw set. Yalat commented that he looked ready to take up the warrior's challenge. Alaban thanked her for the compliment.

"Tomorrow I leave on assignment for Jawlcheen," Alaban said resignedly.

"Tomorrow—I almost forgot. Tomorrow I hear my final statements. I hope we can see each other before you leave. I wouldn't feel right without saying goodbye," I said, giving him a sad smile.

He glanced at me, and then quickly looked down at his hands. "I have to be at the ascension tower at ten-thirty. I'll look for you before I go."

I conceded softly.

He glanced nervously at Yalat. "What I asked you about...Do you remember...?"

"Who carried Sil back to our room when she passed out? Yes, I remembered just now," Yalat intoned.

I sat straight. I hadn't asked how I'd been brought back to my room. "Someone carried me here after the test?" I asked incredulously.

Yalat held up one index finger. "Oh, yes. I'd forgotten to tell you about that. Yes. After you fell unconscious from your vision, no one else seemed to know what to do about it except me. Sub Professor Ocelot was the first one to come to our aid, so I asked him to carry you. I'd forgotten his name until just now." She noticed the amazement on my face. "Well, you didn't expect me to levitate you all the way up here, did you?"

"I...I didn't think about it. I was too affected by that vision," I stuttered. I felt repulsed by the idea that such a horrible person had touched me. I felt infected with evil, wishing I could bathe again to wash away any of his remaining germs.

"That must have been some powerful vision to knock you out like that. What was it?" Alaban asked intently.

I shook my head sadly. "I don't want to remember it. It was more terror than I ever wanted to see."

Alaban took my hand in his. "Don't worry about it." He invited me to walk with him.

"Yes. Why don't you? Go enjoy each other's company for a while," Yalat chimed in, adding that we wouldn't see each other for a long time. She gave Alaban a wink and a nod.

Alaban smiled a little. He bowed.

I looked to Yalat, who waved her claws at me, shooing me out. I suspected a friendly conspiracy between them, but was glad for the distraction to forget about the wicked professor. So I went along with it.

In the hallway, Alaban grabbed my hand. "I have an idea," he said. "Let's go to my room and reenact your dreams. Then maybe you'll figure out what they mean."

I laughed at the strange idea. "What about Trau?"

"Trau's been ordered to stay in Building One for questioning," Alaban said with a satisfied smile. "The guards came for him today. They said he wouldn't be back to this building. He took his things with him."

"I guess Trau is one person you won't miss," I said, wondering just how brutal he'd been to him.

"You're right. Let's not talk about him," Alaban said.

We went to his dormitory. Alaban's traveling box sat at the foot of the bed, already packed. His room was identical to mine. He invited me to make myself at home. I thanked him, but remained standing, each of us feeling awkward.

"Well, I don't have a red uniform or a box of pins, but we can just go through the motions and fake it. What do you say?" He grinned with a shrug.

I couldn't help but smile at him. He had such a likeable manner about him that set me at ease. I agreed with a laugh as I crawled onto his bed and lifted my legs to sit straight. I explained where we had been in my dream. He sat facing me with his feet on the floor.

"So what did I do, start poking you with pins?" He smiled, making tiny stabbing motions over me.

I smiled back, feeling somewhat silly. "Yes, sort of, but every time you stuck me with a pin, you'd leave it there and look me in the eye, like you wanted to see my reaction to it."

He made a face. "That's creepy. Why would you dream of me torturing you like that?"

"I don't know. Let's find out." I lay back on the bed as if frozen, as in the dream.

He pretended to stab me with a pin, snickering at the silliness of it. I propped myself up on my elbows and admitted this probably wouldn't work. It was too absurd. He protested, however, asking for another chance. He promised to try and be serious about it. I agreed to one more try. I lay back again, watching him with a smirk. He closed his eyes, cleared his throat, and stretched his neck to prepare for his acting performance. Then, with forced seriousness, he played out the process of withdrawing a pin from an invisible box. He pretended to press it through my abdomen, checking my face and raising one eyebrow for approval. I nodded, feeling my cheeks draw up in a wanton smile. He smirked a little. He repeated the action. Again he moved the imaginary pin to my abdomen. He stared at me, this time with piercing eyes. He pretended to bring the pin toward my face as if to stab my eye. I thought of a psychological explanation.

"You want control. You're trying to take control of my thoughts," I blurted.

He stopped moving the invisible pin. He sucked in air with a whistle as he dropped his arm to his side. "Human psychology. Very good. I like that." He stared into my eyes intently. "But I don't want to control you. I just want your attention. I want you to focus on me."

I regarded him kindly. "All right. I will."

He smiled. Then he returned to our play. "What next?"

"In the next dream, you were sad. You put all the pins back in their box."

"I'm sorry I tried to control you," he stated immediately.

"Do you think that's all it means?"

"I know exactly what it means. But I'm not giving you the answers. You have to figure it out yourself. I'm just helping you act it out," he said, his smile fading to pleasant insecurity.

I knitted my brow at this, but continued directing the act. Just as in the dream, he put the pins away, pretending to pull them off me and drop them into an imaginary box in his lap. I mentioned the incessant knocking at the door. I asked Alaban who he thought it was, but he only shook his head and asked me to go on.

When I'd finished the details, he stood by the bedside, staring at the door as if it led to an unwanted future. Then he acted out the scene so well, it was almost as if he'd seen the dream himself. He pointed to the door.

"Let them wait," he growled, glaring at the door. Then he threw the imaginary box at the wall and made sound effects to go with it. He spread his hands out toward the floor to indicate the pins falling.

He glared at the door. "I know! I know! Shut up! I know!" he spouted. He looked frustrated. I shuddered from his uncanny representation.

"Okay, I'm looking around," he said as he walked around the room. He pretended to search for something.

"You're looking for an escape route," I realized.

He stopped and looked at me. "You're right. But I can't find one." He froze in a paused step toward the bathroom.

"The people behind the door want to come in and get you?"

"No. I wouldn't be looking for an escape route then. I'd be ready to fight." He left the act to stand purposefully in the center of the room. He coaxed my reasoning. "Why am I looking for a way out?"

"Is it Trau? You want to get away from him?"

"No." He rolled his eyes and shook his head. "You're thinking entirely of me, which I like, but it's confusing you. Who else is here?" His eyes smiled kindly.

"Me? It's someone coming for me. That's why you were looking for an escape route. You wanted to save me from someone."

He nodded, but then shook his head. "Yes and no."

"It's someone who's coming to take me away? Is it someone I'll be assigned to work with?" I asked him. I wedged my elbows into the bed to prop myself up.

He nodded solemnly. "The Organization. Our generals. Your crew. They'll take you away. They'll separate us. We won't see each other for a long time. They want to keep us apart. That's why I'm angry."

"Why would they want to keep us apart? Why would they care?" I asked in confusion.

"We'd be too powerful together. Can you imagine your power and mine together on the same team? There's nothing we couldn't accomplish. We'd put the older warriors to shame. We're easier to manipulate when we're apart. I asked to be assigned to your crew. The General said no way."

I sat abruptly. "And he told you that?" I took this to heart. "Maybe you're right. With our powers together, they'd want to use us for really dangerous missions. They couldn't justify placing a pair of rookies on top level security assignments."

"That's one way of looking at it. I think there's more to it than that." He stopped. He gave me a strange look and shook his head. "I'm getting off track here. Let's finish this dream of yours first. Then we'll talk about something else," he suggested.

I agreed. He asked me what he had said again at the end of the dream. I told him, adding that he'd seemed sad when he said it. I couldn't understand why. I glanced at him with uncertainty as I lay back down. He stood leaning on the wall. He crossed his arms. He became pensive for a moment. I began to think maybe he preferred not to act out the last part of it, or if he did, that it would turn into a joke. But then he returned to sit by me at the bed. He picked me up, just as in the dream. He took me by one arm and slid his other hand under the back of my head. Only this time, he pulled me up slowly and carefully. He gazed into my eyes, not with a mischievous stare, but with a hypnotic one. He seemed to be trying to communicate visually with my very soul. I tried to read the meaning in his eyes, but then he gently pushed my head to his shoulder. He hugged me lightly.

I wondered where he was going with this new seriousness. He carefully touched my face with his hand. He caressed my cheek softly but intently just as in the dream. He traced the line of my cheekbone upward to my temple and brushed my hair back a little. He repeated the action. Then he traced the cheekbone and the outer part of my ear. Ticklish sensations skated over my ear and then the side of my neck and under my jaw. He did this a few more times, tracing a little more carefully into the ear each time. I tensed. A knot formed in my stomach.

Then he began to speak to me, his voice as soft and inviting as his touch.

"Hold on," he whispered. He began to breathe more heavily. He swallowed hard as he rocked me gently. "Promise me, Sil. Promise you'll hold on to me. I'm sorry if I ever hurt you or offended you. You mean so much to me."

A warm, tingling sensation invaded my face and hands. My heart rate increased. My breathing became shallower. The strokes of his hand on my face grew more and more caring and arousing.

"Why am I holding you like this? Why is there no escape for me?"

I consciously fought against his hypnotic act. I forced myself to think. "You don't want us to be separated, but there's no way to avoid it. You're sad that you won't be around to protect me."

"You don't need protecting. You're more powerful than I am. You're just as gifted as me."

"No, Alaban. You were always the most gifted," I said shakily.

"Sh. Sh. You know the answer. You just don't want to say it. You're too shy. You can tell me. You won't be telling me anything I don't already know. I want to hear you say it."

He held me close. He stroked my face and my hair. He rocked me gently. I felt him kiss the top of my head.

"You…" I trailed off. My ears began to burn. My eyes felt glassy. He stopped caressing my face and rubbed my back and sides instead. One of his hands glided over the side of my breast. "You're attracted to me. You want me as a mate," I spoke hesitantly.

"Mmm. You're getting closer." He kissed the top of my head and caressed the back of my neck. "That's not my only motivation. If I want you for my mate, it's more than just attraction. This runs deeper. You know it. Tell me. What do I feel for you?"

I faltered at his inquisition. As his truth crept into my heart, I resisted it. Logically, it was too difficult to believe. We had only been together for a few short days since our separation. How could he have fallen for me in such a short time? Why would he feel so certain as to persuade me to believe it?

"Hold on to me, Sil," he whispered. "Hold on to me forever. You know what I feel for you. What do I feel, Sil? You can say it. I want to hear it from you. It doesn't matter if you feel less for me. Just guess how I feel and I'll be happy. I want you to know it, Sil. Say it."

I began to shake. Alaban hugged me and waited patiently for the shivering to subside. I hugged him tightly. He returned the squeeze and sighed. He ran his hands up and down my spine. He kissed my shoulder. He kissed my neck. He brushed the side of my face with his lips. I finally regained my breath after a series of shudders.

"Tell me," he whispered intently.

"You love me," I said finally.

He pulled away to gaze into my eyes gratefully.

"I love you with all my heart and soul. I know you only think of me as a friend. If I had more time to spend with you I'd change your mind, but we don't have any more time. Not like this. But I'm not giving up. I'll message you every chance I get and I know I'll see you again soon." He brought his hand to my chin and stared at me with glazed eyes. "Maybe the next time we meet you'll feel the same for me." He leaned forward to kiss my cheek, and then my lips.

I didn't know what to say or how to feel. I did love him as a close friend, but not as a mate. His physical chemistry didn't attract me. And yet I felt so many confusing emotions for him. His touch was alluring. His words unlocked an ecstatic feeling in my body.

We embraced each other again. He kissed me around my ear and jaw. Arousal took over. Suddenly I found myself kissing back. Alaban pressed passionately into my mouth, in a way I had not expected. He pushed me backward onto the bed and lay partly on top of me. He moved a hand over my body. I pushed him away.

"No. I can't. This isn't right," I cried.

He let go in disappointment. "It's okay. I won't. I won't touch you if you don't want me to." He moved away from me a little.

I bolted up out of the bed. "I'm sorry, I shouldn't have done that." I backed away from him as if he were a mortal threat to me.

At the bathroom sink, I splashed cold water on my face and rubbed my eyes. I calmed myself as much as possible. I looked at my face in the mirror. My cinnamon skin now appeared rouged and shiny. My eyelashes matted with water. I sighed heavily. I patted my face lightly with a towel. My shoulders felt heavy. My eyes ached.

I turned to find Alaban leaning on the doorway, looking forlorn. He moved aside to let me pass. I walked past him and sat at the edge of the bed. I stared down at the base of the opposite wall. Tentatively, he sat next to me.

I hooked my arm around his and leaned on his shoulder. "I'm sorry, Alaban."

"What are you thinking?" he asked softly.

"I'm not sure what to think," I replied. "I feel close to you, but I can't care for you in the same way and it's not fair. It's not fair to you. You deserve love. There's just something missing from us. I do love you as a dear friend. I just can't stretch that and turn it into something it's not. I feel guilty. I want you to be happy."

Alaban closed his eyes and nodded. He reached out for my hand and kissed it.

"Don't feel sorry for me. That's the last thing I need. I just wanted you to know how much I love you. When we're far out in space and it seems like no one knows you're alive, I want you to think of me. I'll always think of you. I've never forgotten you since we were in school together. When you're ready to start choosing a mate, I want you to think of me first. I know you and I love you more than any other man ever will. Will you do that for me? Just consider me." He rubbed my hand in his. "We're both powerful. Together we would be the envy of all the humans in the galaxy. Imagine what kind of children we'd have. They'd be super powerful." He grinned, lifting my chin. "And they'd have their mother's good looks."

I grinned back, half-heartedly. He read my thoughts.

"I know you don't want a mate yet, but when you do…"

"I'll think of you first," I promised him.

He entwined his fingers with mine and thanked me. He explained that he had challenged me to spar because he wanted to see if I'd be able to take care of myself out in the world. He was glad to know I could. Then he gave me sad news. He had spoken with his contact general about his job. He was advised that he would soon be called upon for assassination work. He felt bad about it, but he hoped it would only be a short-term duty. He asked me not to hold his work against him. He promised to get out of it as soon as he could.

I leaned close to him and told him I understood. I was saddened to hear this, but was not surprised by it. Alaban's ability to get into any code-locked area together with his martial skill made him a perfect candidate for the work. We hugged each other again. We sat quietly for several minutes like this.

"It's late. You have to hear your final statements in the morning," he reminded.

I pulled away from him to check the clock. It was 2308. "You're right, but I don't want to leave you right now."

He stood, pulling my hand. "Come on. If you stay here much longer, I'll have to start kissing on you again." He smiled a little. "I'll see you tomorrow after your final statements. I won't have much time then, but at least we can say goodbye properly. Besides, you're going to need your beauty sleep if you're going to look good for your testing committee in the morning." He paused reflectively. "I wish I'd been there to carry you home instead of that sub professor."

"Me, too," I admitted with a nervous frown.

"You have a bad feeling about him. I don't blame you. He's one of the men behind the door in your dream." Alaban said.

"Sub Professor Ocelot?" I asked.

Alaban nodded. "He's on your crew."

"Oh, no," I muttered. Within my mind, the visionary shards plunged into my surging waves of fear. A report of distant thunder confirmed the eminent danger of a tempest ahead. This sub professor was sure to guide our ship into it.

"Don't worry," Alaban said. "If he or anyone else ever treats you badly, just let me know. I'll show him what the gifted guy can do."

He thrust a fist at the thick stone wall and cracked it five ways all the way to the ends of the wall in some directions and from floor to ceiling in the other direction.

His demonstration distracted my anxiety. "You're very strong, Alaban. In a few years, you'll be even stronger. I won't have to worry about you out among the enemies. They'll all be afraid of you."

"That's okay, as long as you won't be afraid of me."

"I won't be," I vowed, taking his hand gratefully into mine.

Alaban walked me back to my door. I gave him one kiss on the mouth. He hugged me to him tightly. When he released me, he told me he loved me, but covered my lips with his fingers to prevent me from answering him back. He stroked my hair and then backed away, watching me disappear into my doorway. He returned to his room alone.

Chapter 11: Congratulations and Goodbye

That night, I dreamed little. I only remembered one piece of a dream. Alaban and I sat at the edge of his bed. We held each other loosely. He kissed my forehead and my cheek. Then he tucked his face between my jaw and my shoulder resignedly.

The knocking began at the door. This time the door opened. A group of dark figures stood at the doorway. Sub Professor Ocelot entered the room. He wore a combat uniform and was fully armed. He glanced at us briefly and then walked over to the center of the wall, which was still cracked dramatically from Alaban's powerful punch. He placed his hand on the indentation of Alaban's fist. The wall snapped back into its original flat surface. He glanced at us again with disdain, as if blaming us for the damage he'd repaired. Then he left. The other men did not enter. They followed him away from the door. Despite my fears, I felt it was my duty to follow them, but I also wanted to stay with Alaban.

Alaban sat straight. He took my hands, kissed them, and then stood up, pulling to make me stand with him. He turned me around and gently pushed me away from him towards the door.

"Go," he said.

I looked out the doorway. It was now an exterior door. Through it I saw a heavy rain and darkness. I looked back at Alaban. He crossed his arms and looked down at the floor.

"Go," he repeated.

I awoke filled with sadness. I hoped to see Alaban as soon as possible, not to tell him about the dream, but to hug him to me and feel his presence one last time before he had to leave. I missed him already. Perhaps he was right about changing my mind with time. Deep in my heart I did feel something for him, but now was not the time to entertain personal feelings. Everything was happening so fast: my examination, the spider, the Fitmalo case, the vision, and now Alaban's heart. This overwhelming mixture of events affected my well-being. I needed time to refocus. Perhaps after I began my new job things would settle down in my life.

When the official escort came to our door, Yalat and I followed him to the elevator. Alaban was in the hallway, standing at his door. He did not approach us, but gave me a longing gaze and held his fist over his heart. He smiled weakly. I placed one hand over my heart in reply. I waved to him as I boarded the elevator.

Yalat regarded me with sympathy. Maybe she knew. Maybe Alaban had told her. I sighed and straightened my stance. I was about to face all my judges at once, including Ocelot. I resolved not to look at him in the face this time. I didn't want to see any visions like the one I'd suffered before. I hoped desperately that the disastrous terror I'd seen in the shards had not been of unchangeable future events caused by him. I did believe, however, that he would be directly involved with the projected horrors. And to work with a man so cursed would bring me suffering, I knew.

The guard escorted us to the same room where I had performed my personal defense test. I stood in the center of the room as before. Yalat took her seat at the side. The entire committee of twenty professors sat at a curved table, which spanned the length of the room.

Professor Marced, the translucent Torreon, spoke first. "Welcome to your final statements meeting. On the academics test, you only missed four engineering questions and one aerospace question. We found your knowledge and attitude very acceptable. We commend you for your studies."

"Thank you, sir," I said as I bowed to his section, surprised at my score. The last minute practice with Yalat had paid off. But had I passed the whole examination?

Teffen, the Grey spoke next. "The levitation committee agrees that despite the unusual and *life-threatening* experience we witnessed from your test, your levitative abilities surpass any we have witnessed in our collective lives. You have a true gift, one we hope you may use to defend yourself and others and never in a thoughtless manner in the future."

"I give you my word, sir," I said solemnly. My heart swelled. I had passed the levitation test.

Ongeram the Furman was the next to speak. "Those of us on your basic skills committee commend you on your bravery and your ability work in a team. We all know of your experience with the spider. I believe you will be a great warrior."

"Thank you, sir," I answered. I must have passed the whole exam.

Redet spoke next. "Sil, on behalf of the personal defense committee, I must say your performance was truly beautiful."

I *had* passed!

"Reading from my notes here, the reactions from the judges were, and I quote, 'most graceful performance by a human,' 'truly powerful as well as graceful,' 'practically flawless,' 'so well-timed, the performance was almost hypnotic,' and one judge even called it, 'awe-inspiring.' We thought it was truly wonderful."

I had passed with excellent scores! I lifted my face towards the ceiling, closed my eyes, and said a quick prayer of thanks.

"In fact, we'd like to ask you if you wouldn't mind performing form twenty-nine for us right now so the whole panel may see you," Redet continued happily.

I was so overjoyed I'd that I nearly stalled at her statement. This was a highly unusual request, but none of the other judges refused or made any motion against the proposal. I bowed and walked to the center of the room where I assumed a ready stance. I breathed deeply to calm my excitement and concentrate.

"Begin when ready," Redet spoke.

I stepped forward, crossing both arms downward. Then I stepped with a double high block. I changed my stance to follow with an uppercut and simultaneous knee lift on the right. I flipped backwards, twisting and whirling into a low scissor kick. After this came the horizontal levitative whirl, an upward swan, and an upside-down rotating split. I landed with a back flip and glided into a triple palm strike. I dipped my head down in front of me and did a side flip. I threw a forward palm strike with the right and a back fist behind me to the left. I landed on one knee, throwing a double block forward, and then whisked my legs in front of me to fell my imaginary opponent.

I leapt skyward in a whirl, tucking my elbows to my ribs and holding out my forearms and fists to the sides. I curled myself in midair, rolling upward and away from my audience. I fell feet-first towards the floor, arms raised above me. Before hitting the ground, I thrust a ridge hand and low roundhouse kick to the right. I battered the falling invisible opponent with a left front kick to the stomach. Then I twisted him into submission with a double knee clamp around his head, flinging him to the floor. I then levitated myself to the left, guided by an elbow. I followed the momentum of the move and strafed backward to plant a heel between another opponent's feet. I swiveled my body and grabbed high, pulling down to bring a knee to his face. I swirled to fell the imaginary foe. I spun skyward again, flipping upside down to face the back of an opponent's head. I gave two knife hand strikes at his neck and then completed the flip, kicking the air squarely in the back.

I twirled my legs, levitating myself in a vertical whirl. At the top of this whirl, I changed to a backward swan, quickly overturning into a wide spread strike of all arms and legs. I pranced down to the floor and did five consecutive windmills, ending in a double tornado kick. I threw an uppercut and an elbow with the left, and then a jab with the right.

I leaned right, placing one hand on the ground and kicking high with both feet. I let my body fall near the floor and whirled horizontally, almost touching the ground. I lifted myself toward the ceiling and did a toe touch at the height of the climb. I fell to the right in a lateral flip and ended this move by grabbing the invisible enemy around the torso with both legs, and around the throat and head with both arms. I shot myself upward, releasing the foe into the air with an imaginary crack of the neck.

The other moves in this form were repetitions of the same types of moves starting from the left instead of the right. I ended the form at the ready stance. Finally I stood at attention and bowed to the judges.

A hearty round of applause sounded from the tables. Honored to enjoy such approval from a group like this, I stood at attention, but kept my eyes down. The applause continued for a minute. I glanced at Yalat, who nodded and clapped with pride.

Redet clucked for attention from the group. The applause subsided.

"After such a show of ability, I'm sure our panel members will want to say a few words. If any of you would like to make a statement, please wait to be recognized." She paused for a moment. "Yes, Professor Jiao."

Jiao spoke. "I'm sure you know it was a mistake to bring the microship into the building. I'm only glad I was present to disarm the device. Always consider the danger to yourself and others before you act."

I bowed solemnly. "Yes, sir. That was a lesson I'll not forget. I owe you my life and the life of my tutor." I knelt on one knee in reverence.

"Stand at attention. There is no need to kneel. I was glad to be of service," Jiao said.

I rose to my feet again as ordered, but still kept my head down.

"Professor Parsh may speak," Redet said.

"Sil, this mistake has given you humility, but please keep your balance of self-esteem. It is best to never be too proud nor too humble," she said.

I bowed.

"Professor Ongeram," Redet announced.

"Your performance today makes me understand how you could win a sparring match against my new partner, Alaban Jetscuro. He is swift and powerful, but you have greater precision in your flow of energy and psychic power. Professor Pauber told me about your match. I would not have believed it without seeing you perform here today. I congratulate you."

"Thank you, sir," I said.

"I would like to say something to you as a female," Redet interjected. "Apart from being highly skilled and intelligent, you are also a lovely young woman. On your journey through life as a warrior, you will be in contact with males who will not appreciate or respect you as an individual. They will only see you as a healthy member of the opposite sex and a possible mate. They will say and do things to offend you. Please remember to cause them bodily harm only if they become aggressive. Remember that their taunts and threats mean nothing. They are to be considered as simple innocents until they touch you. If they do, aggressively, you may be obligated to seriously injure them. I am sure your tutors have mentioned this to you before."

"Yes, ma'am. I will only use physical defense in reaction to a physical threat. I will try to avoid an attack, but if it happens, I must defend my own life first."

"Very well. Professor Stennet?"

"I would like to know how you are able to move objects through each other without changing their molecular structure," Stennet said.

"Actually, sir, only one object needs to be moved on a molecular level. I spread the molecules out to make a path for the second object. Once the second object passes through the first one, I move the first object back to its original form. It takes a great deal of concentration and practice. It also drains my power quickly."

He raised his eyebrows and nodded in consideration.

"Professor Omeh," Redet called.

"Are you often prone to such debilitating visions as the one you experienced after your personal defense test?"

"No, sir. I have visions often, but I had never seen one so powerful before. I apologize for my behavior. I thank those of you who were concerned for my health. I especially thank Sub Professor Ocelot for taking the time to help return me to my room," I offered, dutifully. No one responded. I wondered if perhaps he had bowed or nodded in my direction.

Redet declared an end to individual statements. Professor Jiao asked for the honor of awarding me my title pin. I stepped forward to his place at the table. He fastened the gold pin to my uniform just above my left collarbone. I bowed and thanked him again as the committee applauded.

There was a shuffle of chairs and a movement of committee members. Some came to congratulate me. Others moved complacently toward the door. Yalat congratulated me with a hug. She then went to mingle with the other Lizards on the committee.

Professor Parsh approached me. She held my right hand in both of her right hands and my left in both of her left hands. Her iridescent green eyes glistened as she commended me. She then gave me her blessing.

"May you always use your talents for the good of others and may God bless you with many followers and friends. May you be protected from evil. May your heart guide you and may your mind be alert to check your heart and body. Peace be with you, my young sister."

"Thank you. That's very beautiful, Professor," I breathed.

She continued. "Whatever you do in your life, I'm sure you will make the best decision for yourself and your loved ones."

I considered this and nodded thoughtfully. She lifted my hands and bowed to me. She smiled sweetly as she moved away.

Professors Jiao and Stennet were the next to approach. Professor Stennet shook my hand. He invited Yalat and me to dinner at his house in the Public Valley. He advertised his wife's good cooking. He also said his daughter would like to meet me. She was a young, aspiring warrior, too. I told them I couldn't speak for Yalat, but I would be honored to accept their invitation. We arranged to meet at the airbuses by the ascension tower at five o'clock.

"I'll be glad to see you this evening," Jiao said with a smile. He squeezed my arm lightly. He bowed and walked away with his father.

I moved toward Yalat to ask her if the dinner invitation would be all right, but I saw Ocelot heading for her as well. I turned on a heel and made for the door. As I hastened out towards the elevator I collided with Alaban just as he rounded the corner to look for me.

We laughed at our accident. Alaban touched my title pin and congratulated me. He kissed me on the cheek and hugged me tight, lifting me up off the ground. He set me down again. He took my hand. He offered to buy me something to celebrate since he was now on salary. He flashed his money card.

"Let me buy you a drink—not alcohol. I know how you feel about that," he said.

"That sounds great," I said, squeezing his hand.

Ongeram and Omeh boarded the elevator with us. They raised their eyebrows and chuckled about us holding hands, but Alaban pretended not to notice. He gazed at me with affection.

When we arrived at the third floor, we strode out quickly to the café. Alaban ordered some tall ice drinks for us. We sat near the garden and sipped the sweet pink liquid. We didn't say as much as we had on our minds. We talked about my final statements meeting. He was impressed that they'd asked me to perform form twenty-nine again for them.

"I wish I could have been there. I'm sure you were great. What I'd really like to see is that Tambuo dancing you used to do on Liricos. Those jingling miniskirts are...inspirational," he said, grinning and giving me a wink.

I smiled. I told him about the dinner invitation from Stennet and Jiao.

"Be careful with Jiao. He may have saved your life, but I'll bet he's looking for something in return," Alaban spoke jealously.

I shook my head and smiled. "I'm not interested in Jiao," I said. "I'm more interested in you."

After gazing into each other's eyes for a few moments, he asked me to walk with him to the ascension tower. We walked arm in arm all the way to the tower. We didn't speak much, but Alaban said as we passed the amphitheater that he really liked this planet and that he hoped to someday come back to it. I agreed it was nice.

At the ascension tower, we saw Ongeram and Zank loading supply boxes on a tram along with a black Lizard pilot. Alaban went to help them. When the tram was full, the two senior officers sat at the front and said something to Alaban about the time. Then they whisked away toward their ship, leaving Alaban alone with me.

"I have to go now," he said sadly. He came close and kissed my forehead. "I love you. I'll message you when I can. Maybe if we keep in touch, the next time you see me you'll learn to love me back."

I nodded. I took his face in my hands and looked deep into his eyes.

"There will always be a place in my heart for you. Good luck, Alaban." I pulled him to me and kissed him goodbye in the way he deserved. I felt dishonest about kissing him this way, but at the same time I felt he understood. We exchanged a few heartfelt goodbyes. He turned and ran toward his ship as I called after him to stay safe. I watched him sadly.

I walked in loneliness to Building Three. Soon I would have to leave Yalat as well. Then I would truly be alone. The part of my life that was dependent youth was now ending. A new chapter was beginning. I marched forward to face it.

Chapter 12: Assassination

I found Yalat in our room, reading information on her palm computer. She still researched the Fitmalo mystery. I ventured to interrupt her, asking what Alaban had said to her last night while I was bathing.

Yalat seemed uneasy. "He said he felt you would soon be in grave danger and that I should look for Sub General Wilbaht to help you. Isn't that strange?"

I blinked in surprise. "That's not what I expected. What kind of danger?"

"He didn't know. He asked me not to tell you unless you asked," she said. "I spoke with Sub General Wilbaht by messaging this morning. Oddly enough, he already knew who you are and that you've been testing here this week."

I shook my head. "Things get stranger around here by the minute. Did Alaban say anything else about me or himself?"

"Ahem. Well, yes. He said he loves you dearly and would someday like to ask you to be his wife! Do you believe that? The boy is too young to be thinking along those lines, I say. Did he tell you that, too?"

"Yes, but I told him I only love him as a friend. I felt bad for him. Now I'm not sure how to feel."

"You did the right thing, Sil. Don't worry about him. I'm sure he will be fine. I dreamed of him last night. I think it was a premonition. I saw he was a general! He seemed very happy."

I took her reassurance to heart, hoping her vision would come true.

As five o'clock approached, we strode out into the warm afternoon to meet Jiao and Stennet at the ascension tower. They greeted us formally and then showed us to our vehicle. The airbus was so small that the cabin looked like a tiny living room area. Yalat and I took the rear seat. Jiao and Stennet took the seat facing us. We made polite conversation while we waited for the pilot to start takeoff procedures. He stepped up to our open door to greet us. He said his name was Rol and that we'd take off in three minutes. He reached up above him to pull down and secure our door and then boarded the cockpit.

The engines sang as we lifted upward, but then we touched back down. We all looked toward the pilot questioningly through the short window between the cabin and cockpit. He shut down completely and got out. He came back around to our door. We wondered if the airbus had some mechanical failure.

Rol lifted open the door. "I'm sorry for the delay, folks. U.G. military has ordered me to allow three more passengers. You may wait for the next airbus or continue with us. They should be here any minute."

Stennet looked annoyed. Jiao whispered something to his father, who nodded. Yalat and I looked at each other.

"It must be an interrogation transfer," Yalat whispered to me. "Sometimes the interrogations generals hold small airbuses to transport informants."

I looked up at Rol, a Torreon. He seemed anxious to get going. Stennet and Yalat agreed to stay on this flight, mostly out of curiosity rather than time-consciousness. Rol bowed gratefully and apologized again for the inconvenience.

From the ascension tower lobby we saw a copper-brown Arborman guard followed by two humans in traveling uniforms. I almost gasped when I saw who they were. Behind the Arborman trudged the infamous Professor Trau. Tired and angry, he held his wrists together in an electrostatic binder. I instantly assumed he had been positively linked to some kind of Fitmalo conspiracy. I wondered why they would allow such a prisoner to board a public airbus.

What was worse, following Trau was my visionary nemesis, Sub Professor Ocelot. I felt my heart sink to my stomach. The presence of either one of these men would have disturbed me, but both together were more than I was willing to handle at the moment. I thought quickly. There wasn't enough space on the empty seat to accommodate the three new passengers comfortably.

"Since I'm the youngest here, I should ride up front with the pilot. Excuse me," I announced, standing.

I quickly stepped out to the right cockpit door. I stood beside Rol, turning my back to the oncoming men. As they passed behind me, I asked Rol permission to sit in the cockpit with him. They boarded the airbus. I glanced over my shoulder to see Ocelot take seat next to Yalat where I'd been. Trau and the Arborman sat in the empty seat at the left of the airbus, facing the door.

The pilot first closed the cabin door, and then opened the right cockpit door for me. I thanked him and climbed in, relieved. I didn't know what the two groups of people in the passenger area would talk about, but I was glad not to be obligated to make small talk with them.

The pilot climbed into the left cockpit seat and started takeoff sequence again. The engines sang. We lifted off. The trees and lakes of the Sor3 landscape sank away below us. The hazy atmosphere cast a pale luminescence over the valley. I thought of Alaban and wondered when he would return to see this landscape again. I took in the serene view to calm my nerves.

We ascended the mountainside to the hammock peaks of the Public Valley. The city slowly came into view. We flew just below the thin cloud cover toward a brightly lit conglomerate of skyscrapers. The foundations of the towers carved deeper and deeper into the valley floor as we advanced over them. I admired the complexity of the cityscape. About two kilometers ahead of us, I spotted our proposed landing site: a marked flat roof decorated with strips of orange landing lights. The pilot slowed the airbus and inclined it toward its docking area.

"What's that?" the pilot asked, turning his head to look out the left window.

I glanced up at him and asked, "What?"

A bright light flashed. I turned away. A loud thud and a sound of ripping metal filled the cabin. The air around me thickened with a bright purple spray. A horrible cracking noise deafened me. Then I only heard a high-pitched ringing in my head. The airbus shuddered violently, but then continued smoothly.

I turned to view what had been our pilot. His chest and face splayed open in a grisly waste. The controls in front of him seared and sparked. His right hand still gripped the steering mechanism. His left hand had been decimated by the blast. The acrid smell of blood and ozone suddenly became pungent. I gaped in horror.

We still headed for the landing site. I realized the airbus would probably either explode from the high-speed impact or miss the platform and crash into the next tall skyscraper. I reached over to try and move what was left of the controls, but they were fried beyond use. I searched my door, but found no manual latch on the inside. I looked to the pilot's door. It was cooked and bubbled through the middle. The wall behind him shone through with exterior light.

I wrestled free from my seatbelt and turned to look out the small window between the cockpit and the passenger area. The left side of the cabin was ripped wide open. Trau and the Arborman were dead. Their mangled bodies gushed blood all over the floor and seat. The other passengers stood, speckled with the cadavers' blood, but appeared unharmed. They gathered at the right side door, probably planning to jump out that way as we approached the landing pad. But that door wouldn't open either. They would have to climb over the remains of Trau and the Arborman to jump out the left side.

I twisted back around to see the landing area. The roof was only a few meters distance from us, but we were coming in too high. If the four survivors in the back were to make their jump, they would have to levitate down to the landing pad roof.

I heard Yalat shout to me. "Jump, Sil!"

I turned to respond to her, but she had leapt out already. As we passed over the building, I watched the others take turns stepping between the two corpses. They bailed out one by one from the gaping hole. They would be all right. Now what about me?

I only had one option if I planned on living. I had to pass my own body through the front window.

The airbus cleared the landing roof and headed for a slightly shorter building about half a kilometer away. I concentrated hard on the window. It took too long to move the glass apart to make a hole big enough for me to fit through. Wind poured in through the hole and stung my eyes and throat. The oncoming rooftop raced toward me. I levitated out the window just as the nose of the airbus began to skid across the roof. I soared up and away from the crashing vehicle as fast as I could, but it wasn't enough. The airbus exploded just a few meters behind me, blasting me forward. The flames torched my back, clothes and hair. Spikes of hot metal and glass shot through my body. I careened toward a signal tower at the edge of the roof.

The tower bludgeoned the right side of my body. I felt the bones shatter in my right arm, shoulder, leg, and hip. Incredible pain jolted through me. The impact to the side sent me spinning off the edge of the roof like a whirling rag doll.

I fought to stay conscious as the city hurtled up at me. I used what remained of my energy to levitate over to the roof of the next building. I reached out to it with my left arm and pulled with all my might. I slowed my descent to land by a signal receiver pole. I grasped the pole, hugging it between my good arm and my face. I stood teetering on my left foot. I concentrated all my effort to hold onto the pole.

During my last years of training, I had learned to deal with different levels of pain, from muscle fatigue on week-long mountain climbs to sharp contusions from the blows of a wooden practice sword to swift kicks to the chest and abdomen in sparring. I had learned to contain my panic to control my physical response for self-defense and survival. But this pain was beyond any I had ever experienced. It passed my threshold of containment, invaded my consciousness. It challenged my will to live. With every beat of my heart, an inescapable wave of pain engulfed my body. A massive throb spread through me. It flared beyond tears or screams. This was a sample of pure hell brought to life in my own flesh. Only a shadow of strength remained in me. Hope wafted in and out of my consciousness.

All sound snuffed out. The city wavered before my eyes. I could only perceive my own heartbeat and the coursing pain. I gripped the pole between my hand and face. I wanted to keep my eyes open. If I closed them I might fall into oblivion. The city became a dark, swirling cloud.

"This isn't the death I wanted," I thought in mortal anguish. "Not now."

I felt a celestial presence around me. The spirits lingered with me, but did not gather me to them. At this moment, I knew Alaban was also with me, on a different level. He urged me to fight for life.

I didn't know how long I stood there. Time and pain battled each other within my own body. I felt myself gritting my teeth against them, but it did no good. I could only grip the pole and pray for an end. My spirit begged for comfort. My soul pleaded to step over into death, but God denied my plea. I had to live a little longer.

Colors and patterns changed before me. Something obstructed the city lights. It touched my face. I made an effort to focus my vision. A form blurred before me: a beige object with diagonal stripes of red and blue.

Something pulled at my crushed arm. Something else grabbed my broken hip. Someone slid pieces of glass and metal from my back. A hint of life seeped back into my body. I still couldn't hear anything, but my vision cleared slightly. The colors clarified. They were the front of someone's traveling uniform. I peered up to see a tall man with dark gray skin.

I finally closed my eyes and shuddered away from my body. I floated above the scene. I saw myself there at the pole. Sub General Wilbaht and Professor Sub General Channol withdrew pieces of metal from my body, which was painted red from head to foot.

The Torreons extruded metal and glass from my flesh, covering each wound with a long set of fingers. They drew out the injury with healing power. Another Torreon stepped in to assist.

The other four survivors gathered close by on the roof: Stennet and Jiao, Yalat and Ocelot. With them stood a variety of security and medical personnel. They all observed, spellbound and horrified, as the three Torreons performed their miracle on this gory body that I hardly recognized as my own.

I watched my body sag against the pole. My broken arm seemed to be fixed. My hip looked normal. A long splinter of metal pervaded my torso. It entered my back on the right side and exited between the ribs below the right breast. Wilbaht stood in front of me. Channol stood behind. They steadied my body between them while the third man slowly pulled out the spike. Suddenly I was sucked back into my body and into consciousness.

The renewed pain awakened my panic. I cried out weakly as I let go of the pole. I fell crumpled to the rooftop. The Torreons scooped me up and prodded the leaking wound. I gasped for air. The desire to live returned to me. As the pain ebbed, I fled into unconsciousness.

When I finally awoke, an entire day had passed. I found myself alone in my dormitory in Building Three. I sat up and was immediately overtaken by a dizzy spell. I lay down again. Next I tried to crawl to the bathroom. I flopped over onto the floor. My hands and knees shuffled sluggishly, but my body seemed to jolt along. I had to lie down in the doorway between the two rooms to catch my breath before going on. I went slowly through my bathroom routine. I crawled with difficulty to my bed again.

I noticed I was dressed in a gauze wrap from beneath my arms to the tops of my thighs. The medical personnel at the rooftop must have taken me to a local hospital. They had checked me over, cleaned me, and given me minimal clothing before releasing me to Yalat. I didn't know how I'd been returned to this room. I only knew I was back here and very thirsty. I peeled off the gauze and slipped on the first uniform I found. I went barefoot. I felt my head. My hair was wildly uneven at the back where it had been burned.

I carefully stood, clinging to the wall. I crept gingerly up the stairs to the small gallery and then to the dining area. I had to stop halfway up, panting and sweating from effort. I heard muffled voices coming from the dining area, but I couldn't make out who was speaking or what they said. My hearing was still affected from the crash, but my pain was gone. The room shifted on its axis several times before I finally reached the top. I stumbled and fell on all fours. I stayed there panting, but someone helped me up. It was Wilbaht.

His long dark gray hands pulled my arms gently. He said something to me, but again, I couldn't hear well enough to understand him. I shook my head and pointed to my ear. He looked surprised. He turned to someone behind him and said something. Then he inserted the tips of his fingers in my ears and wrapped my head with his huge hands. When he released me, my equilibrium and hearing returned. I blinked several times as I looked at him. I fell again to my knees, this time in reverence.

"I owe you my life, sir. How can I repay you and your brothers?" I asked loudly, my forehead nearly touching the ground.

He lifted me with levitation. He smiled kindly. "Regain your strength today and tomorrow. Then you must come with me on assignment."

"With you, sir? Yes, sir, as you command. I am at your service. It will be a great honor to work with you, sir."

He patted me on the shoulder tenderly. He stepped aside to reveal the person standing behind him: Sub Professor Ocelot. He reached out for my hand with both of his. I could not avoid staring into his face. No visions came to me this time, only relief that they did not.

Wilbaht spoke, "Sub Professor Ocelot and I will be your new partners," he said with a grin.

"I'm glad you're alive and well again." Ocelot shook my hand with a serious manner.

I thanked him under my breath, but nausea crept through my stomach. I began to sweat profusely. I pulled my hand away from him. I excused myself and rushed to the kitchen sink, where I turned on the water and splashed my face twice. I leaned over into the sink in case I had to throw up, but my stomach was completely empty. I turned off the water and wiped my face. I breathed heavily and shivered. I turned to see the two men and Yalat staring at me with concern and sympathy. I apologized.

"Let me order something for us all," Yalat said, waddling toward the computer. "Go sit down," she whispered to me as she passed by.

I walked carefully to the table. Wilbaht motioned toward my chair to levitate it out from the table for me. I pressed hard on the table to balance myself and sit. I breathed heavily again.

"How is your right lung?" Wilbaht asked.

I lifted a hand to press on my ribs where the largest metal shard had gone through. It felt as if nothing had ever harmed it.

"It's fine, sir. I have no pain there at all. It's breathing normally. You worked a miracle on me. You and your brothers must have reduced your lives and energy significantly to save me. Why did you? I was practically dead. I was already leaving my body when you got to me."

"We were almost too late, then. Thankfully, you are alive now and capable of recuperation within the next few days. That is as much as we could hope for. To answer your question, I can only tell you that your survival will be important to many people in the future." He grinned at me with a caring face.

"I thank you again, sir. I owe you everything," I said. I felt very tired. He was right about taking some days to recuperate.

I turned to Yalat. "Were you injured in the crash, Yalat?"

"Oh, no, dear. Thank you for asking," she said.

"And you, sir, are you all right?" I asked Ocelot.

"Yes, thank you," he said. He seemed distant.

"Stennet and Jiao?" I asked.

"Stennet took some shrapnel to the arm, but it was nothing serious. Jiao is fine," Wilbaht said.

"Who assassinated Trau? Does anyone know yet?" I probed.

Ocelot and Wilbaht stole glances at each other. "How much do you know about the Fitmalo situation?" asked Wilbaht.

As we ate slowly, Yalat and I revealed everything we'd learned in the last few days. I gave them details about our visions of the spider, how we killed it, what we encountered on the twentieth floor, and the vague information Alaban had given me about Trau and about his own assignment. Yalat mentioned the type of questions they'd asked at interrogation and about her theory of the Fitmalo military being behind the assassination of our unknown official. She also gave them details about the microship.

"Who else have you told about your theory, Yalat?" Ocelot asked.

"Only the people in this room and Alaban," she stated.

"Don't mention it to anyone else. How well do you trust Alaban?" he asked.

"I trust him with my life," I interjected.

Ocelot glanced at me suspiciously. What did he mean by that look? He turned back to Yalat. "And you, Yalat, what do you think of him?" he asked.

She backed me up. "I believe he is a very intelligent young man. He knows this kind of information is sensitive. If he ever mentioned that the three of us had talked about it, he would be implying that we are working on intelligence against the Fitmalo military. He knows better than to do something like that. And I know he would never do anything to harm Sil. He cares as much for her life as I do."

I nodded slightly to Yalat. She had given just enough information about that and not too much. I would miss her ability for tactful expression.

Ocelot remained silent in thought.

Wilbaht suggested that Yalat leave me as soon as possible. "If anyone from Fitmalo military investigations is looking for the two of you as the first ones at the scene of the twentieth floor assassination," he paused. "It will be more difficult for them to find you if you split up. You should both leave as soon as possible."

"You're right, sir," she said. "I'm due for a vacation anyhow. Perhaps I could visit your family, Sil."

"Yes, they'd be glad to see you," I said.

"Then I'll leave tomorrow. I just want to be sure Sil will be fine tonight," she said.

"Thank you," I whispered. I propped my head up with my hand, leaning one elbow in the table.

Exhaustion covered me like a blanket. I'd only eaten a few bites of food. My water glass was empty. I blinked and it was full again. Yalat must have served me more. I reached for it, sipped, and then replaced it. I closed my eyes for what seemed to be just a moment while the others talked.

"Sil." I heard Wilbaht's deep voice say. I felt a broad hand on my shoulder.

"Sir?" I said weakly. I opened my eyes and looked over at him.

"You should get some rest now. Can you get down the stairs on your own?" he asked.

"I'll be fine, sir. Thank you," I said, standing slowly.

I leaned heavily on the table again. I backed away from it on wobbly legs, but then reached for the back of my chair. I stayed there for a few moments struggling against sleep.

"Ocelot, lend her a hand, please," I heard Wilbaht's deep voice say.

Ocelot walked around the table to assist me. He draped my left arm over his neck and strung his right arm around my waist. I tried to resist his help, but my physical state left me too weak to stay alert and stand on my own. My head rolled to face his shoulder. My body sank towards the ground. Ocelot scooped his other arm under my knees to lift me. I found my face pressed into the crook of his neck as my body moved from the kitchen to the stairs. I breathed deeply, suspicion clinging to my nostrils along with his scent. I checked him with my sixth sense. If this was an evil man who would later be involved in the terrible visionary shards I'd seen, he did not emanate that type of aura. I only read neutrality from him. I doubted my clarity of sensitivity as I felt him carry me down the stairs and to my room. He dropped me onto the bed as he probably had the day I'd passed out before the committee. I shivered, as much with distaste as with cold. He held my wrist to take my pulse.

"Are you a medic, sir?" I asked aloud.

"I'm your ship's medic," he answered. "You'll be all right. Your pulse is fine."

Yalat stroked my hair. She asked Ocelot if there was something else she could do. He told her to keep me warm and give me plenty of water for the next few hours.

"You should sleep through the night," Ocelot said, clutching my shoulder to keep me awake for his message. "Don't try to exercise tomorrow. I'll be by to check on you after Yalat leaves."

I tried to reach up and brush his hand away, but sleep engulfed me once more.

Chapter 13: Jiao and Ocelot

"They're inside!" I shouted, bolting up out of bed.

The room felt unusually cold. I breathed in the icy darkness before the motion sensitive lights blinked on. The computer clock read 0300 hours. I swung my legs over the side of the bed. The dream disappeared. My shouts left me wide-awake and wondering what I'd dreamed. All I remembered was being inside a ship.

I went to the bathroom sink where I gulped water. My thirst had increased during the night. I splashed water on my face and neck. I turned to leave the bathroom, but was overcome with thirst again. I slurped greedily from the tap.

I walked down to the main gallery, now fully balanced and alert. Lights danced across the lake beyond the dark amphitheater. Building Two protruded from the ground as a shiny black monolith in the night. A large airbus flashed its colored lights inadvertently before landing at the airfield. Vapor from my breath clung to the glass. I wanted to talk with Yalat, but I didn't want to wake her. She would soon leave for Liricos. I was glad she had chosen to visit my family.

I felt restless. Ocelot had told me not to exercise, but I had to do something to occupy my time. I stretched and practiced a few slow flips. To my surprise, I found myself more nimble than ever. My energy level surged.

I finished all thirty personal defense forms with unparalleled strength. I lifted the levitation stones and swirled them around in the air in various patterns. Then I used them to form a wall in front of me. I punched forward with power, pulverizing one of the stones. The dust scattered in the air. I pulled the dust particles and tiny pieces back together. Destruction of Organization property was punishable by a three-month dock in pay, and I wasn't even on the payroll yet.

I considered the irony in my sudden conscientious feeling. We had destroyed a thick, tall, and very expensive glass window when we battled with the spider. But of course, it wouldn't be charged to us due to the nature of the predicament.

I set the other stones back where they had been, but kept the broken one in my hand. I tried with all my might to compress it so that it would stay together. I left it on the floor next to the other rocks, although bits flecked from it to form a pile of sand.

In my dormitory once more, I meditated to check my psychic energy. I envisioned the Center and all its buildings, rooms, and beings clearly. I saw Wilbaht turning in his bed. I saw Ocelot awake, practicing some advanced fencing techniques with his triblade. I saw the other beings in Building Three sleeping or beginning their morning routine. I saw Yalat snoring in her bed. I saw myself leaning to one side. As I lay down to sleep again, I also sensed a distant presence. I felt Alaban's life pulsing along with my own. His existence comforted me.

I awoke at nine to the touch of a cool hand on my face. Yalat was ready to leave. I sat blinking at her with woe. She reflected the sentiment.

"Don't bother getting out of bed, dear. It would do no good for either of us if you came with me to the ascension tower. Besides, you need rest and you're not fully dressed. Ocelot will come to check on you later. Wilbaht will care for you now. I'm glad to leave you in such good hands. He is a great man. I will contact you from Liricos. I sense that my journey will be a safe one. You've been a great gift to me these many years."

"Thank you for all you've done, Yalat. I'll do my best to make you proud."

"You already have," she said, embracing my arm. I returned the embrace, setting my cheek over the bumps of her closed eyes. When she let go, she waddled to the door for her traveling box. She winked and nodded. Then she went away, levitating her box along beside her.

My caretaker was gone. After a while, I watched out the window to see her ship take off. It zipped through the clouds into the sky. I sighed heavily to see her go without me.

Finally at midday I bathed and changed into my official gray uniform. I packed my travel box. My traveling uniform was gone, since it had been shredded from the explosion. I would have to buy a new one as soon as I was paid.

I messaged my parents to let them know I was all right. I also sent a message to Alaban explaining that I'd been hurt but that I was safe and healthy again thanks to his advice to Yalat. I wished him well. I signed the message, "your loving friend".

After leaving the computer, I went back to the dining area for something to eat. While I sat there contemplating things, Ocelot burst through the door.

"Where is Yalat? Is she here?" he asked nervously.

"No. What happened?" I asked, wondering also how he'd gotten in through our door.

"Where is she?" he demanded.

"She left early this morning," I explained.

He sighed in relief. "Good. There's a military investigator from Fitmalo looking for her. If she left early this morning she should be out of danger. He'll probably come to this room, so we've got to get you out of here."

I left my meal. I levitated down to my dormitory and grabbed my traveling box. I rushed back up the stairs with it and left it on the floor by the table. I got rid of my dishes so there would be no evidence I'd been here alone.

Ocelot grabbed my traveling box. "If anyone asks, I'm the one who's leaving. You're staying to hear the announcement of your first assignment. If any Fitmalos approach us, we'll split up. I'll meet you on the third floor if we get separated, but it may take me a while to get back to you."

I nodded. "Yes, sir," I said, skirting out the door and down the hallway. I paused at the elevator. Ocelot met me there and pressed the button to open. We entered.

Ocelot asked how I was feeling. I said I was fine. I explained my excess energy and commented truthfully about my early morning exercise despite his advice. Ocelot frowned and said I should have gotten more rest. I apologized and changed the subject. I asked him where we were going.

"Sor4 to start. We'll wait for instructions there before moving on."

"I meant now."

"So did I."

I looked at him in surprise. I had expected to stay here another night before leaving on assignment. "So I won't have an official meeting for the announcement of my first assignment?"

"Only by messaged conferencing," he said. We stopped talking. A large Furman and a Fitmalo boarded the elevator at the sixth floor. Ocelot nodded at me to get off at floor three.

I left the elevator and kept to myself while I waited. I perused the shops, explaining to the shopkeepers that I was only looking around. Some became annoyed, but most were complacent. Finally I arrived at the café. I sat fidgeting with a menu for several minutes.

"Sil," I heard someone say quietly behind me. I turned to find Professor Jiao staring at me as if I were a ghost.

I quickly offered him a seat beside me. He pulled his chair close.

"I can't believe you're not in the hospital. I knew the Torreons were good, but I didn't realize how good. You look perfectly fine."

I lowered my voice to keep people from overhearing. I explained to him the highlights of my recovery, but did not mention that Yalat had left. I did tell him I was waiting for Ocelot and why.

"I want to talk with him, too. I'd like to know who was behind the attack."

"Do you think he knows?" I asked.

"He might have an idea. He was on Trau's interrogation team." Jiao said. He stopped to gaze at my back.

"May I?" he asked, stretching out a hand to my shoulder. He rubbed his hand down one side of my back and shook his head. He retracted the hand. "Your back was like a spike grenade. Now it's smooth. I don't know how they did it." He shook his head. "It's too bad Alaban left before the crash. I know it's even harder to handle trauma when your mate is away."

"My mate? No. We're only friends. Don't tell me there've been rumors about us," I said in an agitated voice.

Jiao tilted his head with interest. "You're not mates?"

I reiterated to him that we were not.

He raised his eyebrows. "I apologize. It's only that several people assumed."

"It's not important," I said, shaking my head. I remembered Ongeram and Omeh who had laughed at us holding hands in the elevator. Probably one of them had mentioned something about it.

Jiao scanned our surroundings. "I need to speak with Ocelot soon. I need his help with a code."

"He's a code-breaker?" I asked.

"Yes, a good one."

"How do you know each other, sir?"

"We're cousins, believe it or not," Jiao said with a slight grin.

"But you're not from Liricos?"

"No, I'm from Jain."

"How long have you lived here on Sor3?"

"Not long, about three years. Why so many personal questions?"

"I'm sorry, sir. I'm being too curious," I admitted, bowing my head.

"It's all right. It's good to be open around those we trust," he mentioned.

I considered his statement. I examined his face before revealing my thoughts to him. "Sir, I know it may not be my place to say this, but please be careful. I have a strange feeling that Trau was not the only target on that airbus."

The look in Jiao's eyes changed to guarded apprehension. Then he saw my sincerity. He sat back in his chair and looked from side to side with a knit brow. He glanced at me again.

"Sil, I have to give a recording of some encoded information to Ocelot, but I want him to show it to you once it's translated. It's something you deserve to know. Ask him about it some time. Tell him it's codename 'stagnate'. I appreciate your warning. And I'd say the warning suits you as well. Don't trust anyone but your partners for the next few months. Stay out of harm's way. And do me a favor. Keep an eye out for my cousin. He

102

takes care of himself, but it doesn't hurt to have someone watching his back."

"Yes, sir," I affirmed. "Sir, I want to ask you something. You said a moment ago that people assumed Alaban and I were more than friends. Do you think Sub General Wilbaht heard that rumor?"

"I couldn't say. Why?"

"I don't want him to believe lies about me. I'm not a person who forgets her place in life. I've been a student until now. I've followed the ethical rules of youth. I haven't begun an adult life yet. I know you don't owe me any favors, but I would truly appreciate your help in dispelling those rumors, especially with the Sub General."

"That's a very honorable statement. I wish more students held your ethic."

Just then, Wilbaht himself strode through the café. He stopped to bow and shake hands with us politely. Then he dropped a card between us and kept walking. I picked up the card. It was a money card with an incredibly high credit limit. Attached was a note. It read, "Wear Universe."

I showed the note to Jiao. He stood and motioned that he would come with me. I tucked the card into the neckline pocket of my uniform. We walked together to the Wear Universe boutique, which contained a wide variety of clothing samples. At the back of the store we found Ocelot observing himself in the virtual mirror.

He saw himself wearing clothing typical to the planet Santer. In reality, he wore his traveling uniform, but the virtual mirror showed him with a knee-length leather coat, a pair of heavy brown canvas pants, an off-white buckskin shirt, and thick-soled brown boots. He selected to buy the outfit on the computer and slid his card through the payment slot.

"The attendant will fold and box your purchase. Thank you for shopping at Wear Universe," the computer said.

Ocelot stepped off the virtual mirror platform. He spoke to me without looking my way. "Get something from Santer," he said.

I stepped onto the platform where he had been a moment ago. As I touched the image of the Sant helion on the side screen, Jiao and Ocelot walked toward the front of the store.

I selected the planet Santer, then human species, then female. The virtual mirror blipped on. The first outfit was meant to show a lean, feminine midriff, but I was much too muscular to wear it without drawing negative attention. I said, "Next." The image changed to a cold weather outfit, covering my entire body. Judging from the clothes Ocelot had ordered, I was sure this wasn't right.

"Next," I said. This outfit was lighter than the heavy insulation of the one before it, but it was also designed for an extremely cold climate. "Next," I said again.

This one was about the same weight as the one Ocelot had bought. It consisted of a deep red undershirt, a low cut coral sweater, a knee-length brown leather jacket like the one Ocelot had ordered, and camel-colored slacks and boots. I ordered it.

I stepped down from the platform and went to look for the two cousins. They stood near the front of the store hidden by a clothing rack. They talked quietly. As I approached, Jiao stopped talking and nodded at me. Ocelot turned.

"Go back and order something else: whatever you think you'll need. This may be our only chance to stock up for a few months. If you need something from another store, go buy it now. Get any personal items you want as long as the total is less than fifty kilograms. We'll be around here for a couple of hours. If you don't see me, look for one of us in the café," Ocelot ordered.

"Yes, sir," I nodded.

I went back to the virtual mirror and browsed a little. I was tempted to buy a Liricos outfit, but decided I wouldn't need it. I looked at Tambuo clothing for a few minutes. I found one Tambuo dance outfit, which I felt was stunning. I didn't really need this, but I could use it to practice dancing from time to time. If I could get back to Liricos one day soon, I might be able to visit my family and dance again with my mother and my sisters. I ordered it. I also ordered some exercise clothes, a sweater wrap, and a new travel uniform.

As I collected my boxes from the entrance of the store, I noticed the two men were no longer there. I went to another shop and bought a second traveling box where I stowed my new purchases.

I stopped at a grooming salon for a quick, badly needed haircut. The Vermilion hairstylist nearly shaved the back of my head to offset the damaged hair. She tapered the hair towards the front, leaving me with bangs and hair covering the front of my ears, but almost none at the back. I disliked this look, but there was not much else she could do for it without adding fake hair or shaving the whole thing. I accepted the cut and paid her.

As I neared the café, Jiao approached me alone. When I stepped close to him, he spoke.

"Go to the ascension tower lobby. Sub General Wilbaht will meet you there. I explained about the rumors as you asked. I wish you luck. Don't forget the information I mentioned."

I shook his hand. I thanked him and wished him luck as well. Then I walked away without looking back.

Chapter 14: First Assignment

I stepped through the main ascension tower lobby doors. Some elderly Greys sat together on my left. One slept sitting up. The other two played a virtual board game of some kind. The glass doors ahead opened onto the field.

Several airbuses sat parked nearby. Beyond these were the spaceships. One was an oversized Fitmalo business ship. One was a medium-sized Rybalazar pyramid cruiser. Several other medium ships dotted the field as well. I wondered which we'd be traveling in.

I didn't see Wilbaht or Ocelot anywhere. I walked past the Greys to the glass doors. From an open airbus stepped Wilbaht in his traveling uniform, armed with an auxiliary weapons pack strapped to one thigh. His height was impressive. He stood at more than three meters tall. His curly gray beard showed his age, but he moved with ease and elegance.

He took a few steps toward the lobby and then stopped. He motioned for me to follow him. I trailed behind him as we passed several small ships. When we approached the Rybalazar ship, he stopped and opened its rear platform door. I halted. I felt hesitant about boarding a Rybalazar ship, but I also knew it was the perfect place to hide people from Liricos. Who from Liricos would willingly board a ship that belonged to their sworn enemies?

I hurried my pace to follow Wilbaht into the ship's cargo hold. As soon as I cleared the boarding platform, Wilbaht raised it and sealed the outside door. He took my traveling box and inserted it into a securing net on the ceiling while he welcomed me.

"I'm glad to see you've fully recovered," he said. "Welcome aboard. I'll show you around once we're past the moons' gravity. We need to get going."

He opened a door, which led to a narrow white hallway. We mounted a thin spiral staircase that rose from one end of it. I followed him up two levels of the ship. At the top of the stairs we entered a wide observation deck with five stations. Ocelot sat at the fuel and systems gauge station to the far left. Another human sat up front at the main helm and navigation system station.

Wilbaht had to lean down to avoid the low ceiling. He stepped down and touched the second man's shoulder. The pale-skinned human turned jauntily in his seat. His face was speckled with a short, graying beard. His appearance reminded me of Professor Stennet; only this man had bright blue eyes and a wayward appearance. I felt uneasy as he looked at me.

"Klib, this is our new trainee. Sil, this is Klib, our navigational pilot," Wilbaht said.

I stepped down into the helm area and reached out to shake his hand. He twisted in his seat to return the handshake. He smiled wryly.

"Very nice. Welcome aboard," he said.

"Sir," I said in response.

"Sil, take weapons and defense station. I'm on communications," Wilbaht ordered softly.

"Yes, sir," I replied. I found the chair furthest to the right of the observation screen. Wilbaht sat in front of me and to my left.

I glanced over at Ocelot. We nodded to each other. We all set our seatbelts and safety braces. Klib sent the request for takeoff signal to the tower and waited for a response.

"Rybalazar Sonic Wake two minutes wait time for takeoff," a tower official droned.

Klib boosted the engines and elevated the ship less than a meter from the ground. An airbus passed above us. A moment later, the tower gave us permission to takeoff. Klib brought us up slowly in a direct vertical ascent.

I watched the multiple screens in front of me. Apart from technical stats lists, I viewed eight different angles of the ship's exterior. Two were views from real cameras. The other six were computer-enhanced line diagrams of our surroundings. Thankfully, no targeting points appeared on the screen at this time.

A protective panel covered weapons controls. The tiny computer screen next to it showed eight different weapons ports, all on full. We were equipped with two atomic torpedo ports, three plasma blast ports, two antimatter plasma mine ports, and one nuclear mine port. The heavy armament of the ship reinforced my distrust in Rybalazar. Anyone attacking our ship probably wouldn't live long enough to be sorry they had. I also discovered a triple-layered defense shield, the outermost of which was a plasma dissolution shield. It used a technology I was not familiar with.

Klib took us through the clouds. Then we blasted off at a sixty-degree angle. We sailed on all clear. Our ship cut through the atmosphere and charged toward Sor3's first moon. A few distant ships and orbiting satellites appeared on my screens, but nothing came close to us. I relaxed a little, relieved that no one had followed us.

We spent an hour in relative silence. We only interrupted the dull roar of the engines to check and confirm a few stats. The multiple computer systems did most of the checking themselves. I wondered if this silence would become normal flight procedure. Klib announced when we'd cleared the path of the first moon. Then silence ensued again for an additional hour.

Finally he told us we had passed the path of the second moon. He requested to go to autopilot. Wilbaht granted the request and told everyone to switch to auto watch and auto alert. We unfastened the safety harnesses and stretched our necks.

Wilbaht stood, angling his head to one side to avoid the ceiling. He offered to show me around downstairs. As we descended the stairwell, I heard Klib whistle a single note. He muttered something to Ocelot and laughed. I knew first impressions were sometimes untrustworthy, but I perceived our pilot to be a common type. I hoped our personalities wouldn't clash too badly.

Wilbaht led me to the floor directly below the main observation deck. We stepped into a fairly wide dining area with a table and benches bolted to the floor in its center. At the end of the dining area and to the right, an open door revealed a tiny two-seat observation deck and communications board. Directly in front of the stairwell to the far end of the dining hall spread a row of small rooms with open doors. These were about the size of the closet-like room I had shared with Yalat after our interrogation. The tiny bunks continued in a row down the hall. Wilbaht guided me through a narrow hallway, which turned left at the end of the last small room.

Again to the left, Wilbaht showed me a large bath area. Farther down this hall and also to the left we found an exercise room. At the end of the hall I noticed an emergency medical and cleaning supplies closet.

In the exercise room, a variety of weights and resistance equipment hung secured to one wall. I also saw a treadmill, a cycle, and punching bags. The longest wall was burnished to a pearly sheen to serve as a mirror. The floor was covered with a thin padding. The ceiling contained extra transpiration collectors for sweat to be reprocessed through the black water tank. Embedded in the ceiling by the pearled wall was a smart holographic projector used to create transparent enemies and targets for sparring practice.

He then showed me the water systems in the bathroom. There was a tap from a freshwater tank, an internal recycled water tank for sink and bath water, and a recycled black water tank for filtered, purified, and chemically treated urine and collected transpiration. Solid waste was collected in the reclaim fuel hold, both from the bathroom and the kitchen.

We went back to the rows of rooms. Wilbaht entered one and demonstrated its amenities. The bed was a narrow folding frame attached to the wall. A ceiling net hung at the back corner to hold personal items. On the wall opposite the bed was a foldout chair and desk ledge. A computer receded into a niche in the wall. The back wall of the bunk slid open to hold hanging clothes. Wilbaht told me I could pick any bunk I wanted, since none had been claimed yet.

We walked back into the dining area. Klib had come down from the helm to grab a snack. He slid open one wall next to the table and benches. Inside was a storage closet twice the size of the dormitories filled with food supplies. Klib opened a plastic container of a fruit and flour paste. He snapped off a section of it and closed the container again. He slid the wall panel back together. It clicked shut. He munched his snack and pointed to the opposite wall.

"Sink's on that side," he said.

He walked over and pressed a latch to slide open this panel. It revealed a sink, a food prep area and a few cooking utensils hanging in a net above a burner. He opened a cabinet beneath the counter to show me it held cold storage foods. Then he slid the wall closed again.

I followed Wilbaht again as he ducked into the small observation deck.

"Here we have civilian messaging and reading for research plus auxiliary communications," Wilbaht explained.

Klib leaned into the doorway and spoke to Wilbaht. He asked to take the bunk closest to this deck. Wilbaht allowed it and ordered him to go ahead and unpack.

After Klib yessired him and left to get his things, Wilbaht showed me a few gadgets in the mini deck. Then we went downstairs. Here was a secondary cargo hold I hadn't seen when we'd entered the ship. It contained emergency repair equipment, space suits, oxygen tanks, welding equipment, solar tents, heavy winter coats, and other survival equipment. He briefly indicated a door to the engine and life support systems control at the back of this hold. He also informed me of a recon ship attached to the side of this ship, which was accessible through the external door of this hold. He indicated a layout drawing and safety instructions on the wall for boarding and detaching the recon ship. Then we left the secondary cargo hold and went down the hall to a door opposite the main cargo area. This was a standard quarantine room and medical station.

We returned to the main cargo hold to take our traveling boxes to our dormitories. I found the box I'd brought with me as well as the one Ocelot had carried in. Wilbaht took the dormitory two doors to the left of Klib's room. I claimed the bunk two doors to the left of Wilbaht so there was an empty room between each of us. After we'd unpacked, Wilbaht announced a meeting to discuss duties and schedules. He stepped over to the spiral stairwell and called up to the main observation deck.

"Ocelot. Crew meeting," he called. He then slid into one of the dining table benches. His knees touched the underside of the table, even with his feet extended.

I slid in next to him. Klib left what he was working on and sat diagonally in front of Wilbaht. A moment later, Ocelot trotted down the stairs with a palm computer and projection string. He sat next to Klib and set both objects on the table. He straightened the string to make a large screen area on the table and then turned on the notepad computer. The screen swelled and illuminated. It showed a flight duty master schedule for each of us.

"This is a Sor4 twenty-five hour schedule. I set up the duty roster by rank privilege," he explained.

According to the schedule, we each had one cleaning detail and one secondary duty, a two-hour block in the exercise room, an eight-hour block for sleep, and six hours work time on the main deck. We each had five hours or more of personal time, but Wilbaht indicated we might have to give some of that time up for maintenance checks, and we would be doing research during most of that time. He advised us not to get defensive if we were asked to work those hours.

Wilbaht pointed to a half hour on the schedule that was blacked out on everyone's timetable. "Ocelot, what is this?" he asked.

"I know it's against normal policy, sir, but I was hoping to talk you into allowing a communal meal. It might help us keep our sanity during the long haul between solar systems," Ocelot said.

"And if we have an emergency situation during this communal meal?" Wilbaht asked, arching his thick eyebrow.

"We can set a surveillance robot on deck. Plus there's auto alert. If we practice it, I'll bet we can all make it upstairs in less than fifteen seconds from here. We're right next to the stairs."

Wilbaht considered this for a moment. "If you can set up a convincing surveillance system, I'll approve it."

"Thank you, sir." Ocelot went on to explain the work schedule. "Sil, your schedule will be the hardest to get used to at first. You'll be sleeping at opposite hours from what you're used to."

I said I was willing to work any hours assigned to me. Ocelot went on to explain overlapping schedules on the main deck for crew communication reasons and isolated schedules for exercise and personal time for privacy. We were allowed to work out together whenever personal time and exercise hours overlapped, but only by consent of the other crewmember.

When Ocelot finished his briefing, Wilbaht interjected, "You'll post this on everyone's dorm computer. External maintenance checks will be called periodically, but I'll try to keep it to a need basis. Keep water usage to a minimum. We'll be on Sor4 tomorrow, but we shouldn't have to restock, so the supply we have now has to last more than a month and a half, maybe two months depending on travel time."

Everyone nodded.

"Questions?" asked Wilbaht.

I raised my hand. "Who is the fifth person on the schedule, sir?" I asked of the empty name label on a schedule column.

"We'll pick up another crewmember on Sor4. I don't have confirmation as to the identity of the person, but he or she will board with us the day we leave the planet," Wilbaht said.

I nodded.

Klib raised a finger. "Not really a question, sir, but I think an all-around introduction is in order," he said.

"Good idea. Why don't you go first?" Wilbaht acknowledged.

"Sure," said Klib. "Klib Sarrow: Second level navigational pilot, tank and heavy weapons driver, native of Xiantalix in the Gold Wind helion. No warrior skills whatsoever. I just drive and maintain, but I've never let a ship break down and never lost a crewmember. So you can rest assured I'll keep all you hot shots alive in the air."

We smiled and nodded. Wilbaht spoke next. "Sub General Wilbaht Cordolib: civilian covert intel, former education advisor, war veteran, and seer. I'm a native of Palat in the Firoba helion. I am a father, grandfather, great-grandfather, and soon to be great-great-grandfather. Remind me to show you pictures of my family one day."

"Great-*great*-grandfather?" Klib said in surprise.

"I'm one hundred three years old, only middle-aged for my species," he replied.

This was true. The Torreons were the only intelligent species that lived long enough to achieve the first intelligence ranking. Theirs was the race that had begun space exploration in the first place. They had discovered most of the scientific breakthroughs of the last few millennia, including the discovery and usage of space folds for rapid travel among solar systems, and subparticle rays that allowed communications to travel much faster than light. They had aided other helions to develop their own technologies. They had helped unite the populations of the galaxy to commence trade among helions. This had led to the creation of our financial calendar and eventually to the formation of a standard for all of us under the cooperative government of the United Galaxy.

Next it was Ocelot's turn to introduce himself. "Sub Professor Ocelot Quoren: cryptographer, emergency medic, swordsman, civilian covert intel, chemical weapons certified and, uh, ship systems engineering trainee. I'm from Liricos in the Lapas helion."

"Swordsman," I repeated in a whisper. I remembered seeing him practice with the sword when I was meditating just this morning.

All eyes turned toward me.

"My name is Sil Gretath. I'm a first-year warrior in training. I'm also from Liricos. I've only just finished my entrance exam, so I don't really have an area of expertise yet; well, except levitation."

Klib reacted strangely to this statement. He nearly snorted and laughed. We all stared at him. He stopped, but suppressed a grin. He shook his head and waved us away.

Wilbaht ignored him and touched my arm with the back of his hand. "I've heard you're a seer like me," he said. "You have strong dreams and visions that come true. Yalat told me."

"Yes, sir," I said, bowing my head.

"It's nothing to be ashamed of. I'm glad to have this ability. It has helped me save many lives over the years, as it will help you. You only need to learn how to use it and accept it as part of who you are. You and I will be good company for each other."

"Thank you," I said, flattered. I felt welcomed by Wilbaht, but I couldn't understand Klib's reaction.

"If there's nothing else to be announced, I declare this meeting adjourned. Ocelot, claim your bunk and unpack for a while. Sil, I want to show you some details on the main deck," Wilbaht ordered.

"Yes, sir," we all said in unison.

I followed Wilbaht upstairs. He showed me around the different stations I hadn't seen yet. There was a section detailing internal and external door seals, as well as welding seams and artificial gravity projection. There was a panel for life support: temperature control, air content monitors and internal moisture monitors. The communications station held a detailed atlas of planets, moons, and helions in perspective with our current position and could map out all possible pathways for communication signals to and from us and any major city or space station in the eight helions of the United Galaxy. The engines, air pumps, water pumps, solar energy collection, battery power and electrical distribution, hover pad system and all mechanical maintenance plus statistical readouts were shown at the station where Ocelot had sat during takeoff and at an empty seat, which would soon be filled by our fifth crewmember.

Klib came up to the observation deck with us and showed us some of the basic navigational instruments and controls. Wilbaht ordered me to get a few hours' sleep before my on-deck duty began. He informed me that Ocelot would buzz my dorm to wake me.

Wilbaht descended the stairs to his bunk as well, since his sleep time had already begun. He welcomed Klib and me to the crew once more. We thanked him accordingly. I took a few steps after our commander.

"Hey, Sil," I heard Klib say. I waited for him to speak as Wilbaht disappeared down the stairwell. "So you're good at levitation?"

"Yes," I said simply.

"Well, you can levitate me anytime, baby," he said with a broad grin.

This confused me. I wasn't sure why he would say that. I wasn't sure if he meant it in a sexual way or not.

"It's a joke, a little humor," he said, feeling his punch line lose its momentum.

I took steps back to the stairwell. "I'm sorry. I didn't like that joke. Excuse me." I followed Wilbaht down the stairs.

"Hey, it's nothing personal. Just trying to break the ice," he called.

"It's okay," I said between floors. I wasn't sure why he thought I would enjoy a joke like that, but I let it go.

I went to my bunk and closed the door. I lay down fully clothed and napped lightly.

It seemed only a few minutes later Ocelot buzzed my room. Unfortunately the speaker was just above the bed, so the noise woke me with a start.

"Sil. 0120 hours. Are you awake?" he asked through the speaker. I pressed the button to speak.

"Awake, sir," I said. I yawned as he reminded me to be upstairs by 0130. "Yes, sir," I answered.

I said good morning to Ocelot as I reached the top of the stairs. He scanned the readouts at his station. He turned his head slightly to glance at me.

"Good morning, or evening. It's whatever time you want it to be up here. Sil, can you move an external camera to just below the main cargo hold door? I need to check a faulty reading. It looks like we're losing some air pressure below."

"Yes, sir," I said. I went to my station and moved a camera to show the door. I sent the image from my screen to his.

He spoke to me as he checked the readout. "You don't have to call me 'sir' unless the commander is around. We're on a team. I'm only a few years older than you anyway, and not much higher in rank. I know you're trying to make a good impression, but we'll all get along better with less formality. The only one we need to address by his title is Wilbaht. Just call Klib and me by our names."

112

I hesitated about this idea. I didn't feel familiar enough with him to call him by his first name in person. Apart from this, I still distrusted him. I wasn't comfortable calling him anything but 'sir'. At the same time, I didn't want to seem unnecessarily rigid around him. Maybe I could get away with not addressing him at all.

I helped check and confirm air leakage using a sulfur spray test. Ocelot sealed off the lower hallway and internal doors of the main cargo hold to avoid more air loss. I asked if this ship had ever had sealant problems before. As it turned out, this ship was a new issue. Klib had come with the ship, as recommended by Ocelot's uncle.

I remembered Jiao was his cousin and Stennet was Jiao's father. I asked if he meant Stennet had recommended the ship.

"Yes, how did you know?" Ocelot suddenly turned reproachful.

"Professor Jiao talked with me yesterday," I said.

He narrowed his eyes at me. "Jiao doesn't usually give out family information. You must have gained his trust after the accident."

"I guess so," I said. "He asked me to watch your back."

He blinked and gave me a condescending look. *"You're* going to watch *my* back?" He stared at me intently. His piercing gaze made me nervous.

I swallowed hard. "Yes, sir. I assume that's part of the job."

He smiled skeptically. "We'll all watch each other's backs. No heroes, just a team. And I told you not to call me sir." He turned back to view his screen work.

"All right," I replied, offended by his manner.

"Don't worry about what Jiao says. He gets antsy sometimes," he said without looking at me.

I found out by way of a tentative inquisition that Jiao and Ocelot were close cousins, practically brothers. They had grown up together on the Jain planet after his family was transferred there from Liricos. They had both moved to Sor3 after their trial year abroad. I also learned that Ocelot had already been working with Wilbaht on and off for over a year on intel about the Fitmalo situation. Thinking this was an appropriate time to explain about my own past, I gave him some basic information about my family.

"I have three sisters still at home. I have an older brother, but he moved to Tambuo several years ago. That's where my mother's from. My father runs a school for exceptional students. That's where I had most of my training."

"When I go downstairs, could you keep an eye on this pressure readout?" he rudely interrupted.

Embarrassed, I agreed to stay alert about the readout. I realized he obviously had no interest in my personal history. After all, he had been on my testing committee. He'd seen the general report on my background already. We sat in silence for a while. Then I remembered the information Jiao had mentioned. I asked Ocelot about codename 'stagnate', mentioning that Jiao had wanted me to see it.

"He said it wasn't urgent, but that I shouldn't forget to ask about it," I stated.

Ocelot knit his brow and clenched his teeth. "Did he say why?" he asked with a tone of aggravation.

"No. He wouldn't say what it was about. He just wanted me to know what it said for some reason," I said.

"You don't need to know what's in that file," Ocelot said, turning to the screen once more.

"Oh. If it's something I'm not supposed to see, I'll understand. I'm just a rookie. I don't need to know everything," I said with aggravated apology.

He set his jaw. "Yes. Just forget about it." He sighed. "Jiao," he said, shaking his head.

Disappointed with my first real conversation with a crewmember, I concentrated on my screens, which were all empty except for a scrolling list of ship statistics to the far right. I moved over and checked for any communications updates at Wilbaht's station. It, too, remained empty.

"Don't touch the ship's log. Wilbaht is the only one allowed to do that." Ocelot snapped.

I returned to my station skittishly. "Anything else I need to know?" I asked.

"Most of the time you'll be working on research or stats checks. If you time it right, you can bring something to read up here from messaging on your palm computer. Games are not allowed. Mostly we just check station readouts and compile investigation reports. That's why it's called work," he spoke flatly.

I sat stiffly at my panel, feeling as though I'd been scolded for wrongdoing my first day on the job. I felt repentant, although I couldn't figure out what exactly I'd done wrong. I kept quiet, hoping Ocelot's acid demeanor would settle. I stared out at the planet Sor4 on the main screen. It seemed to be the size of my fist right now. At least we had a planetary arrival to look forward to. Once we left the Soren helion, we would pass through a deep space zone without so much as an outpost or a space station to break the monotony.

"Listen, my time up here is about finished. Why don't you take my seat and watch this gauge? If it increases its cubic cm per hour, buzz me.

Here's a buzz board on this side by my station. I'm in bunk one," he spoke in a dry voice.

He stood to go downstairs. We said goodnight, even though it was morning for me. I went to his chair, which was still warm. The gauge stayed at the same reading.

This wasn't the beginning I'd looked forward to with my new job. I felt awkward around my crew. I wasn't sure how to act around them. Wilbaht was nice enough, but I found Klib difficult to understand. Ocelot was staunch enough and now I had bothered him by asking about Jiao's information. He truly intimidated me. I missed Yalat. Normally I would have gone to her for advice. Here in the observation deck all by myself, I felt perhaps I was not ready to leave her side after all. This voyage was going to be long indeed.

Chapter 15: Distrust

We landed at a Center on Sor4, but didn't start ship checks right away. Wilbaht wanted to meet with a general to discuss details for our assignment and to meet the fifth member of our crew. This left the rest of us with free time. We could stay at the ship or go out as long as we kept near the Center, wore communication patches, and stayed alert and ready to move. Klib suggested a bar and restaurant nearby. Ocelot said it was a good idea. Having no ideas of my own, I tagged along.

The restaurant was a single-story brown box with protruding rafters and was nestled into a gated garden of weedy flowers. Inside, the place was dimly lit and smelled of cooked meats and alcohol. It had a three-sided bar in the middle and tables throughout the rest of the restaurant, each separated by some kind of leafy foliage. We took a seat at the bar, although I would have preferred a regular table. There was something almost familiar about this place, even though I'd never been here.

Klib sat between Ocelot and me. He leaned one elbow up on the bar and waved a finger at the closest waiter. The Kangaroo Lizard was busy mixing a drink, but he leaned toward him to listen to Klib's order.

"Got anything from Xiantalix?" Klib asked him.

The Kangaroo Lizard nodded. He finished mixing the drink, served it to a customer on the side bar, and then reached for a bottle of Xiantalix Red Ale. He showed it to Klib, who nodded. The waiter retracted to pour him a glass of it. He handed Klib the glass, and then turned to me. He hopped backward when he saw my face.

I raised my eyebrows at him. He took a slip of paper from his apron and showed it to me.

"Is this you?" he asked.

The printed photo was a bit wrinkled, but it was clearly a picture of me in the amphitheater at the C.A.T.T. Center on Sor3. I was perplexed.

"Yes. Where did you get this?" I asked him.

"Wait right here," he said, patting the bar.

He snatched the photo away from me and bounded off to the kitchen. The three of us exchanged nervous glances. I waited for some indication of danger. I opened my auxiliary weapons pouch and retracted my laser cutter without turning it on. Ocelot flipped open a pouch on his thigh and kept a hand on his sword handle. Klib clutched his drink and sipped it, pretending to ignore our reactions.

A heavy-set Furman bumbled out of the kitchen with a delighted broad face. The waiter followed him. I stood down from my seat, not knowing what to expect.

"Are you Sil?" the Furman asked me with a grin.

"Yes. What do you want?" I spoke defensively.

"Oh, don't be alarmed. I mean you no harm. A friend of yours left you a message. I am a relative of Ongeram, his partner," he said, gesturing broadly with his hands.

I stepped closer to the bar. The Kangaroo Lizard came back to my spot carrying a pink fruit drink identical to the one Alaban and I had shared the day he left Sor3. The waiter left it at my place, and then went to see what Ocelot wanted. I sat again at the bar and replaced my weapon. The Furman pulled an envelope from his apron and placed it by the drink before me. He smiled broadly. He waved his hands about as he spoke.

"He spoke very highly of you. I've never seen a young man so much in love. He bought us all a round of drinks. He recited poetry about you." The Furman harrumphed before quoting him. "'Oh, where is there a greater woman, in skin of bronze, with hair of silk; with kisses succulent as the first taste of a mother's milk; her body voluptuous, a steeled lioness; with the face of an angelic war goddess'," the Furman boasted.

116

Seeing Klib's blank expression, he explained, "The Ode to a Warrior Maiden."

Klib raised his eyebrows and made a face of recognition, although I doubted he actually knew the poem.

The Furman recited more for us. I vividly imagined Alaban toasting with his new crewmates. I could almost hear his jovial voice resounding from his cunning smile as the Furman quoted. "Oh, to make love to a fair and rippling creature so divine! What man may dream to fall at her feet but in battle and slain? Alas, she only gives her treasures to the man more powerful than she. And see all that I am that man, for she hath lain with me!"

The crowd must have whooped and guffawed from his lively recitation, especially after that line. He'd relished the attention and the freedom to finally celebrate without Trau.

The Furman yammered on. "Oh, bellicose beauty..."

He would have continued, but I gripped his arm and let him know that I was familiar with the classic poem.

"He talked about you all night. He was very entertaining. He told us a lot of dirty jokes and stories. He said you'd be here today. You're lucky to have such a fine young man. Or should I say he's the lucky one? Ha, ha, ha!" the Furman chortled.

He leaned out to me and pounded my shoulder with laughter. "Free drinks for you and your friends. Well, not exactly free—he paid in advance—quite a heavy tipper. Order what you like." He smiled and winked at me. He went back to the kitchen chuckling.

"In that case, bring me the whole bottle," Klib called to the waiter.

I did not see or hear Ocelot's reaction. I sat staring at the envelope. Several questions sailed through my mind at once. How did Alaban know I would be here? Did he foresee it or did he secretly look up my assignment listing and figure it out for himself? Even if he had seen the assignment, how would he know I'd be exactly here, now? It had to be premonition.

Also, why would he be in a bar bragging and reciting old poems about me? What else could he have possibly said? Was he the one who started the rumors about us in the first place? Why did he set this up? I covered my forehead with one hand and touched the envelope with the other. I didn't want to open it there in front of them.

Conscious of the worry on my face, I bit my lip and looked past Klib to Ocelot, who stared back at me with that same look of suspicion he'd given when he questioned Yalat and me about Alaban the other day.

I excused myself, clutching the envelope in my hand. I walked out of the building to sit at a bench close to the entrance gate. I opened the envelope. Inside was a folded paper letter written in Alaban's own scrawl.

It read: "Surprise. I got your message, my 'loving friend'. I know what happened to you. I saw it all. I even felt pain at my back and in my right side when I had the vision. I'm glad Wilbaht was there. I'm sorry you had to be there when Trau got what he deserved. Something tells me there was a Mantis involved in the shooting, but I don't have any other information.

"I'm glad you're alive and well now. I love you so much, Sil. The goodbye kiss you gave me may not have meant you feel the same way, but I'll always remember it.

"You're wondering how I knew you'd be here. I know a lot of things I probably shouldn't. The picture I gave the manager was one I printed out from your interrogation file. Yes, I read it. Your statement was a model of virtue. You did well. Your deposition and mine probably caused Trau's assassination. (Hooray! I thank you for that).

"Why? Men who control the most highly guarded secrets are also the ones who control which secrets get out, and to whom. I trust the people you and I are working with, but not many more. I suggest you do the same.

"Don't try to message me just yet. I won't be able to receive messages for a while anyway. I have a feeling I'll see you again on Jawlcheen. I still wish you and I could have been partners. We'd be great together. Our talents compliment each other. I know you think I'm too aggressive and sneaky sometimes, but that's just the kind of partner a virtuous and honest warrior like you needs. Keep that in mind.

"I dream of you every night. Even though we've never mated, I still feel so close to you, intimate, as if we were mates already. That is my goal, Sil. I would love for you to be my wife someday. There's no one like you.

"It's going to be a long, lonely ride out in space, but I can bear it. I know I'll be able to kiss you and touch your face again. I don't know when, but I'm sure we'll see each other within the next few months. When we do, I'll hold you in my arms and won't let you go for hours.

"Keep this letter with you. Read it whenever you feel alone. You'll never be truly alone as long as I'm alive. I love you more than anyone. Stay safe. Love forever, A."

A warm feeling came over me. I felt honored. No one had ever sent me a paper letter before. No one had ever sent me a love letter before. A part of me wanted to give him a chance. My logical side told me this was a bad idea. I wanted him to be in love and happy, but I did not share his feeling of physical intimacy. A twinge of guilt swept through me.

I folded the letter and replaced it in its envelope. I tucked the envelope into the neckline pocket of my uniform and gazed into the twilight. I said a short prayer for him.

I returned to find Ocelot and Klib still in the same places. Klib's bottle of red ale was nearly empty. They both drank from it. I sat next to Klib again and drank my pink fruit drink quickly. As soon as I finished, Klib offered me a shot of his red ale. He waved at the waiter to bring me a clean glass. I explained I didn't drink alcohol.

"Aw, don't be shy. Just try a little sip. I'll be offended if you don't," he said.

I tried a tiny sip of the bright red liquid just to appease him. It was bitter. It burned my throat. I coughed. I left it on the bar and asked the waiter for another fruit drink. I scowled at the flavor.

"I guess it's an acquired taste," Klib said with a grin.

"I guess," I agreed. I felt a warm hand at the small of my back.

Klib leaned in toward me. "You know, if you're missing your boyfriend, I've got a good shoulder to cry on," he said.

His peppered jaw housed a grin, which I would have found encouraging if it had been offered in innocent friendship, but his aquamarine eyes conveyed other motives.

"I appreciate it, but I don't feel like crying. Thanks anyway," I told him, leaning away from him.

"He got too attached to you, huh? Trying to get rid of him?"

"No. It's a long story," I said.

"Well, tell all. Hey, this is a bar. You're supposed to tell your problems to the guys at the bar," he professed confidently.

I reached for his hand on my back and removed it, placing it firmly on the counter. I held his hand down with both of mine.

"If you want to talk, why don't you go first?" I said, staring determinedly at him.

"Yeah? Actually, I'm glad you asked. I have some pretty good stories. Stick around me long enough and you'll learn a lot. Whatever they didn't teach you in school is what I know," he bragged.

I feigned interest. I took my hands from his to receive the second drink the waiter brought. Ocelot ate from a small plate of food. I asked the waiter to bring me one of the same. Klib reached out to either side of him. He clapped Ocelot and me on the backs of our necks, causing us both to drop a scoop of food.

"Did I tell you the other night about how I met my first wife?" he asked Ocelot.

Ocelot shook his head, regarding him with annoyance. He glanced at me guardedly.

I concentrated on my meal and tried to ignore Klib. He gave a long and convoluted explanation of his relationships with his first and second wives and a variety of other women in between. When the details of the demise of his relationship with his second wife waned, Ocelot ordered Klib a large plate of roasted meat. This shut him up for only about fifteen minutes.

Klib gulped down a chunk of meat and wiped his hands and mouth on a napkin. Then he turned to Ocelot and started talking again. "Hey, Ocelot, did you ever find out what happened to that Vermilion ex-girlfriend of yours? The one who tried to kill you?"

"I don't know and I don't want to know," Ocelot warned him with gleaming eyes.

Klib laughed heartily. He turned to lean toward me. He covered the side of his face nearest Ocelot.

"Some crazy orange girl slit him from shoulder to hip," he said. He leaned back in his seat and laughed some more. I regarded him with disgust.

Ocelot became angry. He gritted his teeth. "I told you not to mention that," he said firmly.

Klib attempted an apology, but his laugh drowned it out.

Ocelot stood, pushing his plate away. "I'll see you back at the ship," he said. He stomped out.

Klib chuckled a moment as he watched Ocelot leave. "Ah, he'll be all right," he assumed aloud.

With the same breath, Klib ordered another bottle. I didn't want to see his personality go from bad to worse. I excused myself and asked him to please not drink anymore. I gestured to the waiter not to give him anything else. Klib tried to convince me to stay, but I insisted on having some time alone. I told him I'd see him at the ship.

This night had been an utter failure. Although my first impressions of Ocelot and Klib were poor, I realized that their image of me was also less than preferable. Judging from the way Alaban had spoken of me, they probably thought I was some kind of wayward tart. I hoped it wouldn't take two months to get from here to Santer. We might hate one another by then. I almost considered going back to Sor3 on the next shuttle to ask for a new assignment altogether. Still, I knew I had to make an effort to get along with my crewmates. I had only been around them a short time. Maybe our misunderstandings could be smoothed out.

I walked out into the cool night air and breathed deeply. The air on this planet had low contamination. It was good to breathe it in. It replenished my energy and gave me strength to plod on. I strolled through the street back to the Center, passing shops and teahouses on the way. Businesses began to shut down for the night. I passed the Center, which was smaller than the one on Sor3. Its courtyard was lighted but empty. I wondered how long Wilbaht would take to find our new crewmate. I hoped she would be a female: someone I could easily get along with. I walked past the Center courtyard, back to the landing field and to our ship.

As I approached the main cargo hold door, I heard a series of swooshing sounds coming from outside, just to the right of the ship. I moved carefully around the landing base to investigate.

At a distance of about twelve meters, I saw Ocelot in the dimly lit field, practicing with his sword. He was carving up a low-hanging branch of a tree at the edge of the landing field, working out his anger. He backed away from it for a moment, and then charged at it again, swirling high in the air and slicing through the branch completely. It collapsed lightly onto the ground. He landed on top of it and then backed away again to start a swordsman's performance I did not recognize. It was a difficult performance that required great upper body strength. I watched out of sight for a few moments, trying to place this particular sword style. As he ended the form, I approached him slowly. Perhaps he wouldn't mind sparring with me a while. This might help to at least convert our unease into acceptance. He stood tensed, sword extended before him, left hand in a spear form over his heart, his back to me. I stepped a little closer.

"Ocelot," I began.

He whipped around, bringing the sword up to my ear with such speed and force that even when he saw me and wanted to slow the blade, it still slipped through the back of my ear. I didn't wince, but stood still, afraid to cause more damage by jerking away. I only stared wide-eyed and held my breath.

He instantly withdrew the sword, slapped the blade closed, and threw it down. He rushed towards me in shock. I breathed. My ear bled hotly over my neck and shoulder.

"Sil! Are you all right? I could have killed you," he panted.

He held my chin gingerly in one hand and the back of my head in the other to observe my sliced ear. I stood still, feeling the burning wound, but after my experience in the airbus explosion, this was like a bee sting. Still, his reckless action offended me.

"I'll get something for it. It'll be okay," he said.

"No," I stated firmly. "Stand aside."

On top of all my disillusion, he had piled on a serious offense. Here stood a fellow warrior, one I was expected to observe as a mentor, who had just broken one of the most important and basic rules of our credo: never let anger lead to the misuse of defense moves or weapons. I had to address this gross misdemeanor whether he intimidated me or not. By Organization law, since he had wounded me with a deadly weapon, I could file a demand of action against him with our commander or seek retribution by challenge. Since this had been an accident, I graciously chose not to report him.

121

"You have wounded me without cause. Prepare to spar hand to hand," I demanded. I stayed still. I stared forward, resilient.

He took two steps backwards. He stared at me, not knowing what to say. We stood like this for several seconds.

The blood at my ear began to coagulate. The pain slowed a little. I closed my eyes and meditated where I stood. Finally Ocelot turned and trudged to a spot several meters in front of me. He stood at attention and bowed. I retuned the bow. We assumed a ready position. He nodded.

I charged forward, feigning an attack to his right, but whirled near the ground to kick his legs out from under him to his left. He crumpled to the ground. I jumped back and returned to ready position. He slowly rolled up to ready position again. He narrowed his eyes at me. I jumped forward, and then bounded upward. I spun to kick him in the chest. He caught my foot and actually threw me forward, moving against the momentum of my kick. His strength impressed me. I flipped to land in ready position. He would not attack.

I edged toward him a little, and then shot my left foot toward his abdomen. He sidestepped and held out an arm to hit me in the face, but I ducked and whirled under his arm and behind him. I caught his ankle to yank him backward, but he did not lose his balance. I did a handstand, levitating myself quickly skyward. I hooked a heel around his neck as he turned around. I lifted him off the ground with levitation and heaved his body into a backwards flip in the air. He landed on his feet.

I tried another power kick toward his abdomen. This time, he didn't even block the strike. He merely braced himself and clenched his abdominal muscles to receive the impact. He skidded backwards about half a meter. I bounced off his stomach as if he were made of tough plastic.

"Fight back," I urged.

I pounced at him from the air with a kick to the upper torso, but he blocked. I tried to fit an uppercut to his jaw, but he caught me by my arm just above the elbow and spun me, pulling my arm behind my back. Before I could turn and wrench away from him, he threaded his other arm between my free arm and my waist. He brought a claw hand up under my chin, squeezing me close to him. The back of my head touched his shoulder. I was caught.

Instead of fighting against the pressure of the claw hand, I levitated upward in that direction, which also helped free my arm. I kicked him in the chin with my heel as I bolted up into the night sky. I flipped and gave him a return kick in the back of the head. He stumbled but didn't fall. We faced each other again.

I flew up and kicked, but he caught me by the leg and flung me to one side with power. I landed on my feet.

He advanced toward me, but didn't attack. I backed away from him. I nearly stumbled on his sword, which still lay on the ground. He let his guard down. He leaned down to retrieve the weapon. Then he retracted it and stored it in its sheath at his thigh.

"I forfeit the match. Your attacks are out of line," he stated. "Report me to the commander if you think you have to." A tone of disgust wavered in his voice.

I stood at attention. "I won't report you. We've already sparred," I said.

He shuffled away from me. I trotted after him.

"Is there some rule I don't know about, sir? Unless I'm wrong, I sparred according to regulation. Why do you say my attacks were out of line?" I called after him.

He paused and turned briefly. "You're a rookie, so I don't expect you to know everything. But it's common sense and common courtesy to accept a simple apology from a crewmate before jumping to extreme actions. You're on a team. Someone in the team makes mistakes. You pick up the slack. If there's an accident, you give an apology. It's overlooked. You don't make a big deal about it. There are rules and then there are priorities. My priority is to keep the team intact. I check the circumstances before the rulebook. If a person can't handle being part of the team, that person needs to be placed elsewhere. You acted as you saw fit. You jumped to regulation regardless of circumstances. That says something about your priorities."

I stood speechless.

"I'll suture the ear if you want, but this challenge is over," he stated.

Resigned and perplexed, I walked next to him to the ship's quarantine and med station, where he cleaned me up and laser-stitched my ear. We didn't speak during the whole process. I'd made a mistake. It was true my suspicion and disliking of this man had driven me to react harshly to his accident. Now I was the one who would be frowned upon. Pride and continued suspicion of him kept me from apologizing as I should have, but I didn't remember him giving an apology for nearly killing me, and that was clearly the worse offense.

I missed Alaban and Yalat badly now. I needed a friend to confide in. My only recourse was to talk with Wilbaht. Although I didn't know him well, he gave an impression of wisdom and patience I did not see in the other two men.

Meanwhile, I had nothing to say to Ocelot. He had nothing to say to me. When he finished with my ear, I checked it in a stainless steel mirror on the quarantine room wall. It already swelled red and ached passively. As Ocelot disposed of the bloody gauze and washed his hands, I left the quarantine area. I scuffed up the spiral stairs to the dining hall. Ocelot followed moments later.

At the table, we found Wilbaht flipping through pages of information on his lap computer. He looked up at us momentarily and smiled.

"Aha, my young ones are back," he said contentedly in his deep, aged voice. "I want to talk with you both before I sleep."

Ocelot and I sat opposite each other at the table. I stayed next to Wilbaht. He passed the lap computer to Ocelot and instructed him to read our assignment summary aloud to us.

Ocelot read from the encoded text as if it were printed in normal script. "Greetings to all warrior members of the Rybalazar Sonic Wake crew. We are honored to once again count on your continuing support..."

"Just skip to the important part," Wilbaht interrupted.

"Yes, sir," he said, scrolling down another page or so. "You have a three-part mission assigned by General Black Agram on Santer. Mission part one: Intercept and report interstellar communications related to Fitmalo rebels and Fitmalo military relations.

Part two: Travel to Santer to assist ongoing investigation of smuggling of chemical firearms. Investigate links between Santer and Jawlcheen/Fitmalo black market. Investigate mid-level Santer government officials in conjunction with same. Assist in any covert ops captures or terminations commanded directly by General or Sub General in same."

I looked over at Wilbaht with anxiety. I wanted to avoid assassination if at all possible. Wilbaht glanced at me. He did a double take when he saw my ear.

"Hold on a moment," he told Ocelot. "What happened to your ear?" He pointed at it.

Ocelot looked up from the screen like a scolded child. "I accidentally cut her, sir," he admitted.

"With what?" Wilbaht's voice carried a tone of warning.

"It was my own fault, sir," I said, covering for him in order to offer a truce. "He was practicing fencing techniques and I stepped in too close. There's no real harm done. It was an accident"

Wilbaht crossed his arms and stared a long while at Ocelot, and then at me. "You're both angry about this. Our new assignment has barely started and already I have problems between crew members," he complained. He eyed us some more. We sat like stones. "Ocelot, where were you fencing and when?"

"Outside, at the edge of the field a few minutes ago," he admitted.

Wilbaht tensed. "You know weapons practice is illegal on a landing field. What were you thinking? It's dark outside. If the ship lights had been off, you could have killed her. You knowingly violated the law. You will not pass this off as a careless accident. I expect a full explanation now." Wilbaht was rightfully stern.

Ocelot set his jaw. "Permission to speak with you alone, sir."

Wilbaht glanced between the two of us. He deliberated about whether to allow him a private audience or not.

"It's all right, sir. I'll go and bathe while you talk, with your permission," I offered.

"Be quick about it. Come back here when you're finished. We're not through with this discussion," Wilbaht spoke with authority.

"Yes, sir."

I got up from the table and went to my bunk for some clothes, and then to the bath. I used as little water as possible, as Wilbaht had ordered. I worried about the outcome of their conversation, but hoped for an improvement in our relations. Suspicion or no suspicion, we had to learn to work together. Life on this ship promised to be completely different from the life I was used to. I felt as though I'd been cast into the middle of the ocean to learn how to swim. I prayed for guidance to do the right thing. I changed into my traveling clothes, remembering to tuck Alaban's letter into the new collar, and washed the blood from the shoulder of my combat uniform.

When I returned to the dining area, Wilbaht sat clutching Ocelot's fist, which he held in the middle of the table. Wilbaht appeared to be saying a prayer for him. When he retracted his hand, I approached them.

"Sit down, Sil. We have much to talk about," Wilbaht said calmly. "Ocelot tells me you received a letter from Alaban at the bar just now."

"Yes, sir," I responded. I sat next to him.

"Did it contain any information related to our investigation?" he asked.

"Mainly it's a personal letter, sir, but he did mention a few things about the assassination." I drew the letter from my collar. I opened it and scanned for the information. "He says he suspects a Mantis was involved in the airbus crash, but he doesn't have any more information than that. He also says my deposition may have influenced Trau's assassination because men at the highest level leaked information about it. He doesn't say who exactly or why."

Wilbaht frowned. "How would he know that?"

"He didn't say, sir, but..." I hesitated. "Alaban is capable of getting into code-locked security. He could have done the same with computer records. You know he broke into Professor Jiao's office."

Ocelot interrupted. "Yes. That's another thing I don't trust about him. If he feels free to break into his superior's office and steal weapons for

125

his own use, what's to stop him from stealing whenever he wants? He could be involved with Trau in the smuggling conspiracy."

"Alaban wouldn't have taken anything if it weren't necessary. I know him. He's not a thief. As far as being close to Trau, he wasn't. Alaban never liked him. He spent as little time with him as possible. When he got his title, he was glad to be free from him. I think the feeling was mutual. I didn't know Trau was involved in smuggling, but I'm sure that Alaban wouldn't have gotten involved with him." I paused to consider the implications of Ocelot's question. If he thought Alaban could be a thief and a smuggler, other people might think so too. "Do you think Alaban is in danger, sir?" I turned to our commander.

"I wouldn't say he's in any life-threatening danger, but he's definitely under close watch. Since he was Trau's pupil, we can only assume that he was exposed to some of his illegal business."

"I can vouch for him, sir. As a close friend and as a witness to his character, I can honestly say he had nothing to do with any conspiracies or any other illegal activities Trau was involved in," I stated.

"How do we know you're not covering for him? You're clearly influenced by the nature of your relationship." Ocelot dared to say.

I contested defensively. "I'm not covering for him. There's nothing to cover. The nature of our relationship is only friendship. Alaban may be interested in me, but I haven't accepted him in that way. We're not mates. Like I told Professor Jiao the other day, I haven't lived an adult life yet." I turned to face Wilbaht. "Sir, all my life I have observed the rules and social ethics of a student. My parents and teachers never left me unsupervised until recently. Yalat has always been protective of me. She's never let me spend time alone with any man until this week. I know the ethical traditions are not always followed these days, but I have followed them." I blushed.

Ocelot leaned on the table with his elbows and spoke gruffly. "We have a problem here, sir. She claims innocence, but witnesses heard Alaban telling risqué stories about her. His side of the story and hers don't match. Then there are several unusual facts surrounding their meeting on Sor3. I believe there is a hidden connection between them. She might have been one of the targets in the assassination on the airbus. I want to know why."

"Why would I be a target? No one knows me. I'm just a trainee," I cried.

"Ocelot, the events surrounding their testing cycles were unusual. However, we'd be overreacting if we jumped to conclusions about them. She was only in contact with Alaban a few days before the assassination. Regardless of her relationship to him, I doubt she would be involved with anyone in the smuggling conspiracy. Her alibis are excellent. She was only with Alaban for a few hours during her testing schedule. She could not change from a well-guided trainee to a corrupt young woman in such a short time. As far as her personal life goes, she is of adult age for her species. She is within her right to choose a mate or not. It's none of our business. In any case, I believe her," Wilbaht spoke firmly.

"Forgive me, sir, but I don't," Ocelot pressed on. "All this information is conflictive. Why would a trainee with such outstanding abilities be held back from testing for three years? And despite her age, she's still treated as a child by her tutor? Now we find out she's involved with a traitor's student who knew exactly where she'd be today. He even left her a secret message at the bar. She says they're not mates, but he bragged about her to everyone in that bar in a sexual connotation. And just now she challenged me in anger. She acted like a totally different person than the one you see here now. Who is she really?"

Overwhelmed by his claims, I could only gape in disbelief. This was a nightmare.

Wilbaht held out a large hand to Ocelot. "Hold on. We'll address one thing at a time. She has the right to contest these accusations. Sil, do you have something to say about this?"

I dug my nails into my palms. "I was angry just now because you nearly killed me, but that's beside the point. You were on my testing committee. You had access to all the personal information ever recorded about me. If you thought there was something wrong with the file, why didn't you mention it then?"

Ocelot clenched his teeth, but made no reply.

"The only people who logged information into my file were my former professors and Yalat. I had no access to it. Why would Yalat lie about my achievements and failures? Are you saying you suspect her, too?"

"No, Sil. No one is accusing Yalat. Her record is impeccable. Ocelot, if you have a suspicion based on proof, we'll address it, but do not implicate someone else without evidence. We must consider Sil's personal record to be accurate. I see no grounds to suspect her otherwise," Wilbaht told him. "It sounds to me that the only base of suspicion you have are the conflicting claims of her personal life. This we cannot demand to investigate. She has a right to privacy as a warrior."

Ocelot tapped the table with frustration, knowing Wilbaht was right. He folded his hands and looked away, ready to spit with anger.

"I promise you I've never been involved in anything illegal and I swear to you again that I've never had a secret relationship with Alaban Jetscuro or anyone else," I stated.

Ocelot crossed his arms, unwilling to bend. Regardless of whether he was trustworthy, I knew if we were to work together in relative peace, I would have to gain his trust. Otherwise he would be reluctant to share important research with me later. Reluctantly, I decided to give up something dear to me just to mend this situation. I looked down at Alaban's letter.

"I can prove what I just said, even though it means breaking the confidence of my best friend," I said.

Ocelot glanced defensively between the letter and me.

I slid Alaban's letter across the table to him with an exasperated sigh.

He took it in his fingers with hesitance, but then turned it to read greedily. He seemed embarrassed to read parts of it, as he should have been. I clenched my teeth onto a thumbnail and waited. He read over the whole letter twice, stopping to concentrate on one section of it several times. He analyzed the handwriting a few moments more. He folded it neatly and pushed it back towards me.

I took the letter and replaced it in its envelope.

"Well?" Wilbaht asked.

"Things are not as they appeared. I believed testimony that was obviously untrue. I apologize," he said, still unwilling to look us in the eye.

"I don't know what you expected from Alaban, but I'm sure he's not involved in any conspiracy and neither am I. I swear I'll be honest with you—with all of you. I am trustworthy. Do you believe me now?"

"Yes," Ocelot said. He closed his eyes a moment, his face sullen.

"Good. Now we can get back to this assignment briefing. Did you finish reading part two, Ocelot?" Wilbaht asked. He acted as if nothing had happened.

Ocelot glanced up at him in surprise, and then quickly found the computerized text again. "Yes, sir. We're at part three now."

"Would you please finish it so we can get going?" Wilbaht pressed.

"Yes, sir," Ocelot spoke. He read again from the encrypted page. "Part three: Three warrior crew members will set up home base in apartment suite in Salumat, capital city of northwest region of Santer. Check in at the Caladia Center to leave ship and receive ID's. Proposed cover: One crewmember traveling professor, two crewmembers husband and wife marketing officials. Fourth warrior crewmember on computer support and information tapping in Salumat brain center. See General Black Agram or Sub General Alaxon at the Caladia Center for briefing. Expected stay at Santer: four to eight months Santer time. (That's about three to six months Sor4 time.) That's the end of the text, sir."

"Yes, our new partner will meet with us in two days. She is an engineer. She'll be training you on intricate ship systems, Ocelot. Sil, you'll be working closely with the three of us on investigative techniques before you start making any reports. I know you've studied them, but our system may differ from your practice."

"Yes, sir," I responded humbly.

Wilbaht looked down at us both before continuing. "Well, now that general assignment briefing is finished, I can get some sleep. You two can either avoid each other or shake hands and get back to work," Wilbaht said.

He slid out of the bench and stood gracefully by the table. The two of us stood as well. Wilbaht waited a moment to observe our reaction.

Somewhat reluctantly, we reached out simultaneously and shook hands firmly, without looking each other in the eye. We were about to let go of the handshake when Wilbaht suddenly grabbed our clasped hands between his. He held our hands together for a moment. He eyed us both patiently.

"Remember this," he told us.

"Yes, sir," we responded, as we all released each other. I caught a glimpse of Ocelot's dark eyes. I wasn't sure, but I thought maybe I saw in them a newfound respect. I hoped it was true.

Chapter 16: Trau's Testimony

During the next two days, the four of us did every procedural check possible on the ship. We checked the hull and door seals twice a day. We repaired the main cargo hold door seal and checked it eight times. Klib went back to the same bar as often as Wilbaht would allow. Ocelot disappeared into the wooded area alone on his hours off. I went to the café inside the Center a couple of times with Wilbaht. He urged me to forgive Ocelot for his distrust and defensive behavior. He asked me to give him time without expecting him to be friendly. I promised not to bother him about it. I found Wilbaht to be a kind but commanding leader. I believed he would soon become a strong father figure for me.

At the end of our second day, Wilbaht called a meeting to introduce our new crewmember. I breathed a sigh of relief when I saw her. She was a six-limbed golden Lizard, slightly taller than Yalat, and several years younger.

"Klib, Ocelot, Sil, this is Professor Yinore. She will be joining us on the crew. I expect you all to fill her in on schedule and procedural information. Please make her feel welcome," he said.

We all introduced ourselves to her in turn. She greeted us in a reserved, yet friendly manner. We found out that Yinore was an expert on deep-space travel and general ship engineering. Her specialty was gravitational deviants. She was also currently studying for her next rank promotion specializing in political mediation. She planned to test on Santer while stationed there. I was impressed with her academic prowess. I hoped to learn a great deal from her.

After Wilbaht showed Yinore around the place, she chose bunk four, between Wilbaht's and mine. While she unpacked her things, I timidly poked my head into her dorm to welcome her personally.

"I'm glad you're here, Yinore. You're an answer to a prayer," I told her.

She angled her orangey eyes at me while she unpacked. She had a pleasant, pretty face, in Lizard terms. "Oh?" she asked. "How so?"

"I was afraid I'd be the only female on board. This is my first assignment. I'm not used to being around only men." I said, feeling a bit foolish.

"Your sponsoring tutor was a Lizard?" Yinore guessed brightly.

"Yes, ma'am. How did you know?" I asked.

"You seem very familiar with me. Most humans are standoffish with us at first. Plus, I read people's thoughts through their eyes. If some day I tell you, 'I know what you mean,' before you even say anything, you'll know why. Don't mind me," she confessed.

We spoke a while longer as she finished her task. Then we were called to the top floor for final stages of ship checks. Yinore took the seat next to Ocelot on the engineering panel. She showed her expertise as we went over statistical readouts. She even corrected some of our gravitational settings around the ship to conserve energy. Yinore's presence on the crew elevated my expectations for the job. I now felt more at ease to concentrate on all the newness around me: the new ship, a new set of daily duties, a new method of gathering data and compiling reports.

I was now able to access a wider range of informational resources, since I was an official Organization intel employee. My warrior partners guided me through these resources with cautionary warnings. Not all of the sources were reliable, and some were rigged with counterintelligence teaser/parasite programs, which, once I accessed their data, would try to latch onto my string of research to absorb any pathways I linked to.

However, our research computers on the ship were protected by nine different smart shields; each one an independent, complex entity used to detect anomalies or undesired glitches. No parasite ever got past the fifth shield.

I also learned much more about the Fitmalo situation. Ocelot and Wilbaht filled me in on what they knew, or at least what they thought I should know. I learned from them that Fitmalo Prime Minister Lock came from a family of former prime ministers. He was the sixth in his line to rise to power. Several of his cabinet members were also distant relatives of his. Also, there were more rebel factions currently active on Fitmalo than I had previously believed. One of these was led by a former Fitmalo military general named Zar. An exiled war hero, Zar now lived on Sor3. His was the most powerful of the rebel groups. We referred to them as the military rebels. Another group drew support from our own U.G. Organization. This one consisted of developmental planning personnel and trade distributionists from the previous cabinet. This group carried the greatest support from the public. It would be necessary to coerce these two groups as well as any others into working together to successfully overturn the current government.

Lock was almost definitely preparing to become dictator, but Organization intelligence had discovered a secret group of his own cabinet members and a few businessmen called the Regime, which planned to seize power from Lock sometime during his proposed dictatorship. They wanted to help keep him in power only long enough to secure a position of advantage. Lock probably knew about the Regime, but we guessed he had a counterstrike set up to fend off the wolves.

The hope of our Organization was to mobilize our own people and the rebels in a covert strike against both Lock and the Regime. However, a rebel revolt couldn't take place until Lock openly seized power. Otherwise, the United Galaxy would never condone the takeover. The planet would be exempted from regular trade until Lock or a member of his cabinet was reinstated. This would render our efforts moot and would cause more chaos.

The crew talked about some possible strategies that might help our cause, but our ideas were full of holes. In the end we resigned ourselves to rely on upper management's ideas for guidance. Wilbaht knew more than he needed to say about this. He had friends in the highest positions of our Organization. He encouraged us to be patient.

I spoke with Wilbaht about the biological weapon Yalat had theorized on. He told me that, sadly, the case had been restricted to military generals only. However, he expected that Yalat had been right when she suspected Fitmalo military agents had been responsible for the assassination and attempted theft of the weapon. Only now he worried that perhaps the

Regime, not Lock, had proposed to take it and that if they had succeeded in getting it, they might use it on Lock and his supporters. I asked if it were possible that the blackmailers could have been Fitmalo rebels in search of a weapon to use against the government, but he dismissed the idea. If the Fitmalo rebels organized themselves well enough, they would not need to steal a weapon from the Organization. The Organization would provide them with arms for the job. Besides this, the only ones privy to the existence of the lab were members of high government and the Organization generals involved in overseeing scientific research.

None of this information gave me a clue about the infamous microship, or why it had followed me to my levitation test. As the interrogator had told me on Sor3, if I were allowed to know about it, I would. I understood I was only a rookie, but I soon found myself wishing for more data privileges than I was permitted.

During our communal meals on the ship, we avoided talk about politics and work-related research. Klib told stories about humorous accidents that he and his copilots had incurred over the course of his career. Yinore and Wilbaht spoke of popular aerospace, including the debate about reverting to micro gravity on short space trips and the affect this would have on the quality of life. Ocelot contributed to the debate now and then, but mostly kept to himself. Klib cut in with various puns. I noticed after a while Yinore avoided looking him in the eye. His thoughts offended her, apparently. I could only add a few anecdotes of my experiences. Mostly I asked questions to try and fit in.

At the end of our second week of travel, Ocelot admitted he had told me everything he'd ever known about Fitmalo, Jawlcheen, and the Thrader helion. He said he could think of no other information pertinent to our mission except the files from codename stagnate. He still hesitated to show them to me.

"Why do you think I shouldn't see them?" I asked.

"It's a file from Trau's interrogations," he said.

"What does that have to do with me?" I asked.

"Trau mentioned you," he said, hinting at a possible link between Trau's interrogation and my relationship with Alaban.

"Now you have to show me," I said frankly.

Reluctantly, he went downstairs for the file. He came back with a lap computer and a peripheral decoding device. He inserted the tape coil into the decoder, plugged the decoder into the computer, and accessed the file. The decoder buzzed.

"Before you read this, you have to know we didn't believe all of his second testimony." He stood staring at me, still considering whether I should see it or not.

I took the computer from him carefully. Ocelot went back to his place at his station, watching me as I read.

The first interrogation file was recorded the night Trau had been taken from his and Alaban's room on Sor3. It was the same night that Alaban had reenacted my dream with me. One interrogator asked him questions, just as my interrogator had with me after the spider incident.

As I read through the questions, I noticed the prompter knew much more about Trau's involvement with the Fitmalos than I had expected. I asked Ocelot about it. The prompters were the General from Xiantalix and his aide: Lam and Samson. On the second interview, Ocelot himself had prompted with Samson. I asked why he had been on the interrogation committee.

"Jiao intercepted an encoded message from someone in the Regime pertaining to weapons and the military scientists' convention. The message was left on the Center's intel main board addressed to a codename. We still don't know whom the codename belonged to or if he ever got the message. Jiao took it off the main board. I decoded it for him. According to the message, Trau and the Fitmalo military rebels in the Public Valley were people to beware of. Since Trau was in for questioning because of your and Alaban's statements about him, I asked to cross-question him, but it turned out to be a waste of time. The most info we got from him came from his first interrogation."

I carefully read through the first few pages to see for myself. After Samson asked Trau his name and station, the interrogation went like this:

Samson: During your time on Fitmalo, who was your reporting general?

Trau: General Swall Jade.

Samson: Has General Swall contacted you recently?

Trau: Not directly.

Samson: Have you been in contact with any of Swall Jade's enemies in recent months?

Trau: None of my recent contacts has expressed an unfriendly position regarding Swall Jade.

Samson: Then why would former Fitmalo General Zar care to meet with you?

Trau: I earned his respect as his bodyguard several years ago on Fitmalo. That's all.

Samson: Choose your words carefully, Trau. You don't want to suffer strikes from the unseen hands. Try again. Be specific.

Trau: The unseen hand does not scare me. I've worn that glove myself.

"What is this? Who are the 'unseen hands' he's talking about?" I asked Ocelot.

"Sometimes spies are sent out to antagonize informants who hold back information. They break in and enter a home, bother relatives, steal personal items. Then the informant usually comes back to give the information willingly. Those spies are the unseen hands," Ocelot explained.

I read on.

Samson: We know about your relationship with "the Daughter". Someone else's hands can be all over her at any moment. Now answer the question truthfully. Why did General Zar ask to meet with you?

Trau: You won't touch the Daughter. Those unseen hands will be cut off along with your heads. If you want to know General Zar's motives, ask him. I guarded him and his family during a time of internal resistance. He's lucky to be alive. He only wanted to thank me for keeping the unseen hands away from him.

Samson: This is your chance to get your story straight, Trau. Next we bring in your former student as a cross witness.

Trau: You can bring him in right now. He knows nothing. I never let him see anything about this. I kept him away from details.

Samson: Do you think you can work both sides at once without anyone knowing about it? Remember, why did General Swall hide you on Fitmalo last year?

Trau: Counterintelligence was after me. He saved my life. I know that. I won't forget it. The Daughter would never let me.

Samson: Why did the Fitmalo government officials here on Sor3 request you for the recent bodyguard assignment?

Trau: They know my reputation. I'm the best choice for the job. I'm here to clear the way for them.

Samson: Did former General Zar ask you to bodyguard for him recently?

Trau: Yes, but I turned him down. He'll have to get his bodyguards through conventional means. He knows where my loyalties lie.

Samson: One moment. General Lam would like to remind you of the military science convention. Do you know who hired the spy microship?

Trau: A close friend. But that has nothing to do with this.

Samson: Did you know what was on the twentieth floor of Building Three?

Trau: Maybe. I know it's gone now.

Samson: Who told you?

Trau: The same grapevine you're on.

Samson: Who did you visit in the Public Valley the day Alaban performed his personal defense test?

Trau: I was bodyguarding for the youngest Fitmalo military general at a private party. It's all documented in my work report.

Samson: Did you leave the party at any time?

Trau: Yes. I ran an errand for him.

Samson: What errand?

Trau: He requested female entertainment.

Samson: Were they safe?

Trau: One might not have been.

Samson: Is she still viable?

Trau: No.

Samson: Did you meet with anyone else that night?

Trau: No.

Samson: What did you do on the night Alaban received his title?

Trau: I took him to the Public Valley to celebrate.

Samson: What did you do after you left him stranded at the bar tower?

Trau: I went to the Red Zone.

Samson: For what?

Trau: I went to visit the women that were at the Fitmalo general's party.

Samson: Why?

Trau: I had to cleanse the one that was questionable.

Samson: Who else was there with you?

Trau: A trader.

Samson: What species?

Trau: Human scum. Spell it out. You know whom I mean.

Samson: What did he want?

Trau: An extra business agreement.

Samson: Did he pay?

Trau: No.

Samson: The General wants to know why you let the man get away without paying.

Trau: There was no reason to bite the hand that feeds. I warned him to stay out of it. All doors are locked for him. He has no choice.

Samson: How well does this human scum know General Zar?

Trau: Some would say too well. I'd say not well enough.

Samson: Where did you go after you left the Red Zone?

Trau: I went back to Building Three.

Samson: You went somewhere else.

Trau: No. I stayed in the Red Zone all night. I went back to Building Three in the morning.

Samson: Did you tell Alaban where you'd been?

Trau: No. I never tell him anything about my personal life.

Samson: Are you sure he hasn't tried to follow you?

Trau: I'm sure. I've conditioned him. He stays out of my way willingly.

Samson: How did he get back to the Center?

Trau: I sent a public driver for him.

Samson: No further questions for today. You'll be cross-questioned in the morning. You'll be quartered here in Building One on the secure interrogation level for the night. End recording.

When I finished reading this section, I asked Ocelot about the Fitmalo general Trau had bodyguarded. He said he had all the related information he was allowed access to. He had a list of the people present at the meeting, how they got there, an overview of what was discussed, the identities of all those present, their backgrounds, and a file on where each partygoer went afterwards. He did not, however, have access to the recording of the meeting itself. Nor did he have access to info on several of the important people who attended the meeting. He also had no trace of Trau's activities in the Public Valley on the night of the bar tower incident. None of the available leads pointed to any information about the twentieth floor, the microship, or Trau's demise.

"Why was Trau taken to the Public Valley after his interrogation?" I asked.

"We were supposed to meet with one of his contacts there, an assistant to General Zar, to try and bargain for information. After the assassination, the Organization personnel on that case reported the contact as missing," Ocelot told me.

"Do you have any idea who 'the Daughter' is?" I asked. "Did Trau have a daughter?"

"No. He had no children. There is a file on 'the Daughter', but it's part of another investigation for generals' eyes only. I'd like to get my hands on it. It could help us crack this case. That's the problem with this job. We're constantly finding leads we're not allowed to follow. 'The Daughter' could be any important female he or the smugglers worked with. There were hundreds. Or it could be a codename for a ship or a weapon or a shipping line. We'll never know as long as the generals sit on the data."

"Lam and Samson know too much. They almost seem to be on Trau's side," I dared to mention.

136

"They probably are, but there's nothing we can do about them right now. They're protected by generals' data security."

"Are you saying they're in on the smuggling and no one can touch them?"

"On the record, I know nothing about any general's involvement in any wrongdoing. I have to assume they gained their positions because of their record of flawless integrity and they can't possibly be involved in anything short of moral perfection. Off the record, I'd guess about two-thirds of the permanently based generals are on the take. No one's allowed access to any records of their actions. The protective cyberwall around them is impenetrable. They're gods. They order us to research crimes and send them the reports. They sit on the info until it's convenient for them to use it."

"But if a general is breaking the law, isn't there someone else we can report him to? Another general we can trust?" I asked, flustered by this abuse of our system.

"How would you know which one to trust? If we go to someone else to report our suspicion, we might be reporting him to his own partner in crime. Then we'd be targets," he replied.

I grew more frustrated.

"Anyway, there's nothing to report without proof. That's what we're here to gather. We continue discreet espionage, comply with orders, and hope there's a balance of just desserts in the universe. White-collar criminals rely on hundreds of others to keep afloat. If we catch their supporters and do away with them on the low end, the bottom should drop out for the kingpins. They lose whether they're arrested or not. That's all the punishment we can give, outside assassination. But we don't get many assignments like that. When you're on intel, it's not your job to affect justice. It's your job to follow directives within the limitations we're given. We do what we can. Then we pass the research on to the boss or some other crew or law enforcement."

This hard-core explanation seemed too jaded, his approximations too high. I had always expected enough checks and balances among our top ranks to curb the corruption. I decided to take his speech with a grain of salt. We had to bring some justice to the system, regardless of the infidelities of a few elite generals. I focused again on the interrogation file.

"I think Alaban knew more than Trau let on. Alaban said my testimony had something to do with his assassination, probably since I told them about Trau's secret meeting when he left Alaban at the bar tower," I mentioned

"You weren't with him at the bar tower, were you?" Ocelot asked me.

"No. Even if he'd invited me I wouldn't have gone with him that day. I was in the middle of testing. Yalat can vouch for me about that."

"Then most of Trau's second testimony is a lie. I believe someone tortured him during the night between interrogations. He was belligerent, incoherent the second day. See for yourself. Only don't take anything he said personally."

Ocelot was right. Trau was belligerent in his second interrogation. He was defensive and cynical. His testimony was filled with expletives. The questions focused on his contact with a variety of smugglers, Fitmalo representatives of current and former cabinets, and others. Some of these questions were answered directly. Some of them were answered in a double meaning. For almost every person he responded about, he added several indecorous descriptions. At one point, it appeared that Ocelot had prompted the interrogator to tell Trau to keep personal opinions of these people out of his testimony, but Trau was unrelenting.

Finally the questions turned to the nature of his relationship with Alaban. Trau let loose with several paragraphs in which he badgered Alaban's personality. I sympathized with Alaban to think his own sponsoring professor, the man who was supposed to serve as a second father to him, would regard him with such disdain, and in fact, hatred. Then I noticed a discrepancy in his rantings against him.

In part of his statement, he focused on Alaban's weakness of character. He called him a beggar for attention, a pouting schoolboy with a worthless outlook on life. He called him a thief. He cited a couple of instances when Alaban had stolen from him and had received a beating and two days without food or water. My heart sank for him.

Then Trau began to complain about Alaban's strengths. He said Alaban was too cocky and competitive, but he also detailed a few abilities he was proud of. He said Alaban thought of himself as a mathematical god because he could get into anything having to do with numbers. He complained that Alaban couldn't keep a personal defense trainer for longer than a month at a time because he always ended up seriously injuring him. He claimed he'd taken Alaban to a smugglers' hideout once where they were met by concubine dancers, but Alaban was more interested in getting in with the smugglers than being entertained by the girls. He called him a conniving, underhanded young clown who would just as easily play a comedy routine for the target as he would kill him.

I looked at Ocelot in anguish. "He's not saying all these things to make Alaban look bad. He's bragging about him. He's communicating with someone through this interrogation. He wants them to recruit Alaban for something. Someone from the Regime is going to try and use Alaban for an illegal assignment." I shook my head. "I could have warned him. Now I can't even message him until we get to Santer."

Ocelot knit his brow. He left his seat to watch the screen with me. He scanned over Trau's statements about Alaban. "If that's true, you'd better be just as careful. Look at the rest."

The next part mentioned me. Trau continued his false complaints about Alaban. He said that Alaban even thought he was the greatest levitator until he had seen me in action. According to Trau, Alaban decided since he couldn't beat me, he'd seduce me instead.

I felt deceived for a moment. I wondered if there was any truth in what he said. On the night he came home drunk, Alaban had tried to get intimate with me but had failed badly. However, on the last night we were together, he had been respectful and understanding when I refused him.

Trau went on to lie about my whereabouts on the night he'd been in the Public Valley bar tower. He said I'd met Alaban there to go to a sex bar of all places, and that I had gone home with him for more when the driver picked him up. He continued by calling me a lot of names. He even said Alaban had invited me to spar with him as some kind of sadomasochistic foreplay. What incredible lies.

I continued reading. General Samson appeared to be listening to a prompt from Ocelot. He asked Trau if he was sure of the accusation he made, in light of my perfect record.

Trau acknowledged that I seemed perfect. "All the more reason for the kid to try her on."

I scowled at his remark.

He told them Alaban knew I was the best at levitation. He even knew I could transpass objects. I immediately thought of the microship, but he did not mention it again. What if Trau had sent the microship to spy on my test? Would he have used its recordings as evidence to promote his idea to someone in the Regime? I couldn't be certain, but this was the best explanation for the microship thus far.

In Trau's next statement, he said Alaban was crazy about me and that I would be the perfect bait for him.

"Bait?" I asked myself aloud. What were the Regime officials planning? Trau obviously had something specific in mind.

"Do you have any idea what they might be planning?" I asked Ocelot, who now peered over my shoulder to re-read the text again.

"I'm guessing grand theft. Trau's saying someone should hold you hostage in return for Alaban's cooperation, or vice-versa. Emotion is the arrow in blackmail's bow, as they say." He eased away from me, but kept his eyes glued to the screen. "It's an ideal set-up."

"That's why he wanted to convince someone that we were more involved than we really are. Who would want to use his plan?" I asked.

"Someone well-organized and powerful enough to arrange it. That could be anyone from Lam or Samson to Prime Minister Lock himself," he admitted. "Again, we have no proof."

Thoroughly miffed, I handed the lap computer back to him. I worried about Alaban. I had to get word to him somehow, but not through the normal currents of communication, and not directly from me.

At 0730 hours, Wilbaht came to relieve me. I spoke to him about the stagnate file and about my worries. He became concerned for Alaban's welfare, too. He offered to contact him indirectly through his own associates to warn him not to believe any blackmail threats he might receive, reassuring him that as long as he was in charge of my welfare, no harm would come to me. Wilbaht asked if he should mention some personal information from me to let him know the warning was legitimate.

"Refer to me as his loving friend. Then he'll know it's from me," I said.

Chapter 17: Klib

After our communal meal, when Klib had returned to the top floor, the rest of the crew stayed together to talk about the meaning of what we'd found out about the stagnate file. We decided not to mention it to anyone else for now, since we couldn't know who was on our side. Lam, Samson, Swall Jade and at least one other high official had to be Fitmalo Regime sympathizers and perhaps overseers of smuggling activity, but how many more? Wilbaht kept a list of suspects, but encouraged us to stay on task with our current investigations and to report all suspicious evidence to him.

After our meeting, Ocelot returned to his schedule to work with Klib, but I stayed behind to speak with Wilbaht and Yinore. I explained my relationship with Alaban to them so there would be no other questions about us regarding Trau's testimony. When I finished the story, Yinore wished me luck with him, but seemed inconvenienced by the elongated meeting. She bustled down the stairs to check the engine room gauges. Wilbaht observed me with glistening, oily blue eyes. He smiled caringly. He told me I reminded him of his youngest granddaughter, Olimbi.

"You are both young and strong minded, but delicate of heart," he said. "Perhaps some day the two of you will meet."

"It will be an honor, sir," I agreed.

Wilbaht patted me on the back and said goodnight before enclosing himself in his quarters.

I hurried to start my cleaning duty. Klib meandered down the stairs. He entered the dining hall just as I turned to go down the hallway. I retrieved some cleaning supplies from the closet and began to clean the bathroom floor. I crawled on my hands and knees to clean along the edge of the wall, backing towards the door.

"Do I make you nervous?" I heard Klib's gruff voice speak from the doorway.

I looked up over my shoulder at him. He leaned into the doorway with crossed arms. I realized his eyes focused on my rear end, which was pointed towards him.

I quickly stood and turned to face him. "Sorry. I can clean later if you need in here," I said.

"Nah, you can finish cleaning," he said. "I can wait."

Hesitantly, I went back to scrubbing the floor. This time I turned with my face in his direction. When I got close to the door where he stood, he spoke again.

"You didn't answer my question."

I stopped and looked up at him.

"I asked you if I make you nervous," he said, now standing over me.

I left the cleaning rag on the floor and stood slowly. I decided to be honest with him. "Sometimes. Why do you ask?"

"You took one look at me back there and ran away," he said, standing his ground, his pale eyes taking me in, descending over my uniform, slowly returning to my face.

"No, sir. I stayed talking too long with Wilbaht. I overran my time for cleaning. That's why I had to hurry." I spoke as formally and respectfully as possible.

"Yeah? How come you get to break the schedule?" he asked, now adopting a more familiar manner.

"I shouldn't. It's just that something came up about our mission."

"Oh, the mission, sure," he said, gazing almost thoughtfully at me. "I'll forgive you this time, but don't let it happen again." He moved to one side of me and advanced to the toilet. He didn't wait for me to leave before he opened his trousers and started to urinate. I stepped quickly out the door and into the hallway.

Although aggravated by this confrontation, I didn't want to make things worse. I decided to behave civilly with him. I leaned on the wall in the hallway next to the door and waited for him to finish. He stepped out, but still kept one foot in the doorway. He motioned for me to return to cleaning duty. I began to sidle past him, but he blocked my path with an arm he strung across the doorway. His fingers held onto its frame.

"You know, you don't have to be nervous around me." He scanned my face up and down. "I can be a nice guy away from the rest of the crew, once you get to know me better. You look like you could use a little…attention."

To my horror, Klib slipped a hand to the back of my thigh and attempted to grab my rear end. I pounded both palms to his chest to push him away. I grimaced.

"Whoa. Maybe not. My mistake," he said with an evil gleam in his aqua eyes.

"If you ever touch me like that again, you'll find my elbow inside your lung in about two seconds."

"Okay. I got the point," he laughed, raising both hands in rendition. He backed away down the hall. "Hey, don't get offended. I just thought you might appreciate a little human touch. You let me know if you change your mind. Deep space can get mighty lonely."

I only glared at him as he disappeared around the corner. A few expletives from Trau's interrogation came to mind. I knew Klib was annoying, but I hadn't thought he would dare to proposition or grope me.

During my time on deck, I didn't mention the incident to Ocelot. I wished I had been partnered with Yinore instead. I wanted to tell her about it, but her schedule was opposite mine. She only worked with Wilbaht and Klib. I saw her only in passing and at our communal meal. I felt embarrassed to seek her out to discuss this, but I wasn't confident that I could handle this on my own.

At the end of my work schedule, I hurried to meet Yinore as she entered the exercise room.

She stepped aside to let me in. She gazed into my eyes and frowned. "Oh. Humph. Klib. Yes. It was only a matter of time with him. He's been thinking of it since you came on board, I'll wager. He's of the third intelligence, I'd say. Thinks with his lower brain mostly. No wonder he had so many foolish accidents during his training years. I'm surprised he was able to rise above his libido long enough to secure a pilot's position."

"What should I do about him?" I asked.

Yinore asked me to explain in detail what happened. She rubbed her chin with one yellow claw and patted her elbow with another as I told her.

She grumbled to herself a few moments, and then said, "Technically, he committed no offense. He had the right to ask. You had the right to say no. You both exercised those rights. He did break protocol by attempting to pursue a sexual relationship with a crewmate, but the rulebook only says it's discouraged, not punishable. The only consequence would be separation. You already have very little contact with one another. I believe your threat will be enough to keep him from trying again."

I gazed at her, considering her words.

"Disappointed? Be careful, girl. Don't seek retribution just because you're angry. Let it go. Ignore him. We have plenty of other things to think about, you know."

"Yes, ma'am. I'm sure you're right. It's just..."

"You feel wronged. I know. I know what you mean. I've been there before myself. Don't take it personally, Sil. This may be the first unwanted offer you've had, but it won't be the last. Just let him know where you stand and ignore him." She observed me resolutely. She opened the door again to show me out.

"I'm sorry I interrupted you, ma'am. Thank you," I muttered with a bow.

"Quite alright, Sil. Glad to be of help," she said, ushering me out.

I realized fully at that moment that Yinore was not Yalat. Just because they were both Lizards did not mean they would react the same way. Yalat would have gone with me to confront Klib, in Wilbaht's presence, if possible. She would have rebuked him, setting him straight about acceptable and unacceptable behavior around me. Then again, I was my own woman now. I didn't need a tutor any more. I would have to rely on myself to resolve personal problems.

The next day, I turned in my first investigative report to Wilbaht. I had used recent records of travel and shipping to Sor3 to find a pattern of cargo weight discrepancies. If the empty ship's weight plus the reported weight of passengers, fuel, fluids, and cargo was significantly different from the measured weight at landing, this pointed to illegal cargo. I narrowed down the types of ships and their points of departure to show heaviest discrepancies on ships from Fitmalo, Jawlcheen, and Santer, all delivering to the Public Valley. I cross-referenced this information with shipping and receiving personnel and all people who had entered the platform more than four times within the time frame I selected. This yielded a long list of names, but I researched the most prominent ones.

Some were names linked to known smugglers. Some were new. Some appeared then disappeared conspicuously. Two pilots, a Captain Hume Nescu and a Captain Duray Bantem, both humans, appeared on the Sor3 Public Valley shipping tarmac twelve to fifteen times in one month and then vanished from all records. Three Vermilion males appeared at the same time during the first half of the month. Then they, too, disappeared. Trau showed up numerous times, as did three Fitmalo females. Several ships' pilots and freight personnel appeared consistently at the same times as Trau and the Fitmalo women. I researched them all as deeply as the current system would allow. I realized my investigation only covered the most obvious information and that I hadn't positively linked anyone to any wrongdoing, but my study could be used as auxiliary proof if any of these people were arrested later.

Wilbaht accepted my report as average. He encouraged me to research more creatively and not to ignore my hunches. Yinore and Ocelot worked fervently on research for Santer-based smuggling and Fitmalo military purchasing. Wilbaht's research mainly involved people associated with Prime Minister Lock and their possible connections to arms laundering.

We grew anxious to put our information to use on Santer. There we would encounter the real smugglers. For several nights, I dreamed of a shootout between Fitmalos over an arms shipment in some kind of bunker. Ocelot was there among them, but ran from the scene, narrowly escaping an explosion. I felt the dream would come true.

At our hour together in the main deck, I asked Ocelot if he had experienced any unusual dreams lately, too. With his back turned to me, he said he tried not to dream, or if he did, he made a conscious effort to put the dreams out of his mind as soon as he woke. He said dreams are only playthings of the subconscious and that he'd rather not take them seriously. I disagreed, but respected his belief.

I ventured to ask him if he ever had visions.

"I've only seen visions twice in my life. I'm not a seer. I just know things sometimes that I can't explain," he informed me. "Wilbaht says he sees them daily. Do you?"

"No, but I do have them often. Sometimes they extend into my dreams. That's why I asked you," I said.

Ocelot twisted in his chair, eyeing me almost cynically.

"Are you sure you can't tell me about that vision you saw at your testing? If it had anything to do with this investigation, you should at least share the information with Wilbaht," he encouraged.

"No. It was too chaotic. I couldn't make sense of it. All I know is that it was more terror than I ever wanted to see."

Ocelot leaned back in his chair and thought. Not receiving any sign of communication from him, I returned awkwardly to my list of stats.

"I saw a vision that day, too," I heard him say.

I glanced at him with curiosity. He gazed across the deck into his memory to recall it. "It was earlier in the day. It was strange, but not terrifying like yours."

"I thought you said you didn't see visions," I said.

"I said I've only seen two. The other one I saw just a few days before my parents were killed. I assumed a second vision meant death for someone close to me, just like the last time. We only had a near-death experience in the airbus crash."

"Did you see a vision of the crash?" I asked.

"No. It was nothing like that. It was a bizarre...aftermath. I saw four bodies," he said. He shifted in his chair uneasily, unwilling to give me more information.

I looked at him inquisitively. "Why do you think we have these visions? I mean, what are we supposed to do about them? I feel I should have some idea of what to do or which direction to go in my life because of them, but I don't. That vision only confused me. Do you know what you're supposed to do about your vision?" I asked.

He shook his head and paused a moment. "Wilbaht would advise us to follow our conscience. That's probably the best advice."

"Wilbaht is very wise," I said. I checked my empty screens again. "I'm sorry to hear about your parents. How did it happen?"

Ocelot swiveled his face to regard me defensively. "They were killed in a terrorist attack when I was twelve. Sub General Channol took me in after they died," he revealed.

"Wilbaht's brother was your sponsor?" I asked.

"Yes. Being paired with Wilbaht is almost like going back to school. They have very different personalities, though. Wilbaht is a lot friendlier, not that I'm criticizing."

I nodded. Despite the depressing topics of our discussion, I felt enlightened. Ocelot wasn't cold with me for once. Maybe he had begun to trust me. Another long silence invaded our conversation before he spoke to me again.

"Sil," Ocelot started. "I know you wake up at 1700 hours. That's my time in the exercise room." He cleared his throat. "You're supposed to go through pressure points training this year. If you're willing, I can instruct you on the holographic projector from 1700 to1740. You can earn certification in six or seven few weeks."

"Yes. That sounds fine. I'll be there at 1700. Just leave the door open for me," I said, brightening.

He nodded in agreement and turned back to his screens.

Chapter 18: The Planet Santer

Every morning for the next sixteen days, I woke up early to meet Ocelot in the exercise room for pressure points training. Ocelot set the holographic projector at the exercise room ceiling with the training program. We started with points on the Torreonoid phylum. Each four-limbed person had a series of thousands of pressure points linked by specific nerve tracks. The Vermilions, having an extra set of arms, also had hundreds more points than the Torreons, humans, Fitmalos, Greys, and Furmen. The Arbormen had a few more points on their tails. The Saurusoid phylum, (the Lizards), had fewer pressure points than the Torreonoids, regardless of whether they were four- or six-limbed, since they had a different kind of nervous system. The Sectoids, (Mantises and Beetles), had only a few dozen points, all difficult to access since their exoskeletons usually included protective coverings to their joints. I hoped never to meet one in combat.

As a student, I had only learned a few key points for emergency knockouts. This program required the knowledge of all points on all intelligent species. I had to study and recite each set of points on the projected opponent, and then practice strikes to attain an imaginary knockout. The holograms were not very realistic, however, providing no physical target to feel. On human targets, the series of strikes was more familiar, but I wanted a real target to touch. I asked Ocelot if he wouldn't mind standing in for arm and torso points so I could get a realistic feel for the strikes, but he reacted as if I had insulted him. The hologram was good enough, according to him, and there was no reason why I should practice an attack on him. I apologized, offended by his high-strung reaction. The whole program seemed cold and fake, but I was required to respect his lead.

He was my superior, after all, and wouldn't let me forget it, even if he didn't allow me to use his title.

In addition to pressure points training, Wilbaht continued to guide me on research techniques. Our research about the Fitmalos led us to vast amounts of information, most of which we were obligated to discard, since most of it contained astronomical lists of names and data. We did, however, follow all information available on large quantities of stolen and recovered goods in order to track possible smuggling activity. The manufacture, sale, and smuggling of unlisted weapons were especially difficult to track, since the people responsible for this trade were adept at covering their trails.

At the end of our journey to Santer, Yinore and I had not grown any closer. Thankfully, Klib did not approach me again. Wilbaht never swayed from his revered pedestal in my mind. Ocelot and I had become complacent coworkers. I was no longer afraid of him. I even ventured to talk with him about personal thoughts from time to time. He remained serious and formal. We stayed away from subjects of conversation that had caused friction between us. I did not talk much about Alaban, although I had to mention him sometimes when discussing our mission. Wilbaht liked to reminisce about his family. We almost never talked about Ocelot's personal life, except when he'd sometimes mention places he'd visited.

With this limited companionship, I missed Alaban badly. I messaged him several times during our journey even though he could only write me twice. His letters consisted of pages and pages of thoughts he'd collected almost daily. He crammed the letters with news and love notes. I hoped our travels would take us to him before our year ended. I didn't want to wait so long to see him again. I often dreamed of him. I wondered at times if I was in love with him or if it was only loneliness that kept him at the forefront of my mind.

When we finally landed at the Caladia Center on Santer, our cabin fever gave way to hyper anticipation. After we finished all standard landing and health checks, we briskly walked out together. The ground and increased gravity felt strange after so many weeks in space. The air tasted sweet and cold.

We all had an automatic two-day leave for post-flight. Klib was free to do whatever he liked for the time he had to wait for us on this planet. He was given an off-flight stipend to stay available for takeoff. He marched past us with a sling bag on his back. He shook hands with Ocelot and Wilbaht happily before he left. He ignored Yinore altogether, which was fine with her. He winked at me as he turned to leave. I'd never been so happy to see someone go away.

Large pink birds flapped through the air nearby. The clouds glowed a beautiful golden orange. The chilly air awakened my body with a burst of energy. Ignoring the opinions of my crew, I sailed upward into a vertical spin with arms outstretched. I flew up into the cool evening air. I took in the view of the gorgeous sunset and let its beauty replenish my spirit.

I turned in all directions to view my surroundings. I saw irrigation canals between systems of agricultural fields, rows of windmills and clusters of trees. Far in the western distance, the glittering towers of a modest city peeked over the hills. To the north, a few low-lying mountains rippled over the land. Several small towns lay scattered among them. To the east at a greater distance stretched a megalopolis. Its towers dotted the entire eastern horizon.

I glanced down at my remaining crewmates. They watched me from a reclined position on the grass. Yinore wrapped herself in a winter coat, since Lizards were cold natured. I landed at their feet.

"It's so good to be on a planet again," I said. The others concurred.

Ocelot leaned his head back on his hands and stared up at the pastel sky. Wilbaht did the same.

"I should probably be doing something official right now, but we're overdue for some relaxation," Wilbaht said.

"I'd love to stay out here with you, but this cool air is not for me. I'm going to the Center for some hot tea. I'll see you all later," Yinore croaked politely. We waved to her as she sped nimbly towards the building.

I jogged in the opposite direction to an empty parking spot. I performed my personal defense forms at last in the open air. I began form one less gracefully than I would have liked, but in a few moments my motions flowed with more precision. I continued with the slow, expressive movements and then threw the rapid punches. As I turned to my left for the next move, I noticed Wilbaht advancing toward me. He took a place a few meters away from me as I ended form one.

When I began form two, he performed it in unison with me. His towering, slender form glided through the movements beautifully. He was clearly a master of personal defense. Halfway through form four, Ocelot took a place beside Wilbaht so that we lined up in the field to practice together. Ocelot's performance emanated a sense of general strength instead of exaction. After form twenty-three, I stepped aside to watch them both.

They ended the form and bowed to each other, then to me. I returned the salute. Ocelot said he'd like to go get his sword to practice the next form. He asked us if we wanted to join him.

"I don't have a sword. I left mine embedded in the brain of a giant spider back on Sor3. I never got it back," I said.

148

"Why didn't you tell me?" Ocelot said. "I've got extras. You can have one of mine." His affable mood took me by surprise. I attributed it to our arrival on viable land.

"You wouldn't mind?" I asked hesitantly.

"I have extra swords. Just pick one from the stash," Ocelot said. I was equally surprised by his generosity.

"Don't use your swords here in the airfield. Remember what happened last time," Wilbaht advised. "I'm going to catch up with Yinore." He walked out into the cool evening and waved to us.

"Yes, sir," we responded.

Ocelot showed me to a large weapons container back in the secondary cargo hold of the ship. He slid it out from under the bottom shelf and opened it. Five folding swords were piled inside among other disassembled weapons. He shuffled through them. One showed an ornate decoration on its handle. He lifted this one carefully and handed it to me.

"This one might be the best weight for you. Try it out," he said.

I unsheathed the sword, held it away from us, and flung it open. Then I jerked it hard with a twist to snap it into its triblade position. It clinked and hummed. This sword was only slightly heavier than my old one had been.

"It's very decorative. It must have some special meaning. I don't want to take it from you if it has personal value," I told him.

"I made it in honor of my parents. It meant a lot to me at the time, but I'd rather let it go. It's actually a burden to me. You can have it. Besides, it looks like a woman's sword. If I went into battle with this thing, no one would take me seriously. It almost looks flowery," he expressed, frowning at the design.

I promised to be more cautious with this sword than I was with my last one. I ogled the glinting weapon and thanked him.

Ocelot stowed the rest of the cache and ambled out of the ship. I followed him to the main courtyard to practice form twenty-five. We attracted a small crowd with the swooping of our swords. A few of our fellow warriors applauded when we finished. We bowed to them respectfully. Twilight fell too soon after our practice. The Center courtyard lights grew brighter. It seemed unusual to be in the dark after living in a ship whose lights dimmed but never turned off. We found a small café near the perimeter of the Center. We ordered some local fruit tea, which had a strong flavor and seemed to be spiked with a little alcohol.

"I'm glad Klib isn't with us this time," I mused, recalling the bar incident on Sor4.

"He's not so bad except when he drinks," Ocelot said.

149

"He just rubs me the wrong way sometimes," I said with double meaning.

We talked about possible dangers of our upcoming assignment. Ocelot assured me that we wouldn't see much action from it. From time to time we would have to infiltrate among our suspects, but they would probably not be aware of us. He told me of similar assignments he'd had over the last few years.

As he spoke, I watched a light rainfall through the window. I recalled the dream I'd had on Sor3 in which Ocelot had walked out of Alaban's room into the rain and darkness. I still wondered what it meant. I contemplated this through the spatters on the glass. When I looked back at Ocelot, he seemed annoyed.

"I'm sorry. I was just remembering something. What were you saying?" I asked him.

"Nothing," he stated. "I was just saying at my first assignment was on Jawlcheen I didn't see any action the whole year. Maybe you'll be as lucky." He downed the rest of his tea.

We walked back to the ship together. It was not very late in the night, but there was nothing else to do around this area. I wondered what we would do on leave for the next two days. I asked Ocelot if he had any ideas. He said he planned on hiking up to a public forest nearby. He said wilderness was therapeutic after long space treks. Then he turned cold and quiet as the night air.

I shivered and commented about the chill. I crossed my arms and rubbed them with my hands. I walked closely to Ocelot, hoping he wouldn't mind going shoulder-to-shoulder for a while. He gave me the same offended look I'd gotten used to from him and moved away from me a couple of paces. I slowed my pace, feeling embarrassed. I kept my distance the rest of the way.

In the middle of the night, Yinore woke me to say she had run into an old friend at the Center and that she'd be staying there for the night. She seemed more nervous than apologetic.

"Is everything all right? You seem upset," I said.

"Oh, no. I'm fine, thank you. It's just so cold here for me, you know. Sleep well," she said. She trumped through the dining area with a large sling bag on her back and a full coat tucked all around her. Even her tail was encased in a padded cone to keep warm.

I went back to bed with disappointment.

When I awoke, I found Ocelot had gone already. I saw Wilbaht as he left to see General Black about our assignment details. Then I was alone. For the first time in my life, I was by myself. No one looked for me. No one called. No one needed me. I had no pending assignments. I had free time and didn't know how to fill it. I did outdoor training and exercise during most of the day. I found a public sparring and archery field behind the Caladia Center where I practiced sparring with an Arborman female. She was friendly and well trained, but lacked innate skill to make the match challenging. I went easy on her. She appreciated this. Wilbaht did not return that night. Ocelot stayed in the forest. I was glad that Klib didn't appear. I imagined he was probably out at a bar somewhere nearby or at a house of ill repute.

The next day, feeling unwanted and lonely, I spent a few hours on messaging. My family's news helped to soothe my mood. My parents gave me a message of continuing support and love. My sisters each wrote a short message to me. My oldest sister, Tamia, was making plans for her wedding party with her fiancé, Jem. My younger sister, Chena, gave me local news. My youngest sister, Grace, said she was tired of being a magnet for boys who had no brains. I hoped she did not have to go through a confrontation like the one I'd had with Klib. I was sure my father kept Grace close to the family as much as he could. She was his last girl, a teenager, and the prettiest in our family. I also believed she was the most intelligent.

I received a message from Alaban. His assignment had changed, but he still remained on Jawlcheen. He was safe. He sent me his love.

I took comfort in their messages. I replied to all of them even though I had little news to tell. I sent them all my love.

In the morning, my warrior crewmates returned. Wilbaht called us to a meeting at the dining table. He briefed us quickly since he was anxious to get started.

"Yinore, you'll be surveying transactions and bulk shipment records on trade registry through the computer system. You'll be underground where it's warm, so you won't have to worry about the weather. You won't even have to leave the foxhole if you don't want to. There is living space available adjacent to the offices."

"I prefer to stay in the Center, but I appreciate the offer just the same, sir," she said.

Wilbaht nodded to her. "The three of us will be above ground, positioned near all surveillance targets on our list, and close to regional government offices at the capitol. We're also three blocks from our inside contact for the smuggling investigation. The place is furnished, so we only need to bring in personal items and documentation equipment. I'll be moving in today. You two will join me tomorrow. We'll have to act like we're meeting each other for the first time. You'll get all the details from General Black today."

Wilbaht then suggested we test and pack all necessary equipment immediately. We followed his orders. Yinore only helped test a few pieces of recording equipment. Then she was off to see the General. A few hours later, Wilbaht left for the apartment while Ocelot and I went to the Center for briefing.

General Black Agram was a short, six-limbed Lizard like Yinore; only his color was a shiny tar black, like his name. He paced back and forth on the top of his desk to peer down on us as he spoke. His movements reminded me of an oversized rooster pacing to defend his roost. I suppressed a smile as he briefed us.

"This assignment may present a high-risk situation for you. At best, you will merely observe and record activities in the smuggling ring and government offices. At worst, the smugglers or government officials will detect you. Either group has the power and connections on this planet to exterminate you in public without reprimand. The outcome depends on you." He paused, frowning between us. He growled and then continued. "You will memorize all information on your new ID's plus all personal history that's been drawn up for you. Please direct all questions to the Sub General."

Suddenly, the General did something very strange. He jumped into the air and smacked me on the arm with his tail, causing me to dodge and bump into Ocelot. Ocelot sidestepped away from me instead of helping my regain my balance. I fell, but pulsed a levitative burst to bring myself to stand once more. I backed away from Ocelot and apologized. We stood again at attention, confused.

He frowned deeply, glaring Ocelot in the eye. "You'll take a thirty-minute role prep course with a personal trainer. You look like a pair of soldiers in an every-man-for-himself ordeal. You'll never pass for husband and wife. Report now to the office at the end of this hall. The Sub General will see you there. Dismissed."

We bowed and left his office. Ocelot gave me a perturbed look.

"It's not my fault." I whispered defensively.

Sub General Alaxon was an old yellowed Grey. He gave us the information to set up our aliases. I was now Kesserelle Timmott. Ocelot was Marchand Drapor. We supposedly worked in import and export taxation for the United Galaxy Santer office. The Sub General gave us each a huge computer file to read on the subject. An aide came in with our fake ID's and took our pictures to adhere to them. They gave us each a personal information file complete with family history, education, work-related achievements, marriage certificate, and prior housing and financial information.

The Grey droned to us. "The export company you'll be working for is entirely ours. It's located in the same city block as our primary smuggling ring contact. If you need to go downtown to the government offices, it will be under the guise of taxation reporting. The people at the export company will fill you in on that. If you think you are found out, report to Sub General Wilbaht first, and then to us. If it's serious, leave whatever you're doing and get back here as fast as possible."

The Sub General regarded us critically. I dared to read his thoughts. He didn't like the looks of us and was concerned that we might fail.

A female Furman trainer entered the room, interrupting my concentration. She showed us to a small training room next door. She explained the purpose for the role prep training. Her squirrel-like cheeks puffed as she spoke.

"You're investigative teammates. On your research vessel, you keep a professional distance from one another. That's appropriate. Now you're going under cover. Think of it as acting. Any time you're in front of an audience, we need you to *act* as husband and wife. When you're away from your audience, you'll resume normal professionalism. We're not asking you to pretend to be affectionate. So many couples are not. However, they wouldn't make a scene out of brushing past each other or bumping into one another. They would barely notice it. That's why the General tested you just now. You failed the test. That's why you're here. In public, you'll need to appear indifferent about close physical contact. I'm here to coach you."

We understood. She told us to stand in the corner of the room. This seemed strange, but we obeyed. I stepped in front of Ocelot and slightly to the side with my back to him. He leaned away from me as much as possible, pressing against the wall. The trainer set up a pair of small folding tables to either side of us. She proposed an exercise involving the sorting of several cards of serial numbers, which she scattered onto both tabletops.

"You are to both work at this task in your confined space until the task is finished. This will help you get used to the idea of being at close quarters with each other," she said.

Since I stood facing one table, I concentrated on sorting the cards in front of me first. I heard Ocelot's shirt rub against the wall each time he reached for a card on the opposite table. He still anchored himself to the wall to keep from touching me.

"Oh, no. This will never do. What's your name, sir?" the trainer asked.

Occlot told her his name and station.

"Sub Professor Ocelot, if you behave this way out there, even in our own offices, you'll risk exposure. Normally, I'd tell you to straighten up, but you're supposed to do just the opposite right now. Relax, man. She's not coated with acid," she said, shaking her head.

I felt Ocelot resist the trainer's suggestions, as I did.

She gave us several other simple tasks to do at these tables, but Ocelot did not improve. After this, the Furman told us to sit together on a short bench. I sat at the edge of it, knowing Ocelot would want to keep his distance. He did the same at the opposite end. He even leaned out over the edge to avoid physical contact with me. The trainer barked at us to sit closer. I obliged, but Ocelot scooted off the bench and stood.

At wit's end, the trainer stated he'd forced her to resort to drastic actions. She ordered us to hold hands. With extreme reluctance and perhaps even disgust, we obeyed. At the touch of his hand, I read his feeling, which was a hateful one. His animosity was directed not only towards the Furman, but towards me as well. Despite my own discomfort around him, I didn't understand why he would feel so abrasive towards me. Ocelot must have sensed my perception, because he cast aside my hand and crossed his arms. The trainer scolded Ocelot brusquely. Ocelot merely apologized stiffly and feigned ignorance.

"If you refuse to cooperate, your only option is to pretend to be angry with each other," she grumbled.

We both stood cross-armed and angry.

"Yes, just like that. Maybe this will work after all," she said.

When we reported back to the General's office, the trainer went with us. She explained our predicament. He was not pleased, but he went along with our new portrayal of the angry couple. He said it seemed to suit us better anyway. He briefly quizzed us on our new identities, and then sent us out to the apartment to meet with its superintendent.

We rode the city airbus to the Blue Zone of the megalopolis, Salumat. At the Blue Zone Suites building, the superintendent greeted us. She was a Vermilion woman. Ocelot behaved coldly with her as well, so I did most of the talking. She showed us the top level of an apartment. We behaved as if truly interested in the place. She then showed us the middle level bath and kitchen, which was shared with the apartment below. Conveniently, Wilbaht sat in the kitchen making a sandwich.

The superintendent introduced us all around. We asked each other about our fake occupations and origins. We said a few pleasantries to him and returned upstairs.

"I'd really love to offer you this apartment. What do you think of it?" the superintendent said with a sales smile.

"Yes, this is exactly what we need. I'd like to sign for it now," Ocelot said.

"Great," the superintendent said with a broad smile, glancing back and forth between us.

"You didn't ask me what I think," I said begrudgingly.

154

"Oh, stop whining. This place is fine. Don't tell me you know of someplace better. I've already said I'm going to sign for it, so I'm going to sign for it," he snapped.

I crossed my arms angrily. The superintendent's smile turned timid.

"Ah, well, if you'd like to talk about it a moment, I can wait downstairs," she offered.

"No, it's fine. Really," I told her flatly. "We'll take it."

"Oh, good," she said. The sales smile returned to her face.

We followed her back downstairs to her office and signed the rent agreement using our fake names and ID's. We kept serious faces, even after our charade was over. We headed back to the ship for our personal effects.

I wished more than ever that Alaban had been my partner instead of Ocelot. Alaban would have made the day into a hilarious adventure. He would have flirted with the superintendent. He would have bounced on the bed to try it out. He would have made sexual jokes about it, or at least innuendos. He would have teased me into giggles and he would have been all over me. There wouldn't have been any physical intimidation for him at all.

I glanced at Ocelot distastefully. I crossed my arms and looked away. He noticed my peeved manner.

"You can cut the act now. You've convinced everyone." His manner lightened.

"You were convincing, too," I spoke in a monotone.

"That didn't sound sincere," he said cautiously.

"I'm sorry. It's just difficult to work with such frigid partner," I admitted.

"I'm frigid for a reason. When there's a job at hand, I can't loosen up and lose focus. Our lives depend on it," he defended.

"It would have been just as easy to play the roles they told us to," I insisted.

"No. There was no reason to break protocol for that kind of act. We're here to concentrate on the assignment as warriors. You're my subordinate and a female. I'm expected to be formal and respectful towards you. I do that. The General had no reason to change that just to make a momentary impression on people who are not even our targets. Maybe I'm not a good actor, but I shouldn't have to be."

His idea seemed narrow-minded and rebellious to me, but at the same time he was right in defending his tenets about the job. Perhaps he really had refused to follow the suggested role-play to stand by his ethic.

"I apologize. I didn't mean any offense," I told him.

He nodded sullenly into the distance, cold as ever. "None taken."

155

If he read my thoughts at that moment, he did not let on about it. I asked him mentally why he would dislike me so strongly. Could it be that he had something to hide from me? What was it?

Part 2: RESILIENCE

Chapter 19: First Kill

For the next two months, we adhered to a rigid and sometimes exhausting routine. Ocelot and I walked to our cover office each morning. We listened in and watched activities at the smugglers' warehouses and screen-recorded activities from the previous night. At the same time, we went through the motions of regular accounting activities to keep up our assumed identities.

During his two-hour lunch and afternoon meeting time, Ocelot would change at a local restaurant, which also belonged to the Organization. He then sneaked out to a smuggler's office, where he played the role of an export tax code expert, which he was. He worked with the smugglers to encode and report fake goods to be taxed by the government to keep their shipping operation going. He obtained more information for us by doing this than we had imagined possible. We learned that, ironically, the Fitmalo rebels shipped chemical arms from Santer to Jawlcheen while the Regime shipped arms from Jawlcheen to Santer to be laundered and then sent to the Keres helion. Ocelot returned every day after his two-hour "break" to continue working with me. Then at the apartment, the three of us worked to compile the most pertinent information into a concise record of the smugglers' activities.

Wilbaht spent most of his day at the capitol, observing procedures and getting into social circles with suspected middle-government officials. He also made contacts at a nearby university where he did research for a phony sabbatical project.

Yinore kept in contact with us daily, through reports of shipping records and underground news directly related to Ocelot's smugglers. We did not see her in person for many weeks.

My job was the least interesting. Sometimes I ran errands between the office and the capitol building. I went there to deliver export taxation reports, but stayed to observe other aspects of the government building and its workers. On occasion, I spoke with several lower level officials during lunch at the capitol. I mostly heard rumors from them, but some information led us to the discovery of monetary links between the smugglers and a few important officials.

After our second month, we had proof of their involvement as well as possible evidence to link arms smuggling to a secret Fitmalo military order: the Regime. We came very close to completing our assignment objectives and moving out. Things seemed to be winding down. Then suddenly our operation was undermined.

Ocelot had gone out to mark double taxation codes on an arms shipment. His contact was there with a group of Santer officials. This was the moment we'd been waiting for to secure complete evidence against them. Unfortunately, the arms shipment arrived with a surprise.

One of General Zar's Fitmalo military rebel groups had overtaken the Regime arms shipment crew. They arrived with the firepower to shut down this branch of the Regime smuggling operation. A battle ensued between the rebels and the Regime and government officials' bodyguards. Ocelot did not try to protect any of his false employers. He fled, barely escaping with his life just as I had dreamed. Worried that he'd been followed by some of the Fitmalo rebels who thought he was one of the enemy, he hid in different public areas until he finally made his way back to the restaurant. The owner kept him there all night.

Ocelot called Wilbaht and me to see if anything had been reported about the battle. Not surprisingly, it hadn't. News had to be approved by the regional government before it could be broadcast and since the ambush involved government officials, they'd cover it up until an approved explanation could be reported.

When some people at the office asked why Ocelot hadn't returned to work after lunch, I told them he'd called to say he wasn't feeling well and that he'd gone home sick.

Wilbaht called to order me back to the apartment. I made the excuse at the office that I wasn't feeling well either and went home. When I arrived, Wilbaht had gone to check in with General Black about the problem. I called Yinore to see if she was in on the battle information. She had only been notified a few minutes earlier. She was now on alert to be ready to move out. She could say no more. I hung up and paced.

Finally, I sat on the sofa, which had been my bed for the last two months. I heard Wilbaht arrive downstairs. I bounded down the steps to meet him in the kitchen where we usually met, but he didn't come up the stairs right away. I heard him talking with a man in his apartment. I didn't know who it could be, but I decided to wait in the kitchen a while. Maybe whoever it was would leave soon so I could talk with Wilbaht alone.

Instead of staying in the downstairs apartment, however, Wilbaht came up the stairs. His visitor followed him. I prepared myself to welcome a neighbor or a friend of Wilbaht's. Wilbaht peeked into the kitchen door briefly, and then turned and told the man to wait a moment.

"Sil, we have a guest," he said with a smile.

He had used my real name. The man must have been someone from the Organization. I stood from the table and advanced toward the door. Wilbaht stepped into the kitchen. A dark, handsome young man in a dark blue combat uniform followed him. He tried to remain formal, but he couldn't hold back a broad, joyous smile when he saw me.

"Alaban!" I cried. I leapt forward to grasp him around the neck. He held me tightly and lifted me off the floor with a gleeful chuckle.

When he lowered me again, we kissed each other lightly on the lips. I smiled more at that moment than I had in the last five months. I looked him up and down.

"Look at you. You must have put on ten kilos of muscle. You're huge, and so handsome. You're a sight for sore eyes. What are you doing here?" I chattered.

He beamed with pride. He took my face in his hands. "I'd love to tell you, but I can only say I'm here on special assignment. I agreed to do it only if I could see you first." He gazed deeply into my eyes.

The smile on my face slowly faded. "They gave you an assassination," I said. "You'll be in danger."

He nodded reluctantly.

I gripped his hands in mine. "I'm so sorry. I pray you'll be all right."

"Actually, I have to be going right now," he said seriously. "Come to the door with me. I can't let you follow me any more than that."

We walked hand in hand down the stairs. Wilbaht followed us.

At the door, Alaban let go of my hand to shake hands with Wilbaht. "Thank you, sir. You can count on me to back you up any day," he said.

"Don't mention it," he said.

Alaban turned to me. Wilbaht walked away to the other end of the room to give us privacy. Alaban touched my face.

"I still love you," he said, caressing my cheek. His eyes reflected the same.

"I love you, too, Alaban. Good luck." I kissed him on the corner of his mouth, wishing we had time to say more.

He glanced up at Wilbaht who had his back turned to us.

"May I have a goodbye kiss?" Alaban whispered to me. "For strength."

I kissed him as I had the last time I saw him. He embraced me and whispered a thank you in my ear. He looked into my eyes and said goodbye again. He blew me another kiss as he stepped out the door.

As the door snapped shut, I felt my heart grow heavy in my chest. I leaned anxiously on the door for a few moments. Wilbaht stared at me with compassion.

"I found him at the Center," he said, folding his hands before him. "He begged to see you."

"Do you know his assignment?" I asked.

"Yes. It's someone I've been working with at the capitol. He has to evade a great deal of security. You must have been right when you said he can get into anything."

"I hope so for his sake. Now we have two men to worry about. What can we do, sir?" I asked.

"Pack. We're being called off the assignment. Yinore's operation is set to shut down as well. I'll go in to get Ocelot in an hour. As soon as we get him back, we're to report to the Caladia Center for end briefing. Then we'll have a few days leave and probably a new assignment elsewhere."

"We'll be flying again?" I asked.

"I expect so," he affirmed.

I paused at the foot of the stairs. "Sir, before I start packing, would you say a prayer with me?" I asked.

"Certainly, child. Come sit with me here."

We sat on his sofa and held hands. We prayed for the safety of our two friends. Then Wilbaht said a strange prayer for me. He asked for peace of mind and strength of character to carry me through the difficult decisions I would soon have to make in my life. I gave him an inquisitive expression, but he didn't explain himself. He patted my hand and told me to go pack. I asked Wilbaht about it if I should help pack some of Ocelot's things as well. He said I should gather up his things and place them on his bed. At least this would make it easier for him to pack quickly once he arrived.

I took the clothes from the closet I shared with Ocelot. After I had packed my own things in the travel box, I folded his extra clothing neatly and placed it in rows on his bed. Out of the pocket of one of his long jackets fell a black plastic envelope. It spilled to the floor, scattering its contents under the bed. I bent down to pick them up.

They were printed photographs of people and places of personal value. I knew I could get in trouble for going through his personal belongings, but curiosity hooked me.

The first picture showed a waterfall and a tropical lagoon. On the back of this picture, he had written only the place: Sor2. The second was an old photo of his parents on a bridge overlooking some tourist center on Jain. His mother resembled Jiao more than Ocelot. Ocelot looked like his father.

The next photo showed a wooded valley strung with mountains. I recognized this as somewhere here on Santer. The next photo showed a landscape dotted with islander huts. This was a vacation spot on Liricos. The next was a photo of Ocelot taken by an unknown photographer. The picture showed him thrusting his sword toward a practice log on Jawlcheen. Another photo showed Jiao and his family on Sor3.

The next picture surprised me. It was a photo of Wilbaht and me here in this apartment. I remembered when it was taken, although I hadn't been aware of him taking our picture. It was a night when the temperature in the apartment had been unusually hot. We had complained about it to maintenance that day. That night I wore only a sleeveless shirt and a light pair of exercise shorts. Wilbaht sat in the chair next to the sofa in similar clothing, sorting through some playing cards. I had fallen asleep after losing my hand in the game.

In the photo, my left arm cradled my head. My face turned away from the camera. I lay on my back with my left leg fully extended. My right knee pointed toward the center of the room. My right hand rested on my thigh, my thumb tucked slightly into the leg of my shorts. Peeved, I wondered if he'd taken the picture as a joke. I would have liked to ask him about it, but he couldn't know I'd seen it.

I put the photos back in their envelope as Wilbaht called me to come downstairs. I jogged down to his apartment where he briefed me on the plan to pick up Ocelot.

"We'll leave separately," he said. "You cover the streets. I'll go inside. Give me a ten-minute lead. Anyone watching won't automatically make a connection between Ocelot and me. If someone's been observing his actions for a while, they may go on alert if you show up. I'm sure he's been followed. They think he's a key to the Regime smuggling operation. They won't leave until they hit their target or until they lose him completely.

I believe we'll find an assassination team waiting around the restaurant for him. These are Fitmalo military rebels, fairly predictable. They'll have one traveler and at least three hidden snipers. The traveler will be moving in and out of the area casually. He may even go into the restaurant. If they're sure of his location, they'll wait him out until nightfall."

"How do you plan on getting him out of there, sir?"

"I'll pay for a public driver to wait around at the back of the building. This is just a distraction for anyone observing. While working at the capitol, I researched city plans for possible escape routes in case any of us needed an alternative exit one day. There is a system of catacombs beneath the downtown area and part of the Blue Zone. It was built many centuries ago, but I believe it will still be open enough for us to make it out."

"How can you get down there from the restaurant?" I asked.

"There's a sewage vault under the restaurant. It doesn't lead directly to the catacombs. We'll have to go a couple of city blocks to the east before we can get to an internal connection. The tunnels of the catacombs end under an anthropology museum. There's a well preserved stairway at that end."

"I won't be able to contact you so far under ground, will I? How will I know if you got through safely?"

"If we're not above ground four hours after I go in, start searching for us starting at the museum entrance. Bring cave equipment and weapons just in case."

"Yes, sir," I said. "Anything else?"

"Keep your distance from me. Scan for any possible hiding spots for the snipers. If you see any starting to congregate in the restaurant or at the cab, be ready to draw weapons and engage. If they start to group, follow them closely. If they suspect we're trying to get him out, they will attack us inside the restaurant. We're trying to avoid a scene and civilian casualties, but if they strike first, we'll have no choice but to fight back."

We wished each other luck before leaving the apartment. I waited ten minutes as he had indicated before following him out.

When I arrived at the street directly across from the restaurant, I stopped at an information stand to get a feel for my surroundings. I felt an antagonistic presence nearby. He passed close behind me, walking from my right to my left. I continued flipping through various screens of information. When I felt this person was far enough away from me to observe him without being caught, I looked up at him.

The Fitmalo strolled to the corner of the street, waited for traffic to stop, and then crossed to the corner in front of the restaurant. This had to be the traveler.

I left the information booth and traced the man's steps. I pretended to wait patiently for the slow of traffic. Afternoon commuters jammed the main causeway with their three-wheeled solar pod vehicles, some blaring music, and some blinking company slogans. I scanned the surrounding area over the tops of the vehicles for possible hiding places of the other Fitmalos on the assassination team. I spotted one.

An advertising booth leaned onto the base of a building that flanked the street to my left. It was a table covered with a plastic display board. It had been used as a free sample booth for the drink it advertised, but now it lay empty. I tried not to stare directly at it. If a sniper waited underneath it, he would be observing the close vicinity of his traveling comrade.

I crossed the street to the sidewalk in front of the restaurant. It was a bluish-gray building with a stone façade and with curling frond-like sculptural effects jutting from its corners at every floor level. At its top flourished a display of oval-shaped stone clocks of ancient design. Red curtains silhouetted the window frames. The place was a respected establishment and a landmark for this section of the city.

The traveler entered the restaurant. Since he was alone, I didn't follow him in. Instead, I continued my straight path between the restaurant and the street where I expected the first Fitmalo sniper hid. I continued up the steep hill, passing the restaurant. I glanced to my right as I passed the building to check for the public driver Wilbaht had mentioned. The back of the restaurant was still empty.

I crossed the next street; continuing straight ahead, and then entered a fruit grocer's at the corner. From the display window, I observed the advertisement booth and the street below. I bought a small bag of fruits from the Arborman grocer and left the store.

This time, I took the street behind the restaurant. The public driver still had not arrived. I scanned the immediate buildings for more hiding places. There was a balcony on the second floor of a building directly in front of me. A Fitmalo man leaned on the railing. He stared down at the vehicles below. This could have been a second sniper. I averted my eyes to concentrate on my own path.

At the corner of this street, I turned right, crossed, and walked downhill with the restaurant again at my right. As I passed the plate window of the restaurant, I checked inside. The traveler sat reading a menu at a booth close to the entrance. I did not catch sight of Wilbaht. He may have been in the kitchen area or in Ocelot's hideout in the back preparing to escape through the sewer line.

As long as the traveler stayed in the front of the restaurant alone, I could be sure they were not aware of the escape. I felt certain I had located the positions of two of the snipers. I was still missing at least one, possibly two more.

I reached the corner of the street in front of the restaurant, facing the information booth where I'd paused before. I had to locate the third or fourth hideout even if it meant staying in one place for a few minutes.

As I crossed the street, I noticed a Fitmalo man sitting in the stairway of the building behind the booth. He read a financial news screen in the wall. He glanced up at me as I stepped onto the curb. Our eyes met momentarily. I read his suspicion.

I moved around the corner of the building and continued down the street nervously. I didn't want to go back to the restaurant block for fear they might discover me. At the same time I had to back up my partners in case something happened. I couldn't be sure if the Fitmalo I'd just seen would take action against me or not. I decided to make a detour around several buildings and then return to the area from behind the restaurant.

As I rounded the corner of a building to try and double back to my target area, I became aware of an unusual noise. A high-pitched whine, like that of a small electronic device, sang behind me. I glanced over one shoulder and scanned the walkway. I caught sight of a flying metallic insect, a robotic camera. It followed me. The Fitmalo at the stairway must have sent it. If I continued my path away from the restaurant, the Fitmalo might give up tracing me, believing he had made a mistake in thinking I was involved. However, he might also be tracking me to close in and take me out. I had to lose the electronic camera and get back to the site.

I walked as quickly as possible. I tried not to become frantic. I felt something was about to happen. I rounded the next corner and shot straight up, leaving the camera confused. It buzzed away into traffic and met its demise beneath the wheel of an electronics delivery truck. I cloaked to avoid attention from the trafficked street. I skimmed over tops of buildings in a semicircle around the restaurant block as fast as I could.

When I finally arrived back at the fruit grocers, a Fitmalo emerged from the advertising booth. I peered around the corner carefully before retracing my steps on the street behind the restaurant.

A public driver's cab parked at the back of the restaurant. A Fitmalo man talked to the driver. Soon a second Fitmalo strolled up alongside the first. I slowed my pace as I walked along the sidewalk opposite them. I kept them in my peripheral vision. I surveyed the area to see how many people were in danger around me. Only a few other people walked on this street. Vehicle traffic was light in this back alley.

I stepped in front of a stairway into the building next to me and dared to check over my shoulder to see the Fitmalos at the cab. The first Fitmalo had cut the driver's throat. The body lagged over the steering instruments of the cab. The second Fitmalo held out an acid pistol aimed at me.

I dropped my bag of fruit and turned to run up the stairs. I ripped open my jacket to retrieve my hand bow. I turned to the left to escape through a side stairway. A spatter of acid hit the corner as I bounded up the stairs. Acid droplets attacked the back of my jacket. I tore it off as I raced up the stairs. A second shot splashed the jacket as it hit the floor. The leather sizzled and steamed.

I fastened the hand bow securely over my left fist as I flew up the stairs to a door. It was locked. I heard a scuffling sound at the entrance of the stairway where I'd come in. With my back to the door, I drew an arrow and shot towards the bottom of the stairs at my desecrated jacket. The arrow impacted and exploded just as one Fitmalo peeked around the corner of the stairwell. He let out a scream and collapsed to the floor. His blue skin melted into a puddle. I could hear a second Fitmalo gurgle in pain behind him. The acid explosion left a swirling cloud of droplets in the air, which the second Fitmalo inhaled. He, too, perished from it.

Pity and remorse hammered me. I had never killed anyone of high intelligence before. The most intelligent creature I'd previously killed was the giant spider on Sor3. The Fitmalos were of the second intelligence. They were my equals. I told myself it had been self-defense. They would have killed me if I hadn't shot first. Still, I felt deeply for their lives.

Once the faint cloud of acid dissipated, I could probably expect at least one other Fitmalo on the stairs with the same intention. I cloaked a blind spot before me and waited.

Just as I'd suspected, a third Fitmalo arrived on the scene. He carefully peeked up the stairwell and then retracted instantly. He stepped into the stairwell, since he hadn't seen me. He advanced rapidly up the stairs to the door. I continued cloaking while I levitated to the ceiling, hoping this man had poor extrasensory perception. I glided along the ceiling of the stairway to the exit.

The Fitmalo tried the door, finding it locked. He hesitated to decide whether to blow it open or to run away from the scene altogether. Tenaciously, he opted to blow it open. He set an explosive on the doorframe, turned, and scampered down the stairs and out to the street. I followed him from above.

The explosive cracked and boomed. It threw debris and ash out onto the street. I levitated up the exterior wall of the building. People on the street and in the nearby vicinity screamed. Solar cars jostled out of the way, blaring their horns. All civilians scattered away from the street.

The Fitmalo who had set the explosive was quickly informed of his mistake by yet a fourth sniper, who approached him running and pointing to me. He had seen me from the side, since the blind spot only worked in one direction.

I soared upside down, my weapon-clad fist extended toward the ground and my enemies. They drew pistols to shoot, leaving me no choice. I had to kill them. I shot two acid arrows at them, ending their lives just as one of them shot at me and missed.

I continued up the wall until I arrived at a high ledge. I perched there, overlooking the street. I had to be sure there wasn't a fifth sniper hiding nearby. At the balcony I'd noticed earlier, a blue figure opened a door and entered, seemingly fleeing for his life. All the other balconies filled with people trying to see what had happened on the street.

The building was a good seventy meters distance from me, but I had to get to him. The rush of adrenaline helped to power my levitative energy. I made for the balcony and touched down running. I burst through a large white room to an open door. I sensed the man descending the stairs. He

167

reached the corridor that led to the street below. I flew down after him, avoiding bypassers, as he rushed out a side door. I pursued him with my bow newly loaded.

For some reason, he had chosen to run up the street toward oncoming traffic instead of going downhill. Too many innocents crowded the street. There was no way I could get a clean shot at him. I had to chase him on foot.

I sprinted after the Fitmalo, dodging pedestrians and jumping over one woman's mewling pets. I overtook my foe within twenty paces, since he was a good deal shorter than me and not so fast. I passed him on his right and then twisted to throw an inside block to his throat. He flipped into the air sideways, somersaulted backwards, and landed with rolling momentum onto the sidewalk. I didn't wait for him to stop rolling. I pounced on his back, pressing one knee into the small of his spine. I grabbed both his arms and pulled back sharply. I was so overwhelmed and scared by the incident that I accidentally yanked the arms out of their sockets.

He howled in pain. Though repentant of my cruel action, I searched him for weapons. He was heavily armed with six different weapons packs. I pulled each one off of him as quickly as possible. I hung them over my right shoulder as I lifted them from him. He continued to wail in pain.

Vehicular traffic veered away from us and nearly stopped. People on the street raced away gasping and shouting. We were a terrible spectacle for the afternoon commuters. I had to get this man and myself out of sight as quickly as possible. Otherwise we'd end up on a local newscast.

I pulled the bottom strap out of my auxiliary weapons pouch and used it to bind the man's hands behind him. Feeling sorry for my overpowered victim, I popped his shoulders back into place one by one. Tears streamed down his blue face. I realized he was the youngest of his colleagues, probably younger than I.

I marched him into the nearest doorway, which happened to be a laundry. I directed him to the back of the place. Employees stared at us in fear. I found a stairway at the back of the building. At the middle of the stairway was a fairly large window. I kicked at its latch. As it flung open with the breeze, I surveyed a heavily trafficked street below. At the top of the opposite building, I spotted an airbus landing roof. I decided to give my captive a choice.

"Fitmalo, you can either die here and now by way of my breaking your neck, or you can fly with me up to that airbus station and stay alive. If you choose to live, you'll be arrested and interrogated by U.G. officials. If you don't answer in ten seconds, I'll decide for you."

"All right. Arrest me. Just don't let me fall," he pleaded.

"Then don't squirm," I said.

I threaded my arm around his waist and picked us both up. I used all the levitative strength I had left to get us to the airbus site. Once there, I commandeered a tiny airbus to transport us the Caladia Center. I asked for a storage box for the Fitmalo's weapons packs. A Mantis gave me a secure box while a human security guard held my prisoner. I locked the items in the box. I asked the security guard for a regular set of wrist binders. I took back my weapons pouch strap and replaced it. I commended the airbus personnel for their help and then boarded the airbus with the Fitmalo. Our Furman pilot took us to the Center at the swiftest speed the airbus would allow.

I sat in a seat opposite my prisoner. He was clearly traumatized by all that had just happened to him and his comrades. Shock warped his face. He muttered to himself softly about what his comrades would do to him if they found out he'd been arrested. He believed he'd let his family down as well as his people. Halfway to the Center, he became louder.

"Let me die. Let me die," he repeated.

I knew I wasn't supposed to talk with prisoners en route to their interrogation, but I felt I owed this one something. "You had your chance," I said. "I'm not going to kill you. The blood of four men on my hands is more than enough for me. I'm sorry I had to do it, but I had to stay alive. Now so do you."

He grew quiet. He stared at the floor, expressionless. He stayed this way for the rest of our flight. When we arrived at Caladia, a group of four military police met us. They escorted the listless Fitmalo to interrogation.

I wanted to report directly to General Black, but he was not available. Instead, I submitted my full report to Sub General Alaxon. He recorded my statement anxiously.

Once I finished my story, he organized a four-man armed escort for me. They were ordered to take me back to Salumat, first to the museum where Ocelot and Wilbaht would emerge, and then to the apartment to retrieve all personal belongings and documentation.

We took a truck to the museum. Our driver stayed behind while the rest of us demanded entry. We also demanded that the building be closed for the rest of the evening. Museum security and their director were both hard to convince, but finally we were allowed access. We went to the stairway to await my partners' arrival. They should have emerged from the catacombs within the hour, but they didn't show up. We waited several minutes more. I decided to go in after them. I asked the three men to stay at the stairway since they did not carry underground equipment. I entered the cave alone.

The stairway down to the catacombs was, of course, as dark as one could imagine. I used the band light generously. The sides and ceiling of the stairway were decorated with an uneven checkerboard design, representing the uneven path through life and death, reminding me of where I was about to tread. I crept carefully down the moist stairs, stepping down more than two hundred times before reaching the bottom. Puddles of stagnant water dotted the floor. Remnants of black and white murals of ancient people lined the sticky walls. The air hung pungent with damp decay. I fitted a breathing tube to my face and turned on the oxygen pack.

The floor sloped downward a little more with each step I took. Rows of tombs and rickety piles of arm and leg bones lay piled on either side of the cave. Soon I reached an arched doorway. This led to a wide chamber filled with piles of skulls of every species, classified according to size. I shivered as the shadows of skulls wavered eerily around the room. Something moved on the ceiling. I angled the light toward it. Furry brown bats clung in bunches to the stalactites. They stirred only a little. I crept forward as silently so as not to disturb them.

The next doorway led to a narrower hallway, which slanted downward even more. The pitch of the floor here was so steep I nearly slid down the shaft. At the bottom of this hall opened another wide chamber. It held large, elaborate tombs of important officials of the Vermilion and Arborman species. The murals showed bright orange four-armed people and hairy-tailed chimpish Arbormen working together to build an ancient city. The next room was filled on either side with skeletons piled one on top of the other. Some carcasses at the top still rotted. I moved through the gruesome stench to the next chamber.

Here I found yet another arched doorway. It led to a natural cave run through by a stream. As I approached it, I noticed large, milky-white fish in the clear water. These fish were eyeless, with tiny phosphorescent blue dots along their sides. One startled me, flapping its tail and splashing when I pointed my light towards it. I jerked backwards, nearly dropping the light.

I found a stone bridge at one end of the open cavern. Before I reached the middle of the bridge, I noticed a doorway directly in front of me and another long, dark hallway. I looked down at the stone slabs of the bridge that connected with the other side of the stream. A ditch separated the end of the bridge and the bank of the stream. The water had eroded into the rock over time. I would have to hop over it to get across, being careful not to slip in the mud.

I stood at the edge of the bridge and looked up at the doorway. I jolted backwards. A white figure stood before me. It was a human man with a face like putty.

I froze where I stood. Goosebumps stood out on my arms. I had the nervous urge to urinate. The light trembled in my hand.

"Who is it?" the man whispered in a rasping voice.

His arms outstretched to touch both sides of the doorway. A dark loincloth hung at his waist. On his feet he wore hand-made cleated sandals. His eyelids rested halfway over his eyes. He was blind, like the fish in this stream. His whole body glowed a pale translucent white under the band light. Muddy ooze covered his hands and fingers from clutching at the walls. He lived, and yet he seemed to belong to the dead of the catacombs.

"Who are you?" he said again in a grating whisper.

I breathed quickly and heavily. "A friend, I hope," I whispered back at him.

He stood swaying his head for a moment.

"What do you want?" he hissed.

"My friends are lost. I think they're down here somewhere," I breathed.

"Who are you?" he repeated.

"My name is Sil," I told him.

He raised his thick, hairless eyebrows and swayed even more. He licked his lips and pressed them together. "They called to you. But you cannot go to them. They are behind the wall at the pool," he said.

I relaxed a little. "Can you take me to it?" I asked.

"Yes, but you cannot get through," he said.

"I'd like to know where they are," I persisted.

"Then come with me if you can," he said, turning his back to me.

I hopped over the ditch and slid in the mud. Then I followed the phantom man carefully down the corridor. He was surefooted and swift. I couldn't keep up with his pace. At the end of the corridor, I saw him turn right. I tried desperately to catch up with him. I turned in the direction where he'd gone, but I only saw an empty chamber with a few murals and tombs.

In front of me, near the ceiling, stretched a painting of a mythical monster. It was almost diamond-shaped, with eight sets of tiny claws jutting out on all sides. Its mouth opened from the middle of its body with two rows of sharp teeth. Its eyes gleamed phosphorescent yellow. I had seen this creature before, in the vision I'd seen the day of my personal defense testing. Only this one wasn't alive. It was just a mural. A sinking feeling gripped me. I knew I would soon face the real thing. I held the band light in my right hand and drew my sword with the other.

The clanking sound of it echoed sharply through the hollow catacombs. The albino blind man reappeared in the chamber.

"Quiet! Please!" he hissed. "Don't make loud noises."

171

"What's your name?" I asked him.

"I am Gult," he said.

"Gult, have you always been blind?" I asked.

"Yes. Always. There is no other way to be down here."

He couldn't have been aware of the mural.

"Are there any large creatures down here? Carnivorous animals?" I asked.

He took a step back and swayed. "Yes. At the pool. They live at the pool. That is why I never go there."

"If you never go to the pool, how do you know my friends are behind a wall there?" I asked.

"There is a safe passageway too small for them to enter. I was near it when I heard men shouting. I believe they are trapped. I don't know how they got there."

"Take me there. Please," I said. "Slowly this time."

He led me through the tunnels until we reached a narrow walkway. It seemed to be walled up at the end with a smooth, waxy film. Gult stopped halfway into the tunnel. He pointed to the end of it, but didn't say anything. He shrunk back to the opposite end.

I turned to face the filmy covering. This was no wall. It was the body of a monster. I lurched forward with my sword. I stabbed the creature three times. It bounced away from the opening of the tunnel and splashed into a large pool below. It bled yellow.

I held my band light up to the opening. Inside I found a vast cave covered with families of these monsters. These manta-like creatures grew to about two and a half meters in diameter. They clung to the walls of the cavern and swam though the deep pool below.

Directly across the cave from the tunnel where I stood was an arched doorway that had been walled up centuries ago. It jutted out above the pool about ten meters away from where I stood. I left the band light on the floor behind me. I pointed it toward the archway.

"Wilbaht! Ocelot!" I called.

The echoes of my voice battered the cave walls and reverberated back to me. The creatures became agitated. They flopped around, some of them splashing into the water, others bounding up at me. I fended them off with my sword. They tried to bite at me with their hideous suctioning mouths. With all the splashing and slapping of fins on the cave walls, I could barely hear my partners calling back to me.

"Stand back as far as you can!" I shouted.

Creatures screeched and flapped at me, attacking the entrance of the tunnel. Some bit each other in anger. Sticky yellow blood painted the tunnel's end. I stabbed and stabbed at the monsters, but they kept coming to the tunnel in droves.

I backed away a few paces, letting the creatures pile upon each other and then fall away from the opening of the tunnel. They had become excited from the sound of my voice. If I remained quiet, maybe they would lose interest and move away. I waited several minutes. Gradually, they stopped flinging themselves at the tunnel. They all fell away but one. I sliced it a few times as quietly as I could. It lobbed away with a slurping sound, but did not attract more.

No voices came from the archway. I assumed my partners had backed away as I had told them. I only had one weapon that could work on the wall. I understood the risk, but I had to get them out. I feared it might cause an implosion somewhere in the cave, but I saw no other way. I set my sword aside. I drew my fan blaster.

I knelt at the opening of the tunnel and aimed. I charged the blaster to low power, counted to five, and let the blast fly. I held the weapon securely to recuperate the ion charge and avoid recoil. The fan zipped open and hit the wall with a deafening boom that spawned a mild earthquake.

The creatures screamed. They floundered around wildly, now uncertain where the sound had come from. Several stalactites fell from the cavern ceiling into the pool, crushing or impaling some of the monsters.

Shuddering sound waves caused the pool to froth. The archway was decimated, as well as part of its main support underneath. Water trickled down the wall from what had been the archway to the pool below. More stalactites cracked and fell. A pile of rock, mud, and sand lay in the archway's tunnel as well as below it at the edge of the pool. A large stone fell into the pool from the arch. Another and another stone hurled into the water. They were clearing the way out.

I put my fan blaster back in its place at my thigh and once again took up my sword against these hideous animals.

"Draw swords!" I called. As soon as I shouted, some creatures leapt up at me. I only fought off the ones that tried to cover the tunnel entrance.

I heard a clatter of swords through the shrieking of the animals. The creatures flopped up the bank of the pool toward Wilbaht and Ocelot. The men swung constantly at the attacking rays as they levitated toward my side of the cave. I backed into the tunnel to give them room. I put away the sword and picked up my light, ready to move.

Wilbaht and Ocelot entered the tunnel breathing heavily, but they were unharmed. I showed them the way out. We did not see Gult on our way back up to the surface. I told the men about him. They said he sounded like a ghost. In a way, I thought he might have been.

Wilbaht said they had been trapped in the walled section of the catacombs when part of a sewer line had broken, flooding a large section of the catacombs behind them. I admitted they smelled almost as bad as the rotting carcasses I'd passed. They were not amused.

As we ascended the stairs to the museum, its usually dim lights seemed bright as day. The soldiers were glad to see us. They were either worried or bored since we had taken so long to get out. Wilbaht ordered them to take us quickly to the apartment suite. It was now nearly one o'clock in the morning, so we hoped few people would be aware of us. We shirked our roles as neighbors and entered Wilbaht's door all together.

At the apartment, Wilbaht and Ocelot bathed to get the sewer smell off them. Then they dressed while I bathed. I still felt the sticky smell of rotten catacombs in my hair. I washed it twice. I dressed and prepared to leave with them. When I went upstairs to collect my traveling boxes, Ocelot met me in the living room.

"Why did you go through my personal items?" Ocelot asked angrily.

"Wilbaht said I could," I said. "I was just trying to help."

"You weren't helping when you went through my photos," he complained.

I shrank. I didn't know how he knew it, but there was clearly no way to deny it now. "I'm sorry. They fell out of your pocket. Besides, what are you doing with a picture of me?" I defended.

"What picture of you? It's a picture of my partners. It's a picture of Wilbaht. It doesn't matter who's in the picture. It doesn't belong to you. You're the one who always follows regulation to the letter. You should know regulation says you don't go through your partner's personal effects unless he's dead. Was I reported dead?"

"No."

"Then why the internal espionage?" he harangued, holding up the envelope as evidence.

"I'm sorry. I wasn't trying to spy on you," I stated. "It was an accident."

He gnashed his teeth at me. "It's a good thing we have a three-day leave coming up. At least I won't have to share a room with you anymore," he barked. He spun with his envelope and returned to pack.

I was taken aback. "Why don't you take your leave time in the woods? Maybe it'll help you calm down," I suggested.

"I can't. It's going to rain all week. But if I could, I'd get as far away from you as possible," he vowed.

174

"What's that supposed to mean? I just saved your ass out there and now you yell at me about an insignificant accident? I don't understand you. I'm going downstairs," I said with exasperation.

Furious and confused, I went with the escort soldiers to the truck. We waited fifteen minutes for Wilbaht and Ocelot. They dragged down with packed boxes.

When we got to Caladia, we were quartered in separate rooms. My frustration with Ocelot nearly drove me to tears before I finally fell asleep.

Chapter 20: Joy and Sulking

The next morning, the three of us reported for voluntary interrogation. We each made a separate statement. My interrogation and Ocelot's took much longer than Wilbaht's since we had battle details to cover. After the long interrogation, we were called into the General's office. He congratulated each of us for our quick-witted solutions to the problems we had faced. I apologized for my sloppy treatment of the Fitmalo snipers. The General said under the circumstances my reaction was completely rational, although he wasn't sure why I had chosen to spare the life of the fifth sniper.

"The next time you're in a situation where you have to flee the scene, don't take hostages unless it's part of your directive," he advised.

"Yes, sir," I said, bowing my head.

When he dismissed us, Wilbaht stayed to speak with him a few minutes in private. Ocelot and I walked out side by side. We shared the elevator down to the floor accessing the quartering building and marched alongside each other in heavy silence until we reached our rooms.

As Ocelot opened his door, I took the initiative to speak.

"Ocelot, wait." I stepped toward him a little. "I'm sorry about the photos. I was out of line. Please forgive me."

He stood in his doorway without reaction.

"Do you have plans? I'm going to eat at that café," I said.

"I have plans," he said flatly. He stepped into his room and practically slammed the door.

I stood transfixed. Even at the beginning of our trip from Sor4 when he'd been angry with me, he hadn't treated me this rudely. I didn't understand him at all. Why couldn't he forgive me for something so trivial, especially in light of all that happened recently? I stood perplexed and offended.

I stomped to my room, entered, and shut the door as forcefully as he had. I didn't like acting this way. I knew I shouldn't react begrudgingly to him. I made up my mind not to retort insults, but to keep my composure and stay solid. I would behave impeccably. His rudeness would only show his own weakness of character, not mine.

I quickly left the room with controlled composure. I shut the door lightly, and then walked down to the café alone. I ate slowly, watching the rain wash down the plate window of the café.

I remembered Alaban. Where was he now? I knew in my heart he was fine. His dangerous assignment was almost finished. I could sense his spirit. He was always with me. As adults, we had only been in each other's company for a few days, but I felt I knew him well. In our years at school together, he was always strong, gifted, and impressive. He made me want to have fun with life. I admired his imaginative boldness and his daring attitude. The transparency of his inner being made his physical beauty seem unimportant to me. It was true I loved him. I loved his soul and its expression. I looked forward to seeing him again.

I finished my meal and returned to my quarters. Gladly, I sensed that Ocelot had gone out. I called Yinore to find out her situation. She, too, was in the process of packing up and preparing her final report for the General. I told her I'd be glad to see her again. She agreed, but I sensed a tension in her voice as in a half-truth.

A few hours later, Wilbaht knocked on my door. I let him in.

"Have you seen Ocelot?" he asked.

"Not since after the interrogation," I replied.

"How did he act around you?" he asked.

"He wasn't very friendly, that's for sure," I said. "He told you about the photos?"

"Which ones? Documentation photos?" he asked.

"No, his personal photos. That's what he's angry about." I explained the incident. "I know I shouldn't have looked through them. I already apologized to him twice, but he's still angry about it. I'm sorry, sir."

"What a convenient pretext," Wilbaht said shaking his head.

"Sir?" I asked.

176

"Don't believe that was the root of his anger. You only added flame to his fire. I'm going to have a heart to heart chat with that boy if he comes out of hiding anytime soon. In fact, I'm going to look for him right now. He's got to stop this childish pouting. This time he was even rude to *me*."

I blinked. Ocelot had never done or said anything to Wilbaht that didn't demonstrate absolute respect. I couldn't imagine what had made him do such a thing. I had never seen Wilbaht angry before, but I was afraid I was about to witness just that.

"My patience is wearing thin." Wilbaht turned a deep purple color. He grumbled. "I don't want to threaten him with suspension, but if he doesn't shape up, I'll have no other choice."

"Sir, is there anything I can do?" I asked him, amazed by the gravity of the situation.

"If he shows up here while I'm out, tell him I have ordered him to stay in his quarters until I get back," he stated.

"Yes, sir."

Wilbaht marched out the door and shut it firmly.

I stood perplexed. Here I was, a seer, and I had no idea of what was going on.

At about ten p.m., Wilbaht knocked on my door again. He'd found Ocelot and had brought him along. Ocelot held his jaw squared. He did not appear sorry for whatever it was he'd done or said.

"Step in, Sub Professor," Wilbaht ordered.

Ocelot stepped into the little room. Wilbaht followed him and shut the door.

"You will face your crewmember and apologize for your behavior. Then you will shake hands in good will. Do it," Wilbaht directed forcefully.

Through gritted teeth, Ocelot did as he was told. I felt sheepish.

"I apologize for my rude behavior," Ocelot said begrudgingly.

He held out a hand to shake mine, but Wilbaht said that wasn't good enough.

Tensely, Ocelot said, "I'm sorry, Sil. Please forgive my rude behavior."

I shook his hand. "I accept your apology," I said.

Just as he was about to pull his hand out of my grip, I held it tighter and placed my other hand on top of his.

"It's okay," I said quietly to him.

The expression on his face changed to nervous embarrassment. I let go of his hand. He turned to face Wilbaht.

"Ahem. I owe you an apology as well, sir," he began.

"You owe me more than that. You will spend your leave time in my direct service. From ten in the morning to ten at night you will not leave my sight. If you want to throw a tantrum, I want to be there to see it. You'll behave as a service soldier and act like you like it. Understood?"

"Yes, sir," Ocelot said gravely. He stood at attention.

"Step out," Wilbaht ordered, opening the door.

"Yes, sir," Ocelot responded. He walked out of the room.

"Go get some sleep."

"Yes, sir," he said in disappointment. He went to his room and did not slam the door this time.

Wilbaht watched him go, and then ducked back into my room with me.

"I'm sorry you had to see that, but he needed to see that you and I are on the same side. I'm afraid he won't be very good company for the next few days. Just be nice to him for a while," Wilbaht said softly.

"Can you tell me what all that was about, sir?" I asked.

"No, I think he'd rather tell you himself," he said. "Good night, Sil."

"Good night, sir," I replied.

I went to bed wracking my brain trying to think of a logical cause for Ocelot's rudeness, but couldn't think of any.

In the morning, at breakfast with Wilbaht, I refrained from digging up the awkward scene from the night before. Instead, I asked him what he knew about our new assignment.

"We'll have a short bodyguarding job on Karnesh," he said. "There's an interstellar convention coming up. It may reveal some more information about the Fitmalo case for us."

"I have to admit, sir, I'm not looking forward to seeing Karnesh. It's a very harsh planet."

He nodded as he chewed.

"Although it is right next to the Jain planet," I said, brightening. "Do you think maybe we could take our leave days on Jain, sir? I'm sure it would do Ocelot some good to see his second home again."

Wilbaht considered this as he finished his breakfast. "Possibly," he said.

I then asked if he'd spoken with Yinore since the catacombs.

"Yes. She's taking her leave time away from the Center. She'll be back with us for ship checks."

"Oh," I sadly.

Wilbaht wisely guessed my thoughts about her. "I'm sorry your female companionship is not what you hoped for. Yinore is an intelligent woman, but she seems to focus more on herself than others. Sometimes people do not live up to our expectations. We should still treat them with courtesy, however."

"I will, sir," I affirmed. I mustered the courage to compliment him. "If I may say so, sir, I think some people exceed our expectations. I think you've been a great commander for us, and a good companion."

He smiled at me lovingly. "Thank you, Sil. I am honored by your compliments. You have also proven to be a good companion. You are certainly welcome on my ship."

I felt uplifted. From that day on, the two of us spoke more openly to one another, although always with respect.

Later in the afternoon, I sat browsing through some information about Karnesh. A knock at the door startled me. I went to open the door, knowing who it was. I flung it open and tackled him in the hallway.

"Whoa!" Alaban shouted with surprise. I hugged him around the neck tightly and laughed with joy.

"I could get used to welcomes like this," he said gleefully. He hugged me back. "I guess I don't have to tell you I'm alive and well."

We let go of each other for a moment. Alaban's eyes gleamed with his smile.

"It's great to see you again," he said. "Come here."

He backed me into my room and closed the door. He picked me up and twirled me around. He tumbled us onto my bed and kissed me.

"Alaban, wait. What are you doing?" I asked, flustered.

"I'm lying in bed with the woman of my dreams. What are you doing?" He grinned.

He held one arm behind my neck and the other at my hand. Our fingers meshed together. He was not forceful with me, only affectionate.

"I'm lying in bed with my best friend, who I've missed so much. I'm so glad you're back," I said.

He gazed at my face lovingly. "You can't imagine how much I've missed you."

He gave me tiny kisses all over my face, which tickled and made me giggle. Then he buried his face in the crook of my neck and sniffed playfully, like a puppy. I laughed and squirmed. He embraced me tenderly, rocking me from side to side with his face in my hair. We held each other like this for a while. I was glad to hold him. We had both missed the comfort of human touch.

"Oh, Sil, you're so warm and wonderful," he whispered to me.

He sounded sleepy. He pulled away from me. I noticed dark circles under his eyes. I asked how long it had been since he'd slept. He hadn't since before the assignment in Salumat.

"Do you feel sorry for me?" he asked with a half-grin.

"Yes," I replied, caressing his forehead.

"Do you feel sorry enough for me to make me feel better?" A sleepy mischief contorted his face.

"That depends. What will it take to make you feel better?" I asked.

"Let me kiss you until I fall asleep?" he said hopefully. "But stay with me."

"I'll stay with you," I said. "I don't want you to leave my side until they drag you away."

He viewed me with grateful eyes. He leaned in and kissed me. I smiled. I sat up to take off his boots and mine. Then I lay back down with him and nestled my head over his arm.

"Oh, Sil, you're so good to me. You've got to be my wife one day," he murmured, already drifting into sleep.

He kissed me twice. Then he was out. He relaxed completely. His arm grew heavy over me. His breathing deepened. I felt so comforted by his closeness that I fell asleep there with him.

About three hours later, Wilbaht knocked on my door. Alaban and I jumped up from the bed groggily. I went to the door and opened it, not thinking of our appearance.

Wilbaht stood outside the door offering me dinner. He apologized for waking me. Alaban stepped forward rubbing one eye. He straightened himself to address Wilbaht, who seemed surprised, but accepted his presence formally.

"Alaban. I'm sorry. I didn't mean to interrupt anything," Wilbaht said.

"No, sir. You didn't interrupt anything. I apologize for our appearance. I hadn't slept since before my mission. Sil let me crash here for a while."

I wondered why he was being so thoroughly sincere with him. He reached out to shake Wilbaht's hand.

"It's good to see you again, sir," he said.

"Well, in that case, I'd be happy to invite you to dinner with us, unless, of course, you need some more sleep."

"No, sir. I'll be honored to have dinner with you. Thank you, sir." They let go of each other's hands.

"Have you met my partner, Sub Professor Ocelot?" Wilbaht asked, stepping aside to reveal Ocelot's sullen form.

Alaban reached for Ocelot's hand. Ocelot nodded, but wouldn't look him in the eye.

"How are you, sir?" Alaban said as he shook hands.

Ocelot only nodded until Wilbaht cleared his throat as a reminder of his behavior. "Fine, thank you," he responded.

Alaban nodded, but regarded him warily. Wilbaht offered to meet us at the café. We agreed. Alaban thanked our elder again. When the two men turned to leave, I closed the door. Alaban leaned on it and blew a sigh of relief. He hooked his arm around my neck and pulled me to him. He kissed my forehead and embraced me.

"I'm sorry about that," I said.

"No, no. That was good. This is a good thing," he said.

"Why? What are you up to?" I asked with a sly grin.

"I'll tell you tonight. But you have to keep your hands off me around your superiors. Do you think you can handle that? Of course, if you can't, I'd like it even more, but you're a strong-willed woman. You can at least pretend not to be mad for my body, right?"

"What are you planning?" I asked.

"Can you keep your hands off me or not?" he persisted.

"Yes."

"Damn," he professed.

"Tell me what's going on," I insisted with a smile.

"Patience, my dear," he said.

He picked me up over his shoulder and carried me to the foot of the bed. He set me down on its edge and replaced my boots onto my feet. I shook my head at him and stroked his face. He turned briefly to kiss my hand. He glinted the same mischievous grin at me that I'd learned to love. Once my boots were on, he stood me up and pointed me towards the bathroom. He patted me on the rear end several times.

"Go make yourself a little less beautiful or *I* might not be able to keep my hands to myself," he said.

He turned to sit where I'd been and pulled his boots on. He wiggled his eyebrows at me. I couldn't help but smile.

All the way to the café, Alaban made me laugh. I'd never had so much fun. At dinner, Alaban turned formal and serious, but gave me an occasional wink. He and Wilbaht chatted continuously over dinner. I interjected a few ideas. Ocelot said nothing unless asked. Even then, his answers remained short. Alaban attempted twice to include him in the conversation, but then gave up. Wilbaht waved him away and told Alaban not to worry about him. They talked about politics, work, Organization centers, Fitmalos, and other related topics. When their conversation waned, Alaban placed his hand over mine.

"I was thinking of checking out a pub close by. They have dancing later. Will you go with me?" he asked.

"I'd love to," I said, squeezing his hand.

"Do you mind if I join you for a few minutes? A tall glass of ale sounds good right now," Wilbaht said.

"Certainly, sir," Alaban said to him. "Glad to have you along."

Ocelot looked to Wilbaht with dismay. He was still acting as serviceman for him until ten. Wherever Wilbaht went, Ocelot was obliged to follow.

We strolled out into the night air. Wilbaht knew the way. Since he was so much taller than the rest of us, he advanced quickly in front of our little group. Alaban and I stayed together in the middle. Ocelot lagged behind on purpose.

Alaban put his arm around me. I did the same for him. He kissed the side of my face. He complimented me several times between stories of our recent assignments.

We met Wilbaht at the front of the pub, which was on a fairly busy street, although it was only one of a handful of establishments open at this hour. Ocelot finally hurried to catch up with us.

We sat at a round booth near the bar at the middle of the pub. Wilbaht ordered a bottle of ale to share. We all took a glass. Even I sipped a little. It was not as bitter as the red ale that Klib had offered me once.

At about nine thirty, Zank, the Grey, one of Alaban's partners, appeared by our table. Alaban introduced us all around. Zank bowed formally. After the introductions, he stood close to Alaban and talked into his ear.

"Right now? All right. Yes, I saw him," Alaban said. All jovial emotion drained from his face.

Zank apologized for leaving right away, but explained that he was on duty. We said goodbye. Alaban became stony. He turned to see the entrance.

"Could you let me know when Professor Ongeram shows up at the door, sir? I'm supposed to meet him about something," he said to Wilbaht, who faced the door.

"You're not being hailed away on assignment, are you?" he asked.

"Not exactly. It will only take a few minutes," he said.

A few uneasy moments passed. Alaban looked at me apologetically, and then faced forward with eyes closed, apparently meditating.

"He's there now," Wilbaht said.

Alaban stood slowly. "I'll be back in a few minutes. Excuse me."

I turned to watch him. Ongeram stood at the door, holding it open. He seemed to be clearing a path.

Alaban passed a few tables of people as he walked to the door. Suddenly, he spun around, grabbed a Vermilion man by the neck with both hands, and jerked the man up out of his seat. The chair scraped on the floor and toppled, drawing attention from most of the customers in the front of the pub. The people at the man's table and around him exclaimed in surprise.

Alaban hauled the man up to stand facing the door. He reached for a gun of some kind, which had been stashed in a holster under the man's jacket. The Vermilion flailed as Alaban held his throat and pressed the weapon into the nape of his neck. He marched him out the door that Ongeram held for him. As Alaban passed through the door with the man, Ongeram flashed his U.G. insignia to the crowd and closed the door behind them.

The people at the table weren't sure what to do. They sat chattering nervously to each other. A disconcerted waiter picked up the overturned chair. Wilbaht frowned. We exchanged disturbed looks. Ocelot stared after the door.

After about five intense minutes, Alaban reentered the pub. He did not approach us, but turned and went upstairs to the restroom. In the short seconds I saw him, I thought I saw blood on his hands.

Chapter 21: The Dance

A few minutes later, Alaban returned to us with an apology. He turned up his glass and refilled it. He downed half of the new glass of ale, sniffed, and looked down at the table. He sighed heavily.

"You killed him," I heard myself say.

Alaban glanced conscientiously at me, then at his glass. He nodded a little. He inhaled the other half of his glass of ale. He kept his eyes down. He reached for the bottle and poured himself another half again.

"I'm sorry," I said, resting a hand on his knee. "Don't drink for it. You'll be bad company soon."

He consciously relaxed his body against the seat cushion. Then he repentantly gave me a half-smile. He lifted my hand to kiss the back of it. "You're right. I'm in good company. I don't want to ruin your evening. I'll be good." He kissed my hand again. I gave him a kiss on the cheek.

When I asked him what the incident was about, he explained the Vermilion man had still been involved in a network child labor scam after final warnings from the Organization and that he'd had to make a spectacle of removing him from a public area so his collaborators would get the message that the Organization wouldn't let it continue and that they meant deadly business. He had forced the man into a containment truck outside so people would think he was only being arrested, but once inside the truck, Alaban had knocked him out and then killed him. He knew the man probably deserved a death sentence, but he didn't like having to carry it out.

"Ahem," said Wilbaht. "Have they given you many assignments like this?" he asked with genuine concern, citing also the fact that this was the second hit he'd been ordered to do in a week's time.

"Only recently, sir. I'm the low man on the totem pole. I get all the jobs no one else wants right now. It's only temporary."

"I hope for your sake the job changes soon," Wilbaht spoke.

"Yes. That's exactly what I was hoping for," Alaban said. His mood brightened somewhat.

Ocelot scowled before he downed the rest of his glass of ale. Whatever his problem was, it still hung with him. He reached for the bottle from in front of Alaban and poured out the last drop into his glass. Wilbaht ordered another bottle of the same. The waiter filled everyone's glass, even though I hadn't finished half of mine. We raised our glasses and toasted, to what we weren't sure. I drank sparingly. I nudged Alaban. He only sipped. Ocelot downed the whole thing and slapped his glass onto the table. He refilled it.

Wilbaht spoke kindly to Alaban. "Don't mourn too long, young warrior. It was, after all, your duty. I believe you have a duty to your lovely friend here as well."

Alaban cheered up a little. We squeezed each other's hands under the table. He gazed at me thankfully and then glanced behind us to the dance floor.

"They're going to start the music in a minute. Will you dance with me?" Alaban asked.

"I didn't know you could dance," I said.

"Only for the most beautiful woman in the universe," he said, beaming. His mild demeanor returned to him.

"Well, when you see her, give her my congratulations," I said.

"Congratulations," he smiled. He gazed into my eyes with admiration.

I blushed and giggled. Alaban's jovial confidence returned to him. Ocelot regarded Alaban as if to say he had to be kidding. Wilbaht chuckled and waved us away to the dance floor.

The music swelled. Several Arbormen and Vermilions were already dancing. The deejay played music we weren't familiar with, but we did our best. We laughed and played on the dance floor. Alaban went to the deejay and asked for Tambuo music for me. The deejay played an upbeat version of a dance I recognized. Alaban somehow knew the man's part of the dance very well. I wondered when and where he had learned it.

We were fantastic dance partners. Other couples gave us room to watch us. I held his hand and stepped around him, sliding my hand across his shoulders. My hip gyrations matched the rhythm of the music. We stepped forwards and backwards closely together. The onlookers whistled as we held each other's arms and did a torso ripple with one hand in the air. The crowd became almost as loud as the music. The dance ended in a suggestive pose. I knelt with one knee between his legs and my chin at his navel. One of my hands rested on his chest. The other wrapped around him to rest at the small of his back. His palms lay open at my shoulders. The crowd applauded. He helped me up as I complimented him.

He said he had learned the dance on Tambuo, where he had lived for nearly a year after he'd left our school. He claimed he'd been invited to a lot a parties while he was there and had to learn to dance so he wouldn't be left out. Apparently, he'd learned as much culture as science while at the university there. I commended him. The music changed and blared. We danced a little more, but the dance floor became crowded.

Soon Alaban shouted to me over the music. He asked to go somewhere to talk outside. I took his hand as we made our way through the crowd on the dance floor and wound a path to the door. I looked back at my crewmates. Wilbaht nodded and waved to us, acknowledging that we should go on our way without him. Then he patted Ocelot on the shoulder and took the bottle away from him. I shook my head about the man. He was supposed to be servicing his commander. Now he'd become a burden to him. Being a kind-hearted soul, I was sure Wilbaht would overlook Ocelot's inebriated pouting to see him home safely before turning in for the night.

Alaban led me out the main door and into the street at the front of the building. The cool night air shifted between us. People meandered in and out of the pub in a steady stream. Alaban pulled me around the east corner of the building into a dimly lit alley. It angled around this building and veered off between two others. We followed its path until we arrived at a dead end without any low-lying windows. A concrete ledge spanned the length of one wall here about a meter off the ground. The alley was empty except for the two of us, the perfect place to talk in secret.

"Have a seat," Alaban said. He lifted me to sit facing him. He kept his hands on my hips as he spoke.

"I've requested a change of placement," he began. "To be reassigned to your crew."

"I thought they'd already denied your request for us to work together," I said.

"This is a new general. He might allow it. Besides, we only have a few more months before we go on permanent assignment. Then we can choose where we prefer to work and with whom. At least we'll have the right to refuse a job and hold out for something better. I told him we'd be a powerhouse together. He's got to consider it at least."

"We would make a great team. Wilbaht likes you. If you join our crew, you'd keep Klib at bay. Yinore is nice enough. You won't have problems with her. I don't know how Ocelot would react, though. I still don't trust him. He's been strange ever since we arrived on this planet. Wilbaht reprimanded him. He said he might have to suspend him if he gets any worse."

"Yeah? Maybe if he gets kicked off the crew, I can replace him," he suggested.

"That's a nice idea, but I don't think he will," I stated. "I would love to work with you, though."

His glistening dark eyes seemed kinder and softer in the dim light. He caressed my hair.

"You dance so well. You were the sexiest woman up there," he said.

I smiled, flattered. "You're not a bad dancer yourself. That stomach ripple was, um…" I wanted to say "sexy", but I bit my lip instead.

"What, this?" he performed one for me. His muscles waved over his abdomen as his spine swayed.

I laughed in embarrassment. I nodded. He smiled hopefully. He stepped in close to me. He gazed at my face with care.

"You once said there was something missing between us. That's why you couldn't think of me as a mate. Do you still feel that way?" he asked.

"Oh." I looked away. "Alaban, I love you as a friend. I don't want to ruin that. But…"

He moved to stand in front of my face. "But?" he said eagerly.

"But I'm so glad to be with you. I hadn't realized how much I missed you until now. I'm not sure how I feel anymore."

Aspiration danced in his eyes. "What would make you feel sure?"

"I don't know." I gave him a shy, but guilty look.

"I love you so much, Sil. I want you to be my mate, for life. I wish you would feel the same about me. Don't you find me the least bit attractive?"

186

"You are attractive. You're a model human male. I'm just not sure I want a mate yet. I feel...I need more time," I said.

"I wish we had more time together too, but we're always being sent away." He held my hand and stared into my eyes. "We're together now," he said softly. He stroked my knuckles. "I want to sleep with you tonight, and tomorrow night, and every night I can get, and not just to sleep."

I observed him nervously. The longing in his eyes touched my heart.

"Oh, Sil, if you would let me make love to you, it would be the best time of my life. You would make me the happiest man in the universe. If you'll be my wife, I'll feel like...a *god*. I'll do anything for you. You know I'm not just some guy begging for sex. We've known each other since I was twelve. We're old friends. You know me. I know you. Ever since I met you, you've been important to me. You've been *the most* important thing. You're the other side to me. We're a perfect match," he said.

"I feel that, too," I suddenly realized aloud. "You're the other side of me. I feel...we're already together, but...inside." I covered his heart with my palm. I looked to him, hoping to find a means to fully express what I meant. "You're a part of my life, my being." I inhaled an encouraging breath. "Our essence. We're together." I faltered with a sigh, not knowing how to say what I meant.

Alaban removed my hand from his chest to kiss it firmly, inspired by my inaccurate speech.

"But I don't feel the need to mate," I clarified. "Not yet."

He viewed me with wanton amazement and then countered my statement. He spoke rapidly. "I do. I feel it every time I think of you. I *want* you. I want you to feel the same way about me. I want to be the man of your life, your dream lover, your pleasure provider, your hot hunk of muscle." He made a silly pose, flexing his bicep. I sniggered. He grasped my arms. "I want to be the father of your children, woman. I know you like the idea of family. You talk about yours all the time. You want that for your future, don't you? A family? So let's start one, just you and me. Then in a few years, we can add kids. Imagine it. I've got it all planned out. You'll love it." He paused to make a frame with his hands. "We'll have a little Alaban and a little Sil. We'll move to a permanent post, quit the violent assignments, do small-time jobs, come home to cute kids, play with them, get them a good education, tuck them in early, and then have sex the rest of the evening. It'll be a great life!"

I almost laughed at his comical babbling. I shook my head, ready to tell him I preferred to put off future plans of that sort for now, but he continued adamantly.

He expressed not just his desire, but also his deep psychological and physical need for sex, reminding me that he was a virile young male. He told me again that he yearningly wanted me for that purpose, but he didn't want to scare me away. He said he would not demand it from me. He wanted me to agree to it willingly. I repeated to him that I felt uncertain about it and that although he was desirous, I still didn't feel ready. Moreover, I simply didn't feel the need he felt.

"You don't know what it's like to mate, do you? You don't know how it feels," he guessed.

"But you do?" I asked with a defensive smile.

"Yes," he said with a shrug.

I shrunk. I did not want to know of his experiences or where or when they occurred, and much less with whom.

He cupped my face in his hand and kissed my forehead sympathetically. He softly told me it was nothing to be afraid of. He assured me that with the necessary precautions, the act would be beautiful and without worries. He even argued that we were meant to do it. We were male and female, soulfully bonded, made to come together.

"Let me convince you," he pushed.

"How?" I asked warily.

"A little seduction technique I read about. It's supposed to make uninterested women turn lusty. I want to see if it really works."

I defensively refused to undergo any kind of hypnosis. He swore it wasn't. He described a pulse massage, meant to relax and stimulate the body. He gave me an example on my arm. He pulsed a concentrated levitational wave into my skin, which felt like a very mild electrical shock combined with pressure.

"You'll like it. I promise," he pleaded. "I won't do anything you don't want." He covered my lower abdomen with his hand. "I'll just touch you right here. That's all. Unless you want more."

I stared at him, seeing his sincere desire to please me. I disliked the idea, but my conscious cited no rules for this kind of proposal. I deliberated a long while. If I asked him to forget about it, he would feel terribly dejected. I didn't want to hurt his feelings. And yet his anxiousness made me feel pressured and nervous. I didn't know what he expected from me. I knew he was dedicated to me. I knew he was in love with me. I knew I loved him. I knew sex was supposed to be an enjoyable experience. Its pleasure was used in advertising all the time. But I didn't feel I was ready.

He adopted a carefree charm. "Just give me a few minutes. If it doesn't work, we can just forget about it and go back to the Center to play cards," he said. He shrugged affably.

I considered this. Perhaps if I let him try and fail, then he would give up and resign himself to an evening of friendly innocence. Timidly, I allowed it, reminding him that we should go back to the Center soon. He promised to have me home by midnight and assured me I would not regret it.

With his fingers touching my hips and his hands fanned out across my abdomen, he pressed gently inward with his thumbs. He kissed me lightly around my face. Then he moved his thumbs, pressing above the pubic bone, pulsing lightly. I closed my eyes. I breathed deeply. I enjoyed the soft massage, but I didn't feel anything out of the ordinary. He repeated the action, but stopped to rest his thumbs directly over the pubic bone. I opened my eyes, ready to tell him it had no seductive effect, but he interrupted me.

"Just relax," he whispered. "You trust me, don't you?"

"Yes," I replied.

He leaned forward to kiss me. He began a stronger, slow, undulating pulse that played through my lower body. I ignored the pulse at first. Then arousal expanded lazily through my body. His mouth caressed my face and neck. The dual stimulation held my attention. The pulsation droned through me, persuading, beckoning. His kisses became more and more seductive. He lightly sucked my lip and then plunged his mouth into mine. I gratefully kissed back.

"*You love him. Enjoy this,*" my body advised me.

I soon followed his direction as a trusting, intoxicated spectator to his magic show, my conscience distracted by his slight of hand. His act directed me beyond my familiar realm. Surging neurons called for more. He redirected the pulsations below the pubic bone, teasing my legs apart. Then he paused the pulsations, leaving my body searching for more stimulation. He whispered a request to me, permission to touch me in other places. I heard myself whisper yes.

"*Be careful, Sil,*" a voice from my conscience warned me.

He caressed my legs, rubbing circles towards the inner thigh. The growing arousal saturated all indecision and resistance. His performance arrested my will. I forgot my surroundings. I forgot my sixth sense. I forgot higher reason. I kissed at him greedily while he pressed against me. His dark magician's hands traveled to caress my breasts. My blood ran hot. He pressed himself to me and pulsed repeatedly between my legs. A fierce alien hunger swam through my lower body. I pulled him to me desperately, panting.

"Oh, yes. You feel it, Sil. Let me mate with you. Tell me yes," he whispered. He embraced me tightly, kissing around my neck and ear passionately.

"No," my muffled conscience tugged at me. *"This isn't right."*

I found myself clutching him to me as if to mate. My hips tilted instinctively to match our genitalia. When I realized our position, my conscience escaped its suppression and flogged my wits with shame. I quickly let go. My arousal snuffed out immediately, like a doused fire. My senses returned to me. I suddenly felt anxious, guilty. I felt I had done something morally wrong. I moved to sit straight before him, confused by my own actions.

"Let me," he whispered breathlessly in my ear. He slid his hands behind and beneath me, pulling me to him again.

I gasped for a breath to tell him no. Then something caught my eye.

"Someone's here," I whispered frantically.

"What?" Alaban asked, retreating a few centimeters from my body.

"Ocelot. He's walking this way," I said in dismay.

Alaban turned his head to see Ocelot trudging along a wall towards us in what appeared to be a nauseated stupor. He stopped momentarily to lean towards the ground as if he would throw up. He regained his composure and stood grasping the wall again.

"Oh, shit," Alaban said with utter frustration. He leaned with his hands on my knees. He swore a few more times. He breathed deeply to calm himself. Then he stood and faced me. He kissed my cheek with apology as I gathered him to me.

"Don't let him see me like this," I said, wrapping my arms around his neck. I buried my head under his chin.

"Why not? We're fully dressed. What does he care?"

"He'll report me. I'll be reprimanded for attempting to mate in public."

Alaban regarded my swaying partner. "He's blind drunk. If anyone needs reprimanding, it's him."

I peeked over Alaban's shoulder at Ocelot, who now sat in the dust with his back to the wall a few meters away. His arms rested on his knees. His head bowed. His body shook loosely with a hiccup.

Realizing he was right, I glared at the collapsing man. "What is he doing here? Damn it." I said, surprised at my own words. Alaban seemed surprised, too. He held my face once more.

"Are you okay?" he asked caringly.

I nodded.

He reached around and embraced me lovingly. We held onto each other for a moment before he helped me down from the ledge. I smoothed my hair briefly and dusted off my uniform. We walked towards Ocelot's sagging body.

Alaban grabbed him by the arm and jerked him into a standing position violently. Ocelot snapped awake. Alaban held him up. Ocelot blinked with difficulty and swayed, bumping into the wall.

"Stand back," Alaban said to me. I stepped back twice.

He punched Ocelot swiftly in the stomach.

"Aw!" Ocelot yelled. Then he leaned forward and threw up repeatedly.

"Why'd you punch him?" I asked, more out of curiosity than reproach.

"He'll sober up faster with less alcohol in his stomach. Besides, he deserved that. Don't you think?" Alaban said.

"Yes, he did," I spoke acidly.

Alaban slapped Ocelot on the back a few times. Ocelot leaned forward, barely balancing himself with his palms on his knees as he spat at the ground. He nearly fell backwards, but Alaban grabbed him by one elbow. I took him by the other. We marched him away from the pungent puddle of vomit and set him against a wall on the opposite side of the alley. He shook his head and rubbed his face.

Our differences in rank disappeared along with the evening's short-lived enchantment. He was not my superior. He was a drunken interloper. I converted my embarrassment into fury.

"Ocelot, what the hell are you doing back here? I can't believe Wilbaht let you drink so much. What is wrong with you? What if Wilbaht comes looking for you and finds you like this? You'll be suspended for public drunkenness, you idiot," I said forcefully.

"Wilbaht? He left already," he slurred. His head bobbed on a rubbery neck.

"Oh, so you had to come looking for me in this state? You couldn't find a ride home yourself? Why didn't you find some other dark alley to lurk around in?" I badgered. "I'm so disgusted with you."

"I drank too much," he stated in his stupor.

"You don't say?" I retorted.

"Come on, Sil. He obviously doesn't know what's going on. Let's just leave him so he can pass out and sleep it off," Alaban said.

He reached out and put his arm around my shoulder. I stepped close to him, glancing back at Ocelot's disheveled body as it sank slowly towards the ground. He blinked and rubbed his face. Just as we were about to round the corner, he called out to us.

"Wait. I'll pay for a driver," he stammered. He uttered some other words, mostly unintelligible, but we got the gist of it. He didn't want to be left alone there to sleep in the dirt. He wanted to go home. He asked us to help him out.

We stopped and looked at each other. Technically, refusal to come to the aid of a crewmate and a superior was frowned upon with nearly the same weight of punishment as performing a sexual act in public. If Ocelot remembered in the morning that we'd left him here, we would both be in trouble. Reluctantly, we turned back. This time, Alaban chastised him.

"You just interrupted something between us. Do you get it?" He made exaggerated motions with his arms between the two of us. "Why should we help you?"

Ocelot seemed like another person entirely. He blinked lazily, his flesh falling clammily around his jaws. He made no sign that he understood what Alaban was saying or that he'd even addressed him at all. This struck a chord of fury with Alaban. He stamped one foot and posed menacingly above him, like a bull preparing to charge.

"He probably followed us back here just to get a look. Drunken loser." Alaban stomped the dust, sending a cloud of it swirling up onto Ocelot's uniform. "Stay here and piss on yourself."

"What?" Ocelot coughed.

Alaban clenched his fists and scowled, more furious than before. "You're a disgrace to your rank. If you could stand on your own, I might challenge you to the death right now," he spat.

"Alaban, Don't say that. Let's just get him to the street. We can throw him in a cab and go back to the Center," I said. I found Alaban's threat truly disturbing. I understood his frustration, but I would never threaten someone in the way he just had.

Reluctantly, Alaban pulled Ocelot to his feet in the same aggressive manner as he had before. He dragged him along by one arm while I took the other. We shuffled with him to the main street by the pub. Alaban hailed a public driver. We dumped Ocelot into the wide seat behind the driver, but Ocelot grabbed onto our arms and wouldn't let go.

"What the...? Let go, you dimwit. You're in the cab already," Alaban interjected.

"No. Don't let them take me back to the Center. I can't show up like this. Take me to the ship," Ocelot begged.

"Are you insane? What if Klib is there? That'll be just as bad. You got yourself into this mess. You live with the consequences," I told him.

"No, please, Sil. I'd do the same for you," he pleaded like a child.

"No, you wouldn't, because I would never get drunk like you in the first place," I stated.

"Yes. Remember the time..." he paused to burp and gasp for air. "I carried you home," he heaved a breath again. "After your defense testing." He strained to blink at me. "Can't you do the same for me?" he spoke with a pitiable whine.

I gawked incredulously.

"I don't want to listen to this. Move over," Alaban said, shoving Ocelot into the corner of the seat. He crushed him into the closed door and helped me in beside him. He told the driver where to go. He put his arms around me and sighed. I stroked his bicep with one hand. Ocelot's head and arms jiggled limply. He appeared to pass out.

We arrived at the airfield and paid the driver with Ocelot's money card. We hauled him to the ship. I opened the cargo hold door. Ocelot woke up and seemed to regain his feet as we marched him up the stairwell to the row of bunks. He took a detour to the bathroom. I shook my head and apologized Alaban.

" "So this is your ship," he said with genuine interest.

I offered to show him around. He commented on the small size of the bunks. I agreed, commenting that I wasn't sure how Wilbaht fit into his. I motioned him to the hall to show him the exercise room.

I looked up at him nervously. My body had responded strongly to his touch, and yet I felt direly confused. I wanted to embrace him, but I didn't want him to experiment on me again. I wanted him to forget about sex altogether. I didn't want it. I felt I was too old to think this way, but it was an honest feeling. He had complained that we didn't have time, but time was exactly what I needed.

"This one is just like ours," he said of the exercise room. He peered into our reflection on the pearly, mirrored wall. He stood behind me, wrapping his arms around my chest and kissing my neck. His hands gently fondled my breasts. I covered his hands with mine and stared at our reflection. He glanced up at us.

At that moment I had an uncanny sensation. The reflection seemed abstract, puzzling. We looked like a husband and wife standing in a portrait, but he seemed to be standing in someone else's place, as if his image were superimposed over that of another: a man I had not yet seen. Whether my perception was altered by premonition or subconscious, I did not know. However, I did know that I could not accept him. Not tonight. Perhaps not any night. I moved his hands to my shoulders. He noticed the sad conviction on my face.

"You feel bad because we were interrupted? So do I. I should have taken you straight home. I'm sorry." He watched me shake my head shamefully. "Don't tell me you didn't like it. What's wrong? I thought you enjoyed it."

I turned to face him. He held me with sadness and frustration. He bent down to kiss me. A wave of guilt covered me. I felt just as I had when we said goodbye on Sor3. I had kissed him goodbye with all the passion he deserved, but in my heart I felt dishonest to myself and to him. This time I

193

could not hide it. He felt it in my kiss. He pulled away sadly. His eyes questioned why.

"Alaban, you're my closest friend in the whole universe. I need you. I just don't want to mate with you. Please don't force me." Warm tears welled in my eyes.

"No. I would never force you. I love you. I just wanted you to want me, that's all." He squeezed me to him and kissed the top of my head. "I would never hurt you, Sil."

"I'm so sorry, Alaban. I made you think I wanted to, but I didn't know. I was ignorant. Forgive me."

Thoroughly disheartened, plagued with needs of his own, he held me there for several minutes. I apologized for the way things had turned out this night. I asked if he wanted to sleep here in the ship instead of going back to the Center, since the hour was so late. He asked to sleep with me. He promised not to try anything. I agreed to it, noting that there wasn't enough room in the tiny bunk to do anything else anyway. After a few more minutes' reconciliation, he strung an arm around my waist and escorted me out of the exercise room.

The bathroom was open now, so Alaban ducked in and motioned to me that he'd meet me at my bunk.

As I walked past the first bunk, it opened with a whoosh. I paused to see Ocelot in clean clothes and with wet hair. He leaned out of his room to speak to me. He had sobered up somewhat, but fought heavy drowsiness.

"Sil. You shouldn't have sex with him," he said hoarsely. He shook his head as if disappointed.

"What? That's none of your business. So what if I do? Why do you care?" I said defensively. I was still disgusted with him.

"I'm ship's medic. I'm partly responsible for your health. I can't let you get sick," he mustered.

"What are you talking about? Go back to bed. You're still drunk," I said.

"No. I followed you out of the bar to warn you. Alaban has been with more women this year than I've been with my whole life," he said.

"You haven't been around much, have you?" Alaban intoned, stepping up behind him.

"How would you know?" I asked, ignoring Alaban's interruption.

"It's just one of those things I know without being able to explain it. I just know." He turned groggily toward Alaban. "If you care about her, you won't put her life in danger." he implored.

"I'm not putting her life in danger. I've always stayed healthy for you, Sil."

"Are you saying Alaban has a serious disease?" I asked fearfully.

"I don't know. I can't be sure," Ocelot murmured. "Take my advice. Go to the Center med station and get a blood test. You'll know in a few seconds if you're infected or not."

"I'm not infected. I'm not even a carrier. I just got checked out by medical a few days ago. You're hallucinating," Alaban said to him.

I stepped over to Alaban and held his hand worriedly.

"Are you sure you're all right?" I asked.

"Positive. I would never do anything to put your life at risk. You know that. This guy doesn't know it, so just ignore him. You trust me, don't you?" he asked.

"With my life," I responded. I held his hand to my cheek. He stroked my chin with his thumb.

"Go back to bed, Ocelot. Maybe you'll be more coherent in the morning," I told him.

Alaban shifted warning eyes at him. Ocelot appeared to be thinking of something else to say, but didn't say it. He retreated once more into his bunk and shut the door behind him.

I led Alaban to my room and extended the bed.

"Was it true what he said?" I asked him.

He paused. "It's a long story," Alaban said, parking himself at the edge of my cot.

As he explained, I felt like a psychiatrist listening to a case of child abuse. I listened with an open mind as much as possible, pausing often to shake my head in disbelief, checking his face and manner with my sixth sense to make sure he was telling the truth, believing he was, and feeling deeply disturbed by each uncomfortable confession.

According to Alaban, after he had spent four good years at school with me, Trau had taken him to Tambuo to a university. After a year of study there, Trau had plunged Alaban into a phony intelligence operative. Trau had supposedly infiltrated a smuggling ring and brought Alaban along as his protégé since he needed to keep Alaban with him as a cover. To the Organization, he pretended to be an honorable professor taking his pupil out to do research and to teach him. In reality, he was part of a smuggling ring, making contacts and buying and selling among the dregs of society. He dragged Alaban along, telling him he had to keep quiet about his real identity and that he had to blend in with the people they had to work with. At their various stops, Trau would perform deals behind closed doors. To keep Alaban from spying on him and finding out the truth, he ordered one of his cohorts to offer him drugs or concubines, or both. Alaban knew it was wrong, but he was afraid if he resisted, he and Trau would be found out by the smugglers. When they arrived on Fitmalo, Trau disappeared because a smuggling faction was looking for him as well as internal affairs. This was what Samson had mentioned in Trau's interrogation. General Swall Jade had hidden Trau for his protection and had given Alaban free room, board, and tuition at the Organization center university on Fitmalo for nearly a year while Trau was in hiding. Alaban was able to live as a protected student during that time. However, when Trau reappeared, he immediately whisked him away to Godel, where the lifestyle became worse. By the time he understood without a doubt that this was not an Organization assignment, it was too late. He saw no way out. He considered running away, but he would have been unable to finish his training and would never have been aloud to test. He relied on Trau for everything. He was practically a slave. When he and Trau returned to the Soren galaxy, Trau forced Alaban to train and study night and day for several months to recuperate the skills he'd lost during his illegal escapade and to study ahead, beyond his recommended level. When he applied to test early, he had regained his strength, but Trau's way of life weighed heavy on him.

"You were the one I thought of to keep me from losing hope. I always remembered you as the opposite of all I hated. That's why I couldn't believe it when I saw you there on Sor3, testing at the same time I was. It was like a sign from heaven." He took my hand in his. "You represent everything I love. Trau was everything I hated. Now he's dead and you're still alive. That's the way it should be. What I lived through was pure evil. I didn't want you to know about it. I didn't want you to think of me as someone who likes to live that way. I don't. Sometimes when I'm near a Red Zone, I'm tempted by the old habit. But I've only gone to the concubines twice since Trau was killed. And they were clean. I checked their health first. Like I said, I kept myself healthy for you. You're the only one I really want to mate with. You know that."

I stared at the floor.

"I don't want to live like Trau. Trau was weak. He was evil. I'm not like that. I'm strong. I'm more powerful now than I ever was, just being here with you." He went on to pledge his undying love for me. He outpoured exaggerated compliments. He expressed again and again that he would do anything for me, anything to make me happy, anything to keep my by him.

I let his words float past me without absorbing their meaning. A profound sadness bottled me. He scanned my face.

"Do you hold it against me?" he asked.

I shook my head, but did not look at him. He waited intently for some response.

The concubines—legal prostitutes, indentured physical servants—these were living pieces of property, like livestock. They signed their free will away to a man who would own them. Then he rented them to others for money. They were young women who had made mistakes early in life, had children before they were adults and needed some way to provide for them, or who had poor or abusive families who could not support them. They signed contracts in which they agreed to absolute submission in return for a place for themselves and their children to live, access to food and potable water. They could not study or read above an elementary level. They could not bear more children unless they were used as breeders. Their rights as living beings were neglected. The contracts bound them for years. Some worked for individuals. Some worked for companies. The company-owned concubines ran the highest health risk. Companies sometimes demanded plastic surgery, rib removal, implants to make their property more attractive and salable. I felt sorry for them as much as I wanted them to disappear.

The smugglers, transient thieves without family ties, must have used them often. It was a commonplace way of life for them: drugs, alcohol, sex with prostitutes, disease, suffering, and then death. The smuggling organizers gained from the ignorance and weak-mindedness of these low-class deliverymen. Trau had tried to be one of the organizers. Alaban had been a lackey to him, forced to experience a pirate's life against his will. He may have regretted his adaptation to the ill-gotten lifestyle, but he carried its remnants with him. He still went with concubines. I wondered what other aspects of this kind of existence he had carried with him.

We sat thinking, turning the moral offenses over in our minds. Alaban stared at my profile.

"Do you blame me for the assassination assignments?" he asked, distracting my drowning thoughts.

I breathed in the dull air. "No. I know it's your job. You were obligated to do it." I stared at the baseboard before me, still deeply disturbed.

He squeezed my hand, wishing for a forgiving, amorous response from me. I only sat in ruffled disappointment. I loved him. I pitied him. I even understood him. But I could not see him in the way he wished me to see him. I did not desire him in a lusty manner, especially not after this confession. I simply wanted him by me. I wanted to hold onto him and keep him safe from these bad experiences. I wanted to lead him out of his pit of regret. I wanted to see him happy, whole, at peace with himself, cleansed of his former habits. I did not know how to express this to him.

I heard Alaban's voice plead for forgiveness as he pulled my hand to rest over his heart. At last I looked into his black, sparkling eyes and saw humble entreaty for acceptance, a dark mirror to my own thoughts. I withdrew my hand from his to embrace him slowly. I forgave him. He thanked me with warmth.

Soon we lay on my bed together. I positioned my head on his chest. He held me gently, resigned and remorseful. I sensed from him a strange relief from telling me his woes. He breathed calmly as we lay loosely entangled, but not in a sexual way. At this moment we were merely kindred spirits holding onto one another for comfort. We drifted off to sleep together, at peace.

Chapter 22: Past and Future Clues

Early in the morning, I awoke contented, feeling Alaban's warmth next to me. I hugged him as if I were a happy child hugging a stuffed animal. I felt his hands encompass my back and could not help but smile a little. I felt his spirit so close to mine. I felt complete, without loneliness or want. Then I felt his hand wander down my backside. I lifted myself off his drowsing body and left the bunk, looking back at him uneasily.

I realized that sleeping together had been a mistake. If I didn't want him for a mate, why did I let him sleep with me? Why had I let him kiss me and touch me the way he had in the alley? What a fool I'd been. He had honorably accepted my refusal, but I had not clearly defined our relationship. I'd left him hoping. Mentally, I had criticized his desires, but in reality I had prolonged his illusion. Still I did not have the heart to turn him down indefinitely. Was it my own selfishness? Cruelty? Was I too naïve? I felt low and cowardly.

I went to the exercise room to meditate a while, hoping to find guidance. When I returned to my bunk, I found Alaban awake, sitting alone, meditating just as I had. He stood when I approached him. I criticized myself, explaining that I wanted to be close to him, but that I was neither ready to become his mate nor even prepared to consider it.

He held my hands. "Do you love me?" he asked.

"Yes, I love you," I answered without blinking. "But..."

He covered my lips with his fingertips. "You don't want a brief encounter and then another separation. I understand. You don't want me to think of you as just another concubine. You're not. You mean the world to me. If you want me to, I'm willing to wait."

I stammered.

"But if you decide you do want me, I'm here. I'll do anything you want." He kissed my knuckles. His eyes sparkled at me, sweet mischief regaining its ground.

I began to speak, but he interrupted again.

"If we're assigned together, you'll be sorry you didn't take this opportunity," he warned with a smile.

"I think it's a good idea to wait," I answered.

"You're sure?" he asked jokingly.

"Yes," I said seriously.

He eyed me cautiously. "You're not still mad at me, are you?"

I assured him I was not. I encouraged him to come with me to breakfast, eager to leave this topic of conversation behind. I felt guilty about not driving home my point, but at the same time I felt more relaxed around him. I felt certain that he would not be assigned to our crew and I did not want him to leave my side in the days we had left together. I wanted to make the most of our remaining leave time.

After breakfast, we took a walk around the gardens of the Center. We spoke seriously about Trau's interrogation file and the prospective danger to us both from someone he had tipped off about our skills. He asked to see the file, so we went back to the ship for it. We woke Ocelot to ask for it, promising the file would be safe and that we wouldn't take it out of the ship. He reluctantly set it up for us on the dining table with the decoder. Alaban forgivingly made small talk with him, offering no hard feelings about last night, seeing as how he'd intervened for a good, but flawed, cause. He again assured Ocelot that neither of us was infected. Then he asked him about a possible hangover, but Ocelot didn't respond clearly. When Ocelot left the ship, Alaban commented on his manner.

"If I didn't know any better, I'd say your partner doesn't like me," he said sarcastically.

"You're in good company," I added. I knew he disliked me now more than ever.

Suddenly we heard a scuffing on the stairs and a Lizard's voice greeting us. Alaban stood to greet Yinore formally. She stopped to shake his hand. I introduced them. Alaban addressed her with the same polite formality as he had used on Wilbaht. Yinore fixed her vision on his eyes. She smiled warmly, reading his thoughts.

"It's a pleasure to finally meet you. Sil has mentioned you often." She looked him up and down. "Oh, what a good strong young man. So, you're hoping to join us on the Sonic Wake? Well, I'll have to bring on another Lizard to even out the demographics. We'll soon be overrun with humans here," she chuckled. "Not that you're unwelcome. I'll be glad to have another friendly crewmate. Oh, I can tell he really loves you, Sil. You won't find a better human male on this ship, I assure you." She focused on my pupils, deciphering my feelings. "Are you sure? I can tell you compliment one another strongly."

I blinked and faltered for a reply, but she turned again to Alaban. She patted his hand. He observed her, perplexed.

"Don't give up hope. She'll definitely consider you. She does love you, you know. I'm sorry for being so bold. I read thoughts through the eyes, you see. Please excuse me. I only came for my official gray uniform. I'm presenting my test today." She hurried to her bunk to change her suit.

Flustered by the odd encounter, we sat again at the table. Alaban said he'd never met someone with her power.

Yinore bustled out of her room once more. We wished her luck on her test. She thanked us as she scurried away. She called up to Alaban that it was nice meeting him as she whisked herself down the stairs. Alaban asked if she was always so high-strung. I told him this was the first time I'd seen her this way. She must have been excited about her testing.

We sat glancing at each other every few seconds, thinking of what Yinore had said about us. We then read through the file together. When he read the second interview, Alaban cursed Trau's condemned soul fiercely. He excused himself and went to the exercise room to pound something for a while. He came back better concentrated.

"Trau told them about our skills so they could use us. For what?" he said.

"You can get through any computerized locking system. I can pass objects through each other. I'd say they want us to break into a high security building and steal something for them," I thought aloud. "Who was Trau working for?"

"Anyone who paid, I'll bet. He was such a dog. I'm sure he would lie at anyone's feet for the right price. He was a picture of greed. Too bad he never shared the wealth," Alaban spoke.

"But he did, didn't he?" I asked. "He said he couldn't keep a personal defense trainer for you for more than a month at a time. That took money. You said he paid several tutors on Sor4 to prepare you for your final examination. What else did he pay for you?"

Alaban shrugged. "Sometimes he'd shove me off on some computer whiz or a math professor. He left me at an aerospace engineering university for almost a whole year on Tambuo. That was without scholarship, so he paid full price. Of course, some of it came from home. My mom sent him the minimum payment for conditional adoption every month. You know my parents signed me over to Trau when I was eight. They couldn't train me as an exceptional student. They were poor." He eyed me hesitantly.

I had known about this before. Alaban had lived on a commercial express ship with Trau until he was awarded the Organization scholarship to attend my father's school. He had never told me of any wrongdoings Trau had committed during that time, so I assumed Trau had turned to crime some time during Alaban's stay with us. Trau had never visited Alaban at the school during the entire four-year stay. He had only appeared to drop him off when he was twelve and to pick him up again when he was sixteen.

"I see your point about the money. He just never let me enjoy it," Alaban stated.

"What about a specialized area of training?" I asked. "Anything that would point to a specific skill he wanted you to learn?"

Alaban paused a moment. He asked me if I'd ever had to kill anyone. I mentioned the Fitmalo snipers. I asked why.

"He trained me on assassinations. They were mostly fake, but the last few were real. That's another reason I hated him so much," he stated.

"So he did take you along on some of his jobs."

"Just three," he said.

"All three required an assassination?" I asked.

"Required? This wasn't a directive from the Organization, Sil. This was a smuggling ring hit. Trau and his associates were taking over. You saw that statement the interrogators made about 'the Daughter'. Guess who she is."

"A leader in the smuggling ring?" I guessed.

"She's more than that. She was Trau's boss and full-time lover. She kept him on a short leash. She's a Fitmalo. Her name is Viga."

"That's unusual. Humans and Fitmalos aren't usually attracted to each other."

"That's not all. I only heard her called 'the Daughter' once before when I was on her planet. Given the circumstances, I'd say she has to be General Swall Jade's daughter. Swall must have hid Trau on Fitmalo during that smuggling investigation because she asked him to. Now a few things start to make sense. General Swall's been covering up the ring from inside the Organization and his daughter is taking care of details on the outside. Trau was working both sides. Swall Jade must have been his contact general. Maybe he really was assigned to infiltrate the ring. They must have planned on keeping me in the two-faced trade until I started making an ass of myself just to piss them off," Alaban said. "I never did anything so bad that Trau would decide to get rid of me. I never exposed his operation to anyone. I never openly disrespected him. I made a point to be the most subtly rebellious prick I could be without getting myself whacked. I'd 'misunderstand' orders and do something he didn't want. I'd pay more attention to the wrong person when I had to show them in for client meetings. 'Oh, *this* is Mr. Red. I'm terribly sorry, sir. I thought this servant was him. He's dressed so well.' Things like that." He mocked himself with toothy cynicism.

His example reminded me of a passage in Trau's testimony. "Trau said he took you to the concubines at the smugglers' den but you were more interested in the smugglers than the girls. Do you know what incident he was referring to?" I asked.

Alaban furrowed his brow. He cursed Trau and his black humor. "We were there to assassinate the smugglers, but they were there with their concubines. Trau said we couldn't leave them as witnesses. He ordered me to get rid of them, but I refused. They didn't know anything. They were just a bunch of poor women. They couldn't even identify us. We wore hoods. I killed the smugglers. I had no remorse for them; they were killers themselves. I wouldn't touch the girls. He cut their heads off. He *beheaded* three innocent women, Sil. Then he threw their heads at me for disobeying orders." Alaban's breath shortened. Alaban flexed his arms and shoulders and then meshed his hands together. He closed his eyes, continuing to breathe shortly until he regained calm.

My mind reeled. In my optimistic beliefs, I could not fathom anyone, smuggler or killer, doing something so obscenely demented. But it had to be true. Alaban would not lie to me.

"I only stayed with him so I could complete my final exam and be rid of him. Do you know what I did the day I found out he was killed? I celebrated. I invited my partners for a drink at that bar on Sor4—the one where I left you the letter, remember?" Alaban said.

"No wonder you bought drinks for everyone," I recalled.

"Yes, I was so relieved, so happy. I knew you would be there after that, so I left you the letter. I felt like rejoicing. The reign of terror was over. Thank God he's dead." He spoke with determination.

"I'm glad you're free from him," I said peacefully.

"Yes, well said. I'm free from him."

"But someone wants you to follow in his footsteps. If he was so close to Swall Jade and the Fitmalos, it may be someone in the Regime."

"They can rot in hell with him," Alaban stated firmly.

"I'm glad to hear you say that. What if they threaten to hurt me? What if I'm captured? Will you still say the same thing?"

Alaban was quiet for a while.

"Alaban?"

"They would have to prove to me that you were in some kind of danger before I'd do anything for them. Then I'd have no choice," he said in realization. "I don't want it to come to that. There's got to be a way to prevent it."

"But how?" I asked rhetorically.

He shook his head. "I'd never pass up the chance to save your life, but I don't want to have to be faced with that. To work with the enemy..." he trailed off.

We sat thinking about this for a long time. Suddenly, Alaban sat up straight. A conniving gleam invaded his face. He shook his head and it fell away. Then the gleam returned. He had a dangerous idea.

"Don't do it," I advised.

"Do what?" he asked with fires of mischief in his eyes.

"Whatever you're thinking. It's got to be dangerous."

"It is risky, but you would stay safe and I would stay alive. What else is there?"

"Peace of mind?" I suggested.

"Now you're speaking a foreign language. I don't know what that is. It doesn't matter. I have an awesome plan."

"I'm afraid to hear it," I said gingerly.

"What's the best way to bust an entire smuggling ring?" he asked.

"That would be almost impossible. It would take years of surveillance and infiltration. You'd need huge amounts of backup to bring the whole thing down," I responded.

"No. You're thinking from the outside in. Think from the inside out. Think structure. Every successful smuggling ring is dependent upon a few puppet masters. They're not smugglers themselves. They're rich socialites with political positions," he said. "*Big* political positions. That politician they sent me to hit the other night—he was connected to the ring. Probably something to do with that Fitmalo surprise attack your team was involved in. He was in a high security area, all computerized. Never trust a machine to do a person's job. His bodyguards were out of range. They weren't even warriors. No sixth sense. They never knew I was coming. Now, if *I* had been in their place, I would have sensed me before I even entered the front gates. No assassin would ever have gotten past me."

I agreed. "So what's your point? How does this man's death affect the hierarchy of the smuggling ring? Surely there's someone else waiting to take his place. The smuggling line is still operational. Even the battle underground didn't make enough of a dent in it to shut it down altogether. There's always someone who'll step in and take over, as long as there's demand and money..."

"There will always be criminals waiting to get in on the high-paying crime. Okay. But how many of them are involved in overthrowing their government? Not many. I can think of one."

"The Regime. You're saying the political powers of the Regime are also the puppet masters of the smuggling lines."

"Absolutely. I'll bet they've got so many illegal investments going on they can't keep up with them all. They've got to be the most paranoid power-hungry bastards alive. They can't trust anybody. Everybody's out to get them or a piece of their stash. That's why the leaders of the Regime need the best bodyguards money can buy." Alaban puffed out his chest and gestured to himself, eyes gleaming.

"No," I stated.

"Why not? Can you imagine the kind of information I would have access to if I got close enough to one of the bigwigs to break into their computers? With one message to every headquarters in the U.G., their whole operation would be exposed: names, transaction lists, government connections, everything. *And* while I'm working as an inside man for the top dogs, no blackmailer would dare touch me, so they would have no reason to approach you."

"That's a great scenario, but it's impossible. No Organization general is going to send a first year warrior into a high-risk job like that. Even if you proposed an op like that, they would have to send somebody else."

Alaban wrinkled his nose and made a face. "I keep forgetting I'm nobody in this Organization. People keep reminding me, though. I'm not supposed to be seen or heard until they need a dirty job done," he said bitterly. "If I don't get a change of assignment soon, they'll turn me into a younger version of the grim reaper." He rested his chin on his left hand and tapped the table with his right. "No. They've got to let me have it. Someone in the Organization would let me. I'm the one they'd least expect."

"Alaban, even if you could be assigned a job like that, it would be even more risky than a blackmail job. You'd be on the inside for months. If anyone in the Regime suspected you, you'd be killed."

"We've got to do *something* to counter their plan. We've got to find out who's planning to set us up and how to keep them from doing it. Whoever they are, they haven't approached us yet. Either they're waiting for something to happen or they're biding their time for a reason." Alaban drummed his fingers harder.

We sat wracking our brains for a possible solution to this imminent problem, but found no other. We could only draw out a plan for research of suspects. We ruled out Viga as our possible blackmailer, since Trau would have told her of our abilities directly prior to his arrest. General Swall Jade was a possibility, but since he was on good terms with Viga, he could have gotten word easily through her. Trau could not have been trying to message him. We could not be certain that Swall Jade was involved directly with any Regime members or if he would share this information with one of them, but even if he was not, the Regime was definitely an entity to be wary of in this case, as with all others we were currently researching. We also considered the Fitmalo military rebels, led by former General Zar, and the young Fitmalo general Trau had bodyguarded in the Public Valley, since both had been mentioned in the testimony.

Soon we realized our discussion had spanned several hours and that it was nearly dark outside. Alaban returned the computer and decoder to Ocelot's bunk. Then we left the confinement of the ship to walk and stretch in the evening air of spring.

At dinnertime, Wilbaht and Ocelot joined us again at the café. Conversation was more serious. Ocelot still didn't say much. This time, instead of holding a grudge, he seemed anxious. He feared we would mention our confrontation from the night before, but of course we did not. After dinner, we all went our separate ways. Alaban and I walked through town together and returned to my room at the Center late in the evening.

I told him I was very tired and preferred to sleep alone tonight. He said he was very tired, too, and promised he would not get in my way. He even offered to sleep on the floor, as long as he could sleep near me. Reluctantly, I accepted. I placed the thin top mattress from my bed onto the floor beside me. He sat on it and kissed me until I had to pull away. I hugged him and pecked him lightly on the cheek, reminding him that we were tired, and advising him to get some sleep. He felt dejected, but still we said I-love-you's and goodnight. I rested my hand over the side of the bed, letting him hold my fingertips between his as we fell asleep.

In the morning, I awoke alone in the room. A note lay on the mattress where Alaban had slept, telling me he'd gone to shower and he would meet me at seven for breakfast. He appeared punctually and lively at my door. His energy level was unusually high. On the way to the café, he clowned and played like a schoolboy. At breakfast, he fidgeted with his utensils and formed little buildings with his food. He made bright conversation with me. I was glad to hear him talk happily again, but even he admitted that his hyper energy bordered on the abnormal. I suggested some kind of exercise after breakfast might help him. He agreed, adding that he'd like to do some fencing.

After returning to our rooms for sparring gear, we went to the practice field, where we found Ocelot practicing sword forms. He viciously cut up an unseen enemy.

Alaban mentioned that perhaps my partner would be sober enough to spar today.

"Be careful. He's an expert swordsman," I advised.

"All the more reason to challenge him." Alaban drew his sword to stretch and parry with it a few minutes.

Ocelot saw us and stopped his practice.

"Care for a match, sir?" Alaban called jovially. His manner this morning contradicted his abrasive attitude from the alley.

I was sure Ocelot would object, but he did not. In fact, he accepted heartily. I volunteered to referee. I grabbed two sets of padded armor for both of them from the storage tent and waited by the centerline of the sparring rectangle for them to gear up. Alaban moved forward to meet his opponent, but then retreated to my side hurriedly. He lifted his screen mask to kiss my cheek and then jumped back to his trajectory to a spot opposite Ocelot. I moved to the fence to observe them. I watched Alaban with a smile. Then I became a serious referee.

"Tags on body armor only," I reminded them. "Time out for every touch. Please don't hurt each other. I don't want to see anyone hospitalized."

"Yes, ma'am," Alaban said. Ocelot didn't react.

"Begin," I called.

Alaban swung and parried, diving forward. Ocelot defended brutally with a triple strike that sent Alaban hopping backward. He attacked again with greater force and speed, but Ocelot beat Alaban's sword with such strength that he dented it on one blade. Ocelot shoved him away and stood ready. Alaban stared in awe at his dented sword.

"Superb," Alaban commented. He decided to take a different strategy.

He whipped around, dodged, thrust and bounded backward to avoid Ocelot's blade. Then, when Ocelot had swept the sword down and across his body, Alaban leapt up toward Ocelot's shoulder with his sword down and slightly back, thinking he could fend of Ocelot's sword and tag him in the chest with one move. But Ocelot brought his sword up laterally and flipped Alaban up over his head into the air. Alaban did a somersault to land on his feet behind him. He quickly turned back to ready stance.

Ocelot turned to a different stance. He held his sword in the air above him and his other arm extended toward his opponent. Suddenly, I felt afraid.

Alaban charged again at Ocelot. This time, Ocelot fended him off easily. He pulled back his sword for an instant and sent it bursting through the extension mechanism of Alaban's sword, chopping it in two. Instead of stopping the match, Ocelot swiped the point of his sword across Alaban's chest.

"Stop!" I shouted in panic, clutching my own sternum, imagining the stinging pain across his chest.

Alaban jerked and fell backwards as his padded armor sagged open. I rushed to him. The severed section of Alaban's sword whooshed through the air and embedded itself in the ground only a meter away from where I had stood. I unhooked the neck protector and peeled away the armor to check Alaban's injury.

A thin trail of blood stood out on Alaban's shirt. It was not a deep cut, but the blood expanded to leave a heavy, dark line on him from the middle of his right pectoral muscle to just above the left clavicle. The padding was meant to protect the body for up to one hundred kilograms of pressure. Ocelot's strike had exceeded that limit. This was not an accident. It was a deliberate strike to maim.

I marched to Ocelot in fury. "What do you think you're doing? That was an illegal move!" I hit him in the chest with a levitative palm strike, causing him to stagger backwards a couple of meters.

"You could have killed him!" I shouted.

"It was a gut reaction. My mistake," he stated emotionlessly.

I whirled to return to Alaban. He cast the riffled padding aside and stood, ignoring the sting of his cut. I observed the wound closely. It would heal without dressing, but I offered to doctor it for him. He lightly petted my shoulder in response. Alaban stood studying his opponent. I turned to scowl at the man for his insolence.

Ocelot folded his sword. He replaced it to its sheath resolutely.

"It's okay, Sil," Alaban said. "I think we can resolve this hand to hand."

Alaban handed me the broken hilt of his sword and kicked aside the fencing armor. I returned to my standing place and picked the blade from the ground. Ocelot would soon be sorry for his belligerent mistake. I leaned back on the fence and dropped the pieces of the sword to the ground, eager to witness the justice Alaban would level on him. Ocelot whipped off his padding and tossed it behind him. The two men posed at ready stance.

"Begin," I said.

Alaban attacked first. He flew forward with a fake high right punch and twisted to give Ocelot a side kick to the lower abdomen. Ocelot tried to block, but he was overwhelmed by the swiftness and agility Alaban displayed. Ocelot stepped back from the impact, but didn't fall. Alaban continued at close range countering Ocelot's moves and gaining three more strikes to Ocelot's chest before he bounded away from him.

Ocelot took only a few steps forward, not certain how to counterattack a man of this speed and skill. He jutted forward to his left to throw a double jab, but he was too slow. Alaban countered his punches by dodging and pounding the underside of Ocelot's arm. At the same time, he kicked forward just above the knee. Ocelot blocked and retracted, but not before Alaban landed a powerful hook punch just below his armpit. In reaction to his pain, Ocelot sideswiped Alaban with an elbow and forearm, sending Alaban faltering off to the side. He stepped lightly into a pirouette and hopped around tauntingly.

Ocelot's anger got the best of him. He stepped forward twice, threw a left roundhouse and then a jab. Then he stepped in to deliver an uppercut toward Alaban's jaw. His fist hit air. Alaban distracted his opponent's arms with quick fists and kicked Ocelot in the stomach, but quickly realized his mistake. Ocelot trapped his leg, turning his back to Alaban's body. He slammed him to the ground and twisted the leg, pressing a sensitive pressure point at the thigh and kicking him in the head. My own leg almost cramped when I saw the injury. Alaban yelled and grunted. Ocelot jumped up, whirling to face him, but Alaban surprised him with a levitating double heel to the face. Ocelot staggered backward. Alaban stood with difficulty, favoring his hurt leg. Ocelot squeezed one eye shut.

Ocelot thrust forward with a spinning kick. Alaban leapt over his leg and levitated to a horizontal position, crossing his feet together and changing his body into a whirling battering ram. He zipped around him to pummel Ocelot's arm and ribs with his feet. Then he broke his form to grab Ocelot around the neck, flinging him to the ground.

Ocelot rolled up and stood to resume fighting stance only to be attacked at full force by one of Alaban's trick combinations. He darted to his left and threw a right punch at Ocelot's face, not meaning to hit him. Ocelot lifted an arm for an inside block as Alaban had hoped. He pressed the blocking fist towards Ocelot's other arm and thrust a knee into Ocelot's lower abdomen. Ocelot cowered backward, unable to trap Alaban's wrists or counterattack during the move. Alaban then opened Ocelot's blocking arms with a trick play of elbows and cross punches. He then delivered a powerful front kick to the base of the sternum. I cringed, impressed with the execution of the debilitating move. Ocelot sailed backward, falling onto his back and into a backwards somersault. He stayed down headfirst for a long while, but then moved slowly to stand.

Ocelot had barely gotten to his feet, hunched over in pain, and was not yet at ready stance when Alaban battered his arms, venturing in close. Despite Ocelot's attempts to trap and strike his opponent at vital pressure points, Alaban dodged and slipped from his traps at lightning speed. He bashed Ocelot with a claw hand to the chin. He swept Ocelot's left foot out from under him as he brought a forearm to his exposed neck. As Ocelot fell diagonally, Alaban punished him with an axe kick to the kidney. I thought surely the match was over. Normally, this would have been a knockout, but Alaban's aim must have slipped enough to miss the pressure point junction. Ocelot stayed awake, in a table position for several seconds. He slowly stumbled to his feet, now bleeding from the mouth.

Alaban bounced around, hopping and distracting him with fake attacks and shouts. Then he leapt into the air, swiping him with a levitative scissor kick to the neck and face. Ocelot blocked, but blocking did no good against this power move. He teetered to the side as Alaban levitated, twirling in a full circle. He hit him in the ribs with a shin. Ocelot somehow refused to fall. He set his stance wide and concentrated on keeping his equilibrium. But he had to know he was worn down. If he had been slow before, he was almost immobile now. His eye was swollen and red. His lip bled. He wavered, injured and tired. Still he wanted to continue.

Alaban advanced with a flurry of punches, only half of which Ocelot blocked. Alaban spun horizontally again, this time close to the ground. He rammed through the backs of Ocelot's knees. My beaten partner went down again.

This time, he hurried to stand, gathering up his remaining strength. He flashed a series of high punches at Alaban's face, followed by kicks to his knees and thighs. Alaban blocked all but one of the punches, which turned his head to the side just long enough for Ocelot to strike him with an elbow to his sliced clavicle and a power side kick to the torso. Alaban flew backward and nearly hit the ground, but he soon found his feet and returned to attack even more fiercely. Ocelot went down yet again.

Alaban bounded backward. Ocelot was clearly done, but Alaban was willing to continue beating him into the ground as long as he kept getting up.

I had to intervene.

Ocelot brought himself up on one knee. He tried to stand, but Alaban pounced after him. Ocelot stood and blocked, punching weakly.

I stepped between them.

"Stop," I commanded. I touched a palm over both of their hearts to stop them.

I gasped. A white blast cut through me like electricity. A frenzied wave of visionary shards traveled from the men's bodies, through my arms, and flickered all together before my face. I saw images that contradicted each other. I saw a huge room—a hangar. I saw Ocelot drive his sword through Alaban's chest. Then I saw the same scene, but in reverse. This time Alaban killed Ocelot. Then a third version of the scene appeared, and a fourth. Alaban held a sword to my throat. Suddenly Ocelot was in my place. Then it was Ocelot who held the sword. Next, we all attacked each other. Fitmalos came from everywhere, shooting at us. I saw Alaban grabbing at my sleeve, telling me to go with them. Then I saw the Fitmalos execute all three of us. Next a bright green light shot from an unseen weapon. I heard myself scream.

Suddenly the vision disappeared. I stood staring out into the quiet practice field, the two men still attached to the ends of my arms. I regarded them angrily, pulsing a powerful levitative burst into both of them with a shout. They hurtled backward and landed with a thud about ten meters away from each other.

"What's wrong with you? You're going to get us all killed!"

I stood holding my head, realizing what I just said would make no sense to them. They forgot their match and moved slowly to me, now curious about what I'd seen.

"Sil? What is it?" Alaban asked in concern. He advanced toward me with arms outstretched.

I stopped him. "Wait. Have to talk to you alone." I turned to Ocelot. "Go help Wilbaht. I'll talk to you later."

"Tell me now," Ocelot insisted. He cringed, fluttering the lid of his swollen eye.

Remembering his rank, I had to oblige. "The three of us will be in battle together, a Fitmalo battle. We could all die. But this vision was different. This time we have a lot of choices. I only know we have to avoid killing each other. I don't understand how it could be, but I saw us battling an army of Fitmalos. I think this vision is a warning. We can choose our deaths or avoid them. This will happen within the year."

"We all fought together?" Alaban asked. "Maybe I'll be assigned to work with you after all."

"Maybe, but I saw something else. I can only tell you. It's personal," I said to him softly.

"There were only the three of us fighting? We had no backup?" Ocelot asked.

"No. We were the only warriors there. We were in a hangar of some kind. I didn't recognize the place," I said. "This will happen. I'm sure of it."

The men looked at me and then glanced tensely at each other.

"Well, I guess since we'll be working together I can't keep beating you to a pulp," Alaban said. "Peace, sir?"

He held out his hand. Ocelot slowly decided to shake it.

"I, uh, have an extra sword you can have," Ocelot said reluctantly.

"In that case, I'd like to take the one you're wearing now, unless it's damaged. Any sword that can cut straight through another one like that is excellent quality. I'll bet you made it yourself," Alaban spoke.

"Yes," Ocelot said, reaching for the sword. His hand trembled from injury and exertion. He ogled the sword fondly with his good eye, and then passed it resignedly to Alaban, who opened and inspected it.

"She's got some nicks around the blades but I can sharpen them down. Looks good. I think you did me a favor by destroying my old one." He whipped the blade around in the air in front of him a few times to get the feel of its weight.

Ocelot regarded his old sword with regret. He turned and walked away from us without another word.

"Thanks for the match, sir," Alaban called after him. He continued to move the sword in the air, delighted with the spoils of his battle.

I watched Ocelot meander up the field and through the gate. I hoped the animosity between the two men had been laid to rest by their short battle. I felt sorry for both of them. I hated to see Alaban injured, but I also didn't like seeing Ocelot beaten bloody. He was my partner, after all, and he had lost badly.

Alaban finally put the sword away. "So what did you want to talk to me about?" he asked.

"The Fitmalos in my vision were on your side. They were fighting for you at one point. They were trying to kill Ocelot and me. If that's what it takes to work with the Regime, then don't do it. I don't care if the head general of the U.G. asks you himself. My partner and I will die if you do. Promise me right now that you won't work with the Fitmalos, Alaban, as a bodyguard or anything else."

"But you said there were a lot of choices. Maybe that was just one possibility. You know I'd never let anything happen to you."

"It's too dangerous, Alaban. I'm afraid we'd all die in a situation like that. This is more than just knowing the risk. This was a premonition. Promise me by the love of your own heart. Promise me that you will not work with the Fitmalos. Tell me now. Our lives depend on you," I insisted.

"All right. I promise I won't. But I don't know that it will do any good if we'll have to battle an army of them. It would be better to have a man on the inside to pull strings for us."

"No, Alaban. Promise me," I demanded.

"I promise I won't then," he said, holding up one hand as if swearing an oath of allegiance.

"Thank you."

"But you know unless we have someone to help us, it will be nearly impossible for all of us to survive. Three warriors don't take on an army.

211

Our only choice would be to fend them off long enough to escape, and that's wishful thinking," Alaban pondered aloud.

"I understand what you're saying, but if we're going to escape together we have to be on the same side," I argued.

"Why would the person on the inside need to escape if he's accepted by the Fitmalos? He would only need to facilitate the escape of the others."

"And be executed for betrayal? No. I don't want you to die any more than you want me to," I countered.

"Yes, but I don't see your logic. You're telling me to refuse to do an assignment you've already said I can't get because we'll be in danger when we face the Fitmalos, which is exactly the kind of thing I'd be doing the assignment for in the first place."

"You've already promised me."

He stood staring me in the eye. "Maybe I shouldn't have."

"We'll just have to find someone else who will infiltrate the Regime for us," I said.

Alaban snorted. "We're first year warriors, remember? Who's going to take us seriously? You want to report this to your contact general? How will we know we can trust him? I don't know about you, but I can count the people I trust on one hand. Even if we could trust him, what would he do about it? Call it in to a higher general? Who's to say that guy's clean? Think about it, Sil. Leave your emotions aside for a moment. Strategically, what would you plan to do?" he asked.

"Strategically, we can't plan anything. We don't know whom to contact in the first place. Anyway, we don't know who's in the Regime and who isn't. The only detailed information we know about them has to do with the arms smuggling ring. Even if one of us got in, it would take months or even a year before we could reach the right target. By then it would be too late."

"Yes, but they want us for something. If I step forward voluntarily, maybe they'll leave you out of it. I've got an idea of how to get in. I know 'the Daughter', Viga. If Trau was trying to contact somebody to set us up, then Viga must know about it. I can find her. I can get close to her. She'll let me in. If I go in willingly, she'll complete the setup. I'll talk her into letting me do the job myself, whatever it is. Once it's done, she'll give me a top job on the smuggling side. Then I'll be able to work my way up from the inside and find out who's in control," Alaban said.

"Why would she accept you?" I asked. "She knows you didn't want that kind of life before. Why would she think you'd want to join them now?"

"She knows my talents with numbers. She had me create sliding-scale rates for clients, all mathematically justified. She liked my work.

Plus, she liked me. She flirted with me all the time. Once she tried to seduce me right there in front of Trau. She would have kept trying if he hadn't called her off. She'd enjoy having me around. She'll make room for me," Alaban said.

"So you're just going to whore yourself out to the enemy?" I asked curtly.

He recoiled. "I didn't say that, but then again, why shouldn't I? Would you give me a reason not to?" he retorted. His eyes reflected anger and hope at the same time.

"That's really devilish of you. Of course if you want to move up from concubines to smugglers, go ahead. Climb the sexual ladder. Next you'll be sleeping with government officials. You'll be able to rob and kill anybody. You'll be a bigger, better Trau. Just walk in and take his place at his bed!" I nearly shouted.

He glared at me incredulously. "How can you say that? You know I hated Trau. I don't want to be anything like Trau. When have I ever suggested something like that? Is this what you really think of me? Now you think I'm an evil bastard just because I asked you to mate with me? That's backwards. I'm in love with you. Haven't you heard what I've been telling you? I'm only considering this to save *you*," he spat.

I closed my eyes a moment. "I'm sorry. I didn't mean it. I'm just so upset about things," I said, shaking my head.

Angry and confused, he asked, "Then what did you mean?"

"I don't see how you could consider approaching Viga. You'll put yourself in a position where she'll think you'll do whatever she demands: theft, smuggling, crimes of all kinds, and even sex? With her? Why would you go to those extremes? Please don't tell me you're that kind of spy. You shouldn't give yourself up like that," I said.

He stepped close to me again. "I wasn't considering it, but why not? Tell me the truth. You're jealous. You want me for yourself. Why is it so difficult for you to admit?"

"I don't know if it's jealousy, but I do know I care about you and what you do to yourself. I don't want you to be with Viga. I don't want you to be with concubines. It's not right for your health. Don't you care about yourself? Don't you care about your honor? Or mine? Alaban, if you want me to be your mate, why do you still go with concubines?"

"This is about concubines?" His face contorted with exasperation.

"It's about you caring about what's right and acting on it. If you hated Trau, why do you still follow his way of life? You drink alcohol. You go with concubines. What else? If I let you have what you want with me, would you still go with them when we're apart? I think you would. If

Viga showed up tomorrow and asked you to join her, I don't know if I could trust you to say no."

Alaban's eyes moved from side to side, searching for a reply.

"I'm sorry, Alaban. I love you dearly, but jealous or not, I cannot in good conscience agree to be your mate. How can I if I can't trust you? I'm sorry." I paused. "You are my best friend. I love your heart. But I will not be your wife."

It seemed as though an internal vortex sucked all glimmering life from Alaban's eyes. He summoned up no apology, no disagreement, no plea for reconsideration. His face fell. I thought for a moment that he might cry. He turned away miserably. He walked away from me, stepping lazily, as if in a trance, his pride stripped from him. I stayed watching after him a moment. Then I ran to him.

"Where are you going?" I asked.

"To the Center. I have to know if we're being reassigned together." He glanced at me sadly, and then turned to face the grassy field. "Don't come with me. I'll find you later," he said in a dull voice.

I grasped his hand in mine and squeezed it lightly. He barely squeezed back, and then let it go. I slowed my pace to a halt. I watched him pass through the gate alone. I felt less guilty than apprehensive. I wasn't sure how things would turn out. I knew we couldn't be assigned together. Only a few hours remained before we would have to say goodbye. The next time we'd meet could be in battle.

Chapter 23: Promise, Offense, and Harassment

Later, I met Wilbaht and Ocelot in Wilbaht's quarters. Wilbaht doctored Ocelot's eye. He changed a bandage and applied an ointment. I tried not to stare at the purple and red bulge on his face, but it was a sight.

I briefly informed Wilbaht of my vision, excluding what I'd said only to Alaban. He considered it gravely.

There came a knock at the door. Wilbaht stepped to it, clearing the room in two strides. Alaban presented himself sternly. He went through the typical formalities with Wilbaht.

"What did the General say?" I asked.

"Request for change of placement respectfully denied," he said. "On grounds of personal affiliation with current crewmember." He folded his arms over his chest.

"If you'd like, I could recommend you to a different crew," Wilbaht offered.

"That's nice of you to offer, sir, but I can't think of anyone else I'd rather work with. Zank and Ongeram are not so bad. I only wanted to work with you and Sil," he said.

Wilbaht placed a long, dark hand atop Alaban's shoulder. "Perhaps it's for the best," he said.

"I don't think so, sir. I get the feeling my worst days are ahead of me," Alaban said. He glimpsed Ocelot's bandaged face and apologized for the damage.

"It's nothing," Ocelot replied. After Wilbaht glared at him and gestured to Alaban, he added, "I apologize for...the chest." He drew a line in the air over his own chest.

Alaban bowed his head solemnly.

Wilbaht wished Alaban well. He thanked him and shook hands formally. Then he asked if I would walk with him. I agreed. We excused ourselves from Wilbaht's presence and walked together quietly out to the courtyard.

We sat on a bench overlooking the airfield. Alaban took my hand and contemplated it seriously. He sighed. He squeezed my hand and brought it to his lips. He kissed it, and then pressed it to his face. I felt a warm moistness at his cheek.

He let go of my hand and pulled me around him to sit sideways on his lap. He embraced me around the waist and buried his face at the crook of my neck. I held him around his shoulders and leaned my face on the top of his head. He held onto me there for a long time. We caressed each other

215

a little, but mostly we sat still. Finally he sat up straight and sighed, taking my hand in his.

"Sil, I'm going to change my ways for you. I'm sorry about the concubines. I didn't consider how you felt. You're right to be angry. I won't do it again. I want you to know I'll wait for you as long as it takes. Just give me a chance. I have to have you, Sil. You're the best thing in my life, and things are only going to get worse for me. I can feel it." He brushed my hair from my face as he spoke endearingly. "You're my sun, my bright star that guides me through the dark moments of my life," he quoted from a love song, breaking a hint of a smile. "Tell me you'll give me a chance. Just an opportunity to court you."

I regarded him with kindness. I believed he would change for me. I conceded. He kissed my cheek and hugged me to him again.

All evening we stayed close together. That night, we slept holding hands, I on the bed, and he on the floor next to me as before. In the morning, our leave days were finished. Alaban walked me to the door of the ship. We held each other without kissing. We said our goodbyes. I boarded the ship walking backwards with my travel box to see him as long as I could. We blew kisses to each other before I lost sight of him. I wept quietly to see him go.

After cleaning my face, I reported to the upper deck. I pushed myself to overcome my emotions and concentrate once more on my job, but it was a difficult task. Wilbaht mentioned I was running late. I apologized humbly. We started inventory and all pre-flight checks, restocking and double-checking all systems, a job that would take all day to finish. Wilbaht was in his element giving orders, checking instruments, helping stock and inventory. Yinore worked diligently, proudly displaying her new title of professor sub general. Klib appeared well rested and feisty. Ocelot's eye probably looked worse than it had the day before, but he kept it covered with a bandage.

Later, Wilbaht gathered the warriors together for the announcement of our new assignment. This time he read the orders himself, since Ocelot's vision was not up to standard. We had a simple two-week bodyguard assignment on Karnesh, where we'd be assigned to protect Fitmalo officials during galactic conferences. Wilbaht took into consideration my suggestion about a day's leave on the Jain planet before taking on the assignment, and also promised a return trip only if we did not run behind schedule on Karnesh due to inclement weather. Our expected travel time between Santer and Karnesh, by our ship's Sor4 schedule, was three weeks exactly. Wilbaht noted that due to the short flight, we would have more leeway with supply usage. We especially wouldn't need to be so sparing with water. Wilbaht scheduled us for takeoff in five hours, but gave us permission to take a break outside for a while with the stipulation that we had to return within the hour for pre-flight set up.

When he dismissed us, Yinore stayed in with Wilbaht, saying she wished to speak with him alone. The rest of us went outside. Ocelot headed for the trees to hike in the open air before our ship's confinement. Klib went to the ascension tower lobby for a drink. I walked around the airfield.

Next to our ship was a large, pearly white one. It was shaped like a rounded box with incut fins. Its name, Thrader Sea Ram, was emblazoned along its side in dark red letters. I passed several smaller ships from Santer and a few others from the Keres helion. At the far corner of the field, I found Alaban's ship, the Jawlcheen Reaper. The Reaper was only slightly larger than our ship, but its shape was more narrow and streamlined. It was a gray and black ship with sparkling purple letters and ID number. It sat silent. No one was aboard.

A mischievous idea popped into my head. I levitated to the ship's crown. Since Alaban was the youngest on his crew, he would have to inspect and clean the outside of their ship, just as I had with ours. I could leave him a note at the very top of the ship and he would be the one to find it. I flecked off a layer of paint to spell "S loves A". I returned to my ship with an encouraging sense of accomplishment.

Once we all were aboard, Wilbaht called a crew meeting again. We sat in our usual seats at the table, but Yinore stood blinking at Wilbaht's side.

"Congratulations are in order for our newly-titled Professor Sub General Yinore Fleetwing," Wilbaht announced. We all applauded and heckled her a while. She smiled affably.

"We should also congratulate her for another accomplishment. Will you tell them, or shall I?" Wilbaht asked her.

"I will, sir, thank you." She cleared her throat and regarded us all happily. "I have found a suitable mate. We have decided to move to the Jain planet to live together. This will be my last journey with the crew."

My smile fell. "Yinore, I'm happy for you, but are you sure you want to leave us?"

Ocelot concurred, adding that we would miss her help on engineering.

"No, no, it's all decided. You'll soon be glad I'm off the ship anyway." She cleared her throat. "I'm pregnant." She smiled excitedly.

We made expressions of astonishment, but then congratulated her.

"So when is this kid going to hatch?" Klib asked warily. "Don't tell me we'll have a baby Lizard on the ship for three weeks."

"No, Klib," Yinore spoke agitatedly. "I have two more weeks before I lay the egg. Then it will take another three weeks to gestate before hatching. We'll be on Jain by then."

"Well, all right, then. Congratulations, mom," Klib said, changing his attitude.

"Thank you. I'll be asking you to check up on me now and then if you don't mind, Sub Professor," Yinore said to Ocelot.

"Any time, ma'am. Congratulations," he answered.

I took Yinore's news uneasily. I wondered how she might expect me to support her as a possible nurse during her labor. I was curious to see the egg. I hoped we would see the baby once it hatched. I wondered if Wilbaht could request a female replacement for Yinore when we arrived in the Keres helion. If not, I would be the only female left on board. I did not look forward to that prospect.

The next week of ship's work went as scheduled and without incident. Working upstairs with Ocelot was a dull affair. We only discussed stats and work-related info. Gladly, he never asked about Alaban. I would have curtly responded that it was none of his business if he had. He no longer intimidated me. He had fallen from his place of respect in my eyes, and I preferred to have as little contact with him as possible. At 1700 hours, when before I had gone early to the pressure points course, I instead stayed in my bunk to meditate, glad that the course had finished before we reached Santer.

During our communal meals, Klib informed us of a wide variety of unusual adventures he'd experienced at different bars and pubs on Santer. It seemed he'd spent the entire two and a half month stay in the company of wayward drunks and had enjoyed himself thoroughly. Yinore explained about her mate. He was a Sub General with whom she had worked a few years ago. Apparently, she had moved in with him as soon as we had arrived on Santer. The rest of us had little to tell, since most of our time had been spent on the job. None of us mentioned the night I had danced with Alaban. Ocelot wouldn't explain about his eye except to say he was wounded in a sparring match. Klib wanted to know if he'd won. Ocelot said it had been a tie. Yinore nearly asked me about Alaban, but I flashed my eyes at her to tell her to speak to me in private.

When we did speak, I gave her only a brief summary of our situation. She had thought perhaps I had experienced a love affair similar to her own. She seemed glad that I had not, however, because she then had more to brag about. Her mate had taken her to expensive restaurants, had given her jewels, had mated beautifully, and had lavished her with gifts. She felt like a queen and to a certain extent, came to feel that she was. She boasted about her testing as well, claiming to have pulled a nearly perfect

218

score on all sections. I congratulated her on her accomplishments, but soon grew tired of her list of gains, as she seemed to wave them in my face.

During my work out on my first week back on board, I viewed myself in the reflective wall. I thought of the sensation I'd had seeing Alaban and me together here. How would he react if he discovered that I was giving him this last chance out of pity? I worked out harder than ever, rethinking all we'd said and done in the past week.

Later that day, I received a message from him. He said he was leaving Santer. He said the similarities between my partner's former job and his new assignment were strikingly similar. I took this to mean that they were sending him into a smuggling operation. I hoped he wouldn't be stationed among Fitmalos. He'd found the message I had scratched at the top of his ship. It was a great surprise gift for him. He repeated the words of love that always accompanied his letters. I wished him well, adding truthfully that I missed him already.

By the end of the week, Ocelot and I spoke more freely, having laid our leave time troubles to rest. We did not yet wish to speak about my vision or the ramifications of it. Seven days into our travels, Ocelot brought up the subject of training once more. This time he'd found a program we could both learn from on evasive strategies. He asked if I'd join him at 1700 for an hour. Since I preferred not to spend so much time with him, I suggested we shorten the time to 1730, complaining that I shouldn't have to give up my sleep time to accommodate an extra training program. He didn't like the idea, but agreed to it anyway.

The next morning, however, I was ready by 1715, so I went ahead and entered the exercise room. Ocelot was doing side crunches. His back was turned to me. I was surprised to see him without a shirt. I had walked in too early. His skin gleamed from exercise. A thin scar ran across his back from his left shoulder to his right hip, just as Klib had said. I remembered his story about the girlfriend who had tried to kill him.

Ocelot stopped his series of crunches and stood to face me. I didn't know why I hadn't expected it, but the musculature on his torso was exquisite. I blinked in alarm. I knew his upper body was massive, but I hadn't imagined he was so well-carved. I almost took a step back in wonder. He apologized, retrieved a shirt from the floor, and donned it. I realized now how he'd been able to break Alaban's sword. It wasn't the quality of his sword but his own brute strength that had gone through it.

"What?" he asked flatly.

I cleared my throat and looked everywhere in the room that he wasn't. I composed my demeanor and told him the truth. "You must work out every chance you get."

"Yeah, it's all bulk. Good for punches and sword strikes, but it doesn't do me any good if I have to move out of the way fast. I didn't fare so well on my second round with your boyfriend. He won because he was agile and I was too slow. I've let myself get out of rapid evasion practice. That's why I ordered this program."

This comment made me snap out of my shy embarrassment and back into reality.

"Anyway, I just previewed the program. It was a waste of money. It isn't worth going through. It's for teenagers, all introductory stuff. The hologram practice that goes with it is below your level and beyond mine. It's all strafe combinations and quick stretches. A lot of long movements for flips and rotate-evasions. I can't do those anymore. Can't move like I used to. My agility is shot. I've got to build it back up."

I frowned at his inadequacy, remembering the proof from his match with Alaban.

He spoke apologetically, but still tried to keep his gruff superiority. "So I was hoping you'd be willing to help me out, maybe coach me on some things. If we're going to be in battle together, we have to be at our best. I know I'll never move like you do. You're very light compared to me, but maybe you can give me a few pointers."

"I'll try," I said with noted doubt. "It's mostly in the legs and waist. Those are the areas that need to be most flexible for dodging in large movements. You'll have to stay off your heels more. Here, let me see you stretch. Can you do this?" I let myself slide to the floor in a split.

"Not recently," he admitted. He tried it, but still stayed several centimeters from the floor. His balance in this position was not very good, either.

"Sit down. Open the stretch." I showed him what I meant. "Now lean down."

Holding my arms behind my back, I touched my chin to the floor in front of me. He couldn't do the same. I sat up and twisted, turning my upper body so that I touched my right hand to my left thigh. "Try a twist," I said.

He tried, but only reached directly behind him.

He definitely needed work. I coached him for the half hour, wondering how he'd allowed himself to become so inflexible.

For the next few days, Ocelot and I continued the exercise routine, but he only improved a little. It would take months of work to get him to his top performance on agility.

Despite our contact in the exercise room, our conversations were still limited. I didn't chat to him the way I used to. He remained staunch and work-focused, rarely mentioning anything other than stats and research.

Likewise, our conversations during the communal meal turned tense. Klib had a bad habit of bringing up unwanted topics, like one evening's embarrassing encounter.

Klib seemed more content than usual that evening. He whistled and danced around as he prepared his food. Ocelot asked him why he was so upbeat.

"I just got a message from a cute little dancing girl I met on Santer. She took a fancy to me because I bought her a few nice things, you know. She just asked me when I'd be back in town. She probably just misses the presents, but I wouldn't mind seeing her dance again just for me. Ha, ha."

"That reminds me. I never did compliment you on your dancing, Sil. I had no idea you had such talent," Wilbaht said with a smile. I thanked him, silently praying that Klib would not jump into the conversation to poke fun at me. Unfortunately, it was too late.

"Hey, now there's something I'd like to see," Klib chimed in. "When was this?"

"Sil and her boyfriend danced Tambuo while we were on leave. They were both very skilled dancers," Wilbaht answered him, innocently feeding Klib's path to an uncouth punch line.

My face went pale.

"Ooh. Sil's boyfriend was in town? If he danced Tambuo with you, he must have gotten lucky. You know what they say about that kind of dancing. It's all foreplay."

"Klib!" Yinore said loudly. I covered my face with one hand.

"What? Hey, I'm not asking for details. I'm just saying. It's none of my business what you do on and off the dance floor, before, after, during. As long as it was good for you." Klib chuckled.

"Don't be crass," Yinore snapped.

"What did I say? Oh, I'm sorry. I didn't mean to offend," he said sarcastically. "But seriously, that Tambuo dancing can get risqué the way they rub up against each other and slide around and lift their legs on each other. Looks like foreplay to me. Did your boyfriend *rub* you the right way, Sil? I'll bet he was glad to *slide* it to you." He snickered convulsively.

I left my meal. "Excuse me," I said softly.

"Of all the disrespectful, rude remarks you've made, that's the worst. I'll not put up with that again," I heard Yinore yap to him. "You keep your nasty, low-life thoughts to yourself, you heathen!"

An argument ensued, but I did not stay around to hear it. I went straight to the exercise room and kicked one of the padded targets repeatedly. I roared with fury. I pounded the target with both legs until they ached. Then I started punching it.

Finally, Wilbaht came looking for me.

"Sil, stand at attention," he ordered.

Panting and sweating, I left the target and stood before him. "Sir."

"I had Klib clear away your dishes. Also, he'll be taking your cleaning duty today," he spoke.

"Thank you, sir," I said.

"Is there something you would like to talk with me about?" he asked patiently.

"No, sir. To be honest, I'd only feel comfortable talking to another female about it. It's not that I'm refusing to talk with you, sir. If you request it, I will."

"There is one thing I have to ask you," he said. "You're not pregnant, too, are you?"

"No, sir! Who suggested that?"

"It's not important. First, calm yourself."

I panted some more and closed my eyes.

"In a few days, we'll reach Jain. Do you remember me talking about my granddaughter Olimbi? She is on Jain now on a peace mission. She might be a good person for you to talk with. I can set up a meeting if you like," Wilbaht said.

"Yes, sir. I look forward to meeting her," I said. "I apologize for my behavior."

"No apology is necessary. You did the right thing by taking your frustrations out on the exercise equipment. I urge you to overlook Klib's joke, even though it insulted you."

"Yes, sir."

"Carry on," he said as he left.

The next day, the heathen himself approached me in the hallway just after our meal.

"Hey, uh, don't stay mad at me about yesterday. All right? I'd like to apologize. Really. Listen. I bought this for that girl on Santer I was telling you about. I meant to give it to her, but I forgot about it. Left it in my pocket. You take it. Call it an apology gift. I know I'm hard to live with sometimes. I just want to say thanks for not bashing me."

He held out a small box wrapped in a pink feminine lace.

He shrugged. "I don't even know what it is. It looked expensive, so I figured it must be something nice. Take it. No hard feelings," he urged me.

"All right, Klib, I'll forget about it this time," I said suspiciously.

"Hey, I don't expect us to be the best of friends, but maybe you could lighten up some, huh?" he offered.

"Yeah, all right," I allowed.

"See you 'round." He paced out of the hall and back upstairs to his duty.

I gently opened the box. It contained a bottle of scented bubble bath and a light skin cream. I was sure then that he'd been telling the truth when he said he didn't know what it was. I couldn't imagine he would give anyone such a gift on purpose, especially not me. I opened the cream and smelled it. Its scent was pleasantly light and flowery.

Later, just as I was about to go into the exercise room, Klib came around the hallway corner towards the bathroom. He paused to ask me what the present was. He was almost polite. Maybe he really had calmed down since he had a girl of his own to think about. Or maybe Yinore and Wilbaht had chastised him to the point that he had finally grown a conscience.

I began my workout routine as usual, but was interrupted by a tap at the door. I answered to find Yinore looking up at me with amber eyes asking for help. She held her slightly swollen belly with her lower hands. Her jaw trembled. I immediately took her by one of her free arms and walked her to the stairwell.

"Did you tell Ocelot yet?" I asked her.

She shook her head. She halted and sniffed violently. A frown of pain contorted her yellow face. She tightened her grip on my arm and whimpered a little.

"It's okay, Yinore. We'll get you downstairs." I said. She nodded briskly, pressing her lips together.

I called to Ocelot from the stairwell. He and Klib were both on deck. Ocelot hammered the stairs with his boots to get to her. He clutched her other arm and helped her slowly down the stairs and into the quarantine room. He asked about her contractions, but she could only nod vigorously. He lowered the bed all the way to the floor and tilted up the sides to resemble a nest for her. I retrieved a couple of blankets to help with the nest effect.

Yinore huddled to me, glancing nervously at Ocelot.

"Maybe you should wait outside the door in case she needs you," I suggested to him. "I think only females attend this kind of thing in her culture. She's not speaking. It must be soon."

She nodded rapidly as she had before. Ocelot agreed to wait outside the door. As soon as he'd left, Yinore quickly slipped off the lower half of her uniform and crawled into the nest. She rested her chin on the upturned side of the bed and crouched like a common lizard, leaving one hand extended for me to hold. I knelt by her face, not knowing what else I could do for her. She squeezed my hand. I stroked the top of it, hoping this would comfort her at least. She squinted and growled. Then she panted. She

223

trembled. She squinted and growled again. I noticed Ocelot's shadow pacing back and forth at the door like an expectant father. Yinore squeaked, panted, and made one last effort. Then she relaxed. The birth was finished.

She released my hand. She pressed all her limbs to the floor of the nest and looked down. She tucked her tail between her legs, scooting the egg beneath her. Then she lay on her side, cuddling her pride to her with four arms. She kept her tail tucked between her legs as she curled up in the nest with her new egg.

"Congratulations," I told her. "You did it."

She observed her creation with joy. "Oh, it's going to be a girl. Look, it has orange spots. Oh, I can't wait to see her." She rubbed its shiny, porous surface lovingly with her hands.

When she allowed Ocelot in with us, he checked her over and gave her a small dosage of pain medication. She inspected every part of the egg, cuddled it, listened to it, and then nearly talked our ears off about her plans for her baby and how her mate would be so proud to see her. Ocelot made the excuse that he had to return upstairs to get out of listening to her ramble. Some minutes later, I interrupted Yinore to say I had to go upstairs as well. I gave her an extra blanket and then said goodnight.

At the next mealtime, Klib joked about it. "So I guess we'll have scrambled eggs for dinner. Where's Yinore? I'm starved."

"That's not funny. Show some manners," I retorted.

"It's called a joke. She's not here to get offended, so what's the problem?" He bristled as he went through the motions of preparing his meal.

"*I'm* offended," I emphasized.

"My apologies," he bowed facetiously.

Wilbaht eyed us warily, but did not intervene, since Klib had apologized. He made polite conversation with us to help us forget the argument. Ocelot excused himself to take Yinore her dinner. I concentrated on what Wilbaht had to say, ignoring Klib altogether.

I visited Yinore whenever I could, although we were now on a four-person schedule for the next few days so she could nest. We all worked an extra two hours on deck to compensate for her absence.

One day after my workout, I decided to use my new peace gift. I filled the tub halfway with hot water and added the bottle of bubbles. I undressed and sat at the edge of the tub, dangling one foot in. I stirred the bath and then immersed myself in the water. The smell and warmth were so relaxing that I forgot all my troubles. I smiled with eager anticipation to see Yinore's daughter hatch in a few weeks. I thought of Yalat and Alaban and of my family. I closed my eyes and dunked myself under to wash my hair. Then I rested my head on my folded combat uniform. The water felt like a warm embrace all over. I relaxed so much that fell asleep for a few moments.

A few seconds after I woke up, I sat up slowly. When I did this, I heard a faint click from the opposite side of the room. It seemed to come from under the sink. I hoped there wasn't a leak somewhere. I rubbed my eyes. A tiny light shone from under the sink. I quickly continued rubbing my eyes and glanced away, knowing what it was: a motion-sensitive camera pointed at me.

"Klib is in for the greatest pain of his life," I thought to myself.

It was a tiny camera used to record and view at a remote location. Klib was probably watching me at this very moment from somewhere else on the ship.

I acted as if I hadn't seen the camera. I continued splashing water over my shoulders. I let the water out of the tub and then stood to grab a towel, drying myself facing away from the sink. I put on my travel uniform as I would normally. I collected my clothes and left the room.

I flew to my bunk, left my things, and went to search for Klib. He wasn't in the cargo hold where he was supposed to be cleaning. He wasn't in his bunk or the lower observation deck. A sinking feeling came to me. He had to be upstairs with Ocelot.

I zipped up the stairs silently to find the two seated side by side at Ocelot's and Yinore's stations. They both watched the screen of a lap computer. The screen showed an image of me stirring the bath water. Klib must have watched the whole episode himself and then came to play it over for Ocelot so he could gloat. Ocelot watched, dumbfounded. Klib chuckled. He was beside himself with pride at his trickery.

I levitated so as not to make a sound. I moved up just behind them and then grabbed each man by the back of the head. I smashed their faces into each other. As they protested, I snatched away the lap computer and closed it.

"You conniving jackass! Do you have any idea how many regulations you've just broken? This is illegal use of recording equipment *and* sexual harassment, not to mention violation of the right to privacy," I bellowed.

Ocelot rubbed his right eyebrow. Klib cringed and nursed his left eye. They appeared shocked as well as pained.

"And you! Pretending to be respectful! You're nothing but a pair of depraved pigs, both of you!" I shouted.

"*Me*? He's the one who filmed you," Ocelot argued.

"Yeah? If you had no part in it, why were you watching instead of telling him to shut it down?" I yelled.

"That's his computer. Give it back," Klib voiced.

"The hell I will! This computer, that camera, and anything else you used to record with is now property of ship investigations headed by your superior. So you can kiss this practical joke of yours goodbye."

Klib swore at me. Then he vowed I'd pay him back for it. "I spent a lot of money on that camera."

"You didn't spend much time planning it, did you? You're about as clandestine as an interstellar bus," I shouted.

"Oh, yeah? Well, it was good enough to get you to take your clothes off in front of the camera," Klib said smugly. "You gave me full frontal, princess."

"Ooh. That does it," I said. I left the lap computer on my chair. Using levitation, I yanked Klib out of his seat and prepared to beat the living daylights out of him.

"Don't!" Ocelot shouted. He leapt from his seat and wedged himself between Klib and me.

"Step off, Ocelot, or you're going to get the same treatment," I warned him.

"He's not a warrior. He's our navigational pilot. He's got to be in good condition to get us to Jain. Don't hurt him," Ocelot said, holding his arm out between us.

I stood my ground but didn't attack. Klib had the audacity to laugh about it. He reached up from under Ocelot's arm and slapped me lightly on the cheek. I jumped forward and swung at him, but Ocelot held me back. Klib backed away cackling again. I wrestled with Ocelot a moment.

"Just let me punch him one time," I growled.

"No, Sil. Let him go," Ocelot demanded.

I shot a claw hand to connect with the underside of Ocelot's chin. He flinched and I got in a right jab to his face. I jumped and kicked him twice in the ribs. This sent him wheeling off to my left just enough to clear my way. I pounced after Klib, who stood wide-eyed. He tried to block me, but I went straight for his throat. I picked him up off the ground and pulled my other fist back to strike him at the groin.

"Stop!" a thundering voice shouted.

I froze with Klib still dangling from my left hand, which clamped tightly around his windpipe.

"Put him down," Wilbaht ordered.

I did as I was commanded. Klib coughed and wheezed when I released him.

"What is going on up here?" Wilbaht articulated loudly.

We all pointed and accused each other at the same time. Cacophony rang through the deck.

"Quiet!" Wilbaht bellowed. We fell silent.

"Let me do this another way. Sil, why were you holding Klib up by the neck?" he asked.

I rapidly explained what had happened, illustrating the proof to him with the lap computer. I opened it to show the part where I was stepping into the bath. I popped the coil tape from the computer. The image froze. I closed the computer and stowed it at my station chair once more.

Wilbaht looked from the computer to Klib. Klib shrugged and held up his hands.

"They were both watching it together." I pointed to Ocelot. "He'll tell you he had nothing to do with it, but he wasn't complaining about it either." I glared at them. I reported to Wilbaht all that had happened.

Wilbaht stared furiously at the two men. "Why did you do this?" he asked slowly.

"Hey, she's always going around showing off. Then she acts all girly and innocent like she's offended by everything I say. I just wanted to put her in her place. She deserved it," Klib dared to say.

Wilbaht questioned what he meant to do with the tape coil after he'd shown it to Ocelot. Klib said he was going to keep it until the end of the journey, maybe to do some broadcasting with it if I was a bitch to him the whole way. He saw it as leverage against me. He behaved as if he were the victim of my rudeness instead of the other way around. Wilbaht asked him if he did not mean for the tape to be used for his own personal sexual entertainment, which was a more serious moral offense. Klib said I might be pretty, but he wouldn't want to see any more of me than he had to. I reminded him of the battleaxe his first wife had been and he certainly didn't want to remember her. I perceived his babblings to be the lame excuses of a penned liar, but Wilbaht did not call him one.

"So you did this out of spite. If you wanted to change the negative dialogue between you, you should have tried a solution recommended by the Organization rulebook. Instead, you committed a crime against a fellow crewmember. Sil is the person you have least contact with on this ship. You had to actively seek her out to trick her into this. This could be considered as evidence of criminal behavioral patterning. Is this the kind of crewmember you want the rest of us to see you as?" Wilbaht's blue pupils stared boldly at him.

"No, sir," Klib responded nervously. He defended that he was no more a criminal than anyone else on board. He re-explained that he had to get back at me for being a tease and a hard-headed rookie. He claimed he wouldn't have done it if he'd seen some way to reconcile and get along with me.

Wilbaht studied him during a strained tension of silence. "If you weren't on dual commission, I'd dismiss you right now," Wilbaht said.

I was surprised to hear this. A dual commission meant Klib was working for two different branches of the Organization at once. It was a position coveted by most senior nav pilots around the U.G. The job was usually temporary, but paid double or more.

Klib stood cross-armed with a bitter frown buried in his bearded face. He clearly felt he'd been judged unfairly. Wilbaht's unquestionable power kept him from protesting further. I stood at attention, waiting for the silent anxiety to pass between the men.

"Your reasons are unacceptable," Wilbaht finally stated. "You'll spend your entire leave time for the next two landings on the airfield or aboard the ship, with an alarm tag. If you break your curfew area, I'll demand a new pilot, despite your contract. Comply with your punishment and I'll let you stay on. Once we fly again, you'll work off your animosity by doing all of Sil's primary cleaning duties in addition to your own for a month. If I don't see one hundred percent improvement from you, you'll be officially dismissed at the end of your contract year."

"Sir," Klib responded hatefully, amazed by the magnitude of the punishment.

"Get to your station," Wilbaht said.

"Yes, sir," he mustered.

Next, Wilbaht turned to Ocelot. He shook his head as if to remind him he'd only just gotten out of trouble and now he was back in it. "Ocelot, no excuses will cover you this time. You failed to uphold the tenets we stand for as warriors. Don't speak," Wilbaht stated.

Ocelot's face turned sallow.

"You will stay on the ship with Klib at first landing. You'll take all of Sil's secondary cleaning duties for a month."

"Yes, sir," Ocelot said in quiet disillusionment.

Then Wilbaht turned and glared at me.

"And you, Sil. This offense against you was not a physical offense. You overstepped your bounds when you attacked Klib. You knew better. You should have come to me first. You're banned from the exercise room for ten days."

"Ten days?" I repeated, looking up at him balefully. "Yes, sir," I said resignedly.

"Listen up all of you," Wilbaht addressed us. "We're not going to land on Jain. We're going directly to Karnesh."

We all made sounds of disappointment.

"You've brought this upon yourselves. Ocelot, go downstairs and search for any recording equipment that doesn't come with the ship. Give me an inventory list of it and secure it in secondary cargo," Wilbaht ordered.

"Yes, sir." Ocelot obeyed, trotting downstairs hurriedly.

"Sil, stay in your bunk until we start pre-landing. Give me the tape. I'll make sure it's destroyed," he said.

"Yes, sir." I handed it to him. Wilbaht stayed upstairs with Klib while I headed for my bunk.

As I passed the table to go to my door, Ocelot marched out of the lower observation deck with a handful of electronic pieces and a visage of bitter frustration. At the door to my bunk, he whipped me around by the arm, backing me into the wall.

"What are you doing?" I cried.

He pointed at me furiously. "I didn't even see two minutes of that tape and you made me look like an accomplice."

"Maybe you were. You didn't do anything about it. You just sat there and watched the show," I retorted.

"Of course I watched. What was I supposed to do, shield my eyes? You expect me to act like I can't stand to see a nude female?"

"Oh, you really are mean. I think you got exactly what you deserved."

"Oh, really? What if it was the other way around? What if Yinore happened to show you images of a male crewmember at his bath? Wouldn't you watch at least for a minute out of curiosity?"

"Yinore would never do that. But no, I wouldn't."

"What if it was your dance partner on the tape?"

"No. I don't want to spy on him in his bath," I grimaced.

"What if it was me?" he asked boldly.

I recalled the time he had been without a shirt in the exercise room. I quickly averted my eyes.

"Of course not," I stated.

Ocelot pressed a hand up against the wall above my left shoulder. He stared at me in anger. He examined my eyes, drawing his face near mine. I faced him uneasily.

"Your eyes betray you," he hissed.

He pushed off the wall, glaring at me with resilience. He marched away down the hall, punching once into the air.

I stood aghast. I remained immobile for a few seconds. Then I retreated into my bunk and slammed the door. How could he have had such gall to imagine something like that, much less suggest it? Fury ripped through my mind. I waited in tense aggravation in my bunk until our landing time.

Chapter 24: The Convention at Karnesh

Turbulence jiggled our ship as we entered the atmosphere of Karnesh. A dust storm ninety kilometers wide swirled about our destination. Judging from the cloud patterns around the planet, this would be followed by a monsoon in another day or so. The deep orangey-brown haze of sand scoured our ship. We set down on a landing field that seemed to shift like waves on a stormy sea. Loaded winds whined all around us.

We went about our post-flight checks, but the sand obstructed our external sensors. We had to wait until we could get a clear reading before we could finish our checks. No one wanted to go out in this weather, but Wilbaht was obligated to present himself to the reporting general's office as soon as possible and I wasn't about to stay in the ship tonight with the two other men. I preferred to brave the stinging sand.

I packed a few things in a sling bag and then trotted downstairs to say goodbye to Yinore. She was now up and about, working with a lap computer while the egg rested snugly in a blanket. She bade us good luck. I joined Wilbaht in the second cargo hold, where I grabbed a protective coat with a sealing hood. I lugged it to the main cargo hold and put it on. It hung loosely around me, but there was no size smaller. Soon Wilbaht appeared dressed in a similar suit awkwardly stretched over his tall frame. Together we looked like a joke.

We stepped into the first airlock door of the cargo hold and shut it. Wilbaht opened the main door. It slowly lowered out to the ground, working against the powerful wind. I worried, as Wilbaht probably did, that the door seals and hydraulics would fill with sand and prevent a perfect seal. This would cause problems with the incoming monsoon rains. It would also keep us from taking off on time. I hoped we wouldn't be delayed. Being stuck on this planet during a monsoon could mean weeks of waiting, and I still hoped we could get to Jain later.

We moved into the second airlock and sealed it. We braced ourselves, holding onto the bars on either side of the secure doors. Wilbaht motioned to me to balance with levitation, since walking straight would be nearly impossible. When he opened the outer airlock door, our bodies were instantly pressed back to the wall of the second airlock. We wrenched ourselves forward. We floated out, teetering in the forceful wind. The roar was deafening. We couldn't see anything through our helmets. I felt as if someone were pounding on my back, my chest, and around my knees. The waves of swirling sand took on mass and strength. A gust shoved against the small of my back and nearly bowled me forward. I used all my strength to move toward the edge of the field.

Unlike the other airfields at Organization centers I'd seen before, this one was bordered on all sides by a heavy concrete corridor with double entryways every few meters. We sensed, rather than saw, where the doors were. We took several minutes to reach them. When we got to the corridor, the first door slid open with effort. We stepped inside and helped shove the door shut again. The howling wind beat fiercely upon its window. The second door receded into the corridor. We entered this one easily. When it zipped shut, the screams from the wind muffled.

Wilbaht removed his protective helmet. I followed his example. The temperature in the corridor was hot compared with the windy outdoors. We quickly began to sweat. My undershirt clung to my perspiring body by the time we reached the entrance to the tower.

To my surprise, the lobby was crowded with warrior bodyguards and lower level dignitaries. Most of them formed welcoming committees who awaited the arrival of high-level officials. A few reporters flitted among the masses interviewing the committees and making the bodyguards nervous. Other people hung about, exasperated and tired. These were probably stranded or unable to take off due to the storm. They would have to wait another thirty hours or so before the dust subsided and the rains moved in.

In one corner of the lobby, almost directly in front of us, stood a gaggle of Mantis. They screeched in complaint to each other. A Beetle crouched near them looking forlorn. A blue-green Kangaroo Lizard accompanied him. He fidgeted with a handheld game of some sort. The buttons on the game were too close together for the Lizard's fingers. He fumbled with it in aggravation. To our right, a group of lemon yellow six-limbed Lizards and Vermilion people chattered anxiously about their itinerary. Beyond these ambled a wide variety of species. I was disturbed by the presence of so many Fitmalos.

There were not many humans, although I glimpsed a small support group from Jain at a distance. I saw no Greys here. There were only a couple of Torreon bodyguards. Most of the other warriors were Furmen and Vermilions.

I felt out of place among so many people. I hung close to Wilbaht as we made our way through the crowd to the underground exit corridor, which led down into the Organization center.

The Shaliot Center lobby displayed a wide reception area lined with imported flowering plants and receptionist stations at several windows across the wall. We approached a Vermilion warrior translator at the window labeled "Check In." Wilbaht spoke to him about seeing the General, but apparently neither he nor any sub generals would be available for several hours due to conference preparations and security. The translator directed us to a professor sub general on underground floor five. Wilbaht thanked him.

I offered to go with him, but he insisted I find a place for both of us to stay. The receptionist told me to speak with Quartermaster Illis on upper floor twelve. Wilbaht lined up at the elevator. I took the stairs to avoid crowds, pausing to slip out of my protective suit. The stairwell was even hotter than the outside corridor. It smelled of insect skin oils, a scent popular among Beetles and Mantises. The smell was too pungent for me. It reminded me of crushed roaches. I held my hand over my face as I ascended the stairs.

At the twelfth floor, I found a quartering reception area. Quartermaster Illis was a tall, weary Vermilion. I explained to him that Wilbaht and I needed a bunk for the next two nights. He checked his computer for anything available, but found only one room with bedding that would accommodate a person of Wilbaht's height. He took our information and then asked a stressed female black Lizard to escort me to the room.

She padded ahead of me through a labyrinth of hallways to a door marked 9A. She opened the door outward into the hall and stepped aside to let me through. A motion sensitive light came on at the ceiling. The narrow room gave me the impression of a long, double-occupancy coffin. From a tiny bathroom to my right jutted a sink almost as small as my hand. Below it, a common drain sunk into the floor in lieu of a toilet. To my left stretched a pair of long, slim cots, separated by only a few centimeters of floor space. The cots were covered with thin, sturdy bedding, but had no pillows or sheets.

"Good luck," the Lizard offered doubtfully. She turned and left the doorway.

I set my protective suit at the foot of one cot. I took off my sling bag and placed it on top of the suit, feeling claustrophobic.

I left the miniscule bunk and found my way back out of the maze of hallways. I boarded an elevator near the reception area with a pair of short Beetles. They selected underground floor three. The Beetles buzzed and chirped together as we rode down. I deciphered the building layout from a diagram on the elevator wall. According to the diagram, this building was much larger than it appeared from the outside. It had twenty floors above ground and twenty more below ground. The second and third underground floors were labeled as public, so I selected the second.

When I arrived, I discovered a crowd only slightly smaller and more spread out than the one at the airfield lobby. This was a public shopping area. The shopkeepers enjoyed a boom in business, although they appeared fatigued as the Lizard who had showed me our room. If I had felt out of place at the airfield lobby, I felt twice as odd now. The whole place was filled with Beetles and Mantises, whose language I could not understand, much less pronounce. Besides these people, I noticed groups of bright blue Fitmalos. Translators or bodyguards or both escorted most of them. I saw only a few Lizards, but no humans or other Torreonoids. This was truly a foreign planet.

I walked through the shopping area self-consciously. The shops here were interstellar, but mainly catered to people with exoskeletons instead of skins. I found a wide café with a leaf sculpture fountain, where I ordered some raw cruciferous vegetables; the only food on their menu edible for humans. I also asked for a glass of water, but they didn't have glasses, only tear-shaped bottles with a cyphening hole at the top. I accepted this and found a dusty box of straws at one corner of the café's takeout counter.

I carried my poor meal to a table by one end of the fountain. The chair was too short for my comfort, so I stood, picking leaves off my plate to eat. Two tables full of Mantises chattered away next to me in their shrill, clacking language. Some of them pointed at me and seemed to laugh. A racket of cackling sounds resonated across several tables of people near me.

I wasn't sure how to react to this, so I ignored them and continued eating. As I finished my meager lunch, three of the warrior Mantises sauntered over to me. The tall female in the middle addressed me, even though she had to know I wasn't able to understand anything she said. She made motions mimicking a fighting stance, and then pointed to herself and then to me. I took this to mean she was interested in sparring.

This was highly unusual, since it was recommended not to allow opposite species to spar under friendly terms. It was too dangerous for both people. If I kicked her with enough force, I might crack her exoskeleton. She could either bleed to death or be handicapped for several weeks. If she hit me just right with the sharp edges of her arms, she could break my bones or cut off one of my limbs. If the strike went to the head or neck, I would die.

I bowed deeply and held the bow to acknowledge her challenge but respectfully decline it. When she screeched loudly, I straightened my stance. The two other Mantises beside her clicked and cackled. The female in the middle bowed to me jauntily. She turned with her friends and walked away, chattering excitedly.

After this strange confrontation, I perused the first and second underground floors. People stared at me distrustfully, especially when I walked into a weapons and tools shop. I decided to move on, even though I was interested in buying a shield orb. I began to dislike this place. It set me ill at ease.

I went back upstairs to floor twelve room 9A. At a late hour, I awoke with the motion sensor light when Wilbaht entered the tiny dormitory. I immediately went back to sleep. Some hours later, I awoke again to droning snores resonating from Wilbaht's throat. I contemplated waking him, but decided to put up with it. It would be disrespectful to complain about an unconscious act of my superior. I covered my ears and attempted to sleep. I managed to doze off for a few hours. When I awoke again, I found myself alone. Wilbaht's bunk only contained his protective suit.

I gave myself a quick sponge bath from the tiny sink and redressed in my travel uniform. Wilbaht returned just as I was putting on my boots.

"Ah, good. You're awake. Our leave time has been cut short. The Fitmalo cabinet members you'll be guarding are scheduled to arrive tonight."

Wilbaht closed the coffin door and sat cross-legged on his cot. His knees jutted out, nearly touching the opposite wall.

"You'll find their choice of guard subjects very interesting. You'll be guarding a military general named Sunderlign. Ocelot is guarding General Salt, the liaison between military and public works of Fitmalo. Both are above suspicion as far as the Regime and rebel factions are concerned, officially speaking. Unofficially, we might discover otherwise," he opined. "They will be housed in a large underground suite near the stadium. You and Ocelot will be quartered with their group."

He then informed me that he'd been put in charge of bodyguards and section security for the entire Fitmalo area of the conference. "I'll be working as your commander, but also I'll have several other warriors to organize, so if you need to reach me for any reason, I may not be as accessible as usual. You're going to have to rely on extra sensory perception to do this job. Don't trust your eyes and ears. I sense a conflict between conference guests. It may escalate to a fight or even an assassination attempt."

"All right, sir. When will I get the file on my subject?"

"General briefing at 1000 hours in the stadium. You'll need to take the subway. There's a boarding platform downstairs on underground level four. Go to the main floor entrance of the stadium and wait at the front row of red seats. There should be a small crowd assembled by nine thirty. I'll see you there. Be early. I want to give you something before the others arrive."

"Yes, sir."

He stood rapidly, grabbing the brown plastic suits. He passed through the door again. He paused outside to give me one last bit of advice. "They may not be happy to see a pair of human bodyguards. Be formal and polite with them. If they insist on someone else, refer them to me. I'll make sure you're not changed from your assignment."

"All right, sir. Thank you."

He disappeared down the hall.

I hurried to change into combat gear, and then went with my sling bag to the elevator. I decided to skip breakfast, even though my stomach grumbled. The cruciferous vegetables I'd eaten yesterday had only left me hungry and undernourished. It would be better to wait for a decent meal. Surely our Fitmalo subjects would eat soon after arriving at their suite. They would offer us something then. I knew the Fitmalos ate more varied foods than the people of Karnesh.

At the subway platform, I found only a few other warriors waiting around, but none I recognized. I stood in the dark cavern by the nearest boarding entrance. Soon I heard a low rumble accompanied by a hiss. The subway train filled the clear plastic tunnel. Lights on its sides blinked twice. A horn sounded. The flickering image of the train stabilized before me. A section of the plastic tube slid below floor as the train doors opened. I stepped on. A melee of glowing advertisements decorated the ceiling. Before I could sit, I was suddenly jerked backward. The metal seatback thudded into my side. I sat rubbing my ribs as unsettling vibrations permeated the train.

A few seconds after the lurch, the train blasted to a halt, forcing me to jump forward from the momentum. The doors opened. Several Mantis bodyguards sauntered in. They ignored me, passing to the back of the train. A Furman warrior ran on after them. I ventured to ask him if he was headed for morning briefing at the stadium He said yes, but gave no other information.

The train whisked us backwards again. This time the ride lasted a few minutes. We all stood at the next stop out of necessity, but also because we had arrived at the stadium. It was only 0900 hours, but we all wanted to get a good look at the place to be extra prepared for our job.

The subway hall led into two separate wide entranceways. One had steps up to the higher observation level of the stadium. The other led to the main floor. The Mantises and the Furman entered through the main level door. I took the upper level entrance. The stairs led to two different levels: a lower mezzanine and a top one. I climbed to the highest section.

The stadium was an oval-shaped cavern. At the center of its floor, a few maintenance workers prepped the elevated stage with a long oval table. This was lined with a row of raised cushioned chairs. Behind each cushioned chair stood a simple folding chair, probably for translators or personal aides. If my general sat at a cushioned chair and his translator sat behind him, I would have to stand off stage in the lower area, below and behind the second chair.

I imagined how the whole meeting would look. A total of two hundred eighteen people would be gathered on stage. One hundred nine bodyguards would stand directly off stage. A wide runway surrounded the stage where reporters, managers, and security personnel could walk. This area would be restricted. Other security and possibly military personnel would guard the pathways between seating and especially the area closest to the stage.

I looked up to the ceiling, which hung with rows of simple tapestries, which hid lighting and recording equipment. I noticed the Mantises below, poking about the main table. I wondered if they would react badly if I levitated around the ceiling. I thought about cloaking, but decided their opinions of me weren't worth the trouble. I bobbed up to the ceiling to get a good look at the lighting and recording mechanisms to make sure no one could hide there or plant any explosives. I especially wanted to see the space directly above the table. From that vantage point, I could observe any possible weaknesses in the stadium's security measures.

In addition to the subway entrances I'd already seen, I noticed three other wide entranceways. Where they led, I couldn't know yet. It seemed to me the biggest crowds would file in from the subway entrances. Perhaps another entrance came in from the housing area for dignitaries. That would be the highest area of threat to our subjects, although I was sure security would be at pique anywhere an official set foot during this conference.

Judging from the size of the stadium, I guessed the spectators would number in the tens of thousands. I understood then what Wilbaht had said about not trusting my eyes and ears. I had a suspicion that from a mass of spectators this large, we could expect to witness a terrorist attack or at least an attempt. This would be the perfect protest event for any Fitmalo or Jawlcheen rebels. The Karneshians might have harbored issues to exploit at the meeting as well. I resented not having researched that possibility before.

I checked the ceiling thoroughly but found nothing out of the ordinary. I then checked the underside of the top mezzanine. I returned to the subway platform area, where more warriors now filed in. I continued my observation of the underside of the lower mezzanine before grouping with them.

At 0940 hours, Wilbaht entered with Ocelot from the subway platform. Wilbaht stopped just ahead of the entrance and scanned his surroundings. He smiled when he saw me. Ocelot stood expressionless. I approached them. We moved to sit in some blue seats at one side of the stage.

"Have a seat here next to me, Sil. I've brought you something," Wilbaht said. "Eat quickly so they won't see you feeding when our briefing starts." He handed me a bag containing a protein-filled bread, a vitamin pill, and a half pint bag of juice.

"That's very kind of you, sir. Thank you. How did you know I didn't eat?"

"Judging from the menu, I assumed you didn't. You'll need some nourishment to get you through the day," he spoke.

I thanked him again. I downed the vitamin and greedily munched the bread. Wilbaht patted me on the back with a warm hand as he stood.

"I'm going to meet some of these bodyguards. While I do, I suggest you two make peace. Fitmalos don't like human bodyguards. They'll be twice as annoyed with humans who don't get along. They don't have to put up with such nonsense. That's what they'll say in a few hours when they ask for another pair of guards. If they have any rational grounds for their complaint, I'll be obligated to honor their request. You have a few minutes to bury the hatchet. I want to see you two at peace by the end of this briefing," he spoke.

"Yes, sir," we replied without conviction.

He turned gracefully and glided away towards the red seats. I eyed Ocelot while I chewed my bread. He gave me a cautious look. He didn't seem angry any more, only stoic. I waited for him to speak. He waited for me to finish my breakfast. I disposed of my trash in a receptacle at the end of the row and returned to sit two seats away from him. We glanced at each other, and then at the group of warriors. Pride kept me from speaking to him. We sat in silence for several minutes with arms crossed. Wilbaht spoke amicably with a few warriors. He turned to see us in this state of stalemate. He squinted at us warningly and tapped his wrist, reminding us about time.

"Let's concentrate on getting this job done right," Ocelot said with a sigh.

"I agree," I said. "About what happened at the ship—if I made a mistake about your involvement with Klib's actions, I'm sorry. And I apologize for attacking you to get to him. Now you owe me two apologies."

"Why is that?" he asked me coarsely.

"First, you should apologize for watching that film in the first place and not backing me up like Wilbaht said. Secondly, you have no right to insinuate that I would watch a film of you in the same situation. If I wouldn't spy on Alaban, the man I love, the man I've *slept* with, why would I want to spy on someone as unimportant as *you*? You must be a real egomaniac to presume that. You disgust me." I spoke coldly.

He glowered. He turned away, probably to curse under his breath. He turned back to me with an ungracious scowl.

"I apologize, even though none of that incident was my fault," he growled. "I want to be able to go to Jain after this is over, if Wilbaht is still willing to let us. So just forget about it and keep your mind on business."

"Why would I concentrate on anything else? Do you think I'm any less professional than any other warrior here today? I'm as capable as anyone else here. That's why I was chosen for the job. I'm on this warrior team because of my abilities and my dedication. I don't care if you are higher ranking. You're no better, in skills or morals. I'll follow your lead while we're guarding the Fitmalo subjects, but every order you give me had better be professional and impersonal. Sir." I peered at him resolutely.

Ocelot stared at me with storms in his eyes. He then leaned back in his seat and nodded. "If you're going to address me as 'sir', you need to back that up with appropriate speech. And before you go praising yourself, just remember you've never done a bodyguarding job before. So you'd better not make a move without my approval," he said.

"Fine," I said, standing. "After you, sir." I motioned him towards the meeting area.

"Sit down. If you're going to play that game, you'll wait until I stand, Warrior."

"It's not a game, sir, it's my job. I apologize for ignoring protocol. It won't happen again." I sat, waiting for him to stand. I glanced out at the rows of bodyguards. Nearly all of them were present now. Wilbaht spoke kindly with several people in the first few rows.

Ocelot finally stood, but stayed in front of his chair. He waited to see if I would step in front of him. I didn't. He seemed satisfied with this and moved to the meeting place. I followed him too closely just to annoy him. We stepped up to the eighth row of seats. We crossed our arms and stared down at Wilbaht. I thought of moving in close to Ocelot so that our elbows would touch just to set him on edge, but I decided it was a childish thing to do.

Wilbaht glanced up at us and squinted. He noticed we were still not on good terms. He frowned momentarily, and then resumed his pleasant manner.

Soon, an elderly Furman sidled up next to Wilbaht. An assistant translator followed him with a box of palm computer tape files to be distributed to us. Two other older generals, both Mantises, joined the group. The four of them greeted each other formally.

Punctually, at 1000 hours, the head general began our meeting. He welcomed us first in his language, and then again through the translator. We learned in briefing that Wilbaht was in charge of all Fitmalo and some Jawlcheen subjects. The Furman was in charge of some Jawlcheen and all Jain guests. The second Mantis general took charge of Karnesh, Godel, and

238

all others. The first Mantis headed the entire conference. He bade us good luck and left our meeting to the other three.

The Furman addressed us next. According to him, we were the group of bodyguards assigned to the second procession of dignitaries. The first dignitaries had already landed and were accommodated in security suites with their entourages. These were people with low security indexes. The group we would be guarding was of middle to high security index. He told us we had been picked specially to defend and guard these highly prestigious people. He admitted the danger level was higher than normal for an interstellar conference of this scale. Several threats had been received by his office as well as by Organization centers across the U.G. We needed to perform at our best with complete awareness and in full armor at all times.

He reassured us that extra security personnel had been assigned to accompany us to and from the arriving ships in armed transport vehicles. Welcoming committees for the various dignitaries would take care of lodgings, meals, and basic necessities. All we had to do was make sure our subjects stayed safe. We were not responsible for the safety of the entourage. We were expected to protect our subjects at all times, going to and from the conference, waiting behind the subjects during the conference, and escorting them to and from any sites away from the conference area during their two-week stay. We would be allowed to rest only within the confines of the security suites while our subjects were there with us.

As far as the subjects were concerned, we were considered part of their own entourage. They would provide us with food, basic needs, and lodgings, but we were not to inquire about these things unless they were denied to us. We were not to initiate conversation with our subjects. Our subjects were neither prohibited from speaking to us nor were they obligated to do so. If they insisted on conversing with us, we were required to decline to speak on certain topics. We were not allowed to give our opinions on politics, sex, race, religion, or culture. We were not allowed to discuss personal appearances or grooming habits. We were not allowed to do or say anything to interfere with the personal freedoms of our subjects. However, if our subjects did or said anything to personally offend one of us, we were expected to put up with it unless the subject became aggressive. In this case, we could call one of our contact team members to switch with us or call a superior to handle the situation.

The General divided us all into contact teams for backup. We were expected to call to check up on each other every three hours when we were not in direct contact with each other just to make sure no fowl play occurred between meetings.

After a brief questions session, the Furman's translator aide called us each to receive the information file on our subjects and to introduce team members. Ocelot and I were paired with an Arborman and a Vermilion, both from Jawlcheen. We greeted each other all around and met together to one side of the stage to exchange information. The Vermilion's subject was a Fitmalo science community representative named Shourat. The Arborman's subject was another Fitmalo named Coldt. He was a cabinet member general, head of intrastellar relations for the Thrader helion. We discovered we'd be staying in adjacent suites and that our subjects would arrive together on the same ship.

The four of us went together to the air tower. Our subjects arrived on time, just as the dust storm subsided and the rains began to fall. We took a large armored security vehicle out to the dignitaries' ship. The Fitmalos greeted our contact teammates in a friendly manner, but seemed disappointed to see Ocelot and me. Still, they greeted us with civility. I felt we would have no trouble with them.

Sunderlign, my subject, was a man accustomed to giving orders. He barked at his group to hurry up and get on the security vehicle. He was a stout, broad-shouldered blue man. His pointy chin bore a shiny purple beard that curled under his jaw in a stately fashion. He wore the points of his ears pinned back near the crown of his head with gold clips, in the rather garish style of the upper class of his race. His female servant was richly, yet scantily dressed. His female translator and personal aide also dressed in revealing costume. Ocelot's subject, Salt, was rather subdued. He only brought a male translator and a well-dressed female aide. The subjects and entourages of our contact teammates were all males. They seemed formal and businesslike.

We rode the security vehicle to the back of the air tower and disembarked cautiously. We bodyguards stepped in front of our subjects to clear the way. We quickly found their welcoming committee. I stayed at Sunderlign's side as the people pressed around us. The Fitmalos chattered together noisily, barely aware of our presence.

When we arrived at our suite, the head of the Fitmalo welcoming committee showed the generals around first and then allowed us to see only the main living area and our own quarters. I was given a tiny room next to Sunderlign's master bedroom. Ocelot was quartered next to Salt. Not surprisingly, Sunderlign's servant stayed in the room with him.

The General's personal aides ordered and served food for the group. We ate together at a large table in a dining and living area of the suite, seated from highest to lowest rank. Subsequently, Ocelot and I sat at one end of the table while our subjects took the other end. The food was edible. I listened to the table conversation with feigned disinterest. The generals talked of whom they'd seen in the lobby of the air tower. Mostly they had noticed other top officials like themselves. They criticized the political viewpoints of each of them.

The next day, Sunderlign received a call from someone. As soon as his call finished, he told Salt he would meet him later and then beckoned me to follow him. I went with the General from the housing area to the subway. We disembarked at the permanent housing station. Sunderlign flashed his credentials at the security gate. A Beetle let us through. We climbed a narrow stairwell to a low security condominium. The General knocked at the door. It opened for him. I tried to step in front of him, but he waved me away.

A heavy set Fitmalo man greeted Sunderlign with laughter and a slap on the back. They let me in the condo with them. Sunderlign told me to stay at the front door. He and the other Fitmalo sauntered into an open dining area together, clearly visible from the doorway. A third man sat smoking a golden cigar. He greeted Sunderlign with less aplomb than the first man. A female servant served them appetizers and drinks.

I stood by the door for more than two hours waiting for the men to finish their discussion. Unfortunately, I was unable to hear much of what they said. I wished I had brought a sound enhancer with me. After the two hours, I received a buzz on my earpiece. One of my teammates asked me to check in. I pressed the sender at the side of my neck.

"Fitmalo subject B secure, sir," I spoke quietly.

When I spoke, the cigar smoker glanced up at me. Then he glanced back at me again. He seemed to recognize me. He tapped the other man on the shoulder and pointed in my direction. The Fitmalo shook his head. Sunderlign twisted in his chair.

"Bodyguard, come here," he ordered.

"Sir?" I stepped to him.

"What is your name and rank?" he asked.

"Sil Gretath, First year Warrior, sir," I answered.

"What do you mean a first year warrior? Since when do generals get the lowest-ranking bodyguards?" he pouted.

The cigar smoker interrupted Sunderlign's complaint. "You were on Sor3 about six months ago, weren't you? You killed the acid spider. I remember that."

"Yes, sir," I admitted. I began to worry about where this conversation would lead.

The cigar smoker filled Sunderlign in on the basic story of the assassination of the Center official, the military science experiments, and the spider. I was surprised to hear he knew as much as I did about the incident, but I dared not ask him about his involvement in it. He said he had been present at the military science conference there, but gave no more personal information.

Sunderlign asked for details about the spider. I told him it was from here at Karnesh. I explained how it had escaped and how we had lured it to its demise. I didn't mention Yalat or Alaban by name. I hoped they wouldn't ask about them specifically. They didn't.

Sunderlign wasn't as impressed with this deed as his friend was. He sent me back to the door again. The three men discussed something anxiously in hushed tones. Several times one or more of the men would gesture in my direction. They didn't call for me again, but continued talking until late in the day. I found myself shifting my weight constantly. My legs ached from standing still so long.

Finally, Sunderlign got up from the table and ambled to the door. He said goodbye to his friends. I exited the door and checked in all directions before escorting him out. We returned to the suite the way we had left. He did not speak to me directly again that day.

The next morning, the conference began. The opening ceremony was followed by an introduction of each dignitary and a brief presentation of works in progress. This took up most of the day. Near the end of the introductions, as a diplomat from Jawlcheen stood to be recognized, a loud bang made everyone jump.

A group of Jawlcheen protesters waved banners that read, "Traitor," and, "Next time sell them your soul instead of our region". One of the protesters had shot a noisemaker of some kind. They presented no physical danger to the dignitaries. They shouted at the diplomat to stay in Karnesh because they didn't want him back on Jawlcheen. They only wanted attention. They peacefully relented when stadium security overtook them. The conference went on without any other distractions that day.

The next two days of the conference consisted of more presentations by guests outlining health care system improvements. Not much was resolved. On the third, fourth, and fifth days, ecological issues were bargained. Some people disagreed loudly with each other, but the conference remained civilized.

On the sixth day, instead of a meeting, there was a gala event with entertainment for officials and guests only. Afterward, another Fitmalo invited the four subjects from our team to a resort an hour's travel from the stadium. We were obligated to accompany them.

At the resort, our party was greeted by the inviting Fitmalo and a committee. They escorted us below ground to a swimming and spa area. All around this were enclosed rooms for saunas, cold rooms, massages, and health stations. There were also a few meeting rooms scattered around the place.

Sunderlign ordered the entourage members to swim or amuse themselves. The four generals met together with two other Fitmalos in a small meeting room. Coldt ordered us to stand outside. I stayed at the door. As one of the men pulled it closed, I prevented it from shutting completely in order to eavesdrop on their conversation.

The meeting was about the implementation of the Thrader Common Law Plan. Apparently the Fitmalos pushed a benevolent common law for Jawlcheen, Fitmalo, and Nitrogen1 that would take effect in the upcoming months. Once the common law was in place, subtle changes could be made in interplanetary relations.

"Whether the common law is successful or not, we should still have the asteroid army do their job. It will seal the public's acceptance of leadership."

"I don't see any cooperation from Karnesh about it this year. There are still so many traditionalists in office here. We need to get some of our own men elected before we can pass any common law deals on this side."

"I'm with you. Let's start getting rid of some of these traditionalist mummies. Give me a Karneshian who's ready to deal in business— someone who's not afraid of money."

"We could speed things along, you know."

"I'm all for it. Let's set this up now."

"All in favor?"

Sleeves rustled as all hands rose.

"Good. Do you know someone for the job?"

"Yes. You just tell me who and when."

"All three of them."

"All three? That's going to cost us."

"It's worth it if we get our own men to replace them. You'll have to secure that first. Get the Godel protesters to help. They want this more than we do."

"Jawlcheen officials are getting antsy. The sooner we present the plan to the conference, the better. If we wait too long, someone will point a finger at our Jawlcheen supporters and their upcoming elections. Our proposal will be killed before it's ever presented."

"I say we announce tomorrow."

"The organizers won't allow us to speak off topic. Tomorrow is science talks."

"Let's request an announcement about it anyway. At least it will give the public a hint about the proposal so they'll be ready for it the next day."

"Let's do it tomorrow, then."

"I smell success, gentlemen."

"We'll be rolling in gold before we know it."

"And the helion will benefit as well."

"Not just ours."

"If we pull this off, we'll have planets begging to get in."

"We'll have to work on a list of membership requirements."

"Number one, pay us off."

Laughter resonated through the room. These devils were Regime members all right. They wanted more than just control of Thrader. Karnesh and Godel were on their list as well. I wished Ocelot had been listening in with me. Now I would have to find a time and place to tell him and Wilbaht about this meeting without being noticed.

During the rest of the day, the Fitmalos vacationed in the resort. Later in the evening, Sunderlign sat in a Jacuzzi with his females and ordered us to sit by at a table to have some refreshment. Gratefully, I sat. My knees and back ached from standing the whole week long. Bodyguarding was an aggravating job.

Ocelot sat across from me but I couldn't speak with him about what I'd just heard. I asked him instead if he would cover for me while I went to the restroom. He nodded. I got up and walked towards it. On my way, I buzzed him.

"Ocelot," he said.

"I have to talk to you about their meeting."

"About?"

"All Regime. Three Karneshians will be killed. Need to notify security."

He didn't answer me. I knew he'd think of a way to cover me at some point so I could get to Wilbaht. When I returned to the table, I did not look at him.

Later, after we had returned to the suite, I hoped to sneak out during the night to go see Wilbaht, but the security lock on the door to the suite was set to alarm. It would go off if opened without an authorization card, which only the generals carried.

At the conference the next morning, Coldt broke from the norm and made the announcement about a great proposal to unite his helion in peace and common law. He said the proposal would be detailed the following day.

The press and the audience whispered and then talked loudly for the next half hour, drowning out part of the science presentation. At the end of the day's conference, security had to hold people back as our group receded into the security suites corridor.

During the night when everyone was asleep, I buzzed Ocelot. I asked him if I could meet him in his room to tell him about what I'd heard. He agreed. I stole through the suite, hoping no one would notice me. Ocelot opened his door for me. Even though the walls were fairly sound proof, I spoke to him in a whisper.

"Our Fitmalos are planning on assassinating three Karneshian officials. They want to replace them with their own supporters. This Common Law Plan is bigger than what they're proposing to the public," I whispered.

"Do you know any names? Do you know when or where?"

"They didn't say. How can we contact Wilbaht about it? We're locked in here and everyone's monitoring the communication waves."

"They wouldn't set up an assassination in the middle of all this. They'll wait until the conference is finished and they're on their way home. We can report this on the last day."

I thought about this and nodded.

"Go get some sleep," he ordered.

I sneaked back to my room undetected.

In the morning at the conference, the Fitmalos pressed for cooperation between planets on various levels, but mostly in trade law and ecological restrictions.

"We already have a common currency. Most of our civil laws are the same. Why not come together in trade law? It will help us regulate import and export validation. Why not come together in criminal law? If a person breaks a law on Fitmalo, he shouldn't be able to escape to Jawlcheen so he is not taken to trial. Why not come together in ecological law? We should not be allowed to harvest more mineral ore on Fitmalo than on Jawlcheen. These inequalities should not occur in our society. We are united in the United Galaxy, but we are not a united solar system. Under the Common Law Plan, we can correct these inequalities," one Fitmalo spoke in conclusion.

Within an hour after the proposal, guests at the table and in the audience shouted at each other. Even though the few Nitrogen1 representatives agreed with the proposal, some of the Jawlcheen representatives fought the idea. Some said it was logical and supported the proposal. Some disagreed outright and fought amongst themselves. Sunderlign stood and pounded his fist on the table. He yelled at a Jawlcheen dignitary across from him.

"If you are loyal to your planet, you will consider this as an opportunity for improvement," Sunderlign yelled at him.

Insults were exchanged. I sensed danger. I flew to the General's side.

"Sir, I feel someone means to harm you. May I escort you to your suite?" I asked.

"No. If we leave now, what will that say for our proposal? I'm not leaving," he responded.

I stayed at the General's side rather than stepping off stage again.

The Mantis general in charge of the conference intervened, proposing that the Jawlcheen dignitaries retire to a meeting room to discuss this in private, since the conference had to continue with statements from Jain and Godel.

The head of the Jawlcheen group agreed, but two of his officials resisted. One pointed accusingly at Salt. The other yelled at Sunderlign.

"You people want to convert Jawlcheen law to Fitmalo law, not a compromise between the two. You want us to adopt your public execution practices. We won't stand for it. You may be able to pay off some of the Jawlcheen politicians, but you will never get the local representatives to agree to that," one complained.

"No. Criminal law is nothing to you. I've read part of your proposal. You want joint commission on public works so you can build up your own military fund. How is that helping us?"

The two Fitmalos held up their hands with reservation. One Jawlcheen member became so outraged with them that picked up his personal aide's chair and threw it across the table at Sunderlign. I stopped it in midair, just as Sunderlign dove to the side. I levitated the chair back to its place as the security guards rushed to hold the two back. Ocelot appeared at Salt's side. All other bodyguards climbed to stand next to their subjects at the table and did not move during the rest of conference.

That night, reports flashed on the news every few minutes about the proposal. The reports included views from the Jawlcheen protesters, but the media sided with Fitmalo on the unification of Thrader.

Ocelot asked Salt for permission to speak with his superior in person about changes in security due to the day's events. Salt allowed it, but sent his aide with him. Ocelot left me in charge of the Fitmalos in the suite.

While he was out, Sunderlign commended me for my insight. He also offered me a job.

"A man in a position of increasing risk such as myself is in need of a capable bodyguard. You've proved yourself today. How would you like to work for me full time? I pay my staff well. The U.G. Organization doesn't pay a third of the salary I'm willing to offer you," he said.

"I am on a one-year contract, sir, of which I've only served six months," I replied. "I'd rather not break contract. It would be unprofessional of me to do so."

"I appreciate your loyalty, warrior, but arrangements can be made to release you from your contract. Of course, if you're truly dedicated to your year's contract, you can always look me up at the end of it for a job. I guarantee you a place on my staff. You'll fit right in with the rest of my ladies. What do you say?" he said with a wry smile.

"I appreciate the offer, sir, but I am a dedicated warrior. I like the job I have now. I don't anticipate making a change any time in the future," I said.

Sunderlign frowned. "I'm sure I can find something to change your mind. Everyone has something they want, monetary or otherwise. Is there anything we can get for you to have you work with us? Don't answer that just yet. I'll leave you to think about it. Let me know in a couple of days."

"All right, sir," I yielded. There was nothing in this world I wanted less than to have to work for a Fitmalo Regime member. Not even for a guarantee of Alaban's safety would I work for these greed-driven bureaucrats. I would rather face them in battle than side with them.

After a few hours, Ocelot and Salt's aide returned. The aide reported to Salt. Ocelot reported to Sunderlign, saying he'd spoken with his superior without mentioning Wilbaht's name. No specific changes were planned for tomorrow, but everyone was to be extra cautious. Also the ending ceremony was cut short. It would only involve entertainment from Jain and Godel. The high level dignitaries were scheduled to leave the planet on the same evening as the closing ceremony.

Ocelot asked permission to speak with me alone a moment. Sunderlign refused. He said we should all be open and transparent at times like these and that anything Ocelot had to say must be appropriate for all ears. Ocelot bowed to him.

"I only wanted to inform her that I spoke with the commander of our ship and there was no significant ship damage from the sandstorm. We will be allowed to depart as scheduled."

"All right. Thank you for the information," I said coldly.

"You see? No harm in that," Sunderlign said, apparently paranoid.

The next two days of the conference were intense. The members of the Jawlcheen official group who had protested were permanently removed from the conference. In the end, the Fitmalo proposal was generally accepted by the convention participants. The head Jawlcheen official announced a meeting to draw up and sign a proposal on his planet in two months. The Fitmalos were pleased, but protesters from the audience became dangerous. Twenty-four people were removed for protesting during the conference.

One pair of protesters brought plastic blowguns to the stadium. They managed to shoot spikes at one of the Fitmalo generals, but his bodyguard had a shield orb. He was sensitive enough to know when to turn it on and protect his subject. I wondered if that general would offer him a job, too. I wondered if the warrior would accept it.

Sunderlign asked me at dinner if I'd reconsidered his job offer. Again I declined it as respectfully as possible. He was displeased to the point of anger.

"Why don't you want to work for us? Do you have something against our race?" he asked.

"No, sir. I'm simply content with the job I have now. I feel it is what I was meant to do. It's what I've trained for all my life."

"Well, working for me would be just like this, only on Fitmalo."

"I'm sorry, sir. My answer is no."

He chomped with spite. "No one refuses an offer from me without living to regret it. And you will. Mark my words," he warned.

"As you say, sir," I said, neither agreeing nor disagreeing with him.

This angered him even more. He ordered me to go stand by the door until he called me. I obeyed.

Ocelot witnessed the episode tensely, but didn't say a word. I stood at the door until everyone had gone to bed except Sunderlign and his hand servant and Ocelot. I waited with true patience for the General to dismiss me. I calmly meditated where I stood. My complacency perturbed the man. Ocelot stayed near Sunderlign and the Fitmalo female watching the news, but I could tell he was waiting for Sunderlign to call me off the door. The General noticed him waiting around like a wanton dog and finally released me from my post as he retired for the night.

I was anxious to speak with Ocelot or Wilbaht or someone about what was going on. Unfortunately, my position here left me isolated. I felt I was working for the enemy.

I suddenly remembered something Yalat had said about Alaban when we were on Sor3. She had perceived that he was destined to work among his enemies and that he would have a trying life. Alaban himself had said on Santer that the worst days of his life were ahead of him. I wondered if he were in a similar situation or worse.

I meditated on his presence. I felt him within my heart. I knew somehow that he was alive and that he was thinking of me at the same moment I thought of him. I felt comforted to sense his powerful spirit linked to mine. Together we could work against these demons. I was sure even if someone in the Regime had approached Alaban with a job offer like the one Sunderlign had proposed to me, that he would refuse as I had. I was glad he had made the promise to me on Santer.

, The next day, the two generals seemed jumpier than before. The stadium was at full capacity, with hundreds of extra security and media standing throughout.

As a youth group of humans, Beetles and Lizards from Jain finished singing an ode to unity and peace, we heard a loud crack. Then we felt the shock waves from an explosion. The boom rumbled from deep within one of the entrance tunnels. A section of the wall next to the entrance crumbled. It flaked apart, leaving chunks of rock scattered around the floor. A haze of dust swirled through the air from the tunnel. People screamed, especially those nearest the blast. We were ordered to stay where we were. The people of the audience jammed all available exits. Panic overtook them. The poor children of the chorus stood terrified as their teachers attempted to calm them and round them up safely to leave the scene. I wished I could help them, but I was obligated to stay at my post.

All bodyguards remained attached to their subjects at the table. We prepared to defend them and ourselves against any possible threat, but the only threat to anyone now was the possibility of getting trampled by the stampeding audience. The raised stage where we stood happened to be the safest location in the stadium.

Once the crowds finally dwindled, the security for the stadium regrouped. The conference leader asked all our subjects to say their goodbyes to each other since the closing ceremonies had been shut down. The normally long-winded politicians gave fairly quick statements to one another. Each set of people retreated once more to their security suites.

As it turned out, a suicidal protester had carried the bomb. How he had gotten so close to the stadium was a mystery. Fortunately, he had only killed himself and seriously injured four security guards.

Sunderlign and Salt were as shaken as anyone else. They also felt anxious to get out of the underground. Salt had the idea to go out with Coldt and Shourat to a small town by the iron mines just north of the stadium where they could meet without attracting media or other unwanted onlookers.

We accompanied them to the site. The hotel was a broad building, partially wedged underground. The style and décor were minimal here, atypical of the generals' tastes, but here was ample space for their meeting and the kitchen smelled of richly prepared meats and breads. Sunderlign insisted that Salt, the two aides, and Ocelot and I should all sit with him at one table while the rest of the party found other tables. A Mantis waiter took orders from the generals by way of their translators.

When the waiter turned to go to the next table, Sunderlign told him to wait a moment. He pointed to the menu and held up two fingers. The

Mantis looked surprised. He glanced fitfully between Ocelot and me, and then apparently asked the translator to clarify. Sunderlign and the translator whispered to each other. The translator gave the waiter a definite command. The waiter then bowed dutifully.

A few minutes later, two Mantis waiters served our table. Ocelot and I received only a plate of stale bread with a cup of water. The others took plates of varied, well-prepared foods.

Sunderlign saw our nearly empty plates and feigned realization. "Well, you don't have much there, do you? We have enough to share. Don't we, Salt?" he said.

"Certainly," Salt replied. "Why don't you try some of this? You won't find a better cut of meat outside Fitmalo."

He pushed a small plate of steaming meat towards Ocelot. Sunderlign did the same with his. He cut into it with his knife.

"You see it's young and tender. Eat," he ordered. He retracted the knife. He sat playing with the food on his plate, pretending to be disinterested in my reaction.

I almost thanked them, but my sixth sense warned me of ill-gotten mischief brewing between them. I picked up my knife and gingerly poked the meat a couple of times. I noticed Ocelot's strained face.

Suddenly, his visage turned to a gawk. He viewed the food with utter disgust. "This is human!" he spat.

I gasped and dropped my knife with a clatter. I immediately regarded the dish with horror.

The generals sputtered with laughter. Their aides covered their mouths and giggled.

"How is this possible? It's illegal in the U.G. to eat meat from animals above the seventh intelligence. How can they do this?" I asked incredulously.

"I'm sure there are some mentally retarded individuals who would fall under that category, don't you think, Sunderlign? They raise them specifically for this purpose somewhere nearby," Salt spoke with delighted confidence.

"Why did you serve this to us?" Ocelot growled defensively.

"We're just letting you know," Salt spoke, only too comfortably. "We'll serve your friends to you on a plate if you decide to cross us. We've given you an opportunity to work with us. You refused. If you refused because you think your Organization is opposed to us, then you were misinformed. If you refused because *you* are opposed to us, be forewarned. We have supporters everywhere, even within your illustrious Organization. If you try to work against us, you will only harm yourselves and your friends. By the way, we know of your secret discussion the other night about plans to replace certain officials. We know you haven't reported anything yet. Now that we have your attention, I'll give you a good reason why you should not report it at all. A close associate of mine on Fitmalo is in possession of a ship called the Jawlcheen Reaper. I think you've heard of it. Everyone aboard is safe for the time being. With your cooperation, I will allow them to continue to live and work safely. However, if you do not wish to cooperate, well, I'm sure you understand."

Fearing this might be the blackmail we'd anticipated, I spoke insolently.

"I don't believe you. A mid-level general like you doesn't have the power to order the seizure of an Organization ship. Even if you did, why would you go to all that trouble just to keep us quiet? I'll bet you didn't set up the capture of that ship, if it is captured. Someone else did. You just happen to know about it. I'll bet you don't even know why your superiors want that ship. It has to do with the theft of a biological weapon. Your associate didn't tell you that because you're not in on the secret. No one's told you about it. Have they? You've played your cards badly, sir. We're already aware of your superiors' plans. Your threats to us are empty," I boldly guessed.

The two generals exchanged looks of shock. Salt glared at my nonconformity.

"What do you know?" Sunderlign demanded.

"Why would I tell you anything now? You've made it obvious we can't trust you. Why don't you check with your leader about it later? He won't be happy that you heard it from us. I'm sure he wants to keep you out of the top secret plans, especially after hearing that sloppy proposal you delivered on his behalf."

I direly hoped calling their bluff was the right thing to do. I could not guess what might happen next. The generals seethed, but did not respond right away. I felt this standoff could become deadly.

"Perhaps we can reach a modified agreement," Ocelot offered. All eyes focused on him. "We'll agree not to go to the press or any of our superiors with your plans to oust the Karneshian officials in exchange for a favor."

The two generals regarded each other tensely.

"What favor?" Sunderlign asked.

"You'll order a press release protesting the sale of human meat. And tell your associate to leave the Jawlcheen Reaper crew alone," Ocelot spoke.

The men considered his request. Their aides searched their faces for a reaction. I remained silent, ready to cloak and escape at any moment.

"How do we know you'll stay quiet about us?" Sunderlign asked cautiously.

"We're trading lives: our men on the Reaper for the Karneshians. We hold no loyalty to the Karnesh government officials. They're probably enemies of ours anyway. The warriors you speak of are our people. Of course we prefer to keep them alive. I give you my word as a warrior," Ocelot said solemnly.

"And you?" Salt asked me.

"My partner speaks for us both. I also give my word," I said. I trusted Ocelot's judgment, though I wasn't sure of his plan.

Sunderlign told his aide to take a message to be sent to specific Karnesh press heads and cabinet members. He dictated a message to her, detailing the appalling experience of being served a dish made of flesh from a being of the third intelligence. He named the place and the alleged farm where the mentally damaged humans were raised for food. He demanded an end to such practices. He urged all parties to look into the matter immediately. Sunderlign's aide sent the message to its various destinations.

I tried not to stare at the plate of meat. I also tried in vain not to imagine human adults and children enclosed in a meat processing plant for slaughter and meat preparation by Mantis workers. I covered the plate with a cloth napkin and turned away. Ocelot did the same.

Salt made a call to someone. He asked whomever it was to keep his distance from the Jawlcheen Reaper. "Continue visual observation only," he said.

I doubted he really had the authority to request such a thing, but we had no proof of this, so I could say nothing. He warned us that if the Karneshian officials were moved or protected by extra security, we could count on losing a member of the Reaper. Ocelot assured them that our deal was set. We sat in agitated formality throughout the rest of their meal. Ocelot and I did not eat.

Back at the suite, the Fitmalos behaved calmly, although I was sure the generals would scramble to contact their associates on Fitmalo to cross check my claims. Even so, they did not bother us anymore. Nor did we approach them. I feared they might attempt to murder us for knowing too much, but thankfully they understood that a bottom rung warrior with this knowledge represented the shared information among countless others in higher positions. Killing us would prevent nothing. We soon prepared to leave the suite and this horrible planet forever.

As the security vehicle connected with the Fitmalos' ship at the airfield, I anticipated some kind of final warning from them. They merely bowed. Their emerald green eyes communicated disdain. When the entire party boarded the ship, I felt a great weight lifted from my shoulders. The security vehicle separated from their ship's portal and the last of the battering rains fell before us.

Chapter 25: Alaban in Trouble

Back on the ship, we found Wilbaht at the dining table with a projection string. He reviewed information from the conference. The Organization had secretly increased hidden security on all Karnesh cabinet members. Ocelot had tipped him off about the Fitmalos' plan some time during the conference, without ever leaving his post. He had apparently written Wilbaht a note, which he handed him as he passed by. It was a clever way. Few people used paper notes anymore. He and Alaban were the only adults I knew who did.

Ocelot gave Wilbaht minimal information about our sickening experience. Wilbaht reacted with disgust as we had. I mentioned the Fitmalos' claim that someone held the Jawlcheen Reaper, possibly in a hostage situation. He told me to make contact with Alaban right away to see if any of their claims were true. In the lower observation deck, I checked first to see if he had already tried to contact me. He had. In fact, he'd sent me nine different messages.

The first was a playful love letter full of jokes, compliments, wishes and little news. The second was another love letter, but he expressed concerns about unnamed Fitmalos he was assigned to interact with. He said he could tell they were up to something secretive.

The third letter carried a different tone entirely. It was short and to the point. It read, "Sil, message me a.s.a.p. Be careful. I love you with all my heart. A."

The fourth and fifth messages were similar to the third. The sixth message was more specific: "I've been approached by someone from the R about bodyguarding. He said the same was happening to you. Is this true? I told him I'd think about it, but you know what I'll say. Send me an encrypted message if you have to. I want to know what's going on. Remember my love. A."

The seventh message unsettled me.

"Sil, I love you. In some ways you are closer to me now than you were, but in another way I feel you drifting farther from me. I've been faithful to you. I've kept my promise. Have you kept yours? Are you really giving me a chance? I am fettered with insecurity. If you feel more for me now, let me know it.

"I'm always restless now. Ongeram wants to give me medication to keep me from fidgeting. I sense something bad is about to happen. I'm going crazy in here. Our assignments were all canceled. We've been put under ship arrest. I don't know why. They won't tell us. They only say it's for a high-level security problem. We haven't been outside now for four days. Every medium-sized ship on the airfield has been sitting here on freeze for some reason.

"We just got word about the Fitmalo proposal to unite Thrader. I know you're at that conference. If you have any information that will help us, let me know about it.

"Actually, I care more about your heart than your knowledge right now. You're always with me. Your very presence is here. Do you feel anything like that for me? What do you feel for me, Sil? I know I'm being impatient, but I don't want to wait until I actually see you again to know your heart. I love you in every way imaginable. Message me as soon as you can. A."

After reading this letter, I dreaded the next two.

The eighth had been written just thirty hours ago. It read: "Sil, I apologize for my last message. I didn't mean to say you wouldn't keep your promise. Please forgive me. I know you love me. I let my dreams affect my everyday life too much. It's easy to do when you have nothing to occupy your time. We are still on ship arrest. This makes nearly a week.

"I see better now what is going to happen with the Fitmalo proposal to unite Thrader. I'm sure you're on top of things there on Karnesh. I wish we could message each other on real time, but I know that's not possible at such distance.

"I expect you'll get this message in a couple of days when the conference is finished. I forgot you couldn't message anyone while on bodyguard duty. Tell me about it when you get the chance. Tell me anything and everything when you can finally message me.

"My love, I would cross the whole universe for you, if only I knew you would be waiting for me on the other side. Even if you refuse me a thousand times and tell me to go live on an ice planet, I'll still keep you here in my heart. I would give my right arm if I had to, just to have you by me for life. Of course, I hope it never comes to that. You wouldn't make things that difficult for me, would you? And what would you do with an extra right arm anyway? More love than you can imagine, A."

He sounded more like himself in this message. I was glad. However, my uplifted spirits soon fell again when I saw the ninth message. It had been sent just a few hours ago. It was short and frightening.

"Sil, I've done something terrible, but I couldn't see any way around it. Today I am sorry for who I am. I've done something very wrong. I can't tell you about it yet. I only hope you'll forgive me. Today I'm glad you're not with me. I wouldn't want to see the reaction on your face. I can only say I'm sorry. You are still my sun, my brightest star. Guide me, Sil. I love you. A."

I sat back in my chair. I didn't know what to respond to him. What could he have possibly done? Had he killed someone I knew? I hated to think it, but I hoped he hadn't taken the Fitmalos up on their offer. He had asked me to guide him. I anticipated his next message, which would surely come soon.

I sent him a reply: "Whatever you've done, I hope you can get to safety if you're not already. Yes, I can feel your presence here in my heart. A warning: our bodyguard subjects were all R. I was offered a job but refused. I was told your ship was in R's possession. I assume your contact general is R. Who is he? If they let your ship go, you'll be watched. I will answer another of your letters after we take off. Take care of yourself. Love, S."

I encrypted the message three ways before sending it. Alaban would be able to read it quickly, but most other people could not without an advanced decoding device. I closed all messages and went back to the dining table where Ocelot and Wilbaht still conversed about the Fitmalo situation. I interrupted their conversation with the news of Alaban's ship arrest on Fitmalo.

"The generals in control of his Organization center must be Regime members or payees of Prime Minister Lock. The Fitmalos mean to oust our Organization centers from their planet or turn them into military centers. Next they'll try to control our bases on Jawlcheen and Nitrogen1," Wilbaht said.

"That will insure their takeover," Ocelot added.

"I didn't know they'd have such wide-reaching support. How could they justify something like that? How can they justify ordering a ship arrest on a whole airfield?" I asked.

"They'll have to file a special report for emergency actions to give their reasons for such a decision. Then we'll know. I'm sure the Fitmalos you guarded were not in a position of control in the Regime. At best they were middlemen. Salt happened to know about the incident and used it to harangue you. We need to find out what was really going on," Wilbaht said.

"Ocelot, did Salt ask you to work for him, too?" I asked.

"Yes, but he wasn't very pressing about it. I think they were after you, mostly."

"They weren't very aggressive about recruiting me. I think these Fitmalos are not the people Trau was trying to contact. If they had been, they would have tried harder."

Wilbaht agreed.

"Whoever they were, we have to keep them guessing about what we know," Ocelot mentioned. He turned to me. "It's a good thing I intervened soon enough. You were leading them into a standoff."

"I wasn't about to pretend to be intimidated by their scare tactics. I was representing the Organization in there, not just myself," I retorted in aggravation.

"Sil, Ocelot is right. Remember your rank. You are not to initiate any negotiations or talks with any representative of a hostile entity without express permission from your commander. Is that clear?" Wilbaht intervened.

"Yes, sir," I replied humbly.

"Put it behind you. And stop bickering." Wilbaht made a sour face. "I thought you two would have smoothed over your differences these last two weeks. If we're all going to be cooped up in the ship together en route to our next assignment, I'll expect you all to treat each other peaceably," Wilbaht interjected.

"You're right, sir. We've been under a lot of stress lately. Could we still take that leave time on Jain? It would do us all good to relax," Ocelot said hopefully.

"Ahem. Yes, we'll be taking off for Jain in a few hours. I've agreed to take Yinore there. In fact, I wanted to ask you where you had lived before so we could get as close to that site as possible," Wilbaht said.

Ocelot reacted with gratitude. He told him he'd lived in Venus Falls. Wilbaht planned to message his granddaughter so she could meet us there. I mentioned I looked forward to meeting her. It would be nice to have a new female companion, even if we only had three days leave.

During ship checks and inventory, Klib informed us he had already taken care of restocking while we were at the convention, since he'd had nothing else to do. This helped speed our procedures. After takeoff, several ships followed our path to Jain. I stayed on alert on weapons just in case. Fortunately, we only took a few short, uneventful hours to reach our destination since Jain and Karnesh were close to each other at this time of the millennium.

We landed at the Palace Center at Venus Falls. Here it was past midnight. Wilbaht suggested that we spend the night on the ship and then report in at the Center at dawn. After landing and post-landing procedures, Ocelot and Klib walked out onto the airfield.

While the two were out, I stayed in the lower observation deck to read Alaban's newest message, which was heavily encrypted. I used Ocelot's decoder to solve its puzzle.

The message read: "I feel like a puppet. The R came for me. All the R members were also O. They wanted a quick job from me. If I didn't do it, they promised to pin it on me anyway. I hit eight warriors to free one prisoner. He was high-ranking Fitmalo military, but I couldn't ID him in the dark. The R members covered me. They want to keep it quiet. Swall Jade is my general here. I had to follow orders from a general. What else could I do? I'm torn up inside. Fellow warriors are dead. A criminal is loose. The O is falling apart here. Help me think of something. Can W help? Can he have another general call us away so we can leave? Encrypt everything you send me. I love you. A."

I immediately answered back.

"W and I will help. Stay strong. I'll message you as soon as I can. Love, S."

I hesitated a moment, and then added, "You asked me what I feel for you. You are the most important man in my life now. No one could ever take your place. I sense your life in my heart as if you were my soul's twin. I believe you and I become more closely linked every day. I don't know if I can guide you, but I will try to help you. I'm sure W's connections can accomplish anything for him. Please stay hopeful, my friend. Love, S."

I encrypted my message five ways before sending it. Then I ran to get Wilbaht. I found him at the door to his bunk preparing a few things to disembark.

"Sir, I need your help. Alaban is in big trouble. So is one of our Centers on Fitmalo," I spoke quickly.

"What happened?" he asked sternly. He stepped out of his bunk. I showed him Alaban's most recent letter.

"We've got to get him out of there. I'll go talk to an old friend of mine here. You stay here and check for any new messages. Call me if anything comes up. I'll tell Ocelot to stay on alert. If I don't call you before dawn, stay at the ship, understood?"

"Yes, sir. I can't tell you how much we appreciate your help," I told him.

His swimming blue eyes gazed into mine. He squeezed my shoulder and nodded. Then he spun to glide through the dining area, down the stairwell and out into the night.

I went to my bunk and closed the door. A feeling of helpless urgency stirred my spirit. I prayed for Alaban's safety with my greatest concentration. Then I changed into exercise clothing and worked out a while to avoid pacing nervously. I ran back and forth from the exercise room to the lower observation deck to check for messages. None appeared. I did three hours of circuit, personal defense, running and stretching. Here on Jain, dawn would arrive in only three hours. I was wide-awake, waiting for news from Wilbaht or Alaban or both.

Ocelot and Klib returned to the ship after their long walk. They caught sight of me jogging towards the exercise room. I didn't stop to explain. I heard Klib's voice say something snide to Ocelot about me. Gladly, I didn't hear much of what he said.

In the exercise room, I set up a virtual opponent. The projection equipment created a shadowy Vermilion figure stepping out from the reflective wall. I fought with this opponent for about half an hour. I killed the shadow several times before I noticed the two men observing me at the door. I spun to shoo them away.

"What?" I asked in aggravation. "Don't tell me you're interested in watching me exercise, too. Why don't you step in here with me? You're not afraid of a little audience participation, are you? I can take you both on stage at once. Step right up." I turned off the hologram. I stood at double hammer position with my shoulders back and my fists slightly down and out to my sides.

Klib nudged Ocelot's arm. "Hey, Ocelot, I didn't know a female could be cocky. I thought you had to have one to act like one. I guess I was wrong."

"You're an ass," I retorted to him.

"Yeah, well, you're a show off, and that's putting it mildly. You didn't learn your lesson the first time, did you? I thought they said you were intelligent. Whose lap did you sit on to get that rumor started?" Klib responded.

"No one's. I earned my reputation with hard work. Who'd you pay off to get your pilot's license?" I asked.

"Oh, you've got me. You're so quick," he joked.

Ocelot leaned in the doorway and crossed his arms like a menacing thug. He stood by Klib's side letting him do all the talking.

"What do you want?" I asked. "Why did you follow me over here?"

"I'm just looking. Hey, this is public space. The door was open. Anyway, it's entertaining to watch a woman with biceps bigger than mine, kind of like a freak show," he said.

"I think our biceps are about the same size, Klib. I just use mine more than you do. Now what do you want? You're supposed to stay away from me, remember?"

"I'm not even in the same room. I'm standing in the doorway. See? We've even got a chaperone. You're not afraid of me, are you?"

"I'm afraid you'll drive me crazy with your mindless drivel. *What do you want?*" I was exasperated with him.

"I just wanted to know how your boyfriend is doing. Wilbaht seemed pretty upset about him. It must be something worth knowing."

"I don't know how he is now. All I know is he's stuck on Fitmalo. I'm waiting for his communication. If you'll excuse me, I'm going to check again to see if he's messaged me yet."

I made a gesture to move the two of them out of the way so I could get through. Ocelot stepped to the side easily, unmoved by our discussion. Klib backed away slowly, making me wait for him to stand back.

"Don't touch me," I reminded him.

As I marched past him and down the hall, he called out, "Your mouth says no, but those hips are begging for it." He giggled.

I threw back a glare at him and muttered. "Sick son of a…"

I returned to check for Alaban's message. Finally it had arrived.

He wrote, "I knew you'd come through for me, Sil. Thank W for me. Tell him I owe him a favor now. Thank you for your note. It meant everything to me. I noticed you still called me 'friend.' I guess pressuring you isn't the right way to go about it. I'll stay constant for you. Just remember that. I can barely wait for the day when the two of us are reunited without having to worry about Fitmalos, partners, or worldly problems. I just want to think of you: beautiful, sexy, sweet, wonderful you. I'll hold you in my arms until my elbow joints lock up. How's that for romantic? I will be alive in the next few weeks because of you and W. Keep me in your heart always. Love, A."

After dealing with the two undesirable men in the ship, Alaban's kindness shone through his letter like precious sunlight. He was my heart's repose.

I replied, "You are my one true friend in this universe. No one else loves or appreciates me like you do. I will never feel alone as long as you are with me in spirit. Know that I am always with you. Stay hopeful. I'm sure help is on the way. I look forward to the day when we'll hold each other again, too. So much love, S."

I decided he would probably receive no immediate help again tonight and that he would most likely not be called to do any more of Swall Jade's bidding so soon after the terrible assignment he'd been given. I let his troubles rest, keeping faith in Wilbaht's power to help. I shut down the lower observation deck board for the evening.

In the dining area, I was annoyed to still find Klib and Ocelot hanging around. They sat at the table playing a virtual card game. Klib looked up at me and spoke.

"Well? Aren't you going to tell us the news? We've been waiting on you half the night," he complained.

I stopped and stared at them. Ocelot seemed disinterested. Klib was bright-eyed and alert, even though this would normally be his time to sleep. I didn't believe they were really waiting for me to tell them about Alaban, but Klib was being a pain about it, so I answered.

"Not that you would need to know, but I believe he's going to be fine. I'm sure Wilbaht will find someone to pull him out of Fitmalo. He's under ship arrest there," I stated.

"Ship arrest? What did he do, kill someone?" Klib asked.

"Maybe," I responded. "It was probably someone who insulted his girlfriend." I crossed my arms and stared at him.

"Heh, heh. Good one. This he-man of yours sounds like a real winner. I'll bet he's got plenty of girlfriends lined up at every Center he stops at."

"I don't think so, Klib. Not that it's any of your business."

"Oh, let me guess. He sends you love letters every week. He tells you he's faithful and you're the only girl in the universe for him. Yeah, I've used that trick before. All it got me was married...twice." Klib folded his hand of virtual cards.

Ocelot snickered.

"Shut up," I muttered.

"Who are you telling to shut up?" Klib asked almost eagerly.

"You, who else?" I told him. I half-turned to continue down the hall, but Ocelot's reaction caught my eye. He gave Klib a Cheshire grin.

I spun on my heel.

"What do you think is so funny? You're supposed to back me up on this. Alaban's safety is important to all of us and you know it. Why are you making fun of the situation? What kind of warrior are you? I thought you were someone honorable when I first met you, but now I don't know what you are," I chastised.

Klib pounded the table in laughter and pointed at him. Ocelot slapped the table with one hand and groaned in disappointment.

260

"You owe me a full case of ale, man! Make it Rybalazar Extra Fine, the one with the goat on the label," Klib shouted between peals of laughter.

"What?" I said in confusion.

Ocelot shook his head and closed the virtual card game. Klib attempted to control his glee to explain.

"We made a bet that you couldn't get pissed at me without yelling at him. I was the one aggravating the hell out of you. He didn't say a word and he still got it!" His face turned red from laughing. He peered at Ocelot through watery eyes. "See? That proves it. It is not just me. She hates us both."

"You mean everything you said was for a bet?" I asked.

Klib nodded with a wide grin. He stood from the table and stretched. "Yep, and a very lucrative one at that."

Ocelot was annoyed, but also slightly amused.

"It was nice doing business with you, Ocelot. I'll be expecting my reward in a few days, sir. Now I'm off to bed. Have a good night," he said, still giggling.

I observed the scene with my arms crossed, not sure how to react.

Klib chuckled as he passed me. "Your bitchy temper is too predictable, princess. Sweet dreams." He waved his fingers at me and smiled in coy triumph. He backed into his bunk and closed the door. I still heard his cackles through the wall.

Ocelot stood to face me. He too moved toward his bunk.

"You should reevaluate your attitude, Warrior," he said wryly as he passed me.

I held my solemn stance in realization. I'd been duped. It was my own fault. I had been unfair—predictably so. They had set this up to teach me a lesson, something Klib had claimed when he'd filmed me in the bath. That lesson had failed. Apart from the fact he'd been caught, it was a vengeful plan, not a didactic one. This lesson was an eye-opener. They were right. Klib wasn't the only spiteful personality on this ship. I'd become one, too. When had I changed my ways? Had I become so distracted by my discomfort around them and the changes in my life that I'd lost my moral focus? Six months ago, I would never have confronted my superiors with such informality or disrespect, no matter what. The credo that Yalat had taught me nagged at my memory. I had to maintain my integrity despite the expectations of others, by my own high expectations of myself. I had lost that. I stood humbled, lesson learned.

Chapter 26: Morality and the Jain Planet

Wilbaht appeared at 0930 hours with good news and a warm greeting. He had spoken with his friend, a covert ops general, who had invited him to stay the night at his home. He assured me that Alaban and the rest of the Jawlcheen Reaper crew would soon be called away urgently to Jawlcheen. I grasped Wilbaht's great hand and shook it emotionally. I thanked him with a broad smile. He returned the gesture.

I ran back to the messaging board to let Alaban know that help was on the way. Almost as soon as I'd sent the letter, I received his reply for the one I'd sent last night.

"If you're right, W will get us out of here in no time. Please thank him for me. I hope someday to be as powerful as he is. I'd like to have a hand in changing this O for the better.

The Fitmalos haven't lifted the ship arrest yet, but they haven't approached us again, either. I sensed from your last letter that you forgave me for what they ordered me to do. I would feel better if I could actually read that from you. You did forgive me, didn't you?" He went on to thank me for my last letter, pouring on syrupy compliments and wishes.

I wrote him a quick reply. I said I had forgiven him for everything. I sent him my love in undying friendship.

When I left the lower observation deck, I found Wilbaht searching for me with more pleasant news. Yinore's egg was hatching.

I followed him to the quarantine room with bubbling excitement. We moved to the edge of the wall to watch while Yinore poised herself on all six limbs in the nest next to her egg, which showed a tiny uneven crack on one side. Ocelot and Klib stayed on the opposite side of the room. Klib rubbed his beard, less interested in the hatching than in leaving the scene. Ocelot stood by with documentation files to fill out for the baby's identification. Yinore tapped the top of the egg gently to communicate with her baby. The baby tapped back, cracking open one side of the egg.

"Oh, she's hatching!" Yinore said with enchantment.

The egg soon split open, breaking in two pieces at the top. The baby shoved with all her might to stretch her neck up and out of the egg. Yinore carefully picked away the extra pieces at her head. The baby blinked and raised her front arms.

"Hello, little girl. I'm your mother. You're so pretty," Yinore babbled to her ecstatically.

The bright yellow baby rested, breathing heavily from her first exertion of energy. Yinore bumped noses with her offspring. She blinked at her all the more. Then she pressed hard with her hind legs to crack open the bottom part of the egg. She lolled out of it, unfurling her tiny limbs and tail. She quickly found one jagged edge of eggshell and chomped it with sharp new teeth. As she ate the shell, she gained energy. She gradually found her feet and stood on all six while she munched the remains of her egg. Within a matter of minutes, she devoured every crumb. She sniffed around to take in her surroundings. She lifted her head to sniff her mother, who sniffed her back.

"Ba!" the little one shouted. We laughed. She wobbled, surprised by her own ability to make sound.

"I'll call you Yeelan, the sunray. You are bright as a sun, my daughter." She nuzzled her.

Yinore picked up her child, who flailed in panic until her mother held her to her chest. Then Yeelan grabbed onto Yinore's clothing with all her fingers. She clung to her, bobbing her head from side to side, observing the shapes and colors around her. Her scales were so tiny and new that she looked as if she were made of bright yellow plastic.

"Ap?" she seemed to ask. She wiggled her tail. Yinore chuckled and coddled her.

Ocelot checked the baby's heartbeat and lung activity. She was healthy.

Yeelan leaned backwards to look at him as he checked her. "Aa-a!" she chirped.

Ocelot grinned. He was about to stroke her chin with a finger when she snapped at it. He quickly withdrew. The others laughed at him heartily.

"You have a lovely child, Yinore. I congratulate you on this blessing. May she grow smart and healthy," Wilbaht boomed.

Yinore nodded and thanked him, turning her attention back to her young. She soon procured a makeshift diaper for her baby while Ocelot typed up a ship's medical report of live hatching. Wilbaht and I signed it as witnesses. Ocelot took a DNA sample from the tip of Yeelan's tail to include in the document. We all helped gather Yinore's personal items for her as she crooned to her daughter. Wilbaht called the ascension tower for a travel cart. He asked if she needed help to a room, but she refused politely. She said her mate would meet them at the tower lobby. We said our goodbyes.

Yeelan peered up at me with pure curiosity. I waved at her and smiled. She squeaked and shouted some kind of infantile gibberish to me. Yinore said thanks and goodbye to us, and then boarded the cart to roll away from us towards the ascension tower and out of our lives. I regretted the impersonal relationship we'd had, but I wished her the best with her new family.

After she'd gone, Wilbaht proposed an outing, excluding Klib, who had to stay in the airfield as his continued punishment. Ocelot offered to show us around, although ten years had passed since he had lived here.

We walked out to the grassy field of the landing area. A thick smell of flowers hung stickily in the humid air. To one side of the airfield, the ground dropped away lazily over lumps of igneous rock. To the other side, a low mountain grew in a knotted snarl. It was grown over with ferns, moss, and small trees. The trees leaned heavily from the weight of the pink blossoms, which perfumed the area.

Looking down the mountain, we saw a deeply carved valley with a narrow river. Similar mountains flanked the river valley, all gnarled and green. Among the rolling mountains nestled a few small towns.

Behind us and beyond the mountain above the airfield lay the city of Venus Falls. We passed between rows of small ships parked all along the mountainous side of the airfield, and then climbed a broad stairway to a street overlooking the city. Buildings scattered throughout the valley like upturned crystals. The tallest buildings stood at the heart of the valley.

Ocelot directed us to a public driver stand. We took the first available cab to a heavily treed area. Here, he showed us his old home. It was an apartment complex with an elaborate garden in its middle. He pointed to the places where he had lived with his parents and where Jiao had lived with his. A wistful nervousness came over him. He told Wilbaht how he had spent his free time climbing trees and throwing nuts and berries at people with his cousin. Ocelot smiled a little. He looked up at the trees and then at the apartment. His smile faded. He still mourned the death of his parents.

He guided us across the shaded walkway to a terraced memorial garden. He stopped before a metal statue. It was a lifelike image of a man and a woman standing, facing one another. They held each other's right hands together between their hearts. Their left hands reached up, touching the right cheek of their partner's face. They gazed at each other lovingly. Ocelot stood before the statue of his lost parents. Memories crept through his mind.

At the base of the statue, a simple epitaph read: "Jan Triol and Leono Quoren—Love transcends life".

"Jiao's mother had this memorial built for them," he explained.

We bowed respectfully. Ocelot reached up to join in the clasped hands between them. He closed his eyes in silent prayer. It was strange to see him in this setting. I hadn't seen Ocelot as anything but a tough, serious, yet sometimes foolhardy, adult. I could hardly picture him as someone's child.

Wilbaht offered to give him time alone with the memorial. Ocelot let go of the metal hands and turned to face us, saying that he would come back later and that he preferred to show Wilbaht some local sights, if they still existed as he'd last seen them.

The two men discussed possibilities as they sauntered slowly away from the statue. Curiously, I moved closer to it. I levitated to eye level with the figure of Ocelot's mother. She was beautiful. She had long, straight hair tied with a flowered string. She wore a long dress with flowing sleeves. His father wore a combat uniform. His weapons strap carried a sword, the handle of which looked a great deal like mine. I realized Ocelot had fashioned my sword using the pattern of his father's. Only Ocelot had added rubies and a double etching, probably a detail honoring his mother. If I hadn't known better, I would have said the statue was of Ocelot himself. I glanced down at him. He and Wilbaht watched. Wilbaht looked pleased. Ocelot seemed pained. I dropped back to the ground.

"I'm sorry. It's just that you look so much like your father," I said.

"Yes, I know. Are you coming with us?" he asked.

"Yes." I bowed to the statue in honor of the deceased before following.

I followed them back up the terraced land, through the gardens of the apartment complex, and out into the street. We walked through a brightly colored marketplace. I marveled at the fresh foods and handmade clothing. Everything here was made for humans and Lizards. Yalat and I could have lived here in luxury. I was intrigued by the variety of products available for humans. I felt like a child in a huge toy store. Every few steps I took led me to something new and fascinating. When we passed a section full of hair adornments, I doubled back and ogled the wares. I let the men move on without me. I chose a set of modest hair clips, since my hair had grown past my shoulders during our flight. The saleslady at the booth tried to sell me more, but I knew to buy little. I always had to travel light.

I turned to follow my crewmates. I saw them at a distance. Wilbaht towered above everyone around him. Now he probably felt out of place.

One of the young women who passed them stopped wide-eyed. She turned and grabbed Ocelot by the arm.

I felt the tiny hairs stand on the back of my neck. I treaded firmly ahead, ready to defend my partner. I saw her jump to throw her arms around Ocelot's neck. She hugged him tightly to her. Ocelot laughed and hugged her back.

I slowed to a halt. I watched as the other young woman who accompanied the first smiled and reached to hug Ocelot as well. She kissed him on the cheek. He kissed her back. I froze. Ocelot, my partner, the man who hated to be touched, now stood ten meters away; touching, hugging, kissing, and welcoming the touch of two women he hadn't seen in ten years.

Tumultuous thoughts ran through my head as I watched the bunch of women multiply to three and then four around him. He was a celebrity among them. He did not move away from them or cast a critical eye at them as he would with me. He turned friendly, warm. This was an unknown person. It suddenly occurred to me that he only showed his cold, rigid demeanor to me. What was it about me he didn't like? Was it my attitude? Was I overly critical? I suddenly felt rejected.

I strode boldly forward to meet his clinging admirers. I joined them closely, but they didn't notice me at all. They all talked at once. One girl invited him to a wedding party.

"I'd love to, but can I invite my partner?" he asked.

The girl turned to crane up at Wilbaht. "Sure. You can bring anyone you want. There's going to be a crowd of people there. It's my cousin's wedding. My uncle is not holding back on any expenses. Everyone is invited," she chimed. She was very feminine and flirtatious. She wore copious amounts of facial makeup.

"Oh, it'll be great to see you again tonight," said another girl.

"Let's go shopping," the other said. "I haven't bought a new outfit for weeks."

"Okay, but I have a hair appointment in a couple of hours," said another.

They gabbed a little more about personal beauty. Then their conversation turned to Ocelot's physique. They shamelessly squeezed his arms, felt his chest, and giggled. Ocelot reddened a little, but laughed. He welcomed this from them. To me it was an abomination. I stood by with disgust. I wanted to pull them away and tell them to show some respect. But it was not my place to do so.

Soon they departed, telling him they'd see him tonight at a banquet hall downtown. They trotted off giggling and talking. They didn't acknowledge my presence at all. Ocelot shook his head and grinned, watching them go.

"They were at the female academy when I was training at the Center here. They haven't changed much." Ocelot turned to squint up at Wilbaht. "Do you want to go to their party, sir?"

"We'll see. Why don't you ask Sil?" he suggested.

Ocelot regarded me half-heartedly. "You don't want to go, do you?"

"Only if Wilbaht goes," I said, equally unenthused. Offhandedly, I added, "It might be interesting to see how large groups of humans behave together."

266

"What do you mean how humans behave? You are human," Ocelot said with a smirk.

I briefly explained that I hadn't grown up in human society. The only humans I knew were my own family and a few classmates.

He looked at me as if I were strange and freakish. He scoffed. "No wonder."

I looked up at Wilbaht. "Maybe I should do something else."

Wilbaht changed the subject to say we had plenty of time to decide and that he was interested now in seeing a museum he'd read about. Ocelot offered to go with him. I trailed resentfully after them.

Back at the Center, we were given three modest quartering rooms, each next to the other. After returning to the ship for some extra clothes, Wilbaht said he'd like to go to the wedding party after all. He encouraged me to come along. I accepted the invitation out of respect for him.

However, I was uncertain about what to wear. The only clothes I had that didn't look militant were my abbreviated wardrobe from Santer and my Tambuo outfit. I was sure there would be no Tambuo dancing on this planet, and I didn't want to draw attention to myself so as to observe discretely, so I wore a pair of understated khaki pants and a blue sleeveless top. I felt self-conscious about my arms, unsure of how people would react to my musculature. Not that their opinions were so important to me; I simply hoped to remain unnoticed.

We followed Ocelot to a tall luxury hotel downtown. The wedding party was held in a huge reception room on the tenth floor. We arrived at the entrance to the room and waited for the four girls to arrive.

Ocelot posed near the door in his thin white dress shirt and gray uniform pants, ready to show off, anticipating his ladies' arrival. I glanced uneasily at Wilbaht, who looked stately his official gray uniform. I began to wonder if I'd chosen the right apparel.

The four women we'd seen earlier bustled through the foyer door. They wore tight, gaudy dresses. Their hair was matted with some kind of sparkling gel. Bright-colored makeup shone garishly on their faces. Their shoes were decorative and difficult to walk in. A pungent perfume wafted into the room with them. I realized then that my Tambuo outfit would have been perfect for the evening. Then again, I wasn't sure I wanted to fit in with these colorful birds.

They fawned over Ocelot. He appreciated their attentions to the point of buffoonery. They invited him to enter the reception room. He gestured toward us.

"You remember my partners. This is Sub General Wilbaht," he indicated.

"Oh, nice to meet you," they all said, obviously impressed with his title. They grasped his hand with the thumb and first two fingers only. I wondered if this was customary here. Wilbaht bowed courteously and returned the salutation.

"And, uh, this is Sil," Ocelot said offhandedly.

They turned to me. I held out my hand to greet them. One of the girls squealed with laughter. The others reacted with delighted surprise. They asked her what she was laughing at.

"I thought you were a man!" she screeched. The brood giggled in unison.

I was taken aback by the girl's mistake, appalled by the fact that she would openly advertise such stupidity. My countenance remained stern as she facetiously apologized. She covered a wicked grin. The girls giggled cruelly, feigning embarrassment. I rested my hands on my hips. What a bunch of idiots. If this was a representation of human society, I was glad I hadn't been a part of it. The foolish lot turned away from me. I stood my ground angrily.

Ocelot actually smiled at them. "Did you start drinking already?" he asked.

"No! I just had one glass of wine," one of them said.

Each of them confessed to having some kind of alcohol before arriving. Ocelot shook his head, grinning at them happily. He held out his arm to brush the silly flamingoes into the reception room. They jostled forward, chattering about who would be at the party. He listened to their prattle with interest.

Wilbaht stepped after them. I remained rooted to the floor. Wilbaht glimpsed over his shoulder inquisitively and then returned to me. I did not change my ostensible discomfort.

"Don't blame ignorant people for their ignorance. Their lack of intelligence reflects poorly on them, not you," he spoke. "You are far lovelier than any of those young ladies. I'm certain there are many men of your species here who will find you attractive. Even if they don't, I know of one human male who thinks you're the most beautiful woman in the universe. I heard him say so." He smiled down at me lovingly.

I remembered the night when Alaban was with us on Santer. Wilbaht was right. I shouldn't have taken the girl's rudeness to heart.

"Thank you, sir," I said. Wilbaht was a wonderful father figure.

We strode in together. The room was elegantly decorated with flowers, ribbons, and fountains. An elaborate buffet of foods overflowed at one side of the room. Tables for guests filled half the area. An empty dance floor gleamed at the other end. Humans gathered in groups around the buffet and their own tables. There were just humans here. Only a couple of Lizard waiters and Wilbaht were not.

The bride and groom sat under a gazebo in the middle of the room. They fed each other sweetly. I looked around at the other women. They all wore short dresses. The men dressed similarly to Ocelot. Wilbaht and I would have to be odd together.

We followed the trail of heavy perfume to the food table. We picked out a few things and then sat with our thick-brained hostesses. We ate tranquilly as the four ladies babbled to Ocelot about all the gossip they could recall from the last ten years. They hardly touched their meals from gabbing so much. They did, however, manage to finish the whole bottle of wine.

Every few minutes, someone came by our table to say hello to one of the girls. One man recognized Ocelot and shook his hand.

"Hey, where have you been? The fencing team hasn't been the same since you left," the man said to him.

They stood and talked about local sports for a while. The girls took the opportunity to bunch together and whisper gossip about both men. I overheard them plotting to set up one of the girls with the man speaking with Ocelot.

I gazed sympathetically at the unsuspecting man. He was nice looking and well groomed. I could see why she liked him. However, I couldn't see why a nice, intelligent man like him would want one of these female nuisances by his side. And to kiss her—I imagined to kiss the lips of one of these made-up faces would be like kissing a vat of colored wax.

The man shook hands with Ocelot again and departed, moving toward his own table. The girl with designs on him waved flirtatiously as he left. He merely nodded in her direction. The chatty girls began their stream of gossip all over again.

Soon the waiters served us dessert, then flavored ice, and finally a warm tea. I ignored the noise from the four birds. Instead, I surveyed the people in the party. For the most part, they were either happy or bored. Little children ran and played hide-and-seek beneath the tables. Older children sat with their parents or stood around the sound and music control area, choosing songs to be played after the meal.

All the adults at the tables around us talked about business or politics. Some had opinions about the Fitmalo proposal. One table of people near us spoke vehemently against the proposal of a common law in Thrader. They all agreed the Fitmalo government was planning some kind of economic monopoly.

I would have liked to listen to more of their conversation, but the music started, drowning out their voices. The newlywed couple danced alone at first. Then their immediate family joined them in a circle.

Ocelot did a double take when he got a good look at them. He asked the gabbing hens if the bride was who he thought she was. Obviously the bride was an old girlfriend of his. The birds informed him that she was.

"I wonder what she'll say if she sees you," one cockatoo said.

"I'll bet she regrets letting you go," said another.

"Did she ever mate with you?" asked the slyest of the bunch.

"I'll bet her husband will be jealous when he finds out one of her ex-boyfriends is here," another said.

"You know what the best cure for jealousy is," chirped the first one.

"Get together with someone they know?" asked the second.

"And make sure they know you did something," said the third. She moved her head like a chicken when she said this.

"Oh, yes. That works. I can testify to that," the fourth one chimed in.

I was ashamed to be seen with them. Wilbaht and I had stayed completely out of their conversation thus far, but their unethical gab grated on me. Fortunately, Ocelot did not feel the need to answer any of their pointed questions since the birds quickly followed the topic of romantic strategies to give personal accounts of idiocy.

At the end of the song, the bride and groom left, waving to the applause of the party. The small children and babies were taken home. Most of the adults and teens remained. More than half the guests had soon left the room.

The music continued. The teenage members of the party had their turn on the dance floor. They were creative and athletic in their dancing. Their music was punchy, high-tempoed and new. Some of the boys did flips and spins. After nearly an hour of youth dancing, the music ended. The teens reluctantly exited the room. Some of the older adults left, too. The waiters and catering personnel withdrew the buffet. One last bottle of heavy wine was delivered to the tables of the remaining guests. The girls immediately poured it all around, but I covered my glass. The girl pouring made a haughty face at me.

A new melody began to play. The four girls immediately became frantic about getting the first girl to dance with her prospective beau. They scampered up to him and somehow convinced him to dance with her. Once these two were set, the other three returned to argue about which one would dance with Ocelot first. I rolled my eyes and shook my head. They were being ridiculous about him.

I watched as other couples filled the dance floor. They all gave each other a kiss on the mouth before dancing. The couples held each other closely. They spun slowly for several steps. Then they separated. The men twirled the women twice. Then they came back together to kiss again. I had never seen this kind of dance before.

The birds scampered to one side of the dance floor. Ocelot quickly escorted the oldest of the three to dance. She grabbed him by the face and pulled him to her forcefully. She kissed him hard. He recoiled in surprise, but smiled at her. She left a smear of lipstick on his face. She wiped it away playfully.

I knitted my brow and turned away. I tried not to look back at them, but I couldn't help it. Something other than my critical conscience tugged at my mind. The second girl cut in to take her turn. She was not as aggressive as the first, but she was more flirtatious. I felt a twinge in my stomach. Something was wrong.

The girl who had gone after Ocelot's acquaintance glued herself to her prey. He did not resist her as I thought he would. Rather he welcomed her attentions. I did not understand it. I looked at Ocelot. He had the same complacent smile on his face as the other man had. The twinge in my stomach became pain. I looked to Wilbaht. He leaned half-asleep, his jaw propped up on his palm. I looked back at the dance floor. The third woman had thrown off the second and was now in a serious lip lock with my partner. I made a face.

I poured myself a glass of wine, stared at it a moment, and then gulped down nearly the entire glass. It tasted awful. I nearly gagged on the stuff. I coughed loudly, waking Wilbaht from his snooze. He slapped me on the back and asked if I was all right. The stomach pain increased with the inflow of alcohol. I cringed. I held my stomach and shook my head.

"It must be the strange food," I replied.

I tried not to watch as the three women took turns dancing and kissing for several minutes. A dark anxiety crept into me. Inexplicably, I wanted to wrest Ocelot from the three women and lead him to safety. I felt they meant him harm. I clamped a hand onto the back of my chair while the other held my stomach. I watched them whirl and kiss, as they clutched at him. Did this song never end?

"Would you like to leave?" Wilbaht asked me.

"I don't want to leave without Ocelot," I confessed. "I feel like he's in some kind of danger. I sense some kind of turmoil. I shouldn't leave until I'm sure of his safety," I said nervously.

"If you'd prefer to leave, I can stay with him," Wilbaht offered. "Although I don't sense any problem."

"What if you fall asleep again?" I asked him.

Wilbaht frowned, perturbed. "I did not fall asleep. I only meditated. If you feel so strongly, go tell him about it."

I looked again at the dancing couples. The least aggressive of the three birds had found herself a more intimate dance partner. His hands moved along her body as if the two were about to mate. She welcomed his touch with a heavy kiss. I hoped the same phenomenon would occur with the other two. Maybe they would find a man who appealed to them more. But there weren't any men left in the room who didn't already have a dance partner. My stomach weighed and sloshed.

Finally, the music ended. I felt relieved. My stomach pain eased a little. Ocelot and the two remaining women returned to the table. One of the flirting girls cleaned his face with a cloth napkin. They all shared smudged pink lips.

Ocelot excused himself to go to the restroom to wash his face. While he was gone, the two birds plotted and argued fiendishly about him.

"I have *got* to take him home," one of them said adamantly to the other.

"No way, girl. I saw him first. He's mine for the night," she defended.

"It doesn't matter who saw him first, sweetie. It matters who's got a room to herself," the first one said. Her voice reminded me of a twittering parrot.

"My roommate is busy dancing with someone. She is not going back to our apartment. Believe me. I've got more space to entertain, *sweetie*."

"Well, let's let him decide, then," the parrot said rudely.

"All right. You'd better plan to tuck yourself in tonight, because no man has passed me up this year," the other retorted.

"That's because you only offer it up to the ones that are already desperate," the parrot mimicked.

"Shut up, he's on his way over here," she spat.

My stomach boiled. Apart from their degenerate attitudes, something was wrong with them. I especially sensed a fetid ambiance from the parrot-like woman, as if she were diseased. Their moral decadence seemed to be reflected in their health. I wondered if the excessive makeup and perfume were meant to hide signs of physical decay. I eyed them carefully, scanning their exposed skin for infection. The dim lighting of the ballroom, however, did not allow for an accurate evaluation.

When Ocelot returned to sit between them, the birds pretended their conversation never took place. They smiled and flirted. They gossiped about their dancing friends. They scanned the room for the second girl's roommate, but both she and her partner were gone.

272

"Oh, she always leaves with somebody," one said.

"They probably ran off to his place to party one-on-one," the other said in a coy tone.

The first girl gave Ocelot a sultry look. "Mmm. I wish someone would invite *me* to a party like that," she said.

Ocelot raised his eyebrows.

She smiled seductively and placed her hand on his thigh. He lifted her hand back to the table.

"You know I have some friends here I have to take care of," he reminded her.

"Well, take care of them and let's go," she encouraged him in a heightened whisper.

"Or you could go with me," her rival interrupted. "I'm going out for a drink in a minute. You wouldn't want me to drink alone, would you? Then we could go back to my place."

My esophagus burned.

I watched with nausea as Ocelot put his arms around both of them. "Why don't we all go out for a drink? We don't have to split up, do we?"

The girls gasped and giggled with delight. The parrot's eyes gleamed wickedly.

I excused myself. I walked carefully to the restroom where I regurgitated my entire dinner. Instead of feeling better afterwards, I felt the same. I washed my face with cold water. I drank from the tap in the sink. I faced myself in the mirror. I looked as bad as I felt. My lips were pale, my face blotchy, my eyes strained with redness.

I had to get Ocelot away from those women. I didn't care why anymore. I would break their painted faces if necessary, but they had to go.

I leaned with my hands against the wall and breathed deeply a few times to try to compose myself. I stood jauntily. I shook out my arms and rolled my head. I marched out of the restroom and back toward the reception room.

As I left the hallway, I saw Wilbaht standing akimbo by our table waiting for me. The rest of them had left. I panicked. I ran to Wilbaht.

"How long ago did they leave?" I asked him.

"Just a minute ago. Are you all right?" he asked.

"No. I've got to stop them," I said, changing directions.

I dashed toward the exit and the elevators. The doors were just closing on Ocelot and his brood. I flew wildly to stop them. I reached the metal slabs and wrenched them apart with a grunt. The three of them started in surprise. I didn't hesitate to grab Ocelot by the collar. I yanked him out of the elevator. He stumbled out, stupefied. Before he could ask what I thought I was doing, I spoke to him in a commanding voice.

273

"I have to talk to you. Official warrior business. It can't wait." I looked him in the eye, communicating my urgency.

"Uh, okay. Girls, I'll meet you downstairs. I'll be just a minute," he assured them.

They oohed at his apparent importance and then pouted and posed for him. The most forward of the two winked at him and blew him a kiss. He winked back and waved absurdly. The elevator doors closed before them.

"This had better be important," Ocelot hissed.

"Ocelot, you're in serious danger. My senses have been going crazy all evening. Those girls—there's something wrong with them. I heard them talking while you were away from the table. They only want you for sex and then afterwards, I don't know. Maybe they mean you some kind of harm. They don't really care about you. And they may be diseased."

"What?" Ocelot balked.

"Listen, I just threw up because I have such a strong feeling against them. They are not your friends," I argued.

"Of course they're not. I hadn't heard from them in ten years. But they're not diseased. I could tell if they were. What harm could they do to me? Even if they were plotting to kill me, which they're not, I can handle myself against two skinny girls. What's your problem?"

"I can't let you go with them," I stated.

He balked again. "Wha...? I can't even enjoy a day's leave without your criticism! Get off my back, Sil! This is none of your business. You stay away from me. I don't want to see or hear from you for the next three days. You will not ruin my leave time. You already screwed it up once. In fact, you've screwed up a lot of things lately. All you do is cause problems and then act like it wasn't you. Klib was right on the money about that." He returned to the elevator door and pushed the button to enter.

I stepped after him. "No. I'm not trying to ruin your leave time. I'm trying to help you."

"I don't need your help. Help with what? Dating advice? Get the hell away from me."

Desperately, I grabbed him by the arm. "Yes, advice, just like the advice you gave me. Remember when we were on Santer, when Alaban was with us? You told me not to sleep with him. You sensed he'd been with a lot of concubines. What you're about to do is worse. At least if they were concubines, they would by tagged for medical history. With these girls, you have no way to track their immunological patterns. You don't know whom they've been with or what they've contracted. You can't pretend you're immune just because you're medical."

He pulled my hand off of his arm as if it were made of slime. He stepped into the elevator, standing in the doorway to try and keep me from following him.

"I remember Santer. You didn't take my advice. You slept with the man anyway." He informed me frankly, "You ignored me. Now I'm ignoring you. Get lost." He retracted his arm to step in and select the ground floor.

I elbowed my way in before the doors closed. He threw his hands up in frustration.

"That's entirely different," I insisted. "Alaban and I love each other. You don't love either of those women. Besides, Alaban was clean. What I'm telling you now doesn't begin to compare with that."

"You made the comparison."

"You missed the point. Their stupidity is rubbing off on you! I'm warning you, as your partner, that you can't trust them. Listen to me. I feel deeply that you should not go with them, Ocelot, please."

I stood solemnly. The doors of the elevator slid open to reveal the two birds posing languidly around each other. Ocelot looked to them and then me.

"You've said what you wanted to say. Now go back with Wilbaht. I don't want to know you exist until we take off. Stay as far away from me as humanly possible. That's an order," he said.

He stepped out to throw his arms around his females and did not look back. The girls flirted excitedly with him. He responded with a proud, willing smile. The flirtatious group made its way to the cab stands outside. The elevator doors closed. I hung like a scarecrow ignored by the crows.

The elevator box rose again to collect Wilbaht. He stepped in quietly. He stared at me, but neither of us spoke until we had left the building.

"It is difficult to help a man with advice if he does not wish to be helped," he advised. "I'm afraid you've learned a poor lesson observing this particular group of humans. You represent one end of the human spectrum. I believe Ocelot's acquaintances represent the other end. Sadly, it seems he's taken advantage of their lack of moral and intellectual value." Wilbaht cleared his throat. "On the other hand, he has the right to enjoy personal freedoms without reprimand. I trust he is capable of taking care of himself. As long as he is not involved with anything publicly unbecoming to a warrior, we must respect his personal decisions."

I disliked Wilbaht's statement, but bowed to him in agreement.

We took a cab back to the Center. Wilbaht said he was not tired. He invited me to a game of chess. I took him up on the offer. We sat in the floor of his room with a virtual chessboard between us. We played the first ten moves quickly and then slowed.

He asked me if I'd heard from Alaban. I told him yes, but I hadn't learned of his escape to Jawlcheen yet. I openly told Wilbaht about the feeling I had of Alaban's presence in my heart. He asked me details about this feeling. I explained. He said he had heard of this kind of extrasensory closeness before. The bearers of this sense were called spiritual twins.

"Some of the old texts say the spiritual twin is one spirit split between two bodies. Some say they are celestial twins," he informed me.

"Yes, I believe that. I feel as if he were really a tangible part of my being," I said. "Sir, do these spiritual twins ever become lifelong mates?"

"I've only read of a few cases, but some have, yes. They seem quite successful. However, I also I remember reading of one couple who produced children with birth defects. One was blind and the other had a syndrome in which he felt no pain. Both children met with an early death. It was a strange case."

I frowned at the story.

The hour grew late. I didn't concentrate well on the chess game. Wilbaht won easily. I congratulated him. Then I said goodnight and went back to my quarters. Before I entered, I observed the door to Ocelot's empty room and wondered about him. Every stop we'd made since Sor3 had shed light on a different side to his personality, each facet less appealing than the one before it. Although earlier in our journey I had set aside the distrust I'd first perceived about him, the feeling had returned often, sloppily painting him as an unpredictable boor. I went to bed, shutting out the notion of his moral inequities. I meditated instead on my spirit's twin, content to have a more specific name for our connection.

The next morning after breakfast, Wilbaht's granddaughter, Olimbi, arrived at the Center. She was a welcome sight for both of us. She wore a long, sleeveless dress that flowed around her gracefully as she moved. She was nearly as tall as Wilbaht, and more lithe. Her skin was a lighter gray than her grandfather's, but her facial features showed the family resemblance.

"Granddaddy," she cried when she saw him. She showed a bright smile as they embraced. Their family love shone on them.

Olimbi and I greeted each other warmly. We bonded instantly.

The three of us spent the day together. I forgot all negativity. We went to the ship to show Olimbi where we'd been for the last six months. She met Klib, but was unimpressed with him. This delighted me.

In the afternoon, we strolled around the city in good conversation. We found the marketplace we had perused the day before. Olimbi and I stopped at many booths of women's apparel. Wilbaht suggested perhaps he should let the two of us shop alone for a while. He offered to meet us at the Center for an evening meal.

We enjoyed each other's company so much that we chattered and giggled almost as badly as the four twits I tried to forget from the night before. We walked the entire length of the market. Then we turned to walk up a broad street, directing ourselves toward the Center. About halfway up the hill, we found a spa and health center for women only. Olimbi convinced me to go in with her. The price of entry was very expensive, but we decided we could afford to splurge this once.

Inside, we were given white robes and a locker to store our clothes. We changed self-consciously among a couple of other women. Then we sat ten minutes in the sauna. Next we ran quickly into the cold room and shivered together. Steam rolled off our bodies as we danced about and giggled in the freezing room. After this, we went to the warm communal bath. It was funny to see so many human and Lizard females, old and young, lounging around completely naked. There were also a couple of Vermilion women and an old yellowed Grey in the wide bath pool. We shyly hung up our robes and joined them. Light conversation wafted among the bathers. The atmosphere was casual and calm.

Olimbi asked me about Alaban, since Wilbaht had mentioned that I might want to talk about him. I explained in general terms the whole convoluted story to her. She understood my dilemma and encouraged me sympathetically not to give up. She believed everything would work out for the best. She also asked about the Fitmalos, but I had to say most of that information was classified. I did mention my disagreement with their common law plan. She sided with me vehemently.

I learned that Olimbi worked at organizing corporate donations to community improvement projects. She said only a few Fitmalo-based companies ever participated in charitable donations, and these corporations demanded tax reduction documentation before they went through with the deal. She said she didn't want to offend anyone, but she considered the Fitmalo society to be viciously competitive and greedy. Jawlcheen was more attuned to cultural needs, although the Fitmalo infiltration into their business sector had tainted the planet's moral balance in recent years. Not that the Vermilion people of Jawlcheen would ever admit to taking cues from the Fitmalos. They attributed the changes to the natural progression of economy.

All species harbored a level of pride in their own ethnicities, but the Fitmalos and the Vermilions were among the proudest. Each was an opposite to the other. Vermilions were strong, tall, four-armed people. The Fitmalos were short, slender and catlike. Even the colors of their skins were opposites. The Fitmalos were blue-skinned. The Vermilions were orange. They had worked and traded together for more than a millennium without significant conflict. But animosity had expanded over the years, especially recently with the proposal to unite their helion in common law. Whether the law would be adopted by both parties or not, I anticipated a problematic decade ahead for both races. Olimbi agreed.

After a two-hour conversation, we dried and redressed ourselves. The hostess gave us preserved flower strings for our hair as we left.

We walked out into the street feeling young and pampered. The hill seemed less steep, the day less humid, and the city less crowded. Olimbi walked with her elbow on my shoulder as a playful gesture of friendship. Our gait was quick and light. We eagerly headed for her grandfather.

We had nearly cleared the top of the mountain pass when a bundle of flowers ran into us. We stepped aside. A traveling warrior bent down to pick up the flowers. When he stood, I realized it was Ocelot. His face showed a lack of sleep. My peaceful feeling vanished. He regarded me with disdain. He peered up at Olimbi and apologized to her. I half-heartedly introduced the two. Ocelot bunched the flowers into his left arm to shake hands with her.

"Oh, I'm very sorry, miss. It's a real honor to work with your grandfather. I'm sure you're very proud of him," he said.

"It's all right. Yes, we're all proud of him. He's told me a lot about you. Who's the lucky lady?" Olimbi asked with a grin. She eyed the flowers.

"Uh, they're for some friends of mine," he said. "It was an honor to meet you."

She returned the salutation. He brushed past me hastily. I shook my head. Olimbi noticed the friction between us. She asked me about it. I explained last night's fiasco. She was even more appalled than I was, especially since Torreons never kiss in public.

We quickly abandoned this disturbing topic to discuss lighter subjects. We spent the rest of the afternoon hiking along a tourist trail with Wilbaht, who directed the conversation cordially. The grandfather and granddaughter had much to discuss regarding family memories and personal projects. Olimbi politely explained her relationship to each family member they mentioned and gave me a brief description of them so I would not feel left out. I appreciated her kindness.

Later in the evening, during our meal with Wilbaht, Olimbi asked him what he thought about last night's incident with Ocelot. Wilbaht grew stern.

"Each of us suffers from our own personality flaws, neuroses, and so on. Ocelot is no exception. I'm alluding not only to his choice of company. Ocelot happens to have a bad habit of holding a grudge. He bottles up anger, then tries to rationalize it." Wilbaht cut into his meal. "He turns it into bad judgment and aggression. On Santer, for example, he was angry with me for punishing him, which incidentally, I did because of another outbreak of his anger." Wilbaht paused to chew his food, angling his swimming blue eyes at me. "So he resented even more the way you and Alaban flaunted your relationship in front of him. In his egocentric perception, he felt you were making fun of him. He was punished and alone and you were not." He paused again to chew and swallow. "I believe he meant to return the insult to you, twofold, last night. Upon reflection, I doubt he would go as far as to lose his senses and mate with such obviously unclean women. I believe he merely used them to set the scene. Although I could be wrong." He muttered calculations of an average human male's hormonal influence on the brain during simulated mating proposals and flirting rituals based on studies he'd seen in a recent Torreonoid physiological journal, but added that Ocelot was not an average, but rather an exceptional intellect, which would alter the parameters for possible error of the study. He began to figure in the likelihood of available protective measures and how this might have swayed his decision. He stabbed another morsel and popped it into his mouth.

"If he held a grudge, why didn't he complain about it before? The only thing he's complained about to me recently is my attitude." I frowned. "He shouldn't turn vindictive all of a sudden, especially not so recklessly."

"True. However, some people would rather lash out recklessly than expose an emotional weakness. He would never admit that you'd hurt his feelings. He wants to appear stronger than you because of rank and gender. All of us in this business are in the habit of projecting a tough image of ourselves to others. At my age, I know well that being tough in adhering to what is right is worth much more than trying to convince others that you're right by acting tough." He winked and nodded at the saying. "In any case, Ocelot's actions should not have caused an argument between the two of you. Now, this is something I have considered deeply. In light of the constant banter I've witnessed between you, I believe a larger problem exists. Even without Klib's influence, the two of you have been sporadically conflictive, almost like young siblings. I've made a decision. If one more significant conflict occurs between any of you, I'm sending in an official reprimand."

"Sir?" I asked in shock. Olimbi blinked at me questioningly.

An official reprimand meant no promotion for an additional year. It also meant conditional suspension. Wilbaht would have to report on our behavior once a month to General Black. Any bad reports would result in an automatic two-month suspension without pay.

279

"You fought with each other on Sor4. You argued incorrigibly on Santer, en route to this solar system, on Karnesh, and now on Jain," he said, counting on his fingers. "Those are five significant instances despite my warnings. I would be within my right to reprimand you just for disobeying orders."

"But sir, most of those were not my fault. You can't blame me for getting angry about the videotape," I argued.

"You physically attacked your crewmates," he countered.

"Well, yes, I forgot about that. But Sor4 was a misunderstanding I had no control over," I said.

"Yes, that's true, but..." he began.

"And on Santer, Ocelot got angry with me for spilling his photos while I was getting his things ready to pack, which *you* told me to do," I continued.

"Perhaps, but..."

"And now I was only trying to protect him and he fought me about it," I stated.

"Stop!" he thundered.

Olimbi and I and the people around us jumped. A waiter near our table asked if everything was all right.

"Yes, yes. I apologize for the disruption," Wilbaht told him. The waiter left.

"Sil, I cannot punish one without the other. It doesn't matter who initiated the arguments or on what pretense. He might have begun these arguments, but you continued them rashly. You must learn when to stand your ground and when to let go," he explained. He said if Ocelot's biggest flaw was mishandling bottled anger, mine was becoming overly defensive and outspoken when I felt I'd been wronged.

I considered this a while. I had to admit he was right. I agreed to try to remain neutral with Ocelot in the future, or at least to keep my head whenever he angered me. Wilbaht encouraged me, saying that one of my noted strengths was humble honor of reason and morality. He urged me to hold onto this virtue. He added that this was a trait he admired in his granddaughter as well. Olimbi smiled gratefully.

In the evening, we said goodbye to Olimbi. We promised to write each other often. The grandfather and granddaughter hugged. Wilbaht swayed her back and forth as he probably had when she was a little girl. I wished her luck.

Back at our quarters, late in the night, I heard Ocelot's door open and close. Finally he had returned to sleep in his own room. Guilt ticked at me for making him think I'd brushed off his advice on Santer. Now I had asked him to beware. Of course he had to remind me of my heedlessness. I turned in my bed, remembering Wilbaht's words and contemplating morality. Soothing nuances of Alaban's life interrupted these thoughts to drift me off to sleep.

Chapter 27: Mixed Messages on the Long Haul through Space

The next morning we were back on the job again. Wilbaht asked us to put off preflight and inventory until after the ship had a good cleaning. We cleaned, threw out garbage, and repaired simple mechanical parts, like the hydraulic door mechanism on the main cargo hold. The sandstorm on Karnesh had done a job on our ship's paint. I hardly needed to scrub away the excess before priming to add a new coat. I used our auto paint robot to fill in the final coating of paint. It slid quietly up and down the sides of the ship, spraying and baking on the enamel. By the end of the afternoon, our ship looked brand new.

At 1700 hours, we began preflight checks of instruments, fuel, water, life support and so on. After only a few checks, we broke for a meeting.

Wilbaht informed us that we didn't have a definite mission yet. Our mission would be announced between the first and second space folds. General Black had merely ordered us to set course for the Soren helion. We were scheduled for takeoff in twenty-seven hours. The bad news for me was that Yinore would not be replaced. I would have no female companion on this journey. If it hadn't been for Wilbaht's comforting presence, I would have slumped into an abysmal depression.

I didn't believe we were actually bound for any of the Soren planets. Even if we had been, this journey would take nearly four months. The maximum travel time for a ship this size was six months, but no one ever wanted to travel under such strenuous time conditions. Water usage would be strictly limited. Power would be conserved more than before. Lighting and gravity projectors would be turned off in intervals. Solar power between helions would be compensated with landing fuel and waste reclaim fuel. The length of the voyage itself would be dangerous.

Wilbaht and Ocelot worked out a plan for emergency extended flight time of five months just in case. We brought in live plants to help produce oxygen, since the reliability of our life support system decreased significantly after ninety days of constant use. Using estimates, we devised a strategy to lighten our load in order to bring in extra water and plant life.

This was bad news for Klib, who had to give up nearly his entire case of ale that he'd won from Ocelot. He shared a bottle of it with us at dinner to enjoy some of it before he had to let it go. He then took the case to the air tower where he sold it to someone. He only kept four bottles for himself.

Ocelot took charge of collecting plants and their necessities for the ship. I picked through our inventory to check for unnecessary surplus of any kind. I calculated the discard weight as slightly under what was needed. Klib relinquished one more bottle of ale. He proposed a party to get rid of it.

The four of us sat outside around a band light as if it were a campfire. Klib offered the ale all around. I drank very little. Klib took my second and third portion for himself. We discussed assignment possibilities. I didn't mention Alaban's premonition about meeting on Jawlcheen, but I felt we were headed that way.

Wilbaht rose, saying he had some messaging to do before bed. Normally I would have gone in with him, but I wanted to take in the planetary atmosphere a little longer. Who knew when we would have the opportunity to breathe real air again?

Klib asked Ocelot if he'd gone out with any pretty girls on his leave time. Ocelot gave him a watered-down account of the wedding party. He told him how the girls had competed for him. Klib called him a lucky son of a bitch. Ocelot bragged that he'd gone home with two.

Klib hooted. "How come you didn't bring them over here? You had ladies to spare. You could have shared the extra one."

"Sorry, Klib. You were the last person on my mind at the time, if you know what I mean," Ocelot said.

"And that's a good thing," Klib admitted with a pout. "But man, I could have used the company. Damn."

"Those girls were diseased. I could sense it," I said to him impulsively. I stopped, checking my behavior, as Wilbaht had advised.

Ocelot gulped down the rest of the ale from his glass and stared at me cynically. "You really think I'll be infected."

This time I kept my voice and temper even. I thought of the best way to answer. "I pray you won't be. I do care about your welfare. You're my partner."

"Tsk. Don't be so dramatic," he complained.

I stood with resolution. "I'm not staying here to fight with you. Didn't Wilbaht tell you what he'd do if we fight anymore?"

He had not. I told him.

"An *official* reprimand?" His glass stopped centimeters from his lips.

"No shit?" asked Klib sincerely.

"I'm going in. Thanks for the drink," I said in a melancholic voice. I left the two undesirables there in the thick humidity, hoping this would be the last discussion we'd have for a long time.

Twenty-one hours later, the interior of our ship looked like a hotel decorated with tropical plants. We set up containment nets all along the walls of the middle and lower levels of the ship to hold the plants in their soil and hydroponics bags. Some of these plants would produce fruit in about two months. I looked forward to fresh food on board for once. The presence of plants would also help ease our stress levels after long months of space travel.

Our takeoff went as normal. I was sorry to see the planets shrink in my screens as we shuttled away from the Keres helion. The crew kept the conversation to business only. In a way, it was good to hear statistical readouts and constant status reports. It was certainly better than arguing about personal ethics, or the lack of them.

As soon as I had time, I checked for messages from Alaban. There was only one. He and the Reaper crew had arrived safely on Jawlcheen. His new contact general had given them all an extra day of leave time, but Alaban had to undergo twelve grueling hours of interrogation.

The Center where he had been held hostage was now under Fitmalo military control. Fitmalo rebel groups had supposedly been linked to the Center. The military took over investigations due to suspicion of possible terrorist plans. They did not accuse our Organization of harboring terrorists. They only stated that they suspected the rebels had infiltrated the Center and they were there to weed them out. This also explained away the temporary ship arrest. Swall Jade had supposedly cooperated with Fitmalo authorities to allow a search of all the ships on the field. However, even he had been moved out of that Center and into another on the opposite hemisphere.

Prime Minister Lock had less than a year and a half left in office. This was our timetable to stop the Regime officials from gaining too much power. However, if they successfully overtook other Centers on their planet, we would have less leeway to curtail their plans. We would practically be shut out. I wondered who the criminal was that Alaban had been forced to help escape on Fitmalo. He may have been one of the Regime officials or he may have been a resource. I looked up a few pages of arrests from Fitmalo-based Centers to try and ID the man, but much of the information was classified. I would have to ask Wilbaht to help me with this.

Since Klib and Ocelot were still being punished and had to do my cleaning duties for at least the next few weeks, I would have plenty of time to work on research for our ongoing investigation of the Regime, and more time to spend with Wilbaht. Unfortunately, I was also punished. I couldn't use the exercise room for ten days. I had to do exercise in the limited space of one of the cargo holds or pushups at my bunk.

I messaged both Alaban and my family about my meeting with Olimbi and about the beauty of Jain. I also messaged Yalat, who I'd not heard from for a long time. Knowing her, she was probably off snooping around for information on the same investigation we were working on.

I received a new message from Alaban. It contained a picture of a flower. He had remembered my birthday. He sent me a long string of compliments and love poems.

I also received birthday wishes from an unknown person. The message simply read, "Happy birthday, Sil. From: Anonymous." I checked the sourced of the message. It came from the Organization main board on Sor3. I thought of all the people who knew me by name in the Soren helion. There were many. I wondered if it was an old acquaintance or if it could be some kind of trick. Since we were still in a safe messaging area and the note would go directly to the main message board, I decided to reply, thanking the person and asking to know his or her identity.

The next day I received birthday wishes from my family. Each of my sisters wrote me a short message. My parents each wrote a page of loving memories, news, and advice. Even my older brother, Blen, who I hadn't seen for years, sent me a short message. My older sister, Tamia, and her husband, Jem, were expecting a baby. I would have a niece or nephew within the year. Grace's skills in aerospace engineering and mathematics had won her top student of her class. My father planned on opening a second school for exceptional students. All my sisters volunteered to help. I wished I could help them, too, but even if I were stationed on Liricos, my time with them would be limited.

My mother wrote a letter full of sweet memories. She said she would love to see me again and asked if I could visit any time soon. I told her I would try to be there after my contract year ended. It would be wonderful to feel like part of the family once more. Mother mentioned Tambuo and asked if I ever practiced the old traditions she had taught me.

She reminded me that each dance had a spiritual message. Each represented a different stage of life. She told me she was practicing the dance of winter. She was feeling old. I reminded her that she was not yet sixty and she had a long life ahead of her, and that she was still so pretty and slim. I sent her a picture of myself in my Tambuo outfit so she could see that I hadn't forgotten. This would warm her heart.

After our communal meal, Wilbaht asked me to work with him in the lower observation deck. This was his personal time before sleeping, and my regular cleaning time. He enclosed us in the little room and spoke as if he were about to tell a delightful secret. He told me he'd like to work with me on honing our skills as seers and levitators. I was flattered. He asked if I received visions during meditation. I explained I usually tended to see my immediate vicinity and that I did not predict or far see during routine meditations. He then asked me to describe how my flash visions appeared to me. I told him the ones I understood best normally appeared before me as if they were real. I then explained the approaching shards as pieces of a broken mirror flying at me from some other dimension.

He responded with interest. His visions were presented to him in a very different way. He felt as though he'd stepped half a meter out of his body into the scene he was meant to witness.

"It's fascinating to know all the different manifestations of premonitions and visions. I've worked with many visionary warriors over the years. Few seem to see with such clarity as I do, but I think you have great potential. Your visions of the spider on Sor3, for example, helped prepare you to face the real animal. Your recent vision of the Fitmalo army will help you prepare to face battle." His swimming pupils examined my face. "You are a gifted seer, but you are much more than that."

His aura changed from casual to intense.

"You are a piece of a puzzle I've been trying to solve for some time. That is why I arranged to have you assigned to my crew," he revealed.

I was taken aback. I'd had no idea he'd requested me. I hadn't even imagined that he knew who I was before we were on Sor3.

His gray cheeks turned blue with purpose. "I had several visions of you before we met. Divine guidance directed me to find you. I told you on Sor3 that my brothers and I healed you because your survival would be important to many people in the future. I did not speak hypothetically. I knew." He smiled warmly. "You didn't really think someone with my credentials would be doing a job like this routinely, did you?"

I stared at him in awe. "Why me, sir?"

He chuckled and patted me heavily on one knee. He reclined in his chair, resuming his relaxed manner. "The entire tide of life sometimes turns on the axis of one grain of sand. We all live and die in a multiplicity of ways. When too many die at once, our balance is lost. Then suffering occurs in all beings. Part of our job as peacekeepers, as well as seers, is to help insure that this imbalance never takes place. You and I are a part of that great mission. It is a considerable responsibility. It is an even greater honor to be tapped by the hand of God. Of course, we ourselves are not special. We were merely given a very special gift."

I remained amazed. Wilbaht continued.

"I have been observing you, Sil. You've faced an unusual array of adversity during this journey. I believe you've reached a level of self-control necessary to begin higher training. You still have much to learn, but I see you have finally gained control of your impulsive reactions to offensive speech. I watched you while I was in meditation during your talk with Ocelot and Klib just before we left Jain. You controlled your temper. I am pleased. I want you to put their actions out of your mind completely. I will be dealing with Ocelot holistically during our time together upstairs and in the exercise room. Klib, on the other hand, is not so open-minded to change, as a warrior would be. It will be best to continue a distanced and formal relationship with him. I would have intervened earlier, but I wanted to give you time to realize the potential dangers of your personal conflicts on your own. Rise above them. They are insignificant in comparison with the serious dangers we will soon face."

"Yes, sir. I promise you won't have any more problems with me, sir. What should I do first?" I asked anxiously.

"First, you must improve your visionary talent." He directed me to focus more clearly before meditating. He guided me through an exercise to help me enter visionary sight more deeply. This hypnotic instruction opened my eyes to a new perspective. As our time ended in this first session, I reflected upon all he had told me. I thought of the times I'd behaved below his expectations. Most of those instances, I realized, involved Ocelot. I asked my leader if I should apologize to him to rectify my misbehavior. Wilbaht suggested an apology for the general misunderstandings and a promise to adhere to strict formality, but warned me not to lay blame on myself or on him for any specific argument, as this would lead to further disagreements.

"Demonstrate to him a forgiving manner, humility. Don't feel too remorseful for your errors. None of us is immune to our own foolishness. Even the highest intellect will react irrationally from time to time. There are no saints here, but we can learn from our mistakes and move on. That is what I would like us all to do."

I took his speech to heart. At my time to share the upper deck with Ocelot, I approached him directly. He twisted in his chair. His face indicated wariness of another argument.

"What now, Sil? Are you ready to pick apart the rest of my morals? What shouldn't I be allowed to do this time? Breathe more than my share of oxygen?" he spoke flatly.

I looked down at the floor. I took a deep breath and then faced him. "I want to apologize for my behavior. I'm sorry for my defensive attitude…and my rudeness with you. I am not here to criticize you. My purpose is to serve as backup for you and Wilbaht as a well-disciplined warrior. I apologize for straying from that purpose. It will not happen again." I bowed my head. "I ask your permission to address you by your title instead of your name to help me remember my place here in this crew. Will you accept this, sir?" I waited for his response.

Ocelot considered my unexpected proposal. "All right. You'll call me by my title and act accordingly."

"Yes, sir," I said to him. It felt unusual calling him this once more. I only needed to get used to the idea. Soon it would become second nature.

"Carry on," he ordered.

"Yes, sir," I repeated, returning to my seat.

We spoke to each other about instrument readouts and ways to care for the tropical plants. Personal information and emotions no longer had a place in this setting. We were neither friends nor enemies. We were simply coworkers.

Wilbaht and I worked on levitation in the main cargo hold. I showed him how I passed one object through the other. After five examples, he tried one. He lifted a coil of life cord and a band light. He brought them together and concentrated very hard for several minutes. He managed to meld them together, but did not pass the cord through the light. The end result was a fairly useless abstraction. Wilbaht set the object down. Exhausted, he was pleased with his accomplishment even though he had not completed the pass. I completed it for him.

After this exercise, we worked on a meditation technique. Wilbaht asked me to concentrate on a point in the ship away from myself, instead of using my own body as the center of my meditation. This was difficult at first, but I learned greatly from the exercise. During the next few days, Wilbaht and I made slow, steady progress on both levitation and visualization. Our time together was enriching to us both.

During these first weeks back on flight, I received several typical messages from Alaban. He was under no threat at this time. I felt relieved for him. Yalat messaged me, but her letter was somewhat dull. She did not inform me of her research, although I had asked about it. My mother began to message me more than she had previously. She seemed very emotional in her letters.

I also continued receiving messages from my anonymous friend. Message two read, "I'd rather not tell you who I am yet, but I'll give you a hint. I saw you here on Sor3. I know about your accident in the Public Valley. I was afraid you would leave us forever. I'm glad you didn't. I cared for you that day as if you were my own sister."

I thought of all the people I knew who had a sister they might compare me with. Jiao had a sister I'd never met. We had been on our way to meet her when Trau was assassinated. I assumed it had to be him.

I wrote back: "I'm flattered by your attention. I never did meet your sister, but I would like to some day. Best wishes to your family."

I remembered Jiao and the airbus crash. I remembered how I'd felt when I saw Trau and his escort board the airbus. The assassins were probably observing the airfield traffic, waiting for him. Or were they? I suddenly hit upon an idea. What if the airbus company had more than an agreement with the Organization to transport warriors to and from the C.A.T.T. Center? What if they had a secret schedule for on-duty armed warriors, with possible prisoner escorts, to accommodate them on exclusive aircraft or on airbuses with the least amount of passengers? It would be a rotating schedule to avoid predictability. Someone outside the Organization could have tapped into the company's computer system to find out the schedule and plan for an attack at the right place and time.

I recalled the satellite recording we'd analyzed of the Public Valley during the day of the airbus crash. The Zhorn missile used to bring us down had been fired from the top of a building by hooded henchmen, (one a Mantis, the other an Arborman), perfectly positioned for the strike. They had disappeared through the office building as soon as the missile was fired. All record of their existence within the building, on the street, and on the planet, for that matter, had been negated. Someone in the Organization knew all: someone purposefully hiding it from us.

I asked Wilbaht permission use his pass code to research the possible secret schedule. He obliged. I discovered it did exist, both on the airbus company database as well as the Organization's transport record. Encouraged, I read through the list of transportation from the C.A.T.T. interrogation department for the days surrounding the crash. I then traced the systems access log to find out who else had researched the same information. I discovered that another warrior, now reported as deceased, had researched this schedule two days before the crash. I pored through his file excitedly, anxious to find one of our suspects connected to him.

After days of research, I found the link. The warrior's work report included numerous bodyguarding assignments, several of which were for former Fitmalo General Zar. He had to have been involved in Trau's assassination. This was proof. Now I needed to find out why.

I shared the information with Wilbaht. He congratulated me on my insight. We considered a few possibilities. If Zar was in fact, behind the assassination, that would mean Trau had somehow been connected to his Fitmalo military rebel group. We knew Trau had served as bodyguard for Zar several years before the assassination, when Zar was still with the Fitmalo cabinet. Trau may have formed some kind of allegiance with Zar during that time. Zar may have wanted Trau dead because he switched loyalties to work with the Regime and Viga. However, a sloppy public assassination seemed too bold and untimely for that motivation.

Trau had, after all, been working with Viga for some years. He'd had no noted contact with Zar since Zar declared his insurgence and proposed to head the Fitmalo military rebels. Trau could not have been a regular cohort of General Zar since he was exiled from Fitmalo. There had to be some other conundrum Trau was involved in to make Zar want him dead. Perhaps some unfinished business? A broken promise? A smuggled weapons sale gone wrong? Something bigger? The spider gurgled in my memory. The assassination of the official on the twentieth floor, the science lab, the biological weapon, the meeting of military scientists, the microship; they all had to fit together. But how? This was the question I'd lived with and researched for nearly seven months.

Of all the reports we had sent to General Black: smuggling information, leads on Fitmalo rebels and Regime affiliates, their military and corporate dealings; none of these had yielded the answers to the questions surrounding the Sor3 incident. Now I had found evidence pointing to General Zar as the conductor of Trau's assassination. But why? And whom else had he targeted?

Zar's military rebels had kept out of the public eye since the incident occurred. Likewise, Viga's smuggling operation in the Soren helion had continued quietly. The Organization knew about them, but did not move against them. Officials involved in the case were either taking bribes to keep the trade open or were involved in the operation itself.

Any of these people could have been enlaced in the mystery of the biological weapon the twentieth floor. Who had it now? What did they propose to do with it? Did the weapon exist in physical form or was it only a formulary recipe? Where was it now? We had been unable to find any record of it. Even Wilbaht's level of clearance was useless in tracking top-secret dealings in the military branch. We would have to investigate secondary evidence that might lead to the priceless data. Like my hunch about the airbus schedule, I believed we could find some gradual, roundabout pathway to evidence surrounding the case. We had to solve the mystery and find the weapon before it could be put to use. Time was counting down and we were still far from a solution.

After my ten days without the exercise room, I returned to it gratefully. I expressed my relief and gratitude to Wilbaht. I told him it would be important for us to start training harder now. An affront with Fitmalo military awaited us in the near future. His guidance in my meditative visions had brought clarity to the timing of the upcoming event. I now held no doubt that the confrontation would occur at the end of this flight. He confirmed my anticipation. He had seen a vision of our Fitmalo battle as well. We compared them. Wilbaht had not seen any Fitmalo execution assembly. He had, however, envisioned Fitmalo soldiers in a hangar of some sort. He had also seen multiple endings to our battle, the fact of which only led us to prayer and more meditation.

One other thing about both our visions disturbed us. Wilbaht himself was not present in them. We were not sure why. We did not sense that he was dead. We wondered how he might be otherwise occupied during our fight.

All this considered, Wilbaht approached Ocelot and me after our next communal meal. He asked us to please recommence sparring and training time during Ocelot's exercise hours. He also used his rank and authority to go against Organization policy and lift the ban on sword practice on the ship. He told us to keep the swords hidden from Klib and only use them in the exercise room while the door was locked. He reminded us both of the safety hazards. We acknowledged them. We all knew now that a battle was eminent.

We had to make the training as realistic as possible and also come up with a few team tactics we had not previously needed. Ocelot had to loosen his rules about no physical contact during mock sparring. This would have to look and feel like the real thing. He proposed that we spar hand to hand the first half of the hour and then practice sword forms and tactics during the second half of the hour. I proposed we spend even more time than that, even though I would lose time for my cleaning duty. We even used some of our time on the upper deck to do a few simple close-quarters grappling techniques. We became obsessed with the training. It became our primary topic of conversation at any hour.

During this time, my anonymous friend continued to message me. Message three read, "It seems you've guessed my identity, but you didn't use my name. Some of the information you gave tells me you think I'm someone I'm not. I'll give you another clue: I've witnessed your levitative power."

I was beginning to enjoy this simple game. I saw no harm in it. As long as this person was Jiao or someone I knew and as long as I kept the information to a minimum, this would be an innocent correspondence.

I replied, "I believe you were on my committee at my testing on Sor3. Am I right? If so, I think you are a good, intelligent man. Give me some more clues so I can be absolutely sure. Tell your sister hello for me."

In the days that followed, Wilbaht helped us with concepts of scope of physical awareness in battle. He was a great resource, since he had been in a heavy battle on Mercury3 many years ago. He even criticized the historical account of it on the information log. He gave us serious and gruesome details to consider. We found his strategies invaluable. We worked so hard physically and mentally during this period of our flight that a month flew by.

Then my anonymous friend wrote me yet again. Message four read, "I don't have a sister. You guessed wrong."

I was confused. If this person wasn't Jiao, then who could it be? I thought of the others from my testing that would still be on Sor3. There was Pauber, the man who judged the sparring match between Alaban and me. There was Stennet, Jiao's father. Who else was there? It seemed there was a middle-aged man in the group, a Professor Krabach, but I couldn't remember having spoken to him outside testing.

I wrote, "I'm sorry. I don't know who you could be. How old are you? Give me more clues."

The very next day, he responded. I was surprised at the speed of his reply. I wondered if, in fact, the messages were coming from the Sor3 main board or if someone had illegally copied its location code to send it to me from a closer site. My sixth sense toyed with my conscience. I read with suspicion. Message five stated, "I'm older than you. I am human. I invited you somewhere once. After that I was wounded. I went somewhere to heal. Guess who I am."

I thought of Professor Stennet. He was the one who invited Yalat and me to dinner the day of the airbus crash. He was wounded in the arm during the crash. Perhaps he was my anonymous messenger.

I replied in a way that would bait an imposter just in case. "It's too bad the way things turned out on the day we were wounded. Tell your children hello for me. What is your reason for writing to me, sir? Are you interested in trading information about the incident? You know I cannot trust a correspondence like this without encoding or proof of your identity." I eagerly awaited a response, but did not receive one for some time.

Two weeks later, I received a few messages from Alaban, but then his messages stopped abruptly. I sent him five letters. They went unanswered. I wondered what kind of assignment he might be working on that did not permit him to send or receive messages. I decided to be patient, although it was becoming more and more difficult with the passage of time and space travel. I missed him, and yet I still felt his presence deep in my heart. I almost felt he was closer to me now. His essence stayed with me always. I prayed I would see him again before our impending conflict.

We were now about half way to the Soren helion, but still we had not received word about our next assignment or which planet would be our destination. We all had fond memories of Sor3 and Sor4, but we felt we would not see either of those planets for a long time. Klib acted as though he didn't care, as long as we arrived on some planet. He became more fidgety than the rest of us. Wilbaht began to worry about him. He told Ocelot to try and cheer him up while they were together on the upper deck.

I received letter after letter from my mother. Yalat communicated a few times with me, but mostly she gave vague information and blessings. My mother's letters were always sweet. She gave me a glimpse of life back on Liricos with each caring note. I vowed to return home with honor for my family. I longed to see them all again.

My anonymous mystery writer finally replied to me. Message six read, "I don't know who you think I am. I have no children. Here's another vague clue: I am taller than you."

Now I felt acridly suspicious. Maybe this was a trick after all. Maybe this was Alaban writing notes to tease me. Or it could have been someone with a sinister motive.

I wrote, "I don't know who you could be. If you don't reveal your identity, I will not respond anymore. I don't trust you."

The next few messages appeared quickly over the course of just a few days, reinforcing my suspicion that someone was hacking the Sor3 message board mail codes to send these notes to me. I read the next three short notes without responding. I found out from the anonymous person only that he or she was a warrior, and that two letters in the person's first name were I and A. I was ready to give up on the correspondence, but I gave my theory about Jiao one last try. I asked if his first name started with J. He only replied yes. Then I asked point blank if he was Jiao.

The person messaged back, "You don't know who I am. Jiao is too busy tracking weapons to message you. I'm glad you're confused about my identity. Don't worry. I'm on your side. I'll give you a piece of my last name: Nero. I don't think you really want to know who I am. If you did, you would have figured it out already. This was a fun game, but you're not trying hard enough."

Aggravated by this distraction, I looked up warriors who had been on Sor3 during my testing. I researched humans, both male and female, who could have come in contact with me during that time. I came up with a short list of only ten people. Of these, I automatically eliminated Jiao and Stennet. Of the eight remaining possibilities, none of the first names contained the letters my anonymous friend had given me. Frustrated, I erased the list. I finally went to Wilbaht with my predicament. He suggested that I discontinue correspondence with this person immediately. It could have been some kind of scam.

I sent the person one last message and a warning. "Name for me at least seven people we both know by name. I don't mean famous people. I mean acquaintances we both know and work with. If you can't, then you are not who you say you are."

The writer replied, "I give up. You ask too much of me. I will comply with your request, even though I'm sure you'll know who I am. People we know or have worked with are Yinore, Yalat, Wilbaht, Stennet, Klib, Jiao, and Alaban. That's seven, although I probably shouldn't mention the last one. I don't trust him. Truthfully, I despise him. You know who I am. The game is over. Too bad it was so short. We could have played this a long time."

I could only think of one person who would say that about Alaban. I forgot my vow of civility. With absolute repugnance, I wrote back. "You don't measure up to any of the warriors you just mentioned, especially the man you hate, *Ocelot*. And here I thought we had made so much progress. Don't write me anymore. If you have something to say, say it to my face. No more hiding behind childish messages. What was the point of this anyway? Never mind, I don't want to know. You're in for a tough sparring practice today, *sir*."

Shortly after I sent this message, I had to go upstairs to work with the fiend. I shuffled up the stairs. As I stepped onto the deck floor, I stood akimbo, boldly staring at him. I shook my head slowly and gave him a reproachful look. I recommended that he check his messages right away. He questioned me about it, but I only told him I'd cover for him while he did. I flopped into my chair. He observed me suspiciously but didn't ask anymore. He trotted down to the lower observation deck to check it. He did not return to work with me that day.

When Wilbaht arrived on deck, he asked about my mood. I explained the whole guessing game to him. His oily eyes glistened brightly as I summarized the messages. He grinned when I told him about the letters of the first name Ocelot had invented.

"Why would Ocelot make up a lie like that?" I asked.

Chuckling, Wilbaht answered. "He didn't. No one ever said Ocelot was his first name."

"It isn't?" I asked.

Wilbaht laughed loudly. Finally he ended in a heavy giggle. He glanced back at me momentarily and started up all over again. I smiled at him weakly. I wasn't sure what was so funny, but obviously the joke was on me.

"What's so funny, sir?" I asked him.

"Oh. I can't tell you," he said, suddenly feigning seriousness. "I won't give you his name. You'll have to research that yourself. It will do you good. I will give you one piece of advice. Don't reproach a man for his deeds until you know his motives." He beamed with a broad smile. "Did you not consider that perhaps he was trying to make amends with you? Not that he'll be willing to admit it now. Poor soul. I advised him to make subtle improvements with you. Something non-confrontational. Apparently he took my advice to the extremes. Cyber-distance was as removed as he could get. Poor misguided fellow. Always trying to be impersonal. Maybe someday he'll learn a more effective way to be sociable. I'll have a talk with him later."

Dumbfounded and driven by new curiosity, I brought up Organization personnel info. I searched for Ocelot's name. I found it on several different logs, but none mentioned a name other than Ocelot Quoren. Quoren; no wonder he had sent me "nero" as part of his last name. But what was his first name? The only place I was sure would have that information was our main ship's log. The only person allowed to access that was Wilbaht. I didn't dare ask his permission to read through it.

While I sifted through pages of information, Wilbaht began to hum contentedly. He reminded me of Yalat. She used to hum or sing softly on long journeys. When I realized which song it was, I stopped flipping through the information and turned to face him.

"I know that song," I said in surprise.

I paused, closing my eyes to remember. I thought of Yalat's scratchy voice singing the words to me. *"A million tomorrooows have come and gone, and stiiill you sing ooon..."*

Wilbaht asked if I knew all the words to the tune. I admitted I only remembered two lines. He suggested we ask Ocelot about the lyrics. Saying this tickled him once more. He chuckled to himself as he scrolled through the ship's log.

Chapter 28: Mortality

Alaban finally replied to me. He said, "Sil, I miss you even though I feel you here in my heart. I sense we are getting closer physically. You must be near the Thrader helion. I'm here in space, too. We stayed on Jawlcheen a long time. I had hoped I'd see you there. Remember my premonition? Now we are en route to our next assignment. If my sense is right, we'll see each other in a month. We must be heading for the Gold Wind helion, and maybe for the Fitmalos in your vision.

"I dreamed this week that I was in chains in a field and you came to rescue me. Will you be my heroine, Sil? I'll repay the rescue with kisses if you'll let me. I'm confident we'll survive the battle. Maybe afterwards they'll finally let us work together. I'd be content with a nice long leave time to spend with you. I'll see you soon. Practice that left swing and parry. Keep thinking of me. I love you. A."

After reading his letter, I began to worry about our next destination. I hoped we weren't heading for Rybalazar or Xiantalix.

I slept fitfully during the night. I dreamed repeatedly of Alaban and Ocelot killing each other in a sword fight. This dream disturbed my psyche too much. I muddled through the day in an altered state because of it.

I went early to practice sparring with Ocelot as usual, the nightmare still fresh in my mind. I walked into the exercise room sleepily. Ocelot was doing repetitions of a part of personal defense form twenty-nine: the windmill kick ending in a wide stance and a triple palm strike. He stood straight when I entered.

I said good morning to him formally in the usual way. Then I immediately asked him about our pending battle.

"Sir, do you think we could be heading for the Gold Wind helion?" I asked him.

He squinted, perplexed. "Gold Wind?"

"Yes. Do you sense anything about that? Alaban said he thinks he's heading that way and that we might have to fight the Fitmalos there."

"Why would a Fitmalo army be way out in the Gold Wind helion? That doesn't seem possible." He shook his head.

"No. It doesn't make sense. Do you have any idea where we're going? I'm starting to have nightmares about it," I glanced up at him, but then quickly looked away, still envisioning Alaban's sword slicing through Ocelot's jaw and his chest.

"We're not headed for Soren. That much I know. We're really in the middle of the galaxy. We're actually closer to the Lapas helion than Gold Wind," he told me.

"Are we?" I asked wistfully, wanting more than ever to go home again. I sighed. We couldn't be going there. A Fitmalo army in Lapas made even less sense than a Fitmalo army in Gold Wind.

"It's my guess we're going to Jawlcheen," Ocelot admitted.

I thought for a moment. If Alaban had just left Jawlcheen, he wouldn't be returning there any time soon, so his premonition about meeting on Jawlcheen couldn't be right. But if we were headed there and Alaban was destined to meet us, and if the Fitmalo army vision was right, it would be more likely that we'd all be sent directly to the planet Fitmalo first. If this were true, why would Alaban be out in deep space if he had just left Jawlcheen, Fitmalo's neighboring planet? I couldn't figure out how we would meet by the end of the upcoming month. I pondered this with my thumbnail between my teeth. I shook my head.

"Are you ready to spar?" Ocelot asked strongly. "You said I'd be in for a tough match today. Let's see what you've got."

Suddenly I remembered the messages. I had been so preoccupied with my nightmare that I'd forgotten. His sudden aggressive attitude jarred me. He had never challenged me before. In sparring he had always been patient, diligent and respectful. I stepped back from him.

"Let me stretch out first," I told him warily.

I went to the opposite end of the room to stretch while he practiced punches on a padded target. When I had finished, I stood at ready stance in the center of the room. I observed him cautiously, uncertain of his new boldness.

"Ready," I stated.

Before I could jump to one side, he was in my face with a whirl of fists. I gasped as I blocked and dodged as hard and as quickly as I could. This surprise attack confused me, but I fought back well. He backed me up against the wall, which I used as an anchor for a double kick. I jumped and kneed him sharply in the chin with one leg and kicked him near the groin simultaneously with the other. He faltered to one side only long enough for me to put a short distance between us. He attacked like never before. His excessive force made me angry. I increased my use of psychic energy to deliver levitative strikes often. Time after time we delivered harsh blows and used tactics we wouldn't normally use against each other.

After more than half an hour of heavy fighting, my arms were so bruised and weakened from blocking and punching that I was forced to fend him off only with kicks and fast dodges. Suddenly, he cornered me. He wrenched my blocking arms out of the way to clutch my throat in his hands. He pressed me hard into the corner of the room. I managed to pull his hands from me by triggering a pressure point in his hands and twisting. I shot downward, levitating myself between his legs and across the floor to the other end of the room. I dodged, kicked, and levitated, hopping to avoid him. He jumped around the walls and ceiling after me, trying to anticipate my moves. Several minutes went by in which we did not touch each other. Finally, our time was nearly finished.

"Time out, sir," I requested, almost breathlessly, crouching upside-down on the ceiling.

He dropped to the floor. "Time out granted."

I drifted to face him. We bowed. Our breathing rasped from the full hour of power drain and endurance. We stood drenched in sweat.

We faced each other for a moment, teetering from exhaustion.

"That was a good match," he said between breaths.

I stared dubiously.

He nodded. "I think we'll be all right out there."

He trudged to the corner for a towel. I sat and stretched out, massaging my aching arms and shins. Ocelot went straight to the bath without another word. I examined my bruises in the reflective wall. The skin on my arms and shins would be blotched with bright colors for several days. I wondered if Ocelot would have the same marks or if he had deflected my strikes more easily than I had his.

At our communal meal, my sore hands and arms shook so badly that I had to steady my utensils and cup with levitation. I noticed Ocelot had trouble with his flatware, too. A welt and a tiny gash decorated one side of his neck where I had punched and accidentally scratched him with the recoil. Wilbaht noticed our state of pain. Instead of chiding us, he smiled.

Klib became defensive, thinking for some reason that Wilbaht was laughing at him instead of us. Wilbaht explained he was just noticing the way we had beaten each other up this morning. Klib fidgeted, embarrassed that he had called attention to himself. He had become more diffident recently, maybe even paranoid. We all felt tense about him.

Later in the evening during my observation deck hours, I apologized to Ocelot for misunderstanding his messages, but explained that they did seem to come from someone who was toying with me cynically instead of from someone who wished to offer friendship. I also said it seemed he'd used a different name to confuse me for fun. He hunkered over his panel and ground his fists into his armpits.

"So what is your real name anyway, sir?" I ventured to ask.

"I've already given you three letters of it. That's all you're getting, especially after that last message you sent me. I didn't appreciate that." He cast a glare at me. "I can understand not measuring up to Wilbaht or Yalat or even Jiao, but don't tell me I'm a worse man than Alaban. I've had to kill in my day, but I'd never agree to do steady assassination duty. You want to talk about a lack of morals..." He shook his head and turned back to his work. "Never mind. I don't understand how you got so angry about a harmless guessing game. It was just something to pass the time and make our long journey less boring. You take unimportant things too seriously."

I ignored his comment about Alaban to resume my promise to Wilbaht about my temper. "I'm sorry. I thought you were lying to me about your name. It was a misunderstanding. Please forgive me, sir." I stood at attention, hoping he would let it go and maybe then we could get back to work as usual.

"Forget about it. We've already settled that hand to hand," he said, staring at his screen.

"Yes, sir," I said cautiously.

I had hoped the brutality of today's sparring match was a test to see how well we could defend ourselves in an actual enemy encounter. Now he indicated a vengeful motive. I hoped he'd only said this as an afterthought. Another question about his messages still nagged at me, but I wasn't about to pick a fight with him. After an awkward silence, I brought up the subject of safety checks and calibration of external instruments instead. We regressed to outward civility and inward repression of grudges yet again.

About two months after we'd left Jain, we finally received word from General Black as to which planet we'd be heading for. It turned out we were all wrong. Our destination was Sor4: to continue our investigation of Viga's smuggling ring. This assignment didn't seem right to me. I was sure something else was involved.

The next day as we prepared for our meal, Wilbaht began to hum the same tune he had sung a few days before. I sang along quietly with him. Ocelot walked up to the table and flinched. He stared at us in amazement.

"You know that song?" Wilbaht asked him pleasantly.

"Yes, sir. I hadn't heard that in years. My mother used to sing that to me," he said.

"Do you know the words?" Wilbaht continued.

Ocelot sat down, blinking. He thought for a moment, mouthing the words he remembered as Wilbaht continued humming.

"Sing it for us. I'd like to know how it goes," Wilbaht said. He hummed the tune again.

"*How long will I stay by your side? A million tomorrows have come and gone and still you sing on. How long will I stay by your side?*" Ocelot sang to Wilbaht's tune. "*Whenever I'm with you, you know I won't run away. Whenever I'm near you, you know that I want to stay.*" He returned to the chorus, which we sang together. Then he continued, "*Forever and ever, my love.*" He stared to an empty space next to him as if he were observing his mother's ghost. "God, it's been years time since I remembered that."

I stared at him in fascination.

Klib commented that he didn't realize we had a choral group in here. We continued our meal without song. Ocelot stared at the empty end of the table, distracted by a flood of memories. Wilbaht prodded him to tell us more about his youth. He relinquished only a few images, and then self-consciously shrugged off their significance, concentrating on his meal. Wilbaht asked Klib about his childhood, too. Klib described a tough life growing up with a single mother, but good memories.

Ocelot's golden voice stuck in my mind. The revealed memory of his youth changed my perspective of him. I glimpsed for a second the trajectory of his life as a boy who'd endeavored to become a warrior. His cold, abrasive shell became momentarily translucent. From that moment, I felt neither intimidation nor criticism for him, but rather a newfound acceptance.

I looked to Wilbaht. He had guided us to this. He was conducting this lesson, just as he conducted my lessons on far seeing. He was clearly trying to orchestrate the change from discord to harmony among us. I wondered if he also had a design for bringing Klib out of his corner to reveal his kinder side as well. What might he have in store, then, for me among the crew?

He glanced at me furtively, guessing my thoughts with approval. I almost believed I saw him wink with his lipid eye before he convinced Klib to keep talking about his young life. I felt more reluctant to open my consideration of friendship to Klib. I was still deeply vexed by the filming incident. Forgiveness was a difficult virtue, I reminded myself. But I was not without blame, either. We had all deserved the punishments assigned to us after that clash. Perhaps a gradual change lay ahead for all of us. Wilbaht's persuasive method certainly set the tempo. Trusting in my commander's wisdom, I set aside my reservations and sat attentively to listen to Klib's story.

Since our assignment had changed to the Soren helion smuggling system, we focused again on our previous research and especially on Viga. We knew she was, in fact, Swall Jade's daughter, and that she also had two clones only a few years younger than she. Swall Jade apparently had planned or foreseen the need for special security around his daughter since she was very small. Perhaps he had been involved in this type of illegal activity most of his life. We considered the idea that theirs might be a family business, dating back several generations. Upon research of this theory, Ocelot discovered that several of Swall's distant relations had been linked to illegal activity, but only on the planet Fitmalo. Swall and Viga were the first to hit the big time.

I correlated the travel patterns of Viga and her clones to match their appearances on Sor3 with Trau's activities just before his death. They were the three Fitmalo females who had appeared with him at the shipment delivery tarmac so many times before his death. I cross-referenced their movements to try and find some moment at which they, too, might have met or communicated with former General Zar, but found none.

Through estimations and hunches as well as concrete data, we drew up a delivery pattern we assumed Viga's group was using to smuggle goods from the Thrader helion to Soren and vice versa. They involved common, legal freight ships and a few passenger craft. Again, using weight discrepancies and ship captains' movements and personal associations, we learned who shipped where. But we couldn't be certain of the contents of their shipments. For some, we identified raw materials and mechanical parts. Some local drug busts that had led to dead ends at the Organization served as red flags for us. We automatically presumed they came from Viga's crew due to the drug type. All were Nitrogen1 mineral drugs, direct from her area of the galaxy.

Another small shipment we knew of came from a known weapons maker on Sor4. He sold specialty arms by request only. Viga had definitely paid him a visit on several occasions. He had used a large amount of basic metals and tools during specific times, a few weeks after which, the delivery ships from Soren to Thrader weighed heavy. The Regimists were stocking up. For what, we wondered. We feared a Fitmalo show of military strength against Jawlcheen sometime in the near future.

One evening after working on the upper deck, I checked my messages as usual. This time terrible news awaited me. My sister, Tamia, wrote me a note about my mother.

"Dear Sil, I'm sorry to have to be the one to tell you about this. We have all been worried for Mother's health for a long time. She'd been going to the local hospital for medication, but then she stopped going. She was diagnosed with terminal cancer. They had removed the errant cells nine times already. They gave her genetic enhancers and tissue replacement, but the cancer kept growing back. Her body resisted all treatment. She didn't tell us until just recently. We knew something was wrong, but she didn't want to worry us. Now she is in the hospital, in terminal care. I'm so sorry I couldn't let you know earlier, Sil. She is in some pain, but the physicians have given her a neural blocker. She has us all around her, but she keeps asking to see you. I'm crying while I write this, Sil. I know she won't be with us much longer. I'm sorry I couldn't tell you before. I'm so sad that she won't be here to see her first grandchild. I am six months pregnant. I wish she could live longer, but I can't stand to see her suffer. She is so thin, Sil. You would not recognize her. This has to be her time to go. I will

300

message you again as soon as something happens. Father, Blen, Chena, and Grace send you their love. Please come to see us whenever you can. Love, Tamia."

I sat staring woefully at the screen. I couldn't believe it. My sweet mother was slipping into infinity and I'd had no idea about it. I saw on my messages list a note from Alaban, but I didn't have the heart or patience to open it now. I dragged myself to my bunk and lay unsleeping on my cot, in shock. I could not cry. I could not believe it. I felt that my mother was alive and well, and yet she was not. After several hours, I finally drifted off to sleep.

In the early morning, I was awakened by a dream. My mother sat beside me in my bunk. She wore her Tambuo outfit, her hair adorned with flowers like those we used for weddings. Her face glowed, radiant and young. She held me to her, tucking my head under her chin as she used to do when I was small. She gave me a blessing of peace. I complimented her on how beautiful she looked. She smiled.

"I give all my beauty to you girls now. May you always carry it with you. I'm so glad I could visit you before I go," she spoke.

"Go where, Mother?" I asked her.

"You'll know when you're called." She held my face in her hands and kissed my forehead. Then she disappeared.

I awoke with a start. I knew she had come to me in her last moments of life on this side of spirituality. I felt shaken, but blessed. She appeared so lovely and angelic. She looked happy. I kept her image in the forefront of my mind as I dressed to begin the day. I didn't want to cry. I didn't want the men to find out I had lost someone close to me. I didn't want them to feel sorry for me. I didn't want to draw their attention to a feminine emotional weakness. I moved through my daily routine as best I could. I shielded my heart with a sense of duty.

When I entered the exercise room, Ocelot was stretching as I had taught him. I smiled a little to cover my grief. I said good morning to him. He was in a dull mood. He asked if I wanted to go over a few moves we hadn't worked on since last month. I agreed.

We went through the movements and then began sparring. Ocelot didn't use exceptionally strong blows, but he punched against me to get a reaction. I wanted to fight back with energy, but couldn't concentrate enough to spar correctly.

Ocelot threw a punch to my abdomen. Instead of blocking and moving away, I accidentally moved forward to receive the blow. I recoiled, staggering backward. I sat and then rolled up to my hands and knees. I placed one foot on the ground. Ocelot grabbed my elbow to help me up, but I didn't stand straight. I hung my head. I sniffled and covered my face.

"Sil, are you all right?" he asked. He stepped in closer to me. I felt him peer down at my covered eyes.

I wiped away a stray tear and stood erect.

"You just walked into the punch. Are you okay?" he apologized.

"I'm not hurt," I admitted.

"You're sure?" he asked. For the first time since we had been on Sor3, Ocelot set a hand on my shoulder and actually caressed it a little.

This simple, caring gesture broke my façade. I crumbled. Tears blazed down my cheeks. "My mother died today. I…" I couldn't continue speaking. I covered my face once more and leaned limply to him. I knew he didn't want to support a sniveling woman's tears, but my emotional fortitude buckled. My childhood's need for nurturing resurged into my adult body. I had to reach out to him for comfort. If he wouldn't afford me this simple act of human compassion now, then he was a lower man than I ever imagined. But he did. He even draped an arm around my back to comfort me. I stood shaking and crying against his chest for a minute.

"I'm sorry for you, Sil. I know what you're going through," he said quietly.

As soon as I could compose myself, I pulled away from him. I wiped my face with shaking hands.

"Thank you. I'm sorry. I'm sorry I touched you," I said, backing away. I walked into the hall and to my bunk.

I enclosed myself in my cell. I sat on my bunk with my face in my hands. I shed more tears. I missed her. I grieved for her, remembering all the times she had taught my sisters and me to dance Tambuo, to make things, to cook, to take care of ourselves. I remembered how hard it was to leave her to sail on my first journey with Yalat. After that trip, Mother had always greeted me with a firm hug and tears of joy. Those few months between journeys had been the most wonderful times in my life. She never let a month go by without messaging me to send her love and news. How I had hoped to see her on Liricos at the end of this first year of my new job. But it was not to be.

I wiped away my tears and sighed. Then a selfish thought occurred to me. What satisfaction I'd felt when Ocelot held me. I could still imagine the feeling of his arm around my back. I still conjured up the smell of him and the feeling of his body against my face. What was wrong with me? I was grieving the loss of my mother and allowing myself to think demented thoughts about my partner at the same time. I needed to meditate in order to let these things pass.

"Oh, Mother, I'm sorry," I whispered to her. I wondered if she knew I spoke to her. "I'll miss you so much." I cried.

I slept through our communal mealtime. At 2200 hours, Wilbaht knocked on my door. He asked me if he and Ocelot should cover for me on deck. I immediately got up and fixed myself as much as possible. I opened the door to speak with him. His old gray face showed pity. I told him I would do my duty as usual. He expressed his sympathy. I thanked him.

At 0130, I climbed the stairwell. Ocelot asked me if I was all right, but seemed standoffish. I said I was fine. I thanked him. He asked me if I wanted to talk about it. I said yes. I told him about the visionary dream I had of my mother. He hadn't seen or felt anything like that when his parents died. He said he was jealous of my vision.

"But you said you did see a vision before they died. What was it?" I asked.

From the look on his face, I could see that he wasn't willing to remember, but given my similar circumstances, he cooperated. "I saw the terrorist. I saw him set the explosives. I watched him walk out of the building as if he were a worker there. There were people everywhere. I knew why he was doing it. It was a protest against the planet's government and the Organization. They were holding prisoners from his radical group and wouldn't negotiate a release. I saw him leave the area. I saw my parents arrive."

Ocelot paused. He stared into the air before him, as if he were watching the vision replayed all over again. He frowned. His brow furrowed.

"I knew what was going to happen to them. It's a terrible feeling when you know a tragedy will happen but you can't prevent it. I must have messaged them fifteen times after I saw it. They had already left their hotel. Nothing could be done for them. I saw the explosion on the news the next day."

Ocelot lowered his eyes in mourning. I, too, mourned in a tearless sadness. If we had been sitting at arm's length from one another, I would have reached out to hold his hand. It was probably better that we sat on opposite sides of the room. He might have felt uneasy about such a gesture.

During the next couple of days, I spoke little. I didn't open my messages or send any. I took time to mourn and to regain my inner strength. However, my emotional recuperation was interrupted by an unsettling vision.

One night as I prepared to sleep, I clearly heard Alaban's voice calling to me in angst. I whipped around to see only my tiny bunk. Then, as I sat on my cot, I was faced with a whirlwind of images. This time, the broken mirrors yanked themselves away from me. The severed panes showed only hands and faces. I was not allowed to see an entire scene. I could not know where they were or what really happened. I only felt

Alaban's dire angst. I saw Fitmalo hands drawing singe guns. I saw Ongeram's face of anger. I saw Zank grinding his teeth as he drew a sonic scythe. Shots were fired. Noises of a battle were swallowed away with the sailing shards. I heard shouts, parts of conversations I could not piece together.

"You won't take him…" I heard one man shout.

"Kill them," a Fitmalo ordered harshly.

The black Lizard pilot shielded his eyes with his front paws.

Ongeram patted the side of Alaban's face with his huge hand sadly. Alaban beheld him with distress. Was Ongeram wounded? Was he dying?

"Get out of here!" Alaban called to the pilot.

The Lizard edged away, mortified.

A pair of Fitmalos fell to the floor, dead.

"Why did they do this?" I heard Alaban ask.

I saw him cover his forehead in distress as he called my name.

The last of the glimmering visions flitted away into their own dimension. I stared at the vortex where they'd disappeared, confused and anxious.

I prayed pleadingly for Alaban's safety and for the safety of his crew, although I felt certain that Ongeram was no more. I slept with clenched fists that night, never relaxing my determination for them.

When I woke at 1700, Wilbaht called an all-crew meeting. As the last of us sat around him, he announced, "Our assignment…has been canceled."

"What?" we gawked.

"Now what?" Klib blurted.

"Our orders are to turn around and head for the Thrader helion. General Black has traded our assignment type to temporary military. Request to transfer came from General Lam of Sor3. He is now our contact general. He is sending us to Jawlcheen for a mass gathering of Organization militia and intelligence agents to cover the Thrader Common Law campaign and declaration signing."

We all complained, since we were already getting an image of Soren on the main screen of the observation deck, and especially since we were sure Lam was a double agent. Klib pointed out that we'd wasted a lot of time traveling for nothing. Suddenly, a thought occurred to me. What if Alaban had experienced a similar order?

I finally checked my messages. In addition to his message I had noticed from the other day, there appeared another from him. There was a new message from Tamia. I already knew what news it contained. There was also a message from Yalat. A shudder crept through me. I opened the messages in order, starting with the most recent.

Yalat's message was foreboding. She wrote, "Sil, my dear child, I have received a strong premonition. You will soon face grave danger. You must keep your partner close to you during a confrontation. Trust Wilbaht to get you out. I have bad news about your companions. You may have to leave them behind with the enemy. I'm afraid if you don't, you will all perish. Fight bravely, my child. This will be the moment you've trained for all these years. Choose the right path, Sil. May the hand of God guide you in battle. Love, Yalat."

As soon as I read this, I did not hesitate, but opened Alaban's more recent letter. It was encrypted. Even when I translated it, the message itself was cryptic. It read: "Remember dream reenactment. Remember everything I said about it. My actions are all about love. Believe in me. Don't try to be my heroine yet. I love you immensely. A."

I tried to figure out what he meant. I got a few parts of his message, but I didn't see how they all fit together. Frantically, I opened and decrypted his first message. This was the most disturbing of all.

Alaban said, "We're not going to Gold Wind. We're not going anywhere. For the first time I am afraid of someone: the man I helped out on Fitmalo. I know now where we'll be. Please know your vision isn't what it seems. Don't trust your swordsman. He is not a friend to us. Please be careful. I love you so much. A."

Alaban must have dreamed of the three of us in battle with Ocelot as his primary opponent. All of our dreams had multiple endings. He must have believed his dream was the right one. I hoped this was the case. I hoped my first horrible vision with Ocelot had not foretold of his own doings of evil. But if Alaban and Yalat were right, I could have to leave Ocelot behind. Or worse. We might have to fight him as my vision had warned. Worried memories and premonitions swamped my sixth sense. I focused to clear it.

Why did Alaban say they weren't going anywhere? He obviously hadn't meant it as a figure of speech. If he was still in space between two helions but not going anywhere, a Fitmalo spacecraft might have intercepted his ship. That would explain the battle in my most recent vision. Would the Fitmalos intercept our ship as well?

What if General Lam was sending us straight into the jaws of the Fitmalo army? I recalled Trau's testimony. He said I would be good bait. If these Fitmalos were under orders from Regimists…Pieces of this inky puzzle floated together in my mind, but I didn't want to see them take shape. A creeping chill oozed down my spine. The icy breath of mortality seeped through the air around me. One sickening probability became clear to me. We would not all survive this battle.

Chapter 29: Enemy at Hand

Despite our foreboding mission, ship life dragged on. In sparring, I became even more serious and formal than before. Strangely, Ocelot had the opposite reaction. He seemed more peaceful, more relaxed in his manner. Still, he sparred masterfully every time. Wilbaht finally passed two simple objects through each other: a tiny metal wire and a plant leaf. He bubbled with pride at his final success. I far saw more clearly than ever before, although my predictive abilities had not improved much. The ship's plants finally yielded fruit. Unfortunately, their flavor was not what we had expected. Klib threw a tantrum about them.

"After waiting all this time for something good it turns out tasting like tar!" he complained.

He threw his silverware down on the table and paced the dining area. He rummaged through the pantry carelessly, spilling containers onto the floor. We tried to ignore his rash behavior, but he ranted on.

"Damned dry food. There's nothing to eat in this can but dried up food substitutes. I'm ready to slice off part of my own arm to have something real to eat. We should have brought poultry with us instead of some of these damned rubber plants."

Wilbaht tried to reason with him. "Poultry doesn't fare well on long space treks. They would have died within a month. We *would* still have some of your favorite foods left if you hadn't served yourself ten eggs a week for the first half of the trip."

Ocelot interrupted him when he saw Klib throw some containers of wheat and barley tack on the floor. "Hey, watch it with those, Klib. They're not the best tasting, but I'd at least like to eat them whole."

Klib scowled at him and threw a few more down, but Wilbaht stopped them from hitting the floor. He levitated them into a stack to one side of the sliding door. Ocelot tried to coax him out of his belligerent fit.

"If you're looking for something with high protein, why don't you take the dried steak strips that are left? I'll let you have my portion for the week if you really need to. It's no big deal."

Klib kicked the base of the shelf repeatedly, causing the whole thing to buzz and shudder. I stood in alarm. He backed away from the shelf after one more swift kick. Wilbaht slowly moved out of his seat. Klib bristled and clenched his fists. He glared at me.

"What are you staring at, woman?" he snarled at me.

"Nothing. I was just going to, um, help clean up here. You can have my portion of meat, too, Klib. Like Ocelot said. It's no big deal. Really," I offered.

Klib observed us like a caged animal. "Oh, so now you're scared I'm going to break something so you give me a little extra food to keep me quiet. Yeah, keep Klib out of the way. That's the way it always is around here. You think I don't know about your little secret meetings, your little 'warriors only' club? Yeah, I'm just the cab driver. You just tell me where to go and I'll take you there. Well, this is the worst ride I've ever been on, I'll tell you right now. If you hadn't told me to turn around and go back the other way, we'd be on Sor4 in a few days. Now we'll be out here another six or seven weeks. Do you think I can put up with this lousy excuse for food for that long?"

I backed a couple of steps away from him towards the row of bunks. Wilbaht stood solid. He slowly raised a hand to calm him.

"Klib, I know you're disappointed about the trip. We all are. Once it's over, you'll get a good long vacation. You've earned it. Just try to be patient with the situation a little longer," Wilbaht crooned.

"You just need some time off to relax, man. Take a break. I'll cover for you after we eat," Ocelot added.

Klib backed down some after this. "Yeah, all right. I'll find some kind of shit to eat later." He folded and then unfolded his arms with nervous aggravation. He swore about the long space trek a few times under his breath.

Wilbaht glided back into his seat. He gestured to me to move back to the table. Klib stomped past me towards the hallway. He continued grumbling complaints.

"I'll be half-alive when we finally get to a goddamned planet. Can't eat, can't drink, can't *fuck*!" I winced, since he announced the word near my ear. "I'll be glad to get to a planet with *real* food, *real* women. This ride is fucking goddamned torture!" He disappeared behind the corner of the hallway.

The rest of us exchanged disturbed glances. Wilbaht advised us to be passively friendly with Klib for the next few days to get him back on track. He calmed down some the next day, but his constant agitation remained.

Several days later, when I entered the exercise room, I found the projected shadowy image of a Fitmalo warrior standing out from the burnished wall. He held a wavy sword. Ocelot paced around in front of him. The Fitmalo changed stances, following Ocelot back and forth.

"Good morning, sir," I said as I customarily did.

"Yes, it is. It's a good morning, Sil. Do you know why?" Ocelot asked me in a rather loud voice. His manner was not a happy one, despite his outcry.

307

"Why, sir?" I asked, reluctantly playing along.

"Because we're alive," he stated firmly. "And he's not." He referred to the holographic Fitmalo.

He swung around and sliced fast and accurately through the shadow's body with three complete blows to the abdomen. The computer did not move the hologram fast enough to counterattack. The image slid apart and dissolved. A new opponent appeared identical to the previous one.

Ocelot turned to face me, leaving his back exposed. Just as the shadow drew back to strike, Ocelot plunged the sword backwards and strafed toward the man's heart. Again, the hologram fizzled away and appeared anew.

"You don't think the Fitmalos will be fighting us with swords, do you?" I asked him.

"No, but I know we'll be at close range, so they won't be using anything more powerful against us than a singe gun." With this he spoke to the computer. "Hologram, change weapon type to singe gun."

The sword disappeared from the Fitmalo's hand. He instead drew a singe gun from a holster at his side. Ocelot cut off his hand before he could ready the gun to fire. He then cut off the hologram's head.

"What other weapons do you have?" I asked him.

"Why, do you think we should practice with a different weapon?" he asked. He continued sweeping the sword at his massless opponent.

"I think we should double up if possible. I can still wield my sword while I'm wearing my hand bow. How about your blade thrower?" I suggested.

"Who knows if we'll have time to strap them on? Besides, the extra weapon on the left hand could get in the way of sword handling. We can try it, but I'd rather stick to the sword. You didn't see any other weapons on us in your vision, did you?"

"No. But I'd rather not trust my visions. All our dreams and visions are conflictive. Alaban had one, too," I mentioned tentatively. "I know how you feel about him, but I'm afraid he feels the same about you. I know I'm not in the position to give you advice, sir, but I hope your opinion of him won't affect your decisions during battle. I don't want to see either of you die."

He stared into my eyes solemnly.

"But you will," he stated.

The muscles around my torso clenched. I swallowed hard.

"Do you know…who?" I asked.

He turned away. "No," he said.

The Fitmalo shadow attempted to strike him with a transparent singe blast. Ocelot swung the hilt of the sword to strike the hologram in the chin, and then cut the man in half. The image dissolved. Another Fitmalo reappeared in his place. Ocelot backed away from him.

He gestured to me. "Here, you kill him for a while."

I reformed all my nervousness and fear into a blood thirst for my opponent. I battled image after image, striking through the empty air swiftly. Ocelot stood behind me to judge and coach my moves. Soon I was killing the holograms faster than the computer could register them. Ocelot called me off.

I stepped back from the image. I returned my sword to its sheath, breathing heavily. Ocelot ordered the hologram to shut down for the day. I watched the shadowy Fitmalo disappear before me. As the image wriggled away into nothingness, I looked past it into the burnished wall.

My eyes grew wide in shock. Then I shut them, resisting the image I had barely seen. Out of the corner of my eye, I imagined a ghostly image of Alaban diving into the room behind Ocelot and swinging a sword high in the air to attack him. I turned and shook my head, attempting to shake the image from my mind.

Another full week of tension sloughed by. Each day filled me with more anxiety. Ocelot fought more roughly than he had before. One morning he attacked me unannounced from behind, flipping me brusquely onto my back and slamming the back of my head into the mat. I immediately levitated him away from me, although he fought my hold on him. My levitative powers had reached their peak thanks to Wilbaht's direction. I kept Ocelot up in the air. My head and neck throbbed. I hadn't been ready for his attack at all. He struggled against me, but only wasted his energy. I stood, massaging the back of my neck. I set him down against the wall. I stayed at the doorway.

"No more," I told him. "I quit."

"I'm sorry I surprised you, but that's a possibility we have to be ready for," he said, finally shaking off my mental grip.

"No, sir. I don't want to fight with you like this anymore. I won't come to spar with you tomorrow. I've had enough," I contested.

"You want to stop training just when we need to sharpen our battle skills the most? Why? What are you thinking?" he retorted.

"What are *you* thinking? We're supposed to be on the same side." I looked at him with resentment. "With attacks like that, you're making me start to doubt your loyalties. I'm not sure if I should fight with you or against you."

He stood straight, shoulders back. He determined to stand his ground, but the expression on his face changed to one of self-doubt and maybe even suspicion against me.

"I'll see you at the meal," I told him quietly. I walked out.

At our duty on the top observation deck, Ocelot apologized. "You were right. It wasn't a fair move. I just want you to know you won't have to work against me in this battle. I will be there to back you up," he promised.

"Likewise, sir," I acknowledged, fearing secretly that this statement could soon prove to be an insincere one.

We sat in menacing silence during the rest of our time together. I bit my thumbnail constantly. Ocelot drummed his fingers on his panel. At his time to leave the deck, he stood by his chair and stretched. He seemed reluctant to move towards the stairs. He took some steps toward them and stopped. I gazed up at him. He wanted to say something, but did not. He grasped the stair railing with one hand, but paused before descending.

"Good night, Sil," he spoke, almost sadly.

"Good night," I replied.

He stayed a moment longer, staring at the floor. Finally he descended the first few stairs. He hesitated as if deliberating about something to tell me. He stared up at me from halfway down the stairwell. He sighed. He raised his hand to wave at me, and then touched the railing that separated us. He let his hand slide down the rail as he turned to go downstairs. I watched the stairwell for a few moments. Why did he do this? Would he be the one to die? I had to steel myself against worry.

"God, give us the strength to work together. I know we can't afford to work against each other. Let us be one unit, one team. Lead us through this battle. Let us move by your will," I prayed in a whisper. "If one of them should fall before me, please give me the strength to carry on in battle without him. If I should die, let Wilbaht live to tell the tale."

After my prayer, I wondered about a lot of things. I questioned Ocelot's motives for his actions today. I questioned my own abilities with the sword. I wondered if I was wrong to actively ignore the fleeting images I had seen this morning in the exercise room. I couldn't think of how to prepare for battle anymore. I was as ready as anyone could have been, and yet I felt I was missing some obvious piece to this imminent battle scene.

I felt, as Alaban had, that he and I were physically closer to each other. I perceived his proximity as well as the body of an army growing closer in the blackness of space. Tonight we would pass through another space ripple. The folds of the galaxy would push us through a buttonhole where we would face the Thrader solar system. A fleet of armed ships could soon interrupt our trajectory. Would the Fitmalo army commandeer our ship? Would we be kidnapped? For the many possibilities I considered, I did not foresee anything definite. Only this battle sense remained. I meditated for two fruitless hours. No peace came to me. My mind and spirit remained in turmoil.

In the morning, I awoke with goose bumps. I dressed in my combat uniform as usual, but I did not go to the exercise room. I stepped out into the quiet dining area. Our ship's hour was 1715.

Suddenly, a piercing blast of sound rang through the ship. Klib had sounded full alert. I zoomed up the stairwell. Wilbaht emerged swiftly from the lower observation deck. Ocelot was the last to arrive. We stood fully awake, each of us at our stations, eager to get this terror over with.

Klib informed us of what was happening. "Fitmalo space station, sir. They're requesting ship's registration, purpose, and crew ID."

"Send the standard communication, Klib," Wilbaht ordered.

"I did, sir, but they're asking for a personal message from a commanding officer. They said we're about to enter Thrader military defense space," Klib continued.

"What? There can't be any such thing until the helion approves a commonwealth defense," Wilbaht said. "That treaty isn't due to be signed until next month."

"I don't know, sir. I'm not about to argue with them. Look at the size of their attack ship door," Klib continued. He brought up an enlarged image on everyone's on-deck screens.

"Sil, I'm going to message them. As soon as I send, put up low-level shields," Wilbaht ordered.

"Yes, sir," I answered. I sat at my post to ready shield one.

Wilbaht typed out a quick identification report.

"Sending," he told me.

I set the shield to full on. Ocelot sat at the edge of his seat, wishing he could do something. A few moments later, Klib informed us of a new message from the space station. Wilbaht sent the image to all our stations so we could all read their correspondence.

The message read, "Welcome, Sub General Wilbaht. We invite you to inspect our new hybrid. Please continue on current course to rendezvous."

Wilbaht leaned back in his chair for a moment. He put a hand to his chin in deep thought. He knitted his brow. We waited anxiously for him to speak. He left us and our probable foes waiting for some minutes before he finally spoke.

"Klib, what is our distance from this space station?" he asked.

"About 200,000 kilometers, sir," Klib responded.

Wilbaht leaned in toward his station panel. He typed for a short while. He accepted the invitation to inspect their hybrid, whatever it was, but requested confirmation of the nature of the inspection.

"Sil, bring up the secondary shield," he said.

"Yes, sir." I flipped on the second shell. It registered as a mesh of blue and yellow film all around the outside of the ship that showed up as a green cast on all outer screens.

We waited again. We wanted to know what Wilbaht was thinking, but we didn't dare to interrupt his thought.

Finally, the space station notified us that we were ordered to stay our course and that the space station personnel would let us know where to dock when we got closer. The inspection requested was of defense facilities.

Wilbaht sat silent for a moment.

The space station looked like some kind of underwater plant life. The body of the hybrid was a polygon of unusual abstraction. On two sides, I noticed large sealing doors for entry and exit of small attack spacecraft. Around the attack ship ports protruded triangular formations connected to arcs of external corridors. At the ends of each of these corridors were four tubes jutting out in different directions. On the ends of each of these tubes were three small retractable tubes. Some of these extended to accommodate spaceships at dock. Most of the docks on one side of the space station were filled while the other was sparsely used. I counted the docking areas. A total of seventy-two medium sized ships could be attached at once. This wasn't the biggest space station I'd seen, but it was the newest and most bizarre.

"I think maybe they called it a hybrid because it's part space station and part military base," Ocelot said. "They have military ships as well as civilian vessels."

I zoomed in on my imaging screen. Ocelot was right. I saw several unmarked white ships with only a serial number to one side, and some multicolored ships openly displaying name as well as serial number. Two of the ships I recognized. One I was sure I had seen on Santer. The other one I knew well.

"The Jawlcheen Reaper," I spoke aloud.

"What's that?" Klib asked.

"It's an Organization ship," Wilbaht explained.

"So is the Sea Ram," I added, pointing to it.

"I know that ship," Wilbaht stated. "I've been on board. Unless it's changed hands since I last saw it, it belongs to a personal assistant to General Swall Jade."

"So we're not the only warriors here after all," I said.

"Those wide doors must lead to an internal hangar full of attack ships. You said in your vision our battle took place in some kind of hangar," Ocelot noticed.

"Whoa. You're talking about battling against these people? You'll get yourselves killed. Where will that leave me? They'll kill me just for being part of your crew. No way. They haven't threatened us yet, and they probably won't. So don't provoke them. We'll get out of this alive if we just play along with them, right sir? Tell me you're not going in there to start a war."

"Klib is right," Wilbaht stated firmly. "We have to go in peacefully to avoid confrontation. Even if they're holding other warriors hostage, we must not fight them. Only use your weapons against a direct attack. We have to give them the chance to explain themselves."

"Somebody had better tell me what's going on. This is some serious shit. I'm not the ship's mascot, am I? I have the right to know about all this," Klib demanded.

Ocelot briefed him with generalized information about the Fitmalo plan to unite Thrader and about our suspicions of the preparation for a military takeover sometime within the next year and a half.

"If this is part of an illegal takeover plan, why are they inviting our commander to inspect their station? Wouldn't they want to keep that kind of thing quiet?" Klib made a face.

"Officially, they're not planning a takeover. They're obviously pretending to police the airspace for the defense of the solar system," Ocelot told him.

Klib made another face. "Defense against what? It's not like there's people lined up to invade this helion from anywhere else. Who would want them?"

"I think it has to do with import taxation," I volunteered.

"And smugglers," Ocelot added in realization.

Wilbaht held up a finger to the air. "Could it be that this proposed defense against import tax evasion and smuggling is actually a station to facilitate such trade? I think we've hit upon something."

"They're just beginning this operation. They're warming up. If this goes as they've planned, they'll use it as an offensive threat against Jawlcheen to insure their takeover," Ocelot spoke with anticipation. "If Jawlcheen saw this as a military outpost, they'd protest and cancel the commonwealth signing."

Wilbaht was with him. "Yes, but as a space policing system, it appears to be an asset to them. If the station is accepted by a neutral entity like the U.G. Organization, the public will consider them beyond suspicion. They will be applauded. That's why we've been invited to inspect their hybrid. They want Organization officials to approve it so they'll have our support. This will ease their takeover in many ways. It might even leave the door open for them to barter with Keres as a second commonwealth," Wilbaht said.

"Why would anybody want to bother dealing with Keres? That place is even more useless than Thrader," Klib said, trying to get into the detective work.

"Keres contains the largest source of raw metal ore and other precious materials. Their mining laws are the loosest in the U.G. I'm referring, of course, to Karnesh and Godel. Jain is another story altogether. They'll find the most resistance from the Jain planet," Wilbaht explained.

"They'll never strike a deal with Keres as long as the Jain planet is aware of it. Not if I can help it," Ocelot vowed defensively.

"Hold on, there, hero. Don't jump the gun. Nobody's threatening to take over anything today. They're just asking Wilbaht to look around. If you're going in there to start something, let me know so I can drop you off and leave. I'd rather live to see a takeover than die trying to run from the Fitmalo army," Klib told him.

"He's right about keeping your senses," Wilbaht said. "We're not going in as aggressors. As far as they know, we're only here to look around and shake hands. Then we'll be on our way."

He gave Ocelot and me a meaningful glance as he said these last words. He stared at us gravely, and then gestured with his head towards Klib. We understood. Klib shouldn't know of the certainty of our premonitions. It would do us no good to have a frantic pilot.

Klib felt reassured by Wilbaht's words. He felt purposeful, glad to finally be let into the loop of warrior secrets. He became eager to communicate with the space station and to dock at one of its tentacles.

"Sil, turn off both shields. We won't be needing them after all," Wilbaht ordered.

"Yes, sir," I said. I complied with the order. The green film subsided.

"Ocelot, Sil, go below. Make sure your uniforms are complete. We want to make a formal impression," he told us.

"Yes, sir," we responded. We knew he meant we should dress in full armor.

We made our way to our respective bunks. I strapped on the shin and forearm guards first. Then I rummaged through my travel box for my flack vest. I attached the adhesive communications device to the back of my ear and at my collar. I rolled my hair into a double clasp and clipped it firmly at the back of my head. I took my weapons out one by one to check them and to give them each one last cleaning. I anchored my mind now

314

around procedures and routines to carry me rigidly to face my most squirming fear.

I took one last look in the mirror on my wall. If my mother had given me her beauty, I did not see it. It was hidden behind the mask of my stern visage, the face of a warrior setting out to the task of war.

I secured all items in my bunk in case I was not meant to return. Regulations were met. Safety standards were complied with. The cold steps of procedure were complete. If I did not come back alive, anyone who inspected my bunk would discover only that a warrior had left everything according to Organization standards. They would not know who I was or what I believed in or what kind of person I had been. They would only see these impersonal clues to a life. I thought perhaps I would feel resentful about this. Strangely, I took comfort in it. My life was not so important to this universe. I was only a grain of sand beneath its vast sea, only a miniscule part of its whole greatness. But I was part of it just the same. For this I was thankful. For this I had a moment of peace. I said a quick prayer of thanks.

I stepped out of my quarters well armed physically and spiritually. Now if only my mind would catch up with the rest of my being. I wished I could grasp all the pieces of the puzzle to finally understand it all before I had to face the enemy.

Chapter 30: The Hangar

"Maybe Wilbaht will let me tour the place with you. They might have a VIP bar in there somewhere," Klib mused while our commander had gone to finish dressing.

"I doubt you'll find any entertainment on this military hybrid, Klib. I'm sure it's all regimental," Ocelot told him with double meaning.

"Yeah, you're probably right, but I'd like to get out of here, even if it is for a few minutes," Klib continued.

"Ask Wilbaht. Maybe he can get you special permission," Ocelot said. I thought it was unfair of Ocelot to set Klib up for disappointment.

Wilbaht returned in his official gray uniform, complete with achievement bars that decorated his shoulders in a glittering array of colors. However, he appeared unarmed. Was he really so confident about his role in what would soon happen?

Wilbaht asked the docking clerk if we were expected to disembark immediately and to whom we should present ourselves. The soldier replied that we were to please stay aboard our ship until further notice.

We docked at an extension tunnel, which was not an airtight structure. In fact, it was only a collapsible framework. We would need our space suits to leave the ship. From his control panel, Ocelot closed the double air lock around the main exit door of the first cargo hold. He then opened the main door so that the space station's docking robot could successfully clip the hooks from the wire mesh tunnel to the frame of our outside door.

We waited a few minutes after docking before a general contacted Wilbaht. He requested real time visual communication. Wilbaht switched on his visual communication screen. We saw a Fitmalo general dressed in a pale gray uniform with bars of accolades on his shoulders not unlike Wilbaht's. He addressed us.

"Welcome to Thrader Defense Space Station One. I am General Helt. On behalf of the commonwealth of Thrader, I welcome you. We appreciate that you've taken time out of your traveling schedule to dock with us, Sub General Wilbaht. It will be an honor to have such a celebrity on board."

"The pleasure is mine, General. I trust this station is in compliance with the recent common law agreement for your solar system. I congratulate your people for your impressive feat of engineering," Wilbaht said.

"Thank you, sir. I'm sure you'll find everything on the inside of the space station impressive as well. How many crewmembers will be joining you in this inspection, sir?"

"Two, sir," Wilbaht responded, but Klib waved at him and pointed to himself. "Or possibly three."

"We would like to offer each of you some refreshment once you disembark. We collect a wide variety of imports on this station. I'm sure you'll find our reception accommodating. I will meet you in person as soon as you all arrive at our lobby of section three. I look forward to meeting you in person." The General and Wilbaht thanked one another. Then the screen went blank.

Wilbaht turned to Klib. "I'll allow you to go with us to their lobby, but you must promise to either stay there once the inspection begins or return to the ship."

"Yes, sir. Any time away from this ship is appreciated," he responded.

Wilbaht ordered us to suit up in secondary cargo. When we finished checking suit seals and temperature and oxygen regulation, we moved to the primary cargo hold.

We could only pass two at a time through the double air locks. Wilbaht and Klib went first. They stepped into the first air lock, sealed it, opened the second air lock, stepped into it, sealed it, and then pumped the air out of the second airlock back into the first one. Once the air vacuumed out, they opened the door and hopped weightlessly through the silvery mesh tunnel to another set of airlocks on the other side. The door shut automatically after them. Next Ocelot and I repeated their procedure. The mesh tunnel contained handles at every meter to ease the trip between ship and space station. We pulled ourselves along to reach the door, which opened automatically. We grabbed onto side handles at the wall. After the door closed, air sprayed into the sealed room. The door to the second lock opened. Gravity projectors brought our feet to the floor. The intermediate door shut. The door to the main corridor opened. We stepped in.

Wilbaht and Klib had already begun to take off their heavy suits. Wide lockers lined the wall here. They did not, however, have locking mechanisms. If anyone wanted to prevent someone from escaping this space station, they only needed to take away the person's space suit. Wilbaht read my thoughts.

"Don't worry about the suits. I sense they will be here when we are ready to leave," he said.

Trusting his instincts, I took off the bulky equipment and stored it all in a locker next to Ocelot's. As we passed the lockers, a computerized voice asked us to spread all limbs for U.V. bacterial cleansing. We each obeyed in turn, stopping and closing our eyes for the intense flash of U.V. light.

Then we walked together up the ramp hallway to another sealed door. This one had double air locks for emergencies only. We passed through these and into the main wing of Section Three. The wide lobby of this wing was a sickly, dull green color. The floor, ceiling and walls all had a slightly different hue, which made the scene even less appealing. We regarded the area with distaste.

We approached a table spread with a variety of fruits from every helion in the United Galaxy. A Fitmalo military cadet stood behind the table. He addressed us formally and offered us refreshment from the table.

317

"We also have a wide variety of fruit and vegetable juices available," he spoke.

"Got anything with alcohol?" Klib asked first.

"I'm sorry, sir. We are not allowed to carry intoxicants on this space station. May I offer you a virgin drink?" he replied.

"Just give me a fruit punch," Klib said as he snatched a shiny plum from the display. Despite his disappointment about the drink, he delighted at the fruit. He smelled it and then sank his teeth into its juicy flesh. His face showed it was good.

Wilbaht asked for the same from the recruit. He nodded to Ocelot and me to go ahead and take something. I picked some grape-like berries from the stack, a fruit native to Takash, the helion farthest from the center of the galaxy. The berries tasted sweet and tangy, as if they had been grown on a natural farm. They were fresh, which meant they were either grown here on the space station or imported from an agricultural ship, as the General had said. I wondered if they had been bought or confiscated by force.

The General we had seen on the communication screens strode up to us with a formal smile. He shook Wilbaht's hand. The two chatted about our current course and what planet we had arrived from. Ocelot and I finished our refreshment quickly. Klib simultaneously ate and pocketed fruits from the tray.

Helt suggested that we begin the tour of the civilian facilities on this wing. Klib obediently stayed in the green lobby. After leaving the atrocious lobby, Helt showed us various communication centers throughout the wing as well as a hydroponics lab, which spanned much of the upper portion of this section. At the top of the wing where the tentacle connected with the body of the space station, we found an exercise area, which wound around through the body of the station and back into the tentacle of section four. In this tentacle we observed customs and import offices and small storage warehouses. The technology at each of these areas was state of the art.

Helt took us through the entire wing even though most of the facilities were the same. After we climbed back up the fourth tentacle, Wilbaht asked Helt if we would be touring the rest of the station as well. Helt informed him that he would be greatly honored if we would see the entire military facility.

"If it will take longer to see the rest of the station than it has taken to see these two wings, we will need to cut this tour short, unless we split up. I could allow my sub professor to inspect half of the area while I inspect the other half," Wilbaht suggested.

"Well, I'm sure I can find a second tour guide for you. We really do want you to see the whole station. We want everyone in the U.G. to know we have nothing to hide," Helt insisted.

He communicated with another officer through a phone in the wall. He called Sub General Navran to report to our section immediately.

Navran met us in a holding area at the wide security door that separated the civilian section from the military section. He was also dressed in a gray suit, but without so many bars on his shoulder. He did not wear a smile as his superior had. He simply presented a no-nonsense front.

"Please show this Sub Professor around section six and the military zone base two," Helt told him.

"Yes, sir," Navran responded. He bowed to him and to Ocelot.

"Sir," I interjected. "Whom should I go with?"

Wilbaht regarded me with gravity. "Stay with Sub Professor Ocelot."

I took a deep breath. "Yes, sir."

We parted company, Helt guiding Wilbaht through a corridor to our left, Navran escorting us to the right. The security officers scrutinized us. They requested to detain us for carrying weapons into the military section, but Navran explained we were not to be bothered or disarmed, by orders of General Helt. We were here for a routine inspection. Besides this fact, we were supposedly on their side, doing the same job of protecting the interests of their helion and those of the U.G.

Navran escorted us through a long corridor with only communications equipment and security locks interrupting the repetitious gray and white paneled area. He only told us it was a tunnel used to bypass the weapons hold. This corridor went on for what seemed like a quarter of a kilometer. If this encompassed the area around the weapons hold, it was the largest weapons hold I'd encountered on any facility, both in space and on land.

When we finally arrived at section six, the topmost tentacle of the station, Navran entered a special code at the door to allow us through. Here we saw military training rooms on either side of the hallway. Some were for combat simulation. Some contained specialized exercise equipment. Others included libraries of military information. There was also a set of internal training classrooms here.

We noticed through a window a class of Fitmalo recruits studying a large hologram of a defense air tank. They went over the anti-recoil system and repair steps. Another group studied pressure points of a male Vermilion. They used a live volunteer. I felt skeptical as to whether the Vermilion man had really volunteered for the job, or if he was prisoner forced into it. The Fitmalo instructor pointed to sinews on the man's neck and proceeded to poke at him until he winced violently. The class laughed. We turned away from this room quickly. Ocelot and I exchanged an uneasy glance.

Navran, unmoved by the scene, ushered us on to another area, which was sealed off by a heavily secured door and three armed guards. Our sullen guide once again quietly argued with the security guards at this post to allow us passage. Finally they agreed but asked to have an armed escort follow us through. Navran permitted the escort, but appeared more peeved than before. He asked the man to please not get in our way.

The door opened to a brightly lit orange and gray area replete with cubicle-like rooms. In the center of this area stood a clerk's desk. The military clerk rose as we entered. He stared at us, offended.

Navran stepped up to him to explain. "These are visiting warriors. They are here to inspect the facilities. There is no need to vary your normal routine. We will not be entering or listening in on any interrogations. We're merely observing the area."

The man did not change his manner, but nodded to us. We returned the formality.

Navran led us around a circling corridor. We viewed a few empty rooms. They were standard, without any visible recording equipment, but we knew these were highly monitored. We looked in on one ongoing interrogation. The subject was a Mantis. He seemed to be denying something. He shook his head and waved his arms. He appeared to be healthy. He had not been tortured. Everything on this side was in order.

"Why would a space station need an interrogations area this large?" Ocelot asked.

Navran did not skip a step or pause when Ocelot asked him this. "We intercept cargo ships. Some of the import ships carry illegal goods. We interrogate the crew of those ships to be sure they are not bulk smugglers. If they are, we have to determine which crewmembers knew about the smuggling and if any of them are wanted for illegal activities already. If we have three or more ships docked at the same time here, we need the extra space to perform the interrogations."

Ocelot did not question him about the explanation.

We circled around to the clerk's desk once again. Navran thanked him and led us out of the area. The armed escort stopped at the security door. He gave us a skeptical glare as we left.

Navran led us back down through the tentacle. This time, instead of taking the narrow corridor back to section four, we entered a bright hallway. The door sealed shut behind us. Another door just a few meters in front of us did not open. We approached it and waited. Navran explained it was only a common security procedure. We were being monitored from every angle and by multiple data recorders. I didn't like this at all.

Finally the door in front of us opened. To either side of its threshold Fitmalo soldiers manned seven monitoring stations. At one screen, we saw our own image from the bright hallway. The other screens showed different sections of the station, inside and out. I found an image of our ship and the Thrader Sea Ram as well as the Jawlcheen Reaper and another ship I didn't recognize.

Navran gave a brief explanation of the area. "This is central monitoring. We can check any personnel activity from here. Just below us is the systems monitoring center for engineering, life support, and so on."

He led us on through this area towards the end of the monitors and a stairwell leading down to the systems monitoring center. Ocelot and I hung back a little, trying to get a good look at every screen on this level. I stopped. My eyes fixed on one wide screen above me and to my left. On this screen I found the hangar from my visions. A wall full of two-passenger attack ships loomed above a platform. There must have been two hundred ships packed tightly into the wall.

The screen next to this one showed a platoon of air soldiers practicing a mock deployment on the platform. Behind them I saw four figures. Two were Fitmalo generals. The other two were warrior bodyguards. One bodyguard was a Mantis. The other was a tall human. The image was not clear enough to discern the faces of these people, but I knew what I did not want to know. The human was Alaban. My eyes could not move from the image. I watched as the four figures moved toward the back of the platform and off the screen.

"Is your underling warrior going to join us?" Navran asked in a perturbed voice.

Ocelot turned to me and ordered me to hurry up.

I took a step towards them, but kept my eyes on the monitoring panel. The next set of screens showed different angles of this hangar and the surrounding areas of bunks, a cafeteria, the lobby of a set of offices, and the doorway to the weapons hold. On one screen showing the hangar, I saw them again exiting the platform.

Unabashedly, I thrust a finger up towards the screen and demanded of the nearest soldier, "What section is this?"

He looked at me, startled, and then sought guidance from his superior. Navran told him to tell me so we could get going.

"That's section one, miss," he informed me.

I scanned the other screens from that section. Wilbaht was supposed to be on that level now. I caught a glimpse of him and Helt passing through the soldiers' bunking area. I did not see another image of Alaban.

"Let's go, Warrior." Ocelot's voice was agitated. Had he seen what I had?

"Yes, sir," I breathed.

The computerized systems analysis readouts of the second monitoring station blinked, shifted, and wavered around us as we passed through this area. Navran spoke a few minutes about the various readouts and the technological perfection of the computer systems. I barely caught a word of it. I searched the screens. If Alaban was here, where was the rest of the Jawlcheen Reaper crew? Even if Ongeram had died, Zank and the Lizard pilot had to be somewhere on this space station.

I found a screen detailing military and civilian docking tubes. They were identified by name and serial number. The list also included quantity of crewmembers and a Fitmalo code for docking purpose. More information could have been accessed, but I didn't have the authority to request it. I quickly scanned the list for the Reaper. It identified the quantity of crewmembers as a blank. What did that mean? I found our own ship on the list. It said the Sonic Wake had four crewmembers. The Sea Ram contained six. The other ship I had not identified previously was the Palat Sun Seeker. It had seven crewmembers. Where were all these people?

I followed Navran and Ocelot like a sleepwalker numbed by a potent dream. My mind struggled to plan some way to meet Alaban or at least to find out precisely where he was and what he was doing here. I felt him very close by.

Our guide led us through the monitoring area, through some simple offices, a secondary bunking commons area, and to a small cafeteria where a few troops ate. I could tell from their uniforms that these were flight personnel. Navran offered us to sit and have a glass of water before we finished our tour. He said we only had a few more things to see and then he would take us back to the docking lobby. He asked Ocelot what he thought of the space station so far.

"It's very impressive, sir. You must be proud to work in such an up-to-date facility." Ocelot's voice was hollow.

We sipped our water as Navran talked about a few other aspects of the station as a policing unit as well as a technological experiment.

"Does that mean you have many experimental weapons on board?" I asked suddenly.

He narrowed his eyes at me. "Only a few. We have a new version of a plasma cannon. We are not so interested in the newness of our arms, but rather our monitoring and communications systems."

"Yes, I could tell they were all state-of-the-art," Ocelot stated. He stomped on my toe under the table in warning.

Navran guided us out of the soldiers' personal area and into a flight prep area, almost like a huge locker room. Flight suits, helmets, and protective gear hung in clear plastic cases all along the walls and in a few aisles. I tried to count them, but we went through the area too quickly to get an accurate number. I guessed there were over two hundred.

Past this stretched a long airlock room. The green lights on the door panel indicated that the room just outside this one was already pressurized so we didn't need protective equipment.

Navran stopped just before this doorway. "You are about to see something most military stations don't usually show to outsiders. Since you are Organization employees and we want to make a good impression on your people, I'll be taking you through the viewing room that oversees one of our reconnaissance ship hangars. Since this space station will be policing a wide range around our planet, we need the extra recon ships to bring in the cargo ships from our surrounding space."

The tiny hairs on the back of my neck stood out like pins. My heart rate increased.

Navran opened the air lock. We stepped into a room with doors to either side of us. A set of stairs angled up to our left. These led to the hangar viewing room. To our right, another door led to the hangar of military zone two. Navran guided us toward the stairs. I hesitated, looking over my shoulder out the glass door to the hangar. I only glimpsed the wall stacked with fighter ships. Ocelot grabbed my arm in a crushing grip and yanked me toward the viewing room doorway. I was offended, but I understood his anxiety. He let go of the arm. I followed him obediently up the stairs.

We walked up ten steps and then turned to the right. We stepped onto a floor tilted at a thirty-degree difference from the stairs. Changing directions of gravity felt awkward. We entered a long, empty hallway furnished with two tiered seats for an audience of soldiers. The viewing room spanned the width of the hangar. At about the center of the deck, we turned to look out the window. I bristled at the whole antagonizing montage.

Directly in front of us loomed the gigantic sealed portal, which was the entrance and exit for the attack ships. The ships fit snugly into the walls like a display of giant rifles. Narrow checkpoint platforms jutted out from the grid every fifteen meters up the wall.

The greatest platform tilted up before us. Here we observed about fifty troops running to regroup together. The troops aligned themselves in formation in full protective gear and helmets. Their leader barked orders to them.

I leaned near the glass to look directly down. Three plasma cannons sat side by side below us. These could later be attached to a ship or could be hauled to a battlefield. They could also be fired from where they stood. If a foreign aircraft tried to invade or retaliate facing the hangar, these would be a good defense for the station.

Navran told us to feel free to watch the soldiers' demonstration. We observed as the squad leader ordered the first row of soldiers to their ships. He held the rest of the troops at ease to time the first set of men. They hustled out to the edge of the wide platform and dropped one by one down a ladder in the center. There must have been even more attack ships hidden from our view on the wall at the edge of the platform. Soon five of the ships hovered close to the platform's edge. The squad leader made a wide gesture with one arm. The five ships lined up in front of the portal and revved their engines. Then one by one, they returned to their niches in the wall. A few short minutes later, the troops reappeared, returning to line up with their comrades. The squad leader seemed satisfied with their time.

The tingling sensation I felt became a buzz of hyper energy. I perceived Alaban's every move now. He was in the large airlock where we had been. He stepped slowly behind a Fitmalo general. He moved through the airlock and then through the door to the hangar: the door we had not taken. I shook with energy. I heard Navran ask if I felt a chill. I shook my head and pressed my hands to the glass. I looked below. I did not yet see him, but I knew he was just around the corner of a ledge that housed the plasma cannons. I shuddered. Static electricity seemed to travel in clashing bolts through my body. Then I felt as if it all collected together in my chest.

Alaban stepped out from behind the corner. My energy closed up like a fist inside my heart. He marched in unison with a Fitmalo general. The other general and a Mantis hung close to them to observe the training. Alaban walked with tightly clenched fists. He felt what I did. He knew where I was. He did not turn to see me. That would arouse suspicion in his subject. Why was he guarding that man?

The party strode out to greet the squad leader, who bowed like a simple lackey. The Fitmalo general closest to Alaban turned so that I got a good look at his face. He was not a general I recognized. He spoke commandingly to the squad leader, who in turn ordered all his men to repeat their practice run. The men dashed off even more quickly than before, sliding two at a time down the ladder and disappearing to the wall of ships below them. The squad leader made an unnecessary fuss in reverence to the General. The General held up a hand to still him. The man finally stood at attention and remained staunchly militant during the rest of the exercise. When the group returned to line up, the General paraded through their ranks, inspecting each with a discerning eye. He returned to the squad leader and mentioned something to him in passing. The squad leader bowed and then shouted to his men.

At this signal, the troops about faced and ran to the airlock room. The squad leader followed them a few paces, but stopped just before we lost sight of him around the corner. He checked his timer. He must have ordered the troops to store uniforms and then go through a full emergency drill to time them for the General.

"Well, it looks like the demonstration is over," Navran suggested. He moved toward the exit.

Ocelot asked, "Who is that general on the platform, sir?"

"That's Head General Teradom Cinc. You may have seen him recently in the news. He was one of the leaders who signed the agreement for the adoption of Thrader common law. He's an honored guest here. The other one is General Sunderlign. I don't think you would know him, but he is also a cabinet member. He spends a good deal of time with us here," our host informed us as he stepped lightly towards the door at the opposite end of the observation area.

I peered down at the man. It was him. I hadn't realized it before. Sunderlign now gestured toward the plasma cannons. I saw his odious wrinkled blue face clearly. I then realized the Mantis looked strikingly similar to the Mantis female who had offered to spar with me on Karnesh. How appropriate that he would have chosen her from the conference there.

Alaban stepped back a few paces to let his subject pass by him, following Sunderlign and his bodyguard. As the General passed him, he looked up at me. His glance lasted only for a moment, but his eyes conveyed turmoil. I pushed off from the glass wall and hurried after our guide, hoping to find some way to communicate with Alaban without being seen by the others.

Ocelot followed Navran closely. He glanced at me over his shoulder in concern. I double-stepped to catch up to him. We passed through the door at the other end of the viewing area, again adjusting our angle of gravity. We found a set of stairs and a choice of exits identical to those we'd passed a few minutes before. At the bottom of the stairs, we glimpsed the hangar from the glass door. Navran paused at the airlock room doorway.

"Would you like to see our new plasma cannons up close? You expressed an interest in our new weaponry just now. I'm sure General Helt would be willing to allow a closer look," he offered proudly. He extended an arm towards the hangar.

I took his offer immediately, without waiting for consent from Ocelot. I turned on a heel and marched lively towards the door.

I heard Ocelot behind me, trying to suppress his aggravation with my reaction, "Yes, I think it's our duty to go in."

His footsteps echoed after mine. Navran paced behind us.

"Aren't you supposed to fall behind, Warrior?" Ocelot nagged me.

I stopped at the door. I stood at attention. "Yes, sir. I apologize." I clenched my teeth.

Ocelot stood next to me to allow Navran through first. He seemed to enjoy this display of rank from us. Navran graciously gestured to us to enter the hangar. Ocelot marched out quickly. He did not slow his pace as he moved toward the Fitmalo leaders. Navran hung back a moment with me, but then quickened his step to keep up with Ocelot. The Fitmalos left the first plasma cannon and turned to face us. Ocelot stopped and stood tall, shoulders back, eyes glaring toward Alaban.

Realizing his mistake in breaking from traditional protocol, Navran hurried to stand between Ocelot and the others. He bowed almost as sweepingly as the squad leader. He apologized for our unannounced entry. He introduced us to the head General as Alaban and I stared longingly at one another. We needed to speak together alone, but our present company couldn't possibly permit it.

Just then, Sunderlign recognized us. He took steps toward me, pushing Navran out of the way. Navran blinked in confusion. Sunderlign gave me an evil grin.

"What a delightful coincidence. My former bodyguard. As you can see, I have found a worthy replacement. She was not hard to convince, although I would have enjoyed twisting her arm a bit." He looked me up and down. "I can always use another talented body on my staff. Perhaps you can indulge me after all."

He jerked his head towards Navran, who didn't know what to make of this. "Report back to General Helt. Tell him I will be personally responsible for these warriors for now."

Navran's face showed confusion and offense, but he was highly outranked, so he could only obey orders. He bowed profusely to both generals and then slightly to both of us before leaving the hangar the way we had entered.

"Sir, if I may speak freely, I stand by what I said to you on Karnesh. I will not leave the Organization for a private bodyguarding position," I told him firmly.

Sunderlign grinned all the more. He retracted to his colleague's side and spoke to him. "These are the warriors Salt and I told you about."

General Teradom took in the conversation with a pleasant, beguiling countenance. "You're right, sir. She is exactly what we're looking for." He advanced a couple of steps towards me.

Although he was shorter than me, his power helped create the illusion of imposing mass. His bright blue skin was well-preserved, his coiled dark indigo hair sensibly groomed, showing his upper class status along with his heavily decorated military garment. His thin diamond-shaped pupils took in my form, read my thoughts, and confidently softened to set me at ease. "State your name and rank for us, Warrior."

"Sil Gretath, First year Warrior, sir," I said automatically.

The corners of his mouth rose. "This is more than coincidence. This is our lucky day—yours and mine," Teradom said to me. "This bodyguard is good. He sensed you approaching since before we met." He motioned with his face toward Alaban. Alaban made a slight gesture as if to bow to the General, but stood stiff-necked when he saw the man was not finished speaking to me. "You've missed this young man. You've cared for each other a long time. I can tell. That's a refreshing sentiment these days." The man paused to smile to himself. "I've been many things in the past, but never a matchmaker. I ought to add that to my list."

"Sir?" I asked, straining.

The corners of the blue cat's mouth tilted upward more. "Allow me to explain. You've been worried that you'll be coerced into working for a Fitmalo general who wants to use your talents for illegal activity." The corners of the blue mouth relaxed. "That general is here."

I stared at the man's cool, hypnotic eyes with a quivering chin. In my peripheral vision, I saw Ocelot's hand glide to his weapons pouch.

"I am not he," Teradom clarified.

Ocelot froze. I blinked.

Teradom's pleasant manner returned. "Sunderlign, I'm sorry to have kept you in the dark, but this young woman is more than bodyguard material. I'm afraid she will never work for you, sir. We may, however, persuade her to stay on with us after we remove her from this station."

I eyed him suspiciously.

He spoke to me in a soothing, overly confident voice. "I had arranged to meet with you after your tour, but I see fate has directed you to me sooner. So much the better. I am here to save you, so to speak." His tone changed to business. "We know you've been sent to Jawlcheen by Organization military General Lam, but you were not meant to arrive there. You were meant to dock here. Your general is working against you. He's moving you around like a pawn. If you had finished your tour of this facility and boarded your ship, you'd soon realize what I mean. Your ship would be commandeered by a Fitmalo Organization general by the name of Swall Jade. He is here at this station as we speak. He outlined his plan to me this morning. Under other circumstances, I would respect his actions and stay out of his way. However, in this case, I had to intervene. I did not oppose his plan in front of him. I prefer to quietly remove you from his temptation altogether. You see they mean to move you to another ship for an entirely different purpose than the one you were meant to do."

"What is she meant to do, according to you, sir?" Ocelot interrupted with noted skepticism.

Teradom gave him a frown, but kept his demure manner. "You are a sub professor, not a general. Don't interrupt, please. I'm coming to that."

Ocelot scowled.

Teradom returned to speak to me. "You are very advanced for a first year warrior, very talented. However, since you are relatively new to your ranks, you cannot be aware of the treachery that is taking place within the Organization, among your generals. The black market is booming, thanks to them. They've allowed smuggling. I should say they've encouraged smuggling to our planet, leaving us with an economic shambles. The United Galaxy is a bureaucracy of charlatans. Its Organization leaders put up an honorable front to make themselves look good. They defend their positions with enthusiasm because they have their hands in the pockets of every planetary government in the galaxy. 'Pay homage to us and we'll subsidize your war,' they say. 'We'll fund your reconstruction. If you have no money, we'll overturn your government and support a reform cabinet that will.' Oh, yes. You're working for men who deal in money and blood—our blood." He pumped a fist over his heart and then pointed to me.

His fingertip pressed onto my sternum as he spoke softly but adamantly. "Your blood." He withdrew the hand. "They've pushed you young warriors around like chess pieces without regard for your welfare. I, on the other hand, do not consider a beginning soldier's life to be less important than the life of any other. My demands for excellence and proper treatment of personnel on every level have brought me to this rank. I have the highest popularity index of any head general in our planet's history because of it. Your Organization I would not work for if they offered me twice the pay. I say this to you because I sense you are a devoted, honest young warrior. Also because this young man has asked for my help, and I for his."

I glanced up at Alaban, who nodded slightly.

"I intercepted his ship as soon as I heard of Swall Jade's plan. I explained the same thing to him as I've explained to you now. He was grateful to leave the Organization behind. In fact, he volunteered to work with us. Of course, after his own crewmembers betrayed him, he was all the more willing to join me. He'll never have to worry about such atrocities with us. As long as he follows the straight and narrow on our staff he'll enjoy a fine salary and job security, no excessive travel time, and a valued position here in the commonwealth. This is what I'd like to offer you as well."

"What?" I barely said.

Had he said Alaban's crew had betrayed him? A shutter clicked in my mind. I remembered the visionary shards sailing away from me, with images of Alaban and Ongeram and the others of his crew with the Fitmalos. I remembered the unsettling messages Alaban had written me. These things had happened weeks before. But just now, Teradom had said Swall Jade had only revealed his plan to him this morning. This man was lying. He was lying and Alaban knew it. This was the man he'd been afraid of, not Swall Jade. This was the man he'd helped escape from the Organization cell on Fitmalo. This general was lying to us. And Alaban was helping him do it. My understanding stamped to halt.

"I am a loyal warrior like any other, sir. Why would I be willing to leave the Organization to work for a new and unstable government?" I asked defensively.

The General stifled offense to continue his truthless persuasion. "I'll get to the point. I am offering you a place in our new government's intelligence task force. Your talents have not gone unnoticed. If you are true to your conscience, you will find it gratifying to leave such an underhanded bureaucracy to join a new and much more honorable cause."

I stared at Alaban, the one man I had believed would never lie to me. "My actions are all about love," he had said. "Remember the dream reenactment." He meant to protect me, to find a way out for us, but with the enemy. Everything we had talked about regarding this situation, the promise he had made to me, all of it had been as dust. Here he stood, guarding a two-faced monster, and lying to me. My heart hardened to a thick lead shell that began to crack within my chest.

"How did his crew betray him?" I demanded.

Teradom's hint of charm nearly evaporated. "Normally I wouldn't abide an ungracious attitude like this, Warrior, but since I understand your emotional duress, I will forgive your reaction. Allow me to explain. When your friend here arrived at our station I offered him a similar position. His crewmates didn't agree with his approval of our offer. They proposed to prevent him from working with us. Since they could not convince him to stay in the Organization, they decided to kill him. Yes, just like that. They had been on the job together, what, ten months? At the first sign of an exercise of free will, they endeavored to end his life. I was a witness to this."

I closed my eyes and shook my head. "I don't believe it. That couldn't have happened. Even if it were true, I wouldn't work for anyone but the Organization. I'm not a traitor!" I opened my eyes to glare at Alaban. His eyes widened. He shook his head.

"I swear upon my birth planet that it is true. They even took up arms against General Sunderlign and myself. I'm sure you know the

329

punishment for firing a weapon at a head general." Teradom stared tensely into my face.

"Execution," I whispered with dread.

"Execution. Absolutely. And who carried out the execution of your back-stabbing crewmates, bodyguard?" Teradom stepped back to present Alaban to me.

Alaban swallowed hard. He responded frankly. "I did, sir."

My jaw dropped. I felt my world tilt on its axis, carved through by this unforgivable blasphemy. My innocent love perished.

Part 3: LOSS

Chapter 31: Betrayal

"No. You're not a murderer. You may be an assassin, but you'd never hurt your own men," I cried. "You promised you'd never work for the enemy."

"The Organization is the enemy. Swall Jade is the enemy. I didn't realize it before. Now I know. This general is different. He's on our side. He can keep us away from General Swall." Alaban stood straight as if hung by a pole. His arms dangled almost lifelessly at his sides as the lies dripped from his mouth.

"So you killed your own crew?" I chided, drawing air into my heaving lungs.

Alaban gave a weak explanation in the most stable voice he could manage. "I had to, Sil. When General Teradom offered me the job, I agreed to work with him. They tried to kill me for it. I had to fight for my life. If I hadn't done it, I'd be dead now. It's not what you think. He didn't blackmail me. He only offered. Look, I want to work on his task force. You want to work with me. Accept his offer and he'll let us stay together. This is our chance, Sil. If we stay with the Organization, Swall Jade will force us to steal for him and then throw us back to the contact generals' pool. They'll keep us apart indefinitely. Come with me. We won't be separated again. We'll be safe."

"Safe from what?" I cried.

"From the Organization."

Suddenly, Ocelot stepped forward and exploded at Alaban. "If you think you can cover your ass with a thin lie like that, you're even more of an incompetent bastard than I thought. If Ongeram and Zank tried to kill you it was in self-defense. You are a murderer. You have no loyalty. You're just like Trau. You want Sil to join you so you can keep her out of the way. If she's on your side, you won't mind killing as many warriors as it takes. You should be burned alive for high treason, you inhuman son of a bitch!" He lurched after him and swung at him wildly with a right hook.

Alaban leaned back just enough to avoid the punch. He blocked and tried to grab Ocelot's arm, but he recoiled quickly. Each man stood his ground. Teradom backed away a step to stand by Sunderlign. The Mantis stepped forward in case she was asked to help separate them.

A fierce glow came alive in Alaban's eyes. His demeanor changed dramatically. "What I'm saying is true, but what do you care? Your loyalties are more skewered than mine. You want to stay close to Sil so when she retrieves the weapon, you'll be the first one to get your hands on it. How much did your uncle offer you for it? Huh? It's tough being the underling in the family, isn't it? Yeah, I've followed your tracks. It's been one failure after another with you. If it weren't for Uncle Stennet and Cousin Jiao, you wouldn't have been on that committee in the first place and you sure as hell wouldn't be her partner," Alaban retorted.

"You know damned well I'm not after the weapon and neither is anyone in my family," Ocelot shouted. "Don't try to turn my partner against me with that bullshit, you lying coward."

I yelled at them to stop it, but Alaban heckled Ocelot. "Who's the coward? I've kicked your ass before. I'll do it again."

Ocelot pounced forward. He swung at Alaban repeatedly, but Alaban blocked perfectly at every strike. He swatted back at Ocelot, but Ocelot blocked high and deflected Alaban's guard to reach up to rake Alaban across the nose with the heel of his hand. Alaban flinched, punching angrily at his slightly shorter opponent. Ocelot got a lucky move, catching one of Alaban's arms and tagging him in the abdomen with a side kick. Alaban slid backwards to a ready stance. Both men glowered with hatred.

Teradom stepped between them swiftly, preventing another attack. He motioned for Alaban to stand down. Ocelot held back, barely controlling his urge to strike again. I stood my ground, sickened.

"Bodyguard," Teradom spoke cautiously, "You are displaying characteristics that we Fitmalos find undesirable in humans. I overlooked your race when I hired you for your unparalleled talent. Please don't play the stereotype, starting a fight with family insults. Let's give this man a chance to leave in peace. He will not have the opportunity to retrieve anything from this woman. She is coming with us."

"I will not..." I began.

Ocelot interrupted me with a guttural shout. "She's staying with the Organization. You will not take her out of here. I will see you dead before I leave my partner behind!"

Teradom cringed his slanted, bulging green eyes at Ocelot.

Alaban tensed, waiting for his new master's command.

Teradom held out a hand towards Alaban's shoulder. "Bodyguard, a new suggestion: kill him."

Teradom stepped away as Alaban drew his sword.

"No!" I shouted.

Ocelot and I drew swords as well. I stood between the two, trying to keep them from dodging around me and pushing me aside.

"You're both wrong! Stop this!" I cried. I slashed at both their swords. "Remember my vision. We can't fight each other!"

Ocelot backed away from me as I sidled a little closer to Alaban. Suddenly, Ocelot jumped into the air behind me and caught my blocking arm and my chest with a spinning hook kick, causing me to stumble away from them. He swung madly at Alaban.

I returned to stand, but the Mantis rushed to detain me. I pushed her away, but she punched back. I soon found myself in danger as she swung at me with her sharp forearms. I defended with the sword, trying not to do her any serious damage.

"Bodyguard!" Sunderlign shouted to her. "Let her go. She mustn't be damaged."

The Mantis said something in her language and backed away from me, disappointed. She drew her sword and approached the fighting men, hoping to assist Alaban. She soon got her chance.

Ocelot beat Alaban's sword fiercely and then kicked him swiftly in the ribs. Alaban faltered off to one side. Ocelot heedlessly drew back to strike while he fell, but the Mantis flew in to intercept the blow. Alaban rolled back up to his feet as the new opponents whisked away at each other. The Mantis was more highly skilled with the sword than I had imagined. Ocelot had met his match in fencing.

While the two swords clanged together repeatedly, I swept toward Alaban to keep him from entering the fight with them. He tried to sidestep me but I kept after him.

"Sil, trust me. If you agree to work with his task force, you can negotiate to let your partner go. They don't want him," Alaban said as he hopped around in front of me.

"Then why are you trying to kill him?" I retorted.

"We just need to get him to surrender," he spoke.

He battered my sword and dove to my right, but then spun me with a kick to the side of my left knee. I whirled to try and catch him but he sprinted out of reach.

Ocelot found a weak point in the Mantis's left swing and took advantage of it. He bowled her over on her side, but didn't injure her. He was about to strike to kill when Alaban flew in. Ocelot parried and twisted just at the right moment.

I moved in to try and separate them again, but the Mantis came after me with a powerful blow. She nearly knocked my sword from my hand. I gawked at her strength. I struggled to keep my balance. Her next three strikes left me skittering backward. Since the first blow she'd delivered, I hadn't fully recuperated my grip on the sword. If Sunderlign shouted to her now, I didn't hear him through the sharp din.

The squadron of Fitmalo fighter pilots re-entered from the airlock room. Their footsteps resounded almost as loudly as our clashing swords. They stopped in position, although their leader hesitated, uncertain of what to do faced with four sword-fighting warriors and two top generals in a normally empty hangar.

Suddenly, the Mantis beat my sword so heavily that I faltered badly. She took the opportunity to deliver a solid kick to my chest. I thumped to the floor. She didn't stay with me to execute another strike, but sailed off to assist Alaban. She attacked Ocelot with unparalleled energy.

Ocelot battled desperately. This was no fair fight, even for an expert swordsman. He couldn't possibly fend off both opponents for long. I thought quickly. The Mantis would have to leave the battle if I threatened her bodyguard subject. I leapt over to Sunderlign, who now cowered near the cannons. I held up the sword to Sunderlign's throat, hoping both Ocelot's opponents would back down.

I shouted and whistled to the woman. "Mantis!"

Sunderlign surprised me by drawing a wavy dagger of his own. "Bodyguard!" he shouted.

Sunderlign lifted his dagger to meet my sword. To my dismay, it was an electrical instrument that threw a shock through my sword and up into my arms. I roared in pain, stumbling backward. I had barely enough time to regain control of my muscles and parry upwards to avoid dismemberment by the Mantis's sword. She forced me to use every sword technique I'd ever learned to fend her off. But all my blows were defensive. I couldn't find a gap in her sword coverage. She leapt about in glee, eagerly anticipating the moment when she would spill my blood. She beat me toward the edge of the platform.

The troops stayed back, as ordered. They watched the show with curiosity. Teradom and Sunderlign now stood before them, daggers drawn.

Soon I found myself at the edge of the platform. I pulsed a blast of levitative energy at the sinewy insect to escape.

Alaban and Ocelot still fought nearby. I jogged toward them, sword raised high in the air. I brought it down to crash into both their blades just as they hit each other. I pulsed them apart, but they quickly marched back in toward each other.

"Please stop!" I shouted.

Alaban dove toward me with wide eyes, shouting my name. He grabbed me by the arm and jerked me to him, fending off the Mantis who meant to stab me from behind. I spun against his chest to see Ocelot engage her once more.

Alaban held me close to him with an arm around my chest. "Stay with me, Sil. Let them fight."

I looked around frantically. Sunderlign and Teradom watched with enjoyment. Teradom spoke to the squad leader, who bowed over and over foolishly. The troops stood slightly out of line to watch the spectacle. The generals observed smugly. How could Alaban work for them?

I gasped and gritted my teeth. "How could you kill your own partners? That's high treason. Why?"

"I had to, Sil. There was no other way. You have to trust me," he said. "I'll tell you everything later. Just come with me. Let this happen. It's right. I know it doesn't feel right to you, but it is."

"No," I cried, pushing away from him.

He held tightly onto my arm. "Wait," he ordered.

Just then, Ocelot gained a touch on the Mantis's leg and took advantage of her injury. He pounded her sword. With a swoosh of his blade he cleanly cut off her head. The body stood, swinging the sword limply until Ocelot severed her abdomen and pushed the body off to one side with a foot.

Alaban pulled me closer to him. I struggled to free myself, but he held me with power. "If you stay in front of me, he'll stop fighting. That's what you want, isn't it? So stop squirming."

I knew he was right, but I couldn't stand to let him tell me what to do after the atrocious crime he'd committed.

"Let go," I protested. I pressed my shoulder hard against his arm, but he was too strong, both physically and psychically.

Ocelot stood over the body of his opponent. He glared at Alaban with pure hatred.

Sunderlign and his superior moved forward slowly, both holding their swiveled daggers to one side.

"Now I'll have to find a new bodyguard," Sunderlign complained.

The General gestured to the squad leader to have his troops surround us. He approached Alaban and me.

He waltzed in close to me as the troops and Sunderlign surrounded Ocelot, weapons drawn. Ocelot pivoted slowly to observe the men around him. All the soldiers pointed singe guns at him, ready to fire. Alaban held me fast.

"One move, Warrior, and we'll give you a full squadron execution," Sunderlign warned Ocelot.

Teradom's manner remained cool despite our sudden violence. Still, he did not turn off or put away his sword. He toyed with it frivolously as he addressed us. "I am a generous man. I am willing to overlook this interruption. You know this man must die. He's killed one of our most trusted staff."

Teradom eyed the rebellious aggressor almost coyly. "To show you my good will, I will allow him to leave unharmed. In return, you will stay with us. Of course, you have the freedom to refuse my offer if you find it necessary. We are not interested in taking you by force. That would be slavery. We want you to work with us willingly. However, if you choose not to join us, you will soon find out for yourself what it means to be held against your will. I'm sure you would find life as a prisoner in Swall Jade's possession to be dull at best, painful and unusually cruel at worst.

"If you come to work for us, we will gladly let your partner go unharmed, start you on a generous salary, and allow you your own comfortable personal quarters in exchange for a somewhat challenging job, which I believe you will come to enjoy. And of course, with us you may count on a certain level of luxury. You will even be allowed personal time to spend in the loving arms of your own mate. That is an attractive offer, don't you think?" Teradom nodded to Alaban. "You see? You have so much to gain by coming with us, so much to lose if you don't. I'm confident that you will select the best path. Life and freedom for you and your partner, or death and imprisonment. This is the easiest choice you'll ever have to make." The fiend smiled confidently.

Ocelot stayed still, not letting go of his sword. He stared at me.

Alaban brushed his face against my ear. "Take his advice, Sil. Stay with me."

"Don't agree to anything, Sil," Ocelot shouted.

Sunderlign intervened. "Quiet. You are a prisoner until the General releases you. If the girl works for him, you live. So let her choose wisely."

I searched my anguished mind for a way out of this, but came up with dead ends every time. With the weight of doom, I resolved to relinquish my integrity to save my partner's life. I was about to ask to see Ocelot safely aboard our ship when suddenly, Ocelot made a move that defied all hope of salvation.

"She can't work for him if he's dead!" he shouted.

He spun around with his greatest force, slicing Sunderlign open through the middle. He then pulsed his most powerful ring of levitative power to fell the soldiers all around him. He leapt into the air towards the General.

Teradom levitated to block him and throw him back to the ground. I'd had no idea he had exceptional power like us. I watched restlessly from Alaban's tight grasp as the two hopped around among the soldiers, who held fire for fear of hitting the General. Ocelot bounced from one soldier to another. Finally he held one in front of him. Teradom stabbed the man through the heart without missing a beat. He yanked the soldier's smoking body to the ground and continued thrusting the dagger at Ocelot. Their swords touched. Ocelot received a jolt of electricity that sent him careening backwards. He collided with another soldier, who fell to the ground with a groan.

Seeing this, the squad commander shouted to his troops to regroup around him near the airlock door.

Ocelot regained his feet just in time to dodge and flip. He changed his approach. He avoided the General's strikes, attempting more kicks and dodges than sword movements.

The General was fast for a man of his age. He quickly backed Ocelot toward the row of plasma cannons. Knowing the General meant to corner him between two cannons, Ocelot flew up over him. He landed closer to the edge of the platform. Alaban backed us away from the sword fighters, still keeping me to him with power despite my fitful struggle.

Suddenly, the troops ran out toward us again, forming a living wall between the line of plasma cannons and the fighting men. I didn't understand this strategy at first. Did the squad leader want the troops to prevent Ocelot from attempting an escape towards the doors? They almost looked as though they were waiting for them to move from the edge of the platform so they could safely descend to their ships. The men at the ends of their line gradually sidled towards the platform's edge, forming a wide semi-circle around the battle, as if to contain them. Since Ocelot had not yet killed any of the troops, perhaps they assumed he wished to spare innocent lives. This was true, but if they enclosed him too tightly, he would be forced to attack them as well. Why would the squad leader put his men at an unnecessary risk?

Ocelot continued to dodge and kick, but he didn't hit his target often. The General was getting in more contact strikes than Ocelot.

As they kicked and swiped at each other, the squad leader stole up to the controls of the second cannon. The soldiers slowly enclosed the sparring pair, weapons drawn. Now I understood. They meant to corral Ocelot into position.

"Ocelot, jump..." I yelled, but Alaban firmly cupped his hand over my mouth.

"Let him die," Alaban said under his breath.

My heartbeat swelled madly. I glanced from the cannon to the soldiers and then to Ocelot, who moved fluidly through the movements we had practiced so many times. The General gained another touch to his sword. It sparked and threw Ocelot back to the railing of the platform's edge. The railing buzzed when he hit. He cringed and growled, but struggled again to his feet. The crowd hung back, allowing the General to approach him.

The General marched to him, sword prepared to strike.

"Ready, General, sir!" I heard the squad leader yell.

I looked frantically between the cannons and the railing. I wrenched my face from Alaban's grip.

"No! Ocelot look out!" I shouted.

The General drew back his sword and charged forward. At the same time, the troops all dropped to the ground in unison.

The next horror I saw came directly from the vision I'd had so long ago at my testing when I'd first laid eyes on Ocelot. I had denied it all these months. I had hoped it wasn't real, but here it was, sickly played out before me.

Ocelot stood by the ladder that led down to the attack ships, sword arm extended, ready to defend against the General's feigned attack, the other arm out to one side to keep balance. He was a perfect target. The General dove in, but then levitated up and away from him.

The squad leader fired the plasma cannon. The blast glowed a wavering hot green. The shot looked like a miniature comet piercing the air. It ripped through Ocelot's left side and kept going until it hit the protective shield of the portal. The comet exploded, leaving a dent in the thick metal seal.

I jerked ferociously against Alaban's grip.

"No!" I shouted and then whimpered. "No. no."

I watched in disbelief as Ocelot dropped his sword to the floor. It clattered sharply. Unnaturally, light shone through the gaping hole in his side. Then the hole filled with gushing crimson. He gazed in shock at his mortal injury. He staggered. He looked up once more to view this awful scene around him. Then he slipped in his own blood and fell backwards at the ladder, vanishing from our sight.

I howled in anguish.

The troops stood. The General turned off and stowed his dagger as he walked up to me. Alaban finally loosened his grip. I stepped away from him on wobbly legs. My psyche begged that this was only a dream or a theatrical play, something that would soon be over and forgotten. Shakily, I moved away from the evil character that approached me. I did not wake up. The curtain did not fall. The dark troops who faced us were real. The devouring evil emanating from this man's blue face was real. My partner was gone. My soul mate had gone mad. My hopes dissipated from my heart like escaping flies.

Teradom spoke icily. "You will come with us now, won't you, Warrior?"

I continued backing away from them, shaking my head in shock.

"Let it go, Sil. Stay with me. Everything will be all right. I'll keep you safe," Alaban dared to say.

Teradom spoke firmly to me. His cool, kindly manner was gone. His determined stare grasped at me. "This is your last chance. Join us now or your ship and all those aboard will be destroyed."

Alaban followed me closely to the edge of the platform. The troops returned to attention. I turned, stepping solidly into the pool of blood. I stared at it in amazement.

Alaban grabbed my arm and gently swung me around to face him. "Let him go, Sil. Stand by me."

I wrenched my elbow from his hand. I glared at him, then at Teradom. I stared into Alaban's dark, reflective eyes. He actually looked hopeful. I shook my head in disbelief. His eyes pleaded with me.

I took a step backward to the very edge of the platform at the ladder. With my ultimate voice of courage, I spoke loudly and resolutely to him.

"I'd rather die with Ocelot than stand by you!"

I watched his colored cheeks of health turn ashen. His vibrant demeanor drained away. His eyes that before conveyed hope now stared forward vacantly. His jaw hung open in a dull expression. I kicked off the edge of the platform and allowed myself to fall down past the wall of ships.

As the boxed ships whizzed up past me, I heard Alaban's sword clank to the ground with a ringing tone. It echoed and blended with the sound of Teradom's swearing protest.

"Damn it! What a fucking waste of time!"

Fifteen meters down, Ocelot lay sprawled in a larger pool of blood. His last spark of life snuffed out before me. I sensed its quavering wisp lift away from his tattered body. I cast aside my sword and knelt in the red puddle beside him. Without thinking of anything but the desire for him to live, I plunged my hands into his wound.

"Bring the life back. Build up these tissues and organs. Build it all back up again. Pull him back together, God. Let him live. Let him live," I chanted. "If the Torreons could bring me back to my body, then so help me I can do the same for him. God help us. Bring him back."

High above me, I heard the General shouting to the troops to move.

"She gets her wish, then. Let her die. We'll find another way to get what we're after," Teradom said. He called to Alaban to clear out. "Now, bodyguard! She's made her choice. Let her freeze to death for it."

I conjured all my healing power and directed it into Ocelot's body. I massaged the slimy texture. I felt the remnants of his pain course through my arms and into my own body. It was almost too much for me, but I determined to bring him back, even if it meant giving him all my reserve energy. I worked his flesh diligently. Another entity's power reached through me, a celestial power. It cooperated with my pleas. I watched in grateful awe as the organs grew back. Most of the blood around us seeped back into his body. I rubbed the organs carefully until they were all back in place. I wrapped one hand under his side and held the other over the top of

341

his wound. I made little circles with both hands, helping his body recreate the muscle tissue. I began to feel heavy, weak, but I would not stop.

Shouted orders rang through the hangar. Troop's footfalls drummed above.

I tried to ignore the noise, concentrating all the more on my healing task. I caressed the muscled areas over the wound until the tissues and skin regrew to their original form. I leaned forward to rest my face over his heart to check his heartbeat and because the healing had left me exhausted. His heartbeat was strained—weak, but improving. His breathing was shallow, but consistent.

I heard above me the clamor of boots on the ladder. The troops descended to their ships above us. They boarded, prepped engines, and began to detach from the wall. A flashing series of lights around the edge of the platforms followed by an alarm told me the hangar was about to depressurize. The portal would open as soon as the attack ships lined up to blast out.

I had to get us out of here or we would freeze and suffocate as Teradom had said, but I didn't have enough energy to haul Ocelot up the ladder with me, and of course once I got there, even if I could pass us through the sealed doors, we would encounter the General again.

I looked around us. The only chance we had was to board one of the empty attack ships and power it up to at least give basic life support. I crawled over to the nearest ship. The hatch was sealed, but could be opened with a code key. I stumbled back to Ocelot and dug through his pockets. I found a multipurpose decoder key.

With a short prayer, I attached the key to the panel on the ship. It opened the hatch right away.

"Oh, thank you," I whispered. I tucked the device into my pocket.

The attack ships were already hovering before the portal. With my remaining strength, I dragged Ocelot's heavy body to the ship. I tried different ways to lift him, but I ended up using all my levitation skill plus worn out muscles to haul him up to the open hatch. I slung his body halfway over the ledge to the cockpit. The first portal door began to open. Filters all around the attack ship niches sucked air out of the hangar at an alarming speed.

I dove back to retrieve my sword, disengaged it, and stored it as quickly as possible. I rushed back to Ocelot's folded body and climbed over it into the cockpit. Tired and beaten, I did not know where I found the energy to pull him into the seat next to me and fold his legs to sit him upright. I barely maintained consciousness as I reached out to the panel in front of me. I ticked the buttons to close and seal the hatch and then boosted on life support.

To the sides of the hangar portal, mechanical arms ground loudly to separate the sections of the door, push them outward and then retract them to the sides. The attack ships zoomed out from the hangar in two rows. The portal stayed open.

I considered flying the ship out with them, but I felt myself slipping into dormancy. Even if I managed to fly out, where would I go? We couldn't survive long in this tiny fighter. It would take weeks to get to the nearest planet. If I tried to fly out and dock the fighter at one of the tentacles, the Fitmalos would either attack or simply deny access to the tunnels by keeping the docking mechanisms retracted and the doors locked. Plus we couldn't leave the ship in zero atmosphere.

The General would think we were dead by now. He would expect me to suffocate and freeze here in the depressurized hangar in a matter of seconds. Alaban would know I was alive, but would he still come after me?

I couldn't think anymore. I couldn't stay awake. I tucked my blood-encrusted hands under my arms and fell asleep with the image of Alaban's ashen face fixed in my mind.

Chapter 32: Escape from the Space Station

A low boom awoke me. The portal had resealed. The air pressure pumps whooshed on all around us. The attack ships returned to their places in the wall above us. A few moments later, I heard the troops clattering up the ladder.

I checked the time on the attack ship's computer. If they had gone out to destroy the Sonic Wake that had not been their only purpose. They had been gone three and a half hours. I ignored the possibility for the time being. The General could have been bluffing. Honesty was clearly not one of his virtues.

The acrid stench of blood hung with us in the tiny cockpit. I felt sick from it. I looked over at Ocelot, who sagged in his seat. I held a thumb to his jugular vein. His pulse was normal. His breathing was quiet, but steady. I was sure if I could keep him alive, he would stay like this for two or three days. I remembered my own recuperation from the airbus incident. That seemed like eons ago.

A new set of boots clamored onto the ladder, then another. Soldiers were coming to look for our bodies. They hopped off the ladder to the bloody platform. I turned off life support. As the men stepped up to peer into the hatch, I leaned over Ocelot's body to project a blind spot. The men shone lights into the ship, but did not see us. One looked right through me.

They walked away to the next ship, and then the next. They came back to this one again. The blood stains trailed up to this ship. They couldn't figure out where we were. They looked all around it. My energy was wearing down.

I heaved a sigh when they finally left. They would continue to look below us and all around the hangar. We would be reported as missing. I wondered if the soldiers would stage an all-hands alert. Or perhaps Teradom would want to keep the incident quiet. And what about Wilbaht and Klib? If our ship was still intact, what would Teradom tell Wilbaht about us?

I leaned back into the seat after rebooting life support. I hoped the quiet whir of the air circulator wouldn't bring the soldiers back to us. I waited and listened sleepily in my chair. I heard voices far above us. I closed my eyes and meditated on their sources. The two soldiers reported to the squad leader and to another man I'd seen during our tour. They argued with each other. One said they hadn't searched well enough. The other promised that they had. The officer ordered them to recheck the whole facility and then clean up the blood on the main platform as well as below. All four men retreated through the airlock room to recruit more help. The hangar was left unattended for the moment.

I took the opportunity to escape from the little ship. I planned to move us to another one nearby. The soldiers would be here momentarily to clean around and inside this one.

I turned off the ship and popped open the hatch. I climbed halfway out and reached back in for Ocelot. I pulled him by his thick arm, but couldn't move him well without levitation. I gave up and pulsed a levitative wave to him, lifting him out of the ship and dropping him awkwardly to a clean spot on the floor.

I checked his uniform to make sure we wouldn't make another tell tale path to our next hideout. The uniform was stained everywhere, but the stains were mostly dry. The seats where we had sat in the attack ship were also smeared with blood. Soon they would know we had been there. I resealed the hatch and lugged him away from the attack ship.

Normally, there would be no point in anyone closely monitoring the security sensors for the hangar at this time. The portal seal was confirmed. The attack ships were secure. But today someone would be checking on the hangar area because of our recent ordeal. They knew where we were. They had merely waited for the hangar to be pressurized to come for us. If Teradom and his cohorts still wanted to collect our bodies, alive or dead, he only needed to scan the hangar for our location and then surround us. The soldiers would be back soon. The only chance we had was to move unpredictably and fast.

I stepped to the edge of the mini platform and looked in all directions. Below us at the bottom of the stack of attack ships was another airlock door. I didn't know where it led, but it was worth a try. It would be easier to fall down and give us a soft, levitated landing than it would be to haul Ocelot's body back up to the top platform. Besides, climbing back up meant unavoidable confrontation with the people looking for us. I had to risk it.

I heaved Ocelot's body up over my back as if he were a huge blanket. Then I clambered over the railing with difficulty. I let us drop. I fought against the gravity projectors to bring us gently to the floor.

At the base of the attack ship grid, I pulled Ocelot over to one side of the airlock doors. I peered through them. An empty corridor led to a set of double doors flanked by a panel of visual monitors. I sensed no one nearby.

I opened the doors using Ocelot's decoder key. Once again, his body became a winter blanket on my back. I leaned forward to balance the weight. At the end of the corridor, I stopped to check the monitor screens. These pinpointed specific parts of the hangar. None of the soldiers were back yet.

I boldly flung our bodies through the double doors at the end of the corridor. This was an auxiliary communications and defense control room. It was unoccupied, dim, and eerie. Not hesitating to ponder why it had been left empty, I bustled through the room to its exit. This led to a long hallway with an elevator, a set of spiral stairs at the far end, and several other doors farther down the hall. I sensed several people in rooms behind some of the doors, but only one person in the room closest to the elevator.

· I hoped no one would walk out into the hallway while I dragged Ocelot to that room. I paced out into the corridor. After twelve steps, the elevator hummed. I jolted us forward as fast as I could. I had to get past the elevator and into the room to hide us.

Just as the elevator doors opened, I bustled into the office. Before he saw me, I knocked out the young Fitmalo recruit at the computer with a fist to the temple. Then I sidestepped to lean Ocelot against the wall just behind the door. As I stood up, the door opened again.

A female Fitmalo and someone behind her stood at the doorway and gasped to see their colleague slumped over to one side, his shoulder pressed to the keyboard of the computer next to him. I couldn't attack the female, knowing that the other Fitmalo behind her would retreat or yell for help as soon as he saw her in peril. I crouched with Ocelot and cloaked a blind spot around us, hoping my power would hold out long enough to get them into the room completely with the door closed so I could execute an attack.

The female behaved as I had hoped, but the male behind her remained at the threshold.

The female grasped her unconscious friend by the shoulder. "Raki? Raki, are you okay? Firo, help me with him."

Firo finally walked into the room. The door nearly closed. I was about to pounce after them, but a voice from the hallway asked what was going on.

"I don't know. He's out cold," the woman said.

Just then, Raki started to come around. He sat up on his own and held his head in his hands. Firo clapped him on the shoulder.

"Oh, what happened? I was just sitting here and I got this pain in my forehead," Raki said groggily.

"You'd better get to the medical station," Firo told him.

"Why don't I go with you? Have you been feeling all right lately?" the woman asked.

Raki stood holding his head. The others escorted him out of the room, but then Firo returned. He turned Raki's computer off and sat at his own, which faced away from us. He clicked it on and began sorting through some kind of numerical data.

I released the blind spot, since his back was to us. As the man leaned back in his chair to stretch, I shot forward to deliver a powerful palm strike to the base of his skull. His body hurtled up diagonally. His face whacked against the wall. He crumpled first over his computer area, and then to the floor, wheeling his chair away from his computer ledge. He jerked a little, but then lay still.

I jumped up and locked the door. I sat with my back to it, focusing to see mentally all around us. Alaban was close by again, two levels above us. I couldn't see whom he was with or what they were doing. If I could get to him, would he still help me? After that episode in the hangar, why would he, especially with the dead body of my partner over my shoulders?

This was his fault, but would he recognize the fact? He somehow believed he was doing the right thing. If he had wanted to keep us alive and together, why hadn't he just assassinated General Teradom to begin with?

346

As Ocelot had said, we couldn't work for him if he was dead. That story about being betrayed by the Organization and his own crew didn't hold water. The idea of Swall Jade enslaving us was even more preposterous.

If Alaban's true motive for his actions was to keep me alive and safe, then he had given up too much for me, blatantly against my will. He had promised he wouldn't work for them. He knew I was adamantly against it. How could he possibly imagine that I'd suddenly change my mind? The charismatic, gifted, trustworthy man who had proposed to be my life-long mate, whose only words to me had been of love and endearing friendship, had now become an incomprehensible, treacherous beast.

I glanced at Firo's computer screen. One of its shells contained an icon for station updates. I selected it to see if we'd been reported. I opened shell after shell of security and systems information, but found no report of alert. I located ship docking and found our ship's crew listed as two, not four. Teradom had already reported us dead. Was he so confident of our demise or was he still planning something?

Assuming Wilbaht and Klib still survived, I entered interrogations records. No Torreons or humans had been taken into custody. Where were they? If everyone assumed Teradom's report was true, Wilbaht and Klib could be at the ship waiting for our remains to be delivered to them. Having no remains to deliver, Teradom would probably either make up a story of the destruction of our bodies or he would finally decide to get rid of Wilbaht and Klib. This was a possibility I did not want to consider, but had to face unemotionally. Such a move would leave us without a viable escape route. I considered other emergency options, like stowing away aboard the Jawlcheen Reaper or hiding out within the space station until we could stow away on some other ship.

In any case, we had to get out of here. I needed to take the elevator up three levels and make my way across a series of hydroponics labs to get back to section three and to the tentacle connecting the Sonic Wake to the space station. When I felt no one occupied the corridor, I unlocked the door and bustled us through it. I carried Ocelot to the elevator. We got on without being seen, but at the next level up, a couple of soldiers waited to get on. I cloaked a blind spot and shoved them both to the floor. They flopped backwards, hitting their heads on the opposite wall. They looked at each other in confusion. They wouldn't report this. What would they report? They couldn't be sure what had just happened to them.

We continued up to the next floor. I felt Alaban not two meters away from me. He felt my presence, too. I was sure of it. He did not move to alert anyone to my whereabouts. He stayed in the same position, waiting.

At the next level, I fastened my hand bow to its place at my fist and stepped out to see a group of Fitmalo soldiers heading away from us. The hydroponics lab entrance was at the end of this hallway.

I hefted Ocelot's body over my shoulders and ran to burst through the nearest door. This was a simple storage room containing a clerk who had been collecting some supplies. She hugged the little boxes to her when she saw us, as if she expected me to try and steal them from her.

"I don't want to hurt you, miss," I began.

She relaxed her shoulders slightly.

"But I will," I stated on second thought.

I swiped at her with a simultaneous thumb to the neck and a fist to the temple. She went down with a clunk.

I leaned Ocelot's body against the shelves. My thighs and back tired from carrying him around.

Now I had to concentrate on getting us through the hydroponics lab. Many people trafficked this area. Soon someone would discover the Fitmalo I'd just knocked out in the office. Then an alert would be enforced. It would be impossible to run, duck, and hide as we'd managed to do so far.

I mentally scanned our immediate vicinity. I searched for air circulation ducts, pipeline housing, back ways through the area. Only one system of air filtration was large enough for us. It spanned the ceiling area above the hydroponics lab, but didn't cover the entire area. It snaked back around towards section four. Plus the air ducts were inaccessible from our current position. We would have to ascend to the next level to get to the air tunnel.

Time was running out for us. I waited until I felt the hallway was clear. I heaved Ocelot onto my back and bolted for the elevator. Once inside, I pressed for the next level up, but the elevator already began to follow a request to go down one floor.

"Oh, no. Please don't," I breathed.

I cowered into a corner of the elevator box, pressing Ocelot to the wall behind me. His head rested at the back of mine. A slight groan escaped from his throat. I pushed his head back so that it lolled into the corner, face up. I knew he wasn't waking up, but involuntary sounds were the last thing we needed now.

The elevator stopped. The doors opened. I cloaked in panic. To my dismay, Sub General Navran, Head General Teradom and Alaban entered the elevator together. Alaban stepped in close and turned his back to me, but said nothing. His face was stony.

Navran spoke to the General. "I had no idea those warriors had anything to do with General Sunderlign, sir. I would never have let them in the hangar."

"No one is blaming you, Sub General. You couldn't have known. Apparently not even Sunderlign knew of their personal vendetta against him," Teradom explained.

"Sir, do we know what it was all about?" Navran asked.

"According to my bodyguard here, Sunderlign served human meat at their table while they were working for him on Karnesh. Apparently they took his faux pas as a mortal offense. They thought he had something to do with the human meat market in Keres, which he did not."

"That's terrible, sir. The General will be missed among us. I'd never known an Organization warrior to attack for personal reasons in public before," Navran continued.

"Yes. That male was a loose cannon, completely uncontrolled, too emotional. The Organization is better off without that one. The female, however...It's too bad she got caught up in the fight," Teradom replied.

At the next floor up, Navran said, "Thank you, sir. I will report to their ship's commander right away." He bowed as the doors closed after him.

"What will you tell Sub General Wilbaht about their bodies, sir?" Alaban asked the General.

Teradom peered at him wisely. "There's nothing left of them. Since they were hiding near the attack ships after they killed Sunderlign, their bodies were sucked out into space. They froze and then burned to cinders from the ship exhaust. There was nothing we could do for them. We express our deepest sympathies. We do not blame the Sub General for the foolish actions of his crew, as we recognize they acted independently. If he doesn't believe us, we'll just show him discretely edited footage from the hangar.

"The sooner he leaves the station, the better. I sense she is still somewhere in the military section. We mustn't let her communicate with him. If she does, she'll be signing her commander's death warrant. At any rate, she's not leaving this space station. I expect she cloaked to sneak back into the lightship barracks. All airmen are advised to report anything unusual. If she is as talented as you say, she could evade them, but this will take time. Any quick movements or attacks will not go unnoticed."

"She'll try to make her way back to the docking arm. We should have the entranceway to the hydroponics lab sealed for a security exercise. At least that's my suggestion, sir," Alaban told him.

Teradom eyed him with a pleasant face and nodded. "Very bright, young friend, but of course I've planned a more comprehensive strategy. I'm ordering a full alert drill on sections three and four as soon as Sub General Wilbaht is set for departure. He will leave before the drill is over. Your woman will be forced to reveal herself. She cannot wander our halls

349

undetected for long. Once her ship is gone, she will have no one to search for but you. I'm sure you anticipate getting your hands on her as much as I do, perhaps more." Teradom turned confidently to face the door.

"Yes, sir." Alaban lifted a hand to his ear as if to adjust his communicator, but then reached just below his shoulder and to his right where I stood. I couldn't avoid his touch. He purposefully caressed my right cheek and jaw.

"Maybe while she's in hiding she'll finally realize what she's missing," Alaban said.

I held my breath, mortified.

Alaban lowered his hand just as Teradom turned toward him. "Her last chance for freedom depends on you. You had better be convincing. Otherwise, you know what her fate will be."

"Yes, sir."

The General stepped off the elevator. Alaban followed him, but cast a haggard glance over his shoulder at me before stepping out.

As the doors closed, I punched the panel to go to the floor just above the hydroponics level. Maybe I could get to the air ducts after all.

I shuddered. So they planned on capturing me still. I couldn't let that happen. I had to get us out of here now.

When the doors opened, I cloaked as two recruits stepped into the elevator. I sidled past them as quietly as I could. The elevator doors shut halfway, but then caught on Ocelot's leg and reopened. The men thought this was strange, but continued talking. As the doors shut, I turned around to find the hallway empty to one side. Unfortunately, I looked back to see a group of Fitmalos—five of them. Two of them faced us.

Before they could run or call for help, I dropped Ocelot to the floor and flew at them. The two men facing me received a hammer blow to the throat. They jolted backward, surprising the three others near them. I flung fists and shins at them. I hurled one man's skull into another's. Then I grabbed the third by the collar and thwacked him in the face with my elbow. One of the men I'd knocked down first stood wheezing. He drew a firearm. I picked up one of his countrymen and threw the body at him. I pounced upon them, tossing the weapon from his hand. Then I kicked the men in the face repeatedly. I pummeled several pressure point combinations on all five of them to make sure they would all stay down.

During the whirlwind fight, I noticed a large panel in the wall not far from us. This had to be a part of the air duct. I whisked back to Ocelot and pulled him awkwardly to lie next to the wall panel. I slid it open and yanked out a filter behind it. I glimpsed the size of the tunnel. I would have to go in backwards first, and then pull Ocelot in after me.

I backed into the shaft. As I reached over to guide Ocelot's body carefully into the tunnel with me, a door at the end of the hallway delivered a new group of Fitmalo soldiers. They sauntered in, unaware of the battle scene. As the last of the group cleared the threshold of the door, the first pair reached for their weapons.

I aimed the hand bow above their heads and fired. The arrow hit the ceiling above the group and popped. It puffed out in a large green ball of acid. It showered the men, who gasped, coughed, and clawed at their faces.

I pulled Ocelot's body with all my might to get him in the tunnel and out of sight as the soldiers reeled, yelping with pain. I stuffed his body into the shaft, squeezed around him, retrieved the filter, and levitated the panel door to close before the cries of the injured brought more soldiers to the scene. I squirmed through the tunnel, listening to the commotion made by the wounded and those who discovered them.

I felt my power had increased during our escape thus far, so I risked a difficult strategy. I wedged myself under my partner's heavy body. I levitated us, holding onto his wrists. With my greatest concentration, I shot us down through the blackness of the air duct with speed and precision. Faintly lit squares from vents whizzed past us along the way. I slowed only when we reached the point in the duct that penetrated furthest into the hydroponics lab.

Here, I carefully shoved Ocelot's body to one side and then perched above a broad circular fan. It spun above a table of seedlings. I extracted my laser cutter from its pouch. Without time to spare to check for people nearby, I cut through the fan's electrical connection. The fan blades slowed as I sliced diligently through the metal arms of its casing. Finally, the fan fell through with a conspicuous crash, crushing the table and all its plant life.

At a distance of about seven meters, I heard a voice ask loudly, "Hey, what did you break now?"

At an equal distance from me, but from the opposite side, I heard a reply. "It wasn't me! I don't know what that was!"

I hopped down to stand atop the fan and the collapsed table. I gathered Ocelot to me. I levitated us to a tall row of bean plants. The two people approached from either side of us, winding their way through long, hanging vines. As the nearest Fitmalo passed us to check the source of the noise, I whisked us along the row of plants, around a hydroponics chemical reserve, and through a series of tented vegetable patches. I cloaked to avoid several lab technicians on the way. They shuddered, spooked by the loud rustle of plant leaves, caused by an unseen source. Finally we reached the end of the greenhouse area. We still had to get through the communications area, the green lobby, and to the locker area where I prayed our spacesuits still hung.

I burst through the main hydroponics lab door and heaved our bodies up to the ceiling. The security personnel turned to the swinging door in confusion. They had not seen us, but someone behind us had.

As we skidded along the ceiling, Ocelot draped over my back, someone shouted, "Did you see that?"

I plummeted us forward with all my strength. An alarm sounded. Fitmalo soldiers hurried to secure the door between the green lobby and the communications area. I zipped through the door just as it closed. I spun us, sliding aground near the exit. I had to seal the door between the communications area and the lobby before we were followed. I let Ocelot's body rest on the carpet while I readied my fan blaster.

I held it firmly and flipped it on to charge. I counted to five. I watched anxiously as several soldiers filtered in through the doorway, firearms pointed at me. They shouted at me to put down the weapon. I fired. The fan beam wobbled along in the air as the Fitmalos shot at me through it. Their shots dissolved in the atomic fan, causing it to expand all the more. When the men realized there was no stopping this, they dove out of its way, scattering to different parts of the room.

The beam divided into three parts. The center of the beam kept going through the door, annihilating anyone in its path. The two parts of the beam that hit on either side of the door impacted and vibrated the structure at a frightening rate. The lights flickered. Green paint shuddered off the walls like tainted snow. A horrible grating sound wove its way through the framework of this end of the tentacle. The security door attempted to close and seal itself, but its glass membranes sprung from its frame, pulverized. The debris prevented the doors from moving together completely. The alarms in the green lobby sputtered off. Half the lights dimmed. The other half flickered. Air circulation slowed and then ceased.

I retreated with Ocelot, backing towards the locker room door, but the remaining Fitmalo soldiers in the lobby opened fire at me. I somehow managed to duck and dodge most of their shots, but two singe gun bullets grazed my right arm and burned badly. I returned fire with the hand bow, but the soldiers scattered again. Some hid under draped tables. Some cowered behind a service area.

I counted seven left alive and ready to fire. I managed to drag Ocelot through the door. I dumped him onto the floor in front of the lockers and ran back to fight off the remaining soldiers.

Fitmalos fired on me from three directions. I cowered in the doorway to avoid their shots. I aimed and fired at three of them near a set of seats to my left. A man to my right shot just before I did. The singe hit my flack vest over my left breast. The impact jerked me backwards. The singe burned a hole in the vest, but I didn't take it off for fear of another hit. The smell of burning flesh and synthetic materials wafted from my sleeve and from my flack vest. My chest and arm burned sharply, but I could do nothing for them now.

I shot at the man who had injured me, but he dove out of the way. The acid blast scalded his legs and hit a man near him. The first man crawled along in agony. There were still two others hiding off to my left somewhere, but I hoped they would stay back for the moment. I swung into the locker side of the door and set it to full lock. It sealed together with a thump.

I raced to fling open the locker that had contained Ocelot's space suit. I was immensely thankful to find it still there. I yanked it out.

I glanced out the final airlock. Our ship still floated where we had left it. It appeared fully intact. If we were lucky, we could get from the tentacle to the ship. Then maybe Wilbaht could negotiate our way out or call for help. We might even be able to blast our way out, although we would have to face the fleet of attack ships to get away. I knew my hopes were based on failing ideas, but I had no other way to turn.

I methodically fit the suit over Ocelot's body as if he were a huge infant. Once the legs and waist were in, I inserted his left arm into the sleeve of the suit. I leaned over to reach the right arm when I heard a whoosh behind me.

As I glanced fearfully over my shoulder, I fell forward over Ocelot's body. Several hot projectiles sliced through me. They penetrated my arm from the elbow towards the shoulder. They dug through the top of my thigh towards my knee. One even scraped across my forehead. The most damaging spike wedged itself up under my vest and buried itself deep beneath my ribs.

I flipped over onto my back and fired my last acid arrow at the remaining Fitmalo soldiers who had managed to unlock and open the door. One of them fired again, but aimed badly in reaction to my shot. The spikes bounced off the ceiling near him and fell clinking to the floor just in front of me. My acid shot blossomed between the two men. They writhed and blubbered into a pair of disheveled heaps.

With difficulty, I returned to tuck Ocelot's right arm into his suit. I rejected the pain of my injuries to zip up the suit and then connect the helmet, which I set to seal and begin life support.

I moved to get my own suit, which also still hung in its place. I knocked it to the floor. My lung cavity ached. My spike wounds already began to swell. I felt their itchy poison agitate my muscles. I stepped gingerly into the boots of the suit.

The room swayed. I leaned onto the lockers. The poison affected my motor skills. I panted with agony and determination. I had to at least save Ocelot before the serum killed me.

The room wavered as I pulled up the suit to my waist. Poison coursed through my veins. It reached around my head and neck like an icy hand. It flooded my brain. My eyesight clouded. My head plunged into a sea of poison.

The suit slipped from my hands, falling again around my ankles. I barely felt the trickles of blood drip from my wounds. I staggered. My vision blurred and then darkened completely.

A strange awareness entered me. I felt my mother with me somewhere nearby, perhaps in a different dimension. I thought I heard her speak to me in a double voice.

"Sil, you can't die now."

I fell backwards into a light sleep even as I fought to stay alive and awake. I felt as though I were sinking. The celestial presence I'd sensed in a dream some time ago arrived at my side. Dark hands caressed my wounded body. My injuries slowly reversed. Someone pulled the spike from my leg, absorbing the poison and the pain. The next spike scraped out through my arm from near the elbow. The pain seeped out with healing strokes.

"You need this life from me. Take it," I heard the double voice say.

My healer inserted a finger into the singe burns at my shoulder and massaged the flesh until it returned to its normal elasticity.

"You need all the good I have left in me. Take it. Take it all," the voices told me.

My vest loosened and fell away. Someone turned me over on my side to extract the two spikes embedded in my ribs. Health returned to my body. A hand pressed over the scar on my forehead.

My mother's voice disappeared, as did her presence. I heard a new, clear voice speak to me as a hand caressed and healed the burn scars at my breast.

"Drain all the power from me. Take it. Live. Use it all up, Sil. Come back."

The soothing voice changed slowly into an agitated voice.

"Pull out all the healing power I have left, Sil. I give it all to you. Take it."

I grabbed the hand away from my chest and bolted upright to see Alaban kneeling over me. I gulped air. We stared into each other's eyes. His dark, handsome face furrowed. His black, expressive eyes sought to comfort me even as I opposed him. With only this conversation of the eyes, we exchanged a long argument. He communicated a plea of desperation. I denied his plea.

Alaban bent even closer to me. I thought he meant to kiss me, but instead he whispered to me slowly and tenderly. "You're not coming with me?"

I clenched my jaw and shook my head slowly without removing my gaze from his eyes.

He pressed his forehead to mine and squeezed his eyes shut. He sighed loudly as he clenched my arms.

Then he jumped to his feet with a growl and pulled me up to stand with him. He shouted at me. I backed away from him, but he grabbed me by the wrist.

"Why couldn't you trust me? I just wanted you to live, Sil! I just wanted you to live! But you'll never live for *me*, will you? I gave you everything I had. I would still give up everything just for you. But you can't see it." He pointed at me in ire.

"You think your honor and your *job* are more important than my love! You're wrong, Sil. You are so wrong." He released my wrist, throwing my arm back at me.

I gasped.

Alaban raged. "I anchored my heart on you. No matter what happened in this goddamned pitiful universe, I could overcome it because you were my sun, my 'bright star'! Now it turns out you're an ungrateful *thief*. You stole my heart just to build *yourself* up and you *never gave anything back*!"

"Alaban, I…" I began shakily.

"*Shut up!*" he bellowed.

I panted. He went on relentlessly.

"I am through waiting for you. I get it now. We will never be mates. I'll never be good enough for you. It's *you* who's not good enough. *You're* the failure. You're the traitor to *me*!"

He grasped my chin between his thumb and forefinger. I groaned and whimpered as I stared, terrified, into his face.

He drew himself close to me, but still yelled. "I loved you more than anyone in this universe and you would rather *die* than live with me? You said you loved me, but *you lied*!" He pushed my chin away, causing me to stumble backward a step. He grimaced in anguish.

I held my chin where his fingers had pinched me. I gaped, transfixed by his fury.

Suddenly he drew his sword. "You want to die?"

I started in disbelief. "No," I whispered.

"Put the suit on!" he shouted, pointing at it with the end of the blade. "Do it!"

With a shudder, I did as he commanded. What would he do? I fitted my arms jerkily into the heavy sleeves. I zipped up the suit. I was about to pick up the helmet, but he told me to leave it on the floor. I searched his eyes for an explanation.

He raised and parried the sword so that the blade rested across his left shoulder. His eyes glowered fiercely.

With frightening speed, he rushed at me, grabbing me by the back of the head with his left arm. He tucked two of his fingers from his right hand into the collar of my space suit even as he held the sword. I panted in fear.

His chest heaved. The frown that carved through his dark face deepened. His eyes lost their terrifying glow for a moment. He whispered to me again. "I'll see you again on Jawlcheen." He touched his nose to mine. "Forgive me."

I froze. He spread a tear across my cheek with his lips. He pressed his face into mine so tightly that the sword began to cut into my neck. Then he grasped my hair and jerked his face away from me.

He took a deep breath. His eyes turned fearsome once again. He growled loudly, pronouncing every word with powerful clarity.

"I release you!"

My eyes grew wide. I cried out. He swiped the sword between us without cutting either of us, but to anyone watching the monitor for this room, it would appear as though he had cut my throat. I gasped. He toppled me to the floor as his sword smacked the base of the opposite wall. From within his vest, he retrieved a vial. He popped its top, spilling its contents onto the floor near my head as he reached for my helmet. The vial had been filled with blood. He pressed on my chest to keep me down. He fumbled with the vial in his left hand as he reached for my helmet with his right. He swallowed nervously. He stowed the vial into my collar and kissed my face quickly three times before he covered my head and secured the helmet. He covered me with his full weight and hugged my padded body with a shout of anguish.

The whole charade happened so quickly. I stared at him in shock. When his weight lifted away from my body, I panicked. My heart begged to stay with him even as my mind's convictions pushed him away. I could do nothing inside my dark, heavy equipment. Alaban hit the airlock release. He levitated Ocelot's body and mine rapidly into the first airlock. He turned me to face him.

"I love you," I saw him say as he pressed the panel to seal the door. A lone tear fell from his crazed face.

The door slammed between us. He pulsed us away from him as the second airlock door opened and closed, and then the third. Alaban sent us all the way to the end of the wire mesh tunnel, where our ship's door received us into the main cargo hold of the Sonic Wake. As soon as we were inside the cargo hold, the docking robot disengaged the wire tunnel and retracted it back to the door where Alaban stood.

I watched his dimly silhouetted image for the brief second before he was snatched from me as the outer door to the cargo hold shut and sealed itself. I felt the engines of the Sonic Wake rev up to detach and cruise away from the leering hydra. I sat shell-shocked and grief-stricken on the floor. My sobs echoed loudly inside my helmet.

Chapter 33: Transition to Suffering

When the gravity projectors turned off for the standard internal power down for departure, my tears abated. I slowly solidified into a conglomerate of maddening emotions. My conscience twisted into a mass of flickering nightmares. The part of my mind that controlled my motor skills and routine movement still functioned, but my reason and psyche seemed to float apart from my body. I watched myself guide Ocelot's body through the first cargo hold, pass the hallway, and enter the secondary hold.

Images and sound fragments tunneled relentlessly into my brain. I saw myself pull off my suit. My hands stored the space suit to its holding net. I went through the motions of removing Ocelot's space suit and returning it to its place. I watched myself pull our bodies along to the end of the hallway and into the quarantine room. I pressed Ocelot's body to the gurney bed. My hands zipped the white elastic straps to secure him to the bed. My floating body performed the procedures, but my mind and heart had fled somewhere, searching for safety.

The vital signs monitor read a normal pulse. It showed no irregularities in the heart or lungs. A brain scan showed a slight concussion. I unstrapped him from the gurney and guided him weightlessly out of the quarantine station, down the hall, and up through the spiral stairway. I floated us both all the way to the main observation deck.

"Resuming internal gravity systems," I heard Klib say.

I draped Ocelot over my back once more. I'd almost gotten used to carrying him this way. When Klib flipped the switch, my boots thudded to the floor. I leaned forward and grunted from the sudden weight.

Klib swung around to see us. He flinched rashly. Then he unstrapped himself from the chair and jumped to his feet swearing loudly.

I stared listlessly at Wilbaht, who wrenched himself from his straps.

He leapt to us, exclaiming that I was alive. He lifted Ocelot from my back. He held his head as he sat the body against the railing of the stairway. I knelt with him. Wilbaht felt Ocelot's face and neck.

"He's all right," he spoke with surprise and relief. He turned to me. "Are you?"

"Okay," I whispered expressionlessly. I stared at Ocelot's sleeping face.

Wilbaht analyzed Ocelot's bloodstained uniform. He placed a hand over the huge hole in it. Then he wrapped his long hand around Ocelot's back to feel the same kind of hole there. He gazed at me with realization.

"You healed this," he spoke incredulously.

I nodded weakly.

He reached over to me to touch the burn holes at my sleeve.

"Who healed you?" he asked.

"Alaban," I whispered, almost without sound. I stared forward dully.

"Is Alaban dead?" he asked gingerly.

Klib moved in close to us to see the evidence of our battle.

"No," I said aloud. I heard my voice babble to him in an attempt to comply with my duty to answer my commander, but my delivery of the news was sidetracked by the aftershock of our trauma. In a nonsensically emotionless voice, my mouth spoke. "He killed his crew. He works for Regime now, wanted me to join. Fought Ocelot. Killed...Sunderlign. M-Mantis, beheaded. F-Fought. Swords. In the h-hangar, n, Ocelot shot, dead." I felt myself becoming incoherent. I sat heavily onto the small floor space.

I struggled to regain some form of clarity. I inhaled deeply. "Ocelot fell. He has a c-concussion," I exhaled.

Wilbaht set a heavy hand on my left shoulder. He peered into my dull eyes.

"It's okay, Sil," he spoke patiently. "We'll take him from here."

"It's okay, Sil," I heard myself repeat absurdly.

Klib whistled a single note. "This bird is cooked," he said.

"Help me carry Ocelot downstairs," Wilbaht ordered.

I stood awkwardly, wavering.

"Not you, Sil. You follow us," Wilbaht clarified.

The two men grabbed the heavy body. Wilbaht took him around the shoulders. Klib held his ankles. I followed them slowly down the stairs and through the dining area to his bunk. I watched them carefully lay him on his bed.

"We'll leave him there for a while. I'll check on him in a minute," Wilbaht said.

"Damn. I've never seen anything like this." Klib pointed to the bloody uniform.

"Come here, Sil," Wilbaht said to me. He put his arm around me and escorted me to my bunk, where he pulled down my bed from the wall. He sat me down and squatted next to me. He looked into my eyes, felt my throat, and took my pulse.

"Klib, get us a glass of water. They'll both be dehydrated. If Ocelot doesn't wake up soon I'll have to inject him."

Klib arrived at my door with the glass. He handed it to Wilbaht, who gave it to me. I gulped it down with a thirst I hadn't felt in months. Wilbaht urged me to take it slowly. I didn't listen.

"So it was your boyfriend who did that to Ocelot? I told you he was no good. He was just pulling your strings the whole time," Klib said.

My eyes widened to a mad glare. I leapt to my feet in a blind fury, knocking the glass to the floor and trembling violently. "Y-You told me? You didn't tell me anything about him. You don't know anything!" My voice grew more powerful with every menacing step towards him. He paced backwards.

My thumb closed around the activation button of my laser cutter, which was still attached to my right hand. I snatched Klib by the collar and moved the laser close to his throat. His eyes showed panic.

"Say it again. What the hell did you tell me about him? *What did you tell me?* I will kill you, you son of a bitch. I will *kill you*," I growled loudly.

Wilbaht's hands landed on my shoulders. "Sil! Put it down."

I glared at Klib's blurry face.

"Sil, put it down," Wilbaht repeated. "I don't want to have to hurt you."

I heard myself swear at Klib a couple more times with words I never thought I'd hear myself say. I raised the laser cutter to his face.

A splitting pain ripped through my head as Wilbaht pressed painful pressure points around the sides and back of my neck. I let go of the laser cutter. Klib's collar slipped from my grasp. I held an arm to my head. I swayed to one side, nearly losing consciousness. Wilbaht moved me to my bed and pulled my weapons from my hands and thighs.

"Here, put these in storage," he said to Klib.

"Yes, sir," Klib said firmly.

The headache subsided.

"Sil, I'm ordering you to stay in your bunk for the next six hours. You are to leave Klib alone. Don't talk to him. Don't approach him. Do you understand what I just told you?" Wilbaht said. I nodded. He made me repeat back to him what he'd said to make sure I understood. Then the men left me alone with my strife.

I lay blinking slowly, watching twisted images of the last few hours replay themselves over and over. I stared forward half-awake. I saw true events as well as warped versions of them. The cruel images invaded my conscience for hours. I became vaguely aware of Klib standing at the door to my bunk. I heard him speak to Wilbaht.

"She's been like this the whole time I was on watch, sir. Doesn't move. Doesn't say a word. Ocelot's still out, too."

"All right, Klib. Go check upstairs for vital stats and then get some rest," I heard Wilbaht say.

Wilbaht's great hand darkened my vision. "Sleep, child. Sleep."

I slept. But my sleep was interrupted by nightmares and regretful memories. I saw Alaban and myself back at the Center on Sor3 throwing rocks into the water. I saw us as teenagers working on a robotics project with other students at school. I saw us dancing together on Santer. I saw him kissing the tears from my face at the space station. I saw him with the sword between our throats. I dreamed he sliced us both with the sword, leaving us both bleeding to death.

"Yes, let me die with you," I said aloud. I reached out to clutch him to me, but I only grasped the air in my bunk.

I lay down again. I returned to a different dream. We stood in the hangar once more. Teradom offered to let Ocelot go free. This time I agreed to work with him.

"All right. I'll do it. Just let him go," I said.

"No, Sil. You don't know what they'll make you do," Ocelot pleaded.

"It doesn't matter what happens to me. Just go. Don't try to come back for me. Go with Wilbaht. I won't side with them until I see you safely board the ship," I told him.

Teradom was pleased. He sent Ocelot away with the entire squadron as an escort. I watched from a surveillance screen as the Sonic Wake detached from the station and sailed away towards Jawlcheen with my three former crewmembers aboard. Teradom allowed Alaban and me to share quarters for the night in a regal suite on the space station. Once we were alone, Alaban explained to me that he was just working for them to spy on their operation. He said he hadn't really killed Ongeram and Zank. He told me they were fine, but in hiding. He held me close to him. I felt relieved.

"They expect us to be mates now. Let's not disappoint them," he said.

He kissed me and pushed me down on his bed. Suddenly, he was pulling off our lower clothing to mate with me before I had said yes or no. I pushed him away frantically.

"Don't you love me, Sil?" he asked.

"I love you, but this is all wrong. I don't want this," I told him.

He became angry and clutched me by the back of my hair. He drew the sword and held it between us, pressing it against my throat. He continued pulling at my clothes. I squirmed beneath his crushing weight and the piercing pain of the sword. He prepared to rape me despite my struggle.

"Why shouldn't I have you, Sil? *Why?*" He shouted.

The blade cut into my throat until I couldn't breathe or make a sound.

I awoke with a start. I sat staring forward at the blank wall. Then I lay back down again.

"That would never happen," I whispered to myself. "That would never happen."

I shivered and then slept again. This time I dreamed that my reality was the dream. I dreamed I woke up next to Alaban in the bed we had shared in my temporary quarters on Santer.

"Bad dreams?" he asked me.

"Yes. It was terrible," I told him.

"It's just a dream, sweetheart. Here, sleep on your other side. Maybe you were just snoring," Alaban said.

"I don't snore," I told him. I turned so that my back was to him.

He snuggled close to me, resting his face by the back of my head. He imitated a snore. I smiled and pulled his arm around me. He kissed my cheek, and then rested again beside me.

Then I felt a nudge at my shoulder. I opened my eyes to see Ocelot standing in front of me with the gaping hole in his side. He stood half-dead, sword drawn.

"Move out of the way, Sil. He's got to pay for what he's done," Ocelot said.

I leaned back over Alaban, shielding him with one arm. "No. Don't hurt him, Ocelot. He didn't mean it. Let him go."

Ocelot grabbed at my shoulder again. I slapped his hand away. He knelt at my bedside. He stared into my face with worry. I knocked away his wrist as he moved his hand toward me again.

"Sil, it's okay," he crooned. He gently clutched my hand.

"No. No. Please don't hurt him," I whispered, wild-eyed.

"Sil, it's me. It's Ocelot." He stood up next to Wilbaht. He was healed again, his uniform just as it had been when we returned to the ship.

"Be patient with her," Wilbaht told him. "Sil, do you know where you are?"

I felt behind me for what I thought had been Alaban, but there was only the wall to my bunk. "Where is he? He's gone."

I scrambled to sit up and look around me. I wasn't dreaming now. I looked up at them both. I drew my knees up to my chest and pulled a sheet around me. I felt I was being spied on. I felt embarrassed, childish, lost. The dull stare crept back into my face.

"She's been like this off and on since she got back," I heard Wilbaht say.

He offered me a glass of water. I took it gratefully, downing its contents in just seconds.

Ocelot knelt again before me. "Sil, I don't know how you did it, but you saved my life when I was already dead. I owe you my life. I can't imagine how you got us out of there. You must have carried me the whole way even after you gave me so much of your energy."

I blinked. "Yes. I carried you on my back. You were heavy."

He smiled a little, but then grew worried again as my dull stare came back. He stood and looked for guidance from Wilbaht, who only shook his head.

I threw the sheet from me and stood with them, wobbly. Ocelot reached out to my right arm to help steady me, but I winced. The arm was still swollen from the poison spikes despite Alaban's cure. Ocelot released my arm with an apology.

"I have to go now," I said.

"Go where?" Wilbaht asked.

"Bathroom," I responded.

"Oh. I'll get out of your way, then," he said with a slight grin. The two men sidled out of my bunk and into the dining area as I grabbed some clean clothes and made my way to the bath.

I bathed twice to get the smell of blood off of me and then donned my travel uniform. I trashed my combat uniform in solid waste fuel reclaim. I only kept my boots and the arm and shin guards, which I scrubbed thoroughly. I went through all these motions in a haggard daze. All I could think about was Alaban.

I returned to my bunk, but only sat staring again.

Wilbaht passed by before going to sleep. He told me to get plenty of water and asked how I was feeling.

"I feel...empty," I said honestly.

He stepped into the bunk with me. He lifted my chin to catch my gaze.

"Sil, I know this is a time of great sadness for you, but we still need you to stay alive and healthy. Please remember that."

"Yes, sir," I spoke half-heartedly.

His shiny eyes conveyed sympathy but also firmness. He nodded to me. He left me to turn in at his own bunk.

I sat thinking of what I had just said. I felt empty. It was true. It was a feeling I'd not experienced. Not ever. Especially recently, I had felt Alaban's presence in my heart as part of my own being. Now I suddenly realized he was gone. I tried to control myself and meditate on his whereabouts, but I couldn't find him. I couldn't see or sense him anywhere. I panicked. Where could he be? Why had his spirit left me?

I ran to the door of my bunk. I looked around. Klib had to be upstairs. Wilbaht was in his bunk. Ocelot was bathing. I felt a chill. I shivered. The room blurred for a moment. I sneaked softly to the lower observation deck.

I looked up docking and departure information from import tax authorities to see if the space station had allowed the Reaper to go on its way. No such information existed. I prodded my muffled logic to think of where Alaban could be.

Another chill wove its way through my body. The room grew cold. The lights seemed to dim. Panic ensued again. I brought up my own personal communications screen. Did I dare message him? If I encrypted it many times and bounced the source of the message, perhaps no one would know I'd written to him. A wave of desperation pushed me to write.

With a lump of yet unswallowed pride in my throat, I typed a plea of mercy. My hands shook and my head throbbed, but I was driven by a singular unnerving fear: the fear of accidental self-injury, the fear of unintentional suicide. I had accidentally extracted him from my soul. I felt as if I were dying without him.

My head swam. I felt again as if I were in a daydream. My hands typed furiously. I blinked groggily at the screen as my pride slid down my throat along with stray tears.

I wrote: "Alaban, I don't know where you are. I can't feel your presence. Where are you? Why did you leave me? Are you cloaking yourself from me? Are you alive? You have to be alive. You are the one man in this universe who understands me. Please come back.

"I am sorry for what I said to you in the hangar. I do want to stand with you. I need you. I should have accepted you from the beginning. No one will ever love me like you have. I am so lonely without you. Please forgive me. Come back to my heart. I will be your mate for life. I will be anything you want. I love you more than anyone in this world. Please love me again. Your desperate, loving mate."

Sobs of grief overtook my body. The room melted around me in a dim watercolor of tears. My head and neck throbbed. I reached the send button with a limp and trembling hand. I sent the message over and over, hoping that he would read at least one endearing line of it. Maybe he would change his mind. Maybe he would come back to me. As I sent the message time after time, I felt myself slip farther and farther into failure. My mind and heart agreed I had lost him. My soul's twin had not only released me, as he had said. He had abandoned me.

I lost all control. I recoiled into the chair like a wounded animal. I heard loud wails escape from my throat. I pulled my knees to my body. My lungs shuddered in my chest. I gasped for huge gulps of air. I covered my head with my arms. A hollow cavern expanded in my chest where my heart should have been. I cried madly.

I reluctantly became aware of other noises close by. Wilbaht had come to see what had happened to me.

"Sil, what have you done? You've just messaged someone in a nonsecure area. If anyone from the space station is surveying this band, they'll realize you're alive." He touched my back, which still heaved with sobs. "Oh, dear God, child, you're burning with fever. Ocelot!"

Ocelot arrived before Wilbaht could finish calling his name. He stumbled over Wilbaht's feet and braced himself by the arms of my chair.

"What happened?" he asked.

"She's consumed with fever," Wilbaht said.

Ocelot thrust a hand to my neck to feel the fever for himself.

"Holy God. We've got to get her to quarantine," Ocelot said. He tried to pull me out of the chair, but I resisted.

"No! Don't touch me! The only one who can touch me is gone! *He left me*!" I shrieked. I kicked and slapped at him wildly.

Ocelot still grabbed at my arms, but I flailed loosely. Then my aggression changed to a cowering whimper. I cried like a little child. I felt the world teeter and fall out from under me. My body collapsed forward out of the chair. Ocelot caught me.

I felt Ocelot's arm around me, then his shoulder in my stomach. Then my hair was out of my face and hanging above my head. I lolled upside-down, staring at the back of Ocelot's uniform. Tears ran over my forehead and into my scalp.

Somehow, despite his weakened state, Ocelot got me downstairs and onto the quarantine bed. I sniffled and shivered. Ocelot pulled out a med kit from the wall. He brought an adhesive thermometer and placed it on my forehead. Wilbaht appeared at my side. He held my hand.

I heard Ocelot complain that the temperature was over forty-one. He retrieved a cold blanket from the refrigerated panel, unfolded it and packed it around me. It stung and made me shiver all the more. I groaned as the icy burn skittered over my skin. I squeezed my eyes shut. My body went limp.

"Sil, can you hear me?" Ocelot asked as he rubbed my face with a cold cloth.

I jerked awake, gasping. "Don't heal me. I curse the man who tries to heal me. If I'm to die, let me die," I spoke shakily.

"We won't let you die, Sil, but if you want to heal by conventional methods, you have to help us. Look at my eyes. Listen. Wilbaht said you were hit. What weapon was it?" Ocelot said clearly.

"Singe guns. Fitmalo spike guns," I slurred.

"Where?" he asked as patiently as he could.

I clumsily lifted my left arm to point to my right side and right arm, which still ached from the under-cured wound.

"I need to see," Ocelot informed us.

Wilbaht carefully helped pull off my top shirt, which seemed to be wet, probably with sweat. I trembled and complained of the cold while the two examined me.

Ocelot went to the med box for a shot of something, a power clamp and a scalpel. "Sil, your arm is swollen because you've got a spike still stuck in it. It's buried right along the bone."

"Those spikes have serrated edges. They tear the flesh when they're pulled out. They secrete more poison when compressed," Wilbaht told him.

"We've got to pull it. I'll hit her with an antivenin as soon as it's out. Just keep her calm and awake while I find it," Ocelot said. He retreated to the med dispenser computer and searched the quarantine room inventory bank for the cure.

Wilbaht held my hand in his. He petted my hair to calm me. "Sil. Remember your meditation training. Focus on your breathing."

I attempted to follow his instructions.

Ocelot returned to adhere a sleeper patch at my temple. He said something about finding the antivenin and that he needed Wilbaht's help. The men turned me gently onto my stomach and strapped me down tightly. I turned my head away from the sore arm. I preferred not to watch the operation. I was still awake when Ocelot pierced the top of my elbow with the scalpel a few quick times. I tried to remain still. Then he put the scalpel aside and picked up the clamp.

"I'm going to insert plastic rods around the spike to offset the serrated edges. After I pull it, I'll have to squeeze out as much poison as possible. It's going to hurt like hell if you're still awake, but I have to."

"Fine," I whispered.

I felt an unnerving pressure at my elbow. The power clamp pressed in to grip the end of the spike. The anesthesia and the sleeper from the patch began to circulate, dulling the pain.

Ocelot pressed the rods one by one up against the three serrated edges of the spike, jostling them into the wound as gently as possible. They felt like alien creatures burrowing into my bone. I clenched my jaw and grunted.

"Okay, I'm ready to pull it," he cautioned.

"Do it," I said through my teeth.

As I pronounced these words, a shock sliced through my arm. I jerked once, and then relaxed panting on the bed. I heard a sizzling noise coming from the wound. The poison from the spike foamed from the exposure to oxygen. The spike and the rods clinked to the floor. Ocelot threw the power clamp to a ledge behind him. The poison smelled of spoiled vinegar. Wilbaht switched on the ventilation fan to absorb the gas. Then I felt him tuck a towel under my elbow. Ocelot wrapped a plastic band around my arm near the shoulder. He tightened the band and used it to squeeze brutally from my shoulder down to my elbow, but I did not move. The medication quieted all sensation. Then I was out.

When I awoke, I found myself alone in quarantine. Wilbaht had set my traveling box by the wall for me. I bathed in the shower behind the quarantine lab and redressed myself with difficulty.

Ocelot returned later to change my bandage. The arm swelled, so he wrapped it loosely and set it in a canvas sling. Ocelot and Wilbaht took turns pushing me to drink glass after glass of water to help speed my body's expulsion of the remaining poison. Ocelot checked my fever often. I slept on and off for days in quarantine. This new ordeal kept many thoughts from my mind, but my emotional scars ran deep. My heart became jaded to my rescue instead of thankful.

The next time I awoke, I determined to fight the physical weakness. I couldn't stand being cared for like an invalid anymore. I had to toughen up, march forward through this job, cast off the shadowy events that had blackened my youthful illusion. I had to keep working. Wilbaht had told me someday people would need my help. I couldn't help them if I allowed myself to waste away.

I carried my box up the stairs to my quarters. I squinted and skulked at my thin reflection in my wall mirror. At 1900 hours, after five days in quarantine, I appeared at the table with the rest of the crew.

Chapter 34: Recovery

Wilbaht welcomed me back. Ocelot said it was good to see me on my feet again. Klib mentioned it would be good to get back to our regular schedule since the extra three hours of duties in my absence were wearing him out.

I asked if anyone had messaged us about the space station. No one had. Secretly, I wanted to ask was if Alaban had replied to me, but I knew he hadn't. I also knew I was wrong to want to hear from him after what he had done. I couldn't help myself. Try as I might, my tough outer shell could not ward off the innate desire to sense his existence.

Stonily, I apologized for my behavior during my fever and thanked them all for their help. Ocelot assured me that no apology was necessary, but then he hadn't seen the way I'd treated Klib. I informed them that I would return to my regular schedule immediately and that I would submit a full report to Wilbaht about the space station as soon as possible. Wilbaht advised me to take my time on it.

I cast an ill glance at Ocelot, certain that he would remark about the impending report. He only looked back at me with uncertainty and then turned his attention to his plate. I wasn't looking forward to working alone with him again. I knew we would both end up making some kind of dutiful speech about it all, concluding in awkward silence.

"Are we still under orders from General Lam, sir?" I asked our commander.

"No. All assignments have been terminated, as have you. You've been reported dead. For your own safety, I suggest you stay that way until you're out of danger. That may be indefinitely," Wilbaht said.

His eyes skirted between Ocelot's face and mine. "Since you've both been pronounced dead, and assuming you wish to continue working for the Organization, you'll have to change your names and build new identities. That means creating from scratch all official documentation from your birth, your education, all the way through your testing and your assignments. It will be impossible to place you on this ship with this crew as your new persona. When we land, the only people who will officially disembark this ship will be Klib and me. We may be able to reestablish you as warriors by your new names once we check in on Jawlcheen, but that, too will take some auspicious finagling. It's a good thing we have a computer records expert on board to facilitate such a plan." Wilbaht nodded at Ocelot. "Also, being dead, you won't be using your own access codes anymore. They've been discontinued. You'll have to use mine. I don't have to remind you what that means to your research boundaries. Use caution and your best judgment."

I considered the ramifications of what he'd said. I asked if my family had been notified of my death. Wilbaht said he was able to contact Yalat about it and that she had explained to my family that I had been mistakenly confused with another warrior and that I was actually alive and well. I quickly muttered my thanks to him.

As Wilbaht stood to clear his dishes, he patted my shoulder in sympathy and moral support. I raked the last morsel of flatbread across the drops of broth in my plate without recognizing his gesture. I knew Klib and Ocelot regarded me uneasily, but they managed to deflect the mood by discussing our approach to Jawlcheen. Forty-two days remained before our next landing.

For me, they may have been forty-two years. No ray of hope waited for me at the end of this journey. Alaban was no longer a source of joy in my life, whether he planned to meet me there or not. His deplorable actions had made him an untouchable to me. I shamefully regretted having written him that letter.

At 0130 I climbed the stairs to the observation deck. Ocelot stood at attention when I stepped onto the floor, forcing me to face him. I imitated his formality, ready to salute if necessary. Instead of paying some kind of tribute, he asked permission to check my arm.

"Yes, sir," I replied solidly.

I unhooked the sling and removed the bandage. I held my arm out to the side as straight as I could. He gently pressed my elbow to lift the arm a little more. I winced. He did not apologize, but turned my hand to observe my palm. He held it closer to his face to examine it.

368

"No signs of anemia. Your hand is cold. Has it given you any problems?" he asked.

"No, sir. I still have full mobility in it," I replied. I opened and closed my fist to prove it.

He replaced the bandage. He rubbed the veins on the top of my hand with his thumb and then rotated the hand to hold it in both of his. He gazed at me seriously. He didn't let go as I had expected him to.

"Sil, I know I thanked you already for what you did, but I think you weren't well enough to understand. You gave me back my life. I can never thank you enough," he said. He was about to say something else, but I pulled my hand from him.

"You saved my life, too. We're even. You don't owe me anything. We have no debts to each other, sir," I said firmly.

He again stood at attention, staring at my adamant features. He bowed. I repeated the ritual. Stiffly, we returned to our stations. Then ensued the awkward silence I had hoped against. I stubbornly refused to make small talk. We went through the tired motions of stats checks like robots following routine directions.

Later, I started a watered-down version of my old workout routine. I did not work out with Ocelot. I was afraid he would treat me like a physical therapy patient. I challenged my arm daily on my own. I didn't anticipate regaining the strength I'd had going into the space station. I believed I had passed my physical peak. I would never again train to become a machine of war.

The next day, Ocelot was ready to work on altering our personal data with a retro dating program. I knew a complete ID change was necessary, but I didn't feel right about giving up my name. I explained that I didn't want to dishonor my family.

Ocelot made a suggestion. "If you want to retain your name and family's honor, why don't you keep your first name and change from your mother's last name to your father's? There are millions of people with similar names in the Lapas helion. Any variation from the original would be enough to create a new persona without alerting suspicion," he told me.

I considered this. It was human tradition for females to keep their mother's last name. I was sure my mother would encourage the change had I been able to ask her advice about it. I agreed to the solution.

"What's your father's last name, then? I can go ahead and start the data today," he said, almost anxiously.

"It's Rayfenix, sir," I told him.

He thought for a moment, and then smiled slightly. "That's appropriate. The phoenix is reborn."

"I guess you're right," I mused. I asked him about his ID as well.

"Actually, I didn't have to change my name much. I changed my identity once several years ago. All I had to do this time is go back and revive my original name as if it belonged to a separate person."

I looked at him, perplexed. "How is that?"

"I changed my name when I was about fourteen years old. I nagged Channol for a long time about it before he gave in. Remember the anonymous messages I used to send you?"

"Yes. You said your first name starts with J," I said.

"You guessed it started with a J. You thought I was Jiao. Actually, that was an interesting game. It's too bad it had to end so soon, but you started to think I was some kind of con artist. I like suspense games. That's partly why I got into encoding. Every code is like a puzzle to be unraveled," he said.

Annoyed, I retorted, "You're trying to avoid telling me your real name by throwing a lot of idle chatter at me. If you don't want anyone to know what your real name is, don't use it. If someone asks me who you are, I won't be able to answer. Then we may be in trouble all over again. So what is it, sir? Are you going to tell me or not?"

Ocelot frowned. "I'm sorry you think this is all idle chatter. I thought you might be interested in more than dry facts."

"My interests are irrelevant to this mission, sir. Dry facts are all I need." I squared my shoulders. I was sure I gave the impression of a soldier not yet ready to at ease.

He narrowed his eyes at me, still offended. "If anyone asks, just tell them you've only heard me called J. You don't know my name. The only one who knows my name is my superior."

"Sub Professor J? That's not believable, sir. Wouldn't I have seen your title pin on your official uniform? The one you're wearing now that says Sub Professor Ocelot Quoren? You've got to reprogram these title pins sometime. Why not tell me now?"

"I'll reprogram mine with the first initial only. On yours I'll have to redo the whole last name. Anything else, warrior?" He spoke defensively.

I turned away from him, buzzing to myself, "How could he be so paranoid about his own name?"

"What did you say?" he demanded.

I swiveled around to show him only the left side of my face. "Never mind, sir."

"No. I want to know what you said, Warrior."

I raised my voice. "It doesn't matter, sir. I'm sorry I said anything. It's your decision about your name, but you're creating more problems for yourself. I don't understand why you can't tell me the simplest information."

"You should accept the fact that I'm not willing to tell you. There are two levels of rank between us, Warrior. Remember that. I know what I'm doing. Why can't you trust me?" he retorted.

His last question made me quiver with déjà vu. I immediately saw Alaban standing before me, shouting, *"Why couldn't you trust me?"* I felt the uncontrollable urge to escape. I stood shaking. I breathed heavily. I clutched the back of my chair. Anxiety gripped me.

Ocelot stood at my unexpected reaction.

I turned away from him, battling myself to keep it together. I closed my eyes and meditated. I controlled my breathing. I carefully returned to my chair, rubbing my forehead with my palm. I closed my eyes again and reclined onto the seat back. When I finally opened my eyes again, Ocelot peered at me with concern.

"I'm sorry," I spoke resignedly.

"What happened?" he asked.

"It's nothing." I tried my best to steel myself again. "I apologize for raising my voice to you, sir. I shouldn't have. You're my crewmate and my superior. If you don't tell me your name, it's your call. I'll say whatever you command about it," I said out of duty rather than sincerity.

"It's all right. I thought I was seeing the old you come back for a minute there. We used to have some pretty good arguments." His face showed uncertainty.

I nodded profusely. "You wanted to know some personal information so you can rebuild my identity. What did you need to know?"

He studied me. I hated this. He thought I was struggling more than I really was. I wanted him to look away, mind his business, and leave me to sulk. Instead, he kept after me about the ID data, forcing a friendly patience, altering his manner to accommodate mine. He asked me questions about my quadrant of Liricos and my early schooling to get an idea for the new string of data about Sil Rayfenix. Then he looked up schools in my area of Liricos and picked one to create my parallel history. By the end of the hour, he behaved as if my strange episode was forgotten.

Over the next couple of days, however, it became apparent that Ocelot and Wilbaht were using my mental health as a pet project. They gave me pep talks in passing. In normal conversation, they only discussed neutral topics, ship statistics, and things that would remind me of the positive side of life. It became annoying. Finally, after our communal meal, I addressed this.

"Wilbaht, Ocelot, sirs, I know you're encouraging me to be stronger, but I can tell you expect me not to be. You're plotting what to say or not to say to me behind my back. If anything, you're making me more self-conscious. I'm fine. I will continue to be fine. And I'm not afraid to talk about the space station."

The two glanced at each other. Wilbaht smiled compassionately. "I'm glad to hear you say this."

"I'll have my report ready to turn in tomorrow, sir."

"I look forward to reviewing it with both of you, if you feel up to it," Wilbaht said.

"Absolutely, sir," I replied, bowing to each of them.

Later, Ocelot and I worked again on my new persona. I was now Sil Rayfenix. I was still a native of Liricos. Both parents were from Tambuo instead of just one. I had two sisters instead of three. I went to schools in the same region as my real hometown. In academics, I excelled in statistics and numerical expression. My sponsoring professor was a yellow Lizard from Jain. I had barely passed my entrance test. I had no unusual abilities. I was assigned to a crew of two Lizards and two Greys. We had not traveled much. We mostly worked on simple data espionage on Santer and on Jain. Now I traveled to Jawlcheen to finish my first year and await reassignment. Once all the false information was patched in, the officials at our Center on Jawlcheen would expect the new me to arrive on a ship called the Santer Phase Orbiter, which Wilbaht had found on a ship arrival schedule. The Phase Orbiter would arrive at the Loam Center on the same day as ours. There was no guarantee that our charade would work, but it was elaborate enough to at least earn us a fighting chance.

Ocelot still didn't share his new, (or old), information with me. I didn't ask about it, although it was unfair that he knew all of my new information but I didn't know any of his. To ask him would probably put him on the defensive again and I wasn't willing to start any more arguments, although his staunch refusal seeded a restless distrust in my mind.

The next day, after our meal, the three of us sat down as promised to discuss the space station incident. I was not nervous about it. Wilbaht was a trusted guide. He knew when to curtail a conversation when things became too emotional. However, as we revived the conflict in the hangar, I felt pressured to give more information than I had included in the report, and more than I wanted to remember.

"So this General Teradom used Swall Jade's ship to convince you that he was there waiting for you," Wilbaht said.

"He had Alaban convinced," Ocelot said spitefully.

"I don't believe he did, sir." I explained about the recent vision and Alaban's last messages to me. I explained how I'd deduced that he and Teradom had been lying. Wilbaht said he understood.

"But *I* still don't understand," I said. "Alaban said he had to kill his own crewmembers because they tried to kill him first. I can't imagine that about Ongeram and Zank."

"I'm sure they didn't attack first. Alaban probably killed them to keep them from reporting him," Ocelot said.

"No, that whole story seems wrong. I don't even know if it's true that he killed them."

"They have been reported dead, Sil, officially," Wilbaht said.

"So have we. What was their listed cause of death?" I asked hopefully.

"The cause of death is not available. Their bodies are being delivered to family members. The remains have been positively identified," Wilbaht said.

I shook my head in distress. In my mind, I traveled back to the moment when Alaban had confessed to executing them. Next Ocelot had yelled at him. I had mentioned this in my report, but I hadn't mentioned the fact that I disagreed with Ocelot's approach. Why had he lost his cool so quickly? I did not hold back my opinion now.

"Why didn't you try to get us out of there instead of starting a fight?" I asked him point blank. "You swung at him before he even started arguing."

"There was no way they were going to let us go. It was better to fight them off than pretend to deal with them," he said.

I bristled. "I told you the day before we went to the space station. I told you to hold back from antagonizing him. You did exactly the opposite. Maybe Teradom was right about you being a loose cannon."

"Hold on, Sil," Wilbaht intervened. "Ocelot paid for his mistakes in bloodshed. You were a witness to that. Don't forget we're discussing this to find out how to counteract the Fitmalo Regime, not to lay blame on anyone in our own crew."

Ocelot's face grew penitent. Maybe now he would take his own emotional health more seriously. I held back, but living cells of suspicion divided within my mind.

Wilbaht continued. "However, we do need to address the incongruence between your reports. Ocelot does not mention it, but Sil reports that Alaban insulted Ocelot and his family. He said Ocelot's uncle Stennet offered to pay for the weapon once Sil retrieved it. Is that true?"

Ocelot shifted restlessly. "Yes, Alaban said that."

"Did your uncle make such an offer?" Wilbaht pursued.

"No," Ocelot stated. "Alaban only said that to throw us off."

I interjected. "How well do you know your uncle, sir? Could he be after the weapon without your knowledge?" The suspicion doubled, invading my conscience. "Or do you know something about it?"

"No. That accusation was completely unfounded. Besides, why would my uncle want a weapon like that? He's loyal to the Organization. He would never get involved in weapons deals. Even if he wanted to, he's only a professor. His rank isn't high enough to put him in a position to know the location of secret weapons. That data would be far outside his reach," Ocelot said.

"Stennet may not have close access to weapons, but Jiao does," I countered.

"Don't buy into that story of his. He would have said anything to put you on his side. You can research my whole family and never find anyone disloyal to the Organization. My family has been with the Organization for generations. Our integrity is rock solid," Ocelot retorted.

Wilbaht interrupted. "I trust your integrity, Ocelot. However, one man cannot assume responsibility for the integrity of his whole family. Let's set aside this possibility to be discussed later."

Ocelot stared. He silently ingested his mentor's stricture with difficulty. He crossed his arms.

"What I would most like to understand," Wilbaht added, "is Alaban's reason for siding with the General in the first place. He did not seem the type of person who would leave his guiding Organization. I did not perceive him to be a traitor."

My suspicion shriveled with the influx of remorse. Stoically, I admitted to Wilbaht that Alaban had played along with Teradom's setup in order to impose his imagined sanctuary on me: to have me with him for life. Had he succeeded, we would have lived as slaves whose only glimpse of freedom would have been Teradom's permission to sleep together and to mate. Our purpose in this world would have been squelched. We would have been no better than the humans caged on Karnesh for meat production. His ludicrous plan never had a chance. I could not fathom why he hadn't understood that from the beginning.

I closed my eyes momentarily. Watercolor images blended through my memory: images of Alaban caressing my face in the elevator while I cloaked, of the hangar, and of the sword parody he'd acted out so masterfully. He had pretended to slay me in order to save me. I would rather have seen him slip out alive to escape with us on the Sonic Wake. But he had stayed behind to serve the devil. I skulked at fate's cruel puppeteering. I leaned rigidly against the table without another word.

When the men realized that I was not willing to go on, they complimented me on being able to get so far with Ocelot's body as a handicap. Our meeting ended, although Wilbaht planned to speak with us individually later.

He encouraged us to do as much creative research as possible regarding the Fitmalo space station and the generals in question. I also began investigating Jiao and Stennet's possible connection with the Regime. I wasn't about to let that possibility go. Stennet wasn't a high official. This was true. But he was in a useful position to anyone wanting clues to locations of people in charge of military science deals. Jiao was another strong possibility. Despite his relative youth, he could have been just as useful because of his specialized expertise. If the two were working together in selling secret intel, they would be twice as attractive to a criminal buyer. I knew Ocelot held Jiao in high esteem, but if Alaban accused them, there must have been at least some truth to it.

In thinking of the Regime's covert networking and their hidden roots within the Organization, I wondered about the purpose of Teradom's task force. Who were they and what were they meant to do? What did he want Alaban and me for specifically? Was it only the weapon he was after or were we meant to pose a constant menacing threat to anyone opposing the Regime? How would Alaban be treated now that his other half was no longer available? Would they use him as a simple assassin? I was sure that was a part of their plan for him. I made a mental note to watch the news and obituaries to see what Fitmalo and Jawlcheen officials might meet with tragic accidents in the upcoming weeks.

I had been on the job for nearly ten months now. Upon our arrival on Jawlcheen, I would still have another two months with this crew, or with Sil Rayfenix's fake crew. The end of this contract year would bring changes for us all. I had already undergone so many changes with this crew. I paused to recall our adventures and arguments that had shaped our relationships to one another: my harmony with Wilbaht, my discord with Klib.

Then there was Ocelot, the one I simply put up with: the go-between. He somehow supported Klib's boorish personality while at the same time holding a place of esteem with Wilbaht. How could he adapt so readily to the opinions of one so morally right and at the same time befriend one so obviously sunken? Perhaps he meant to pacify the tensions between them. If so, his motives and efforts were admirable. If not, he could have been appeasing their personalities to insure his place with them and to draw information from them. At worst, he could have been a double agent among us, now equipped with a Sub General's access code. I considered the damage he could do even if he were not.

I weighed his pros and cons. Since Yinore left us, we had become almost dependent on him to deal with minor engineering problems on the ship. He had high-level abilities with informational systems and encoding. His behavior towards me had improved greatly since we were on Jain. He had helped me train well for the battle at the space station. He had refused to leave me behind at our time of battle.

Then again, Ocelot was difficult to understand. His personality had changed unpredictably during our leave times. Otherwise, he was closed and secretive. I still had no idea why he was so protective of his name. His temper had a breaking point unbound by reason.

I reviewed all the instances in which I'd sensed some form of distrust towards him. They were numerous. His recklessly vindictive actions on Jain had always disturbed me. His fencing match with Alaban on Santer had been uncontrolled. I remembered his fights with me, the way he had sliced open my ear and nearly killed me on Sor4, the time he had willingly watched Klib's illegal film, his bets with the man, his drunken stupor on Santer, his temporary insubordination with Wilbaht. I even recalled the time when Yinore had met Alaban on board the ship on Santer. She had said I would not find a better man than Alaban on this ship. I knew she had disliked Klib, not only for his uncouth commentaries, but also for the distasteful thoughts that gleamed from his eyes. I wondered what she had read from Ocelot's eyes during her stay here. If I were still alive officially, I would have contacted her about it. What might she know about him that we didn't? How well did any of us know him? What if Alaban was right? What if Stennet did ask Ocelot to steer me towards the weapon in exchange for some kind of reward? My suspicion thrived.

Chapter 35: Accusation

On the upper deck I had limited information at my disposal: only commercial and official Organization information. Still, I looked up a great deal of documentation on Ocelot's warrior family. I did this in plain view of him. The first day I started looking up data on Jiao, Ocelot leaned so far out of his chair to try to see what I was reading that he nearly fell out of it.

I jerked my head around to see him stagger to his feet. I arched an eyebrow at him and asked what he was doing. He stood straight and pointed at my screen.

"So you are researching my family," he said.

"Yes, sir," I told him frankly. "You invited me to research them."

He seemed a bit flustered, but didn't object to it. "Have you found anything I should know?"

"I'm sure you're already aware of everything I've found so far, sir. This is official Organization information. I'm just doing my homework so I can cross-reference their official locations and actions with any conflicting data I may find downstairs. I'm sorry to have to do it, sir, but I have reasonable doubt about them."

He blinked and clenched his jaw. He made two fists.

"I'm being transparent about this," I continued. "I'll report anything out of the ordinary to my superiors as per standard procedures."

He stayed watching over my shoulder. His presence agitated my nerves, but I had to keep researching this. Plus, the fact that he now knew about it might draw out some reaction from him to indicate his involvement.

"Your research will move a lot faster if we both work on it together," he said finally.

"You can't be impartial about it, sir," I informed him, hoping he might trip.

"I'll share the data with you as professional courtesy. My partiality won't affect it. Anyway, if there is something illegal going on in my family, I'd like to be the first to know about it," he said.

Outwardly, I accepted, although I planned on double-checking all his research myself. We divided the work. I looked up all information from the Soren helion about them, which was the information I needed most anyway. He took all information from Jain, which encompassed a longer time span, but mostly dealt with Stennet since Jiao was too young to be useful to anyone in a subverted position then.

Secretly, I also looked up information about Ocelot himself. Each day during my personal time, I used the communications board on the lower observation deck to browse through a wider variety of resources. I found discrepancies in Ocelot's childhood information that didn't coincide with personal facts he had told me. His parents, for example, were reported deceased by way of a space ferry accident instead of a terrorist attack. This may have been part of his second identity's history that he'd made up when he was fourteen. His parents' names were also different from those I had seen on their memorial on Jain. He had switched their first names. Jan was now his father's name and Leona was his mother. It would be difficult to find out his real childhood history without knowing his birth name.

The information about him after fourteen years of age matched my previously gathered evidence. He was adopted and tutored by Channol until he was nineteen. He failed his first Organization admissions exam due to a low grade in levitation, which was probably one thing Alaban had been talking about when he mentioned Ocelot's failures. He had passed the testing on the second try, however. His first year crew was composed of five people I didn't know, but I saved their names and ID's on my notepad to cross-reference them later. Ocelot had lived on Sor3 on and off for the past five years working in decoding and covert espionage. The frequent intervals in which he had not been present on Sor3 showed only ship travel, although I knew he had spent tours on Jawlcheen and perhaps Santer. According to this data, he was now nearly twenty-seven years old, although I had believed he was older. I wasn't allowed access to any of the files or cases he had worked on because they were all classified. Soon I gave up researching Ocelot's adult information. Too much of it was blocked. I was sure Wilbaht's code should have given me access to most of the vacant information. So why was I unable to access much of it? Ocelot could have infiltrated the system before me to block the data himself. I bit my lip in disconcertion.

I decided to research through a different route. I traced him from early childhood by researching his parents. I looked up Leono Quoren. I could only access a few housing records on him. All other information was blocked. Still, with this simple data, I found an alternative route to the facts. I found that Leono and his wife were housed near an Organization center on Liricos between twenty-four and thirty years ago. I looked up clinic and hospital archives in the immediate vicinity from this time period to search for human birth records. This search yielded lists of thousands. I selected last names beginning with Q. Thirty-nine sets of parents' names appeared. I found three Quorens.

The first Quoren I selected turned out to be a mother, not a father. She had given birth to a girl. The next Quoren was a father, but his name was Chorm and he also had a daughter, Angelique, by a wife named Kimber. The third Quoren I selected brought up a sign stating that this information could not be found. It had to be Ocelot. Had he anticipated the path of my research or had he covered this up previously to protect himself from someone else?

I tapped my fingers loudly. If Ocelot recently blocked this information so I wouldn't get to it, he could also have been researching just a few steps ahead of me on anything else I searched for. He could have changed or blocked whatever he thought I shouldn't find. If this was true, he had just rendered my whole plan of investigation useless.

I turned off the board with a growl and marched out of the lower observation deck to the exercise room where he would just be finishing his workout. I rapped on the door impatiently.

The door opened to reveal not Ocelot, but Wilbaht. He sweated and smiled in a lively manner. He opened the door wide to invite me in.

"Sil, come in. We were just finishing," he spoke winningly.

"Thank you, sir. I was just..." I began.

"Five minutes," Wilbaht said, raising a hand to pause me.

Ocelot stood at one end of the room. I stepped in and sidled to my right, keeping my back to the wall. Wilbaht hopped gracefully to the opposite end of the room. Both men displayed a lighthearted manner. They had been playing.

Wilbaht bobbed about, ready to take on his younger, shorter opponent. Ocelot edged toward him. Wilbaht cleared the room in two broad steps and swung a leg toward Ocelot so swiftly I thought I was imagining things. Ocelot barely managed to duck under the leg and actually attempted to counterattack with an uppercut to the underside of Wilbaht's knee. Wilbaht brought the leg around into a hook and swept Ocelot backwards with it. Ocelot rolled, bumping into the burnished wall. He sprung away from it. Wilbaht leaned down to punch at Ocelot a couple of times. Then he hopped backward. He faked a front kick, stepped forward, faked a couple of punches, and finally walloped him with a roundhouse kick to his blocking arm. Ocelot tried to duck, but the leg moved across his shoulder and hit him just above the ear. Wilbaht whirled about, hopping all the more.

Although hit, Ocelot was delighted. Both men neared the point of laughter. Ocelot somehow managed to move in to tag Wilbaht at the side of his lower ribs with a foot, but Wilbaht grabbed it. He jerked Ocelot towards him. Ocelot lost his balance completely. He ended up looking like a prize animal strung up by his ankle, held by Wilbaht the hunter. A guffaw escaped Wilbaht's throat. He dropped Ocelot to the padded floor. Ocelot rolled up to try and kick Wilbaht's leg out from under him, but Wilbaht was too sturdy. He punched Ocelot, who deflected the blow to the left shoulder. Ocelot levitated to strike Wilbaht with a double kick to the chest and face, but again Wilbaht made himself swift to dodge him. Instead, Ocelot got in a kick to his thigh, but this strike did no damage whatsoever.

The two danced around each other for nearly a minute without contact. Then Wilbaht zipped toward Ocelot, slung his upper body around him diagonally, grabbed him by the back of one thigh despite sustaining a solid knee to the ribs, and snapped back to stand, whirling Ocelot around, and throwing him to the ground with a loud whop. Ocelot lost all his breath at once. Wilbaht pinned him to the mat.

He beamed triumphantly. "I may be old, but I'm not slow yet."

Ocelot groaned from under Wilbaht's knee.

Wilbaht stood and helped Ocelot to his feet. He asked if he'd caught his breath yet. Ocelot shook his head no. Wilbaht slapped him on the back a couple of times. He chuckled.

"It was a good round," he said.

"Yes, sir. I don't think I want to do that again for a while," Ocelot panted.

They both exchanged smiles and handshakes.

"Hey, Sil. What did you need?" Wilbaht asked me.

"I have something to ask Ocelot, sir, regarding some information I'd been looking up," I told him.

"Oh? Did you find something about our case?" he asked me.

"No. That's the problem. Someone's been tampering with the archives. I can't tell if the little information I've found is true or not. Most every path I've searched is blocked," I told them.

"Really? What line of data is it?" Wilbaht asked.

"It's information on family members of one of our crew," I stated, indicating Ocelot with a cold stare.

All pleasantry disappeared from Ocelot's face.

"So you're investigating Professors Stennet and Jiao. I suspected you would. You're finding blocked information on them? That's definitely suspicious," Wilbaht said. He looked apologetically at Ocelot.

"It's not just Stennet or Jiao, sir. I keep hitting a block or missing information about other members of his family. I think Ocelot is blocking the information before I can get to it. Who else would want to keep common data about them a secret?" I stated boldly.

The two men were taken aback.

"That's a steep accusation you're making, Sil," Wilbaht cautioned.

"Yes, sir, it is. I openly challenge Ocelot to prove me wrong," I said. Ocelot returned my cold stare. "You offered to work on the research with me; you said to speed things along. You really meant to slow my investigation or lead me to false data to protect yourself and them. I can only guess what you're protecting them from. If Stennet and Jiao are involved in something illegal, you know about it, and I'm willing to bet you're in on it with them." I spilled my whole theory then and there, since Wilbaht was standing by as a witness. It was better to have all this out in the open once and for all.

"If they're in on anything illegal, I don't know about it. Why would I block information? I'm trying to research the same as you. You're acting paranoid," Ocelot retorted.

"Maybe I am paranoid, but I have good reason to be. You keep too many secrets for me to trust you. You won't even tell me your real name," I replied.

Ocelot's jowls drooped. "It's not my uncle or Jiao that you can't find information about. It's me, isn't it? You're looking up my history, not theirs."

Wilbaht set his fists against his hips. He regarded us patiently.

"I'm researching all three of you. I can't tell which information is valid and which is newly patched in. You've tampered with so many files I might as well just contact Stennet and Jiao directly and *ask* them if they're doing any double agent work. At least I might get a decisive answer that way." I took one step towards him. "Maybe I'll ask Jiao what your real name is while I'm at it."

Ocelot gestured at me and searched for support from Wilbaht. "This is preposterous. I never blocked any of their information. I never changed anything about them on any information log. I've erased some information about myself, but that had to do with building my new identity."

"Aha! Why would you need to erase anything if you're building a totally separate identity from your own? Your old identity would stay the same. You wouldn't have to change anything about that. What are you doing meddling with your own birth record?" I challenged.

"My birth record? I didn't change that," he stammered.

"Oh, really? Then why did I find a 'no information' sign on a birth document for a child born to your parents on Liricos twenty-seven years ago?" I countered.

Ocelot shifted his eyes and his stance. He stepped back nervously. He shook his head with self-criticism. His face showed guilt. He knew he was caught.

Wilbaht criticized him. "Ocelot! Why did you erase your own birth record?"

"I didn't know what I was doing. I was too inexperienced with programming back then. I was only fourteen. I was still learning data patching. Channol can vouch for me, sir. He supervised most of the reworking of my personal information. If you don't trust me, ask him about it. I'll go back in and redo the file. My new retro dating program is a lot better than the old one. I can get back in and change it today with no problem."

"Yes, that would be very convenient for you, wouldn't it?" I spat.

"Why are you suddenly against me? You distrust me that much?" He made a face.

"Yes, and I won't trust you until you prove your innocence. This is evidence enough for me."

"Lack of evidence is not evidence. Why do you presume I'm guilty without proof?" he demanded.

"Suspicion from the heart condemns a man regardless of proof," Wilbaht interrupted. He gently pressed his dark hands against our arms to move us apart. He stood observing us gravely for a moment. He pursed his lips. We waited for his response.

"In a case like this, I suggest an old-fashioned lie detector test," Wilbaht decided.

"Yes. All right. I'll do it just to set the record straight," Ocelot said.

"What kind of lie detector, sir?" I asked.

"We can use the vital signs monitor from the quarantine room. I'll ask the questions and read the output. You give me a list of questions to read. I'll give you fifteen minutes to prepare. Meet me downstairs."

"Yes, sir," we responded. Wilbaht led me out by the arm. I shuffled along next to him. Ocelot dragged behind.

As promised, fifteen minutes later, I presented my list of questions to Wilbaht in the quarantine room. He hooked up the vital signs monitor to record stats on Ocelot's responses. Ocelot arrived with a quick step and a bitter face. He hadn't even put on his top shirt after his bath. He brought it with him folded over one arm. He leapt up onto the gurney bed, leaned back against the headrest, and thrust out an arm so that Wilbaht could attach a sensor to him. Wilbaht ignored Ocelot's behavior. He placed sensors on his arm, neck, temples, and over his heart.

"Ready when you are, sir," Ocelot said restlessly. He stared straight ahead, avoiding eye contact with either of us.

Wilbaht reminded him to answer yes or no only. He asked him a few trivial questions to begin with, like if Jain was the last planet we were on and if there were twenty-one helions in the U.G. and if he was human. He calibrated the readout. Then he began with my questions.

According to Ocelot's answers, his real name was not Ocelot Quoren, but he was born on Liricos. His father was Leono Quoren. His mother was Jan Triol. Within the last ten months, he admitted he had altered data about his childhood in permanent records, but not his birth record. Again he professed that Channol had overseen the identity change

382

he'd carried out as a teenager. He swore he had not blocked or altered any personal records or information about Jiao or Stennet and that no one had offered him any kind of reward for his involvement in the retrieval of a weapon.

Wilbaht asked if he was aware if Professor Stennet was ever involved in any dealings with Fitmalo rebels, Fitmalo military officials or military scientists. Ocelot answered that he had no knowledge of it. He also claimed that Stennet had never expressed an interest in me or my abilities outside my testing and that Stennet had never worked or communicated with Trau, as far as he knew. Wilbaht went on to ask the same series of questions about Jiao. Ocelot answered the same way for all the questions about him.

"All right. Those were all of Sil's questions. Now I have a few of my own," Wilbaht crossed his arms in staunch formality.

"Do you trust your uncle Stennet not to deal with the Fitmalo Regime?"

Ocelot paused to think. He wanted to say yes, but his answer was, "I don't know. I can't be certain. I don't think he would."

"And Jiao?"

"Yes, I trust him," he said without hesitation.

"Do you trust Sil?"

He paused. "Could you be more specific, sir?"

"Do you trust her not to deal with the Fitmalos?"

"Yes."

"Do you trust her to research information about you?"

Ocelot paused again. "I don't want her to research me."

"That's not the question. Do you trust her with the information she may find out about you? In other words, do you think she is responsible and loyal enough to handle any sensitive information in a way that will not divulge your secrets to others?"

Ocelot didn't like this rewording, but he answered yes.

"Do you realize that by keeping simple information from her you have caused her to distrust you deeply?"

"Yes," he said unapologetically.

"Do you realize this accusation she has made against you is well evidenced? Blocked and altered records are not a lack of evidence, as you said. They *are* evidence. You know this, don't you?"

Ocelot sighed. "Yes."

"Do you realize this young woman probably gave up more than twenty years of her life span by healing you?"

He paused a while longer. "No. I didn't think it would be so much."

"Do you feel indebted to her?"

"Yes."

"As a sign of your gratitude, will you tell her your name so she can research your background properly?"

"No," Ocelot pronounced through his teeth.

Wilbaht pursed his lips. "Do you realize that you are very stubborn for no good reason?"

"No, sir. I think it is a good reason. You know my name, sir. If any research needs to be done about my past, I'd prefer you to do it. I don't see the need to make private information available to anyone who asks. I'm claiming personal rights to privacy on premise of rank."

Wilbaht shook his head at him in aggravation. "Hand me those sensors. Get down from there."

Ocelot plucked the sensors from his body and face and handed them back to Wilbaht.

Wilbaht turned. "All right, Sil. It's your turn."

"Me?" I asked.

"Yes, you. I didn't say Ocelot would be the only one on the chopping block. Hop up here," he ordered.

Hesitantly, I did as he commanded. I rolled up my sleeve. Wilbaht attached the sensor to my arm, face and neck. He let me attach the one over the heart. Ocelot donned his overshirt. He viewed me with vengeful pleasure now that I sat in the hot seat. I narrowed my eyes at him. He set his jaw and stared back.

Wilbaht asked me a few questions to calibrate my readings. He asked me if my real name was Sil Gretath, if I was born on Fitmalo, and if I was a crewmember of the Rybalazar Sonic Wake. Then he asked me some unsettling questions.

"Sil, when you had a fever you wrote a message to Alaban. Did you send him that message to lead him to our location?"

"No, sir," I said firmly.

"When you sent it to him, were you aware that you were putting yourself and the rest of us at risk?"

"No, sir. I was too dazed to think clearly. I apologize again for doing that. I did encode the message several times. I also bounced it from another location. I don't remember now where I bounced it from."

"Yes or no will suffice," Wilbaht said.

"Sir." I flexed my hands nervously.

"Did you know that you left that message without closing it before you were taken down to here to quarantine?"

"No, I don't remember."

"Everyone on this ship saw that message. If it had been written under normal circumstances, we would have doubted your loyalty to us. Do you see why?"

I swallowed before answering. "Yes."

"When you wrote the message to Alaban, you told him you should have accepted him from the beginning. Did you mean that you should have accepted the proposal to work with General Teradom?"

"No."

"Did you mean it on a personal level?"

"Yes."

"Would you say Alaban is an ambitious person, interested in attaining a certain level of power?"

I remembered that Alaban had once said he would like to have Wilbaht's level of power one day. "Yes."

"Would you say he is overconfident or perhaps egotistical about his own abilities?"

I stared at the white wall in front of me. "Yes."

"Do you think Alaban was aware of the task force Teradom spoke of before Teradom offered him the job?"

"He might have been. I can't be sure. He never mentioned anything like that before."

"Did Alaban ever blame the Organization or any of its members for keeping the two of you apart?"

"Yes."

"Did he ever complain about Organization practices or scoff at any regulations?"

I paused stiffly. "Yes."

"When you were in the space station, you saw Alaban bodyguarding the Head General. Is that correct?"

"Yes."

"Did he ask the General permission before speaking or acting on his own?"

I blinked. I hadn't thought of it as being unusual before. "No."

"Then one might assume that he was more than just a privileged bodyguard. His membership on the task force must give him a certain level of prominence. Would you agree with that?"

"Yes."

"Did you trust Alaban completely before you saw him at the space station?"

I searched my heart. "Almost completely."

"Had you trusted him not to join the Fitmalos?"

"Yes. He promised me he wouldn't."

"When he promised you this, did he promise of his own ideas and free will?"

"No," I said sadly. "I asked him to promise not to."

"Do you think Alaban may have joined the Fitmalos without coercion?"

"No."

"Do you think Alaban was sincere about his emotions for you?"

"Yes."

"Were you sincere with him in the same way?"

"Yes."

"All right. Let's change the subject. Alaban implied that Stennet and possibly Jiao were trying to get the weapon through Ocelot and that Ocelot expected you to retrieve it for him. Do you believe that?"

"I believe it's possible, sir."

"Do you have any other reason to suspect Stennet and Jiao other than what you've already mentioned?"

"Yes. I recall seeing them escorted to interrogations on the day after the acid spider incident on Sor3. I believe they were questioned about facts surrounding the incident, sir."

"Why didn't you mention that before?" Ocelot intervened.

"I had no reason to suspect them before," I replied.

"Have you found anything else suspicious about them in your research?" Wilbaht continued.

"Not yet, sir. Only blocked pages from case files."

"Have you found anything suspicious about Ocelot in your research?"

"Yes. More than two thirds of the personal information I've looked up about him and his parents has been altered or blocked. Some information I've cross-referenced contradicts itself."

"Do you think he's done this to hide something from his fellow warriors?"

"Yes."

"Do you really believe in your heart that Ocelot is disloyal to us?"

"I don't know, sir."

"Has he said or done anything else to make you distrust him as a warrior?"

"Yes, but not specifically." I mentioned he was always secretive.

"Have you had any visions that might influence your judgment about him?"

"Yes. The first time I saw him. Part of what I saw was from the space station. Part of it hasn't happened yet. I had hoped he was not the source of the events I saw, but I'm starting to think he was."

"Did this vision make you distrust him from the beginning?"

"Yes."

"If Ocelot tells you his real name and openly shows you all the information he covered up, would you trust him then?"

"No, sir. I have no way of knowing if he is telling the truth."

"If the information could be confirmed by someone you do trust, would you change your mind?"

"Yes."

"All right. You can get down from there."

I pulled the sensors from my skin.

"Ocelot, I'm sorry, but I'm going to have to ask you to stay off the computers until further notice."

Ocelot unfolded his arms jauntily. "But, sir, our new identities are still incomplete."

"I'm sorry. My order stands. In the mean time, I'll be doing research on my own. I'll contact my brother and a few associates of mine to get to the bottom of this. Consider yourself on temporary suspension."

"What? Why? You think I'm guilty, too?" Ocelot chagrined.

"My opinion does not outweigh the facts. You have been accused of a form of conspiracy against the Organization. Evidence has been presented against you. The lie detector was inconclusive on your statements. As much as I would like this accusation to be untrue, I cannot ignore the evidence. You are temporarily suspended and you will switch schedules with Klib starting tomorrow. When Sil goes upstairs to relieve you, you will leave the upper deck immediately." Wilbaht told him.

"But..." Ocelot shook his head and stammered. He clenched his fists and his jaw. His eyes grew fiery with contempt.

"If all evidence against you is cleared up, the suspension will be lifted and you can return to your regular schedule. Meanwhile you are to keep your distance from Sil and don't touch any computer on this ship. Understood?" Wilbaht ordered.

"I understand, sir," he responded. He gritted his teeth. He pouted bitterly.

At our mealtime, Klib came down to the dining area asking about him.

"What's going on with superboy? He says he's suspended. Went upstairs to sulk. What'd he do?" Klib asked.

Wilbaht explained the general problem.

"Hold on. You got him suspended, didn't you?" Klib asked of me.

"Yes, I did," I answered frankly.

"Okay, so maybe I'm a little slower than the rest of you, but if a man is working on changing information that pertains to himself, he's not bothering anybody else with it. Why is that any of your business?" Klib asked.

"The charge is conspiracy against the Organization. That kind of offense nullifies certain personal rights to privacy," Wilbaht explained.

"Conspiracy against the Organization," Klib scoffed. "Now I've heard everything. Where I stand it looks like the only one around here doing anything against the Organization is this witch. Yes, you, precious. If you hadn't been so anxious to get that turncoat boyfriend of yours back in your pants, Ocelot never would have been wounded in the first place. Then he wouldn't have to be reworking his own files, would he? Looks like this little girl just set him up to pull the wool over your eyes, sir."

I stood, flustered. "You don't know what you're talking about, Klib."

"It's more than just her accusation that made me decide to put Ocelot on suspension. Don't jump to conclusions," Wilbaht told him.

"Who's jumping to conclusions here? Have you got cold, hard evidence against him or just somebody's word? I wouldn't believe that even if Ocelot told me himself. Just because she's cute and acts innocent she's got you believing anything she wants. Ocelot is the straightest warrior I ever met. If you're out to get him jailed for something he didn't do then you can find yourself another pilot. I'm going on strike. You can land this tin can yourself."

"Klib, if I suspended him, it's for a good reason. This is not personal. There is evidence to consider. Do not question my authority." Wilbaht replied gruffly.

"I'm not questioning your authority, sir. I'm questioning your thinking. This kid's playing the 'daddy's little girl' routine and you're going along with it. I don't care what kind of evidence you've got going. It's all bullshit. She probably planted evidence against him. She's just taking her sexual frustration out on us. Her boyfriend's got the key to her chastity belt and now he'd rather kiss Fitmalo ass than fuck her. Bitch." Klib edged his way back toward the stairwell.

I turned red. Wilbaht stood defensively. The air trembled around him as he emanated powerful waves of fury.

"You will not use profanity against a crewmember. This level of disrespect will not be tolerated." Wilbaht boomed. "Consider yourself on temporary suspension as well."

Klib cowered to the safety of the stairwell, but continued his protest. "Oh, right. I see how it is. You won't put up with it from me, but you'll let her get away with it. She cusses me out and nearly burns a hole through my throat and all you do is put her to bed. I speak my mind and I'm on suspension. That's what I'm talking about. I may as well not even bother. You two are probably hot for each other, too."

"You've overstepped your boundaries far enough. If you have anything else to say, you'll direct yourself to me formally and with respect," Wilbaht bellowed, standing at his full height and slowly skimming the floor towards the insurgent, yapping dog.

Klib gripped the railing for support, but continued with a self-righteous air about him. "Yeah, all right, sir. I have something to say, with your permission. I refuse to work or eat with that female any more. And if she doesn't like what she just heard, she'd better cover her ears every time she sees me because that's the kind of thing I'll have to say to her from now on. And I dare her to lay a hand on me. She's not the only one around here who can file a complaint. I'm going upstairs with Ocelot. We'll make our own schedule to keep away from this bitch. Sir." He rounded the stairwell to the top floor, sneering at me.

Wilbaht growled with frustration. "Could anything get any worse around here?" He stood akimbo and grumbled in disgust. The quavering air around him cooled. He turned to see my flushed appearance.

His voice still grated with anger. "Finish your meal and go take inventory in the quarantine room." He trudged up to the main observation deck to continue the argument.

"Yes, sir," I said quietly.

Chapter 36: Revenge

I continued my regular routine, but mealtime was cut short. Wilbaht ate with me only fifteen minutes. We did not sit to chat after finishing our meals. I gave him only updates on information I'd researched, but none of it concretely indicated any wrongdoing. Wilbaht's research concurred with mine. He waited to receive word from his brother, Channol, from Yinore by my request, and from various other personal acquaintances he had messaged. Since Ocelot was now on a different schedule, I almost never saw him. He wouldn't eat with us. He probably ate with Klib sometime at the end of his duty.

Klib kept his promise. He refused to work with me even though our schedules were supposed to overlap. At my time to go upstairs, he always anticipated my arrival. He'd wait at the top of the stairwell until he heard me start to climb it. Then he would trot down the stairs and elbow me or bump into me on his way down. He always muttered some rude comment as he did this. The first time I ignored him. The second time I told him to leave me alone. He flipped me off as he left the stairwell. As furious as he made me, there was little I could do about his attitude unless I was willing to physically fight him.

The third time, I avoided physical contact and cleared my throat as he said his indecencies. The fourth time I started up the stairs. I heard him walking down, so I dismounted the steps and waited for him to pass by before I went up. He blew a kiss to me as he walked out into the dining area.

All alone on the upper deck, I rethought the evidence against Ocelot. Just like his lie detector test, all factors added together about him were also inconclusive. I viewed his empty chair and wondered what he did up here without being able to use a computer. If he was innocent, I would feel ashamed of my accusation against him. I would have to make it up to him somehow. If guilty, he would deserve dismissal. Wilbaht might even erase his new identity and prohibit him from ever entering Organization facilities again.

Guilty or not, and despite his secrecy, I did miss his company. I remembered how he'd reacted when my mother died. He had been a real comfort to me. He was certainly more bearable than Klib. I was sorry Wilbaht had changed their schedules.

As the quiet days dragged on, I felt more and more ostracized by the rest of the crew. Even Wilbaht had little to say to me. He did try to cheer me up every now and then, but we didn't talk the way we used to. He probably believed I had made a mistake in accusing Ocelot and that I had been unfair in the way I had confronted him. I had forced him to punish his own confidant and he was resentful for it.

One day we had a mandatory external hull check. I volunteered to go outside. Ocelot monitored internal mechanical tests. Klib stayed at the helm to assist communications of internal and external balance checks. Wilbaht monitored communications as well as weapons and seals. I cleaned the external weapons casings and the shield projectors. We all heard each other on the earphones. Somehow I felt less alone hearing their voices as I floated around the ship, facing the blackness of space, than I had felt inside the ship with all of them around me. Even so, Klib's insults weren't any more bearable.

"Hey, Sil, you sure your doggy leash is secure?"

"Yes, Klib. Why?"

"I wouldn't want you do go floating away from us or anything," he said.

"I'm strapped onto the main cord and a security bungee, so quit daydreaming," I retorted.

"Oh, I'm not sure if I'm daydreaming, but I think I see some cord fibers unraveling out there. Why don't you double check to make sure?" Klib teased.

"I already checked everything three times by standard procedure, Klib. I'm not going anywhere. I'm sure you're sorry to hear that."

"Well, now that you mention it. Hey, speaking of daydreams, can you picture what I'm daydreaming right now? You are a seer, aren't you? If I imagine something, can you automatically picture it?"

"No. I can't read your mind right now. To be honest, I'd rather not."

"Have you ever pictured yourself skinny dipping?" he asked.

"No, Klib."

"Well, if you could read my mind you would," he chuckled.

Ocelot's voice came on the communications set. "Hey, you'd better leave her alone, Klib. She might report you to the boss and get you grounded from your porno sites."

"Yeah, you're probably right. I don't want to lose that privilege. I especially like the flicks with human women from Liricos...in bondage," Klib taunted.

Wilbaht interrupted just in time. "All right, everybody, get back to work. I don't want to hear anything communicated between any of you except stat reports and ship information, understood?"

"Yes, sir," we all said in turn.

I wanted to go inside and kick Klib in the face. I could just imagine him sitting in his chair laughing it up. He would never have dared say anything to me if Alaban had been here with us. If only he had been assigned to our crew back on Santer, everything would be different. A knot formed in my throat just thinking about him.

I looked out across the blackness. It was punctured with stray stars and smeared with nebulae. Thrader's sun burned brightly in the distance. In twenty-one days we would be on Jawlcheen. Then we would be rid of Klib. I said a silent prayer asking for the patience to put up with him just this short while longer.

When all checks finished, I returned to the main cargo hold. I closed the outer door and moved through the airlocks. Wilbaht and I both confirmed a complete seal. I traipsed back through the second cargo hold. I saw Ocelot at the interior door to the engine and life support systems area, just finishing his checks. He closed the door to the blue-lit room. I turned my back to him to take off my helmet. I swallowed to keep my ears from popping from the slight difference in pressure between my suit and the cargo hold. On the communicator, Wilbaht called an all-crew meeting to the main observation deck in fifteen minutes. We all responded.

Ocelot didn't pause to say anything to me. He went straight to the hallway door. I watched from the corner of my eye as he slipped out and tramped up the stairwell. I realized I missed Ocelot in much the same way I missed Alaban. Alaban was far away. I had gotten used to that fact over the long months. Ocelot was here in the ship with me, close enough to speak to, and yet he might as well have been millions of kilometers away in some distant solar system.

It suddenly occurred to me what terrible luck I had with men in general. Every man I had come in close contact with over the last ten months had rejected me in some way. On a day like this, I would have liked to speak with Yalat at length over a meal. She would have some kind of blue beetle dish that she enjoyed so much. I would have fresh fruits and vegetables at last. We would talk about everything we had missed in each other's lives during the better part of this past year. She would tell me not to worry about silly men, but to continue being the best warrior I could be despite all their foolishness. I found some comfort in this idea.

I unzipped my space suit and slipped it off. I felt something rattle inside it. I remembered what it was before I saw it. I reached down inside the suit by the ankle to retrieve the vial from the blood Alaban had used to fake my death. To my amazement, it was not empty. It contained a rolled paper note. I scarcely comprehended how he had been able to spill the blood, insert the note in the vial, and then slip the vial into my suit. He had

392

breezed through the parody so rapidly. I stepped out of the boots. I tucked the vial into my pocket while I quickly put away the suit and helmet.

I exited the dimly lit cargo hold to perch at the stairs where the lighting was better. I withdrew the paper carefully from the vial. It was stained with blood, but the words were still legible. Alaban had written them in the smallest letters he could write. I held my breath as I extended the note and read.

"Sil, if you're reading this note, I have failed and you are presumed dead. Know this: Ongeram planned to sacrifice himself so I could infiltrate the Regime. He said this was the best opportunity the Organization could ever hope for. He's a martyr. Zank's death was an accident. He was supposed to live to report against me but only our pilot survived. I couldn't keep my promise to you and follow Ongeram's orders at the same time. I'm sorry. I couldn't tell you any of this in front of Teradom, but I didn't think I'd have to.

"If you don't come with me, I will be stuck doing menial jobs for him. I can't do the big job without you. I'll tip off a few warriors about Regime news when I can like Ongeram wanted, but I'll have to say goodbye to the Organization. I should say good riddance. You were the only good thing about it. Working for these killers won't be much different. Even though we're on different sides now, when I see you again on Jawlcheen, no matter what the circumstances, we can still be together even if Teradom doesn't want you anymore.

"If I have to give you this note, I will hide myself from you. You'll know what I mean. I have to do it for your own safety, and mine. Destroy this note as soon as you read it. Don't let anyone know about it, not even Wilbaht.

"One more thing: I want you to know you tore my heart to shreds when you said you'd rather die with your partner than stand by me. I hope you did that for show. Please tell me you didn't mean it from the heart. You can tell me when I see you on Jawlcheen. Don't ever message me. Take care of yourself. I'll love you forever. Alaban."

I read the miniscule words over and over in disbelief. So that was what had really happened. So this was why I couldn't feel him in my heart anymore. But the worst of the truth still remained. He was theirs. He was with them. He would not come back to the Organization.

He still wanted me. I stared at the message in awe. I read it again and again. I forgot everything else.

"Sil, where are you? We're waiting," Wilbaht's voice spoke in my ear.

"I'm sorry, sir. I'm coming," I replied to him.

I rolled the paper again, returned it to the vial, and stuffed it into my pocket as I ran upstairs.

I stepped onto the upper observation deck feeling taller and stronger. I had been cured of two plagues: the mysteries of Alaban's purpose at the space station and why he had abandoned my heart and spirit. My mind was clear, my self-control restored.

"What kept you, Sil? Too busy changing your tampon?" Klib started.

I pointed a finger at him and proclaimed, "I will not put up with any form of harassment from you anymore. You have no right to talk down to me. You may think I was unfair with Ocelot, but I'm obligated to do my job. You probably think the space station was my fault. It wasn't. And just because I'm female you think I should act like a public concubine? Your sexual cravings are not my problem. I don't owe you anything. I am a warrior and an investigator. That's all.

"You are nothing but a beggar for attention and a coward. My patience with you is gone, just like the girl you picked on and harassed. Sil Gretath is dead. My name is Sil Rayfenix and I will kick your sorry ass from here to Jawlcheen if I have to. And there'll be no way to press charges against me for it, because officially, I'm not even on this ship. So back off!"

He scoffed, but regarded me with confusion. For the first time, Klib kept his mouth shut.

"Are you finished?" Wilbaht asked me. His voice carried a tone of aggravation.

"Yes, sir," I replied. I marched to my seat.

Wilbaht took a deep breath and then sighed. "This problem is exactly why I called this meeting. This crew has suffered more personal disputes than any other crew I've ever experienced in my eighty-one years with the Organization. Combining genders on a crew is supposed to ease tensions. However, among the three of you, this has actually caused more stress. I have wasted time and effort trying to smooth the conflicts among you. I have hinted, prodded, and pleaded with you to accept one another. I even threatened and punished. In all my experience, I have not found a more disastrous crew.

"I confess that before we left Sor3, I had another crewmember in mind, a Vermilion female. However, when Ocelot expressed his personal objections toward Vermilion females because of a recently failed romance, I dropped her from the list. Now I regret not hiring her. She would have been the perfect translator for the Beetle pilot I had chosen. But without the Vermilion, the Beetle could not fly for us. When Professor Stennet recommended Klib, my sixth sense brought me doubt, but there was no other pilot available since we had to leave the planet right after Sil's exam.

394

"I had hoped Ocelot and Sil would work well together because of a similarity in age and that Klib would be old enough to give balance to the group. However, age has not turned out to be a factor at all among the three of you. Apparently you've chosen sides by gender. You all see the opposite sex as competition for some reason. This was meant to be an important covert ops mission, not a flying sociology experiment!" He gave a sour face.

"I am your leader and an experienced warrior, but I am not infallible. I admit I erred in not demanding a change of pilot when we were on Karnesh. The whole idea of sexual harassment is contradictory to our purpose as warriors and as employees of the Organization. It also causes a breakdown in communication. It causes strife. God knows we've had enough of that on this flight.

"I have filed a general report to all pilot referral personnel in the Organization informing that Klib Sarrow should not be included in any ship's crew containing females of similar species. He has demonstrated a significant lack of respect towards a female coworker as well as his superior and should therefore be suspended from Organization flying for a time period to be determined by pilot referral personnel."

Klib scowled at Wilbaht, but said nothing. Ocelot cast a sympathetic eye after him.

"Any further insults, social conspiracy, or demonstrated lack of respect amongst you will result in a temporary incarceration in the quarantine room with electrostatic binders. That goes for all of you." He surveyed us sternly.

Wilbaht then altered our current schedules so that no two top floor schedules overlapped. Each person would leave the main deck ten minutes before the next assigned crewmember in order to deter the misuse of personal communication time. Wilbaht cited the tendency to take sides against one another when we had excessive time to talk. The two human men stole furtive glances at one another.

Wilbaht then ordered a mandatory communal meal, at which every word we spoke would be scrutinized. If anyone was found guilty of insult at the table, Wilbaht announced he or she would be taken by him, conscious or not, to the quarantine room for jail time. He reminded us that our basic goals here were survival and a successful landing on Jawlcheen. He ended the meeting by ordering Klib to the helm and the rest of us to our regular duties. I obeyed willingly, knowing Wilbaht's extreme decree was justified.

Two days later, Wilbaht went upstairs to relieve me early to tell me Yinore had replied to him. She had reported nothing corrupt about Ocelot, but noted the fact that he had the tendency to avoid direct eye contact, so her judgment could not be a reliable source of evidence.

He also warned me that Klib was now in the dining area drinking alone. He had asked him if he was going to bed soon, but he told him he couldn't sleep. He was depressed, and with good reason. Wilbaht advised me to ignore him, but to let him know if he did or said anything he shouldn't.

When I went downstairs, Klib was still there drowning himself in his sorrows. He crooned to himself softly. His last bottle of Rybalazar Red Ale decorated the center of the table. Several glasses formed an arc in front of him as if he had served imaginary friends who were sharing the ale with him. As I passed near the table, he addressed me as if I were an old friend.

"Hey, man. I hadn't seen you for while. Come sit over here. I'll buy you a drink. Just got a prrromotion," he gurgled.

He held up another bottle in his right hand. He set it down awkwardly. It rolled out of his hand and across the table. I jumped over to catch it before it fell. I set it back on the table again.

"Whee-ooh. 'S a good catch. Hey, wha's yer name again? Paul? Or is it Jaren? Aw, whatever yer name is, I'll buy y' a drink. Have a seat." He slumped at such an angle that his bearded chin nearly touched the tabletop. He wasn't even looking at me. I wondered if he was talking to me or to one of the people he had imagined.

"Hey, have you ever been to Xiantalix? There's a city there called Agate. I think's Agate. Got this great restaurant. Forget the name of it. 'S got the best roast meat in the galaxy. I don't know how they do it, but it tastes even better than roast meat my mom used to make. This place here, food's fershit. But, hey, don't tell the manager I said that."

I paused in front of him wondering if he had completely lost his mind or if he was just drunk. "Klib, don't you want to get some sleep?" I asked him tentatively.

"Naw, I'm good for one more round, boys. Pour me one last shot, would you, chief?" He lazily slung one hand out in front of him to grasp a glass, but knocked it over. I grabbed it and handed it to him. I cleared the other glasses over to one end of the table along with the bottles.

"No good food on this planet. I'm ready to set sail for home and get some real food." He sighed heavily, expelling a stench of alcoholic breath. "Just wanna go home. Y' know? There comes a time in every man's life...when he's ready to just...go home." He swaggered and blinked before sitting straight once more. "Hey, pour me a little shot. Let's give one last toast to my home planet."

I decided to play along so he would take this one last drink and go to bed. "All right. But this is your last drink. The bar is closed, okay?"

"Yeah. All right. Just pour me one more drink. Gotta drink one last one to Xiantalix," he slurred.

I poured him a tiny amount of ale into his glass. He peered at it with squinting, bloodshot eyes. He clutched the glass and stared into it for a moment. He tried to sit up straight again, but wavered limply.

"Well you've got to have a glass with me, man. How'm I supposed to toast this by myself? Here, let me pour you one."

He reached for the bottle that had less than half the ale left. He gripped a glass and poured the ale as carefully as he could under the circumstances. He spilled a little, but managed to fill the glass almost three quarters full. I helped him set the bottle back to its place. He raised his glass. I clinked mine together with his.

"To Xiantalix, the best planet...for guys like me," he proclaimed.

"To Xiantalix," I repeated.

He gulped down the liquid, choking a little on the last drops of it. I pretended to drink, but then set my glass down. I cleared away the extra glasses. I found the cork to the bottles and replaced them. Klib reached over and stopped me from taking them away.

"Hey, leave me the bottle. I collect these. This is a good brand." He blinked heavily. He pulled the bottle from my hand and hugged it to one shoulder.

"The bar is closed, sir. It's time to go. Do you need some help to your room?" I asked, still trying to play along for his sake.

He blinked at my glass in front of him. "One more drink, what do you say?"

"No, sir. The bar is closed. You've got to go."

"Are you going to drink that? If you're not, I'll take it." He pointed a floppy hand at my glass.

"I'm drinking it. It's time for you to go home."

"Naw, you're not. Come on. You know I need that drink more than you," he coaxed.

"I'm drinking it. Look." I took a swig of the bitter stuff and nearly coughed it back up. I tried not to make a face, but the taste was terrible.

"Good stuff, ain't it?" he asked.

"Yeah. Great brand," I lied. I reminded him again that he had to leave.

He still wanted the rest of my drink. I finally agreed to let him have it if he would just go. He thanked me and reached for it, but ended up bumping the glass. He tipped it so that it fell over, splashing my hands with the putrid red stuff. He swore. I picked up the glass and put it away. Then I cleaned up the spill while he blubbered some more obscenities.

My throat tingled from the alcohol. I repeated for the last time that he had to leave. He loosely removed himself from the table. I squeezed the alcohol from the cleaning rag into the sink and rinsed it. The water seemed colder than normal. Klib shuffled unsteadily past the table and nearly fell over. I caught him and guided the tripping, humming sot towards his bunk. His body heat should have warmed me, but instead I felt a spreading chill.

The freezing sensation edged its way through my arms, my throat, and my stomach. I couldn't speak. I stood blinking in panic. Klib regained his balance and stature with sudden confidence. Realization seeped through me with the cold. He had poisoned me.

Soon my whole upper body seized up, iced over from the inside. Next my legs gave out from under me. Before I knew it, I couldn't move. I could only blink my eyes, but just barely. I was fully awake, but must have looked asleep. Klib lifted me to a cradle position and grinned evilly.

The hallway passed us by, then the corner. I concentrated all my thought to mentally call Wilbaht for help. Klib carried me past the bathroom to the exercise room. As we crossed its threshold, I heard a noise in the hall. Klib heard it, too. He dumped me onto the padded floor and made for the door. He tried to close it, but someone stopped him.

"Hey, Ocelot. Get in here and lock that door behind you," Klib said with relief.

My body remained frozen, but my mind reeled.

"What happened?" Ocelot asked.

"She's on Bane's powder," Klib said proudly.

Ocelot knelt by me and covered my face with his hand. "She's cold," he said.

"Yeah. Don't worry. It won't kill her. Trust me. I know my drugs. It'll just knock her out for a few hours. The old man's going to be on deck for a while. This is the perfect pay back time."

Ocelot stood. Klib bent down over me. He lifted the front flap of my tunic and tucked a hand into the waistline of my uniform pants.

"Oh, yeah. This will pay me back plenty. Go close that door, man," he spoke as he pulled open the front closure of my pants.

I felt a tear stream from one eye. I shouted silently to Wilbaht to help me.

Ocelot pulled Klib back up to his feet. He fell to his knees over me. I felt his hands where Klib's had been.

"Well, hey, you know if you really want her, you can go first," Klib said to him.

I felt the waistline of my pants tighten again.

"Hold on. I'm going to get something. Don't close the door. Wait." Ocelot hurried away to the supply closet. I heard him rummage around for something while Klib stayed by me.

He chuckled. "Lucky for you somebody around here thinks of safe sex." He kicked at my knee.

Ocelot came back with a medical kit. He threw the case next to my head. He got down on all fours over the case and fumbled with some things inside it. Then he pierced my arm with a shot.

"Hey, what're you doing? You don't think I gave her too much, do you?" Klib asked.

"She could go into a coma," Ocelot told him.

"No way. I've used this stuff before. The only thing it does is knock them out for three hours, tops. No one's ever gone comatose from it. Hey, just don't wake her up yet," Klib said.

Ocelot inserted his hand below my neck, turning my head to face him. He leaned down to put an ear to my mouth and nose.

"She'll live. Now hurry up," Klib said.

Ocelot pulled my eyelids open to examine my pupils.

"She's out cold. She won't come to for another couple of hours at least. I'm telling you," Klib insisted.

Ocelot left me on the floor and stood to face Klib.

"Do you know what the penalty is for rape on Organization property?" Ocelot asked him. "It's death or voluntary castration."

"Don't worry about it. I set a loop on the surveillance for this room. Wilbaht will just see an empty floor. He won't find out...unless one of us tells him. Hey, you've been complaining about her ever since I can remember. She got us suspended. Don't tell me you don't want a piece of this." Klib retorted.

"I don't give a damn about the suspension. This girl brought me back from the dead. Nobody touches her."

"Well ain't this a turn of events? Hey, you're in on it now, whether you want it or not. It took me weeks to plan this. I don't care if she's your mother. This is justice. She's been asking for it since she boarded this goddamned ship. I'm not leaving here until I get mine, so you can either get some or get out of the way," the sinister weasel told him.

"It's not going to happen, Klib. Let her go."

The shot Ocelot gave me slowly reversed the effects of the Bane's powder. I started to regain mobility.

"Aw, shit. Now you're letting her wake up," Klib complained. He backed away from me.

I gyrated twice before sitting up on my own. I pushed up from the floor and stumbled. Ocelot helped me find my feet. I lifted my hands to Ocelot's chest and pushed myself away from him. He held onto my arms.

"Hey, you had a strange spell there. You must've been sleep walking," Klib fumbled.

I staggered a couple of steps away from Ocelot. He held onto my elbow as I put my head in my hands to contain the dizziness.

"Hey, Ocelot, why don't you take her back to her bunk? This time lock your door so you won't go wandering around," Klib babbled.

I released my head from my hands. I pushed Ocelot's hand from my elbow. I blinked at the contemptuous ogre.

I shouted as I leapt forward. I levitated with power, leaning down to thrust a two-fisted punch into Klib's lower abdomen. He doubled over and sailed backwards, hitting the corner of the room with a thud. I tried to land in an extended forward stance, but I fell sideways. I returned to stand, wobbling. Klib cringed and groaned in the floor. Ocelot took my wrist to steady me, but I withdrew my arm from his hand. I spat at Klib's writhing form before I ambled away.

"Where are you going?" Ocelot asked me.

"Grr. She's going to go tell on us like she always does," Klib retched.

I stood at the threshold of the exercise room. "Yes, but I don't need help from a higher power this time. You just gave me full authority to kill you. It looks like you'll have blood in your urine for the next few days. If you come near me again, you'll have a much more serious accident."

Klib gurgled a few lame obscenities.

I walked away from the pathetic scene. Ocelot followed me down the hallway.

"I owe you one," I said firmly.

I trudged to my bunk where I sat heavily on my cot.

"I'll go report to Wilbaht," he said.

We exchanged an uneasy glance. I stood again to face him. I stuck out my hand. He shook it. I squeezed firmly.

"Thank you," I told him.

He nodded. I returned to my bed. He reminded me to be sure and lock my door as he closed it. I did.

Jagged hatred raked across my soul. Klib's sickening image hung maliciously in my mind. I could have killed him in self-defense, but my conscience wouldn't allow it. Besides this, I wanted him to suffer a little longer for what he tried to do. I had always thought revenge was not in my nature, but this ire burned in me. I imagined myself kicking the heathen down the stairwell, breaking his jaw, beating him in the chest until his heart nearly stopped. Then I imagined Ocelot holding me back.

"Let him go, Sil," he would say. "What good will it do to have a dead pilot on our hands?"

I let myself slip into a dream.

"He's going to pay for what he did," I replied to him.

"He'll never fly again. He's got a life of suffering ahead of him. Let him go," Ocelot argued.

I watched Klib limp away, withered and groaning. I saw Wilbaht escort him towards the quarantine room.

"For a minute there, I thought you were in on it with him," I admitted.

"I would never do anything to hurt you, Sil." Ocelot stepped close to me.

As I looked up at him, his face changed. Suddenly it was Alaban standing with me. I forgot the incident to embrace him.

"Alaban, I missed you so much." I tightened my grip around his chest.

He hugged me back and held my head to his shoulder. "You know I'll never let anything happen to you."

He lifted my chin to bring my mouth to his. He kissed me lightly on the lips, then on my cheek and on my forehead. He held my face in his hand as he hugged me to him again. He stroked my cheek. I moved to look up at him fondly.

But it wasn't Alaban anymore. It was Ocelot.

I blushed hotly and moved away from him. "I'm sorry. I thought you were someone else."

"I just wanted to make sure you were all right." He turned away, disgusted.

"No, wait. It was my fault. You don't have to leave." I went after him.

"Actually, I do. I have a new assignment," he spoke. He descended the stairs. I followed him closely.

"But our year isn't finished yet," I said. We left the stairwell together.

"It has to do with my new identity. I have to leave right away," he said as we entered the main cargo hold. He hit the panel to open the main door. It lowered onto a landing field on a grassy planet. Another ship stood a few hundred meters from ours.

"So I guess this is goodbye. It was nice knowing you, Sil Rayfenix," he said. He held out his hand for me to shake it.

"Is there any way you can stay?" I asked him.

"No." He retracted his hand and walked quickly out into the field.

I followed him, running.

"How will I contact you?"

"You won't. Why would you need to?" he asked.

"Why shouldn't I contact you? I'm your friend."

He stopped in the middle of the field. "What do you mean friend? You accused me of conspiracy."

"It was all a mistake. I'm sorry. I brought you back to life in the space station. I am your friend," I stammered.

"I have to go." He gestured toward the other ship. A pair of Greys waited for him at the door. Ocelot's face seemed sadly resigned. He tried to shake my hand again.

"Please contact me," I begged.

"I wouldn't know what to say," he answered. He put down his hand. "I'm sorry. Goodbye, Sil."

As he turned to leave, I grabbed him by his shirt. I hopped in front of him. I felt the urgent need to make him stay by any means. I put my hands to the sides of his inquisitive face. I reached up and kissed him. I didn't want to let go of him. I didn't want to see his reaction. I felt surely he would feel repulsed.

When I finally let him go, I saw once again he had changed back into Alaban. We were on Sor3. He was getting ready to leave with Zank and Ongeram.

"Goodbye, Sil," he said sadly. He stroked my cheek and kissed me one last time. He turned and ran off to his ship. I stood in the lobby of the U-shaped ascension tower at the C.A.T.T. Center on Sor3, utterly confused.

I sat up in my bunk, half-awake in the darkness. I shook off the bizarre sensation.

"Crazy dreams. They don't make any sense," I said.

Chapter 37: Falling

In the morning, I was awakened by a buzz by my head scant seconds before my alarm went off. I switched off the alarm and stood, still in my uniform. Wilbaht rumbled to me on the speaker that I was to report upstairs. I reported aloft as ordered. Wilbaht and Ocelot both stood near the stairwell, formally awaiting my presence. Wilbaht stood between us and crossed his arms.

"We will discuss what happened in private. I will tell you that Klib will not leave the quarantine room for the duration of the trip. We can't press charges because of your identity change, but he'll never fly for the Organization again."

I nodded.

"We're close to Jawlcheen," he continued. "We have less than three weeks left on this journey. Let's make them as bearable as possible."

"Yes, sir," I replied.

His demeanor lightened. He then gave me the news I had been hoping for. "On a positive note, I received word from Channol and from a mutual friend of ours. Ocelot's story checks out one hundred percent. I also received a message from another trusted friend, a character witness if you will, regarding both Ocelot and Jiao. He says they are both above suspicion in any way." He turned to Ocelot. "Your suspension is lifted."

Ocelot returned the fond gaze to our commander. "Thank you, sir. I'll be twice as careful about handling data in the future."

Wilbaht laid a hand on both our shoulders. His face showed satisfaction.

"Sil, I believe you have something to say?" Wilbaht said to me.

I faced my partner and recited the apology speech I had memorized. "I owe you an apology, sir. I can't think of how to make it up to you, but if you ever need anything, you can call on me first. You've proven your loyalty in more ways than one. I'm truly sorry I caused you so much trouble. If there is anything I can do for you, just name it."

He smiled a little. "Now that you mention it, there is something I'd like you to do for me."

"Absolutely, sir," I responded.

"Don't ever call me 'sir' again. You make me feel old," he said with a smile.

Wilbaht laughed heartily. I grinned a little.

"All right, sir. I mean…all right," I stuttered.

He thrust a hand toward me, just like in my dream. This time I took it and shook it firmly.

"No hard feelings," he said in his golden voice.

Wilbaht chuckled. "This calls for a group hug. Come here my children." He hugged us both tightly under his arms.

Ocelot and I were taken by surprise, but went along with him. We hung our arms around each other clumsily. Wilbaht slapped us both on the back twice. He beamed down at us with a full smile. He did love us as if we were his own children.

"It's good to have the three of us back together again," he said proudly.

Later that day at our three-person communal meal, our conversation regained its old friendly tone. The atmosphere among us was warm. We exchanged a few smiles. It seemed the worst was behind us. Klib would never bother us again.

On the upper deck later that evening, I felt relieved to see Ocelot once again poring over text on his computer.

"Hello, s...I mean...hi," I sputtered.

He glanced up from his work to view me with glad eyes. "Hey. I was just writing about you. We never did complete the data for your new identity. I'd like to finish that up this week. That is, if you trust me to do that now." He eyed me knowingly.

I responded seriously. "Yes, I trust you. I'm sorry I put you through all that. And, um, thanks for standing up for me last night."

"You gave twenty years of your lifespan to save mine. That's a gift no one can fully repay. I won't forget that. I'll back you up any day. That's a promise. Just tell me you won't accuse me of anything again without at least talking to me about it first," Ocelot said.

"You have my word," I replied solemnly.

"I think we'll have smooth sailing from now on." He returned to type at the computer.

He stopped tapping to check my sullen face.

"Can I ask you something?" he began.

I didn't answer, but lifted my chin inquisitively.

"Why didn't you kill him?" he asked.

"It wasn't my right to take his life if he wasn't threatening mine."

"He gave you an unauthorized, potentially lethal drug in an unknown dosage. That was life-threatening enough." He squinted at me with criticism.

"I shouldn't take a life unless I have to. Life is sacred. It belongs to God. It's not mine to destroy," I told him.

"You think Klib's life belongs to God? I'd say he belongs to someone else," he said.

I shrugged.

He changed the subject. "I'm glad to be back on regular schedule again. I nearly went crazy from boredom."

I brightened a little. "Me too."

Placidity returned to Ocelot's face.

When Wilbaht came upstairs to join me, he confessed something to me.

"Sil, I would like you to know that I did hear you calling me last night. I alerted Ocelot to help you instead. I believe he was the best man to intervene in the problem. I knew seeing him on your side would help you realize his true loyalty."

"Thank you, sir. You were right, as usual. I don't know what we'd ever do without you."

Wilbaht grinned, flattered. "You'll get along without me soon enough. We'll be on Jawlcheen before you know it. You'll be on your own soon after that. You'll only have a month left in my care. Time passes quickly, especially for an old man like me.

"You two have caused me plenty of headaches. But you've also filled my heart. If you were Torreons, I would start calling you by the names of my own grandchildren. You remind me so much of Olimbi. She's coming to Jawlcheen, by the way, with my son, Gatterand, her father. We'll have a little family reunion. I'm looking forward to it."

"I'll be glad to see Olimbi again, too. Sir, is there any way we might continue on together after the year is over?" I asked him hopefully. He had guided me through so many difficulties and still I felt I had so much to learn from him. "I know a rookie is supposed to leave the initial training crew after the first year on the job. But on the record, Ocelot and I weren't part of your crew this year. We're different people now."

"Hmm. You certainly are. I'll give it some thought." He regarded me lovingly.

In the morning, I sat up and blinked as my alarm sounded. Routinely, I tried to put the dreams of Alaban behind me. The afterimage of his face of animalistic rage still floated before my drooping eyelids. I rubbed my eyes to rid myself of the streaking image. I considered working out with Ocelot, but I felt I would be imposing without an invitation. I moved dutifully through my work routine instead.

After a couple of days of improved peace among the three of us, Ocelot announced that he had finally completed my new identity. He asked me to look over all the files to double check them. He passed the whole file to my station so I could read it. I skimmed through document after document. Everything seemed to be all right, except for one thing. My parents' marriage documentation said the marriage rights were performed by the Liricos Proof of Love Ceremony, witnessed by my imaginary aunts and uncles. I had to explain this error to Ocelot so it could be fixed before the database changes went into affect.

"It's not a set of official marriage vows that you see in documentation. It has more of a religious value," I explained. "Besides, the Ceremony ends in a mating ritual. To have spectators at a ceremony like that would go against Liricos ethical traditions."

"Well, that shows you what I know about culture. What should I change it to?" he asked.

I told him to say the signed documentation was witnessed, but not the ritual. He fixed the error. I didn't find any other mistakes. His faux pas struck my curiosity.

I asked Ocelot about similar traditions on Jain. He asked about Tambuo. We talked about other family customs and family in general. I explained my father's role as director at his school. We discussed our education. Ocelot mentioned the most interesting studies in his year at med training. We finished with the topic of genetic engineering, realizing we shared similar opinions on limitations to genetic testing.

Ocelot glanced at the clock. This can't be right. Is it 0350 already?"

I opened my eyes wide. "Yes. It is. I'm sorry. I've kept you awake."

Ocelot moved quickly to the stairwell. "It's okay. We can continue our conversation tomorrow. I enjoyed it," he actually said.

"Me, too," I confessed reluctantly.

Our discussion spilled over into our next communal meal and even the next day when we sat together in the observation deck. I felt full of heart when I talked with him. His knowledge impressed me, but he didn't show it off. He included me in the conversation as often as himself. He asked intriguing questions, brought up pertinent topics, and generally became a valuable source of information and encouragement. We almost forgot about Klib entirely.

I asked Ocelot about his own identity documentation, which he soon finished as well. He had even gone back and double-checked all the information he had patched in or erased as a teenager. He felt proud to have finally repaired it all.

"Listen, I don't want to pry about your name, Ocelot, but could you at least tell me why you don't want me to know it?" I asked him, hoping he would respond well in his good mood.

He turned almost sullen. "I changed my name the first time because kids used to make fun of me for it. Imagine starting at a new school when you're only five or six years old and the whole class is making fun of you."

"Was it really that bad?" I asked him.

"Yes! It happened every time we moved. My parents finally started calling me by a different name. After they died, I begged Channol to let me change it on official record." He crossed his arms and leaned back in his chair, recalling his frustration.

I asked how he'd gotten the nickname. He recounted a story from his early youth in the tropics of Liricos. Ocelot described the area where they had lived at the time—rainforest territory—populated towns invaded by nature reserves and zoological gardens. He described their home and neighborhood. His family was close-knit. Since his father's name was Leono, meaning "lion", and since Ocelot looked like a tiny copy of him, his family called the two "Big Lion" and "Little Lion". These pet names inspired games between them. I delighted in imagining them playing together, although he did not give details. He then said one day his parents took him to a local zoo, where he saw some cats he thought were small lions. He'd pointed to them and said they were like him: little lions. His father corrected him, explaining they were ocelots, but went along with his comparison, saying they were about his size. The young boy liked the name of the newly discovered animals, and decried that he was one. His parents honored his declaration. From then on, his family called him Ocelot.

"It was a lot less embarrassing than my real name," he concluded.

"Why would your parents give you a name that would embarrass you?" I asked.

"Their intentions were good, but the result was not. I still don't want to tell it to anyone. I don't want to relive the humiliation." He drummed his fingers on the edge of his panel.

I thought about this and about his guarded personality for a moment. "That explains a lot."

He looked over at me apprehensively, regretting having divulged the snapshot of his youth to me. He became taciturn again. I would have apologized, but I didn't want to draw attention to his discomfort.

When it was time for him to go downstairs, he finally spoke to me. He asked if I wouldn't mind working with him on some levitation techniques during his exercise time since he was getting rusty. Glad to accept this forgiving gesture, I agreed to help him. We exchanged a friendly smile as he traipsed down the stairwell.

I stared after where he'd gone, still smiling. I felt anxious, almost giddy. I mentally criticized myself for such a juvenile reaction. It was silly. I tried to calm myself, but I kept experiencing the same lighthearted feeling. Even during my work time alone, I found myself smiling over and over. I wasn't sure what was wrong with me.

Later, Wilbaht noticed my distracted state. He asked me if I was feeling all right. I told him I was fine. I was just feeling energetic.

I went to bed still restless. I tried to relax and sleep. This time, all I could think of was Ocelot: his new friendly manner of conversation, his vulnerability because of his name, his kinder face, the way he so generously held nothing against me for accusing him. My self-criticism increased as my thoughts swirled around him. I felt short of breath. I sighed repeatedly. Finally at a very late hour, I drifted off to sleep.

At 1730 hours, I awoke feeling more like myself again. However, when I left my bunk to walk towards the exercise room, I began to feel anxiety. As I rounded the corner of the hall, I glanced at Ocelot's door. I felt a swelling pressure around my heart. I approached the exercise room with a kind of hyper nervousness. I knocked on the door. Ocelot opened it.

Perspiration trickled down his face. He ushered me into the room as usual.

He turned his back to me as soon as I entered. If he hadn't, he would have seen a nervous grin on my face. He replaced the weights he'd been working with to their slots in the wall. Conscious of my strange behavior, I stepped to the middle of the room and inserted a thumbnail between my teeth.

He turned back again to see me this way. "What's wrong? You look worried. Don't tell me you're still thinking about Klib."

"No, I'm just feeling strange lately. Maybe I should check my blood for chemical imbalances. I keep getting this weird nervous energy," I told him.

"Maybe you're sensing something's about to happen."

"Maybe. Maybe I'll have a vision later." I smiled at him a little.

He nodded. He observed me warily. "I hope we don't have to go through anything like the space station again."

I shook my head. "No, I'm sure I would have sensed something like that before. It must be something minor. I don't feel anything bad is going to happen. Really, I feel…good."

"Ah, well. Maybe you're anticipating good weather and a week's vacation when we get to Jawlcheen," he said with a smile.

I smiled back and laughed a little. That ridiculous giddiness came back again. Ocelot looked at me with curiosity, but didn't criticize me. I made an effort to control myself.

We worked on some levitation exercises together as promised. We used the weights to practice double-, triple-, and quadruple helixing around us. Ocelot had trouble with the triple helix. He admitted levitation had always been his weak point. His weights kept colliding in midair. He didn't try the quadruple helix.

I told him how Yalat and I had worked together a few times by holding hands and channeling our energies together to combine levitative power. He was willing to try it. I held my hands up in front of me, shoulder width apart, palms towards my face. Ocelot held up his hands in the same way. I felt anxious standing so close to him. We intertwined our fingers. A mild tingling sensation engulfed me, like a low voltage of electrical current. I had never felt this so clearly when I had worked with Yalat. I tried to find a physiological explanation for it.

"Do you feel a flow of energy?" I asked him.

He regarded our hands doubtfully. "Maybe a little," he said, just to go along with me. "So what now?"

I shook off the feeling. "We can start moving the weights. If we take turns lifting and orbiting, we should be able to spin them all," I said.

"All? I can barely orbit three," he said incredulously.

"Combined energy is always stronger than the individual. You can use three or four times your own strength. At least, it always worked that way when I connected with Yalat. It can't hurt to try." I stared nervously into his brown eyes.

He nodded at me. He lifted one weight. He brought it in fairly close to us. He swirled it around us at the waist. He watched it pass us to the left and right.

"Don't look at it directly. Your eye movement distracts your mental concentration. Just stare at a fixed point or close your eyes," I suggested.

He closed his eyes. I lifted another weight, swirling it at a slightly different angle from the first. I told him it was his turn. He brought up the third weight. He swung it around us at the shoulder level. I lifted the fourth and made an orbit from my left ear to my right hip. He moved the fifth in a similar, but opposite pattern. I pulled the sixth about our ankles. He started to smile. He moved the seventh in a vertical pattern, zipping it between our feet and sailing above our heads. I grinned. I moved the eighth in a sporadic path, bouncing from elbow to elbow between us. He spun the ninth in a halo above us. I suppressed a giggle. I swung the tenth in a wide oval around our knees. He picked up the eleventh weight, but sent it away from us. He made it orbit the entire length of the room. He grinned broadly. I picked up the twelfth weight. With this weight I drew a swiveled line all around the other weights. This twelfth weight wiggled close to its comrades, then listed away in a squiggly pattern.

As he moved the thirteenth weight, he shook his head. "This is great," he whispered.

I wasn't sure if his words distracted me or if it was my own chemical imbalance that caused things to go haywire. I stared at his face as he said these words. Something strange happened. I looked at his mouth.

An unfamiliar desire gripped me. It was stronger than my own levitative abilities. I blinked and clenched my teeth. I struggled against this feeling, shifting my concentration away from the orbiting weights.

Suddenly, three of the weights clinked together, bumping each other out of orbit. These collided with two others. Then the whole lot of them went clattering to the floor.

Ocelot opened his eyes to find me staring into his face. At that moment, it seemed to me that his were the most beautiful eyes I'd ever seen.

Just then, the weight that had spun above us fell, knocking Ocelot in the head. He winced. The strange spell was broken. He released my hands to rub his injured crown.

"Oh, I'm sorry. Are you all right?" I collected the weights around me.

"I'll be fine. What happened? I thought the combined energy was working great." He still massaged the top of his head.

"I don't know. Maybe I do have a chemical imbalance. I lost my concentration altogether. That's never happened before." I replaced all the weights shakily.

"Yeah, you don't look so good all of a sudden," Ocelot said.

"I don't?" I touched my forehead and my cheeks to check for fever. I wasn't aware of any.

"Why don't I go down to quarantine right now and get a blood scanner?" he suggested.

I agreed to wait for him in the dining area. He went downstairs momentarily. He returned with the scanner, which he strapped to my arm. He told me to hold still as the box scanned me from head to foot. He looked over the readout on his hand held computer.

"All readings are within normal range. You do have a high level of endorphins in the brain. That explains the nervous energy you were talking about. That would also cause a lack of concentration. It'll probably go away in a few minutes or a couple of hours at the most. These things don't last long. There's no need for medication. It's a natural physiological occurrence." He paused. "I know what it is. You've experienced so much negativity lately, your body's gotten used to a deficiency in positive energy. You probably regained it all so quickly that it feels like an imbalance."

I moved to see the readout with him. "I think you're right."

He nodded. "You'll be back to normal in a day or two."

He turned off the monitor and the scanner. I thanked him. I apologized again for dropping the weight on him. He assured me it was no big deal.

"I'll just keep this with me. I'd rather not have to see Klib again today. He keeps asking for more food every time I go down there." He

410

tucked the scanner and his palm computer into a shirt pocket. He brushed by my shoulder. A tingling sensation ran through me.

I watched him saunter down the hallway as I went to stand by my door. I admired him completely. I stepped into my bunk and sat staring at my computer cubby even though I was supposed to start my cleaning duty. My mind was awash.

I pushed myself to do my necessary chores. I felt as though I were moving through a dream. I wanted to believe that Ocelot was right about my feeling, but I sensed the truth stalking me from the shadows of my mind, waiting for the right moment to spring upon me. My happy nervousness turned to staunch denial.

At our meal that day, I avoided looking Ocelot in the eye. Seeing his face before me, his eyes full of kindness, made me hold my breath. He asked me if I was feeling better. I told him I was still feeling a little restless, but that I was sure I'd be fine. I convinced him he was right about it. Now if I could only convince myself.

Ocelot told Wilbaht about the weights and how one had crowned him. Wilbaht laughed about the incident. He concurred with Ocelot about its cause. He noticed I was biting my lip.

"Don't worry about it, child. These things happen from time to time. None of us is infallible. You'll regain your concentration in no time. I'm certain of it," he said. "Speaking of the exercise room, Ocelot, I'd like to take time off one day this week to do some sparring with you. We won't have many chances again before we reach the planet."

I listened to Wilbaht's voice and Ocelot's as they harmonized in conversation. Wilbaht's reassurance comforted me somewhat. I directed my focus to him instead of Ocelot, although I became more and more aware of Ocelot's presence and his every move. His life permeated the air around me. I basked in his pungent energy. My better, more logical conscience resisted. But the more I resisted, the more I felt myself falling.

In the upper observation deck, Ocelot tried to make conversation with me, but I was too distracted to talk intelligently about any topic he brought up. He interpreted my behavior as embarrassment for having hit him on the head.

"Don't worry about dropping those weights. You know how thick-skulled I am." He smiled at me. I smiled back, but quickly looked away.

We spent a few minutes in silence. When he stood to go downstairs, he stopped just behind my chair. He attracted my senses. I half-turned timidly towards him.

"Why don't you work with me again in the morning? We can do some sparring," he invited.

"I don't think I'll be much help to you," I said weakly.

"Come on. Don't be so hard on yourself. Sparring with a real person is always better than fighting against the hologram. Hey, I'll show you some new grappling techniques I learned for sparring against Saurusoids." He waited for a response from me.

I sat deliberating. I fidgeted with a loose string on my uniform.

He tried one more time. "I'll make a deal with you. If you can drop me five times in sparring, I promise I'll tell you my name."

I whirled around to face him. He smirked.

"I'll be there," I said definitely.

All night, intrigue played raucously inside my mind. I made a failing attempt to focus on plans of attack to use against him in sparring. My mind shifted to relaxation and tempting images of him standing with me, staring into my eyes. I dreamed of kissing him, but he disappeared every time.

Once I dreamed Ocelot disappeared just as Alaban walked into the room. He asked me what I was doing. I said I was getting ready to work out. He scanned me suspiciously and then drew his sword to investigate the hall outside the exercise room. I awoke perturbed. Reluctantly, I dressed and went to spar with him.

He greeted me with enthusiasm. "So are you ready to win or are you ready to taste the mat?"

"I'll do my best," is all I could manage.

"Aw, you need to wake up," he complained.

"Just let me warm up a while," I responded.

I stretched out and did a few practice punches and kicks. We sparred. I went down within the first two minutes, and then again a few seconds later.

"Come on. You're not putting your heart into it," Ocelot grated. "Imagine I'm someone you really hate, like Teradom. Hey, Warrior, why don't you come work with me and my psycho task force?" He swiped at my face.

I remembered my disdain for Teradom. I skidded past him and tried to dump him onto the floor. I missed, but just barely. He saw this was working.

"Yeah, you know you don't want to work for that old back-stabbing Organization anymore. Come help me steal some weapons of mass destruction."

I whirled my legs at him. Then I faked a punch and hooked him around the neck. At the same time, I kicked into his knee and threw him to the floor with power.

"That's one," he said as I helped him up.

I jerked his arm and levitated him to roll him over my back and then hit him with an elbow as he spun. I clutched his wrist and twisted while I kicked him on the outside of the thigh at the hip rotator. He pulled away and swiped at me, but I wrenched him forward to bring him down again, nearly falling with him.

"That's two," I spoke. Stability returned to my voice.

He tried to catch me to retaliate, but I hopped to my right. I confused him with a barrage of punches targeting his blocking wrists. Then I slipped diagonally, inserted my ankles between his and opened in a split to knock his legs out from under him. He fell to the mat again.

"That's three," I announced.

He didn't wait until he got up this time to attack. He went straight for my knees. I struggled, but ended up on the floor.

We both jumped up. He kicked at me with two roundhouses on the left. I pounced for his raised leg and levitated to deliver a double kick to his chin. We both flopped to the floor.

"That's four," I breathed.

He got up slowly, shaking his head. He massaged his jaw. He grunted. I thought maybe he was more seriously injured than I had hoped. I took a step to him. He bounded like a bullet to wedge a shoulder into my chest. I buckled. He brought me down to the mat and then leapt to his feet.

I rushed at him, but then I strafed to the side. He grabbed at me but I moved around him. I jumped, kicked, and struck. He successfully grasped my arm to fling me with incredible strength to the floor, facedown.

"I guess you did come to taste the mat," he teased.

I groaned. I followed his example of pretending to be injured. I staggered, holding the side of my mouth. I acted as though I'd lost a tooth. He didn't believe my act.

"Here, let me see that," he said. He reached out and jerked me by the arm, throwing me to the mat again.

This time I scissor-kicked to knock him off balance. He stumbled, but regained his balance. I back-flipped up to my feet. I attacked him three times. I use many skills I had not practiced in months. He fended me off well.

Finally, I tired of slugging at him. I lifted him into the air with levitation. He struggled a while, but then realized he wasn't going anywhere.

"Now what?" he asked cautiously.

I didn't answer. I moved him so that he lay parallel to the floor, just a centimeter from the mat. I meant to release him and pin him down with a knee pressed to his back, but when I let him go, he reversed the levitation. He tried to bounce back up from the floor, but I realized his purpose

413

quickly. I caught him by the arm, flipped him on his back, and smacked him to the floor, pressing my right forearm to his windpipe and my left elbow to his torso.

He growled in disappointment. I remained atop his chest. I leaned on the arm at his throat for a moment.

"That was five," I told him.

I slowly withdrew my arms from his chest. I sat back on my heels. I expected him to relent and finally tell me his name. Instead he bolted upright, nabbed my ear, and hauled us both up to stand. I complained. He let go of the ear, but strung an arm snugly around my throat. He stood behind me and held two fingers near the base of my neck. He pressed in. The muscles began to throb. I asked him what he was doing.

"This is insurance. If you laugh at my name or make fun of it in any way, I'll twist in right here. I'm sure you feel that. If I press in just right, you'll have migraine headaches for at least a week," he said.

I struggled to speak. "Ocelot, you know I won't make fun of you. If you don't trust me, then don't tell me. Just don't threaten me."

He eased the pressure at my neck. He apologized briefly, but still kept me pinned to him. He briskly massaged the muscles in my neck that he had poked. He let go of my throat finally, but grabbed me by the arms just above the elbows.

We stood for one painstaking minute in silence. I felt Ocelot's breath at the nape of my neck. I felt his body heat at my back. His hands still clenched tightly around my arms. I moved my hands slowly across my chest to gently touch his knuckles. He loosened his grip, but kept his hands bound to me.

I closed my eyes. Despite my moral turmoil, I did not reject my physical instincts this time. I allowed myself to enjoy this simple closeness. Ocelot sighed. His breath tickled the back of my neck. He slid his hands up slowly to my shoulders. The tenderness of his touch sent invisible sparks through my body. My breathing grew shallow. He leaned his forehead onto the back of my head.

I battled myself to remain still. My face flushed. Arousal begged me to turn and kiss him, but I wouldn't let it happen. He was my partner and my superior, not my lover. Throughout most of the year, he had barely accepted me as a fellow human being. I couldn't imagine how he might react to any amorous gestures from me now. I had to honor my position as a warrior. I had taken that oath into my heart and made it a part of my being. I would live by it as long as my integrity held out. But if this feeling grew much stronger, I was afraid that would not be long.

Ocelot stood straight again, moving his forehead away from me. He sighed again.

"Okay. I'll give you a blatant hint. I'm named after a planet." He tightened his grip on my shoulders.

I opened my eyes, leaving my imagination to flounder. The letters of the name he had hinted at anonymously fit together.

"Jain. You're named after the Jain planet. It looks like a boy's name, but it sounds like a girl's name. No wonder you didn't like it." I smiled. "I'm not making fun of you. I'm not laughing at you. I'm glad you told me. I'm sorry you had to live with that."

He relaxed his hands at my shoulders.

"I guess you think I kept it a secret for nothing," he said.

I assured him I probably would have done the same thing.

I watched our reflection as he looked up at it, too. Suddenly, an uncanny realization struck me. We were standing almost exactly as Alaban and I had stood together when he had come to see our ship on Santer. I remembered seeing our reflection. I remembered the feeling I'd had at that moment, that Alaban had been standing in another man's place. Now I saw Ocelot here in almost the same stance. Our bodies, our aura, everything about us seemed to match together, complimenting each other. I was spellbound.

Then, as if this wasn't enough to leave me disconcerted, a sizzling crack of light extruded itself from the reflection. The sinister shards of vision buckled out from the wall. They crept toward my frozen form in slow motion.

The first shard clarified our reflection, but changed it. I saw Ocelot move his face to my cheek. As soon as this happened, the shard shot through me. I gasped. The second shard widened to show us in the same position, but a third person appeared in the scene. I watched as Alaban strode through the door to find us this way. His face showed shock and fury. The shard shattered backward towards the wall into thousands of jagged pieces and then slowed to a stop. Then the pieces sprung back at me and plummeted through my heart. I cried out in agony.

Ocelot gripped my shoulders more tightly than ever. I heard him ask me if I was all right, but I could not answer. This other dimension absorbed my attention.

The next shard showed us here in the same place. Alaban entered again, this time drawing his sword when he saw us. The next one showed him leaping through the air, aiming the sword. In the next shard, Alaban swung the sword toward Ocelot's neck. I winced as blood showered us. I refused to see anymore.

I shouted. "Stop! Stop it! You can't kill him. That can't happen! I won't let you!"

415

The shards combusted all at once. They hurled themselves through me like a million needles. I fruitlessly shielded my face from the flying terrors.

Ocelot now stood facing me. He peered at me with genuine concern. He asked me something, but I was too distraught to listen. I flailed my elbows at the remaining specks of vision as if they were swarming insects. They abandoned me to the thin comfort of reality. I headed straight for the padded target. I beat the tough object fiercely. I bludgeoned it harder and harder until my energy waned.

My shouts had awoken Wilbaht, who arrived disheveled from his sleep. He still wore his pajamas. Ocelot explained to him that I'd had some kind of vision. I punched the target one last time. Wilbaht advanced to my side. I stood gripping the target, panting.

"It was a bad one," he spoke, knowingly.

I held onto the sides of the target and locked my arms against it, panting. "Yes, sir. I'm sorry I woke you," I told him through gritted teeth. I attempted to calm myself at least to a presentable state.

"Is there anything we can do?" he asked kindly. "What was it?"

I shook my head. All I could say was, "It was Alaban...again."

I reached out to punch and kick the target some more. I fought against it, but gained nothing. I turned again to see them waiting for further explanation.

"He wants to kill someone I know," I told them. "Someone...close to me."

"Someone in your family?" Wilbaht asked.

"A close friend, sir," I said.

"Do we know him?" Wilbaht asked.

"No, sir," I lied. I stamped a forearm onto the target and then leaned my head to my fist.

During our meal, I stayed in the lower observation deck. I told them I urgently needed to research something. In reality, I only flipped idly through pages of previous research. I pondered my new predicament. I was sure this vision was not accurate. I didn't believe Alaban would ever board this ship again. I didn't believe Ocelot would ever want to kiss my cheek. I did believe this vision was a clue to what would happen if Alaban ever found the two of us together or ever suspected I was involved with him romantically. Nothing would stand in Alaban's way. He would murder him without forethought.

What sickening luck I had, to barely have glimpsed the serendipity of falling in love only to have all illusion shattered before me. I sank into my seat and into self-pity. Despite my heart's downfall, I retained one beacon of hope: I resolved to protect Ocelot from Alaban at all costs. As soon as we arrived on Jawlcheen, I would separate myself from him. I would ask Wilbaht not to consider keeping us all together after all. I would say goodbye to them both.

In the upper deck, Ocelot asked me if I'd found the data I was looking for. I told him no. He offered to help. I said I'd rather look for it myself. He was hurt that I would refuse his help. I changed the subject to cheer him up.

"At least I didn't laugh when you told me your name."

He brightened a bit. "Yes, well, it never evoked screams before. That was a first."

I smiled a little. "So why did you change your name back to Jain if it's caused you so many problems?"

"I still wanted to honor my parents by observing a name they gave me," he responded.

"That's a noble reason…Jain," I told him.

"Ocelot. Please don't call me Jain," he responded with a distasteful shudder.

After a while, I bravely made a suggestion. "What if you combine the two names? Then you could use both together. It would sound more masculine."

"What do you mean?" he asked.

"You could make it all one word: Jainocelot. That way you could have both. It's probably a silly idea. Never mind," I said.

He repeated the name. "I like that idea. Thanks. I'm going to use it. I'll change that right now." He complimented me on my creative thinking.

I observed him with yearning while he busied himself with his task. I longed to approach him. I had to keep myself as far away from him as possible on this little ship.

Less than a month and a half remained of our year together. In a way, it seemed like such a long time. Every hour I spent in his company would bring greater temptation. I couldn't bear to spar with him anymore. I would lose my nerve at close contact. I decided to give the excuse that my vision had affected me too much. This was true. And yet I yearned all the more to spend time with him. This month and a half would go by too quickly.

My heavy heart left me weary. Ocelot noticed my despondence. He didn't try to cheer me up this time. He only mentioned that I was looking blue. He asked if I'd like to talk about it. I said no. He shrugged and turned back to his work. Sadness gripped me.

After Ocelot finished redoing his name on all his documentation, he said he was ready to change our title pins. He ran downstairs for something.

Then he trotted back up with a tiny adaptor and his hand-held computer. He asked me to stand. I stood, turning my face toward my right shoulder so I wouldn't have to face him. He attached the adaptor to my title pin at my left collarbone. If he reacted to my apparent coldness, I didn't know it.

I felt the impersonal touch of his fingertips near my shoulder as he attached the adaptor. I closed my eyes a moment, wishing those fingertips would travel uninhibited over my body. This painful temptation was short lived, however. The title pin changed in the blink of an eye. The daydream ended as quickly as it had begun.

"All right. You are now officially Sil Rayfenix, first year status warrior. Congratulations," he said in a friendly tone.

I looked down at the pin. The aquamarine letters sank into the golden gel as if they had always been there.

Ocelot set the next name to go on his own pin. He asked me to insert the adaptor for him. I took the device from him gently. I reached up to his shirt. I sensed that he glanced at me, but I wouldn't look at him. Nervously, I inserted the tiny adaptor plug into one side of his pin. The title didn't change. I told him this.

He held the palm computer up so he could see it better. He poked a few things on it. "Take the plug out and try it again."

I did as he asked. This time I made sure the plug went the right way. He looked at his computer and then at me. I stared only at his title pin. I felt him staring at my face, probably wondering why I was so skittish suddenly.

I watched the mold of his pin rescramble to say "Sub Professor Jainocelot Quoren". I let him know that it had worked this time. I reached up to disconnect the plug, but so did he. We bumped hands. He jerked his hand away from mine.

"Excuse me," he said. He took the plug away.

He still did not want to touch me. He had held my arms in the exercise room as part of his attempt at intimidation to protect himself from being made fun of. It hadn't been a caring, tender touch as I had imagined. I felt rejected, but his formality was rightful. This would make it easier to follow through with my plan.

Still, I wanted to be friendly to him. I didn't want to make him hate me. We could easily be friends. We just couldn't be more. I lightened the atmosphere for his sake.

"You're now officially Sub Professor Jainocelot Quoren. Congratulations. I'm sure you'll make full professor in another year."

He grinned a little. "I don't know. Two or three years is more likely."

"Then I'll be calling you 'sir' again," I reminded him.

"Only in public," he maintained. He said goodnight and left me to my lonesome desires.

I remembered the night before the space station encounter when he had looked up at me as he had gone down the stairs. He had reached up towards me as if to give me a final farewell. I was convinced now that he had known he would be killed. I thanked God for the healing power to save him. I thanked Him for the opportunity to fall in love, even if I could not receive love in return. I still counted many blessings in my life. I had to be strong.

That night just before sleeping, I envisioned Ocelot's title pin. I whispered his name over and over. It sounded like the trickle of water over stones. The soothing melody served as a lullaby for me. As I sank into sleep, I imagined him lying next to me near a clear stream in some unknown woods. I was so in love with him.

Chapter 38: Sabotage

At 1600 hours, I was awakened by a strange, guttural sound. It almost sounded like a giant gulping down a glass of water. As I sat up, a second, more unnerving sound vibrated through the ship. This was a zip and a clank from the exterior wall below, just beside the secondary cargo hold. Then came a high-pitched blasting shriek. If we had been close to a planet or moon, I would have expected this had come from the two-passenger recon ship located just outside our secondary cargo hold. I crammed my feet into my boots and grabbed my top shirt from its hangar. Suddenly, the fire alarm blared on.

As I flung open the door, Wilbaht and Ocelot dashed past me and up the stairs. They had both been in the exercise room. The upper deck had been left unmanned. I hurried after them. On deck, warning signs flashed on every screen.

"Assess your station readouts. Just tell me the most important damage," Wilbaht bellowed.

I blinked and rubbed my eyes to focus. We all sat at our stations. I saw our recon ship slipping off towards the closest planet: Fitmalo. It was four days away. The recon ship could support life up to eighty-five hours, but if Klib filled the extra seat with oxygen tanks, he could easily add another two days. How did he get out?

"He's ejected our entire water supply: fresh water and black water. Plus he's turned on emergency moisture expulsion," Ocelot called to Wilbaht.

"Well, shut it off!" he yelled.

"I can't, sir! He's infiltrated a saboteur program into the main control system!" Ocelot retorted.

"The secondary cargo hold is open, sir. The outer door is jammed. The fire was in that cargo hold. It looks like he bombed it," I said.

"No. It wasn't a bomb. He didn't fire on us; our entire lower level would be destroyed. He must have left the outer door open and turned the recon ship's propulsion exhaust to blast into it. There's no hull breach. The fire alarms were reading heat, not fire. It's zero atmosphere in there. Any other life support damage?" Wilbaht spoke quickly.

"Not yet, sir, but whatever this saboteur program is, it's trained to depressurize and open the main cargo hold in one hour," Ocelot spoke.

"What the hell?" Wilbaht had barely said this when he jumped out of his seat and sprang to the main helm.

"Ocelot, get over here," he shouted.

Ocelot ran to his side.

"Try to get in here and override this."

"Yes, sir." Ocelot sounded amazed.

I wanted to ask what it was they'd found, but I didn't want to interrupt. I set all weapons to follow the recon ship, but an error warning showed up.

"Sir, he's jammed weapons control, too," I said, just as the fire alarm shut down.

"Ignore the weapons, Sil. Focus on the two cargo holds. Look for a bomb or a auxiliary program control box," he told me. "Ocelot, how is it?"

Wilbaht spoke to us as he bobbed back and forth between Ocelot's station and his own.

"It's got a trip lock on it, sir. It's definitely originating from the open cargo hold. I'll try to get into it from here, but it'll take a while," Ocelot responded.

"Why does he want the main cargo hold to open if his control system is in the secondary hold?" Wilbaht asked aloud.

I scanned the entire lower level of the ship. The main engine and life support control center was intact. The secondary cargo hold showed a high level of damage nearest the open door. The remaining space suits were partially turned to dust, seared by the recon ship's plasma-based propulsion unit. A few of the holding nets were melted through entirely along with their contents. Some of the protective cold-weather clothing near the interior door was burned through. A few titanium crates sustained damage as well. The door between the secondary cargo hold and the lower corridor, however, still remained intact and completely sealed.

Next to the door between the engine control room and the secondary cargo hold, a panel lay open. This panel contained an extruding black box: Klib's saboteur program bank. With the cargo hold jammed open from the outside and all our remaining space suits in it, we couldn't get in to remove the box.

I continued checking the lower deck. The door between the main cargo hold and the corridor showed seal damage. I zoomed in on the sealing pads around this door. They had been corroded with some kind of acid paint.

"I can't get into it, sir. Everything I try sends me to a new message about a deactivation or a door opening. It automatically steps up the countdown every time I access something. Our external communications shut down two minutes ago. The main cargo hold will open in less than twenty minutes. Life support's temperature maintenance is set to deactivate in two hours. Lower level corridor and stairwell will open in three hours. Central floor opens if five hours. All life support shuts down in six hours. And if that's not enough, we're on a collision course with Fitmalo's outermost moon," Ocelot told us with frustration.

Wilbaht stood gripping the back of his chair. "Lower level stairwell and corridor open in three hours. That means we have less than three hours to shut the secondary cargo hold and get to the main control system to restart it," Wilbaht said.

"No, sir. We have less than twenty minutes. If the main cargo hold opens, the whole lower level depressurizes. He's destroyed part of the seal on the door between the hallway and the cargo hold," I told him.

Wilbaht hissed and rubbed his beard. "Sil, focus on the secondary cargo hold door. What's jamming it?"

"It's a spool of metal cable and a metal wedge, sir. It looks like he wound the cable around both door extenders," I replied.

Wilbaht sat at his station. "How are you at passing objects through each other and levitating by remote vision?"

"I don't know, sir. That's one thing I've never tried," I confessed.

"You're not just trying this time. You're doing it. We'll combine efforts and pull those things out of there. Let's go downstairs. We'll get as close to the target as we can even though we won't be able to see it with the eyes. Ocelot, you stay here and confirm door seals. Wear communication patches."

We hurried down to the hallway cargo hold door. A haze of debris floated away from us in the blackness several meters from the open exterior. A few stars shone through it. We couldn't see the exterior door itself or its obstruction since it opened completely outward.

Wilbaht covered my hands with both of his. "Concentrate on the cable. I'll remove the metal wedge and the spool," he told me.

"Yes, sir," I replied.

I closed my eyes to better envision the door. I sensed its size, shape, and open angle. I found the cable. It was caught in the hydraulic bars of the closing mechanism. Apparently, the door had tried to close, reopen, and then close again. Its force had caused the cable to fray. Some of the fibers stuck snugly into the greased shaft of the bar. Removing them would be a true test of ability. I decided to make one heaving effort to move the winding cable as a whole instead of bit by bit to save time.

Wilbaht lifted out the wedge easily. Then the spool jiggled free. I concentrated first on passing the stray fibers through the shaft. Then I slowly moved the cable through the hydraulic system, scattering the molecules of the cable around the bar. I carefully fit them back together again once they had passed through.

"Sil, we're running out of time. Don't worry about putting the cable back together again. Just pull it out of the door closure," Wilbaht advised me.

I didn't answer, but followed his instructions. When the cable disintegrated around the door, Wilbaht helped me close and seal it. He mentally scanned the door and the room just to be safe. A moment later, he released my hands and called Ocelot.

"Is it sealed?" he asked.

"Yes, sir. We've got five minutes," Ocelot responded.

"Can you repressurize the second cargo hold?" Wilbaht asked.

"No, sir. I can't control anything. I can only read," he replied.

"Get down here. We'll have to let the existing pressure fill the room. Be ready to breathe thin air," Wilbaht said.

As soon as he finished speaking, Ocelot appeared. We all hung onto the stairwell as we pulsed open the door between the hallway and the secondary cargo hold. Air sucked past us. We gripped the stair rail to avoid being sucked in along with it. I held open my jaw to ease the pressure on my ears. We puffed heavily for oxygen. I felt as if we'd suddenly been deposited onto a mountaintop. Not only was the air thin, but the temperature was below freezing. Even after the warm air from the hallway and stairwell mixed with the nearly inexistent atmosphere of the second

422

cargo hold, the exposure to space after the blast from the recon ship had cooled it off fast.

Once the pressure leveled off, we moved into the cargo hold. Ocelot studied the box at the systems panel. He pulled the box out of its socket and punched a few buttons.

We all breathed deeply for a few moments, but to our glad surprise, the automatic respiration feeders were still working. The room filled with warm air from auxiliary compressed oxygen.

"Sir, we need to hit both switches at the same time to power down and then power back up. The second switch is there in the control room," Ocelot told him. "Sil, go back upstairs and tell me when you see all lights off."

I flew out of the room, making sure to close and seal the secondary cargo hall door on my way out just in case the deactivation didn't work.

"One minute," Ocelot said.

"On zero," Wilbaht spoke. "Three, two, one, zero."

The main lights, air circulation, gravity projectors, propulsion; everything shut down at zero. I edged my way up the stairwell in total darkness.

"Disabling battery backup power," I heard Ocelot say.

I reached the upper observation deck, which still contained a few lights warning about the main power outage. They flickered for about a minute and a half. When these clicked off, I let them know.

The two men turned the power back on. The computer at the helm still warned about life support temperature deactivation in less than two hours, but it had skipped the opening of the main cargo hold. According to its clock, the time for that task had already passed. The door remained sealed.

"The computer is still reading the saboteur program's orders, but the downstairs level should be secure," I told them.

"Can you reprogram now?" Wilbaht asked Ocelot.

"I'll do all I can, sir," Ocelot said to him.

Ocelot stayed downstairs to work with system control. Wilbaht came upstairs to help at the helm. I confirmed readouts for them. Ocelot restored control of all door seals within minutes.

At the indicated time, the temperature maintenance shut down. The temperature throughout the ship dropped quickly. Wilbaht and I soon shivered in our seats. Fortunately, Ocelot was able to get life support back on line within half an hour. The temperature gradually returned to normal.

Emergency moisture expulsion was finally disabled. Ocelot's and Wilbaht's clothing, which had been sweat-soaked at the onset of this disaster had quickly dried. The skin on my hands and face felt dry. My eyes itched as if I had been out in high winds all day. Then there was thirst. We didn't dare mention this yet.

Communications and weapons control were still down, but Ocelot assured us they would be easy to reset. The disturbing problem now was that the navigational program had been affected.

"I'm going to check food supply and storage for any extra water or moisture-rich contents we can use. Ocelot, any luck?" Wilbaht said.

"No, sir. Some of the basic operational directives are corrupted. If I can't repair them all within the next few hours, I'll have to destroy the entire nav system and reinstall it from scratch," he said.

"How long will that take?" Wilbaht asked him.

"Anywhere from ten to thirty-eight hours, sir," Ocelot told him.

"Start on it. Don't wait to find out you can't fix it and then reinstall. Start reinstalling now. That moon is less than three days away. We don't want any near misses," Wilbaht told him.

"Yes, sir," Ocelot replied.

Wilbaht asked me to scan the quarantine room for any unwanted surprises. I checked it thoroughly, but didn't find anything alarming. Klib had left the room in disarray, but there didn't appear to be any weaponry there. I reported this to Wilbaht. He sent me to investigate the quarantine room and Klib's quarters myself.

I double-checked quarantine visually: the ceiling, every corner, under the gurney bed, the bathroom, cabinets, and cold storage. Klib had left no bombs here, no messages, nothing to indicate his plan. I investigated the area around the quarantine door to see if he'd forced it open. It showed no signs of tampering. I moved upstairs.

I passed Wilbaht as he headed for the bathroom and the water tanks. I combed the lower observation deck. It was clean. I went reluctantly to Klib's door. I pressed my forehead against it, meditating on the contents of the room. It held plenty of evidence, but no live weapons or trip sensors. I was only mildly surprised to see my weapons packs stuffed in a discarded traveling box at the back in a holding net.

I flung open the door. A variety of electronic equipment and extra clothing lay scattered about. He had obviously come here before escaping to grab only the things he needed most. He must have done this between 1630 and 1700, when Wilbaht had taken off his upstairs duty to spar with Ocelot. I had been asleep the whole time. Why hadn't my sixth sense awakened me?

I scanned the room. A few pornographic pictures decorated the wall and ceiling around Klib's bed. One was a picture of a nude human female, presenting herself to mate. Klib had covered her face with a picture of me. I ripped the picture from the wall and crumpled it. I decided to grab my weapons and leave the investigating to one of the men. I knew I wasn't supposed to tamper with evidence, but I had the urge to tear all the pictures down. My hatred for Klib nearly choked me. I stomped out of the room.

I went to my own room and examined my weapons to make sure they were all still functional. The fan blaster looked like it hadn't been touched since I'd used it at the space station. The hand bow had been emptied, so there was no danger of misfiring it. It seemed to be fine. The laser cutter had been stuffed into its pocket upside-down. I tested it just to make sure. The red line sang between the two horns as normal. My sword hadn't been opened. I assumed it was all right. I opened it with a clack. I felt a prick at my hand.

I turned the sword to examine the handle. Klib had tried to extrude one of the rubies. He had failed, but he'd left splintery effects in the metal. Maybe Ocelot could repair it later. I touched the well-crafted design. Ocelot would be as disheartened as I was to see his creation defiled. At least the damage was minimal. I stored it and rushed back to help upstairs.

Ten hours later, Ocelot still hadn't been able to reset the nav program. Wilbaht grew tired, since he was working during his sleep time. At 0500 hours, he finally called Ocelot off the task for a brief meeting. I noticed their red eyes. Ocelot's stress level was extreme. We were all counting on him to get us out of this.

Wilbaht concentrated first on the positive. "We're all still alive. Our ship is intact. Klib is no longer a threat to us. We have everything we need to stay alive for the time being.

"We will need to ration water from reprocessed black water. I was also able to salvage about a cup and a half of ice from cold storage facilities. I want to make sure at least a third of our plant life survives as well to keep our oxygen level strong. I suggest that we all exercise less for the remainder of the flight and lower the internal temperature. Each of us will be assigned a specific time of day to drink water. I suspect we only have about three to five cups of reprocessable water left on the whole ship. They will not all be available at once.

"Ocelot, we have confidence in you. You mustn't hinder your own abilities by trying to work through your entire sleep schedule.

"Sil, if he overruns his sleep time by more than three hours, tell him to go to bed. If he doesn't do it, you alert me. Understood?"

Reluctantly, we conceded. Wilbaht told us he was going to bed right away. He asked us not to wake him unless it was an emergency. He told me to follow Ocelot's orders to the letter. I bowed to him. He didn't ask or address the questions that hung in all our minds: how did Klib get out in the first place and how did he accomplish this sabotage? But Wilbaht was right to focus our concentration on saving ourselves first.

I went to sit at Ocelot's station to read the most important statistics to him. He sat at the helm, still struggling with the reinstallation. I helped confirm and double-check readouts from all aspects of ship navigation control, from ballast to propulsion. Ocelot successfully restarted various pieces of the massive program only to cancel and reinstall what he had started six times. Each time, he had miscalibrated something or one aspect of the program wasn't properly synchronized with another part. Each mistake fueled his frustration and anxiety.

"Ocelot, it's 0900. You've got to get some sleep," I told him.

"Wait. I'm in the middle of reprogramming solar feed to the helm control. Give me ten minutes," he said.

Fifteen minutes later, he still hadn't finished. I asked him if he was nearly through. He assured me he was. I waited patiently, although I knew he was buying time.

At 0935, I asked him what he was working on now.

"I'm just starting on raw fuel and stored energy balancing on propulsion. This is what keeps screwing up," he said.

"Ocelot, you said you were just going to finish solar feed. Now you're working on something else. Wilbaht was right. You've got to get your sleep. Otherwise you're more likely to make an error. Just leave it for now," I coaxed.

"I can't sleep now. This has to work. I won't sleep until it's done. Anyway, I'm too thirsty. I won't be able to sleep for more than an hour. Wilbaht told you to follow my instructions to the letter. I'm ordering you to let me finish this," he said. His aggravation was subdued by his exhaustion.

Instead of arguing with him, I slipped out of the room for a few minutes. I returned with my hands full. I stepped down to the main helm where Ocelot still worked fervently. His reddened eyes squinted at the screens. His brow furrowed.

I handed him a glass of water and a finger-sized flask of eye drops. "Take it," I told him.

Ocelot blinked at me with uncertainty. I moved the glass closer to him. He took it and drank gratefully. He handed me the empty glass. Then he used the eye medication. He rubbed his face. He handed this back to me as well. He thanked me and immediately returned to his task. He seemed to relax a little.

"Now go to bed," I told him.

He frowned at me. He looked back at the screen.

"I have to finish this. The energy balancing is going through the right way this time. I just have eight or nine steps to install," he said.

"That's a nine hour job minimum, Ocelot. Forget it. Listen, if it takes two hours or twelve hours, you still have time. Go to sleep. It can't

426

get any more screwed up than it is already, right? Leaving it for a few hours is not going to make things any worse. Let yourself rest for a while. Take care of yourself." I hoped this speech would sway his opinion.

He let his arms drop to his sides. He blinked heavily.

I went back to my station. I watched him. He tapped at the computer a moment. Then he meandered out of the helm area up to the stairwell. He glanced at the empty glass and medication beside me. Then he reluctantly traipsed downstairs.

In the time between Ocelot's departure and Wilbaht's arrival at 1100, I, too, became tired, but I wanted to try and figure out a few things about Klib. I researched him thoroughly. Although his record appeared clean, something about it troubled me. Wilbaht asked me to report all findings to his station. Then he ordered me to sleep, much as I had ushered Ocelot out earlier.

At 1900 hours, Wilbaht woke me for a meeting and a meal. Ocelot had woken himself at only 1600 hours and had successfully completed the propulsion part of the program. He had also finished two other installation tasks necessary for the nav system. He had seven more to go. The good thing was that even if the next parts were installed badly, they were independent of the major bulk of the operation, so there was no danger in having to scrap the whole system again.

During our meal, we each had less than half a glass of water and a packet of fresh-water-packed fish, plus the last of the fruits from our tropical plant life.

Wilbaht informed us of what he had found out about Klib's escape based on physical evidence from his bunk, his computers, and de facto evidence from the escape itself.

"He did not force the door to the quarantine room. He did not unlock the door. Someone left it open unwittingly. I fed him at 0500. I know for a fact that I locked the door behind me," Wilbaht stated.

Ocelot acted sheepish. "I saw him at 1300, sir. I went down to return the body scanner to the quarantine room. I thought I locked the door behind me."

"Maybe he jammed it with something when you left," I suggested.

Wilbaht asked why Ocelot had the scanner out of quarantine in the first place. He explained about my chemical imbalance. Wilbaht suggested perhaps I had felt strange because I'd felt a premonition about the sabotage.

"I don't think so, sir. I'm sure I didn't foresee this," I told him. "Maybe I was too distracted by my other vision to receive any hint about this," I admitted.

"*I* should have seen this coming," Wilbaht said. "I had no distractions."

I looked to him kindly. "None of us is infallible, sir."

He gave me a half-smile. "It's easier to give that advice than to receive it, isn't it?" I nodded.

Wilbaht took a deep breath. "Klib was a spy among us, up until the space station incident. One of his contacts met with him while we were touring the facility. Apparently, this contact told him he wasn't needed anymore, but didn't tell him why. I expect the contact assumed the two of you were dead. He must have given him the saboteur program to get rid of me. I would have gone the way of the martyr if it hadn't been for you two."

"Whoever it was must be your archenemy, sir. That saboteur program was designed to scare the hell out of someone before killing him," Ocelot said.

"Indeed. Although I'm fairly sure his contact was not the one who wrote the program. I believe he was only a courier," Wilbaht told us.

"Why couldn't we see him as our enemy to begin with?" I asked.

"I believe he was being protected, enchanted, if you will, by another warrior, or perhaps by multiple warriors. I suspect General Swall Jade or one of his close associates masterminded this, but I have no proof against them. I do have evidence to identify the man Klib met with on the space station. I researched the Organization ships that were docked there with us. The Palat Sun Seeker was a recent purchase. Its record showed it changed hands on Sor3. Klib had sent messages directly to that ship before we arrived at the space station. He left behind a set of scrambled ID codes to communicate with his contact. From the Sun Seeker's crew listing, I immediately deduced who it was. I cross-referenced Klib's scrambled codes through the communications access listings for Organization personnel stationed at the C.A.T.T. Center where the ship was purchased. The codes and the Sun Seeker belong to the same person. Proof positive. I'm sorry, Ocelot. His contact was your uncle Stennet," Wilbaht divulged.

"I was afraid you'd say that," Ocelot said, bowing his head. He rubbed his nails together. "Damn him."

"Does anyone in your family know you're still alive?" I asked him.

"Not yet. And to think I was about to message Jiao just yesterday. It's a good thing I didn't. His father probably reads his mail."

"Why did he need Klib to spy on us? Why didn't he just ask you what we were doing?" I asked.

"He knew I wouldn't send any unauthorized messages to him about our mission. He knew I'd be suspicious of him."

"Klib was cyphening information out of the official ship's log and from the personal messaging center. Apparently he relayed the information to more than one of his contacts," Wilbaht told us.

"Personal information from messaging? How much?" Ocelot asked.

"It appears that he secretly recorded everything we sent on our journey, from Sor4 to the space station. All our personal messages were read by someone else, both messages sent and received," Wilbaht said.

I instantly thought of Alaban and the messages we had sent each other, especially those we sent when he was stranded on Fitmalo. If the wrong people accessed those messages, they would believe he was prone to disloyalty to his new Fitmalo liege. I worried, but didn't say anything. Surprisingly, it was Ocelot who voiced angst about the shared messages.

"They could try and use personal information against us as blackmail," he said. Panic sprung to his bloodshot eyes. "If Klib is caught, he'll rat us out. He might even do it voluntarily. Then our cover will be completely blown. All that identity replacement will have been for nothing."

"As far as we know, Klib still thinks his trap will work. He won't be in a hurry to confess to murder. He's on his way to Fitmalo. He probably won't cross paths with us again. He'll only show up to the Center to collect his pay and to sign his resignation forms," Wilbaht suggested.

"He'll probably tell them he escaped just before the ship crashed," I added.

Ocelot still rubbed his chin nervously.

"Don't worry, son. If Stennet believed you died, then Klib had no reason to continue sending material. I only found evidence of the informational espionage up to the day we encountered the space station. No one else will know about your second identities. As far as they know, Ocelot Quoren and Sil Gretath are dead," Wilbaht attempted to reassure him.

"By this time tomorrow we will have died twice," I mused.

"I'd better make sure we don't. Sir, may I continue with the installations now?" he asked.

"Yes, by all means," Wilbaht said.

Ocelot hurried up the stairs again without clearing his plate.

At 0200 hours, Ocelot completed the last of the navigational setup.

"Now all I have to do is learn to fly this thing," he said.

"Doesn't Wilbaht have a pilot's license?" I asked.

"I don't know." Ocelot buzzed him. "Sir, I'm sorry to wake you, but can you fly this ship?"

"Why, can't you?" I heard him reply.

"Uh, not really, sir. I could go by the manuals and try it, but that will take a while and..."

"Ocelot," Wilbaht interrupted.

"We'll be approaching the moon in less than three hours."

"Son, I can fly it. Wake me at 0430."

"Oh, thank you, sir. I'm sorry I woke you." Ocelot released the buzz board.

He reclined dramatically in his chair. "Oh, thank you, God! We're going to live through this!"

"We never doubted you," I said truthfully.

At 0435, Wilbaht arrived on the scene. He bade us good morning as if this were a day like any other. Fitmalo Moon Eighteen expanded onto our screens. Wilbaht sat squarely in Klib's old seat.

"Sil, ready our plasma guns," he ordered.

"Sir?" I asked.

"We're going to hit it with a blast the size of our ship, just in case Klib watches for confirmation of our crash," he informed me.

"Yes, sir," I responded.

At the correct angle and distance from the icy moon, Wilbaht ordered a double hit. I fired starboard plasma guns. As planned, the blast made a convincing impact. It looked like the crater of a crash site.

We swung around Moon Eighteen. Wilbaht planned to move us through the field of moons to the nearest Fitmalo Center. I asked him why.

"If I'm deceased now, I won't be showing up on Jawlcheen as scheduled. More importantly, we're leaking more landing fuel than before."

He explained that when Klib turned the recon ship to burn out secondary cargo, the heat and vibrations of the blast had warped the tiff valve, leaving a fissure for the fuel to escape. The leak had been negligible at first, but now it became our primary concern.

"By the time we get to Jawlcheen, there may be none left. I hope there's still an Organization Center left on Fitmalo that can supply us with a new drum."

We were not safe yet.

Chapter 39: The Planet Fitmalo

"Trilobite Center, this is Sub General Wilbaht Cordolib of the Rybalazar Sonic Wake requesting permission for emergency landing and ship repair," Wilbaht spoke to the descent tower.

Moments later, a voice responded. "This is Trilobite Center. We are not currently receiving Organization ships. We suggest a public air field eight kilometers east of your present course."

"This is Sub General Wilbaht repeating. We have an emergency. Our ship requires immediate repair. We are only authorized to receive replacement parts from an Organization facility."

"What kind of repair, sir?" the voice asked.

"Our fuel drum is punctured. We've lost nearly the whole tank. We only need a replacement drum. Then we'll be on our way," he explained.

We waited anxiously for a reply. We neared the Center airfield. No response came. Wilbaht hovered close to the air towers.

This Center was set in a shallow valley surrounded by low-lying, blue mountains. The outdoor temperature was hot, nearing thirty-eight degrees. This was a desert area of the southern tropics. The lack of iron on this planet caused a bluish color throughout the entire landscape and its people. Only a few plants that dotted the mountain glowed green and gold. The planet Jawlcheen was the only planet of this helion blessed with high iron. Its land was reddish, as were the skins of its people.

The white buildings of the Trilobite Center glinted in the sunlight. Only two other ships rested on the airfield. One was a Fitmalo dignitary's ship. The other appeared to be an abandoned Organization ship from Sor2. Fitmalo military guards paced lazily around the broad square courtyard in front of the main building. This building looked like a wide, tapering oval, flanked by two vertical prisms on either side. The building itself did abstractly resemble a trilobite. The courtyard before it was bare, devoid of any decoration or plant life. It, too, was flanked at either end by a dual pair of rectangular prisms. These were the guards' posts. In front of these stretched a wide set of stairs leading down to the airfield. The air towers were three tall white rectangles, much like the prisms around the courtyard.

Only a few homes and businesses could be seen from this Center. It was practically isolated. This is why I was distracted by activity at the crest of the mountain closest to the air towers. A large group of Fitmalos congregated there in what appeared to be a couple of makeshift tents next to a housing construction site. I assumed these were construction workers, but they were too numerous. I felt suspicious of them. I didn't feel they posed any danger to us, but found their presence disturbing.

Then I noticed some of the Fitmalos of this group making a trail down the mountain to the air towers. I was sure the construction on the hill above had nothing to do with the Organization Center. These people were up to something. I was about to mention them when the tower control man finally replied to us.

"Sonic Wake, you may set down in the second quad. Stay in your ship. Someone will be out to help with your repairs in a few minutes," he said.

We didn't cheer or even release a sigh of relief. We knew landing on Fitmalo soil was dangerous to us. If the tower personnel contacted their superiors about our ship, Wilbaht might be taken for questioning. Or worse, they might seize the ship and we'd be discovered.

Wilbaht set us down in the second quad. We went through full shut down procedures and waited. No one approached our ship. Ocelot asked Wilbaht if he would ask for water.

"I'd rather not call attention to that. If they allow me, I'll go to the tower and drink some and fill a canteen or two. Jawlcheen is only four days away. If I can get just two cups of water, we'll be comfortable until we can land there," Wilbaht explained.

We waited pensively for some sign of repair workers. We remained parked for more than forty minutes. No one contacted us or arrived at the ship. Wilbaht finally called the tower again.

"Tower, this is the Sonic Wake. When can we expect a replacement drum?" Wilbaht asked.

We waited a few more minutes.

"This is the tower. Say again?" This voice was different from the first. This voice sounded young and inexperienced.

Wilbaht knitted his brow.

"This is the Rybalazar Sonic Wake. Your tower personnel directed us to land forty minutes ago for emergency repair. We haven't seen any maintenance personnel yet. When can we expect them?"

"Is this an Organization ship?" The voice sounded surprised.

"Yes. Your coworker allowed us to land for repairs only. We're waiting for a fuel drum," Wilbaht told him.

"Who is this?" the voice asked excitedly.

Wilbaht gave him his name and title.

"Oh, yes! We've got an Organization fighter ship on the field!" The man seemed to speak to others around him. "This is Blue Rebel. We're taking over the Center. Will you help us?"

"What?" we all responded at once.

"Blue Rebel, identify your rebel group and your purpose," Wilbaht barked.

432

"Tune in to frequency 10.01.05 through 10.02.07. We're broadcasting in thirty seconds," the man said.

Then there was silence.

We all brought up the Center local news site on our station screens. A young Fitmalo, flanked by rebel comrades appeared holding an old Fitmalo flag.

He asked a technician if they were ready. They were. He animatedly professed his group's purpose and rallied the local Fitmalo people to rebel against a military takeover.

"The Fitmalo military is not your friend. They are driving our guardian warriors out. The Organization was our only protection from the military leaders. They don't care about defending your freedom. They don't care about protecting you. They only want to take your freedom away from you. They've raised our taxes over and over to pay for the military improvements, they say. I say bullshit! They raised taxes to line their pockets. Bring our warriors back to us. Get these soldiers off our streets and out of the Organization Centers!"

His party cheered around him.

He continued. "We have taken the air towers at the Trilobite Center. We've got heavy artillery and chemical weapons and we're not afraid to use them. Any soldier who stands in our way dies today!"

At the end of his speech, he claimed the Free Economy Blue Rebels had begun the takeover of the main Center building already. Then he said something that caused Wilbaht to jump up and bump his gray head on the ceiling.

"And if any other military comes looking for a fight, they'll have to answer to our allies from the Organization. We have an Organization fighter ship on our field ready to back us up as we speak. We are armed and ready!" the rebel claimed. Then the transmission ended.

"What! Is he insane?" Wilbaht thundered.

He grabbed the communicator. "Are you insane? We never agreed to fight with you. We're sitting ducks out here. Didn't you hear me tell you we're waiting for repairs? We can't take off. We have no fuel. What are you thinking?"

Blue Rebel apologized, but reinforced his proclamation. "If you want those repairs you're going to have to help us. We're taking the Center back for warriors like you. So be a warrior and help us out."

"Do not expect me to fire on Organization property. I will not be responsible for any damage you do to that Center. If we have to retaliate against Fitmalo military ships, those lives are your responsibility. So are our lives, for that matter. You will have to answer for any deaths you cause today," Wilbaht said firmly.

"I am prepared and willing to do that, sir. Blue Rebel out," he stated.

Wilbaht pounded the top of the communications panel.

"Young fool! Damn it!" He cringed in anger.

"Sil, pass half of the plasma blast controls to Ocelot's station. Both of you be ready to fire on any incoming military ships. I'm powering back up for mock takeoff. Sil, put up full shields. Give us all peripheral defense screens," he shouted. His powerful voice echoed through the deck.

I scrambled to comply with his orders.

"If we get out of this alive, I want to wring that boy's neck myself," Wilbaht hissed.

We watched nervously as the rebels successfully killed the courtyard guards, blasted open the main doors to the Trilobite Center and penetrated the main building. About one hundred rebels entered the building while several others covered the perimeter.

"Incoming military ship north, northeast, sir," Ocelot called out.

Wilbaht hailed it. "This is the Rybalazar Sonic Wake. We are stranded at the Trilobite Center. We are not allied with this rebel group. I repeat. We are *not* allied with this rebel group. We do not wish to exchange fire."

"Sonic Wake, we see you. If you're not with this rebellion, power down," the military commander said.

"We can't do that, sir. They'll destroy us. I know it," Ocelot told him frantically.

"We'll be glad to comply if you'll show us you mean us no harm. When your ship lands out of firing range to us, we will power down," Wilbaht volunteered.

"You are in no position to negotiate. We are ordering you to power down or prepare to be fired upon," the commander retorted.

"We cannot power down until you assure us we will not be attacked," he responded. "Ready and aim," he hissed at us.

We flipped up the protective cover on weapons control at our panels.

"Prepare to engage," Wilbaht spoke to us.

As the military ship hovered in front of the steps to the Center courtyard, it brought up shields and turned its weapons to fire on us.

Wilbaht gripped one arm of his chair. "All plasma weapons fire on their weapons casings and main door. Fire at will."

Ocelot and I fired repeatedly. The military ship returned fire, but we got a lucky shot. One of their weapons ports fired just as one of our plasma blasts met it. This caused an explosion at the weapons port itself. Their ship shuddered, but didn't lose altitude.

"Ocelot, aim for their hover pad," Wilbaht ordered. "Sil, keep firing for effect."

We did as ordered. Suddenly our ship rocked.

"We've lost the outermost shield on the crown of the ship, sir. No serious damage," I reported.

"Focus all fire on their main door and the hover pad," Wilbaht ordered.

The military ship skirted most of our shots. It moved out into the landing field, just above the abandoned Organization ship. Its hover pad began to spark and sizzle. Soon a loud crack echoed from the enemy ship. Then it fell heavily, as the entire hover pad turned off at once. It collided onto the raised end of the Sor2 ship, decimating it and causing an impact that shook the ground like a mild earthquake.

As dust swirled around the crippled ships, gangs of Fitmalo rebels bounded out from hiding. They ran after the mass of metal in celebration.

"The whole group is insane," Ocelot said.

"Two more military ships coming in from the north!" I yelled.

Wilbaht attempted to contact the rebel leader. "Blue Rebel, this is the Sonic Wake. Call back your volunteers. We cannot protect them if they scatter out on foot!"

"Does the order to fire at will still stand, sir?" Ocelot asked him.

"Yes. Fire first. Go!" he yelled.

We fired every plasma weapon we had at the oncoming ships before they could return fire. One of them was hit and spun off to one side right away. It landed diagonally, skidding into the dirt along half of the landing field. It finally stopped at its farthest corner. The ship was grounded, but continued firing as soon as it stopped. We received heavy fire from the ship that still flew in circles around us. It concentrated most of its hits to our ship's crown, since they saw we only had two shields left on it.

The grounded ship fired constantly, but the weapons available on its firing side were not as much of a threat to us as they were to the rebel fighters on the ground. The rebels who weren't shot cowered in small groups around the wreckage.

"Sir, we've lost the second shield on the crown and the outer shield on the lower right side. Requesting atomic weapon usage, sir!" I shouted in panic.

"Pass me the control to atomic weapons, Sil. You concentrate on plasma shots," he told me.

"Yes, sir," I panted. I carried out the order, typing in the control share codes with my left hand while I continued firing with my right.

"When they move above their downed ship that's firing, I want you both to cease fire," Wilbaht ordered.

Just as we lost the entire outer shield, the hovering ship turned in the field just above its companion.

"God forgive me," Wilbaht breathed as he fired one low-level atomic blast.

It impacted the top of the grounded ship, but obliterated both ships. Even though the explosion's center was only ten meters in diameter, its major repercussion billowed out to one hundred meters. The explosion created a horrible puff of red fire and black ash. The air and ground vibrated violently. Thick smoke climbed through the sky above the wreckage. Wind blew the debris away from us to the southeast of the airfield.

The Fitmalo people on the field around us escaped toward the Center's main building and the air towers.

"Any other ships on screens?" Wilbaht asked.

"No, sir," I said solemnly.

Wilbaht increased communications range. "This is Organization ship Rybalazar Sonic Wake. We are calling all military centers in the Trilobite Center area. We surrender. We do not wish to engage military ships. We surrender. We are now shutting down and abandoning ship." He let go of the communication board. "Sil, track wide range ship activity. Ocelot, find the nearest military outposts. We're not shutting down."

As we began the tasks he ordered, he hailed the rebel group once more. "Stay away from the destroyed ships at the end of the airfield. There will be radiation damage. If you have any sense at all, you'll abandon the Center now. Other military ships will be on the way, probably to destroy the whole Center."

There was no answer on behalf of the Free Economy Rebels.

"There are five military outposts in our local range, sir. The closest two are twenty-four and thirty-three kilometers away," Ocelot said.

"I don't read any more military ships in the air, sir," I said.

"Sonic Wake, you did great. You're heroes. Don't worry. There's no more military around here. They're all at the big generals' procession on the other side of the planet. Why do you think we chose today to take over? We did it! We took the Center back. Now what part was it you needed for your ship?" Blue Rebel announced.

"Should we believe him, sir?" I asked.

He shook his head. "We need a fuel drum and fast. Someone will try to attack us again. It's just a matter of time."

"Hey, we'll help you get that left over drum out of the good side of the Sor2 ship. It's got to have plenty left. It's been sitting here for months," Blue Rebel suggested. "If we all work together, we should be able to replace it pretty quickly. How many men do you have on board?"

Wilbaht looked at us. "Any ships approaching?"

"No, sir," we responded.

Wilbaht replied to the rebel leader. "I only have two men on board: myself and one other. We'll need all the help we can get."

He pointed and snapped his fingers at Ocelot. "Take off your tunic. They can't see your title pin."

Ocelot quickly pulled off his top shirt and dumped it inside out onto his chair as he stood.

"Sil, stay here and watch out for incoming ships. Close the main door and put up shields if you have to. If we're on the ground while you have to fire, trust us to find safety. Defend yourself at full power. We'll be back with that fuel drum as soon as we can," Wilbaht called to me as he and Ocelot descended the stairs,

"Yes, sir," I didn't want to say. I was terrified. They were leaving me here alone in the ship. They were going out to risk their lives. I stared into the various screens at my station, searching for even the slightest danger as I muttered to myself to stay calm.

A news reporter's ship ventured close to the crash site at the far end of the field. Then came two others. They did not attempt to communicate with us. Local authorities wouldn't come into the Center area until radiation levels could be measured and confirmed. I watched the ground activity anxiously.

Ocelot and Wilbaht and a group of healthy Fitmalos ran to the broken Organization ship. They managed to open the double panel covering the landing fuel drum. They disconnected the fuel line with some difficulty. One Fitmalo used a motorized lift to move the drum. Apparently it was nearly full, because the whole group heaved and struggled with it.

I checked the monitors for any ships departing Fitmalo military outposts. So far none appeared. The men had been gone eight minutes. The Fitmalos loaded the drum onto the lift. One Fitmalo drove it over to the base of our ship. I heard the reverberating clanks of the panels opening on our own ship. The empty drum squeaked out of its space near the landing pad. I felt the thumps of the new drum being inserted. The screens remained clear. The ground activity involved only my allies. I heard and felt the two protective panels slap shut on the outside of the ship.

Suddenly, I felt a warning from my sixth sense. I scanned the immediate vicinity for danger. The first ship we had hit, the one on top of the Organization ship, still showed activity. It was almost completely collapsed on one side, but its upper level still remained, barely cracked. One weapons casing glided in its socket to aim at the group of Fitmalos and my partners at the side of the ship.

I shouted a warning at them using the communication patches. "Take cover! They're ready to fire on you!"

My partners alerted the Fitmalos around them. The group fanned out, some running the wrong direction. They didn't know where the danger was coming from. I hadn't told them.

"It's the crashed ship!" I yelled too late.

The ship fired stout laser blades on a group of Fitmalos a few meters away from the front of our ship. Seeing their comrades again in peril, another bunch of Fitmalos boarded our ship to find shelter. Ocelot and Wilbaht made for the air towers while other Fitmalos cowered behind our ship.

"Shields up, Sil! Shoot back!" Wilbaht called to me.

I had to shut the main cargo hold door to boost on the remaining shields. I fumbled for the door control, aimed plasma weapons at the dilapidated ship, and readied shields. I heard a clamor coming from downstairs from the few Fitmalos who had jumped aboard at the last minute. When the door finally closed, I hit the shields button and fired seven blasts. Since the damaged ship had no shields, its weapons port was easily destroyed. As soon as my last blast took effect, the crippled ship caught fire.

The noise from the Fitmalo rebels in the ship grew louder. Surely they weren't coming up the stairs. One of them shouted in pain.

"It's over here," one of them called to the others.

I scanned our lower level of the ship. They were looking for the quarantine room. Two of the Fitmalos were injured, one seriously. His left leg was twisted and bloody. The other had severe burns and scrapes on one arm and hip. The three healthy Fitmalos helped them into quarantine. They went straight for the water to wash the burn victim's arm.

"Don't use up our water," I thought.

But they did just that. The tap that ran from the reclaimed black water tank emptied out fast. They complained about it as the burn victim moaned and the man with the mangled leg wailed in utter pain. One of the healthy Fitmalos argued with another about what to do with their suffering friend.

"We've got to get him a splint or wrap it in something," he said.

"How do you know? What if we're not supposed to do that? He could lose his leg," a female said.

"He could die! We've got to get him to a hospital or at least a doctor," the male said.

"Isn't there supposed to be medical personnel on these ships?" the female asked.

438

"Somebody's got to be here. Someone had to close that door and fire. I'm going to look upstairs for help. You stay with him," the male spoke.

"Oh, no. Now what am I supposed to do?" I asked myself.

I contacted Wilbaht. "Sir, some of the rebels boarded our ship. One of them is coming up here. What should I do?"

"Blind spot. They shouldn't see you," he ordered.

"Yes, sir," I answered too late. Just as I cloaked, the Fitmalo peered up over the opening of the stairwell. He froze as he watched me disappear. His eyes widened.

"It's okay. I'm not military. I'm with the rebel group," he said. "I already saw you."

I released the blind spot. The Fitmalo climbed the rest of the stairs. When he faced me, we both recoiled from déjà vu.

"I know you," he said. "You were on Santer. Your name is Sil. You let me live."

I remembered immediately. He had been one of the snipers after Ocelot. I had taken him prisoner.

"How did you get here? Are you really a rebel or are you a military spy?" I asked. I hoped to at least read his reaction to guess the truth.

"I am a rebel. I swear. The Organization agreed to let me go if I worked as a contact between them and the rebel groups. We've got an injured friend in your medical room. He needs a doctor. Can any of your crew on board help him?" he asked. He appeared sincere.

"No, sir. I'm the only one on board. It would be best if you got him to a hospital. Listen. It's important that you keep quiet about me. I'm not supposed to be here. Please. I spared your life once. Please don't let anyone know I'm here. Tell your friends the ship is empty. Tell them the commander is remote controlling the ship. Tell them whatever you want. Just don't tell anyone you saw me and don't ever mention my name. My life depends on it."

I felt ridiculous begging him like this, but we were in the middle of a battle. I didn't have time to be subtle. He was surprised by my plea, but he consented.

"All right. I never saw you. I won't tell anyone. You saved a lot of rebel lives today, including mine. That's twice I owe you my life. God bless you," he said. He ran back down the stairs.

Finally I felt some relief. I truly felt I received the blessing he gave me. Meeting precisely this man again at this moment was more than a coincidence. I watched and listened to his party in the quarantine room. I learned his name was Hallon. I would definitely keep this man in my prayers.

439

I shut down shields and reopened the main cargo hold door. The Fitmalos left the ship.

"All clear. Come aboard," I called to my partners.

Wilbaht and Ocelot ran towards the ship. Emergency medical teams arrived and landed near the air towers to help evacuate the injured. Peacekeeping authorities ventured closer to the scene. Several meters in front of our ship, a couple of Fitmalos struggled, half-buried under some rocks and debris. Ocelot stopped to help a few rebels pull them out so they could be removed to a medical facility. He waved Wilbaht away towards our ship.

Suddenly, two more military ships showed up on the screen, coming in from the southwest.

I shouted to Ocelot to come on, but at that moment, the burning Fitmalo military ship nearest us exploded from its top. The roar of the explosion and blazing fire drowned out my calls to him. Wilbaht neared the main door. The incoming ships were almost at firing range. If I took the time to close the door, I could put up shields and fire, but Wilbaht would have just entered the ship and Ocelot would be stranded right in front of the military ship's main target. I took a foolish risk.

I rushed to my bunk for my fan blaster. I flew down the stairs and out of the ship just as Wilbaht entered.

"Incoming warships!" I shouted as I passed him.

He dashed past me, reached the ship controls and started firing without shields.

I sprinted through the intense heat over unlevel ground to where Ocelot and the others had finally helped the trapped Fitmalos to an emergency vehicle. A haze of thick smoke mixed with dust and ash shrouded me as I ran. The roar of flames was so great that I barely heard our ship firing. I grabbed Ocelot by his slick, sweat-covered wrist and pulled him toward the ship.

"We're under attack! Let's go!" I shouted to him.

He ran with me towards the ship, but a military shot pounded a crater between the closing door and us. We fell into the rocky dust. I watched the ship above us through the cloud of cinders as it moved away from the air towers. It continued firing on Wilbaht. He closed the door completely and raised the remaining shields just in time.

Ocelot and I were in the worst place possible. We darted to the nose of what was once the abandoned Organization ship, closer to the searing heat from the fire. I stood to one side of the nose. I aimed my fan blaster at an imaginary point in the air: the axis one of the enemy ships was using to move and strike against the Sonic Wake. I prepped the gun to fire. I counted down. Ocelot ogled my weapon with wide eyes.

"It's malfunctioning!" he yelled.

I tilted the fan blaster to see its right side. It sparked. It would explode in my hands if I didn't do something quick. In a wave of panic, I let go of the deadly weapon. I levitated it straight up into the axis of the ship's path. It burst into a huge circular fan, which cut right through the side of one Fitmalo ship.

The second ship that had just come into the immediate airspace was also affected. The atomic fan knocked it off its course so badly that it nearly crash-landed next to the Sonic Wake. It skittered, wobbling up over our ship. It tried to gain altitude, but instead sliced through the tops of all three air towers.

The severed sections of the towers shattered and plunged violently onto a domed waiting area at the ground level around them. Several people escaped from the dome before it collapsed. The ship itself took an acute turn and embedded itself in the side of the mountain with an enormous thud.

The ship that had been cut in two spun momentarily and then separated into two parts, each with its own trajectory. The top half of the ship whizzed round and round as it fell. It ended up in the Trilobite Center courtyard, centimeters from the door to the main building. It smacked to the concrete and screeched madly before coming to a stop, pulverizing the courtyard floor.

The bottom of the ship spun elliptically and tipped on its side as it touched the ground, rolling past the Center's main building. The disc crashed into the mountainside behind the Center, throwing a shower of rock into the sky.

The noise from the crashes nearly deafened us. The dust and debris grew too thick to breathe through. We held the neckline of our shirts over our faces and squinted to get through the disastrous atmosphere and back to our ship. Wilbaht turned off shields. He lowered the door for us. We boarded coughing, covered with dust.

Our commander didn't wait for us to climb the stairwell before initiating preflight hovering. When we got to our stations, our ship was already halfway out of the planet's atmosphere. As soon as we locked ourselves into our seats, Wilbaht punched the ship to take off.

He chose a sporadic pathway towards Jawlcheen just in case someone tried to anticipate our moves. When it appeared that no one had followed us, I asked him if he had gotten any water.

"I did," Ocelot said. He pulled a borrowed Fitmalo canteen from his pocket and tossed it to me. "Drink up."

I gulped the sweet liquid, but left half for Wilbaht.

"Let Ocelot have it. I got some at the towers," he said.

Something about the way he said it made me doubt him, but I tossed the canteen back to Ocelot. I thanked him as he drank the rest of it.

This canteen only held two cups of water. I calculated that between the water the Fitmalos had used or soaked up on their clothing and the amount of sweat we had expelled in the Fitmalo heat, the canteen probably saved our lives. With all the water lost, we now had less on board that we'd had before we landed. It would take us four days to get to Jawlcheen. I hoped we wouldn't all experience dehydration symptoms by then.

"So much for our fake crash on moon eighteen," Ocelot said bitterly. "Everyone in the U.G. is going to hear about this."

"I only hope we can find an Organization Center on Jawlcheen that will grant us clemency before a trial can be arranged. To the people of this solar system, we're war criminals now." Wilbaht spoke, imitating Ocelot's tone.

Mortal fear overtook the atmosphere among us. Our chances of survival were slimmer than ever. We all thought frantically. Even if Wilbaht was allowed to land on Jawlcheen, the ship might be confiscated by Thrader Commonwealth authorities. Could Ocelot and I evade them long enough to escape undetected? Could we save Wilbaht from an unfair trial? A horrible idea tugged at my attention. Alaban had said we would meet again on Jawlcheen. Would General Teradom ask to question Wilbaht himself? Or would he prefer to put him to death? I strategized deeply. If the situation I imagined did arise, I might be able to reappear and negotiate Wilbaht's release, claiming that he had practically brought me back to life through healing after Alaban slit my throat. Then I would have no choice but to follow Teradom in exchange for Wilbaht's freedom. Even if this plan were possible, what would happen to Ocelot? I scrapped the idea entirely. I saw no way out.

Chapter 40: Prayer of War

A few hours later, we took turns sponging ourselves off with a tiny amount of water mixed with an oil-based cleaner. We then rubbed our skin with an ointment to help keep in the moisture. Even so, my skin itched constantly. I found myself rubbing my face and arms often.

Since I couldn't wash my uniform, I just bagged it and wore my civilian clothing from Santer. The temperature was a little too cold for me now that Wilbaht kept it cool to avoid unnecessary transpiration, so I wore my sweater shawl. I looked like a brightly colored bird compared to the men, who still wore uniforms.

We no longer shared meals since we were in a high-risk area. We did take a few minutes together after we were all clean to say a prayer for the souls of the people we had killed in battle. We asked for forgiveness from our maker and guidance for the upcoming dangers we would face.

That night, I dreamed of Alaban on Jawlcheen. He led me by the arm through a maze of dark corridors. My hands were bound. He whistled an old, upbeat tune. His manner was casual, even carefree. He took me to a wide dining hall where Teradom and several other generals sat at dinner. Alaban presented me to the group cheerfully.

"Here she is, sir, ready and willing to do her duty," Alaban said.

"So she's agreed, then?" Teradom asked him.

I was about to object, but Alaban put his hand over my mouth. He smiled at the General. "Absolutely, sir."

"Good. Take those cuffs off her," Teradom said with his mouth full of food.

Two guards stepped up and removed the binders. I rubbed my chaffed wrists. Alaban put his arm around me.

"We'll see you in the morning, sir," he said.

Teradom nodded and waved his fork at us.

I searched Alaban's face for an explanation to what was going on. He put a finger to his lips to keep me quiet. He led me back through the dark corridors to a richly furnished bedroom. He shut the door behind us. We were alone.

"Where are my partners?" I asked him frantically.

"They're dead. Teradom beheaded them himself. He wanted me to do it, but I told him I felt too much respect for Wilbaht. I'm sorry he had to die like that. What was the other guy's name?" he spoke frankly.

"Ocelot," I breathed.

"Yeah. Wasn't he supposed to be dead before? Anyway, he's dead now. I'm glad Teradom let me keep you. Don't cry for them. They're just warriors. They're easily replaceable." He waltzed over to the bed and sat on it, then reclined lazily.

I woke up whispering. "No, not Ocelot. No."

I stood and left my bunk, even though I had only slept three hours. I wrapped my shawl around me tightly. I went to the dining area for a little water. It only amounted to two small swallows. I went upstairs groggily, still affected by my dream.

Wilbaht sat at his post rubbing the back of his neck. He was experiencing the same skin problems that I was. I walked up to him and grasped his hand as if I were a small child seeking reassurance from her father.

He looked at me with concern, but then hardened his visage.

"Sil, I know you've been through a lot recently. So have we all, but you must clear your mind and focus."

I removed my hand from his. I stood blinking. "Yes, sir."

He spoke again. "We are powerful seers. We must repress all fear to see clearly. You know this. We have the power to evade them, come what may. Know it. Make yourself fearless. Prove your strength. Show me that I did not choose wrongly when I brought you onto this ship. Arm yourself," he spoke. He curled his massive hand into a fist and placed his knuckles gently over my heart. "Arm yourself. You are not a weak and vulnerable young woman. You are a determined and powerful warrior. Say it."

I stood straight. Confidence flowed through me once more. "Yes, sir. I am a determined...and powerful...warrior."

We clasped hands in a warrior's handshake.

"Listen to me, Sil. When we encounter resistance, focus on the thoughts of those in command." He gave me a warning look. "I know we will need to avoid greater opposition this time. Be ready."

"Yes, sir." I stood at attention.

Wilbaht dismissed me from the deck. He asked me not to return until my normal time. I obeyed. I jogged down to my bunk. I threw off the shawl.

I remembered how to build up my strength of spirit, perhaps not in the way Wilbaht had expected. I searched for my Tambuo outfit. I stripped quickly and then slipped it on. The glittery newness of the dress gave me a feeling of power, perhaps even beauty. I was a Tambuo dancer, a dancer of prayers, a talisman of spiritual power.

I pounded the cold floor in bare feet to the exercise room. I sensed Ocelot in his room. I was glad not to run into him. He would gawk if he saw me like this, my feminine form brazenly displayed before him. Once the door closed behind me, I saw myself in the burnished wall, barely

444

covered with the tiny wavering rectangles of blue mica sewn onto the golden gauze dress. I remembered my mother and sisters in similar costume. I remembered where I came from, who I was.

I moved through the steps slowly at first. I recalled each movement with effort. It had been at least two years since I had last seen this dance performed. I still remembered most of it. It told a story of battle. I started again. This time I spoke the warrior chants and the ancient prayer for protection. This was typically a men's dance, but during the pauses of the men's steps, I included the hip movements of the women's chorus.

I drew a huge circle in the air in front of me with the left hand. Then I stomped forward, stabbing through the center of it with an invisible sword.

"Come death! I sneer at thee!" I announced.

I stomped forward with the other foot. I punctured the air with a spear hand, and then whirled in a diagonal leap. I stepped forward and knelt. I pointed both hands together high above my head in an exaggerated warrior's stance.

"Warrior ancestors, come to my aid. Be as a shield at my back."

I repeated the movement to the opposite side.

"God on high, I beg your favor. Be as a beacon to my mind. Lead me through this battle as you will."

I stood straight again, brandishing two imaginary weapons.

"May these weapons kill those who strike to kill us. May we strike fear in the hearts of those who would harm our kin. May we live another day for the good of all our people. Guide these acts of war."

I felt around me the spirits of my people as if they celebrated this dance with me. I struck imaginary enemies to my left and right. I raised my arms to heaven. I struck enemies before and behind me. I scooped my arms from the ground to the air, offering a slain comrade to the heavens. I stomped and struck with the spear hand five times in a circle. Spirit warriors flickered in dimensions around me. They moved with me through the other whirling hops, intimidating warrior stances, and stomps of victory.

Finally I finished with the women's prayer for protection. I knelt, holding an imaginary bouquet of flowers at a warrior's feet. I imagined, perhaps selfishly, that the warrior was Ocelot. Ancestral women of my tribe gathered near me, carrying flowers, ripe and pungent as the late summer blossoms of Liricos. The Tambuo drums knocked in time as I moved my bouquet to my warrior's heart. I stood and shook my hips in a tight figure eight rotation. The spirit women's skirts jingled in unison with mine as I touched either shoulder of the warrior with the bouquet. Then I bowed to him. The drums halted as I gave my warrior the bouquet.

I did the final step to shake away all evil. I shook at the shoulders, chest, and hips, jingling along with my women ancestors. I made a low bow. Then I leaned into a kneeling position. My ancient family slowly bowed and exited to a distant dimension. Normally, the warrior would help the woman stand, but I stood alone.

I faced myself at the mirrored wall, blessed and whole. I closed my eyes and quickly recited the prayer of war. "We are marching into battle. Guide our steps to your door. Guide our hands to strike rightfully. Accept our hearts we surrender to you. Give us strength to defend our lives. Grant peace to the dying. Grant forgiveness to the victors. May our honor please you. Our lives are in your hands." I bowed, and then added a personal request. "Please protect Wilbaht. Protect Ocelot." I breathed deeply. "Protect Alaban. I love them all."

Twenty-four hours later, we all gripped the arms of our chairs with anticipation. Wilbaht headed for the Loam Center near the planet's equator. By now everyone knew Wilbaht was an interplanetary fugitive, or at least a suspect on the run. By Fitmalo law, he was already guilty of mass murder. By Jawlcheen law, he was a suspect to be apprehended and tried immediately at a court of law. By the new Thrader Common Law, he would be jailed without counsel until sentenced. This at least meant that officially, no one had free license to kill him on sight.

He called down to the air tower at the Center. "Loam Center, this is the Rybalazar Sonic Wake. We are requesting permission to land at your Center and seek communication with police authorities."

"Rybalazar Sonic Wake, continue on your present course. You will be allowed to land with us," was all the air tower man said.

"That was too easy," Ocelot mentioned.

"Sil, you know what to concentrate on. Ocelot, stay on monitors. Be ready to act. Sil, give us all weapons control." Wilbaht spoke evenly.

We complied with his order.

The ship slowly immersed us into the golden clouds. We passed an isthmus, and then sailed over an ocean. Several commercial ships passed us. Then we were alone over the water. Less than a year ago, this kaleidoscope of sea and sky would have been a welcome sight. Now it was only a beguiling calm.

Suddenly, a pair of rocket torpedoes appeared on our screens. They came from a submarine behind us. The rockets closed in on us fast.

"Counterstrike!" Wilbaht called to us.

We hit the warheads with plasma blasts. They exploded almost directly beneath us. The ship shuddered. Wilbaht pulled us up.

Two more torpedoes zoomed towards us. We hit these with more distance between us. There was no time to express opinions about this. Five Fitmalo military ships took off from the isthmus to meet us in the air. We were in for a dogfight. I concentrated on the ships and their leaders. I sensed their purpose.

"They want to shoot us down over the ocean, sir. They have two more squadrons ready to attack us," I said.

"We're leaving the atmosphere," Wilbaht said.

He took us straight up, dangerously close to a few passenger ships that were just entering or leaving the clouds. The military ships did not fire while civilians traveled nearby. They waited until we broke through to the darkness between Jawlcheen and its first moon.

"We've got all three squadrons after us now, sir," Ocelot spoke.

"If you go around the moon, they'll be ready for us on all sides. They've planned on splitting up and reconvening for a swarm attack," I said.

"Then we'll lead them to their plan of attack and reverse directions. Return all fire," Wilbaht spoke.

We traveled at illegal velocity toward the closest moon, barely missing three barge ships. The first squadron closed in on us too slowly for any of their medium-range weapons to reach us. They held fire as they gave chase. We reached the moon's thin atmosphere. Pockmarks and craters whisked past us.

"Wait. They're anticipating our moves. There's a seer helping them. They know we're planning on doubling back," I said.

"I feel it, too. Get ready for anything," Wilbaht told us. "Ready atomic ports."

Wilbaht bolted us around to the dark side of the moon. The initial five military ships traveled in V-formation several kilometers behind us. The other two sets of five headed for the other side of the moon.

"Ocelot, on my mark, fire two atomic hits," Wilbaht ordered.

"Ready, sir." Ocelot sat poised at his station.

Wilbaht took us frighteningly close to a mountain range. He slowed just enough to bring the enemy to our firing range. He sparked up one side of a mountain, and then swirled us down its slope. The enemy leader fired at us, but hit the mountain ridge instead. Rock hurled from the blast in all directions behind us. Wilbaht pulled us up just as the squadron peeked over the ridge behind us.

"Fire," he ordered.

Ocelot punched the sensor button for two blasts. One hit the second ship in the row. The other hit the fourth. Both were destroyed. Their comrades just behind them and at their sides were also blown apart as they smashed into each other and then into the ground, which billowed up into a

447

wall of dust. The center ship stayed on our tail, firing constantly and causing massive clouds of debris on the moon's surface.

Wilbaht dipped us into a broad crater. The enemy ship blasted the cliffs at the mouth of the crater and then shot towards a spot at the middle of the basin where we should have passed, but Wilbaht pulled back on the controls to bring us straight up.

"Fire," he said.

Ocelot fired towards the crater we'd just left. The enemy ship cruised right into the blast. Our ship shook with the reverberation.

I was amazed. "Excellent maneuver," I said.

"Five down, ten to go," Ocelot replied.

Wilbaht reversed directions as planned, but then skewered off to the left. He increased speed and pulled the ship up a little.

"Let's fly to meet them," Wilbaht said.

We burst onto the bright side of the moon. He aimed us towards the oncoming ships, in a path that would bypass them my several kilometers. Then he turned us to a perpendicular trajectory.

"We should pass right in front of them," he calculated aloud. "All atomic weapons portside up and ready. Count us down, Ocelot."

"Contact in twenty…fifteen…ten…five, four, three, two."

"Fire portside," Wilbaht ordered.

We shot without seeing what we were meant to hit. The squadron must have seen us coming but held their positions, probably thinking they'd cut us off as we tried to retreat. As we passed directly in front of the oncoming ships, our atomic blasts turned them into a fiery wake that blazed up behind us, nearly engulfing our own ship in the blossoming wreckage. The ships' outlines disappeared from our screens. I gaped in morose wonder.

Wilbaht took off away from the moon. "If the others are meant to live, they'll assume we collided and will stop looking for us. Otherwise we'll be in for another run. We're heading for Moon Three."

We flew again through a section of space commonly traveled by commercial traffic. We kept on alert for possible collision courses. The last squadron appeared over the first moon's horizon. They spotted us. I realized the seer was on board one of these ships. He knew which path we'd take. The squadron headed our direction at top speed, narrowly avoiding several bulk vehicles. Just as the first group, this squadron closed in slowly.

"How long before they get close enough to fire on us?" Wilbaht asked.

"Three point five minutes," Ocelot told him.

"They'll reach us before we leave public space. How many atomic shots do we have left?" he asked.

"Four, sir. All starboard," I told him.

"Nuclear?" he asked.

"Three, sir. All center crown," I replied.

"What are they armed with?" Ocelot asked.

"They have a lot more weaponry than we do, that's for sure," I told him.

"Sil, Ocelot, I want you to meditate. Concentrate on making the squadron break apart. We need them to separate," Wilbaht ordered.

I did as I was told. Meanwhile, I sensed someone reading my thoughts: someone in a command position on board one of the ships. We passed an interstellar bus on its way to Jawlcheen. It changed its course to avoid us. Once it was safely out of the way, I knew the lead ship behind us would prepare to fire. Moon Three's oblong body expanded to cover our entire front screen. The squadron did not break up. In fact, they merged even closer together. I was about to mention this to Wilbaht when he fired two nuclear weapons.

Ocelot and I looked up in surprise. I was sure this was the same reaction our foes had before meeting their demise. They never even fired a shot. An incredible force from the explosion, like a solar wind, pushed us forward at a higher speed than this ship was supposed to be capable of.

Moon Three jabbed itself towards us. Wilbaht struggled with the controls. We barely missed the moon's surface. I concentrated all my levitative abilities on pushing us away from the rock. When I opened my eyes, we faced only the glittering dust cloud that separated the space between Jawlcheen and the ice planet of Nitrogen2. I sensed no other ships following us. I searched the skies. We sailed alone.

"You did it, sir. We're free," Ocelot told him.

"Yes." Wilbaht's voice was sad.

"You knew they were focusing on our thoughts. That's why you asked us to separate them," I said.

"Yes, Sil." He swiveled his chair to face us. "We are out of danger for the moment, but we caused many deaths today. There were one hundred forty-one people on those ships. We are accountable for those lives. Someone will make sure we pay for them." Wilbaht grumbled heavily. "There is no balancing of scales between life and death. We can only pretend that the good we propose to do will somehow make up for the lives we have snuffed out. We owe their families a livelihood we can never repay. The people of Jawlcheen will hate us fiercely, forever."

I bowed my head gravely.

Wilbaht paused, thinking. "They will hate *me*. I pray they will never find out about you. I accept all responsibility and the curses they will cast. We must split up as soon as we can."

We watched him with sullen anticipation. He closed his eyes in meditation, and then addressed us boldly. "Our supplies are dwindling. We can't run from this solar system. We have to go back to Jawlcheen. If the deaths of those soldiers are to be justified, we must do everything in our power to stop the Fitmalo commonwealth takeover of Jawlcheen. I only know of one group of benevolent people who will forgive this slaughter. They are the only ones who will take us in without reporting us now."

"Where are they?" Ocelot ventured to ask.

"In the southwestern quadrant of Jawlcheen there is a city of worship. I don't know them directly, but I know someone who does," he replied.

"But, sir, we can't go back now. We'll encounter the same confrontation we just ran from," I said.

"We're not going back yet. We're going to Nitrogen2. There we can hide a while. They'll think we've gone on to Gold Wind. We'll stay on Nitrogen2 until our ship is renamed and repainted," Wilbaht said.

"We can replenish our water supply while we're there," I added.

Wilbaht agreed.

After letting us off primary alert, Wilbaht stood carefully from his chair. Ocelot stood with him. Wilbaht looked down at him and reached out to pat him on the shoulder.

"Happy birthday, son. At least you're alive and well," Wilbaht told him.

I raised my eyebrows at them. I stood as Ocelot thanked our leader. I strode forward to shake his hand. I congratulated him as well. He returned the handshake firmly, but his countenance remained sad. When they left the upper deck, lamentation hung in the ship's tired air.

Chapter 41: The Planet Nitrogen2

We followed a trajectory that would lead anyone tracking us to believe we were heading for the Gold Wind helion. No other ships followed us closely enough to become a significant threat. After we'd passed the planet, we backtracked to turn and land on the dark face of Nitrogen2. Wilbaht landed us at the equator on a rocky mesa coated with several meters of ice. Daytime temperatures were expected to rise to only ten degrees below zero. Current temperatures measured between negative fifty and negative sixty degrees. A light snow swirled about us.

We met to evaluate our remaining inventory. By accurately rationing food, we would have enough to supply each of us with only a third of our recommended calories each day up until a day before we proposed to land again on Jawlcheen. Two of our cold weather suits were useless from the sabotage. The other two were slightly damaged. The only space suit that could maintain perfect seals was Wilbaht's. The rest of our supplies had dwindled from use or had been destroyed by the recon ship blast.

Fortunately, the robots we used for exterior ship maintenance were located in the main cargo hold and had not been damaged. As soon as the daytime temperatures reached their peak, we set a heat pack on the robot that would do the scouring on the ship's surface. I donned one of the body parkas and a facemask with oxygen tank. I sealed the suit's burn holes with a quick-drying foam epoxy and went outside to set the robot on its way. The cold wind stung even through my protective suit. I levitated up to hook the robot to the crown of the ship. Then I used a pickaxe to collect some ice and snow in a sample bucket. I returned to the ship panting and shaking.

Ocelot received the bucket from me gratefully. We set up a complex filtering system for the ice. Since this planet had a high content of mercury and lead, we lined the underside of the bucket with an electromagnet to attract the particles of metal to the bottom. We skimmed the melted water at the top then ran it through the same process in a separate container before actual filtering took place. It took eight hours to get four cups of questionably drinkable water from the ice.

However, Ocelot informed me that Wilbaht had to adhere to the existent water supply since his species was even more sensitive to traces of these metals than humans. Ocelot served the two of us a cup of highly filtered ice water. He assured me that he had run tests on it to make sure the contamination was well below toxic level for us. We toasted to survival and drank slowly.

We let the scouring robot work for three hours. It had only finished the left side of the ship, but the outdoor temperature dropped quickly. The heat pack kept the robot from freezing over completely, but it was wearing out. When I went to retrieve it, it was moving very slowly, barely able to perform its task. I unhooked it from the crown and brought it into the ship as quickly as I could.

The next day, both robots went to work. The scouring robot worked on the right side of the ship while the painter painted on our new serial number in reflective black and white. Wilbaht used some extra ship energy to keep the outer hull warm while it was being painted. Ocelot volunteered to remote control the robot, but Wilbaht took that job. Instead, he made Ocelot reprogram our serial number signal so it would match the newly painted number. Ocelot pouted somewhat, since he would have liked to play with the robot. Wilbaht was content with this technical toy. His sadness lifted a little.

Later, a new water problem faced us. The filtering system for our new water supply clogged quickly. If we replaced filters for this water system, we wouldn't have enough extras to replace filters on the black water reclaim system, which was also in need of repair. We decided to scrap the ice water system and fix the black water filters instead. Ocelot harvested only three cups more of drinkable water from the Nitrogen2 ice. This left us with a more comfortable amount of water for all of us, but Ocelot felt guilty. He seemed apologetic and more humble than ever around Wilbaht, as if he had failed. Wilbaht reacted solemnly.

I tried to distract their melancholy by discussing the new name for our ship. Wilbaht suggested we brainstorm for ideas. He advised that it should be a ship from a different helion, one that did regular commerce with Thrader.

"Why not Liricos?" Ocelot suggested.

We agreed. Our ship would be named the Liricos…something. We enjoyed brainstorming together. Some names we came up with were very good. Some were silly. Some made us laugh. Others were already taken by ships we'd seen before. Wilbaht suggested perhaps a nondescript, common name would be best, like the Bounty, or the Star Survivor. Ocelot suggested it should be something that would please our religious hosts, like the God Speed or the Miracle. However, this sounded too self-righteous. I suggested maybe the name should reflect the three of us in some way, like the Triblade or the Triple Crown.

"Maybe since we're all supposed to be dead we should call it the Ghost Rider," Ocelot said.

"No, that's too morbid. Maybe we should call it the Mirage. When people see us again, they'll think they're imagining things," I said. Ocelot smiled and shook his head.

Wilbaht raised his eyebrows and held up one finger to show he'd had an idea. Then he scratched the side of his head. He raised the index finger again.

"How about the Liricos Apparition?" he asked in his gravelly base voice.

"That's profound," I said.

"That would go over well at the city of worship," Ocelot said.

We agreed heartily.

"The Liricos Apparition it is. We'll repaint the name tomorrow and take off as soon as it's done," Wilbaht said.

I was glad to see him pleased about something again. He reached out to both of us to squeeze our hands on the table. Suddenly, he tightened his grip. He glanced between the two of us in surprise. He slowly turned to stare me in the eye. He read my thoughts and emotions. He knew. I turned away nervously.

"What is it, sir?" Ocelot asked.

Wilbaht loosened his grip on our hands. He cleared his throat. I bit my lip.

"May we all set foot on Jawlcheen as free warriors," he said.

"Amen," Ocelot spoke.

"Amen," I repeated.

Wilbaht stood to go upstairs. He did not ask to speak with me. He did not look at me again or indicate in any way that he had discovered how I felt. I wondered if perhaps he had actually seen something else. After Wilbaht climbed the stairs, Ocelot stood to go the opposite direction.

"Sil, can I talk to you a minute?" Ocelot spoke in a low tone. He gestured toward the hallway.

I followed him to his bunk. I felt out of place there. I wasn't supposed to enter another person's bunk unless I was asked to. I paused at the door. His computer was on. I saw a screen full of commercial pictures and generic information, but he quickly got rid of these. Underneath was a page of medical information on Torreons.

"Come in. I want to show you this. I don't want to talk about it out loud since Wilbaht has a tendency to hear everything. Sorry, sir," he said, just in case he was listening.

I shuffled into the dorm. I noticed the walls were bare except for one picture above his bed. It was a printed picture of the Venus Falls Center and its surrounding mountains on the Jain planet. I immediately thought of the contrast between this dwelling and Klib's. Ocelot was a good, decent man. I wished things could be different between us. I felt uncomfortable sitting next to him, so I remained standing. I crossed my arms to shield myself from my own temptation to reach down and caress his brown hair.

I looked at the computer screen to read the medical information.

"Oh, no. Why didn't he tell us about this?" I asked softly.

"Would you if you were in his position?" he asked back.

I shook my head. "What can we do?"

"Take as little water as you can without risking your own health. Pray that we'll reach our destination in time." Ocelot paused. "He doesn't want you to know."

I nodded. I read the information again.

"The recommended daily intake of water for the Torreon species is between ten to fifteen glasses daily. The blood cells and tissues of this species absorb clean water and expulse wastewater more quickly than those of any other non-aquatic being. The Torreon body continuously rejuvenates using this hydro-cleansing method. This causes the lifespan of a Torreon to surpass that of all other known mammals. With a continuous supply of water, a normal Torreon will reach the age of 220 for females and 240 for males. If the Torreon is denied a reliable water supply for more than ten days, the rejuvenation process stops and the body reverts to a self-preservation mode. If the Torreon goes without a significant water supply for more that two weeks, the rejuvenation process begins to reverse. In most cases of Torreons who have experienced extreme drought, even after the water supply was replenished, the body did not regain its ability to rejuvenate."

The next passage gave examples of natural disasters and space accidents in which several Torreons had beat the odds and survived several weeks with limited water. Tragically, they all died from health complications within five years of the incident.

We had been without a normal supply of water for three weeks. The last ten days had been severe. Even with the added water from the Nitrogen2 ice, our water supply was significantly less than the Torreons' recommended minimum. Wilbaht was the oldest and strongest man I'd ever met, but he wasn't immortal.

I sat solemnly next to Ocelot after all. A terrible thought came to mind.

I whispered to him. "Remember when he said I probably gave you twenty years of my life by saving you? How many years of his life did he give to me when he saved me from the airbus crash? If his rejuvenation reverses…" I trailed off, certain that he would understand.

Ocelot stared woefully into the computer screen.

Wilbaht was dying.

Chapter 42: The Planet Jawlcheen and the Holy City of Angoran

During our short trek to Jawlcheen, Ocelot came up with several ideas to help Wilbaht's health. He and I took a diuretic, which increased our own dehydration, but supplied Wilbaht with more water. He also took the emergency blood supply from cold storage in the quarantine room and slowly gave each of us an extra liter of our own blood. This helped us all, although Wilbaht's health still seemed to decline.

He became more noticeably tired. Two days away from our destination, Wilbaht overslept. He had never done that before. I waited for him upstairs for two extra hours before finally going downstairs to wake him.

I knocked at his door lightly. I waited. He did not stir. I knocked again. I called to him. Finally, I heard a noise within. He came to the door a bit more unkempt than normal. He asked me what I needed. He was unaware of the time. I offered to stay on upstairs a little longer, although I was sure he would politely refuse. To my surprise, he did not.

"Yes. I need a few minutes. I'll be there soon," he answered.

He looked ill. His skin seemed more leathery and sagging than I'd seen it before. I asked him if I could bring him something, but he said no. He seemed to have difficulty with his back and knee and hip joints. He didn't stand straight as he usually did. He moved slowly.

When I returned upstairs, I buzzed Ocelot. I apologized for waking him. I alerted him about Wilbaht's physical state. He said he would go in to work with him a little early to check on him.

Later, Ocelot told me Wilbaht was suffering from acute arthritis. His rejuvenation had definitely reversed. He was suffering symptoms of old age, symptoms that should only have shown up in a Torreon eighty years older than Wilbaht. Ocelot grew frustrated with him.

"He's deliberately refusing to drink all the water he can. He thinks his time is near and we shouldn't waste our resources on him. I've argued with him. I bring him water constantly. He doesn't always accept it. I don't know what to do with him. I can't cure an unwilling patient. I don't know that I could cure him at all, but he's not even letting me try. You convince him. I've done all I know to do," Ocelot complained.

I agreed to at least try.

Wilbaht overslept a second time, this time by over three hours. I did not go to wake him. Eventually, I heard him laboring to climb the stairs. He apologized as he struggled against the decay of his joints. He sat in his seat with difficulty. I immediately brought him a full glass of water.

455

"Sir, please drink this. If you allow your health to decline much more, you'll have trouble landing us. We need you to be healthy enough to get us to Jawlcheen. You can't just retire yourself like this. We need you," I pleaded.

I set a hand on his sagging shoulder. He regarded the water stoically before finally accepting it. He did not reply to my plea. He only appeared reluctant. A few minutes later, he asked for another half a glass. I gladly obliged. Only one glass of water would be left at mealtime, but we could easily split it three ways.

A few hours before we prepared to move into Jawlcheen airspace, the three of us manned the upper deck for pre-entry checks. Wilbaht stooped forward, no longer touching the ceiling with his full height. The wrinkles on his face had grown deeper. His skin quality was less elastic. His nails were turning brown. I tried not to show him how moved I was by his illness. He sat carefully in the helm chair.

"I told you I have a contact who knows some of the head nuns at Angoran. You'll be pleased to know that she will be there to meet us. She is setting up preparations for our arrival. I think you'll be glad to see her as well," he told us. He smiled to think of her. I was sure he meant Olimbi.

As we entered Jawlcheen's airspace, Wilbaht fought against his infirmity. Once, the ship listed to the right so much that warning signals flashed. He had gotten too close to a freighter. The other ship's captain hailed us.

"Liricos Apparition, this is Star Steamer 2874. Whoever is flying your ship needs to wake up. You almost bought ten thousand kilos of metal ore."

Wilbaht returned the man's call. "Star Steamer, this is Liricos Apparition. We apologize for that close call. It won't happen again."

Ocelot offered to assist in piloting through a congested area. Wilbaht refused firmly. He breathed with a slight rasp. He gripped the controls fervently. When we flew over the mountain range, Wilbaht kept the ship high to avoid maneuvering closely around the peaks. When we descended to Angoran, he lost some of his equilibrium. The ship wobbled, but remained air born.

There was not an actual landing field here at the city of worship, only several large empty squares scattered among the pines and longhouses of the holy city. Wilbaht aimed for the closest square, but overshot it and pulled up awkwardly to circle around again.

He hovered us too close to the treetops before descending to the square. We felt a jolt from beneath us. We tipped dangerously forward before the tree under us snapped. We tilted back to our upright position, but the tree trunk had damaged the hover pad. The ship sagged backward and then hit the ground with a massive thud. Wilbaht did not pause to discuss the awkward landing. Instead, he quickly led us through shut down procedures.

We felt his resistance to the debilitating weakness that inflicted his body. He was not like this. He was our solid, powerful leader. The whole Organization knew him as a symbol of our status in the galaxy. He was a picture of integrity and candor. He was our friend and protector. We would make sure the people here treated him as such. I prayed they could help him replenish his health and that he would not lack water again. We moved as fast as we could to get him out of the ship and into their care.

Wilbaht ordered us to bring all our personal belongings, which we had packed by his command earlier in the flight. He asked us to carry his boxes as well.

"What about Klib's personal things?" Ocelot remembered.

"I already cleaned out his bunk. All his personal effects are in a holding net in main cargo. I'll see what my colleagues have to say about him before we destroy his things. He also had an extensive amount of electronic and recording equipment. It's in an evidence case in secondary cargo," he told us through his discomfort.

He then became even more melancholy. "I've entered access codes for both of you to get into the official ship's log. I also copied my personal ship's log into your own handheld computers."

We thanked him as if we were thanking the highest-ranking official for a medal of valor. He levitated himself down the stairwell and out of the ship. He preferred levitation to muscle movement now. At least he still had his mental power. Ocelot and I avoided looking at each other. We refused to conspire against our noble leader at his time of weakness, even by exchanging scandalous glances. We silently split the amount of boxes between us, and then followed Wilbaht out into the chilly, sunlit square.

The felled tree lay smashed and broken around the rear of the ship. A group of Vermilions greeted us: ten monks to our left and seven nuns to our right. They dressed in dark, flowing clothes and soft fur caps.

The men gathered Wilbaht to them with care. They escorted him towards a longhouse nearby. Ocelot was also ushered away by the men. I tried to hand one of them Wilbaht's extra box I carried, but the man held up his hands in resistance.

One of the nuns kindly explained that he was not allowed to touch anything handled by a female unless it was cleansed first. Ocelot noticed this dilemma. He came back to get the box himself. The man bowed to him.

I took charge of closing the main door to the ship. Then the women escorted me in the opposite direction from my partners. I gazed longingly over my shoulder. Ocelot returned my gaze. He nodded to me to let me know he would look after Wilbaht.

The fur-capped women showed me to the door of a triple-stacked longhouse of thick wooden beams covered with evergreen thatch. Two women took my boxes to a cell at the end of a long hallway. Another led me to a cleansing room.

All activity in the room revolved around a circular stone tub. Two nuns busied themselves with filling the tub with buckets of water from a rudimentary pump. A pot of hot water steamed over a centuries-old iron stove nearby. Another nun brought in a long linen robe, a towel, and a long fur wrap. One strong woman hefted the pot of steaming water and waddled with it to the tub, where she emptied it briskly. Another lady stirred it in with the cold water.

A slender woman asked me to disrobe before them so that they could take my clothes to be washed. I did so self-consciously. I stepped in and sat in the tub. The comforting warmth of the water was not enough to ease my self-consciousness. I sat hugging my knees to my chest. I found no soap or washing materials. I only rubbed the skin on my legs with my hands.

"This should do the trick," a burly woman said as she stomped towards me.

She brusquely attacked my back and shoulders with a large horsehair brush. It foamed with a flowery-smelling liquid.

"I'd rather wash myself, if I may," I protested.

"Yes, let her do that herself, Dorya. She knows how to bathe," a thin nun added.

Dorya stopped scrubbing at me momentarily to whisper loudly to her companion. "Well, she doesn't *smell* like she knows how."

"Excuse me, but we've been without sufficient water for about a month," I explained. "I do know how to take care of myself. It's just that I couldn't."

"Oh, well, that's different. What an ordeal that must have been. Here you are, dear." Dorya passed me the handle of the brush.

She stood by with arms crossed, still observing me. "Well, go on."

"She's shy. She's not used to people around her when she's bathing," another woman added.

"Well, I should hope not. She was on that ship with two men," the thin woman said.

"Oh. You didn't let them touch you, did you?" the hefty woman asked.

"What do you mean?" I asked. I scrubbed my left arm as they spoke.

458

"Oh, really, Dorya. She's not like us." The woman holding my towel stepped near the tub. "You'll have to excuse her. She's lived here most of her life. She doesn't remember any other way."

"It wouldn't hurt to cleanse her with windflower spray," Dorya pronounced. "And look at this girl's hair. We'll have to wash it three times."

They shampooed my hair for me and rinsed it, three times, just as the large woman said. Soon the tub nearly overflowed with the fluff of white bubbles. The other nuns dipped buckets of soapy water out of the bath and returned with clean water to rinse me. I drank from the rinsing water as they dumped it over my head.

Dorya returned once more when my bath was finished. She ordered me to stand in the tub. I was reluctant to do this, but she insisted. She and the other women were unmoved by my naked body and my embarrassment. They went about their respective tasks as if this were perfectly normal. Dorya sprayed me all over with a fine, cold mist of water mixed with windflower pollen. The pungent mixture made me sneeze several times. She blessed my sneezes heartily and handed me a cloth for my nose.

Cela, the thin nun, held out a hand to help me out of the tub. I stood on the cold wooden floor and rubbed myself dry with the large fleece towel. I then slipped on the linen robe and the fur wrap. The youngest nun escorted me to the bare cell where they had left my travel boxes.

Here I found a cot of woven reeds, my boxes, and a tiny wardrobe, nothing more. An oval-shaped symbol of the universe hung on the wall. Opposite this, a tiny square window near the ceiling allowed a faint light to the room. The nun told me I would be called upon in two hours for dinner. I thanked her. She also asked for any other laundry that needed tending. I hesitantly opened my travel box and gave her my traveling uniform, which was still imbibed with dust and sand from our battle on Fitmalo.

I dressed myself in the only clean civilian clothing I owned: a knee-length blue dress I had bought on Santer. This dress was too thin for the cool, open longhouse, so I kept the fur wrap around me.

In a few minutes, a different nun came in to bring me simple bedding and a heavy blanket. She retrieved the linen robe and brought me a glass of water. I bowed and thanked her. She nodded to me, but did not speak.

I dozed lightly for a while. The same thin nun who had been present at my public bath woke me.

"There is someone here to see you. She is an old friend of ours. She says she has known you during most of your life," the nun hinted.

"Yes, I'd like to see her," I said.

She nodded with a smile. She returned momentarily with a blue Lizard female in a warrior's traveling uniform.

"Yalat!" I cried joyfully. I stepped forward to embrace my old teacher.

Yalat laughed heartily. "Oh, my dear girl. How wonderful it is to see you again. I'm so glad you're alive and well!"

Our happy greeting soon turned solemn as we discussed the recent sabotage and battles we had faced. She said she had spoken at length with Wilbaht just a few minutes ago. He had outlined some important facts to her regarding Klib and our new identities. She informed me that the Fitmalo military had, of course, recaptured the Trilobite Center. The leader of the Free Economy rebels and most of his followers were still at large.

I asked Yalat how the local news was handling our battles. She confirmed my fears. The authorities had labeled Wilbaht as a rebel sympathizer and a rogue. They were also after Klib, since they believed it had been he instead of Ocelot who had aided Wilbaht with the fuel drum on Fitmalo. As far as we could tell, Klib had not come forward to debunk the rumor of our death. Nor had he alerted anyone about our new identities. If he had been caught and used the information against us to gain clemency, no one had reported it. Even if this were the case, his claims against us would probably appear as hollow attempts to save his own skin.

According to Yalat, Wilbaht was planning a public announcement that would make Klib a high-level wanted criminal and at the same time would ameliorate his own position. This sounded too good to be true. I hoped he wasn't going to try and make a martyr of himself. If he accepted the blame for the whole Trilobite Center battle and the battle around the moons of Jawlcheen, he and his family would be cursed by the supporters of the Common Law movement and by many natives of this planet, not to mention anyone associated with the secret Regime. I worried that Wilbaht might think since he was dying anyway that he should openly take all the blame.

I spoke with her about my concerns over Wilbaht's sinking health. She agreed that he looked withered. She, too, sensed that at least he believed his time to die was very near.

Yalat turned my thoughts to something positive. She gave me good news about my family. I had a new niece named Kaycha. Tamia and Jem were proud parents. My younger sister, Chena, was finishing her last year of administrative studies and my youngest sister, Grace, was still at the top of her class in aerospace sciences. My father missed my mother very much, but with three daughters and a new granddaughter around him, he was never alone. His plans to begin a new school were almost complete. Chena had promised to work for him when it opened. Yalat confirmed that she had notified them of the error in the report of my death and had assured them I was fine.

I asked her how Wilbaht had contacted her about me being alive without running the risk of exposure. She explained that before she had left Sor3, she and Wilbaht had agreed to communicate about my well being using color codes. I was white. Healthy was red. Ill was purple. Safe was green. Dead was black. After we left the space station, he had told her that white was red and green. When he needed her help with our safe house here at Angoran, he had told her that white was not green and that we needed holy help to keep from turning black. She figured out the message right away, since she had seen the news of the destruction of the Fitmalo squadrons. She reminded me that the simplest codes were sometimes the most difficult to break.

She also informed me that she had done a great deal of unconventional research, as usual. She was now stationed at the Red Mesa Center here on Jawlcheen, which lay southeast of Angoran. I was surprised to hear that she had been working off and on with Wilbaht's brother, Channol, through messaging. Yalat had not yet notified him of Wilbaht's whereabouts, since Wilbaht had asked her to tell no one else about our plans to land here.

I remembered that Wilbaht had said Olimbi and her father would be on this planet. I hoped the press would not discover them, since they were directly related to the man who had destroyed three squadrons of this planet's military fighters.

Cela returned to announce our dinnertime. We followed her into a long dining area. A fire crackled soothingly to one side of the hall. The nuns lined up on either side of the great table. They waited for their head nun to lead the prayer in an ancient tongue. Then we were allowed to sit and eat. The meal consisted of a single chunk of meat in a thin soup and a hand-sized loaf of bread. We followed the nuns' example and did not speak during dinner. At the end of our meal, however, when the nuns cleared away the dishes, the whole group got up from the table chattering. They all went away to the kitchen or stayed to clean the table, benches, and floor.

Yalat showed me upstairs to a sunlit room beside a greenhouse at the top floor. In this relaxing, warm setting, I told Yalat what had happened at the space station.

"I'm sorry Alaban has put himself in such a terrible position. I always liked that boy. My heart aches to know that he has chosen this path," Yalat said. She shook her head sadly.

"Yes. Mine, too," I concurred.

Yalat gazed into my eyes. She examined the look on my face.

"There is something else bothering you. You're distracted by some other emotion. Tell me what it is, dear. Unload your problems on your old tutor."

I hesitated. I couldn't hide my feelings from her. She knew me too well. I sighed.

"I know I shouldn't have, but I let myself..." My throat constricted with timidity.

She leaned in close to me and set a warm paw at my back.

"I'm in love, Yalat." I looked down shamefully.

"Oh." She smiled sympathetically. "I suspected as much." She patted my back, poking me lightly with her claws. "I thought I saw love in those little eyes of yours."

"You did?" I asked. "I didn't think it was obvious."

"Don't feel ashamed." She covered my knee with her other hand. "I understand why you must feel this way. The heart sometimes leads where the mind does not wish to tread. I understand."

"I haven't told him. I can't approach him about it. He'll be in danger," I told her solemnly.

"I know, dear. You cannot be together." Yalat crooned sympathetically.

"You know? Did you have a vision, too?" I asked her.

"Several, yes. I'm glad you accept the fact you can't be with him. Your life would be in danger more than ever." Yalat looked me in the eye warningly.

"What do you mean?"

"I sneaked in and spoke with him. I had to disguise myself to do it. You know how jumpy they are over there about visitors, especially females."

"You spoke with him after you talked with Wilbaht?" I asked.

"Yes. After Wilbaht messaged me, I had to speak with him myself. It's as bad as I'd feared. He just left for Fitmalo. He said to tell you he'll return in six months."

I stood abruptly. "He left? What about Wilbaht? He wouldn't leave him when he's sick. Did Wilbaht send him away for something?"

Yalat blinked at me in confusion.

"When did he leave?" I demanded.

"Two days ago, dear. I'd no idea he had any connection to Wilbaht."

It was my turn to blink, perplexed. "Who are you talking about?"

"Alaban, of course. Who are you talking about?" Her throat puffed.

"You saw Alaban, here on Jawlcheen?" I asked incredulously.

"Wait just a moment. You're not in love with Alaban?" Yalat asked, perturbed.

"No," I said simply.

"Then who…" Her shiny black eyes widened. "Oh," she said.

I regarded her nervously.

"Oh, my," she said with a frown. She scraped her claws together in thought. "He doesn't know, you say?"

I wasn't sure again which man she was talking about. "Neither of them knows. They can't."

I explained to her about my vision, my nightmares, and my fears that Alaban might kill him. She comprehended my problem.

Yalat scratched her chin. "Yes, I see. You'll do well to follow your plan. My dear girl, are you sure it's not just a passing crush?" She suggested I might have been influenced by the lack of exposure to other eligible males of my species.

"No. I love him as a lifelong mate. But it can't happen." I stood soberly. "He shouldn't even suspect me. If he found out, he would feel…deceived. He would think of me as a weak-hearted female. Right now he thinks I'm a strong warrior," I said to her.

"You are a strong warrior. Your emotions make you no less. We are not machines. I don't disagree with your plan, but don't make faulty excuses," Yalat told me smartly.

"Yes, ma'am," I responded humbly.

"This is all very frustrating. And I thought we had enough to worry about without these heart-felt problems. I don't mean to seem insensitive, but can't you put your heart to rest for a while? You'll need to rely on your brains and your extrasensory perception to carry you through these perilous moments, for the sake of your survival and theirs," she advised me.

I outwardly accepted her advice, but my inquietude lived on. I changed the subject. "How did you meet Alaban here?"

"I disguised myself as a Jain dignitary touring the capitol. I knew Teradom and a few other officials would be there for the signing of the new mining law treaty for the proposed commonwealth. Naturally, Alaban was there with Teradom. I approached the General to ask him questions about the treaty just when he was about to speak with another official. I interrupted him, in other words. This gave him a dilemma as to which of us to ignore and which to speak with. He chose to speak with the Fitmalo official, of course. He had more allegiance to him. But he wanted to make a good impression on the people of my planet, so he had Alaban speak to me about it, as I hoped he would. Of course I probed Alaban to find out a few more tidbits of information."

On afterthought, she added, "He looked peaked, beaten. And yet he is much stronger now than I remembered him before. He's grown. How old is he now?"

"He's twenty-one," I mused.

"So young and already at the heart of danger. I pity him." She scanned my face. "Don't let yourself turn bitter. Perhaps after all this is over, then you will be able to approach your beau," she said.

Her idea gave me hope. Maybe if I could get Alaban out of his present situation and back on track, then I could let him down easily. Afterwards, I could look for Ocelot again. Perhaps he would be more receptive to me in a few months. I took courage in her suggestion.

Cela appeared. She held a paper note in one hand.

"This is from your friends in the men's quarters," she said.

I opened the note. It read, "Sil, we have to move Wilbaht to a hospital right away. He has kidney failure. The monks have arranged to transport him to a general hospital northeast of here at a town called Sun Lake. They already sent word to his son and granddaughter to meet him there. Wilbaht advised us not to follow him right away. Someone might be suspicious of us. Please ask Yalat to help arrange for security around him. He suggests a warrior bodyguard and escort for Olimbi and Gatterand; also someone to guard his hospital cell once he's admitted."

Yalat sprung from the bench. "Has the airbus left yet, Cela?"

"I think you can still catch them. They are at the south plaza," Cela answered.

"I'll contact you when it's safe to go in," Yalat told me. She dashed off.

In the morning, I received word that it would be safe for me to go to see him at the hospital. I took a brief breakfast with the nuns and then went to the south plaza to an old airbus. Ocelot was also there, dressed in Santer clothing. He did a double take when he saw me. He thought I was someone else since he was not used to seeing me in a dress. He mentioned it was a good disguise. He quickly overlooked the mistake to fill me in on Wilbaht's symptoms.

We sat in separate seats on the airbus, facing perpendicular directions. He said it was good to finally have water again. It was only too bad that we had to enjoy our arrival at relative safety with such a dark cloud over us. We wanted Wilbaht to recover. We realized we had grown dependent on him on many levels. Without him, we would be left unfocused for a while, like orphaned children.

Our melancholy was distracted upon arriving at Sun Lake. The town was small, but modernized. The main buildings huddled together on a rocky hill overlooking the lake of its namesake. Reflections on the water glinted sharply below us. A few blocks from the airbus landing site stood the town's glassy hospital, surrounded by green tiered gardens.

Once inside, I asked for Wilbaht by physical description instead of by name. A nurse directed us to the private wing of the fifth floor.

There we found Olimbi and Gatterand in a secluded waiting area, flanked by four bodyguards and a general from the nearby Red Mesa Center. Yalat was not present, but she had certainly taken care of security as Wilbaht requested. Olimbi spotted us and ushered us to her.

She looked harrowed as expected, but received us with hugs and a smile. She introduced us to her father, who looked like Wilbaht, only much younger. We shook hands with him.

Gatterand explained to us that the surgeon had just finished the kidney eradication and hyper-reconstruction, and that we could see Wilbaht in a few minutes.

"The doctors say his case is terminal. They can only keep him comfortable for the rest of his time here," he said. He paused a moment and gave a sad smile.

"I always worried that he'd be killed on the job and that I wouldn't get a chance to say goodbye. I'm thankful at least for the opportunity to be with him in his last days," Gatterand explained.

Olimbi leaned her head on her father's shoulder. He held her and patted her back solemnly. The Vermilion doctor left Wilbaht's room and said quietly that we could see him now. Ocelot turned on his heel and went straight to him. He stayed there alone with him for half an hour. When he emerged, he told Gatterand that Wilbaht had asked for him. Gatterand left us as Ocelot approached Olimbi and me.

"He's going to record a statement for the press in an hour, but he won't make it public until after..." Ocelot trailed off. He cleared his throat. "He needs to speak with some warriors from the local Center, so I'm going to find them now. He asked the two of you to stay at a specific hotel for the night. He gave me the address. You only need to mention your name and the hotel personnel will take care of you."

"What about my father?" Olimbi asked.

"He wants him to stay here tonight," Ocelot told us.

We conceded. Anything Wilbaht ordered us to do at this point, we would do without question. Ocelot handed her the slip of paper with the hotel address. He bowed briefly to us and then marched away down the hall. I wanted to help him with his task, but Wilbaht had told me to stay with Olimbi. I was glad to see her again. If only the circumstances had been different.

The hotel was very small and had minimal security. We approached the run-down building doubtfully. When Olimbi told her name to the clerk at the desk, he summoned a pair of warriors who escorted us to a luxury suite. There we found a food cart laden with fresh foods and beverages and two beds, big enough for three people each. Our warrior guards told us their orders were to stand at our door through the night and to escort us back to the hospital in the morning. We accepted the attentions graciously.

After a few minutes of looking over the place and its amenities, we sat on our respective beds and talked about Wilbaht. She told me of a few nice things he had done for her and her cousins when she was small. I mentioned several admirable memories. Soon we agreed that the earlier we slept, the earlier we could wake up to return to the hospital and see him again, hopefully not for the last time.

Chapter 43: Deathbed

We returned to the hospital at 0800. As soon as we arrived at Wilbaht's private area, Gatterand approached us. He hugged Olimbi tightly. He looked content, or at least peaceful. He told us Wilbaht had actually improved overnight. He said he had received a slow and steady stream of visitors since very early in the morning. He seemed to be in good spirits.

I asked to see him next. When an elderly Arborman exited his room, I stepped lightly to the door. I knocked softly before entering. The room was tiny, with only a chair at one corner, a sink and life equipment, and the long bed in which Wilbaht lay.

He sat propped up by cushions. An intravenous tube ran to his arm. His neck and forearms were dotted with wireless monitor patches. He smiled at me a little when I entered the room. I forced myself to return a smile, but it quickly faded. Wilbaht gazed at me lovingly through tired eyes. His breathing was deliberated. His skin hung loosely on his face and arms.

"Sil," he said in his gravelly voice. "You don't look like the tough warrior I've seen these past few weeks."

His kind, elderly presence warmed my soul. "I'm not a warrior today, sir. I'm just a girl...who doesn't want to say goodbye to a father figure. One I love very much," I managed.

He grinned. The tops of his cheeks wrinkled around his eyes. "You know I am too old to be your father."

I smiled and laughed a little. His humor was still good. "Well, father or grandfather, I love you just the same, sir."

"And I love you, my child." He reached a long, withering hand towards me. I held his cool, dry digits in mine. "How easily these words of love are spoken at the end of a life. Wouldn't they have been better celebrated if the end were nowhere in sight?" he hinted wisely.

"You're right, sir," I told him. Grief sank with my shoulders.

"Those few short words," his deep voice hummed. "They disappear as they're spoken, but stay in our hearts forever. When spoken sincerely, they can be the greatest gift in a person's life."

I bowed my head. "Yes. That's true."

"Why haven't you told him yet?" he asked in a soothing, patient tone.

"Sir?"

"Don't pretend to think I don't know it. You love him. Why haven't you let him know it?" he asked.

Wormholes tunneled through my chest.

"I am afraid, sir," I said in a broken voice.

His soothing voice melted my heart. "There will always be something to fear. What could be worse than the trials you've already experienced? You know how to face fear. What's keeping you from being open with him?"

"I know he can't possibly love me the way I love him," I sniffled.

"What if you only think he doesn't want this? What if he loves you as well?" Wilbaht suggested.

"No, I'm sure he doesn't," I said, fighting back a hint of a tear. I stood straight and refitted the defensive shield around my heart. "Even if he did, I can't involve him. I love him too much to lead him to his death."

I explained to Wilbaht what I had told Yalat. He comprehended sadly.

"Please tell me he's never said he felt something for me," I stated, beginning to lose hold on my shield. I inhaled deeply.

"No, my child," Wilbaht admitted. "He has expressed admiration for your abilities, but he has never indicated any...amorous intentions."

I fought to hold back tears. I swallowed hard.

Wilbaht reached up to pet my arm with pity. "It would warm my fading heart to see you both united. You were my two brightest prodigies. I had planned to encourage him, with your permission, in my last days among you."

"That's very kind of you, sir, but I can't hope for that." A tear escaped me, then another.

"If it means death to him…perhaps you're right." Wilbaht offered me a cloth for my face.

I released my sorrow there before him as he caressed my arm to comfort me. He patiently let me cry before him, spending his precious, fleeting time watching a young woman shed lovelorn tears instead of arranging important details with his family and close companions. I appreciated his patience as much as his words of wisdom. Finally, I forced myself to control my feelings. I wiped my face and straightened myself with a sniffle.

"It pains me to see you this way, Sil. Why don't you take a day away from the city to relax and collect your thoughts in meditation?"

I hesitated to respond. He read my face.

"This body and mind will still be alive and functioning when you get back. It will be better for you if you're not seen with me constantly right now. I don't want the wrong people to recognize you."

I nodded. I held his great hand in mine and pressed it to my face. I closed my eyes a moment, and then let him go.

"When you go out, will you please tell Ocelot I'd like to speak with him. He needs a day off as well," he said.

"Yes, sir," I spoke dutifully.

He blinked slowly at me. I squeezed his hand once more before I turned to leave the little room and retrieve Ocelot for him. I wondered if Wilbaht would say anything to him about our conversation, but I trusted him to keep my secret to himself.

I waited with Olimbi and Gatterand nearly twenty minutes before Ocelot left the room. He walked out with sagging shoulders and a forlorn visage. He stepped up to me and spoke without looking at me directly.

"He told me to take a day off and get away from the populated areas. I guess he told you the same," he said, wrenching a fist disconcertedly.

"Yes. I'll take his advice, although I don't know where to go."

"There's a public forest reserve not far from here. It has a waterfall and some caves I'd like to explore," he explained.

"I'm sure it will rejuvenate your spirits." My voice grew tired.

"He told me I shouldn't leave you alone right now. Would you mind coming with me?" he asked.

I considered his idea with surprise, concerned that maybe Wilbaht had divulged my feelings after all. However, Ocelot's face only showed dutiful seriousness and grief, no disturbed sentiments toward me. I accepted his offer.

We went back to Angoran to pick up some supplies from the ship. We lugged out two undamaged tent packs and temporary camping equipment. Ocelot suggested we meet at the airbus at 1100.

I stayed the night again among the nuns. One brought me my clean clothing. It was perfectly pressed and smelled of windflowers. I thanked her, asking how I might repay their kindness. She said they needed nothing. They were self-sufficient. They asked for no recompense from us at all. I told her how much we appreciated their help. She merely smiled and nodded to me.

At 1100 hours, dressed for the hike, we took an airbus piloted by one of the monks to the entrance of the reserve. Ocelot guided us over white striated rocks among evergreen trees for several kilometers. The tent pack grew heavy, but the journey was worth the effort. At around 0500, we heard the roar of a high waterfall. It plunged into a stream by a wide, picturesque pond. We made camp below the trees a few meters above it. We poked around the area in opposite directions to explore a while. The air flowed fresh and sweet. The temperature was cool. The late afternoon sun danced through the needles of evergreens and onto the surface of the water.

At the pond, I crouched on one of the white rocks to peer into the water. In the shallow area, I found a cluster of unusual creatures. They seemed to be a plant and animal hybrid. I asked Ocelot if he knew what they were.

His boots ground the pebbles of the shore as he came over to observe. He hopped onto the dry face of a stepping-stone boulder and wound his way down to the miniature inlet. He knelt on a stone facing mine.

"Oh, yes. These are freshwater anemone. They look like walking flowers, don't they?"

"Do they sting?" I asked.

"I don't think so. I believe they live on an algae diet. No need to sting for food collection." Ocelot leaned down and dipped his hand gently into the cold water. "They may use a mild sting for defense."

He picked one up to find out. It immediately curled into a ball to protect itself, but did not sting him. He cupped his hand, letting the creature rest in his palm, centimeters from the surface. Eventually, the creature opened itself again. Its petals waved a bluish white with a pink edge.

"It's harmless. Here. Do you want to hold it?" he offered.

I inserted a hand into the cold water. I cupped my hand and placed it just under his. He emptied the anemone into my hand. It bounced into my palm, soft and delicate. He touched it lightly with his index finger. It curled up again. I let it slip back down to the sand at the bottom of the pond.

I glanced up at Ocelot. His face was close to mine. His beauty almost overpowered my self-control. I stood too fast, nearly toppling over into the water. I levitated back onto the shore. I didn't stop there, but continued walking up to my tent. I told him I was feeling tired. I suggested we sleep early to wake up early. He said he wasn't tired yet and that he was going to climb to the top of the waterfall. He said it must have a great view and asked if I was sure I didn't want to go with him.

I imagined standing by him watching the colorful sunset in such a romantic setting. I also imagined losing my self-composure. Flatly, I said I preferred to stay here and get some rest, and that I'd see him in the morning.

I zipped myself up in my tent, where I stayed all night, although I didn't sleep well at all. The temperature dropped near freezing. To make matters worse, my heating lamp ran low on energy. I huddled shivering under a fluff-filled blanket until after dawn.

At about 0730 hours, I emerged from my tent. Ocelot sat fishing on a boulder near the waterfall. Without greeting him, I meandered off in the other direction downstream for a while. When I returned to the campsite, Ocelot had caught a large fish and was cooking it on a makeshift spit. I complimented him on his catch. He offered to share it with me. I thanked him and sat on a boulder opposite him.

I surveyed our perfect surroundings. The roaring lull of the waterfall and the crisp, pristine surroundings seemed like paradise. Here I was, alone in the wilderness with the man of my infatuation. It seemed like a cruel and thrilling dream. I reminded myself silently not to be fooled by this seductive calm. I knew it would only last a little while. I thought instead of Wilbaht and what he might have mentioned to Ocelot. I asked about it. His answer eased my mind.

"He asked me to give a correlated report for his final review of your first year performance," he said.

"On me? Which one? Gretath or Rayfenix?" I asked with curiosity.

"On both. He didn't forget about that. He logged in as a different commander when he reported on Sil Rayfenix," Ocelot reassured me.

"So what did you say? Or can you not tell me?"

Ocelot poked at the fire with a stick and then sat with his hands dangling over his knees. "I can tell you. I said, uh, you started out a gifted beginner, eager to work, exceptionally talented, but you were, of course, young and inexperienced. Since then, you've learned ship's maintenance well. You've improved all your warrior skills. You've lived through tough experiences. You, um, you've had a lot of hard knocks this year. You're not the young rookie anymore. You seem much older now. No offense."

"None taken," I said with a nod.

He continued formally, as if giving a report to a committee. "We agreed it's unfortunate that the physical wounds you've endured this year match the emotional wounds you've sustained. Your eagerness to work is not so fresh anymore, but you have demonstrated great loyalty and dedication despite your hardships. We hope you don't become disillusioned with your job and decide to seek employment elsewhere."

"I won't. This is what I should do. I am dedicated. Anyway, I don't know what else I would do," I spoke.

"I'm sure with your academic record you could do anything you want." He punctuated this comment with a reassuring nod. "After everything that's happened this year, I'd say you deserve a double promotion. You're one tough warrior. You remind me of the image of the warrior maiden on the U.G. Organization symbol—a sword in one hand and a shield in the other—always ready for battle," he said with a slight smirk.

I wasn't sure if I should feel flattered or disturbed by this comment. I only smiled quickly to acknowledge his comparison.

"That's the kind of fierce determination that will carry you through life. I think you'll be very successful," he said, like a true academic professor. He glanced at me and then at the fish, which was nearly done.

I thanked him. "So what about you? How have you changed this year? What's going to get you through life?" I asked him out of genuine curiosity.

He seemed unprepared to turn the conversation to himself. "I can't be objective about that." He tilted his head and poked at the fire. "How I've changed? I don't know. I've tried not to be so hotheaded anymore. I've learned to value life better. Getting killed and brought back to life will do that to a person." He jutted the stick he was poking with into the fire and left it to the flames. "What's going to get me through life? Perseverance. Patience. I don't know. I was hoping maybe it would be something else."

"Like what?" I probed.

He shrugged uneasily, but then answered me. "The typical dream. I'd like to find a permanent mate someday, maybe have a family, but I know that's not likely being a traveling warrior."

"You could request a stable position on a planet. I'm sure your code breaking abilities would make you attractive to any Center as a permanent resident employee," I suggested.

"Maybe," he said.

He jiggled the steaming fish. Then he glanced up at me conscientiously. "What about you? What are your plans for the future?"

471

I shook my head. "My future is blurry. I'm afraid to hope for anything."

"You sound bitter," he told me.

I stared into the fire. "The only thing I want for my near future is to find Alaban when he arrives here on Jawlcheen and try to get him out of the Regime."

Ocelot's eyes grew large. "When he arrives here? Did you have another vision about him?"

"Yalat said she was able to speak with him. She says he'll be on Jawlcheen in about six months. I have to meet him then. He's going to give me one last chance," I spoke in a distant voice. "I only hope I can get him away from Teradom long enough to confront him."

"I don't believe it," Ocelot said.

"It will happen," I predicted.

"That's too much of a risk, Sil. Can't you try to avoid him?" Ocelot said.

"No. I don't want to avoid him. I have to help him. I owe it to him," I stated.

"You *owe* it to him? He may have saved your life, but it was his fault you were nearly killed in the first place. And he didn't pull the last spike from your arm. You still could have died after he let you go."

I shook my head. "I have to. He's still there because of me."

Ocelot spoke rashly. "He is *not* there because of you. He's the one who screwed up. He betrayed and killed his own crew."

"Alaban didn't kill Ongeram and Zank willingly. Ongeram told him to do it so Alaban would be accepted by the Regime. He was supposed to be a spy on the inside. He didn't really join the Fitmalos until after I let him down. He stayed with the Regime so I wouldn't have to."

The fish smoked on the spit. Ocelot noticed it burning and yanked it off onto a metal plate. He left the steaming dish on the ground.

"I don't believe that about Ongeram. Alaban is a traitor. He made those decisions himself. Don't try to rationalize his actions. He's not there because of you. He's not your responsibility."

"Alaban is my celestial twin. We're like two branches of the same tree. He's always been a part of me, and no matter what he did, he always will be and I will always love him," I told him plainly, knowing this would cover any hint of affection he might notice from me. "That is why I have a responsibility to him."

Ocelot protested incredulously. "How can a loyalist like you love a murderous traitor?"

I didn't look at him. I only shook my head. I rested my forehead on my knuckles.

"If you must face him, let me go with you for backup," Ocelot stated.

"No." I sat straight. "He thinks you're dead. If you show up with me, he'll realize we played a trick on him. He'll kill you by any means necessary," I insisted.

"Why do you think he would kill me? What makes you think he would win?" Ocelot asked.

"You only want to go with me to challenge him again. Why would I let that happen? I don't want to watch either of you die. Why should I have to see you die twice? And Alaban has to live. I owe it to him to give him his life back."

"Why do you think you owe him something? How did *you* betray *him*?" He spoke with frustration.

I stood and paced back and forth on the pebbled shore, refusing to answer.

"You didn't set him up to work for them did you?" he asked bitterly.

"No, of course not," I replied.

"You're not a double agent yourself, are you?" he balked.

"No. Why are you asking me this?" I complained.

"Then how did you betray him?" he asked finally.

"I can't tell you."

"Then I can't help you," he blurted with exasperation.

"No one can. That's what I've been trying to say. I have to face him alone. I've got to convince him to get out of there. I sent him to that hell. I have to pull him out."

Ocelot opened his knife with a "thwick". He pressed into the fish with a pronged utensil and stabbed it with knife, causing the dead thing to flop as if it were still alive. He jostled the blade through it recklessly, and then gave up, clanking the metal instruments onto the plate.

He faced me. "So you're out to save him and pay penance for sending him to hell."

"Yes," I confessed.

"How do you plan on doing that without getting caught or killed?"

I shook my head and shrugged. I paced faster. "I don't know."

"Even if he does turn around and leaves the Regime, then what? He can't go back to the Organization. He's a deserter and a murderer. Are you willing to live in hiding with him? How many years will you last before they'd find you? Then you'd be tried for harboring a criminal and he'd be executed. What good would that do?"

"I need to meditate," I spoke hastily.

I stepped away from the water's edge. I turned to him briefly.

"Ocelot, you have been a good partner and a friend, but this is something you cannot help me with. I know your intentions are to protect your partner, but in a couple of weeks, we won't be partners anymore. Remember that."

He glared insolently, but said no more.

I trudged off into the woods and found a rocky knoll to sit on. I closed my eyes. Although I meditated for more than an hour, I realized nothing new.

We did not discuss this again during the rest of the day. Ocelot disappeared in the woods for a few hours with a band light to explore the caves. He did not invite me to go with him. Late in the afternoon, we packed up and hiked back to the entrance. We left the calming scenery with as much tension as we had brought with us.

We took an airbus back to the hospital, but were told not to bother Wilbaht until the next morning. We returned to Angoran and to our respective cloisters.

Lying in my cell, I touched the wall that faced the monks' longhouse where Ocelot slept. I knew his argument was valid. I knew I had only betrayed Alaban in my heart. I hadn't required him to continue working with the enemy. If he really wanted out, he would have sneaked out easily. I wished he would return to the Organization to divulge the information he had learned from his evil commander in exchange for clemency. But how could I ever convince Alaban to leave his diabolical associates at my behest if he knew that Ocelot was very much alive and rested with me as a permanent fixture in my heart? Would Alaban see visions of him? Would he read my mind when I saw him again? I turned fitfully in my bed.

I had to keep Ocelot alive above all else. What I would have given to share my life with him, to sleep next to him, to feel the warmth of his body, to feel his touch, and to love him openly. But I could only dream.

The next morning, we went together to see Wilbaht. A larger crowd of people shifted anxiously in the waiting area, hoping for a chance to see him. His end was near. A nurse saw us and ushered us in right away.

Wilbaht lay flat on his back now. His life diminished before us. He gingerly grasped our hands. He did not attempt to smile at us. We looked down at him sadly. Despite his fleeting energy, he spoke to us.

"I have set up an assignment for you. You won't be separated until your goals are met or unless you voluntarily end the mission," he rumbled.

We looked at each other. We wouldn't have to say goodbye when our year was finished after all. We had a little more time together. I wondered if Wilbaht had done this because of how I felt or if it was the assignment itself that needed our attention.

"General Croso at Red Mesa will fill you in on the details. This assignment is of great importance to me. If the mission goes badly, (and I pray it will not), go back to the Center and ask to process the second set of files. You'll see what I mean. Promise me that you will do this assignment for me as a last request."

"Yes, sir. I promise," we said together shakily.

"Take care of each other. Make the best of the time you have left. There is a gift waiting for both of you with the General. Ask him about it at briefing. I love you both. You've enriched my life. Go save the world, my fine warriors. Please ask Gatterand and Olimbi to come in next," he said.

I kissed the old man on his fist and his forehead. Ocelot shook his hand with both of his. He stood staring at Wilbaht's face eagerly. He did not want to let him go. I gently pulled him away. Wilbaht seemed to smile a little. Olimbi skirted in past the nurse. Her father followed her and closed the door.

Ocelot and I sat on a bench together, transfixed. I soon realized our fingers were intertwined, but not from affection. We braced ourselves, white-knuckled, against the jarring reality of death.

A tall, lanky, shadow swept past us. Ocelot whispered his name as he passed us. "Channol."

He disappeared into Wilbaht's room. A few minutes later, Olimbi emerged crying. Ocelot moved to the open door with Channol and Gatterand. Olimbi and I cried together like sisters.

Chapter 44: Letting go

Even though our funerary services for Wilbaht were held in secret, a large crowd assembled with us. All the nuns and monks we had met at Angoran gathered with us on opposite sides of the square: men on the east side, women on the west. Yalat and several other trusted Organization members from Red Mesa attended. Of course Channol and his current partners were there. In total, we counted more than one hundred at the Angoran memorial square.

We all revered the image of Wilbaht, which was set upon the rectangular golden box containing his ashes. Olimbi gave out gold silk scarves. We draped them over our shoulders to acknowledge the life of the spirit.

Channol began the memorial service with words to honor Wilbaht as a brother as well as a warrior. Then he invited his nephew and grandniece to say a few words. Olimbi spoke little. She only said he was the best grandfather anyone could have. Channol invited any others to say something in his honor as well. All who spoke reiterated the fact that he was one of the great warriors of his time, and that he had inspired countless people throughout the U.G. We sang a dirge in Wilbaht's honor, as he had requested. Ocelot comforted my grief with his lovely tenor voice.

We sang, "*Hear this life calling you. Please remember me. In your life, passing through, please remember me. Take the time to follow through with dreams along the way. If you will remember me, I'll live another day. I'll live another day. I'll live another day.*"

As I sang the words, I reflected on Wilbaht's leadership. We would always remember him. His dreams would live through us.

After the head monk led the closing prayer, Gatterand and Olimbi retrieved the box of Wilbaht's ashes and his picture from the altar. They had to leave right away. Wilbaht's announcement was to be broadcast in the morning. They needed to be away from Jawlcheen when it happened just in case the media and some unruly citizens of this planet wanted to hound or insult them; or worse.

We shook hands with Gatterand and told him how honored we were to have met him. Ocelot shook hands with Olimbi. He gave her his best wishes. I embraced her tightly. We strolled together hand in hand to her airbus.

After their departure, Channol turned to Ocelot and me.

"Gatterand and Olimbi are not the only ones in danger of bad publicity. As soon as the announcement is broadcast, investigators will want to know where Wilbaht landed and who helped him get to the hospital.

I can stay safely in the Red Mesa Center. The two of you should be nowhere around when they find this ship." He gestured to the Liricos Apparition. "You shouldn't even show up at the Center for now."

Yalat chimed in. "Anything aboard that ship that might lead them to suspect you're still alive must be eradicated."

"My partners and I will help comb the ship and its documentation for anything that will appear suspicious to them. If you have any information that needs to be extracted, do it now," Channol told us.

"Yes, sir," we responded. I felt as if I were talking to a newer version of my old commander.

I asked Yalat if we would see her in the ship, too, but she said she had some important errands to run for security by Wilbaht's request. She assured us, however, that she would see us again soon.

Once inside the Apparition, we headed for our bunks to clean them out completely. In the event of a warrior's death, his or her bunk would be stripped and sanitized. The personal belongings would either be sent to family members or incinerated. I removed my pillow from the bed and tossed it into a biohazard bag. I vacuumed and scrubbed down the entire bunk and then emptied the cleaning elements into the biohazard bag as well. I did the same in the bathroom and exercise room to get rid of any hair or skin cells left there recently. Ocelot cleaned out his room and then headed for the upper deck to check all communication files to make absolutely sure nothing was on record that had been communicated from, to, or about either of us in the entire data bank since the space station incident. He also checked all of Klib's and Wilbaht's personal correspondence for any words referring to us by name or description. I did the same in the lower observation deck.

Channol and his men searched the downstairs area for anything that might indicate our continued presence on the ship. They bagged several items, including the cold suit I had mended. They also took care of the plants and checked the dining area, pantry and cold storage for any half-eaten food or items that would leave behind time-traceable fingerprints or lip prints. The five men cleaned the ship professionally. We worked fervently until very late in the evening. Channol offered to incinerate the bags of materials we'd collected in the Red Mesa Center evidence incinerator. Finally, Channol asked us to leave the ship with our bags so that he could do a last check by himself. He emerged fifteen minutes later.

"I left only life support and lighting for the plant life. It should be fine now. The ship will be seized by the Organization in a few days," he told us.

He asked us to turn in our automatic door openers for the main cargo hold. He polished them with a cloth right when we handed them to him, and then deposited the cloth in one of the evidence bags to be destroyed along with the rest.

"Communications patches?" he asked.

"I got rid of mine," I said.

"Me too," Ocelot added. Channol seemed satisfied.

"Wilbaht asked me to take all the recording equipment your former pilot had used, so all that is safe. Is there anything else you want from the ship?" Channol asked us.

Ocelot responded no right away.

I peered up at my former home regretfully before answering, "No, sir."

"Remember not to leave anything behind here." Channol gestured to the longhouses.

We agreed.

"You can spend the night here, but then you should make yourselves invisible for the next three days. I don't want to see or hear from you at all until the end of the week. Then you can show up at the Red Mesa Center, just not together. Understood?" Channol spoke sharply.

"Yes, sir," we told him.

"Good luck to you." He bowed to us both. He did not pat us on the shoulder, as Wilbaht would have. He and his men marched off down the hill to their own ship, which sat parked at another landing square past the women's longhouse.

I turned back to observe what had been our ship. This hulking mass of metal had earned its own personality in my mind. It was a giant pet, a beast of burden that had carried us safely through unthinkable dangers.

Ocelot interrupted my thoughts. "I don't know about you, but I'm planning on going back to the waterfall. This time I'm going to go in through a different entrance. I'm sure no one will think to look there, even if they do suspect we're alive."

"I think you're right. That's probably the best place to go right now. Do you mind if I go with you?" I asked seriously.

"It's probably a good idea to stick together for now," he agreed.

After my meal with the nuns, I expressed to Cela my profound appreciation for allowing us to stay here and for the hospitality they had offered us. She promised me that she and the people of Angoran would not divulge the fact that Ocelot and I had been here. I thanked her all the more.

That night I purged from my mind all anxieties I harbored about Alaban and Ocelot. I concentrated on Wilbaht. I searched for his presence but only found memories. I said a prayer of thanks to him. Even though he was no longer here to guide me, he had certainly pointed me in the right

478

direction as an adult warrior. Yalat had begun the training and he had finished it. I vowed quietly to his ghost that I would continue on the path he had shown me.

In five days, my first year would end. My contact general would change my title pin to show my full-fledged rank as Warrior. I would then have the right to accept, refuse, or choose any assignment available for my rank. In another three years I could be a sub professor like Ocelot. I wondered where we would find ourselves in those three years and under what conditions.

In the morning, I carried my two travel boxes in my hands and my tent pack on my back. It was a heavy load, but I had to take it all with me. Ocelot approached the airbus with the same kind of burden. He asked the monk driver if he could take us to a different landing pad this time. For a small fee to cover the extra fuel, the man agreed. He flew us to a spot close to the north entrance to the nature reserve.

We trudged through the brush and undergrowth with effort. The heavy boxes slowed our pace, but neither of us wanted to stop and rest until the time for Wilbaht's announcement. Five kilometers from our destination, a single beep sounded from one of Ocelot's boxes. He jerked to a halt. It was time.

We let our boxes thump to the ground. Ocelot opened one of his. He withdrew his palm computer and then closed the box once more. He set the computer on the broad side of the travel box and extended the projection string to make a square viewing screen. He turned the signal receiver to the local Jawlcheen news station.

A plump Vermilion newscaster appeared on the box. He spoke stuffily. "...Announcement from Sub General Wilbaht Cordolib. Some believe he was not working on his own; that there were others involved in his rogue escape. Now we have learned that Sub General Wilbaht did not leave our helion after this most recent battle. He instead returned to our planet. He came home...to die. Keep watching this channel for our collective forum to review the facts and opinions surrounding this man after his speech."

The man's image flickered off. An image of Wilbaht appeared. He sat propped up in his hospital bed as he had when I'd first seen him there. A middle-aged Vermilion interviewed him. I knew this man was a warrior, but he wore civilian clothes to give the impression of an impartial interview. He introduced himself briefly and then presented Wilbaht. He asked him to give his main statement about recent events.

"I would like to extend my heart-felt apology to the people of Jawlcheen and of Fitmalo. It was not my intention to end the lives of your

479

soldiers. I know their families have lost an important financial provider and loved one. I do not ask for your forgiveness. I only pray that you may find peace and financial stability despite your loved one's absence. I am deeply sorry that this great tragedy has occurred.

"I ask your permission, however, to allow me to explain the reasons why I fully defended my ship against them."

I then listened in an affected state to my honest commander as he produced a bauble of lies strung together with truth in order to lead the eyes of the world away from Ocelot and me.

He said, "My pilot and I were on our way to Jawlcheen when a stray asteroid hit our ship. It punctured both our main water supply pipeline and our landing fuel drum. We were leaking badly. We asked to set down on Fitmalo for a replacement fuel drum and for an emergency water supply. We had no idea the Trilobite Center was under attack. When the rebel leader learned that ours was an Organization ship, he wrongly announced that we were there to defend his cause. We resisted his allegations, but Fitmalo military ships fired on us. We had no choice but to defend ourselves. We barely managed to get a new fuel drum from a wrecked ship in order to take off.

"I knew few people would believe my story at the time, but I hoped Jawlcheen would at least adhere to its traditional law and give us a chance to explain once we landed. Unfortunately, even though we were given clearance to land at the Loam Center, we received heavy fire from torpedoes. Apparently, we were judged and sentenced before we could ever land to argue our case.

"Either Jawlcheen or Thrader forces sent three full squadrons of ships after us. I implore the people of Jawlcheen. Ask yourselves why that might be. Even if we had been willing participants in the Fitmalo rebellion, why would two men in a damaged spacecraft pose such a threat as to warrant a chase from fifteen military ships? We had no prior warrants against us. No one questioned us about our episode on Fitmalo. I urge you to ask this of those in charge. I won't go into details about our battle. I'm sure everyone is aware of it. However, I would like you to know what happened afterward.

"We flew to Nitrogen2 to rename and re-encode our ship. It is now labeled the Liricos Apparition and is parked in the holy city of Angoran. I came back because I had to bring a message to your people. This information is dangerous enough for certain people of political importance that they wanted me dead.

"Even my own pilot turned against me for it. When we came close enough to Jawlcheen, he installed a sabotage program in the main ship and stole our reconnaissance ship to escape. He meant for the main ship to crash into Jawlcheen Moon Two. Fortunately I was able to override his program.

"I arrived on Jawlcheen three days ago. However, as I had almost no water supply left on the ship, my health has deteriorated. I have little time left in this world. Therefore, it is imperative that I deliver this message to the people of Jawlcheen now.

"There are those who would have you believe that a united helion is a step towards greater prosperity for all. To be honest, I applaud the idea. However, this solar system is in the process of uniting for the good of a few top officials and businessmen at the expense of the masses. What's worse, your proposed commonwealth is not based on improvement for your helion. You have all heard the argument for improved law enforcement. However, whose laws are to be enforced? Why would you need such a strong military to enforce them? I'm sure you have heard this criticism already from several people who have stated opinions without proof.

"I possess recorded information that will prove the involvement of several Fitmalo officials in a plan to create an economic funnel leading to their own pockets. I have asked my loyal assistants at the Organization to make public my own list of information. I ask you all to follow up on this incriminating evidence and to resist approval of the new commonwealth. If you want local improvements, do not look to management from outside your own planet. Jawlcheen was my home for fifty-eight years. I do not want to see it destroyed by greed. Please consider my request.

"I am glad to have this opportunity to speak to you, although it is from my deathbed. I prefer to pass into the next world peaceably. I believe that if I had not escaped these recent battles, I would have been assassinated upon my attempt to deliver this message to you. I would have died in moral turmoil and your people would have suffered needlessly."

Wilbaht turned to the interviewer. The interviewer asked him a few simple questions about his research and about Klib. Then he asked about us. He asked if our deaths on the space station might have had something to do with the information against the Fitmalo military.

"I believe the general who was killed at the space station was suspicious of their involvement in an investigation against him. It's my guess that he attempted to kill them for this reason and that they reacted in self-defense. I believe his bodyguards killed my warriors in the General's defense," Wilbaht responded. "The strange thing was the personnel at the space station returned their bodies to us, although they had reported them as having been sucked out into space and burned by fighter ship exhaust. Their bodies were completely intact. They showed neither freeze symptoms nor burns. My male warrior was struck through the abdomen by an unknown weapon and my female's throat was cut. Whatever really happened is a mystery: one that General Sunderlign's former staff members may be able to answer," he mentioned cleverly.

"Are their bodies available for autopsy?" the interviewer asked on cue.

"No. They were cremated as per standard Organization procedure. The monks at Angoran have sent their remains to their families," Wilbaht explained.

The interviewer covered a few more questions and reviewed Wilbaht's warrior history briefly as evidence of his character.

"Sir, if all you say is true, then you have been falsely accused and we owe you an apology. I'm honored to speak with you. Thank you, sir," the interviewer said before shaking Wilbaht's hand.

The image flickered away. The stuffy reporter reappeared to recap his statement. Ocelot turned off the device.

"They'll believe him," I said with relief.

"I just hope the Regime doesn't block most of the investigations. Jawlcheen will stage a huge protest. We might end up seeing war after all," Ocelot mused.

I agreed. "Let's hope it doesn't end up that way."

We continued our trek through the rocky woodland. By the time we heard the waterfall, we both half-levitated our burdens. We arrived at our earlier campsite exhausted. When we finished setting up camp, we watched more of the news surrounding Wilbaht's announcement. Opinions varied greatly. Many reporters had attempted to contact Channol, but of course he was unavailable for comment. The monks and nuns at Angoran kept their promise. They only acknowledged the arrival of Wilbaht and no one else. They told the press they had sent two boxes on express ships to Liricos and Sor3 by Wilbaht's request, which was probably true. I imagined they had filled the boxes with common ashes from the fireplace. Yalat would intercept or reroute the delivery of my ashes to keep my family unaware. Stennet and Jiao would receive Ocelot's box with mourning. Ocelot and I were safe for the time being.

Ocelot wandered off downstream to a lower waterfall to bathe. I stayed to bathe at the main waterfall by our camp. The hike had left me grimy with sweat despite the cold temperatures of early winter. My nerve endings shrieked with the stimulation of the icy water. After my bath, I changed into the warmest clothing I had topped with padded leggings and a thick hooded jacket. I curled up in my knapsack to sleep.

I awoke when the temperature dropped well below freezing. My faulty heating lamp was supposed to heat the layer of air between the interior of the tent and the exterior lining as well as the interior living space, but it was barely heating at all. I toyed with it a little, but since my mechanical skills hadn't improved much this year, I left it in a worse state than it had been. I shivered the rest of the night.

Late in the morning, I awoke to milder temperatures. I removed myself from my bedding and knelt at my tent flap to peek outside. A chilling breeze swayed the tops of the evergreens. Bright sunlight warmed the rocky shore.

Ocelot crouched atop the boulder where he had fished the last time. He cast his line into the deep end of the water. I peered out at his broad back. I admired him dreamily. Suddenly, his face swiveled to meet my gaze. Startled, I retreated once more into my tent. I realized how foolish my reaction must have looked. I emerged from the tent and stepped to the water's edge, acting as though nothing unusual had happened. I knelt to cup some water into my hand. I rubbed my face with it.

"Sleep well?" he asked.

"Not exactly," I replied. I explained about the temperature control.

"You slept in long enough. It's almost noon. Do you want some fish?" he offered.

I said yes.

"Then get over here and help fish for them," he said sarcastically.

"Very funny," I said.

"It's not a joke. I've been sitting here for an hour and all I've caught is a cold." He sniffled to illustrate his point.

I levitated over the water to stand beneath him. "How many do you want?" I asked.

He scoffed. "That's not fair."

"Why?" I asked.

"You just took all the sportsmanship out of it," he contested.

"What's the point of fishing if you're not really trying to catch the fish?" I asked.

He sniffled a couple of times. He set down his fishing pole resignedly and picked up the net. He held it out to me. "Get two, if you can. They're probably too cold to come near the surface."

I looked down into the water as far as I could see. I saw no fish, but I searched for them mentally. I found a small school of them huddled together under a cluster of freshwater coral. I pulled up the two largest, much to their distress. I lifted the wriggling fishes into Ocelot's net. They flopped and jerked wildly. I squinted against the spattering water.

"Thanks," Ocelot said flatly.

He got up from the boulder and wandered back to the campfire spot. He had already gathered a heap of small branches into a pile. I did the lighting for him. I sat on the rock facing the firewood while Ocelot killed and cleaned the fish. I concentrated on the smallest pieces of bark at the bottom of the pile. I moved the molecules around so that the friction became explosive. The wood burst into flames. Ocelot jumped.

"Sorry," I said. "I should have warned you."

Ocelot pointed at the fire with his cleaning knife. "You did that?"

"It's a form of molecular levitation," I explained apologetically.

He sat back on his haunches, staring at the flames for a moment. Then he squinted at me.

"You could heat the wood to the point of ignition, but you couldn't keep yourself warm in your tent last night. How is that?" he asked.

"If I'd used this kind of friction, my tent would have caught fire. Besides, I don't have enough power to move a large area of molecules for longer than a few minutes."

He eyed me. "I'll fix your heating lamp before nightfall…unless you want to sleep in my tent," he offered.

I frowned, perturbed that he would say it like that. "Of course not," I retorted bitterly. We exchanged uneasy looks.

"I didn't mean it like that. I meant we could trade tents," he stated reproachfully.

"I'm sorry," I said abashedly.

"Forget I said anything. I'll have to watch what I say around you. You have a tendency to take things the wrong way. I'll fix your heater as soon as I can. Please don't read any double meanings into that." He frowned and jabbed at the fish.

"I didn't mean to insinuate…" I spoke strongly.

"Forget it. It's not important." He finished cleaning the fish and skewered them onto a stick. He wrapped them with a strip of green bark. He glanced up at me again. "Don't you have some objects to pass through each other or something? Why don't you go watch the news? This is going to take a while."

Feeling rightly scolded, I retreated to my tent. Later in the afternoon, Ocelot successfully repaired my heating lamp. That night, I curled up comfortably next to it while frigid winds brought snow.

I dreamed Ocelot was in the tent with me. I dreamed erotic, forbidden dreams. But these dreams were disturbed by the presence of others. Soon my nightmares of Alaban resumed. Alaban the wicked ruled my nightmares. He was no longer my friend. He was an evil assassin bent on ripping my would-be lover's heart from his body.

Even so, I could not retrain my heart to hate him.

Chapter 45: Year's End, A New Assignment

"Go on in. The General is waiting for you," the friendly Arborman clerk said.

I thanked her before moving down the hallway to the office on the right. General Croso's door was closed. I knocked softly. He beckoned me to enter. I stepped through the door to see a burly red Vermilion general leaning heavily on his desk and Ocelot sitting straight-backed at the edge of a thin chair. I greeted the General and bowed to him. He waved me to an available chair. I closed the door behind me.

General Croso resumed the briefing. He passed me a screen with a copy of the information he had already given Ocelot. A list of businesses and addresses appeared along with names, physical descriptions and general data of spy targets.

"You are to keep track of illegal trade activities in the following locations, especially those related to chemical arms. Wilbaht said you two completed a spy tour on Santer together. You'll be doing the same kind of work here, except you won't have to pretend to work for some other company. You're posing as Red Mesa Center computer personnel. If anyone asks, that's all you can tell them. You're not at liberty to disclose any details about your work since it has to do with the handling of sensitive information. If you've memorized your new identities, you should have no problem starting right away."

He noticed my apprehension.

"Yes, I know who you really are. You're safe with me. Wilbaht was a former partner of mine. We went through some tough times together. Not as tough as your latest battles, but he saved my hide on more than one occasion. I owed him a favor to say the least."

I relaxed.

General Croso fidgeted with a stylus as he spoke. "We're placing you in the middle of your target area. We've managed to put our foot in the door with a housing specialist in the Silver Zone, upper middle class. He's reserved an empty house for us, but we only have a couple of days to transact. We've scheduled an appointment for you both tomorrow morning at 0930 with the agent. His business address and info are in your data pack.

"This is high-priced real estate. You'll need a couple of million to qualify for purchase. The Organization doesn't supply that kind of monetary support to individual accounts on a midlevel assignment. That's why Wilbaht left you a little gift, or I should say a rather large gift. Show her."

The General motioned to Ocelot to show me the screen he was holding. Ocelot poked at it and then turned it to show me.

I gaped. "One point eight million to each of us? Is this a computer trick?"

The General chuckled. His round cheeks nearly buried his eyes when he laughed.

"No, my friend. Wilbaht always sent the real thing. He was one of a kind. Never will be another like him. There is a catch, though, about the housing. The real estate laws in the Silver Zone are very strict. You have to leave an eighty percent deposit upon signing for the house. By contract, only twenty percent can be refunded before the housing is paid in full. The cost is two point four million. You could pay the whole thing at once, but that would look suspicious. No underclass warrior has that kind of money. We'll front you a financing scheme.

"Now, the housing department won't allow any dual party purchase without a financial security agreement. Since you'll be playing husband and wife, they'll be looking for a financial marriage contract with your own signatures. The signatures have to match every housing document you sign before the agent.

"Once you're in, you can expect a five to seven month stay unless we need you for a final stakeout. You'll be reporting to me directly or to General Crane in my absence."

Ocelot asked, "Sir, is it really necessary to use our real names? Our new names, I mean? If anything goes wrong, we'll have to change our identities all over again."

"To set up a new set of names and ID's with all this banking and legal documentation would take more time than we have. Unless you can guarantee that you can set up a complete ID change for both of you between now and 0900 hours, I'd say yes, it is necessary. You're not in space anymore, Sub Professor. Time is not on your side. And you're not the one calling the shots here. Remember that." The General was perturbed.

"I'm sorry, sir. I got used to being part of the planning process. I didn't mean that I doubted your work," Ocelot hurried to say.

"It's not only my work. Sub Generals Wilbaht and Channol had a hand in this, too. I'm sure you'll want to honor their efforts," he added.

"Yes, sir," Ocelot pronounced humbly.

The General seemed satisfied with him.

Ocelot's question awakened my curiosity. "Sir, did Sub General Wilbaht say why he wanted us to do this particular assignment? He told us it was of personal importance to him, but didn't give us specific reasons."

"Yes. He said you've had direct experience with arms smuggling and that you would be the best ones to pick up on the movement of a particularly dangerous weapon you've been investigating. He suspected it would be moved here to Jawlcheen and trafficked through the mid-level smugglers, who won't know what it is they're moving. You see we've discovered the Regime keeps a few regional Jawlcheen businessmen in charge of local dealings. If we monitor the right man's communications, we can catch the weapon, and at the same time establish a thread of contacts up the line of the Regime's hierarchy. Our goal is to eliminate any threat from the weapon and to bring the whole Regime-related smuggling ring down on this planet with publicized evidence. Red Mesa and Boldoy have the highest level of arms dealings. We have Boldoy covered, but this town still has holes in our net at the business level. Since the best place to find a regional businessman around here is the Silver Zone, that's where we'll station you." The General tapped his twenty fingers together rhythmically. "In other words, in addition to the regular smuggling investigation, you'll be observing and tracking your neighbors. I hope you have a good sixth sense for this. We need evidence on the right people at the right place and time to make this work."

I sat straighter, eager to follow Wilbaht's hunch. If he'd sensed the weapon would pass through this region soon, I wanted to be there to see it happen and to clamp down on its proposed users so fast and hard that the whole Regime would squirm. The prospect of victory lit my mind.

"Sir, who will we be teamed with?" Ocelot asked.

"Physically, no one. You're on your own at the Silver Zone house. As far as a communications team, you'll be contacting both your former tutors and myself. We won't assign other warriors to your area. We're stretching our resources to cover normal needs as well as Regime espionage as it is." General Croso seemed edgy. "Sub Professor, you'll set up a work schedule for the two of you as soon as you're in the house. I expect an evenly divided workload."

Ocelot yielded formally.

"Sir, there won't be any role prep training with this assignment, will there?" I asked, recalling the uncomfortable ordeal on Santer.

"No. People in the Silver Zone tend to distance themselves from each other anyway. You'll fit in perfectly. Anything else? We're running short on time," Croso blurted.

"No, sir," I told him.

"Now all I need is a confirmation. Do you both accept this assignment?"

"Yes, sir," we both said solemnly.

"Good. Sub Professor Jainocelot, report to legal records office three. Go ahead and order the documents for signing. Warrior Sil, step forward. I'll change your pin."

I stood at his command. Ocelot bowed to him. He walked out of the room. The General attached the pin-encoding device to the side of my title pin and changed it to the appropriate title: Warrior Sil Rayfenix.

"Congratulations, Warrior. Wilbaht said you're an exceptional find. We're glad to have you with us," the General spoke warmly.

"Thank you, sir," I said to him.

We shook hands firmly.

In the legal records office, I found Ocelot waiting at a counter. Three busy clerks sifted through documentation on computers in the office behind it. Ocelot still read the projection screen on the white countertop in front of him. The legal clerk asked us for our names and identification. We used our fake work records and birth certificates on our palm computers as proof. The clerk scanned them and inserted their microcopies onto the face of the document. He read the agreement portion to us aloud.

"The undersigned individuals agree to all stipulations of this contract herein, witnessed by an authorized legal consultant of the planet Jawlcheen. We (the undersigned), do hereby promise to comply with the laws of financial marriage in which each undersigned party is responsible for payment of all collective monetary debts shared by said undersigned parties until the date of official dissolution of this same contract, which must be processed through a divorce contract procedure witnessed and approved by authorized legal consultant upon its signature. We, (the undersigned), do hereby promise to share legal residence and financial responsibilities for ourselves and any legal dependents of either party. We promise to adhere to these laws as dictated by the planet of Jawlcheen. Negligence or abuse of this law is subject to dual party financial arrest as dictated by Jawlcheen economic law of File MCLII Section 2349J.

"Please sign in the box below your name." The clerk held out a stylus for either of us to use.

Ocelot hesitated. I took the stylus from the man and signed under my new name: Sil Rayfenix of Liricos. I handed the stylus to Ocelot. He took it unwillingly. He deliberated a moment. Then he signed under his name: Jainocelot Quoren of Liricos. He handed the stylus back to the clerk.

He spoke to us again, this time informally. "Just come back whenever your assignment is up. Any of the legal clerks here is authorized to witness your second set of documents for you. It just takes one of you to sign and dissolve the original contract if you have no pending debts. Here's your copy of the screen. Good luck."

He linked the legal computer to each of our palm computers momentarily to give us each a copy of the document we had just signed. A pair of Vermilion warriors shuffled behind us in line, so we moved to let them by. They were apparently here for the same documentation.

"Talk about strange marriage rites," I murmured. "That was easier than applying for a shopping card."

"Something doesn't feel right about this. If Wilbaht hadn't requested it, I would ask for another assignment," Ocelot suddenly confessed.

I halted. "Do you think the General could be a double agent?"

"No. I trust him. I just don't like using my real name on that document. If either of us has to pay damages on something, we'll both end up paying for it by law. That doesn't seem fair if we were obligated to sign the contract as part of our job. And Wilbaht gave us that money for the purchase of the house. That means we'll be the actual owners of it, not the Organization. When our assignment is up, we'll have to deal with it as our own financial obligation. That's unheard of in Organization protocol."

"That's true, but this was an unusual request. Wilbaht asked us all to do this from his deathbed. They're making an exception for him. I'm honored that he would trust us with this level of responsibility," I reasoned.

"I wish he were still around. I'd like to ask him a few questions about it right now," Ocelot mused.

Sincerely, I agreed with Ocelot's reluctance about the assignment. If Wilbaht had not requested it, I wouldn't have accepted this assignment at all. I wanted to carry out my plan of staying away from Ocelot for his own protection. But I had to honor Wilbaht's last request. Like Ocelot, I too, thought of a few questions I wanted to ask him about it, if only he were still alive.

Croso said we could expect a five to seven month job. However, before his death, Wilbaht had told us the assignment had an undetermined time period and that we only needed to file the second set of documents when we wanted out. If Croso allowed me, I would end the job whenever I felt Alaban was near. Surely he would reveal his presence to me when he returned to Jawlcheen in six months or so. If I was still assigned as Ocelot's partner at that time, my vile dreams and visions could still come true. I hoped I was destined to find Alaban and not the other way around.

The next morning, we went together to meet with the housing specialist. He was a gaunt Vermilion in a dark red suit with pointy shoulders. He moved quickly and jauntily, as if he had consumed too much caffeine recently. He spoke in a heightened whisper. Each time he began a sentence, he squinted his eyes. By the end of each sentence, his eyes widened dramatically. I wasn't sure if I should feel sorry for the man or laugh at him.

The pointy man escorted us in a cab to the Silver Zone and to the house. The streets here were of cobblestone. High, white walls and security gates surrounded all the homes. From the tops of the walls hung vines of multicolored flowers. Some gates were decorated with wide viewing windows protected with intertwined metal bars. The housing specialist took us to one such gate. He opened it with an electronic bar key and led us through.

To either side of us, we saw a green garden three meters deep and nine meters wide. Before us stood the gleaming white house. Its shape reminded me of an elongated version of our ship, except it did not lean to one side. It was a square-based pyramid with a flat top. A metal security frame similar to the one at the gate protected the deep blue front door.

The red man opened the blue door for us and then handed us each a key. Inside and to our right, a platform stepped down to a kitchen and dining area. A simple table and chairs graced the center of the red floor. In front of us, through the open wall of the kitchen area and beyond the platform where we stood, more steps led to a broad, sunlit room. The sunroom contained benches and potted plants. Through the glass wall of the sunroom, we saw another small garden and a high, white exterior wall. The sunroom was wide enough to practice personal defense forms. I looked forward to using it. To our left was a small bathroom. Slightly to our left and in front of us was a stairway leading up to the second floor. Underneath the stairway was a door. The man showed us it led to a master bedroom and connected bath.

Upstairs, he showed us a second and third bedroom, each with its own bath as well. There was also a small den or office in the upstairs area with a stairway leading to the roof. The roof was a flat patio area with concave walls and a few pieces of simple furniture. The man then showed us the water recycling system, which watered and fertilized the garden. He also showed us air circulation systems; solar power collectors above the sunroom, garbage disposal and waste reclaim systems, which fed the house electrical generator, and a few other simple amenities. The house was completely furnished but not decorated. We only needed to bring our personal effects to move in.

This house rivaled the testing preparation apartments at the C.A.T.T. Center on Sor3. I hoped I would not become spoiled with such luxury.

"Now, we have all the required information from the Red Mesa Organization Center Finance Department here. All we need to do is sign these agreement documents." The man pursed his lips in what I thought was supposed to be his version of a smile.

He went over each document page with us briefly before we signed them. There were a total of fifty-four different document screens to sign, detailing everything from banking information to pet and garden care

490

agreements. When we finally finished the ordeal, the housing specialist pursed his lips at us compassionately. He left us with congratulations.

We returned to the Center for our things. Ocelot took the master bedroom downstairs. I took a room upstairs. We turned the upstairs den into a computer center and home base office for spy work. Ocelot set up a work schedule for us both, as Croso had specified, which ended up looking almost like a ship's schedule, only with an extra hour of free time and without a mandatory time for meals and exercise.

During the next few weeks, we systematically met our neighbors. Most of them invited us into their homes for a few minutes. We successfully bugged each house we visited. Some neighbors politely examined us, said a few niceties and then made an excuse to get rid of us. Others were intrigued by our jobs and invited us to dinners where they scrutinized us about our political opinions as warriors.

Apart from neighborhood social drills, we concentrated heavily on our possible targets and locations through informational espionage. There was too much information to sort through by ourselves, especially with a wide variety of possible targets around town and twenty-seven neighborhood houses on full-time detection. Ocelot set up a multiple scanning computer system, which "listened" for key words or phrases. Even so, we ended up with several pages of conversation bytes every day.

Additionally, we were expected to go out to inspect all target areas in person. Each day we left the office to scour an area on our list in order to get a feel for the smuggling locations, relying on sixth sense to know if we were following a good lead. I covered certain areas and people on one side of town while he observed others.

We also went almost daily to the Center, where we enjoyed contact with our former tutors. General Croso became a friendly, yet time-conscious guide for us as well. Ocelot and I did not spend much more time together than we had on the ship, since I tried hard to keep away from him, especially in the house.

During our first few weeks on the new assignment, we spent time together in the kitchen cooking and cleaning or in the garden tending the plants. Our physical closeness in the kitchen became too tempting for me, so I started exercising while he cooked and ate. I explained away my change of habit by saying I had more energy at that hour of the day, so it would be better for me to eat later. He complained that he would be bored without conversation during his meal. He offered to change his afternoon schedule to match mine. I rudely refused, adding that I preferred to work out alone.

Once a week, we ate together at a café close to a point on our list. Here, we kept conversation to non-work related topics to blend with those around us. Too often I found myself gazing at him with absolute love and admiration. Each time I caught myself doing this, I worried that he would notice. Finally, I suggested we limit our conversations and concentrate on the people around us, which was what we were being paid to do. He became offended. He pouted and complained that nothing was happening anyway.

We came up with several leads during the next weeks, but these only brought us to dead ends. I remained patient, but Ocelot became frustrated. He suggested that we rotate our area schedule so we could each go out to read the atmosphere of the locations that the other had already checked. Again, our espionage was wasted. We sensed that nothing out of the ordinary had happened, was happening, nor would happen in any of the places we scoured. None of our neighbors engaged in any lascivious activities, except a few underhanded business deals, but none of these had to do with our Regime targets or smuggling.

The only successful research we did was on the computer. Just as on Santer and Sor3, I discovered import cargo discrepancies, some of which involved small amounts of chemicals used for conventional bombing, but none of which would be used on a large scale. We traced this chemical theft, not to a Regimist, but to a Fitmalo military rebel. Although this fell outside our directive, I typed a report on it anyway, just to have some work to show. Ocelot became even more exasperated.

The next afternoon, we tried a café close to the house. It was lavishly decorated with projected scenery on every wall and fake plants between each row of tables. It was meant to be a romantic spot. Our table stood near a fake window overlooking the projected green valley and a puffing volcano. I liked the scene, even though it was completely contrived. Pre-recorded birds flew through the picture. The image glowed, illuminating everyone around it with an unnatural purple and green light.

We observed the people in the café. There were not many at this hour of the third day of the week, but I stayed alert in case a suspect showed up. I sensed a few bad vibes from some of the beings in the room, but I did not feel suspicious of any of them. I commented this to Ocelot. He agreed with me.

A Vermilion waiter brought us our food and drinks. He made small talk about the weather and how we liked the atmosphere here. He hoped we would become regular customers. He was overly friendly.

"You are 'together', right?" he asked nosily.

"Yes. We're married," Ocelot said, annoyed by his chattiness.

"To each other, I hope," the waiter kidded with a smile.

"Yes, to each other," Ocelot retorted.

492

"I'm just playing. I didn't mean to make you mad. Please enjoy your meal," he said brightly.

"Thank you," I said firmly, hoping he would leave us alone.

We ate slowly. The café filled with business people from the office building nearby. We watched them sensitively. The same waiter cajoled and annoyed most other patrons as well. None seemed to be people we needed to keep tabs on. I began to wonder about it all. Ocelot seemed uneasy, too. We finished our meal and ordered a light fruit dessert. The waiter asked about the food. I told him it was delicious, which was true. He was delighted. He brought our desserts and water, showering us with unwanted attention. Finally, Ocelot asked him to please leave us alone for a while.

"Certainly, sir. Just wave if you want anything," the waiter said with a smile.

We were glad to be rid of him. We waited around for half an hour. The café would close in a few minutes. The business crowd had dwindled to a few late drinkers and some young couples on dates. The place was totally devoid of smugglers or evil agents. It was a simple café without dramatics or intrigue. Once again, we had waited all evening for nothing. I told Ocelot what I was thinking. He agreed.

"Wilbaht invested millions in this project and we still have nothing to show for it. We're just waiting for the criminals to cross our path." His voice showed he was tired and depressed. I had noticed his face had become more and more resentful during the evening.

"This whole setup is ironic." He cast a dull eye on the sparsely filled café. "We were ordered to do a job that keeps leading us in circles. We were ordered to continue on as partners. We were ordered to buy a house. We were ordered to sign legal documents using our real names. For what? All so we can sit here and wait for the Regime to show up under our noses?" He pouted.

"Then we have to deal with people like that waiter," he added, glaring after the flagrant man and scoffing at what he'd said. "'Are we married to each other?' 'Yes, we are.' We have to tell that to everyone we meet. You know what the irony is? The irony is we think we're lying about it to keep our cover. But we're not fooling anyone. The joke's not on them. Those documents were real. The joke is on us. We are legally bound by financial marriage. They're not the suckers. We are. We're stuck with each other. We're trapped in this contract and it's driving me *crazy*." He flexed both arms and squeezed his fists tightly to illustrate his exasperation. Then he pounded his chest once and let the fists rest solidly on the tabletop. "I'm sick and tired of waiting," he announced.

I was hurt. He felt he had been tricked into an unwanted obligation with me. I suppressed my emotions to reassure him.

"Hey, don't worry about it. You know surveillance can sometimes take months. As far as the financial agreement goes, if you're worried about money, don't be. Wilbaht left us more than we'll ever need. At the end of the job, we'll be able to sign the dissolution document with no problem. We're not in debt. Besides, even if you had outstanding debts I'd be willing to help pay them off. You're my partner. You would do the same for me. Wouldn't you?"

"Well, yes. Not just because you're my partner. You saved my life. I'm indebted to you. And more than that, it's...This past year..." He stopped and started to speak again, but then sat quiet and pensive before me.

"We've been through a lot together," I suggested. I felt satisfied that my words would cheer him up a little. Instead, he changed his manner entirely. He became aggravated.

"What do you want, Sil? If you don't want to be partnered with me anymore, why don't you sign off on the contract and apply for a new assignment?"

I opened my eyes wide to him, and then slowly looked down abashedly. "Is that what you want?"

"No. I just get the idea that you want to get away from me...forever," he said gruffly.

"What? No. Look. I have to stay with you right now. It was my last promise to Wilbaht. Besides, you've been..." I searched for unemotional words, "...instrumental in shaping my career this past year. You helped me through hard times. You're a good partner. Why would I want to get away from you? We get along fine. We're friends."

"We're *friends*? If we're friends, then why do you refuse to talk to me anymore?" he demanded.

"What do you mean? I'm talking to you right now." I pretended innocence.

"The only reason you're talking to me is because all our possible targets have left the building and we're still on the clock." He grated on. "Are my opinions so beneath you that you can't stand to carry on a conversation with me off the job?"

"No. I respect your opinions. I just don't want to argue with you, that's all," I countered. "If I've acted that way, I apologize."

He stared at me in frustration. "So we're friends."

"Yes."

"You're sure?"

"Yes. Look, if you want to talk about something, go ahead," I offered, genuinely miffed.

He sat staring at me for many uncomfortable seconds. I began to think perhaps he didn't really have anything to say after all. Then his eyes grew fiery. I worried what cataclysmic argument brewed behind them.

"Would you still say we're friends if the space station had never happened?" he asked.

I leaned back in my seat. I thought unblinkingly for a moment before replying.

"I'd like to think we'd be friends and not enemies. I remember you didn't like me so well before I brought you back from the dead."

"When didn't I like you?" Ocelot asked sternly.

I knitted my brow. "Obviously you have a poor memory," I evaded.

"When didn't I like you? I always liked you." Ocelot clenched his fists on the tabletop as if he were preparing to strike out at me.

I regarded him as if he'd just told a stupid joke. "What are you talking about? You used to treat me like I was some kind of repulsive monster." I reminded him of the pre-op training on Santer, the way he'd acted like a jerk to me in the Keres helion, and his extremist views against physical contact outside sparring.

I crossed my arms indignantly. "You won't even sit in the same seat with me in a cab. You act like I'm contagious, or inferior." I tossed my hands up and then rested them at the sides of my empty plate. "I don't know why I'm saying this. I'm not going to cancel the contract. All right? I'm sorry if you thought so. Just forget I said anything. We should get going."

I laid my napkin to one side and nearly pushed my chair away to stand when I saw his ill temper draw away from his face like a lifted veil. He leaned forward, sliding one hand over the table toward me to stop my motion.

"I never meant it like that." He stammered, trying to find a good explanation. "Listen, I'm sorry I was a jerk to you, Sil. Didn't you ever wonder why I acted that way?" he asked.

"Daily," I stated.

Ocelot leaned forward. "Alaban," he said.

I regarded him inquisitively but defensively. "Alaban? What about him?"

"From the time I saw him on Sor3, I knew he was trouble. Then he kept reappearing in messages and in the investigation, always influencing you. I wanted to warn you about him, but I couldn't prove anything then. Then he showed up on Santer. He was like a damned plague. When I was trapped in the catacombs with Wilbaht, he told me he'd taken Alaban to see you at the apartment. I couldn't believe it. This *plague* was invading my life. And Wilbaht, the man I trusted most in the world; *he* was the one who let him in. He let him into my apartment. He encouraged him to go out with my partner. He let him get away with murder, *literally*, and still accepted him. I knew he was wrong but I couldn't convince him otherwise. I warned him. I almost *threatened* him to keep him away from us." He sighed, shaking his head.

"I overstepped my boundaries with him. That's why he punished me during our leave time. But Wilbaht of all people should have known he was bad news. And you," he sneered. "'The talented and virtuous rookie.' He played you. He played you for everything he could get. He betrayed us all and tried to drag you down with him."

I stared at him in awe. This was why he hadn't come near me. I wasn't the one who repelled him. It was Alaban. Just knowing I was so closely associated with the man he hated most had kept him at a distasteful distance.

He ranted on. "I cannot comprehend how you could be in love with a *sick, evil* bastard like that. Even if he did accept the job with Teradom to protect you, I can't imagine why in God's name you would still want him. He's done more damage to you this year than any accident or battle. He is a snake from Hell. How can you be in love with him?"

"I'm not," I said simply.

Ocelot gave me an excruciating look. "You said…"

"I said I'd always love him." I faced down at the table. "I'm not *in* love with him. I never was," I admitted.

"What?" Ocelot mouthed silently.

"I'm sorry I wasn't completely honest with you before. I love Alaban as a friend and a spiritual twin. I know you only see him as a killer, but there is so much about him you don't know. He's not evil. He can be a good man. Yes, he's an assassin. That's the job he was given. He didn't want it. He couldn't get out of it, at least not alive. But he's not what you think. The Alaban I know is tempered and kind-hearted. He's funny. He's affectionate. He…"

Ocelot cut into my speech. "No. He wasn't affectionate. He was possessive. He was power-hungry. I saw how he hung on you all the time on Santer. He only wanted to control you."

"You're wrong. I liked the way he hung onto me. It wasn't control. It was need. And I needed him. He was my best friend."

I paused to swallow and frown sadly. I confessed something else to myself as well as Ocelot. "But now…I'm afraid of him. And I'm afraid *for* him. I'm afraid he'll never find peace and he'll always blame me. But Ocelot, even though you're my partner, I don't want you to feel obligated to protect me from him. When he comes back to Jawlcheen, I have to face him alone. It's the only way to get him out of there."

496

Ocelot buried his face in his hands in frustration. "Oh, this is craziness," he muttered. He ran his fingers through his hair and then slapped the table with his palms angrily.

"Sil, listen to me," he ordered. "Let him go. If you're afraid of him, it's for a good reason. He is dangerous to you. Don't you get it? It was a mistake for you to get involved with him in the first place. Maybe you want to set things right, but you can't undo that mistake by risking your life. You're talking about attempting to rescue the Regime leader's top bodyguard from the job that he chose. By Organization rules, you'd have to climb three ranks to even propose an operation like that. Even then, it would never be approved. Your odds of a successful mission would be close to none. They'd send a sniper team after him before they'd let any single warrior try something like that. What you're wishing for can't happen. Will you please accept the fact and let it go?"

I resisted sternly, silently.

"Don't wrap your whole life around one mistake you made. Listen, I've made huge mistakes, but I put them behind me. I had to. And so do you."

A strained curiosity rose in me. "What huge mistakes?"

Ocelot reclined again in his chair. He stared into the prerecorded volcanic scene to collect his thoughts. When he turned back to me, his face showed determined control. He recounted the story, shaking his head in regret from time to time.

"All right. I'll tell you one. I had a girlfriend on Sor3. I was stupid. I wanted to prove I was independent enough to live away from Organization housing and have her live with me. She was a different species: Vermilion. The whole thing was destined to fail from the beginning. She was always jealous, obsessive to the point of insanity. She would accuse me of having other girlfriends. We fought constantly. It was hell with her. She finally took up my own sword against me. If she'd been much stronger, I could have been paralyzed or killed. She left that day and never contacted me again. It took that crazed act of violence to make me realize that she and I had no reason to be together. We were just pretending to have a life we wished we could have with someone else. The whole affair was a huge mistake, but I didn't dwell on it long. Yes, I was angry and I felt like an imbecile. But I took it. I learned the hard way. I picked myself up. I kept going—without looking back." He ended the story with a hint of pride.

Ocelot's frustration abated. He sat with his hands on the table as if he had just folded a hand of cards. "Look, when you make mistakes in your personal life, don't beat yourself up over them. Learn from them and move on. That episode of your life is over. It's time to start something new."

A calm settled in around us. He gazed at me with kind eyes that reminded me of our fatherly advisor.

"Do you understand what I mean?" he asked.

I nodded. We sat quietly for a few moments. I felt proud of him for finally revealing the story of his scar. I also felt that he was right about starting something new.

I folded my hands together and leaned my cheek on them. I watched the birds fly through the computer-generated scenery for the fifteenth time. Their existence was patterned in a repetitive loop. Their never-ending passage reminded me of my own recurring nightmares of Alaban. Like the repetitious scene before me, they would not end unless they were shut off completely. They needed a source of energy to exist. The source of my dreams was my own fear of the inevitable. To cut this source of energy, I needed to defeat the fear. The only way I could do that would be to face the fear once and for all; to set out on my own to find Alaban and end this right away, in spite of Ocelot's advice. Logically, he was right, but my celestial bond to Alaban hailed from an authority greater than the entire Organization. I decided to leave this cycle of misery tonight. I sat straight, motivated by this new prospect. I rested my hands on the table.

"Ocelot, I think you're right. We should end this contract and move on. It's for the best," I said tentatively.

His reaction startled me. He recoiled and seemed to panic. "No, I didn't mean that you should quit the assignment." His nervousness and frustration returned to him.

I poised at my seat, perplexed.

"Listen, I have to tell you something. I don't know how you'll react, but you have to hear it because it's the truth."

He had my attention and curiosity, although I was wary of something dangerous that might come from his next words.

"Wilbaht was the greatest warrior of our time," he began.

I agreed.

"But he also set us up," he continued.

"What do you mean?" I asked rigidly.

"The order to sign the marriage contract using our real names, the house, the money, this assignment; all this he set up because he wanted us to stay together. He...He loved us as if we were his own family." Ocelot leaned forward to confess further. "Sil, he wanted us to be married, not just as a cover for this assignment, but for real."

My skin crawled. "I don't believe it. He couldn't have told you that."

498

"No, he didn't tell me that. He just told me to adhere to the contract, but after seeing what the contract really is, what am I supposed to think?" Ocelot asked, flustered.

"No. Wilbaht would never make decisions for us about matters of the heart. He wouldn't set us up like that."

"I'm sure he did," Ocelot stated.

"I'm sure he *didn't*. As much as I cared for Wilbaht, even if he had given an order like that, which I know he didn't, I wouldn't feel obligated to follow it. I'm not giving up my personal rights. That's completely unfair!" I said, speaking a little louder with each statement.

Ocelot held up a hand to me to tell me to quiet down.

I hissed at him, "If Wilbaht had wanted that, he would have said so, and he didn't. He would never force us to do something that would infringe upon our personal rights. He did love us as his own family, and because of that he respected our rights to free will. Don't tell me you think we should follow those orders, because they don't exist."

Utterly distressed, I felt Ocelot might be right, but I had already made plans to be alone and with good reason. If this was a test of temptation, it was a very treacherous one.

Ocelot's face showed indecision.

"Anyway, why would he assign us to do something like that? Just because he cared about us and we're the same species? I don't think so," I continued, realizing I'd left a loophole in my argument. I stood quickly, behaving as if I were offended by the whole conversation.

"I'm going home," I told him. I marched off towards the exit. He followed, but had to pay the waiter first. I did not stop to wait for him.

I left the café and ran down the stone steps to the sidewalk below. Ocelot ran after me. We walked several meters distance from each other through the dark, dusty, cobbled streets. As we rounded the corner to one narrow, deserted road, Ocelot moved in close to me. I shuddered.

"Sil," he spoke. He lightly touched my shoulder.

I held up my fist as if to block him. I quickened my pace. His hand slid from me. He slowed his steps. I hurried faster. I could feel him staring after me. I shuddered again. When I saw he was not in a hurry to catch up with me, I slowed down a little.

We arrived at the street of our house. Our house—it seemed unbelievable to think of it that way. I wondered if Wilbaht really meant for it to be ours. I wondered if he really was forcing us together. I unlocked the main gate to let us in. Ocelot followed slowly. He closed the gate as I opened the interior door. I left it open for him and quickly ran up the stairs into my room.

I hurriedly locked myself in my bathroom to insure that he wouldn't follow me. I knew I couldn't avoid him for long, but it was too late in the evening to start any discussions. I heard him enter my room and then leave it again. Soon I heard water running to the downstairs bath. I sighed heavily with relief.

I stayed in the bath for a very long time, hoping he would bathe quickly and go to bed without finding me available to talk. As the water drained away to the garden reserve tank, I tried to imagine the water as my anxiety leaving me, but this only helped to calm me a little. I dried myself and left the bath in a white robe.

I took five paces into my room. I stopped abruptly. Ocelot stood before me in a T-shirt and exercise pants. His hair was still wet from his bath. He looked so handsome despite his attire. I continued toweling my hair. He stared at me with piercing eyes. I hung the towel around my shoulders. He said nothing. He only studied my face.

"Ocelot, it's late. I thought we finished this discussion. You're not supposed to be in my room." I stepped toward my wardrobe, which was just past him in front of me.

He caught me by the wrist. He stopped me. I stood tensely gazing into his face. I almost pulled away from him but his eyes implored me not to. His touch softened. A chill flew through me.

Chapter 46: The Beast

He spoke to me somewhat nervously, but his presence was commanding. "Stop. Don't run away from me. You stand here and listen. Wilbaht did want us together. He knew something about us that we didn't want to admit."

He held my wrist in one hand and then cupped my knuckles gently in the other. I gritted my teeth in resistance as he spoke. "I didn't want to admit it. I thought you were in love with Alaban. Now you say you're not.

But you are in love. You won't admit it, but I know you are. I know it. If you're not in love with Alaban, then who are you in love with?"

My throat constricted, prohibiting speech.

He began to caress my hand tenderly. "You think I only see you as a partner. You think I don't want to touch you. Is that why you've stayed away from me?"

My nerve endings cringed in fear and anticipation. I stared at him with dread. My face flushed in horror.

"You're more than just a partner to me, Sil. Believe me, I do want to touch you." He pulled my hand close to his heart. "I do. That's why this assignment is driving me crazy. I don't want to front a phony marriage with you. I don't want a financial marriage by Jawlcheen law. It's not real. I want it to be real. I want to be married to you, truthfully. I want *you*, body and soul. Sil, I love you. I'm in love with you. I want to touch you. I want to kiss you. I want to mate with you. I want to touch you every day of my life." He brought my hand up to his face and kissed my knuckles. "Sil, do you love me? Will you be my wife? My real wife. Be my partner for life. I'll be the perfect mate for you. I'll make love to you. God knows how much I want to touch you. I'll prove it to you right now."

I stood, statuesque before him. I could not speak. My eyes burned. My face tingled. My stomach felt as if I had swallowed a large rock. He saw my insecurity.

"I love you." He turned my hand and pressed my palm and then my wrist to his mouth with passion. He pressed the hand to his jaw. I couldn't believe this. Tears budded at the corners of my eyes.

He looked into my rouged face nervously, but with kind, sensitive, and loving eyes. He lifted a hand to caress my face. Was this just another vision? He stepped in close to me. His hand held my cheek while his thumb followed the form of my lips. His eyes changed from kind nervousness to driven arousal. He leaned down to kiss me, but I took a step backwards.

"Sil?" Nervousness returned to his eyes. He turned my hand at his cheek to kiss it again, but I wrenched away from him in blind madness.

"No! You can't be in love with me! You only want to follow orders from Wilbaht!" I watched his disillusioned face recede from me as I stumbled backward, weakly grasping the wall to keep my trembling balance.

I panted, fighting to keep my mind. "You are my partner as a warrior. I forbid you to follow Wilbaht's order! You stay away from me!" I retched.

I flew resiliently to my wardrobe and yanked out my combat uniform. I pulled the pants on under my robe and quickly turned my back to him to throw off the robe and don the uniform shirt as fast as I could.

Opposing sides of my conscience tore at each other. I grabbed my weapons and boots. I blinked back the wanton tears. I strapped the boots on as fast as I could.

"I'm not following orders from Wilbaht. I'm telling you the truth. Why...? Where are you going?" he asked, sorely disheartened.

"I'm going downstairs to practice my forms," I said, realizing how ridiculous it sounded after a confession of this proportion. "Don't follow me. Just leave! I do not want to see you again tonight or any other night. This assignment is over!" I roared.

I left the wardrobe open. I left my robe on the floor. I passed Ocelot with broad steps, repeating to him not to follow me and that I didn't want to see him. My voice quavered as I sailed down the stairs. Despite my warning, Ocelot's footsteps pattered on the stairs after me. My skin felt as if it were infested with writhing centipedes. I jittered with fear. My gasping breath drowned out his attempt to reason with me. I heard him call my name. I scarcely heard him ask me again not to run from him. Still I raced away from him at full speed. At the foot of the stairs, I turned and pounded the floor toward the practice room. As I neared his doorway, he caught me by the arm. I leapt away from his grasp. He clutched at me again. This time I whisked around to face him in a fighting stance.

"Touch me with that hand again and I'll cut it off!" I roared.

A pitiable, desperate visage showed before me. "This is not a directive. I'm acting on my own. I'm being honest with you," he said.

"No, you're not! You're lying! Stop it! If you come any closer, I will draw weapons and fight you until you leave or die!"

"You don't want that," he said.

"No. I don't want any part of this! I never thought I'd have to defend myself against my own partner!" I yelled between shuddering breaths. "You were the last man I could trust. Now it turns out this was a hoax, too! You have offended me to no end! I refuse to work with you anymore! You either leave this house tonight or I will! I will not stay in the same living space with you."

He took another step toward me. I retreated, baring my fists at him.

His eyes reflected the wounds of his heart. "Sil, I'm not against you. I want you..."

"I don't care what you want! I don't want you!" I lied forcefully. "Stay away from me! Get out!" I spun and dashed away from him.

I touched down on the sunroom floor and pitched the benches and chairs up into the air above me. I flipped them into a pile, walling up the landing that led from the foyer to the sunroom. I levitated the potted plants from the sunroom corners to the base of the makeshift wall.

"Get out!" I thundered again.

I stood vibrating in the middle of the room, watching after the pile of benches to make sure he didn't remove them. He stood, stricken, behind the barricade. I could almost hear the sound of his heart breaking along with my own. If only he would break down the wall and defeat my pretended rage. But I had shoved him away at his most vulnerable moment. My forbidden dream had come true. He had opened his heart to me. But in this accursed entrapment I could not embrace him.

"If you don't leave, I will," I pronounced once more.

My chest heaved with duress. I wanted to tear apart the barricade, collapse at his feet, and beg forgiveness, but my terrible decision was definite. I remained, trembling, in the middle of the sunroom, watching the object of my greatest temptation sadly fade away.

His shadow pivoted and then paused in his doorway. He did not chase me again. A sliver of relief dissolved into my fear, but angst and hope still bubbled together in my mind. My heart frothed with unrequited yearning for him. I stifled it as best I could as I turned my back to him and assumed a ready position.

He entered his bedroom as I began a mockery of my personal defense forms. I sensed him gather a few things into a sling bag as I pushed my worthless body to perform the routine. I skipped forms one and two. I ran through forms three through five sloppily. Bitterness pulsed through my veins and squeezed through my heart's valves as self-hatred.

I felt him stand again at his door, sling bag over one slumped shoulder. He deliberated at his threshold. Nervousness and fear lapped at my mind. He stayed watching me for a few moments. Opposing sides of my being clashed. My emotions begged him to come to me, yet my sense of duty still supported the wall between us. I heard him rustle his bag and tread to the front door. Again, he paused to look back. Sadness and grief ebbed and rose like a tide inside me. The front door conspicuously opened and closed, depositing him into the lonesome night. Regret swam through me. Anguish splashed inside me as I moved.

"He's gone," I whispered to myself, first in reassurance, and then in lament. "He's gone."

I moved badly through the rest of the hand and foot techniques, daunted by this torment. In forms six and seven, I forced myself to give more attention to my movements. By form ten, I controlled my body, but my heart and mind were as spilling liquid. At the beginning of the first sword form, I drew the silvery weapon and stopped. I gazed at it tearfully. A droning sound of crashing waves filled my mind. The inset rubies, the etched designs, the fine craftsmanship...Ocelot had given so much of himself to make this lethal beauty, and he had given it to me. I dropped the fantastic sword to the floor. It smacked loudly as it hit. I felt as if I were drowning. The current of overwhelming defeat sucked me under into an ocean of despair.

I knelt before the sword. I stared through wavering tears at the blades.

"Oh, God! What do you want from me? What do you want me to do? Command me. Tell me where to go, what to say and do. I am lost. Is there no sign to guide me through this? Should I suffer? Is that what you need me to do? Because I am suffering, dear God. I am. What should I do? What?"

I rested my forehead on the floor just short of the sword. I let my tears shower the wooden floor. My chest heaved. Echoing sobs escaped by throat. I reached out and touched the flat blade of the sword. My cries ceased, spooked by a bright flash.

A swirling burst of glittering sunlight blazed up at me. The broken pane of glass I'd seen so many times before fitted its jagged crystals together into one solid circle, which sailed up at me from within the sword. It engulfed my body. It swallowed me into a surreal dimension.

Suddenly, I found myself standing at the edge of a dirt path, quiet and still. My familiar reality, like my tears, was temporarily suspended. I observed my surroundings like a newborn creature, wide-eyed and bewildered. All heartsick ailment was cast aside. This was a realm apart, far above all worldly conundrums, and yet I perceived that these new surroundings held the solution to my troubles.

The path before me wound off into a thick bracken of forest. I stood alone. I looked around me. A high wall of granite soared above and behind me. To either side along the base of the wall grew snarls of poisonous thorn bushes. The path snaked in front of me. The sky above glowed in a bright red sunset, but it soon darkened to twilight. No stars hung in this sky. The forest blackened before me.

I stepped forward. I closed my eyes to better sense my surroundings, but I sensed nothing. I opened my eyes again. The forest shifted in a breeze. Noises of animals played through the canopy like a rain of sound bursts. Their cacophony muffled my crunching footsteps. I heard monkeys, owls, bats, frogs, and other night animals, although I could not perceive their whereabouts. I edged my way down the path carefully. The forest was pitch black now. I stumbled on a tree root and nearly fell. As I caught my balance, a strong breeze jiggled the branches of the trees. The leaves made a thunderous whisper as they all brushed together at once. Tree trunks groaned. Animals shrieked. Darkness began to give way to dawn.

My eyes adjusted to the changing light. The path was narrow but easy to follow. Noises from night creatures faded. Day creatures took their cue. Birds squawked and twittered around me. The undergrowth shrouded parts of the path. I picked my way through it as daylight filtered through the branches.

From up ahead I heard a loud moan from a large animal. It sounded injured. I quickened my pace. I rounded a cluster of tree trunks to find a huge lion, larger than life size. He was nearly as tall as my shoulder. His golden brown fur rippled over sharply defined muscles. He groaned in agony.

He was caught around one front paw by a poacher's string snare. The harder the lion pulled, the tighter the loop became. He jerked it backward with his full weight, causing himself more pain and distress. Above him, nestled in the crook of a tree, jutted the handle of a sharp knife.

I approached the lion. He looked at me with the strangest longing eyes. He knew I wanted to help him. He stayed still as I moved around him to the tree. I grabbed the knife. I held out my hand to show him I meant him no harm. He already knew. Gently, I cut through the cord and pulled it from his foot. When he saw he was free, he lay down beside me to lick the hurt paw. I embedded the knife in the dirt and knelt by him, hoping he was meant to be my guide through this vision. The sun rose high above. I ventured to pet the creature, but he flinched and regarded me with wild eyes. A low growl resonated from his throat.

Suddenly, a loud cry rang through the branches above. A large speckled owl alighted near us on a low-hanging branch. It hooted at us. The lion stood. It gave a guttural set of short calls to the owl. The owl flew at my face. I ducked. The owl disappeared into the woods behind me.

The lion walked to me. He nudged my hand with his nose. I slowly lifted the hand to stroke his mane between his ears. Then I gently retracted my hand. The lion licked it. I had a flashing memory of Ocelot kissing my hand. This lion was meant to represent him. I watched the lion in awe. He backed away from me. He sat down, straight as a statue. He stared at me, waiting.

I wasn't sure what he was waiting for me to do, but I felt I had to keep going along the path. I stepped towards it. The lion stood to follow me. He would not be my guide, then, but a companion. We stepped through the underbrush along the winding path. The light began to fade again.

Soon we heard a bellow from a creature even larger than the lion. Fearfully, I continued on the path. The lion followed a few paces behind until we approached a clearing. The lion leapt in front of me, preventing me from advancing too quickly. He crouched in a hunting position and sneaked forward silently. Another loud bellow resounded from the clearing. I followed the lion to hide behind a tree.

I peered around the trunk to survey the clearing. The new sunset left an orange glow on the nightmarish scene. In the center of the clearing sat a monster, part bull, part dragon. The face and body were like those of a bull, but massive scaly wings branched out from his back and a long spiked tail whipped around him. He was at least twice as tall as me, and more muscular and foreboding than the lion.

Blue monkeys gathered all around him. They pawed at each other and at him. They sat on him, climbed on his back, taunted him, surrounded him, and chattered carelessly. A monkey on his shoulder screamed to the monster, and pointed furiously at one nearby. The bull dragon bent his head down and pierced the second monkey fast through the middle with one sharp horn. It died almost instantly, crumpling to the ground. The first monkey cackled with glee. The monster looked skyward and bellowed in sadness. It was Alaban, in complete misery. I covered my mouth in shock.

Time after time, the monkey on his shoulder ordered him to kill. He always obeyed. He always grieved. The monster stood to reach another victim, but could not step far. He was fettered by a heavy shackle, which was chained to a ring and post in the ground. Around the king monkey's neck hung the key. I had to get it.

I tried to levitate, but could not. Here, I had no power. Suddenly, my sword appeared in my hand. I turned to the lion. He remained crouched in the brush. Twilight set in. I retraced our steps back to the thick woods. The lion followed me. When I stopped, he stopped. I caressed his ear lovingly.

"You stay here. I have to face him alone," I spoke.

The lion growled.

"Please don't follow me," I told him.

The lion lay down and rolled onto his side. He moaned sadly. I knelt to pat his shoulder.

"I do love you, but I'm afraid for your life."

Just then, the owl returned. It hooted loudly. The lion lifted himself to face it. The wise owl flapped its wings but did not call again. Who could this be but Wilbaht? I spoke his name. The owl bobbed its head. The lion moaned sadly, but stayed put. The woods blackened.

I turned back to the clearing, which was now lined with torches. The monkeys huddled restlessly around the bull dragon. The poor, miserable beast swung his head sadly from side to side and groaned. The king monkey rested atop his shoulders.

I crept forward into the clearing as carefully as possible, but dry leaves cracked beneath me. Sentinel monkeys around the perimeter of the clearing screeched an alert to my presence. I charged forward desperately, attacking all who got in my way. I ran toward my old friend fearlessly. He stood excitedly when he saw me. He tossed away the apes that clung to him. He roared at them and sliced through many with his horns and tail. Soon every monkey in the clearing and in the woods came after us. They pounced at me from every side. Some clung to my uniform, scratching and biting madly. I flung them off, defending myself with the sword.

I finally arrived at the bull dragon's side. He bellowed wildly. He raked away the monkeys that clung to me. I wound up standing below him, sheltered by his mass. We fought against the attacking apes together. We stood strong, but the apes kept coming. We were outnumbered. Soon I realized I had little chance of saving myself. How could I save my friend? He protected me as best he could, but even he could not fend off all these creatures. They were too small and quick for us.

Suddenly we heard the lion's roar. He attacked with claws and fangs. He rolled and crushed the monkeys that dared to jump on his back. He zipped through the clearing, frightening all that survived. He disappeared into the woods. The monkeys left me momentarily, wary of an attack from the lion. He reappeared from a different angle to render the same destruction on another bunch of the sinister creatures. Again he disappeared into the trees. Again he attacked from a different spot.

I ventured out from the monster's protection to slice at several apes near us. The bull dragon defended me. Soon the crowd of monkeys dwindled. At last a high-pitched scream echoed amongst the remaining creatures. This was their sound to retreat. They scattered out into the tops of the trees.

The lion paraded forward with the king monkey in his mouth. The bull monster backed away despite his shackles. He lowed at him menacingly. The lion dropped the monkey, its broken neck sagging in a twisted curve. The lion roared at the giant beast before him. The monster stamped the ground. I ran to retrieve the key from the monkey's neck. The lion paced back and forth before the bull dragon. I brought the key to the iron ring around his leg. He stood still, turning his head down to gaze at me.

"You can't hurt him. I'll set you free, but you can't touch him," I warned.

The bull lowed. He turned to face the lion. The lion slowed his pacing and grumbled. The bull dragon turned to nuzzle me. He crooned and gurgled as if crying. I hugged him around his broad face. Tears ran down my cheeks. I let go of him and raced to the fetter. I unlocked the mechanism and threw it open. He stepped out of it gladly. I returned to hold his face in my arms. The lion approached us with a jealous roar and flashing fangs. The bull dragon bellowed to him. He opened his wings to shelter me. He swished his tail. Still, the lion advanced towards him. I

507

ducked out from under the dragon's wing and ran to stand between the two animals.

"Stop. Come here peacefully, both of you," I ordered.

The bull dragon folded his wings. The lion closed his jaws. Reluctantly, the two stepped slowly to me. I grasped the bull around his muzzle. I held the lion around his mane. I leaned my head onto the bull's face and rubbed the lion's wiry fur.

"I love you both," I said finally. "But you will be stronger without me, my old friend." I turned to the bull and stroked his nose.

The monster backed away from me. He regarded the lion silently. The lion stepped in front of me and returned his gaze. He swished his tail and nudged my hand. I patted his back. He licked my other hand. The bull dragon backed away from us, groaning.

"I'm sorry," I told him.

He hesitated, shifting his weight from side to side. He moaned. Then he stepped up to us, sniffing at Ocelot questioningly. He nuzzled my hair and snorted. Then he backed away and opened his massive wings. He flapped hard against the air. He deafened us with a powerful roar. He lifted himself into the sky, which quickly dawned. He hovered above us before flying off towards the sun. The lion leaned his head against me and purred. I hung my arms around his thick mane. I closed my eyes.

My prayer had been answered. I had been foolish to think I could approach Alaban alone. The Fitmalo apes were too numerous for me to handle on my own. Ocelot would have to help me or Alaban and I would both die and the Fitmalos would never be defeated.

Soon I felt as if I had been dipped out of a pool of warm water. I lay suspended in emptiness. I felt warm. I felt peace. A gift of long overdue rest was bestowed upon me. My whole being relaxed.

When I finally awoke, I found myself lying on my back. My hand rested over the hilt of my sword, which still lay open next to me. Sunlight poured into the room from the broad window. Plants from the garden swayed in the afternoon breeze. I had slept through the night and most of the day.

I hopped to my feet, closed the sword with a snap, and stowed it in its sheath. I listened. The house was quiet. Only a few outdoor noises wafted through. Ocelot was not home.

I quickly removed the obstructing furniture and plants from the landing and climbed the stairs to the foyer. As I neared the stairs, I heard a high-pitched repeating beep from my room. It came from my computer, alerting me that I had four new messages. Hoping they were from Ocelot, I hurried to check them. I touched the projection screen above my desk to wake the computer. The screen puffed out like a translucent, breathing chest. It displayed four urgent messages from Ocelot, and one from Channol.

I selected the first message from Ocelot with swelling excitement. He had written from a hotel nearby.

He said, "Sil. Please forgive me. You are such a strong woman. I forgot you're also a very sensitive woman. I forgot women don't usually accept aggressive proposals. I intimidated you. I'm sorry. I was thinking with an affected mind. Testosterone floods a man's logic when he's so hopeful about a chance to mate. I didn't stop to think. I should have known I was moving too fast. You looked terrified. That's the last thing I wanted you to feel. Don't fear me. Don't see me as a rash, impulsive man that you can't trust. I'm not that way. You've seen the evidence. I've wanted for so long to tell you what I said just now, but I held back. I held back so much that you thought I didn't want to touch you at all. I couldn't risk being too close to you on the ship. I would have broken down and tried to kiss you. I nearly fell to that temptation countless times. If I had, we would have been separated. I had to keep my distance to keep you close. I've bided my time, hoping some day you'd let go of Alaban and see me as more than a partner. Now you see me. I've given you the truth. Now you tell me the truth.

"Don't be afraid of me. I won't force myself on you. You don't have to mate with me right away. I know you are more cultured than I am. If you're waiting for a real marriage, I'll do it whole-heartedly. I'll swear the Liricos Proof of Love ceremony with you. You deserve an honorable marriage. I'll memorize the marriage vows for you. I will be your honored husband.

"Call me. Answer my message. Answer your phone. Just tell me to come home. We'll take things slowly. I'll behave myself with more respect this time. Please forgive me for scaring you. Your partner who loves and adores you, Ocelot."

My heart swelled to my throat. I cast my eyes heavenward and laughed with joy.

"Oh, yes! Thank you!" I cried with fists over my heart.

I opened the next note right away. As I read the message, I felt Ocelot's confidence begin to slip, almost to the point of begging.

It read, "I've been thinking of everything you said before I left. I don't believe you sent me away just because I offended you. I think you're afraid that Alaban will try to kill me if he finds out you love me and not him. If that's your reason, please reconsider. I do not believe I'm to die by his hand, even if you say it must be true. Even if it were, why live in misery until then? Wilbaht once said, 'a life lived in fear of death is a poor life indeed.' He was right. I've watched you suffer over this for too long.

Agonizing over what might happen on the day you see Alaban again will only curse all the days before it. Does he have such control over you that he has to ruin your life? If that's true, I will hunt him down and slay him myself before he ever gets to you. I'm not afraid to do that.

"The only thing I fear now is having to live without you. I'm tired of being independent. I'm not so tough like I used to be. That wall is wearing down. I'm not content to be only a piece of Organization property anymore. I'd rather be a regular human being, someone with a life, a place to call home, and a woman by my side. I don't want just any woman. I want you. No other woman compares to you.

"Sil, you are everything to me. I have no one else. I have no heirs. My only living family thinks I'm dead. You're the only one I have left. But that's okay, because you're the one who matters most. I will defend you and love you against all challenges in this life. Don't let fear stand between us. Let me come home to you. Love, Ocelot."

I sighed, enamored. I opened his next message, expecting perhaps a proposed rendezvous. However, his next words were even less optimistic and without any such proposal.

He said, "Sil, please answer your phone or reply to my message. It doesn't matter what time. I can't sleep. I've called you twelve times today. I know your phone is on. I sense you have not left the house. If you feel any loyalty to me, even as a partner, you will at least speak to me."

Guilt thumped at the back of my mind. I bit a thumbnail and selected to read the next message, which was from Channol.

He said, "Sil. Ocelot came to see me today in regards to your recent argument. I know this is a personal matter, but if you do not answer your phone or respond to his messages, I will consider this a refusal to receive intra-Organization communications. This is a misdemeanor punishable by Organization law. You are still under warrior's oath. You are obligated to respond accordingly.

"Since this is a personal matter, I will give personal advice. Wilbaht advised Croso and me under the strictest confidence to allow the two of you to stay on the assignment regardless of whether or not you became mates. Therefore, do not concern yourself about dismissal or separation. This will not happen. I urge you to accept him. He is an honorable young man with your best interest at heart.

"You will respond to this message from me within twenty hours or I will report your misdemeanor to Gen. Croso. If I must report you, you may expect a mandatory mediation in which you will be forced to confront Ocelot before two counselors in a much more stressful atmosphere. I trust you'll decide wisely. Sub Gen. Channol Cordolib."

Channol's staunch warning confused me. Although I took heart in the fact that Wilbaht had explicitly given us permission to follow through with my secret hopes, this message disturbed me. Why had Ocelot gone to see Channol about this so quickly? Usually he did not ask for help from anyone, especially not concerning personal matters, and certainly not from someone as stiff and formal as Channol.

I wrote Channol a quick reply, thanking him for his advice. I promised him I would contact Ocelot right away. I read Ocelot's last message, hoping to find an explanation, but was swayed instead by a tone of hopelessness.

He said, "I don't know what you want. I don't know how to appeal to you. If you really meant what you said about this assignment being over, I have no choice but to go along with you. If you don't contact me by the sixth, I'll go to the Center and ask for an appointment for reassignment. I'll sign the second set of documents: both the divorce and the discontinuation of contract. If you care at all, you won't let that happen. If you don't contact me, I'll only go back to the house for my personal items. I wish I knew what else to say. Ocelot."

I scratched my head, wondering why he would propose such desperate measures. I checked the time on the desk computer. It was nearly five o'clock in the afternoon. Why had he become so anxious about my lack of communication after just eighteen hours? Then something else on the computer caught my eye. My heart skipped a beat. My head swam. I nearly fell unconscious. Today was the sixth day of the week. I had slept for three days.

Chapter 47: Love

I reeled. The sunrises and sunsets of my vision had reflected the course of real time. I stood in a panic. Ocelot had gone to Channol for advice as a last resort. If Ocelot was serious about what he'd said in his last message, then he had to be at the Center now. I dove back to the computer and immediately messaged the Center's main board clerk on real time.

"Has Sub Professor Jainocelot Quoren passed through security today? I am his partner, Sil Rayfenix. I need to locate him immediately. It's urgent."

The clerk replied, "Identification codes required for such information, Warrior."

I typed the ID codes required. He replied, "Yes. Sub Professor Jainocelot entered the building at 1420 hours today."

"Can you get an image of him on a security screen? I need an exact location and I need to know who he's been talking with." I felt desperate.

"One moment," the clerk replied.

I waited fidgeting for the clerk to trace him.

He replied, "I have him in the main lobby. He's speaking with a Lizard professor, female blue."

I groaned. Yalat was likely to give up all the information I'd told her, feeling it was her duty to respond to him with full honesty. If she felt particularly spry today, she would probably inundate him with romantic advice. I asked the clerk to page her.

I tapped my feet double-time, waiting for her to pick up the message string where the clerk had left off. Finally I saw her ID blink on, and then her image.

"Yalat. I know you've been talking to Ocelot."

She interrupted. "If the General had seen him today, he would be on his way to Godel or some other godforsaken place. Why are you making him suffer? I thought I taught you to be a better person than this. Tell me right now what is going on."

Glad that he hadn't gone to the General for reassignment, I described to Yalat what had happened. She interjected a few matronly exclamations about it. I demanded to know what she'd told him about me. She promised she'd only encouraged him to try once more before giving up entirely.

"Sil, darling, listen to me," she added. "I've never heard of anything like the vision you had. But beware. You should not base your life's decisions on visions. They are subject to our own misinterpretations. No one has ever made perfect predictions with visions, not even the greatest seers, because no future is mapped out and carved in stone. We have free will to change our future. That's what makes life worth living. Think of that."

"Yes, ma'am," I said quickly. "Will you please tell Ocelot to come home?"

"He's already left. The poor boy is terribly depressed. He thinks his efforts are not good enough to change your stubborn ways. Frankly, I agreed with him about the stubbornness. You are a bit mulish from time to time. I'm sorry, darling, but it's true. Now be stubborn about not letting him go. Convince him that he did the right thing. Let him know you appreciate his efforts. He's endured a great deal to win you over."

"I will, Yalat. Thank you."

Her critical manner turned warm and bubbly. "Oh, my dear, I know you'll make each other very happy. I congratulate you on your choice for a mate. I couldn't have picked a better man for you." She showed her sharp teeth proudly in a chuckle. "Ah, pretty soon you'll be laying eggs and hatching young. Oh, no, your species doesn't lay eggs, do you? Well, you know what I mean. I'm sure you'll have a lovely family. I don't expect to hear from you any time soon. Don't worry. I'll stay out of trouble if you will."

I smiled at her. "If he's on his way now, I have to go. Thank you, Yalat."

"You're welcome, dear. Go pounce on him," she said heartily. Her image blinked off.

I turned off the computer with a grin. I had to think fast of how to deal with him once he arrived. What would be the best way to approach him? How soon would he be here?

I ran to the main foyer and looked out the window. I bounced with excitement. He was there in the street nearing the front gate. I felt I would die of nervousness. I turned to lean with my back against the wall. I took several deep breaths. I went again to the window. He arrived at the gate. He set his bag down beside him. He stood leaning on the gate without opening it. He gazed at the house with a melancholy I had not seen in him before. My excitement slowly vaporized.

He stared at the house a while longer. Then he opened the gate and walked through. I retracted from the window. I couldn't just spring upon him as he entered the door. He was in a rough state.

I opened the door just as he attempted to unlock it. The uneasiness of his manner and the sadness on his face were contagious. We stared at each other like this for one difficult moment. Then he looked down and refused to look at my face.

513

"Sil," he began. He cleared his throat as he walked into the foyer. "I, um, I made an appointment to speak to the General tomorrow. I came to pack, but I'd like to spend the night here so I can leave early in the morning. You don't have to leave. I won't be in your way. I'll just stay in my room." He shuffled past me.

I stood speechless. All the words I wanted to say to him jammed together in my throat, not letting any through. Instead, the words slid down to my stomach as I swallowed, where they became fluttering winged insects.

He dragged himself along, completely defeated. He had waited for me for three days. Now he had to face me, believing all was lost. I could not find the words to adequately express my regret and sympathy for him. I stared at my brave lion, caged by a cruel trick of fate. I had to set him free, but carefully.

I noticed he hadn't shaved since the day he left. His face showed the lack of sleep he had indicated. He would go straight to his bath, I was sure. He probably hadn't eaten well, either. I hadn't eaten for three days. An idea came to me.

"Ocelot, will you have dinner with me?" I asked tentatively.

He stopped near his door. He turned his face in my direction, but wouldn't look at me. He thought for a moment. "Where?"

"Just here. I need to talk to you." I held my breath.

He froze, contemplating. Then he said uneasily that we could talk after his shower.

"Okay," I almost whispered. He enclosed himself in his room.

I waited, staring after where he had stood. I heard the water run in his bath. I flew upstairs to my room as butterflies hectically battered my stomach. I threw off my uniform to slip on my blue dress: the one that had caught his attention when we were in Angoran. I even sprayed myself with essence of windflowers, hoping he would notice me as completely changed and willing to please him.

I scurried down to the kitchen where I prepared the best meal I knew how to make. I fidgeted when it was done. Was he taking a long time or was I too impatient? I left the dining area to tiptoe to his door. I leaned in and listened. I heard no sound. I deliberated a moment. I was about to knock, but the door opened. I stepped backward jauntily.

"Oh. I'm sorry. I thought maybe you'd fallen asleep. I just wanted to tell you I made extra food if you want some. I thought maybe since you were tired, you wouldn't feel like preparing something for yourself, so I made enough for two. I don't know if you'll like it. It's pasta with reed flowers. If you don't want any, that's okay. You don't have to. I'll just..." I pointed to the kitchen foolishly. I felt childish, knowing I was babbling. The frenzy of butterflies nearly escaped through my esophagus.

A light, musky perfume drifted around him. He was dressed in his gray uniform pants and a thin white shirt. He was clean-shaven. His aura intoxicated my senses. Nervousness choked me. I almost cried there in front of him. I turned around to face the dining area. I breathed heavily. I had to walk cautiously so as not to stumble.

He followed me slowly. I served my plate carefully. I trembled. I stopped a moment. I set the plate on the countertop and closed my eyes, leaning my hands on the counter. I took a few deep breaths and concentrated on controlling my anxiety. I went to the table, avoiding eye contact with this male siren.

"It looks good. I'd like some," he said. His voice was no longer gruff. He had noticed my nervousness.

"Oh. Good. Here, you can have this plate. I'll get another one." I left the plate at his place at the table and turned to get everything else he would need: water, silverware, and spices.

He sat down slowly at his place. "Thank you," I heard him say. I felt him staring at me, reading my emotion, rebuilding his hopes.

I sat opposite him, but then realized I hadn't served myself at all. I jumped up to collect the other things and finally sat again. Ocelot ate at a methodical pace, watching me, thinking probably that I was the most confounding woman he'd ever met.

I ate too quickly. I consciously slowed myself. Still, I finished my meal before he was half done. I cleared my plate, but returned with a glass of water.

"What did you want to say?" he asked at last.

I inhaled and sighed deeply, still unable to look him in the eye. "I want to apologize for the way I treated you the other night." A spinning ball of nervous energy fluttered in my chest, competing with the incessant butterflies in my stomach. "You were right about...I was afraid that Alaban would kill you. I had visions and nightmares about it."

He stirred the contents of his plate while he studied me. His manner became grave.

"This connection of yours with Alaban. Did it...compel you to mate with him? I ask because you said you never were in love with him. But the last time you were with him on Santer, you slept with him even after I warned you about his infidelity." He glanced at me worriedly. "If you do see him again, will you be...driven to mate with him again?"

I shook my head anxiously. "Ocelot, I say this honestly. I swear I have never mated with him and I never will. I never wanted to. I'm sorry I led you to believe that in the first place. That night on Santer, we only slept. We didn't do anything."

Ocelot's confused face washed over with hope and relief.

515

"I never…I never have." I divulged, reddening. I glimpsed his eyes. Hope flourished. My face lightened. "I should have told you all this when we were on the Jain planet, after the wedding party. Those girls…"

"You said they were infected. You were right."

I looked to him with worry. "Were you?"

"No. It was 750G. Not carried by saliva. I didn't touch them after the party. I knew you were right. I was just trying to make you jealous."

It was my turn to smile with relief.

Ocelot explained he'd taken them to a local clinic for testing. They had both been in the advanced stages of the disease. So had the other two.

"I spent the rest of my leave time investigating their trail of infection. The main clinic started a vaccination campaign based on my research."

I raised my eyebrows. "No wonder you carried flowers to them," I said, remembering how he had run into Olimbi with the bouquet.

"Flowers? Oh, yes. Some were for them. Some were for my parents' memorial," he explained.

I stared at him with a hint of a smile. His beautiful, tired face showed indecision.

"Why didn't you call me?" he asked.

"I would have, but I couldn't." I spoke to him excitedly. "I had a new vision, one I can trust. Alaban won't kill you even if he wants to. The Fitmalos are the ones to beware of, not him." I anxiously leaned toward him. "Ocelot, that vision knocked me out for three days!"

His fork clanked abruptly onto his plate.

"You were unconscious for three days?" He stared at me in amazement. Even with the lack of sleep, he never looked so handsome.

My face brightened. "Yes! As soon as I woke up I wanted to contact you. I would have told you to come home right away," I confessed.

"You would have?" he asked hopefully.

"Yes. Then I realized what day it was and where you were. Did Yalat stop you in time? You didn't ask for reassignment, but did you cancel the contract?"

"No. I wanted one more chance to talk to you."

We smiled.

I wasn't sure what else to say. We sat there idly for a few moments without speaking. Butterflies clumped together, wedging themselves under my ribs. I couldn't sit still anymore. I took my glass to the sink and cleaned it while he quickly finished his meal. He stood with his dishes. I moved to let him by. I retreated to stand behind my place at the table. He cleaned his dishes and turned to face me. My nervousness returned. He stepped around to the other side of the table, his mood reflecting my own.

516

After a strained moment, he said, "You look great."

"Oh. Thanks. You like this dress?" I asked shyly. Butterflies flapped from their resting place.

"Not the dress. I mean it's nice, but mostly I like you in it," he replied with a loving smile.

I felt light, almost weightless with so much flapping.

"You look great, too, only…" I stopped to catch my breath. "You look tired. I'm sorry you didn't sleep."

"I should have come back sooner," he replied.

I fumbled for words again. He stood speechless as well.

"Why don't you go ahead and get some sleep? I don't want to keep you awake if you're tired. We can talk in the morning," I finally suggested.

He shook his head. "I want you to keep me awake."

I began to breathe, but my lungs seemed compressed. My whole body warmed to his implication. The butterflies fanned.

"Even if it's just to talk," he added.

I felt thrilled and deathly nervous at the same time. He kindly distracted me.

"I bought something for you," he offered.

He gestured to me to follow him. He returned to his room. I walked a few steps behind him. He grasped a small box from the top of his desk. I stopped at the middle of his room, fraught with nervous energy. He opened the box and withdrew a shiny object. It was a band bracelet, the kind that hugs the arm but doesn't close all the way around. He gently held the ornament between us. He showed me a large chip in the middle, which displayed a hologram of a freshwater anemone. I held up my arm for him to attach the glittering bracelet. I stared down at it, flattered and amazed, moving my arm to see the different stages of the hologram.

"It's just like the one we found at the waterfall. This is beautiful, Ocelot. Thank you." I admired the precious token.

"Do you remember when we found it?" he asked. His tired, loving eyes gazed into mine.

I nodded, entranced. He had noticed, then. I had come so close that day to falling to his temptation. Now the reasons to keep my distance had been swept away.

My hands traced the form of his hands and wrists, and snaked up his arms to his shoulders as our faces met. He moved to clutch my body in his warm hands. I pressed my mouth and tongue to his. His kiss felt like the warm flesh of a succulent fruit, broken through by the perfect pressure of lips. I savored the delicious succulence tentatively at first, but then pursued the provocative delight with passion. I embraced his beloved body.

Nervousness shrunk away from this kiss. Dreams long repressed now overflowed to freedom.

Between breaths and kisses, I told him that I loved him. He repeated my words earnestly. After minutes of languid expression of the mouth, we were no longer shy. In a burst of elation, I wrenched the shirt from his body. He tossed it away with gusto. I gladly felt the undulations of muscles over his torso. He clawed at my hips to gather up my dress and then lifted it from me. We covered each other's skin with traveling hands. I greedily welcomed the sensation of his flesh on mine. He kissed along my neck and down my shoulder as he clumsily removed his shoes. My heart throbbed joyously. I told him I had craved his touch for so long. He squeezed me to him and replied softly but excitedly that he would never deny me his touch again.

We kissed around each other's faces as he loosened his pants. We relished the moment, kissing over and over for a pinnacle of time. He began to strip away my underclothing, but my conscience encumbered the action. I firmly arrested his hands with mine.

"Wait," I told him. "Will you say the ritual with me? Will you be my husband, before God?"

"Of course," he breathed. "Of course I will."

I thanked him, interrupting a kiss. I held his handsome face. He gazed into my eyes with endearing desire and love. We paused to recite the ancient Liricosian marriage vows.

Nose-to-nose, voices quavering, we called each other by name and pledged our dedication. "I swear that I love you. I swear that God has paired us. I promise to love you my whole life. If your body should die before mine, I will keep you in my heart until we are reunited in heaven. I swear that I love you. I swear that God has paired us. I promise to love you through joy and suffering."

Then Ocelot spoke alone. "I promise to love you and any children that grow from your womb." He placed a hand over my abdomen. "As God knows my heart, I swear I am your loyal husband."

I spoke. "I promise to love you and any children that grow from your seed." I moved my hand just to his inner thigh. "As God knows my heart, I swear I am your loyal wife."

He moved my hand to the right place as he stared seriously into my eyes. My face flushed, but we continued the ritual.

We spoke together. "I swear that I love you. I swear that God has paired us. Having sworn together three times, we make this true. I am your mate for life."

As the last words left our lips, we kissed together with greater passion. If I had longed for him before, it had been a distant longing. Now my desire for him blossomed throughout my entire being. Love and lust became one. Our remaining clothing found its way to the floor as we moved to his bed. Soon I found myself boldly naked before his bare form. Inhibition gave way to sensual expression. I moved to worship him, marveling at his body, so different from my own. I relished his attentions in return. I felt sensations I had never imagined. Teasing sensations flitted through me like drunken butterflies. Ecstatic pins and needles painlessly pressed through my arms and legs. Instinct led us. I gladly allowed him to break my last seal of innocence, enthralled to take him in. Each pelting dosage of fulfillment coaxed joyous noises from my voice. Heaving sensations billowed through my lower body. Twinges and sparks and sizzling whirlwinds careened through me. Soon, we were mating desperately. I owned his flesh and he owned mine. Together we repeated confessions of love and ecstasy.

I gave all my heart and energy to please this lion of strength. His voice broke as he said my name and words of love among groans and gasps. Then he nearly roared at the rush of power. He was my lion. He was the right one. As he released his energy into me, I learned a new level of love and admiration for him. Our strengths and vulnerabilities swam together as the fluids of our bodies, and as the unison of our desire. I would love only him. I would never touch another. I would never want to. I felt a selfish pride for having waited for him. For me, he was the greatest man in all existence.

After a long while, our explosion of sexual energy gave way to a lull, like the soothing laps of gentle waves on the beach after a storm. He cradled me. My head rested over his powerful chest. My knee rested over his thigh. Our arms still held each other's bodies tightly. He kissed the top of my forehead tenderly.

"I love you," we whispered together.

At last he slept. I listened to the rhythms of his heartbeat and his breathing. No other music could have been so beautiful. I nestled my head below his chin and slept for the first time, no longer as my own woman, but as his.

The magic stayed with us the next day and the next. Ocelot remembered to cancel the meeting with the General and asked the clerk to please never reschedule him. We took time off to honeymoon in our own house. When we went out, we flirted with each other like the newlyweds we were. We didn't spy on anyone. We wouldn't have been able to keep our eyes on them anyway. When we passed through the market on the way home, Ocelot stopped to buy me flowers. He made me feel so wonderful. All our emotional suffering and frustration were fully healed.

He openly answered all my questions about his behavior throughout the past year. He had felt enticed by my presence since the moment he saw me, but had resisted the idea as long as he could, which he admitted, was a losing battle from the start.

He framed the picture he had taken of me sleeping in our apartment on Santer. He said liked the picture because my thumb was tucked slightly into the leg of my shorts and this made him think erotic thoughts about me. If he had told me that back on Santer I would have charged him with sexual harassment. Now I was flattered. We laughed about it.

I urged him to frame all his pictures and set them around the house. I suggested he hang the picture of the Center on Jain in the foyer, but he disagreed with a laugh.

"I'd rather keep it here in the bedroom," he said with a broad smile.

I asked him why.

"Promise you won't get mad." He grasped my fists in his hands and kissed them.

I eyed him with suspicion. He rolled out of bed and went to his desk. He removed the old black envelope full of pictures he'd taken. He extracted the picture of the Center on Jain that I had seen in his bunk.

"Remember when Klib filmed you in the bath?" He paused to check my curious suspicion. "Klib played the tape on my computer. Wilbaht destroyed the tape, but that last image on the screen was still salvageable. I printed it." He flipped the picture. On the back was an image of me stepping into the bath. I gaped and blinked at it.

"You had this on your wall the whole time?" I asked accusingly.

"You're not mad?" he asked hopefully.

I grinned at him. "No." I kissed him softly.

Next I asked him about the anonymous messages he'd sent me. In one of the messages, he had said he cared for me as if I were a sister after the airbus crash. He explained it was because he'd waited in the hospital with Yalat until I was discharged. Then he had helped transport me from the hospital back to my room. I asked about the message in which he'd said he invited me somewhere and then was wounded. He'd said afterward he went someplace to heal. He explained all.

"The first time we were on Santer, I invited you to that café. I know you didn't think of it as a date, but I was hoping maybe you would at least show some interest in me. All you did was stare out the window. You ignored me like boring news," he admitted.

"I hurt your feelings. I'm sorry, my love." I gave him a peck on the cheek.

He chuckled as he hugged me to him with forgiveness and compliments. He asked me when had I fallen in love with him. I reminded

520

him about the time I'd dropped the weight on his head. We laughed together blissfully.

"Actually, I think I loved you before then," I told him. "When we were at the space station, right after you were shot, Alaban tried to get me to leave you there. Do you know what I told him?" I was ready to say it.

I moved away from him to look him in the face. He looked at me with tense interest.

"I'd rather die with Ocelot than stand by you," I quoted.

Ocelot's face showed victorious emotion.

"Then I jumped off the platform to save you. You were practically gone. I put my hands inside you...here." I showed him where I had regenerated his flesh.

He stared at me, amazed.

I thought sadly of Alaban's reaction to my statement. He had been heartbroken. He would feel the same again whenever he found out I was married to Ocelot. I felt guilt and sorrow for him still. I tried to set those thoughts aside. Ocelot didn't have to know about them. I gazed into his brown eyes.

"Then what happened?" he asked.

I recounted with detail a lot of the space station information, especially the part about hiding us in the attack ship and maneuvering around the various Fitmalo soldiers in the space station. When I neared the end of my story, I began to falter.

"I know you don't want to know what Alaban said to me at the end, but maybe we need to talk about it. Otherwise it'll just cause a rift between us. I don't want that. I want you to know I have nothing to hide from you. I love you." I kissed him solidly on the mouth.

He tensed, but listened with curiosity. I spoke emotionally about what Alaban had said to me, his letter he'd stowed into the vial, and what Yalat had gotten out of him when she'd seen him last. I tried my best to explain to Ocelot how I truly felt about Alaban. I was afraid he wouldn't accept my explanation. He became stony during my account. When I had said all I needed to say, he remained taciturn. He struggled with his own jealousy and hatred of Alaban to try and see my perspective. In the end, jealousy reigned. He clenched his fists in despite.

"You want to kill him," I said.

"I want to kill him twice." Ocelot sat up and leaned his elbows on his knees.

"He won't come between us. I am your loyal wife. I owe you a lifetime. I don't owe him that. I don't owe him at all. I know that now. I just can't help wishing he would leave the enemy. I would still like to be a part of his rescue. I want to see him turn around." I spoke resolutely.

"You're a good woman, Sil. You have a good heart. That's one thing I've always admired about you." He took my hand to kiss it. "Don't ever leave me."

"I won't," I promised him.

I kissed him passionately, but his kiss conveyed doubt. I tried to communicate my endearing love for him. At some point during the night he accepted my dedication to him. We finally communicated with kisses of true love and trust.

Chapter 48: Aftermath

We lived peacefully, enchanted by the newness and fascination of our love, for nearly two months. We tried to get back into our job, but our concentration was distracted by constant, welcome interruptions of passion. Our dedication to the assignment was no longer our top priority. We felt more relaxed about the lack of clues. We perused the lists of information and scanned the bugged areas almost carelessly. I began to think if the assignment failed altogether, that we'd sit back and laugh about it while planning our vacation.

We picked up on some minor smuggling misdemeanors, but these were actions that the local law authorities would need to deal with, not the Organization. We continued our research without positive results. We watched the news closely, as did everyone else on the planet. The Fitmalo generals that Wilbaht had indicated in his announced list were all thoroughly investigated. Several, like Sunderlign, were accused post-mortem. Salt, Sunderlign's close companion, was nailed for double conspiracy against his own government and his business partners in mining rights falsifications. A few others fell from power as well.

Teradom was never mentioned. We got the feeling that since the other accused generals were falling all around him, this only left him with more power for himself and his own close associates, and that probably someone within the Organization was facilitating this vacuum of evidence around him.

We saw his image on the news several times. Each time, we glimpsed Alaban's uniform either directly behind or to the side of the General. Ocelot bristled every time he had to look at him. I tried to pretend I didn't notice it, but he knew I read his body language well.

The people of Jawlcheen did heed Wilbaht's warning. All new commonwealth proposals were delayed. The Jawlcheen government demanded detailed proof of finance and projected spending for all proposed ship building for Thrader peacekeeping purposes. No financing proposals were successfully negotiated. The movement to unite the Thrader helion stood at a stalemate.

One of the lower Jawlcheen officials against the commonwealth lived here in our own neighborhood. Ocelot made a point to meet and associate with him often. Soon Lieutenant Adder and his wife, Aysha, were common guests in our house. On one occasion, Adder even got us into a dinner convention of Jawlcheen traditionalists. We learned a great deal at the convention. We even spotted a few men who we believed were actually spies for the opposition. We researched them and found we were right. We reported them immediately. We were happy to finally have something to report. Apart from this incident, life outside the house went on dully.

I thought about this fact one day while observing the street below a bridge. I was supposed to be watching for possible smuggling transactions at a repair shop, but I kept thinking of my lovely husband. After an hour or so, I left my post. I wandered through the streets, past the marketplace, and up a road where Ocelot was supposed to be. I then searched for him, but he was not there. I checked around the immediate vicinity, but found no sign of him. I called at the Center to see if he had gone in to see Channol or Croso. He had not. I was perturbed. More specifically, I missed him. I felt the need to be with him just then. It was a strange feeling I'd had before, but never so intensely.

On a whim, I climbed the cobbled hill to our house. As I approached the house, I knew Ocelot was there. I also felt the presence of someone else inside, a female. Immediately I was overtaken by a fierce jealousy. I chagrined with fury. My logical side could not contain it.

I entered the main door. I moved swiftly, catlike, towards the sunroom. Here I found Ocelot standing at the window next to our neighbor, Aysha. They both pointed to one of the flowering plants in our back garden. They did not touch. They did not even stand close together. My mind could not compete with my emotion. I glowered at the scene. I stepped down towards them. Ocelot sensed me behind him. He turned to greet me pleasantly. I attempted to contain my senseless anger, but it still showed on my face.

"Sil. What happened?" he asked innocently.

"I felt I had to come home for some reason," I told him guardedly.

Aysha turned to greet me happily. "Oh, Sil. I'm glad you're here. I thought I was going to have to listen to a lot of men's talk on my own." She noticed my cold stare, but interpreted it as some kind of problem with Ocelot and not with her.

Just then, Adder arrived at the sunroom with three of his hands full. He carried drinks for them. He spoke to me warmly.

"Sil. I was just telling your husband that he should call you. We have some celebrating to do. The Southeast quadrant vote went through this morning. We voted no on the bill to unite Thrader in further common law. The Northeast quadrant is predicted to follow suit, so it doesn't matter what the rest of the planet thinks. Even if they're opposed, we still live on free soil. Here, you have my drink. I'll get another," he offered.

"Congratulations, sir," I said humbly. I fully realized my foolish mistake. I accepted the drink with a slight bow.

When Adder had gone back upstairs, Ocelot eyed me warily. Aysha chattered about some of the details of the vote. I overcame my earlier rashness and joined in the celebration.

The couple took us out to dinner at a high-priced place overlooking the city. Moons One and Two shone brilliantly above the rows of white buildings. Moon Three's oblong crescent peeked over the hillside. Their glow was alluring. I felt again the intense urge to be alone with Ocelot. I held hands with him under the table after our meal was done. Then I let my hand wander a little. He snatched my hand into his once more. He didn't look at me, but he squeezed my fingers to keep me in line. Eventually, Adder stood to greet a coworker who sat in another part of the dining room. Aysha excused herself to go to the ladies' room. In their absence, I leaned to Ocelot's face and kissed him. He smiled at me lovingly, but I wasn't interested in love at the moment. My lower brain struggled to take over my actions. I stared into his dark amber eyes and kissed him again. He seemed self-conscious from the public display of affection.

Our hosts soon returned. They chuckled when they caught us kissing. Ocelot jerked away from me when he heard them. He reacted with embarrassment. I behaved nervously, but not for the same reason. I felt offended that we were being spied upon.

We left in a cab. Ocelot and I stayed glued together at the hands. We sat with Aysha in the back seat. Adder sat in front with the driver. Again I felt an irrational jealousy from having to share the space around my husband with her. I struggled not to show it. We made polite conversation all the way back to our house. They invited us over for dessert, but I quickly said no thank you since we had to wake up very early in the morning. Ocelot looked down at me questioningly, but he stood by my reason. We said goodbye to them politely.

After passing through the gate, I stood in front of Ocelot and walked backwards towards the main door of the house. I pulled him towards me by the waistline of his pants.

"What's gotten into you?" he asked me.

"Nothing yet," I responded like a vixen.

At the first step up to the door, I stopped and kissed him with absolute desire. He half-responded, but was too taken aback to imitate my willful approach. He trudged up the stairs to the door, dragging me along. I left him alone long enough to get us through the door and into the foyer. Then I attacked him again.

I begged him for sex. The deep physical need that Alaban had mentioned so long ago had finally budded in me.

Ocelot continued his reaction of surprise, but did not resist. He was turned on by my aggressive love. I pulled him down the stairs to the sunroom, where I stripped us both as fast as I could. I ignored him when he asked me who I was.

I did not just make love to him. I mated coarsely, driven to attain something; something I profoundly needed from him, though I knew not what. Only my body knew the secret. After I had ridden him to the point of his climax, I began to feel a massive power. It expanded through my body as an immense elliptical wave. If I cried out, I did not hear my own voice. If Ocelot spoke to me, I did not know it. I only heard an ocean of life. I only saw the light of colliding stars. Then the flash absorbed into my body. An involuntary tremor of levitative energy jiggled through the air around us. Clothing, chairs, plants, kitchen objects, tables, everything that wasn't secured to the walls or ceilings floated weightlessly in the air, including our own bodies. I clung to my husband. I panted and kissed him. Then I lowered us to the floor by the window. Objects still floated around us and past us through the room. He observed all this with wonder.

"Wow," I heard him say as I fell asleep by his side.

Late the next morning, I awoke from the aftermath to find Ocelot still by my side on the floor of the sunroom, distraught. He stared, confused, at our reflection in the glass window.

"What's wrong, my love?" I asked him dreamily.

"This is what I saw," he said.

I turned to look with him at our reflection. I saw nothing out of the ordinary, only that we were still naked here. Light came in from the side window, causing the glass before us to act as a mirror.

"This was the vision I had when I first saw you. I saw four bodies lying in a row. I didn't know who they were. They were us," he explained. He pointed to himself and me, then my reflection and his. "Why did I see this?"

I had no answer for him. I only knew that I felt a physical and emotional satisfaction that seemed to span generations of time. I showed him appreciation by waiting on him all day. I massaged his back. I made him a large lunch with all his favorite foods. I bathed him. I gave him love and caring. He felt confused, but privileged.

During the week, I began to feel a change in myself. Noises that had never distracted me before suddenly drew my attention. Scents that I had taken for granted now became pungent. Foods I had enjoyed suddenly lost their flavor. I tried foods I had never liked before and enjoyed them. The next week, I became violently ill in the morning. I threw up even though I had almost nothing in my stomach. I returned to throw up bile twice. When I stepped out of the bathroom, I found Ocelot near the door, waiting with an anxious smile.

"Sil, you're pregnant," he beamed.

"But I'm on infertility medicine," I said.

"So am I," he admitted. "It's supposed to be only a thousandth of a percent shy of absolute accuracy. We're both taking it. That decreases the chances even more."

"Then how could I be?" I asked.

"I don't know," he said excitedly. "But you are."

He slid a hand to my belly. He stared at me in amazement. I resisted the idea at first, but then realized he must be right.

"Maybe your aim is more precise than the medication," I joked.

He smiled, still trying to get used to the idea himself. "Forget the aim. I didn't even know the gun was loaded."

I retorted with a smile. "I didn't know I had a target to hit."

Ocelot held my face in his hand lovingly. He lowered his voice and spoke to me seductively. "The other night was pretty explosive. I think the target went looking for the bullet."

"Well, the gun didn't exactly stay in its holster," I said defensively.

"I wasn't the one who took it out," he accused tenderly.

I blushed a little. I looked into his eyes seriously once more. "I guess that bullet was meant to be fired."

"I'm glad it had a target to hit," he said kindly.

"Me too," I admitted.

We wrapped our arms around each other.

"We're going to have a baby, Sil. He's a boy. We're going to have a son," Ocelot spoke in an enchanted whisper.

526

"Are you sure?" I whispered back in wonder.

"Yes. I know it. He's a son. The odds are astronomically against conception, but it happened. That means it's got to be a miracle. You were meant to get pregnant now."

"I guess so," I whispered with uncertainty. I hugged his body to mine all the more. "Can we really do this?"

He released me to peer into my face. "What do you mean? Of course we can."

I spoke quickly. "I mean can we continue this assignment? This place is politically unstable. We can't raise a child here. What about when the baby is born? I can't have my sisters come here. It's too dangerous for them. And what about Alaban? I don't want any harm to come to our son. Our son. I can't believe it. What are we going to do?" I spoke quickly.

"Whoa, slow down. Let's take one thing at a time. Why are you still worried about Alaban? Just put him out of your mind."

I peered up at him almost incredulously. "Why do you say that? You know I can't."

His kind manner turned sour. "Yes, you can."

He glared at me for a disconcerting moment. I looked away nervously. He took my chin in his hand and turned my face toward his. He remained firm in his request.

"What if he comes looking for me?" I asked tentatively.

"He dies," Ocelot spoke resolutely.

I cowered from his hatred. I tried to move away from him, but he held my arm. I decided to forgive his words. I embraced him, feeling even more insecure with our new situation. We held each other there silently for a long while.

Finally, Ocelot spoke to me softly again. "Don't worry. We'll find a solution for everything. We just need to take it one step at a time. I love you."

"I love you, too," I told him whole-heartedly.

During the next few weeks, we communicated more often during the day. Ocelot was more careful with me than he had been before. He checked me every two or three days for vitamin deficiencies or minor health problems. He cautioned me not to work out too roughly. He stopped sparring with me altogether. He listened to my womb every night before sleeping. He was eager to be a father to our baby. I admired him for his caring ways.

One night, we started thinking of names for our son. I mentioned that I was sure he didn't want to name the baby after himself after all he had gone through as a child. He agreed with me heartily. We went through a lot of other names of men in our families, but none interested us.

"If we had a girl, we could name her after you. Any girl would be happy with the name Jain. Maybe we'll have a daughter some day." I turned to him hopefully.

He agreed. "Well, if we're going to name our girl after me, then we should name our boy after you."

"Sil isn't a boy's name. At least not on Liricos."

"Maybe not Sil, but what about Sal?" I shook my head. "Saul? Sul?" He suggested with a silly grin.

"Saul is a nice name," I interjected. "It's strong and masculine. I think he will like it." We exchanged a look of approval. We agreed.

Ocelot knelt to speak to the child inside my abdomen. "Hey, little boy, you have a name now. You're Saul Quoren." He kissed my belly. I smiled at him.

For the next few months, whenever Ocelot called to check on me, he would also ask me, "How is Saul?" I always covered my abdomen happily and answered that he was fine.

As the days passed, we aided in a few minor smuggling busts and finally located three Regime cohorts, but we never approached any of these people directly. We only helped set them up. Other warriors carried out the directives of action against them. We stayed safe. It was as if this were our golden age.

Ocelot's only regret was that he was still unable to contact his cousin, Jiao. He wanted to be able to share the news of our marriage and our baby on the way to his favorite relative. As for me, I communicated frequently through Yalat with my father and sisters—especially with Tamia, since she already had a baby. She gave me advice and encouragement.

After more than three months, I began to feel the baby move. We were both amazed at his tiny life. He was barely more than a living idea, and already we loved him dearly.

As the six-month anniversary of Wilbaht's death approached, I became more and more distracted. Alaban was near. He was on Jawlcheen now. He had lifted the shroud from his spirit. He beckoned to me. I painfully and reluctantly obeyed my husband's request. I did not go out to look for him, but I prayed for him every day.

Chapter 49: Clues to the Regime Plan

One day, while remote spying on an arms smuggling deal, I noticed a new individual I had not seen before. He seemed to be wealthy, but he was followed by a smuggler of ill repute. I looked up his face in the Organization data log. He was an associate of Teradom himself. I immediately alerted Ocelot. We moved quickly to follow the man and his entourage. We tracked him to a ritzy, high-security hotel downtown. We tapped his communications from his room through Organization networking. He sent and received few messages, but they were all encoded. Ocelot hurried to decode them while I stayed on observation. We learned that he was a regional businessman in town for a few days to check on shipment preparations for both legal and illegal goods. In his communications, we found a memo to Teradom's aide. It confirmed that he would be present at a meeting in Hammerstead, a small town west of Boldoy.

I looked up the town right away. It was a sparsely populated town on the canyons of Maiy. It was primarily a tourist site, not just because of the canyons, but also because Maiy was home to several ancient castles, many of which were still operational as hotels or homes of wealthy Jawlcheen families. Knowing the expensive tastes of the Regime generals, I was sure they would want to be pampered and waited on in one of these old palaces. We passed our information on to Croso. He commended us on our lead.

The next day, I met with Yalat at the Center. I asked her for help with the investigation of Hammerstead castles and their owners. She asked why I had such a keen interest in the place. I explained. She assured me she would research as much as possible.

Ocelot was pleased at our findings, but I became disturbed. Alaban and his boss had to be there in Hammerstead. Croso would send spies to monitor all activity there, especially at the meeting. Perhaps he already had someone on the inside, but I knew Alaban and any other assassin on his so-called task force would be able to sense a spy. I also knew the spy's fate if Alaban caught him. I wished I could be trusted with the information about the case. Of course I was not allowed to know who would be sent in from the Organization. If our directors had done their job right, there were probably already several dozen agents scattered throughout the echelons of the Regime in Boldoy and Hammerstead.

I imagined what the Regime members might discuss at their upcoming meeting. Financial deals, power plays, and political atrocities would be high on their agenda. I wondered if they were planning to build a second space station.

I recalled Thrader Defense Space Station One. The main purpose of the craft was to detain possible smugglers and interrogate them, probably for any type of information they deemed lucrative. What other plans did the Regime have for the space station? I considered the power and money necessary to create the spacecraft.

Teradom and the rest of the Regime had to be carried financially by a broad base of both legal and illegal activity. The space station, built on Fitmalo military funds and commonwealth contributions, was an investment for them. It now provided a flow of income, partially to the defense department and partially to their own cause. I found it easy to believe that both independent and Regime-related smugglers were being taxed or robbed at the space station. If the tariffs were high enough, they would cripple the smugglers' business. Knowing the black market distributors needed to retain a cut of their own to stay afloat, and assuming the smugglers would pass their losses on to their customers as a higher price, I realized the price of black market goods could be expected to rise sharply. Soon the price of smuggled goods could be comparable with the price of legal goods.

Perhaps Teradom had hinted at the truth when he told me the Organization encouraged smuggling to keep his planet in economic shambles. If his plan moved forward, fewer people would be willing to risk buying illegal goods, especially with so little difference between the prices of legal and illegal imports. Overall legal trade would increase. People would buy more of the officially taxed and recorded goods -on the open market. If my supposition were true, the economy of the planet Fitmalo would actually improve. It would stabilize, at least. Prime Minister Lock would be given credit for turning his planet around in his last year in office. His popularity would skyrocket. If the economy improved significantly, the people of Fitmalo might even rally to break their planet's constitutional law of terms of leadership. The new commonwealth supporters would claim sovereignty to elect him for an additional term. The traditionalists would protest, saying this was an unconstitutional attempt at dictatorship. This was exactly what the Regime was waiting for. Lock only needed to be reelected by the new commonwealth and then stay in office for his new term long enough for the Regime to create some kind of planetary catastrophe on Jawlcheen, blame it on Lock, and then overthrow him for it.

"The weapon," I thought aloud.

I paced fervently, stunned by the logistics of this theory. I wracked my brain, contemplating this possibility all the more.

If the Regime secretly planted the weapon, set it off, and then framed Lock for it, they could just as easily blame any other government officials on Lock's cabinet and do away with them as well, leaving every previously untouchable government position open for their own Regime members. Their takeover would be complete. People around the galaxy would support the move to oust Lock. Even the United Galaxy Organization would openly accept the takeover. The U.G. might even fund the fledgling government for its startup years. How cunning. How daring. I thought deeply about this plan for several minutes.

If I was only now beginning to see this possible pattern in Teradom's scheme, other investigators in the Organization must also have seen it long before. I had only worked on this case for little over a year. Some warriors had been investigating related information for decades. The Organization knew about this. They had to. But what steps had they taken to prevent it? The only positive reaction I'd noticed from the Organization on this case was the fact that someone had hidden the Sor3 weapon, probably before the Regime could get it. All other Regime plans had been allowed to thrive. Aside from Wilbaht's final renegade action of publicizing his list, (which the Organization edited before it reached the public), the only people who seemed to take definite action against the Regime were the Fitmalo rebels themselves.

I remembered Hallon and his perseverance as a rebel despite arrests and battles. I wondered just how much or how little the Organization's covert ops program was helping him and his comrades in the struggle to overturn the current government and the Regime. Pessimistically, I expected Hallon and his people received very little help at this point, if any.

I understood that the Organization hadn't intervened aggressively to avoid a public uproar. The political eccentrics would fly their flags of conspiracy theories to the world. The Organization would risk subjection to a galactic audit and a sharp decline in power. Anarchy could ensue from individual planets. The prospect was a nightmare. However, conspiracy was real. It caused our Organization's authority to stagnate. Many Organization generals and sub generals held double allegiances. Some were steeped so deeply into the muck of greed that they no longer had reason to wear the warriors' uniform.

I thought specifically of several such culprits. One of these traitors was Swall Jade. Another was Trau, now deceased. Of course Generals Lam and Samson were involved. There must have been dozens, perhaps hundreds of others at high levels, pulling strings on both sides of the curtain.

Then there was Stennet. His relationship to the others was still a disturbing mystery. Ocelot and Wilbaht and I had kicked around a few ideas about him, but we had concluded he must have been some sort of go-between, possibly for Swall Jade and the Sor3 turncoats. And yet, apart from the evidence Wilbaht found in Klib's recording equipment, we had no proof of his involvement. Still, the fact that Klib had worked for him under our noses and that he used the saboteur program against Wilbaht led me to believe there might be even more complexity in this cold war than we had previously thought.

Just then, Ocelot interrupted my thoughts. He had decoded the rest of our target's messages. He'd found a second blurb in one of the communications indicating a specific time and place for our new target's Regime meeting. The meeting would be held in Hammerstead at a castle, although he hadn't specified which. This would be easy to pinpoint by researching ownership of the towers. The date was set for a week and a half from now.

"Congratulations, partner," I said with a smile. "Now we're getting somewhere."

He met my compliment with a kiss on my cheek and a warm embrace. He rubbed my belly contentedly. I outlined for him my theory about the space station and Fitmalo economy. He stood by me, impressed with the idea. I then told him of my ideas about their plan to do away with Lock.

"Someone on our side had better keep that weapon under wraps. Whoever hid it must have top clearance. There's not even a record of its existence on Sor3," he said.

"I wish we could have stayed there longer to investigate the case in person," I replied.

"I wish I could contact Jiao, or at least find out what he's been researching. He might have some good data," Ocelot mused.

"Hmm. We're doing more wishing than investigating," I told him.

He hugged me to him. "I don't need to wish for anything. I have everything I ever wanted right here." He tugged at my ear playfully with his lips, which brought a smile. He kissed me firmly on my temple. "Are you happy?"

"I've never been so happy," I confessed. "But I do wish for something," I said teasingly.

"What's that?" He gazed into my eyes with care.

"I wish I had some palm fruit bread and pickled wedge root," I smiled.

He held me and laughed a little. "Sil, I think you're pregnant."

We chuckled together. I convinced him to go with me to buy the foods I craved. I selfishly enjoyed his attention. I wished to never be parted from him, even for a day. I knew our shell of perfect happiness would not last forever, but I planned to do everything within my power to keep us together within its protection..

Later in the week, I considered our conversation more seriously. Memories of Sor3 kept returning to my mind: the military science convention, the assassination on the twentieth floor, Viga and Trau's smuggling operation, the microship, General Zar, Stennet, Klib. They all had to be connected somehow.

I considered the research we'd done. The facts surrounding Trau's death didn't add up. There were so many questions I couldn't answer. Mostly, I kept stumbling on Stennet's involvement with the others. Feasibly, he could have worked with Trau at some point. Also I had felt for some time that Stennet might have been Zar's second target on the airbus, but something bothered me about the idea. I reviewed the information I knew about the case.

Trau was with the Regime. So were Lam and Samson, his interrogators. So if they were all on the same side, why did they torture him during the night between his first and second interrogations? Did they suspect he still worked for Zar or that he had passed information to him? What did they think Zar wanted from him? And if they had suspected foul play with Zar, why didn't they have Zar assassinated?

I paced as I attempted to untwist this confusion aloud. "Trau was in the Regime. Lam and Samson are in the Regime. Stennet is in with the Regime. He was controlling Klib. But Stennet had no connection to Zar. Why would Zar want him dead?" I stopped a moment. "Did *Klib* ever work with Zar?"

If Klib had worked for Zar, he would have access to Fitmalo military rebel plans. Perhaps he was even a *part* of Zar's plans. Did Stennet perhaps blackmail Klib about a crime he'd committed for Zar in order to force him to do his bidding?"

I thought of the research I'd done on Klib after the sabotage. He had trained to be a pilot on Xiantalix. He had flown Organization ships from the three major trade helions for more than a decade. He had arrived on Sor3 several weeks before we had. He was on Sor3 during Alaban's exam schedule and mine. He was there during the military science convention. He was there during our encounters with the microship. If Klib knew and worked for Zar, (but that didn't seem possible), did *he* send the microship to spy for Zar about the weapon? The clumsiness with which the microship had approached the C.A.T.T. Center reminded me of Klib's flawed mentality. If this were true, what would Klib, a top pay level Organization pilot without any record of illegal affiliation, be doing in such a situation?

I suddenly felt like a dunce. "Of course he has no record. Someone altered it, just like Ocelot altered our records. Who else works with retrodating programs?" I chagrined. "Jiao."

I hated to think of him like this. I couldn't tell Ocelot. I had no proof, only speculation. I thought of the irony in Jiao's warning to me back on Sor3 when he had advised me to trust no one. But then he had asked me to read Trau's interrogation file. Why? I felt very close to unraveling this part of the mystery, but I became entwined in superficial facts.

I thought fervently for the better part of an hour. In the end, I decided that my discovery of the truth pivoted on a set of variable possibilities. If Zar really meant for Stennet to die on the airbus, and if Stennet and the Regime were against Zar, then why were both Stennet and Zar still alive? Any of these opposing entities would have snuffed out their undesired foes by now, no matter how many tries it took them. At least one of these possibilities had to be incorrect. If I could find out which was wrong and why, I believed I could move us closer to solving our puzzle.

If Wilbaht had still been alive, I would have gone straight to him with my ideas. I was sure if I told all my thoughts to Ocelot, he would first become offended at my implication of Jiao, and then he would go to Channol for advice. I was reluctant to have him do that. Channol was certainly trustworthy, but he was neither as open nor as caring as his older brother had been. I was afraid he would take our information and stifle it to keep us low-ranking warriors from forming a full assessment of the facts. It was not supposed to be our privilege to do so.

I wasn't in a hurry to tell Yalat about my theories, either, since she had the habit of saying she already knew most of what I had to tell her. Then she would throw in a few other bits of information that were either directly or indirectly related to what I had mentioned to her. Eventually, she would take my information and continue investigating on her own without sharing unless I persisted about it. I decided I had done the right thing by requesting information from her instead of giving it.

My only other available ally was my own contact general, Croso, to whom I was supposed to report all my findings in the first place. I wasn't sure if Croso comprehended the intricacies of the personal relationships involved in my ideas. However, since I was withheld from action, I believed it was time to let someone know about the full montage from my perspective, and Croso would have to be that privileged individual.

The next morning, I informed Ocelot that I was going to the Center to speak with the General about our recent findings in person. He doubted I'd be able to get an audience with him on such short notice, but I was determined to try.

The Arborman clerk at the General's office asked me about the nature of my request to see him. I told her I had found some important clues to an intrastellar conspiracy he was familiar with. Even with my emphasis on important clues, she could only schedule me for a ten-minute meeting before the General had to leave. He was bound for the southwestern quadrant on a three-day visit to another Organization Center. Resignedly, I waited around for over two hours to see him.

When I was finally allowed in his office, I felt as though I were imposing. Croso was in the middle of some light facial grooming before his trip.

"Give me the most important details in as few words as possible, Sil. I'm off to Southwest in ten. Let's hear it," he said as he combed his wispy white eyebrows before a palm-sized mirror.

I decided to put off my theories about Sor3 to explain only what would interest the General most. "The Regime meeting place at Hammerstead. Alaban Jetscuro is there with Fitmalo General Teradom and probably the rest of his taskforce," I spoke quickly.

"And?" he asked. He clipped a few unruly whiskers from his chin as he listened.

"You know that Teradom wanted Alaban and me to work together to steal a secret weapon for him because our powers are compatible. Alaban cloaked his spirit from me since the space station incident, but now he's revealed himself again. He's calling me. He wants me to meet with him. If I could communicate with him, I think I could get information about Teradom's plan for the weapon. I have an idea of what he plans to do with it, sir. I believe he wants to use it against Jawlcheen. I just don't know where or when."

Croso's seat creaked as he turned to face me. He set down his grooming tools. His face was stern, but not surprised.

"Is Alaban calling you so you can work together to get this weapon now?" His steel eyes drilled through the air between us.

"No, sir."

"Then what?"

"I'm not sure, sir."

"I don't have time for this, Warrior. What do you suspect he wants?"

"It may be a call for help, sir."

The General scowled. "A man in a cushioned job like his does not call for help. You're thinking emotionally, not practically. Consider your physical state, Warrior. Check to make sure your ideas are rational before you make appointments to discuss them. Next time speak with Yalat or Ocelot before you ask to see me." I nearly contested him when he added, "You haven't made contact with him, have you?"

"No, sir."

"Good. Don't. I don't care how much you want to speak with him. You stay incommunicado." His nostrils flared as his eyes threatened me.

"Yes, sir," I said. His stark demeanor affronted my purpose.

He smoothed his silvery moustache. "Does Ocelot know everything about the two of you?" Croso asked pointedly.

"Yes, sir. I haven't kept anything from him," I answered.

General Croso drummed two sets of right fingers on the desk as he examined me. Then he stood, put away his grooming tools in his desk drawer, and straightened his uniform. He stepped around his desk to the door, but paused before opening it.

"Go home. Don't do anything until I get back. Don't even sightsee. I'll return in a week. Type a report about this compatibility of yours with Alaban. I want to know exactly what they're hoping you'll do together to retrieve that weapon. Don't leave out anything I should know, but make it as brief as possible. Deliver it to my secretary. I want it on my desk when I get back. Give me some background information to go with it and a list of references."

"Yes, sir," I told him. I followed the heavy-set man out into the hallway and to his reception office. I stepped aside to allow the secretarial clerk to pass him his itinerary.

"Have a good flight, sir," she said.

"Thank you, Miss Armiss. Make sure this warrior's report gets to the top of my desk while I'm away," he spoke to her.

"Yes, sir." Miss Armiss scanned my face to make sure she'd remember who I was.

"God speed, sir," I offered.

The General barely saluted us as he trudged away. He disappeared through the security doors and towards the airfield. My shoulders relaxed, but not my conscience. His criticism of my rationale insulted me. He had brushed off my concerns altogether. I would have to create an unemotional, regulation-formatted memo for him to take it seriously.

Now I had to go home and explain to Ocelot that Croso had demanded a report about the topic he disliked most. I marched home with dissatisfaction.

536

Chapter 50: The Foreboding Mission

I skimmed the three-page report for any excess information. Croso had wanted it as brief as possible. I tried to avoid expressing my own opinions too often, but part of the report dealt with the soul-felt relationship between Alaban and me, so it was sometimes necessary. I ended the report with my theory about the Regime's purpose for the weapon.

I tensed as I felt my husband approach, reading over my shoulder. He said nothing for a few strained moments. I scrolled through to the end of my report.

"It's a good report. I wonder what he's going to do with it," Ocelot spoke, unable to hide his agitation.

"Maybe he'll find out where the weapon and its formula are kept so they can increase security around it," I suggested.

"Why would they need to do that? I'm sure wherever it is, it's under the highest level security money can buy. Unless Teradom's task force has connections inside the fortress, even the best warriors couldn't get in," he said.

I turned sharply to stare him in the eye. "Why do you say 'fortress'? Are you saying you know where it is?"

He glanced at me hesitantly. "I have an idea."

I stood from my work to face him.

"I've been tracking the movements of hermetically sealed biohazard containment parcels from the Soren helion and records of new admittances to labs and strongholds since we left there. Jiao has been researching the same thing. I ghosted all his tracking information."

"From the ship?" I asked.

"Partly from the ship, partly from here," he admitted.

"What if Jiao discovers the ghost program and traces it to you?" I spoke anxiously.

"Don't worry. I've coded in from different phantom sites. He won't get a positive ID on it," he assured me.

"He'll know it's you. He knows how you work. His sixth sense has to confirm it," I bantered.

Ocelot shook his head. "Even if he knows, there's no proof. No one else would find out."

I gripped the back of the chair with one hand nervously. "Why did you keep this from me?"

"I didn't find anything definite. If I had, I would have told you," he defended.

"What little did you find out?" I asked doubtfully.

"I traced the movement of parcels to this helion and correlated that with secure item reception plans at high-security fortresses and labs. Recently, I found a courier's correspondence about a package that I think might be our weapon. The courier referred to it as the spider's egg."

"*Spider's egg*," I repeated, vividly remembering the Sor3 yellow spider.

"He arrived with it here on Jawlcheen, but I couldn't follow his trail. I tried to research all passengers on incoming flights just before his communication time, but one list of passengers from Gold Wind was set to trigger a spy chaser program. I had to log off and destroy my computer right away. I only caught part of the spy chaser codename."

"Whose was it?"

"Organization. Top-level codename. There's no way to research it. They'd track my inquiry and send U.G. military to arrest me for it," he said.

"I'd say that's more than just limited information. Why didn't you let me know about it?"

Ocelot sighed as he crossed his arms. "You know why."

I whirled to grasp the tail of the tape coil as I popped it out of the computer. I pocketed the object before turning again to bypass him. "Tell me more later. I have to turn this in," I began.

Ocelot clutched my arm. "Sil, I'm sorry I didn't tell you before. I won't hide my research from you. Just promise me you won't do anything about it on your own."

"You really think I would do that?" I clenched my jaw.

"I don't know. You've been acting awfully secretive lately," he said honestly.

I froze. We had lived through too much distrust already. I shrank from his grip. "I won't act on any information you show me, Ocelot. Croso would never approve of my involvement right now anyway."

He regarded me dubiously. He leaned down toward the computer desk drawer. It slid open. He reached inside to the back of it, angling his hand to unclip something from the underside of the desk. His hand retrieved a boxed tape coil. I kept my feelings of reproach to myself as he went through the motions of accessing the information. He pulled up a long list of strongholds and maps of the three inhabited planets of the Thrader helion.

"Eight hundred thirty-seven possible high-security fortresses and labs in the helion. Three hundred nine are Organization owned or associated. Only about half of these have received new biohazard secure items in the past few months. Forty-eight have received items in the time surrounding my suspect's communiqué. Three are in Boldoy," he outlined.

538

"You're right.   That's not much information at all," I spat sarcastically. "Why don't we go over this together when I get back? I have to turn this in before Croso gets back to his office."

I stomped past him, but he paced after me. He slowed me with levitative power and then held me by the arms.

"Don't walk out angry. I haven't narrowed it down yet. There's not enough information."

He wrapped his arms around me to try and soothe my anger, but I only bristled more. I wanted to push away from him, but I knew he was right. I shouldn't have turned my back on him to leave in anger. Instead I turned to embrace him, but spoke bitterly.

"Ocelot, I love you more than anything, but you cannot keep this kind of information from me. You shouldn't treat me like a weak, pregnant wife you have to protect from herself. I am still a warrior. I haven't lost my strength or my ability to reason."

"You haven't lost your stubbornness, either.   You're still determined to contact him, aren't you?" he countered, tightening his grip around me.

I dropped my shoulders in defeat.

"I kept this from you for your own good, Sil. What are you keeping from me?" he asked pointedly.

"My report was complete. You read it. That's all I know right now," I retorted.

"That's all you know and can prove. What else do you know that you can't report yet?" Ocelot dug his fingertips into my back.

"All I know is that he's searching for me through meditation. But he doesn't want me to work with Teradom's task force. He only wants my help."

"He wants *you*," he pronounced bitterly.

"Yes, he docs, but he won't find us. I won't lead him here," I promised.

"How badly do you want to contact him?" Ocelot asked as he released me.

"It doesn't matter. I won't contact him unless Croso tells me to," I spoke.

"Croso would never ask you to, but it does matter. If your urge to contact him is strong enough, your psychic energy will act as a beacon to him whether you're fully conscious of it or not. You'll lead him right to us," he stated.

"No. He's not coming here. He can't leave his post. Teradom won't trust him anymore if he does. He can't risk that," I blabbed.

"Keep talking," Ocelot coaxed as if he were performing an interrogation.

"He needs my help for some reason. I don't know why. I know it's not to retrieve the weapon."

"He wants you with him," Ocelot hissed.

"He wants out," I told him.

"If he's so strong, he'll get himself out." He grasped my shoulders. "Listen, you said he hid himself from you. Can you do the same thing? Can you hide your existence from him?" he rasped.

I shook my head. "I don't know how. Anyway, what good would it do? He's not coming here, Ocelot, and I'm not going to him." I panted. "I will never betray you."

"I know you don't want to," he said.

"*I won't!*" Now confused and upset, I kissed him quickly. "I have to go," I breathed.

He stared sullenly after me as I trotted out.

Ocelot's words reverberated through my mind as I made my way through the streets of Red Mesa and to our Center. I juggled my emotions and my logic. My rational side understood and forgave the fact that he had withheld information from me. At the same time, I felt myself pout. I also felt afraid. Ocelot sensed danger to us. I could argue away the feeling, but the foreboding remained.

Once inside the Center's main building, I traipsed down a wide hallway that led to General Croso's office. My worries abated momentarily when I spotted Yalat walking up the hallway towards me, chatting with a short Grey. As soon as she noticed me, she hopped in front of the man, grabbed him by the arm and attempted to turn him around for some urgent, yet phony, reason. It was too late. He had already recognized me. Instead of turning on my heel to avoid the scene, I decided to accept my fate head-on. I strode up to them bravely. The Grey was Banjil, our testing host from Sor3.

Although flustered by his discovery, he wisely held his tongue. His face indicated, however, that he expected an explanation.

"Professor Banjil, it's good to see you again. You may not remember me. My name is Sil…Rayfenix." I bowed.

He took my hand. "Yes, of course. Sil Rayfenix, did you say? My memory is not as good as it used to be. I could have sworn you were Sil Gretath."

"No, sir. That warrior was killed in battle, I've heard." I wondered what he expected from me. I was not willing to spill any more of the story to him.

He raised his thick eyebrows. "Indeed? I'm sorry to hear that."

Yalat and I exchanged formal greetings before him. Then I explained to them both that I was on my way to the General's office with a report. We parted company with cold formality. I distrusted Banjil fiercely, but trusted Yalat to set him straight. I remembered with disdain the gossip he had incited about the acid spider on Sor3.

I turned to watch the backs of his uniform and Yalat's disappear around the corner of the hallway. They spoke easily to each other. A paranoid idea sprang to mind. What if he had been sent here by someone on Sor3 for the purpose of observing and reporting on the coincidental likenesses between the deceased Sil Gretath and the current warrior Sil Rayfenix, the deceased Ocelot Quoren and the current warrior Jainocelot Quoren? If my fear was right, and if the person who had sent him was one of our suspects on Sor3, we were in deep trouble; unless Yalat could curtail his communication or perhaps even interrogate him to obtain counter information. I was sure she was one step ahead of me.

I had known our precarious position of false identities would be exposed eventually. Too many warriors traveled and communicated amongst planets and Organization Centers for us to hide forever. Still, I hadn't expected our aliases would be discovered so soon. This was a bad time for it. Too much was still at stake in our relationship with the Regime and Alaban to let the farce unravel for those outside our little circle of trusted friends.

I used a systems-independent wall computer to access my report. At the end of it, I tagged a quick note detailing my run-in with Banjil and my suspicions of him. I saved the report and continued on my way to the General's office. As promised, Miss Armiss delivered the boxed, labeled tape coil to the top of the pile on the General's desk. I asked her if it would be all right to wait for him so I could get in a word before he sat down to go through his work. She advised against it, since the General was usually grumpy after returning from abroad. He probably would be angry that I wanted to speak with him before his morning tea. I took her advice, although I planned on returning later in the day. I decided to go speak with Ocelot instead.

Before I had climbed the street three blocks from the Center, I received an urgent call from Croso himself. He told me to return to his office at once. I immediately rushed back to see him. His desk was a disheveled mess. His computer displayed a map of the area surrounding Hammerstead along with several windows of text. The box where my report had been stored lay open and empty in the middle of the pile on his desk. Croso himself was well dressed and proper as always, but his demeanor set me on edge. He interrupted me as I greeted him.

"Sit, Warrior. I have a new assignment for you, and I'll tell you right now: if you don't accept it, you'll be shipped off the planet and out of this solar system tomorrow."

I sat down hurriedly without interrupting him with formalities.

He continued aggressively. "You are to go to Hammerstead in person. I want you to contact Alaban Jetscuro directly. All our other contacts have gone missing. I don't have to explain to you what that means. Unfortunately, you are the only warrior we have left with connections on the inside. You are to extract as much information from Alaban as you can about the weapon and any other plans the Regime has been forming there in Hammerstead. Give him a final warning. Tell him the Fitmalo boss plans on doing away with all task force members as soon as the weapon is in their possession. Tell him if he comes back to this Center in time, we'll shelter him as a witness. If not, he's on his own.

"The Fitmalo generals' meeting will be held tonight. We suspect the topic for discussion will be their plans for the weapon. Castle security will be at its max. Tomorrow some of the generals leave. In three days, only Teradom and two other generals should still be in the building. Security won't be easy, but as long as they have no distractions during the meeting and the day after, they should let their guard down some. If you can't get to Alaban alone and away from the castle, you'll have to infiltrate the castle yourself.

"This is not a cloak and dagger mission. It's cloak and escape. If they know you're there, or if they discover you've been there, you know what will happen to you. Get in and out as fast as you can. Report back here as soon as you're out. Do you accept the job?" Croso leaned his lower set of fists onto his desk. The other set of arms rested akimbo.

My skin crawled. A million thoughts jammed into my brain at once. I was overwhelmed with excitement and self-doubt. Promises I'd made clashed. My conscience reeled. Croso now presented me with the most monumental proposition of my life.

"What about Ocelot?" I asked madly. "Will he be allowed to go with me?"

Croso nearly bellowed, "Of course not. If he goes with you, he'll hinder your performance. You go in alone. You'll concentrate on the job. I don't want a husband and wife team up there checking on each other every few minutes or calling off the operation just because they're worried about each other. Think independently, Warrior. You worry about yourself and your mission. I'll keep Ocelot busy while you're gone. He'll be cracking a code we'll urgently need done overnight. You'll leave at midmorning. Let Ocelot think you're on your regular routine. Take all evening to infiltrate if you need to. Get out of there by midday the following day. We'll hold Ocelot here until then. Fly back and be home for dinner."

Images of Alaban and Ocelot wrestled in my mind. Then I remembered the lion and the bull dragon. I had to save Alaban. Ocelot had to help me do it.

"Sir, I will take the job, but I need you to promise me something," I told him.

He grimaced, offended by a request from such a low-level warrior. "Don't try my patience, Sil."

"It's imperative, sir. If I don't contact you by the morning after I start this mission, please tell Ocelot what's going on. I might need his help to get out of there. I had a vision. You understand, sir," I spoke.

The General grumbled as he considered this. "I'll agree to it if you'll agree not to let him know about this at all. Don't even hint at it. If he asks, we spoke today only of Professor Banjil. Speaking of the Grey, I've put him under house arrest until he can be properly interrogated.

"I'm not giving you a file on the mission this time, just a few words of advice. Travel incognito, carry no traceable identification or noticeable weapons, travel light, and take only minimal recording equipment. I trust you've researched the area sufficiently."

"Yes, sir."

"Call in just before starting the mission. I'll see you back here in four days. Good luck, Sil." He offered me a hand to shake.

I shook his hand and sealed our fate.

Chapter 51: The Attempted Cloak and Escape

My next two days were filled with determined anticipation. Ocelot and I made amends from our argument, although I felt guilty for having to suppress the information about my new assignment. I had faith that he would find out at the right time. On the morning before I had to leave for Hammerstead, Ocelot went out to the Center to speak with Channol. I held him a little longer before saying goodbye. I kissed him more tenderly. I stared into his lovely brown eyes as I told him how much I loved him. He caressed my belly and smiled fondly at me. The baby squirmed as he did this. We chuckled together and kissed again. Silently, I prayed for his safety.

An hour later, I prepared for the journey that I believed would set us all free from the chains of fear. Alaban would leave the Regime under Organization protection. He would sadly accept the fact that I was a married woman now and an expectant mother. Ocelot would no longer dread Alaban's intervention in our lives. The terrible weapon would be the responsibility of the Organization here on Jawlcheen. Ocelot and I could move on to another planet: perhaps Liricos. Saul would grow up close to his extended family. My confidence coasted into my future's horizon.

I called in to Croso's office to let him know I was heading out from Red Mesa at 1000 hours. I changed into a black, understated pantsuit that appeared businesslike and at the same time allowed sufficient mobility for any personal defense moves I might need to make. It also hid the fact that I was pregnant, although I barely showed, now nearing my fifth month of pregnancy. I packed only a few things into my pockets: my laser cutter, a small pad of micro recorders, and a palm computer.

I remembered my bracelet. I didn't want it to fall into the wrong hands if I was caught. I took it off carefully and set it in our desk drawer where Ocelot was sure not to find it right away. I also left my clip-on phone next to it. I would use my computer or public communication to call Croso in the case of an emergency.

Before leaving, I called Ocelot to check on him and to tell him I loved him. He appreciated the attention. He said he'd see me later for dinner. I told him that sounded great, but didn't agree or disagree with him. I knew in the afternoon he would receive a call from Croso to report immediately for an urgent decoding. Croso would probably assure him that he had first called me at home and that Ocelot didn't need to notify me of his whereabouts since I already knew. I wondered what kind of decoding they could dig up for him that would keep him there all night.

From the interquad airbus terminal at Red Mesa, I flew to Boldoy. From Boldoy, I took a small airbus to Hammerstead. I arrived at the historical town at 1215. I stopped at an information booth outside the terminal to look up visitor information for the town, selecting a detailed map and historical guide to the ancient castles. I checked the skyline.

The pointy towers lined the canyon. They rose high in the air, impiously anchored to the red cliffs. One was older and more run down than the others. It was also the tallest and the one furthest removed from the rest of the town. Its full tower, measuring from its foundation in the base of the ravine to its pinnacle, stood fifteen stories high. Its observation room at the top of the tower lay agape. Its conical roof had broken away long ago and had not been repaired. Its main living space grew out onto the flat shelf of the cliff as if it had oozed onto it. Up close, it probably didn't have the same effect, but from this distance, it looked like a weird growth of fungus.

I meditated, focusing on the castles. My psychic energy suddenly surged. I was able to see who was inside the castle and what they were doing. Several people within the castle engaged in some kind of party on its ground level, catered by an extensive kitchen staff. On a different level of the castle, two generals sat at a game of virtual chess in a foyer connecting their suites. Bodyguards and security guards dotted the hallways and doorways of the place. A muscular black human female lifted weights in a large room on the fifth level. In a room near her, a pair of Vermilion females and one human female chattered to each other while painting their nails. In other rooms, I spied Fitmalos and Vermilions engaged in mating rituals or showering or sleeping. I counted fifty-seven people in the castle in more than one hundred rooms. Alaban and Teradom were not there at the moment. I anticipated their arrival later in the evening. Judging from the layout of the ancient palace, unless the automated security system was near perfect, I would have little trouble getting in undiscovered.

Then quickly, my energy diminished. I felt tired and nauseated. The baby kicked at my bladder. I returned to the terminal restroom briefly before moving on.

I took the first available cab to a castle open to the public as an historical site. I took a walk-through tour of the place to get a feel for what I might expect upon entering the lair of my foes. The long, winding halls and rooms were immense, lavishly decorated, and decidedly old. Modern amenities had been added to the castle, but none of the original walls had been altered. I expected the same from the castle on the hill.

After the tour, I climbed the hill on foot. Few people passed me on the street. When I finally arrived at the hilltop, I saw that the castle in question was actually several hundred meters from the main road. An invisible security fence beamed from handsome brick monoliths at the driveway.

The main street turned sharply and wound back down the hill in the opposite direction. I dropped a tiny recorder onto a windowsill across the street from the castle's gate and kept walking.

I stopped in at a computer and information shop. I rented time at a stationary computer and sat before it. I flipped through information about the town's history, but in reality I still meditated, waiting for the moment when Alaban would return with his boss. Finally, they arrived. I watched from the miniature screen on the micro recorder pad to see where the vehicle went through the fence.

I mentally called to Alaban. "I am here."

I felt a tremor of psychic energy. He seemed to be telling me to be careful.

"Come out to meet me," I attempted.

"I can't leave tonight," I understood.

"I'm coming for you," I thought.

I waited a long while for his response.

He flashed me an image of the open tower that overhung the body of the castle. He suggested this as the best path to him.

"Dark," I seemed to hear.

I agreed. He showed me images of security detectors at various points inside the castle. He also flashed me images of areas in the castle that I would need to pass through. He indicated a living room area service closet where I could hide. Then he seemed to close communication with me.

At twilight, I climbed the hill. I basked in Alaban's close presence. His power emanated from him like a beacon. I quickened my pace with anticipation. I imagined the warm embrace we would enjoy at our meeting. Our twin souls would be united again. Peace could be reached between us no matter what we had experienced. He had to accept Croso's offer for protection. He had to come back to the Organization.

I crossed the street to a small park overlooking the canyon. I walked through the shadowy, winding pathway, passing a couple of young lovers kissing on a bench. They didn't notice me at all. I moved to the railing at the edge of the cliff. During the day, this would have been the perfect place to take tourist photos, but now it was utterly dark. I checked once more behind me, but the couple was completely unaware of anything but their own kisses and touches from their eight hands. I smiled at them briefly. I felt my strength and levitative power escalate to an unbelievable level. I hopped up on the top of the railing and flew out over the canyon.

The warm summer wind tapered around me as I moved through the darkness, past the tree-filled park, past the security fencing surrounding the castle grounds, and up to the top of the castle tower. Although I could barely see it, I maneuvered my body into the gaping hole in its roof. Within the tower, no light flickered at all. I sensed my way down the spiraling stairs in absolute blackness.

By the time I reached the sealed door that led to the main section of the castle, I felt dizzy. I stood still for a few moments. My pregnancy affected my equilibrium, but my power still surged. After I regained my balance, I worked on parting the door. Despite my queasiness, I was able to spread the door open easily. I moved myself through to stand in a dark room. This was a community living room. Several other rooms emptied into it, although the doors to all these rooms were closed.

My level of power fluctuated. It lulled back to normal. Then I felt helpless and weak. I was thankful for the surge of ability moments before. If I had lost my power over the canyon, Saul and I would have perished.

Now unable to sense my surroundings, I sidled along the wall past a huge fireplace and to a door Alaban had indicated to me. I opened the unlocked door by hand, since I was now powerless to pass through it by other means. The lights here were not on motion sensors. The refurbishers of the castle must have wanted the palace to retain its ancient charm in every way possible. This appeared to be a long, unoccupied foyer. A curtained window at the end of this hallway only allowed dull gray light to filter through. I discerned the edges of three doorframes and their shiny handles here.

My psychic power swooned in and out of me, but I was able to perceive empty bedrooms on this hall. I levitated as best I could to step lightly on the carpet to the room nearest the covered window. I entered. Two thinly curtained windows here allowed sufficient light to make out the main objects in the room. This was a luxury suite, probably better furnished than the other rooms on this hallway. A set of tall, decorative wooden slats concealed a service elevator in one of the walls. I opened the slats to find a black square. This was the shaft of the service elevator.

I waited a few moments before it, attempting to gather all my strength to me before entering the shaft. When I felt ready, I entered the black square and levitated downward. Musty dampness of the ancient castle mixed with the smells of boiled vegetables and smoked meats from the kitchen below. The odors aggravated my nausea, but I contained it. As I neared the kitchen level, the soles of my shoes tapped the top of the service elevator box.

This simple vibration awakened the incredible force of power in me once more. I suddenly sensed the layout of the kitchen, the dining hall beyond it, the guards on the main entertainment room floor and doorway, the kitchen staff and servicemen bustling about, cleaning up after the party, preparing dishes to be washed, and organizing the prep area for the next work day. I slipped my body through the service elevator box. I cloaked a blind spot as I exited the kitchen service elevator slats. I hovered near the ceiling as I observed a pair of portly Vermilion women scrubbing down the long kitchen prep counter.

I glimpsed the doors at either side of the great fireplace and oven center of the kitchen. The door on the right led to the dining area. The door on the left was the one I needed to reach. It opened into a short hallway and a stairwell, which led to the castle staff housing. The staff housing area consisted of several interconnected bedrooms, a community bath, and an additional foyer. This foyer would guide me to the wide living room space Alaban had shown me earlier.

As I cleared most of the ceiling, the kitchen workers put away their scrubbing rags and sauntered back out into the dining area. Their work was almost done for the evening. As their swishing, black skirts left the kitchen, I felt my body sink into the room. My power had become untrustworthy. I barely cleared a rack of cooking pots and utensils before the levitation gave out altogether. I knelt on the countertop. My cloaking power faded. Dizziness tipped me over. I bumped into bowl of fresh fruits, which spilled conspicuously. I gripped the edge of the countertop and swung my feet to the floor. The room wavered around me. I attempted to recloak, but couldn't. My power had left me.

The pair of Vermilion kitchen workers returned to the prep area, each carrying a folded, soiled tablecloth. They recoiled when they saw me. I was caught.

Chapter 52: Caught

I had to think fast. I didn't want to injure or kill them. They would be missed almost immediately. I couldn't get rid of them without forcing myself into a one-woman attack on the whole castle. Then I realized I might be able to use this dilemma to my advantage. I decided to play-act my way through this.

I hurriedly picked up the fruits and plunked them back into the bowl. I acted embarrassed.

One of the workers barked, "What are you doing down here? Who are you?"

I clutched one of the fruits to my chest. "Please let me take one. He hasn't let me eat anything all day. Please don't tell on me. I'll work it off if you'll just let me have one. I'm starving."

The other worker turned to the first one. "She's a concubine. What should we do?"

"She's not supposed to be down here. I'm reporting her to the guard," the first one replied.

"Okay, report me, but can I have just one? Please," I begged.

The second worker felt sorry for me, but the first woman snatched the fruit from my hand. She put it back in the bowl.

"No. If you want to be fed, you'll have to work for it with your man. You're supposed to feed with him or the other concubines, not us. You don't exactly look starved. You stay here and don't touch anything. I'm going up for the guard. You watch her."

She stamped out of the kitchen. The second woman grabbed a pear from the bowl and shoved it at me as she looked over her shoulder.

"Here. Eat this quick, before she comes back."

I thanked her and gulped down the fruit as if I were truly starving. I disposed of the core and rinsed my fingers and mouth moments before the hateful woman returned with the guard. I hoped he didn't know all the castle concubines by heart.

"Whose girl are you?" the burly Vermilion demanded.

"I don't know his name, sir. He just bought my contract yesterday, sir." I made myself as humbled as possible.

"Oh, you're one of Ryker's girls. He's gonna be pissed when he hears you got out. I'm gonna do you a favor. Then you'll have to owe me something. You understand?"

I nodded shamefully.

"I'm gonna tell him where I found you. If I take you to him, he'll beat the shit out of you in front of me. I don't like to get in the way of that domestic shit. You wait here." He stamped back out of the kitchen.

I bowed my head. I prayed this would work. The kitchen ladies exchanged glances against me and went about collecting the remaining food service laundry without another word. They moved to the door that should have been my escape route. The haughty one paused to keep an eye on me until the guard returned. I pretended to feel sorry for myself. A few moments later, the guard returned with disgust on his face. He grabbed me by the hair with his red clutches and marched me through the kitchen. I whimpered miserably, keeping my hands clasped before me subserviently.

"Looks like you won't be doing me any favors after all," he muttered angrily.

He yanked an empty cloth sack from the kitchen counter and stuffed it over my head. Then he continued pulling me along by the wrist. I didn't panic. I felt surely Alaban would be able to get me out of this or I would fight my way out.

"Where are you taking me?" I whined as I shuffled along beside him.

"Just come on and keep your trap shut," he said. "If you're lucky, he'll change his mind."

He opened a door in front of us. A sickly stench floated through the air.

"Ugh. What is that smell?" I asked him. I slid a little on the slimy floor.

I couldn't contain the nausea I felt from the pungent odor. I bent over to throw up. The sack fell from my head, imbibed with the regurgitated pear. I gasped and coughed. He made a sound of disgust, but yanked me along with him. My hair fell over my eyes. I could barely see around me, but I found the source of the smell. Dried blood and bits of raw meat covered the floor.

The man slapped a pair of electrostatic binders around my wrists. These were connected to a pulley. He cranked the pulley from the wall so that the binders tightened and lifted me off the ground. I quickly grabbed onto the chain so the binders wouldn't cut off my circulation. I jerked and kicked.

"No! No, please don't leave me here. I was just hungry. What did I do? I promise I won't wander out again, please! Let me go. I'll do anything you want," I wailed.

He only frowned and shook his head. He paced out the way he entered. I squirmed and panted. As soon as he left, I stopped. I levitated

550

just enough to keep the chain and binders from cutting into my skin. A few moments later, the automatic lights dimmed. Then they snapped off.

I concentrated to communicate my basic situation to Alaban, but I did not sense him call back to me. I waited patiently in this malodorous place for what seemed like half an hour in the darkness. I called to Alaban again. I let him know I was in a bloody room near the kitchen and that Ryker and a guard thought I was one of Ryker's escaped concubines. Again, Alaban neglected to answer my call.

Almost another half hour later, the kitchen door scraped open. The lights flashed on. Heavy, dragging footsteps entered the room. Whoever it was grumbled when he breathed. He carried a load of some kind. I heard him near the wall behind me. He slung his burden down on what must have been a wooden table, which screeched on the tile floor as he bumped it. I heard him withdraw a metal instrument from a holder on the wall. I shuddered as I heard the weapon swoosh through the air and thwack onto the table. He repeated this action two more times. Then he moved a wooden bench. He sat heavily. He growled a sigh as he settled into the seat. The metal instrument he had used clattered to the table where he let it go. Next I heard a gnawing and a crunching sound.

I meditated to perceive who the person was, but I didn't believe what I perceived. I turned my head slowly. I still could not see the source of the noise. I turned my body slightly to glimpse a hideous creature. He sat at the wooden table, which was spread with raw meat. The creature held a few ribs in his claws. He smacked his lips together and grumbled almost melodiously as he chewed.

His skin was an unnatural dark pinkish color with a few tufts of dull brown fur around his head and neck. His body was massive. He must have weighed five times my own body weight. He had the cranial shape of a bipedal man of the second or third intelligence, but his jaw and snout were formed like those of a carnivorous animal. Four sharp canine teeth protruded from his mouth. He bit easily into the ribs, crushing them apart. He consumed his grisly meal, bones and all.

I looked away. The smell of fresh blood and entrails turned my stomach. I concentrated on keeping the bile down as I listened to the creature munch the discarded body parts.

I checked to my left. Two other humans—males—also hung along the ceiling rack. I sensed they were dead. I barely contained my urge to regurgitate the liquid in my stomach.

Just then, I heard footsteps from outside the meat room. They were strong, purposeful steps. The door behind me slid open. I heard the creature's wooden bench creak as he turned to see his visitor. To my amazement, the creature spoke.

"Bahn," he growled deeply.

"Hey, Sangrol, how's it drooling?" Alaban said to him cynically.

The creature grumbled. "Can't complain." He spoke slowly.

"They told me you have a human female in here. Oh, yes. There she is. Can I make a trade with you?" he asked.

The creature grumbled again. "You can have her, Bahn. You feed me good. Take."

"Hey, that's very generous of you, Sangrol. Remind me to send you a cow later," I heard Alaban reply.

"Mmm. Like cow. Better than Grey," Sangrol growled contentedly.

Alaban stepped to me from behind. I felt the binders release my wrists. He immediately stood me up in front of him and jerked one arm up behind my back. He held my other forearm up to my neck with his own as he forced me out of the little room. I groaned but did not struggle. Alaban turned me so I got a good look at the creature. He kept his warped back to us as we left. The fur around his neck was matted with blood. I almost lost control of my stomach. The animal bade Alaban goodbye as we moved through the door, but Alaban did not reply this time.

After stepping through the threshold, Alaban immediately turned me to the right to ascend a set of stone steps. He shoved me up the stairs violently. I protested, but he told me to keep quiet. His voice was agitated.

He walked me out into a wide living room, much like the one I had first entered after coming in through the tower. Several rough-looking characters lounged around on the sofas smoking some kind of drug. They looked completely out of place in this luxurious palace. One of them whooped when he saw Alaban with me. One asked if he had any more like me downstairs.

"I want a piece of that," another hacked with enthusiasm.

"Hey, let me know when you're finished with her. I'll take whatever's left," a bony, red-eyed Arborman called facetiously.

The garishly dressed Fitmalo girl on his left slapped him viciously. He turned to grab her by the hair, twisting her neck until she whined loudly and then screamed.

The others laughed. One of them made a lewd gesture. I knew Alaban was in the den of the beast, but I had no idea it would be like this.

"This ain't a public well. Go find your own pipeline to drill," Alaban retorted.

They whooped and guffawed all the more. Some cheered him on. I groaned.

"Bastards," Alaban said under his breath.

552

He pulled me along to another set of stairs. He did not relax his grip on me or show me any mercy while we marched up the steps. Instead he prodded me along aggressively. I expected he did this for the security cameras on us.

At the top of this flight of stairs, we encountered a balconied hallway with three doors. At the end of the hallway sat a fat Grey. He flirted with a slim Vermilion female. She stood facing him with all four arms crossed. His hand ran up the back of her leg under her miniskirt. She seemed unmoved by this gesture. When the Grey saw us, he jerked his hand away from the woman. He became mortally nervous.

"Hey, there, Bahn. I see you've got a new female," he said shakily.

"You keep your nasty gray paws off my property. If I so much as smell you on her, I'll break your oversized neck. Now get the fuck off my floor," Alaban told him unabashedly.

The Grey squirmed out of his seat.

"Now!" Alaban shouted, momentarily dulling my hearing.

The Grey waddled hurriedly past us and down the stairs without another word. The Vermilion stared at Alaban with a mixture of fear and triumph.

"If I see you with any of these bastards again, I will send you back out on the street. Do you understand?" he said to her evenly.

She suddenly became repentant of her actions. Fear seized her over entirely.

"Do you understand?" he repeated through gritted teeth.

She nodded childishly. Her green quicksilver eyes widened. She meekly uttered a "yes sir" to him. She hunched forward slightly. Her crossed arms, which moments before had formed a wall of defiance, now hugged her upper body as a thin protection.

"I won't require your services tonight, so get to your room and lock yourself in. Do it." His voice was frigid.

She hung her head. She turned obediently to the door behind her and entered. As she closed her door, Alaban released my forearm. He pulled up on the arm behind my back. I groaned with real pain. I struggled as he unlocked his door.

"Oh, so now you're ready to put up a fight? Huh? Let's see what you've got," he pronounced.

His manner turned sinister. He pushed me rashly through the door and clicked the lights on. This was a room I had seen in one of my dreams. A broad royal blue bed stood in the center of the room. The other furnishings were antiques or made to look like them. I stopped just short of the bed to observe the room.

Alaban slammed the door heavily behind him. I hoped that now he would cut the act and behave like the friend I knew. But I was in for a shock.

Before I could turn around, Alaban grabbed me by the back of the neck and cast me onto the bed. I bounced twice before I turned onto my back. I gasped. This was not the man I knew and loved.

"What? What are you?" I heard myself ask in a panic.

His eyelids and cheekbones were covered with black ashes. His eyes shone with the glow of pale, iridescent contact lenses. His hair stood out in five gelled rows of short spikes tipped with silver paint. He tore open his black jacket, which hung with sharp pins on the shoulders. He glowered at me with a mania I had never seen in him before. He threw the jacket hatefully to the floor. His sleeveless T-shirt was white with red bloodstain designs all over it. The muscles on his shoulders glittered with skin-implanted metal studs. He wore jagged lightning-shaped nose rings and earrings. A thick silver necklace displayed what looked like the claw or tooth of some large animal. I recognized it as a leg spike from the acid spider on Sor3. He snarled at me. I backed away from him towards the head of the bed. He whipped off his broad weapons belt. It clattered to the floor.

"What are you running from, Sil?" he asked me in a sinister voice.

"You're not Alaban. Who are you?" I asked.

"It's Bahn. Not Alaban, just Bahn. Like the planet, red-hot." He kicked off his boots and then removed his shirt to reveal more metal studs in a flame pattern along his pectoral muscles.

Frightened, I thought maybe he was high on some kind of drug like his associates downstairs. He wasn't himself at all. I tried desperately to reason with him.

"Bahn, stop. What are you doing?" I asked him.

He stopped and rolled his head. His neck cracked twice. He hung his thumbs in the top of his black pants. He tapped his fingers menacingly around his groin.

"What, you don't like my new look?" he said gruffly.

He dove briskly after me to catch my ankles. He yanked my legs toward him as he leapt to the bed. He pinned me down. I tried to slap and punch him in the face. He pressed into my biceps with his elbows and leaned on top of me. He rested his spiked head next to mine and attempted to bite my ear, but I jerked my head away from him.

"Why are you so weak, Sil?" he asked in aggravation.

His weight hurt my belly. I pushed him off of me with levitation, but his power was even stronger than mine. He pressed his knees onto my thighs and held my arms in a tight grip. He searched my eyes. We challenged each other's power until I began to weaken. His weight came down on top of me again.

"No, Alaban. Don't do this. Get off. You're hurting me."

"How am I hurting you? I'm just lying here," he said, suddenly in his normal voice.

"Get off, Alaban, please," I begged him.

He only blinked at me in confusion.

"I'm pregnant!" I finally told him.

He recoiled immediately to his knees. I panted and heaved myself up to sit and massage the sides of my abdomen while I scooted away from him.

"No. You can't be. That's not true. It was just a dream. It was just a bad dream. You can't be pregnant," he spoke nervously. "Can you? Tell me it's not true."

He sat before me, shaking his head. He blinked heavily. He staggered backward to stand on the floor. He stared at me with an emotion I couldn't decipher. His face was so different from what I was used to.

I crouched in the center of the bed, ready to run if necessary. He was the most awesome and frightening human I'd ever seen.

He staggered backward a few steps. He closed his eyes. Then he turned his back to me, still shaking his head. He stumbled off to his bathroom, which was adjacent to the bedroom. I heard water running. He came back with water droplets all over his face and chest. He leaned in the doorway for a moment. He breathed heavily.

Alaban staggered to the bedside. He knelt awkwardly. His decorated face cringed. He reached out to me slowly, gently. This time he meant me no harm. I let him grasp my hand. He spoke almost breathlessly.

"I saw a vision of you, almost five months ago. It gave me the most powerful craving. I had to mate. I couldn't stop myself. I took my concubine to my bed with me but I only saw you—in the most fantastic orgasm—and I was there with you."

My face reddened. I wanted to look away, but his crazed stare held my attention. He spoke adamantly.

"It was like you and I were the same person. I felt it right along with you: body, spirit and soul. It was like a supernova. Everything in the room was levitating for hours. And you…you conceived."

He reached toward my abdomen to try and touch my belly, but I backed away from him in panic. He panted for a moment before pushing himself back up to stand facing me.

"It was real. You did mate. I wasn't going crazy." He paused. "Or maybe I was. I thought you said you'd do anything to have me back. You said…that you should have accepted me from the beginning." He pointed at me limply. "You said in your letter that you would me *my* mate for life."

I didn't answer him. I trembled as I stepped down from the bed away from him. His jaw clenched in a tight frown. Then the frown relaxed. His jowls hung sadly.

"Why, Sil? You changed your mind? You couldn't wait?" He spoke quietly but vindictively. He stood rigid as a painted totem.

I opened my mouth to speak to this mythical creature, but I was unsure how to start. He stared eerily at my face with his unnatural eyes. I almost expected fangs to appear at his mouth. He eventually reacted to my fear.

"You don't like the new me," he said. "Neither do I."

He sauntered backwards to the bathroom once more. He whisked off his earrings as he entered.

Suddenly, someone pounded on the door to the hallway. A muffled voice called to Bahn. Alaban left the bathroom without earrings or nose rings. He was only slightly more recognizable. He padded agitatedly across the floor. He shot a glance at me and pointed to the bed.

"Don't let him see your face," he said in a low voice.

I sat near the head of the bed. I removed my shoes and my outer jacket. I turned away from the door.

Alaban opened it.

"Sorry to bother you." The man obviously lied. "You didn't pick up one of my concubines from downstairs, did you?" It must have been Ryker.

"No way, man. You know I don't touch your women and you don't touch mine. What are you talking about?" Alaban asked, noticeably agitated, attempting to suppress his distress.

"Damned stupid guard said my new human female got out and they found her in the kitchen. I told him to string her up in the meat room to teach her a lesson. But my human girl is still in my room. Says she's been there since breakfast. Then one of the guys from the hive tells me you had her. What's going on?"

"No, she wasn't yours. She's mine, see?" He paused, apparently to point to me.

I pretended to button up my blouse.

"When did you get a new girl?" Ryker asked suspiciously.

"Couple of days ago. I left her here last night. Forgot to feed her. Lucky I found her before Sangrol made a meal out of her. I paid a high price for this one."

"Hmm." Ryker stayed in the doorway observing me. I smoothed my hair and reached for my jacket.

"So do you want something else or what?" Alaban asked him.

"No, man. I just thought some foul play was going on here. This job will make you paranoid," Ryker complained.

"No shit," Alaban said flatly.

"Yeah, I'll see you later," Ryker replied in a similar tone.

Alaban shut the door. I turned to him. He was despondent. He stared at the floor. A dreary minute passed before his frosted eyes.

"Alaban?" I said softly.

He barely acknowledged me. He walked lazily to his wardrobe. He opened it to retrieve a simple black T-shirt. He shoved his spiked head through the neck of the shirt and pulled it down over him. He closed the wardrobe and moved to pick up his clothing he had left at the foot of the bed. He rested the jacket over his desk chair. He set his boots next to his wardrobe. He folded the blood shirt as if it were a military uniform and set it on top of the boots. All this he seemed to do in a mock routine to avoid facing me.

I decided to start with unemotional questions to hopefully bring him back to me slowly. "What is the hive?" I asked.

"What's the hive? They're a cover gang for smuggling ops. They're scum. They're our eyes and ears on the underground."

"Were those men in the meat room two of them?" I asked.

"Yeah, a couple of back stabbers."

"Did you kill them?"

"No." He shuffled across the floor towards the bed once more.

"Why did you change the way you look?" I asked him.

"For their own good. Some of the guys used to try and pick on me because they thought I didn't look so tough. I wound up breaking a lot of arms. I figured if I looked worse than them, they wouldn't mess with me to begin with."

He pointed to the ashes around his eyes. "See this? I keep a jar of ashes from my victims," he spoke, imitating the sly drone he would have used to convince a hive member. Then he relaxed into a flat tone of disappointment. "That's what I tell them. They're just coal ashes, but it freaks people out enough to make them think it's true. Looks scary, huh? I didn't mean to scare you. I was just playing around. I guess I can't do that anymore. I didn't mean to hurt you." His darkened face fell into a visage of sagging depression.

I poised tensely near the bed. Alaban disappeared into his bathroom once more. I heard him pound the sink with a fist, swear, punch the sink again, and then release a guttural cry of anguish. Then he was quiet. When he emerged minutes later, his eyes were back to normal. I watched his stoic black form as he paced to the bedside near me.

"Is that better?" he asked, scarcely containing his angst.

557

I nodded.

"Sit with me," he ordered.

He sat at the edge of the bed next to me and planted his fists over his thighs. I sat close to him. He glanced at me and then looked away, sniffling. He breathed deeply and then faced forward.

"I knew," he barely annunciated.

I waited for him to continue. He stared ahead with summoned determination.

"I knew the whole time." He looked at me with a tough façade. "Think back to Sor3. You had a dream. I induced it."

"The pins?" I asked softly.

"Yeah. I blinded you."

The nearly forgotten image of the acupuncture pin through my eye returned to me in a foggy memory. The needle sewed through the memory to bring the past and present together. Two seemingly disconnected moments in time were suddenly united to reveal a clear pattern.

"You knew? You knew about Ocelot before I did," I exclaimed.

Alaban turned his face toward me, but his eyes avoided me, seeking moral support from the impartial wooden floor. "I met him the day before my exam. I saw a vision of the two of you...kissing." He waved his hand in a disgusted gesture. The corners of his lips pulled downward as he professed. "I couldn't let him have you. I couldn't give you up before I'd even had a chance with you. But I couldn't touch him without risking everything I'd worked for. I couldn't get rid of him. I couldn't blind him. But you. You and I share a spirit. I could walk into your dreams and blind you to him. I tried over and over. Finally, when you told me about your dream, I thought it actually worked."

My heart beat heavily. I realized what he had done. The fogged memory cleared. I recalled Alaban with the acupuncture pins saying, "Stay blind. Don't see." He had sent me the dream to keep me blind, so I would not see Ocelot through the eyes of love.

I regarded him gravely. "It did work."

He shook his head in spite. "It wasn't good enough. You chose him anyway. At the space station, you chose him even though he was a dead man. You still didn't see who he was, but you chose him anyway. I didn't understand until then. I was out of my league. I couldn't control the plan of the cosmos. I was wrong. I was wrong to screw with your psyche. It didn't do me any good. It didn't bring us together. It just left you confused.

"Then when I saw you trying to leave, I realized what you'd done for him. It just about killed me, but I knew I had to release you from that spell."

His words to me in the space station echoed through my head: "*I release you.*"

"I just hoped you would realize which one of us loved you more. I knew it had to be me." He would not look me in the eye. He trembled with duress. "When I got your letter after the space station, I thought you'd decided on me. Then I started having dreams of you with him. I thought they were just nightmares. But they were real. Weren't they, Sil? You're in love with him?"

Bravely, I replied, "Yes."

He grasped the tops of his ears in his hands as he leaned down to cringe and grieve to himself. I moved to crouch behind him.

"Are you happy with him?" he asked loudly.

"Yes, Alaban. He is a good man. I love him. He is my husband," I told him.

"*Husband?*" he thundered. Alaban retched furiously, vibrating his pawed hands near his head. "He can't possibly love you as much as I have, Sil. What I did for you…" He cringed all the more, growling sharply against his failure. "He can't love you like I do!"

"I believe he does," I said softly, but resolutely. I wanted to comfort Alaban, but I knew the only comfort he would accept would be my denial of the man I had to defend.

"He is my husband because I chose him, not for what he's done for me, but for who he is and how he makes me feel. He makes me happy. I want to make him happy. I am glad to be his wife. I know this is the last thing you want to hear, but you have to. Things were never right between you and me. Even if he didn't exist, you and I could never be mates. I am sorry I sent you that letter. I panicked when I couldn't sense you anymore. I wrote things I normally wouldn't have. I was fevered. I still had a poison spike in my arm. It nearly killed me."

Alaban dropped his hands from his face. He turned slightly. "I thought I'd taken them all out of you."

"I know you did. You did the best you could. You saved my life. You gave me the greatest gift. You sacrificed your dream for me." I ventured to touch him on his shoulder blade. "You let me decide. I have decided. Now respect my decision, I beg you. You know I love you, my friend. I have always called you that and that's what I pray you'll always be. If you love me as a spiritual twin, you will let him stay alive. I cannot live in peace without him." Tears ran past my nose and salted my lips. I sniffled and then waited anxiously for his response.

Alaban sat motionless, barely breathing. Then his body shuddered. He cried as quietly as he could. He would not turn around to see me. He wept for a few minutes this way. Finally, I leaned my cheek between his shoulder blades and covered his Braille shoulders with my hands. He groaned and sucked air as he sobbed. I hugged him as best I could in this position to comfort him. At last he sniffed deeply and pulled himself together. After another minute of labored sighs and sniffles, he sat straight. I retracted from his shoulders, hoping for a sign of peace.

He spoke deeply, "I won't kill him." He breathed forcefully. "For you."

I sighed my thanks to him.

"You're sure you're happy with him?" He wrung his hands.

"With every fiber of my being I am happy with him, and with our baby," I told him.

I slipped a hand into his. He squeezed my hand to his face and smeared his tear-streaked ashes onto the back of it. He sniffed loudly, and then began to talk again to combat his emotion.

"It's good you didn't come with me. I'm not what I used to be. All I do now is kill for a living," he professed.

"You don't want to," I said to him.

"No, I don't want to. But I do whatever he tells me to. I'm Teradom's pet dragon," he pronounced despicably. He exhaled profoundly.

"He holds the key to your chains," I added.

"Yes," Alaban spoke with exhausted anger.

"Why, Alaban?" I asked. I rested a hand atop his studded shoulder.

"I'm his scare tactic. He uses me all the time. Now I think I hate him more than I hated Trau." He paused to glance around his room. "He advertised all this luxury to us. But it's just for show. We're not high class. We're the dregs of all civilization. The rich image is just to impress buyers. All this priceless stuff is worthless."

"You have a Vermilion concubine, I see," I mentioned.

He nodded. "When Teradom thought I'd killed you, he bought her for me as a consolation gift. Actually, I think she was my reward for being coldhearted enough to kill you. Her name is Willa. She either hates me or she's scared to death of me. I didn't touch her until that night I saw you in the vision. I kept my promise to you as long as I could."

"Do you want to keep her?" I asked.

"Why?"

"I came to get you out of here. We could take her with us if you want," I told him.

Alaban twisted abruptly. He blinked and squinted at me. I sat straight with him.

"What are you saying?" he asked.

"I am here as a spy. I was sent to get as much information from you as I can and then get out of here, but I'm also here to offer you a truce. My contact general is offering you amnesty. I trust him. He said Teradom would eliminate everyone in the task force once he has the weapon. If you stay here, your life will be in danger. Come back with me. We're close to finding the weapon and exposing the Regime. If you don't come back to the Organization now, what's going to happen when Teradom and his associates get busted for conspiracy?" I asked him pointedly.

"I'll get a new assignment and a promotion," he whispered.

My face turned to stone.

"I never left the Organization, Sil," he continued in hushed tones.

Chapter 53: Moment of Truth

I grasped his studded shoulder. "But you said in your letter that you'd have to say goodbye to the Organization."

"I only meant that I couldn't work with the Organization openly. I told you Ongeram sent me here. I'm isolated: deep covert. I can't show up at any Centers. I can't use a ship. I can't message Organization personnel. I'm on my own. I only feed data to secret contacts whenever they show up. I don't know who they are or where they'll be. This is an Organization op. I told you. I'm not a traitor." He frowned and gazed at his hands. "I'm just an idiot. I shouldn't have done anything to keep you from trusting me in the first place. Then everything would have turned out differently at the space station. Would you have gone with me then if you had known?"

"Yes. In a heartbeat," I whispered in awe.

He gave me a pained expression, and then shook his head spitefully. "It's good you didn't come with me. They would have turned you into a killing machine just like the rest of us. If you refused to do an assassination, one of us would be assigned to get rid of you. I would have ended up killing the whole lot of them just to get you out of here. I was wrong, Sil. This is a hundred times worse than the Organization. If I saw any dependable way out of here, I'd take it."

I held his muscular arm as I peered into his coal black eyes. "Then consider this your rescue."

He stared at me anxiously, analyzing the poRID01□□□OTIHe stood rapidly. He paced the room, clenching and unclenching his fists in hyper thought. His eyes searched his mind frantically. I stood to follow him.

He whirled on one heel as he pointed to the ceiling with an idea. Then he shook and snapped the finger. He ended the motion with his hands together in a prayer position. He pointed the hands at me as he spoke adamantly.

"I can't go right now. I will. I just need to do a few things here first. I can be out by the end of the month. It won't be too late. Don't worry." He gently wrapped his hands around my shoulders. "I'll bring Willa with me. She's my responsibility. If I can't get her out, I'll have to kill her. If she stays here, she'll just be passed around the hive until they get tired of her. As far as I can tell, she's clean. She's young. She can still have a decent life after this."

I nodded to him with admiration.

"If you have a computer on you, I'll pass you a few files of meetings and smuggling directives. They'll keep your boss happy for a while. Then we have to find a way to get you out of here."

"Are you sure no one's listening in on us right now?" I asked him.

"I've got a macro wave pulse device in here. It generates interference to keep this room from being bugged," he assured me.

"Let's go by worst case scenario and work our way up," I suggested. "I can get out the way I came in, but then you're left with a lot of impossible explaining to do."

"Right. Let me think a while."

Alaban retrieved a stack of tape coils from a hiding place in his bathroom. He loaded some information onto my palm computer as we schemed.

Teradom knew Alaban hadn't gone anywhere to buy a second concubine within the last few days. If Ryker mentioned it to him, he would automatically turn on Alaban. We had to come up with a plausible explanation for my appearance here. Alaban arrived at a thinly defendable, yet believable idea. He tried out the speech to me.

"Willa isn't the right kind of mate for me. She's a Vermilion. She's pretty, but I always wanted a woRID01□□□OTIwn species. So I found a make-to-order concubine service in Boldoy. I asked for a human female, about my age, reddish-brown skin, dark, straight hair. The cost was more than I usually spend on weapons and ammo in two years, but if she was the kind I was looking for, I figured she'd be worth it. I had her delivered to that park just down the street. I sneaked out to get her. I didn't want anyone in the hive to know about her. They'd try to get to her while I was out.

"Then I had to go out with Teradom to do an all-day job and we didn't get in until late. I had to stand by him while he met with the other generals, so she was left alone for more than fourteen hours. She didn't have anything to eat all day. She's not like the common concubines that sit around starving and wait for their man to feed them. She's used to better treatment. So she went looking for food for herself. That's when the staff caught her and thought she was Ryker's girl." He paced near the foot of his bed as he animated his explanation with hand gestures.

"So then how are you going to justify letting me out?" I asked.

Alaban continued. "It turns out this girl was everything I asked for and more. She's really a breeding concubine. And get this: she was already pregnant when they sent her to me. I called the company back to complain and they said they'd made a mistake. Now I have to go meet with the trader and give her back. They'd better pay me back everything I paid for her, too."

"Do you think they'll let you out long enough to make a trade like that?" I asked.

He stopped in his tracks and sighed. "No."

"What if I call Croso and ask for someone to pick me up in plainclothes? Will that work?" I asked.

"Maybe, but any transmissions from this castle will be recorded and monitored, not to mention the fact that you can't transmit anything from this room," he added.

An unnerving thought occurred to me. "Croso promised to notify Ocelot if I take more than a day on this job," I told him. I explained the whole situation.

Alaban was surprised at my clandestine actions. He worried, as I did, about Ocelot's possible brute reaction to something like this. If Croso notified Ocelot, he would certainly come to Hammerstead. He would approach the castle right away, possibly with intent to attack and kill anyone in his way. We had to think of a different way to get me out under the guise Alaban had outlined.

"Why don't I leave the castle through the tower to notify Croso, and then sneak back in the same way?" I suggested.

Alaban liked the idea. He devised a quick plan to get us past security.

He escorted me with an arm around my growing waistline to an upper stairwell. This led to the broad living area, which contained the door to the tower. A guard blocked the stairway between this and the top floor.

Alaban explained languidly that he was looking for a different setting where we could be alone in the castle. The entire upper floor was empty. He suggested it would be a great place to play around. The guard smiled naughtily. I looked away. He said he would make an exception for us. He stepped aside to let us through.

At the top of the stairs, Alaban turned the lights on. The living area glowed a lavish red and black. I moved to the door of the tower. Alaban reminded me with hand signals that we were being monitored, so I couldn't say anything about what I was about to do. He revealed a sound device he held in his hand. He signed to me that I had nine minutes by the tape he'd brought. I nodded. I parted the molecules of the door as he watched me.

"Amazing," he said.

"Thank you," I replied.

I disappeared through the dark stairwell as he turned on the recording, probably of himself and Willa. I ignored the sounds and voices. I flew through the open hatch of the tower to message Croso from my palm computer. I gave only minimal information. I asked him to send someone for me here at the castle and to stock the person with a money card to make a phony exchange. I asked him not to notify Ocelot unless the pickup went bad. He agreed.

I stayed at the exposed top floor of the tower for a few moments, observing the lights of the town below, planning. I would get out of this situation tomorrow. Alaban would soon leave the Fitmalos behind. Ocelot and I would go home and patch things over. He would be angry that I had left, but he would feel relieved that I would never again venture to put Alaban's safety before my own. We might argue, but he would forgive me. Peace settled in my heart.

I passed again through the door and into the wide living room. Alaban sat on a sofa in haggard boredom. He pounded his fist rhythmically onto the back of the sofa along with the recording to make the reverberations sound convincing to the guard downstairs. At the same time, he browsed through a file of information on a palm computer. When I appeared at his side, he stopped pounding and turned the recording down slowly. Then he turned it off. I nodded to him to let him know the call was successful.

"Stay with me here a minute," he said. He snatched the recorder from the cushion next to him and pocketed it within his pin-spiked jacket.

I sat next to him. We stayed there long enough to convince the guard that we were still involved in some kind of intimacy. We looked through some of the information on his palm computer. It contained lists of smuggling deals, dates, and inventory. It would certainly please the Organization generals as he'd promised.

After enough time had passed, he put away the computer. He mussed my hair to make me look more disheveled. I smiled. He held my face in his hands and shook his head. He forced a visage of gladness. He kissed my forehead. Wistfulness pervaded his face. He kissed my forehead over and over endearingly. He embraced me shakily. I rubbed his back with pity.

"Ahem," we heard from the hallway.

Alaban jerked away from me. I gazed at the man as I picked my hair out of my eyes.

The guard had come to check on us. "I'm sorry, folks, but the boss downstairs was complaining about the noise. I'm going to have to ask you to leave this floor," he explained.

Alaban stamped towards him in anger. The man backed away from him as I followed. "You'd better be glad you didn't walk in on us in the act. The last man who interrupted me when I was with a woman was in the hospital for a month." Alaban seethed at the man.

The guard panicked. "I'm sorry, sir. I'm just following orders from the boss downstairs."

"Yeah, aren't we all? We were just about to leave anyway," Alaban stated gruffly. I hurried behind him. The guard allowed a wide berth to let us by. Alaban cast one last frightening scowl at him before he hauled me down the stairs by the elbow.

We took the stairs down to the main dining hall, avoiding the hive, and then entered the kitchen. We found the night staff more accommodating and pleasant than the Vermilion women who had caught me. The fidgety pale Furman gave us a pair of sandwiches and some juice. Alaban asked for an extra for Willa. We brought our meal with us to his room. He stopped to take Willa her meal. I heard him ask her how she was. She didn't answer.

"You eat this. I want to see you healthy, okay?" I heard him tell her.

Again I heard no reply from her.

When we returned to his room, we shared the remaining food over a long conversation. I learned of a few sickening assassinations Teradom had ordered in the last few months. Most involved political rivals or smuggling kingpins.

I also learned about the five members of the task force. Besides Alaban and Ryker, who turned out to be a Vermilion, the group also contained a black human female nicknamed Paleface, (the one I had seen when I first scanned the building from the terminal); a strong-arm Furman named Oso, and a male Mantis whose real name no one but Ryker could pronounce. The others called him Scythe. Several other members had come and gone by way of their own fatal errors. Two had been identified in public at the scene of an assassination and had been dealt with by Paleface, who Alaban said was an excellent shot with a long-barrel laser gun. Others had shown weaknesses detrimental to the job and had been eliminated in a similar way.

I asked Alaban about the weapon. He was sure Teradom knew of its location. He and his associates had planned well for its theft. However, he had been told not to ask about it. He would receive the information at the designated time. The meeting Croso had mentioned had not been about the weapon after all. It was about strengthening the brotherhood of the Regime on Fitmalo through tests of loyalty and handsome payoffs by way of illegal business deals. The meeting about the weapon would take place within the week, and with fewer members. Alaban promised to memorize as much of the meeting as possible to later divulge the information to the Organization.

Alaban asked me what had really happened with Wilbaht. I told him the whole story. Alaban had seen Wilbaht's message to Jawlcheen. Teradom had killed three guards out of fury when he'd seen it. He had cursed Wilbaht repeatedly over the past few months, especially when Jawlcheen voted not to unite Thrader in full common law. The vote had occurred just over four months ago.

"I guess you were celebrating that night," Alaban said, remembering melancholically the night I had conceived the baby.

I would have resented him mentioning it, but I was too tired. We had spent half the night just talking.

Alaban lay on his back with his hands crossed behind his head. He turned to face me. He propped himself up on one elbow.

"Did you miss me at all?" He spoke in a depressed tone.

"Yes, I missed you," I admitted. He reached out with his other hand to stroke the side of my face. I gazed at him resignedly.

"I missed you." He traced the form of my shoulder and my arm. "So much." He rested his hand gingerly at my hip. "I know I'm not supposed to, but I still want you. Just touching you is the most delicious sin." He spoke hesitantly. He watched his hand as his thumb caressed my upper thigh.

I took his hand away gently. "Then don't touch me," I told him solidly.

Emotional pain flooded his face. "Why did you have to fall in love with him? Why don't you feel for me what I feel for you? Is God evil? Why did He link us? Why did he plant this desire in my soul to have you if you were meant to be with someone else? Where does that leave me? I didn't choose to suffer this way. I can't stop this feeling that I need you and that I need to mate with you. I'm in hell."

I sat straight. I tucked my legs under me. He lifted himself to sit by me, face to face.

"Alaban, you have to let this obsession go. We are not mates. We never were. We were never meant to be. We are linked by spirit, not body. I don't know why you feel attraction and I don't. I don't want you to feel tortured. I would like nothing better than to see you happy. You have sacrificed more for me than anyone should ever have. You deserve a mate who will bring you happiness, but that woman cannot be me. Imagine what would happen if I decided to leave Ocelot for you. What would our life be like?"

He raised an eyebrow. He looked down at my belly. He reached out and squeezed my hand.

"I'd leave this place for you right away. We could go to some other planet. I would do *anything* to make you happy. I would raise your child as my own. I would protect you both from harm. I would love you more every day. We could work together." His voice faded. He stared into my face a long while, my words to him tunneling through his heart. His face fell in remorse. "You would never be happy again. You would never want to mate...and I always would."

He paused for one agonizing moment. "I never did have a chance with you, did I? You tried to tell me a hundred times. I wouldn't listen."

I held his arm as I spoke to him. "I wish I could set you free from this suffering. I want you to find peace." I fixed my vision on his eyes.

Looking into his eyes was like looking into a dark mirror. He stared at me woefully, but then peered into my eyes with concentration, as if he had spotted some shimmering object deep within them. I watched his pupils. A glimmer, a hint of some kind of quavering life attracted my curiosity. I moved closer, analyzing the phantom light. He aligned his face with mine, compelled by the intrigue of discovery.

Alaban then moved to sit in a strange position facing me. I stayed cross-legged. He set his legs around me. We held each other's shoulders. He touched his nose and forehead to mine. We strained our eyes to see deeper.

Something fantastic happened at that moment. It was as if each of us passed through the mirror into the other one's world. All our thoughts, emotions, memories, and nuances of being mixed together at once.

I saw the steps of death he had rendered on Teradom's victims. I felt his pity for them. I felt his resentment and grief. I saw his view of me: his physical attraction, his infatuation. I saw him with Willa, whom he pitied, but truly cared for. I saw and felt how he pushed himself daily to his physical and mental best despite the inhumane trials he endured. I felt his loyalty to the Organization despite Trau and despite his current situation.

567

He perceived my life as well. He traced the thoughts and emotions in my mind with eager curiosity. He understood my love for his spirit. He saw the barrier I drew between us to keep us from mating. He saw my complete love for Ocelot. He finally understood why we could never be mates.

We saw bits of visions of our future together and apart. We knew at this moment that we would always be one complete spirit no matter where we found ourselves physically in this universe. He would always carry my light of being as a spherical essence within him. I would always hold a sphere of dark power from his being within me.

Above all, we comprehended each other's power. I revealed to him how to pass objects through each other. He showed me his internal cloaking ability and numerical sight. The explanation of these strengths empowered our abilities more than before. He saw a glimpse of my past visions, broken shards and all. I saw his visions that appeared to him as a mist, a cloud projected with images.

This strange, immaculate communication only lasted a second. When we moved our faces apart, we both understood more about each other and ourselves than we ever could have spoken. A calm moment passed between us. We embraced each other for an unknown amount of time. We had made peace at last.

Minutes later, we rested together side by side. Alaban placed a hand curiously over my womb. I felt a ticklish flutter from inside. Alaban flinched. I smiled and held his hand to feel with him. Then came a bump and another flutter, and then a light pressure. Then the fetus went back to sleep.

"He'll be a strong boy. I see a bright future for him. I wish I could help raise him. I feel like he's part of my family."

"You can be a godfather to him," I said.

"I'd like that. Do you think Ocelot would allow it?" he asked.

"I don't know. You know how he feels about you."

"People hate and fear what they don't understand. Ongeram told me that. If he's right, I just need to make him understand me in some way. I don't hate him, you know. As much as I wanted to, I never could. I think your opinion contaminated me."

"I think we'll be all right, all of us," I told him.

He nodded complacently. We fell asleep holding hands.

In the morning, Alaban told me to stay put while he went to check on the castle activities and to collect some breakfast for us.

I knew Ocelot was probably finishing work on the bogus decoding job by now. If he tried to contact me soon, he would worry that I didn't answer him. I hoped Croso's men didn't let Ocelot out if he finished early.

568

Surely they would find some pretense to keep him at the Center. If he went home to look for me, he would try to contact me from there. He would find my phone buzzing in the desk. He would open the desk to find not only my phone, but also my bracelet, which I had worn every day since he'd given it to me. He would know that Croso had set him up to be at the Center all night. He would know where I'd gone and why.

I did not want Ocelot to leave Red Mesa to come to Hammerstead now. My vision of the lion and the dragon did not seem to fit this situation. Now I felt sure it would happen on a separate occasion, perhaps when Alaban planned to leave the castle himself.

I bit a thumbnail and waited for Alaban to come back. When he returned to the room, I explained. We hoped the warrior Croso was planning on sending for me would arrive here before Ocelot. If they showed up the same time, or if Ocelot arrived first, things would become difficult. At about 0100 hours, however, the terrible possibility became truth.

Chapter 54: Terror

Ryker pounded on the door. Alaban flung it open recklessly. I did not try to hide this time. I lounged in feigned carelessness on the bed.

"Now what?" Alaban asked with caution and anger. He wore his tough disguise once more.

"There's a human man out at the gate looking for a runaway human female. He brought this picture with him." Ryker handed the photo to Alaban and glared at me in distaste.

I sat nervously.

"What do you mean runaway? Who is this guy?" Alaban asked.

Ryker described Ocelot in plainclothes. Alaban pretended to look at me suspiciously.

"You stay here," he warned me.

"I didn't run away. I swear," I said.

"Shut up!" he snapped. "I'm going to talk to this guy." He and Ryker left the room gruffly.

I meditated to watch them. As my power swelled, I saw Ocelot at the outer gate to the castle. He stared menacingly at one of the guards. I wasn't sure what he was planning. I prayed Alaban could negotiate with him without calling attention to the fact that they knew each other. I felt the tension increase between the two as Alaban approached the gate.

The guard stood in Alaban's way, so he grabbed him by the back of his uniform and shoved him rudely to the side.

"Take a walk," he growled to the man.

He glared at the guard's comrade at the opposite side of the gate. Both guards glanced at each other in hesitation before obeying his order. They strolled toward the main entryway to the castle, the first man cursing Alaban under his breath. Ryker stood a few paces behind Alaban to witness the discussion. He squinted at them intently.

Alaban held up the photo of me as he spoke to Ocelot. His voice rang in a threatening tone, but his eyes communicated a willingness to help. "I bought this concubine three days ago from the Boldoy Ready Partners Company. I've got a contract to prove it. If she didn't finish her contract with you, go take it up with them." He handed the photo back to him.

Ocelot was not surprised, as I had been, about Alaban's appearance. Nor was he surprised about the scheme Alaban used. He got the gist of the play right away. Maybe he knew of the call I'd made to Croso. He went along with the act.

"I already went to the company. They gave me this address. They made a mistake. She was not salable. She's mine. I just missed a couple of payments is all," he told him.

"That's your problem, not mine. Now beat it," Alaban said coldly.

"You don't understand. She's pregnant. She's carrying my child. She's a breeder," Ocelot said nervously.

"She's a what?" Alaban pretended to be shocked.

Ryker believed the act. "That sucks for you, Bahn."

Alaban spun at him. "Fuck off, Ryk," he blustered.

Ryker scoffed at him before turning to walk back towards the castle.

"Do you have any idea how much I paid for that woman?" Alaban shouted.

"I'll pay you back. Just tell me how much," Ocelot told him loudly.

"Five hundred thousand," Alaban barked.

"I'll bring it to you today," Ocelot spoke.

"Yeah, you do that. Until you do, she's still mine, so if you really want her, you'll get the money fast. If I have to wait a long time, she might not look so pretty when you get her back," he threatened.

570

"I'll be back in two hours, tops. Just don't hurt her," Ocelot spoke.

"Yeah, that's sweet. Now get out of here and get back with the cash before I change my mind," Alaban said as he backed away from the gate.

Ocelot retreated down the hill to the main street and the cab that had waited for him. Alaban did not return to his room with me right away. Instead he went to an exercise room.

Two of his task force teammates were busy sparring when he stomped in. He roared as he riveted a hanging punching bag with hundreds of punches. Paleface and Oso tried to ignore him, but he made a scene. He gave no explanation, but continued pummeling the bag until the ceiling beam creaked and rained dust on the room. Finally, he left the way he had entered. Again, he avoided me. He went to the kitchen for water. He was curt and impatient with the staff.

I stopped envisioning him. Once more my power seemed to disappear. My baby stretched before we both fell asleep from true exhaustion.

When I awoke, I found Alaban at my side. He knelt on the floor by the bed.

"It's almost time," he whispered.

I leapt to my feet. We faced each other. Alaban kissed me firmly on the mouth. I reacted uneasily.

"I'll see you in a few weeks at the Red Mesa Center," he told me.

I regained my stamina. "I'll be waiting for the day. I love you, my friend."

Suddenly he smiled. It was a smile I'd not seen in so long. It meant freedom was in sight. "It's great to hear that again. You know I love you back. Are you ready?"

"Yes," I responded.

"I've got to make it look like I roughed you up," he said.

"Punch me in the face, just not the nose," I suggested.

"You're sure?" he asked. I nodded. "I'll go easy on you."

I steadied my head. He popped me squarely under the cheekbone with an ox jaw strike. I jolted back only a little. The hit was not very powerful, but the cheekbone ached sharply. He sank his thumb into the point of contact and rubbed it hard all around to give it a better effect.

When he finished the task, we held both hands together. "Did you notice our power increases a lot when we do this?" he spoke.

"Yes. I can see Ocelot coming up the street. Can you?" I asked.

"He's about five kilometers away," he replied. "Maybe when I get out of here, we can work together."

"That will be great. I think I should have a busted lip, too," I mentioned. I held a tiny bit of my lower lip between my incisors and jutted my chin out him.

He thwacked me with an upper cut. The lip bled. I smeared the blood down my face.

"I think that's enough," he advised. He tousled my hair a little. We clasped our hands together before heading out.

We began our act at his door. I whimpered and limped as he held my arm tightly. He charged me down the stairs, ramming my shoulder into the wall at the landing. He swore, but not directly at me. He still couldn't bring himself to call me names or belittle me with curses. He only complained about the company and the money they owed him.

We passed a few hive members on our way out. Some of them made snide comments, but most people just stared and stepped out of the way. Alaban dragged me to the main entrance and out the door. The afternoon summer heat in the sparsely treed front garden brought me sweat and nausea. Alaban led me to the edge of the reception patio. The sentry guards on either side of the entrance directed their attention to us.

Ocelot left the cab at the street to hike up the hill towards the castle gate. Alaban jerked my face towards him.

"Does that guy look familiar to you? Huh?" he demanded.

I whined.

"Answer me, damn it," Alaban yelled.

"Yes," I cried.

"He was your last owner, wasn't he?" he bellowed.

"Yes," I bawled.

He released my face and struck me with the back of his hand on my chin. I fell to my knees. He quickly hauled me up from the ground.

"Get over here," he ordered.

I skittered beside him as he marched with broad steps. He jostled me to a halt next to the base of a dry fountain about ten meters from the gate. Ocelot approached the gate wild-eyed from the rough treatment I received.

Alaban shouted to the guard he had shoved out of the way earlier. "You! Get over here and watch her. Don't let her go anywhere."

The guard turned from the gate to frown at us. He regarded us odiously. Alaban let go of my arm to approach the gate where the guard had stood. As Alaban and the guard passed each other, I felt an ominous warning from my sixth sense. This was a bearded human male, one I was sure I had seen in a vision before. I bowed my head as he passed me. Suddenly I felt afraid. The man moved to stand behind me. He dug his nails into my arm. I felt his hatred for Alaban in his touch. Besides this

572

hatred, I sensed he was also a drug-addict with less self-control than he showed.

Nausea engulfed me. Saul squirmed within my womb. If he were out in the open, I was sure he would be crying now. He knew something was wrong. Frightened, I raised my head to watch Alaban and the other guard open the gate and search Ocelot for weapons. He had not brought any.

As Ocelot and Alaban made the money exchange, I felt my power leave me once again. Only this time, I felt a terrible sense of loss. I faltered. I fell to my knees. The man left scratches on my arm as he released me. I groped the ledge of the fountain base. Not only had I lost all my own power, but the power I had perceived from my growing baby escaped my body as well. Confusion and panic swept through me as I coughed up bile. I was barely aware of Alaban's order to the guard to get me up off the ground and bring me to them.

Saul was afraid. His bright spirit cried out for help. I became aware of other benevolent spirits among us. They gathered him to them. He seemed to warn me and say goodbye at the same time.

"No!" I cried out in terror.

A pain jutted into my abdomen along with the bearded guard's foot as he yelled at me to get up. Raw, blinding sunlight shrouded my eyes when my head and back hit the ground. I flipped over to push myself up to all fours again. The guard ignored my men's shouts to stop. He kicked me even more forcefully in the same manner. Again I rolled away from him. This time I curled up on my side with pain. Ocelot lifted me from the ground as Alaban attacked the petulant guard.

"Oh, God, no," Ocelot uttered.

He dragged me up to stand, urgently demanding us to go. He backed us away from the scene. I clutched my aching belly as I watched Alaban strike the man repeatedly in the face and stomach until he fell.

Alaban kicked the man around on the ground. Then he lifted him into a standing position with the left hand while his right hand and elbow punched the man bloody. At last, he broke the man's neck and threw the body to the ground, where he proceeded to kick it even more.

As we passed through the gate, Ocelot knocked the second guard out of our path. Alaban paced madly toward him. The second guard raced away towards the safety of the castle. Alaban looked at me once more in anguish before following the man. The other guards took a cue from their friend and entered as well, leaving the front of the castle defenseless.

I slipped from Ocelot's grip onto the stony ground. I heard myself cry out before I felt the full effect of the labor pain. I felt as though a large vice were wedged between my hips, prying me open from the inside. Then the intense pain was gone. Ocelot scooped me up from the ground. He ran with me down the hill to the spot where he had left the cab, but the cab driver had obviously witnessed the murder of the guard and had fled. Ocelot swore. He knelt to set me down on the curb as he phoned for an emergency vehicle. When he told the person on the other end of the line where we were, another horrible pain cramped my womb.

I panicked, unable to lift myself from the pain. Ocelot cradled my head and neck in the crook of one arm and felt my abdomen with the other hand, asking God to let Saul be all right.

Moments later, I felt as though I had urinated myself. Blood and amniotic fluid soaked through my clothes to the ground. I covered my face in shame. Ocelot told me not to panic and that I would only make things worse. He said the medical team would be here any minute. They would take us to the hospital. They would take care of us. Another, more painful, contraction hit me before the emergency hover vehicle finally arrived. Ocelot begged God for more time.

Once inside the emergency vehicle, two Vermilion nurses helped Ocelot strip me and put me in a hospital robe. One of the women prepared to coach me through a birth, but Ocelot argued with her, saying we had to wait until we arrived at the hospital to provide life support to the baby. The other nurse pierced my arm with an injection, which put me to sleep.

The next thing I knew, the afternoon sun had waned to a dull sunset that filtered through the high windows of a hospital room. Three Vermilion nurses were dressing me in my newly cleaned clothes. I lay on a gurney bed in a long room with other female patients in beds lining the wall. My abdomen ached constantly. I touched my lower body, searching for an answer to my panicked question. The baby was gone.

I looked frantically around at the Vermilion nurses. One was a kindly middle-aged lady. She held my hand sympathetically. She spoke in a soothing voice, but her message brought no comfort.

"We're very sorry, dear. Your baby had already died when you arrived. Your husband is filling out documentation right now. He should be in to take you home soon." She uttered something about pain medication and personal care, but my attention had drowned. She let go of my hand and then scooted out of the room while the others moved to check other patients.

Ocelot marched in. He immediately slipped an arm under my shoulders to help lift me off the bed. I winced in pain as I sat, then again when I stretched my legs to the floor to stand.

"Come on," he urged. He hurried me out despite my groans.

I hobbled next to him to the hospital lobby and out to the front. A cab awaited us. Ocelot tumbled me into the back of the vehicle despite my protests. He closed the hatch and ran to the front of the cab to sit with the driver. I contained my grief long enough to realize the possibility that someone might have followed us from the castle. Ocelot seemed to be running.

The cab took us to an airbus station at the edge of Boldoy. Ocelot paid the driver and snatched me out of the back. The aching nagged at me worse than before. I tried to walk slowly, but Ocelot was adamant about our escape. He got us onto a large airbus where people stared at my disheveled state. Ocelot jammed us both into the only empty seat next to a window as the airbus lifted off. Every tremor of turbulence sent throbs through my lower body. I tried to hold back tears to avoid attention from the people around us, but my cheeks remained wet throughout our flight.

Ocelot stared forward like an angry statue. I reached for his hand, searching for some empathy from him. He did not hold my hand or even acknowledge my attempt. I shrank to the window once again, overwhelmed with grief and regret.

When we finally arrived at Red Mesa, we took a cab in a painfully bumpy ride back to our house. Ocelot allowed me to lean on his arm. He carried my hospital bag on the other arm. We passed through the gate and front door among my helpless groans of pain.

I looked around at our once happy home. It seemed like weeks since I had been here last. Ocelot pulled me into our room and sat me on the bed. He tossed the bag to the floor by my feet. In vexed silence, he went to bathe.

In the bag, I found an absorbent sheet, which I unfolded onto the bed. I also found a packet of pain medication. I slowly removed my jacket and pulled the palm computer from its pocket. Despite our trauma, I kept the recent assignment in mind. I knew I had to give the palm computer to Croso as soon as possible, but my physical condition now would not allow it. Perhaps Ocelot could deliver it for me.

I carefully entered the bathroom with him, hoping to speak to him, but he finished his bath and brushed by me in a towel without a word.

I prepared to bathe myself. I found a laser incision over my abdomen and a swelling purple bruise from the guard's boot. I realized as I undressed that the nurses had placed a sponge gauze between my legs. As I removed it and saw the blood that had been meant for my child, another wave of remorse consumed me. I cried hoarsely in the bath, watching the reddened water swirl away from me down the drain.

Terrible lament broke my dreaming heart. All my optimistic aspirations for our future bled from my vacant womb. The wholesome bond between mother and child had been profaned. Saul was denied the blessings that should have been lived between conception and death. He had only known a beginning and an end without a life story of his own. I gnashed my teeth tighter, bringing pain into my jaw as well. I cried out in angst. I realized how selfish and fruitless my tears were. They would not bring him back. Our baby was not to be comforted in this world.

The only person I had a chance to comfort now was my mourning husband. But I feared his wrath against this mortal shame.

When I finally returned to the room, I saw Ocelot had changed into his traveling uniform. He poked at my palm computer irritably. I changed into a soft nightshirt and prepared to put myself back to bed, knowing I would bleed heavily for the next few hours.

I dared to speak to my ireful husband. "Can you take that to Croso?"

Ocelot spun viciously.

"You did know he sent me," I suggested in a spent voice. "I had to go."

"You *had* to go? You didn't *have* to go!" He bared his teeth at me like a defensive animal. "You had a choice! Croso didn't force the job on you. You had to accept it." Ocelot ranted. "I'm sorry you're in pain, Sil, but you deserve it. Maybe this will finally convince you of the facts. You *did* betray me. You betrayed our family. You *killed* your own son, *my* son! And for *what*? To save an assassin? Did you *have* to do that, Sil? Don't give me this bullshit that you had to go. Admit it. You care more about Alaban than you care about us! You're pathetic. Why don't you just call him up and ask him to take you back?"

"Ocelot, stop," I spoke hollowly.

He backed away to the wardrobe. He yanked out his travel box from the top shelf and a handful of hangers of clothes from the rack. He filled the box with the clothes and a few items from the drawer. I spoke his name, but he refused to look at me.

"I'm going to temporary housing at the Center. I can't stand to be in this house with you. I can't stand the sight of you. I can't stand to smell the blood from our child on you. I don't want to hear your moaning. I've had enough. Don't ask me not to leave. I'm already gone."

He pounded the floor on his way out. The door resounded fiercely throughout the house as it slammed.

Unexpectedly, I did not sob. Nor did I kneel in the floor to wail for him. I gazed after him in grave shock. Then I put myself back to bed. I positioned the flat absorbent square and rested my hips on it. I felt another hot trickle of blood leave my body as I reclined in discomfort. I lay on my back, listless. I placed a painkiller patch on my arm, but the only hint of relief I felt was in knowing that Ocelot did love me despite his angry words and that he needed time to heal just as I did.

In the morning, I phoned Ocelot repeatedly, but he would not answer. He did not reappear the next day or the next. He did not call. No one did. Not Croso or Yalat or even Channol; their lives went on as usual. My life…was at a pause.

The hormonal readjustment in my body brought me to an emotional wall. My body asked repeatedly where the baby had gone. I had prepared to care for this offspring in every way. He had truly become a part of me. To my body, it was as if I had lost a hand or a foot. An important part of me was gone, unnaturally. Tears escaped my careworn eyes. I spoke his name through quivering lips before beginning my chain of prayers once more.

PART 4: ATONEMENT

Chapter 55: Hope Remains

Four days after Hammerstead, I wandered though the streets of Red Mesa unnoticed, invisible to the world. I was no longer a talented warrior. I was not an attractive young woman. No lively step decorated my demeanor. No youthful aspiration brightened my face. I wore no laurel of purpose over my sagging shoulders. I lagged behind all my old expectations. I walked for hours with the gloom of one who had altogether forgotten her direction in life.

Ocelot had not contacted me at all despite my messages to him. Croso, although responsible for my mission in Hammerstead, would not make himself available for another two days. No one looked for me. I was shunned by those I had esteemed so highly.

In the late afternoon, I found myself on a deserted, cobbled street. The unobstructed sunlight turned the walls bright orange. The cobbles clunked under my boots as I shuffled and nearly tripped along to an alleyway of the poor, residential section of town. Here a few lines of laundry hung between the tops of buildings. Family conversations and noises wafted from the apartments. The alley emptied into a wide causeway. I stopped in the alley, observing the crowds. I leaned onto the stuccoed wall, feeling the hot wind tangle my hair around my neck. I stared listlessly towards the causeway, watching the stream of people hurry by.

Here my road seemed to end. Behind me lay the road home, the road to familiarity, positive goals; life with a purpose in the service of the Organization and in support of my now unwilling husband. Before me spread the road to the unknown, replete with teeming, maddening life.

People with every moral and immoral quality in existence sloshed by like chunks of ice in a flowing river: all of them with unique identities, all of them on a separate, but similar, path, all crystallized in their own time. They slipped by, destined to melt into the vast ocean of life and death. These were the masses, the general public, the ones we strove not to be. We warriors endeavored to be different, like glittering icebergs of strength. Yet we, too, would melt with time to end up as these. How were we any different?

"You are different. You will make a difference," a familiar voice seemed to say in my mind.

I pushed myself away from the wall, but remained still. A presence warmer than my surroundings approached me from behind. My best friend's dark hands appeared at my shoulders. His arms wrapped around me. I gently caressed his comforting arms as he pressed his chin above my ear. His low voice stole away in the wind.

"You are a strong warrior, the best. You will help change their lives." He gestured with his chin towards the flowing masses. "I know you will. You've already changed mine." He hugged me closer. "I never meant for you to suffer for my mistakes. This was all my fault."

"No. You shouldn't have to suffer any more," I told him.

Alaban kissed my hair. He squeezed me to him. "I wish I could make it up to you."

I withdrew his arms from me. I turned to face him. I blinked in surprise.

"Alaban. You've changed your looks again. You look like a model human warrior. You look so strong."

He flashed a flattered smile, but then became serious. "Is there anything I can do for you?"

I gripped his hands in mine. I told him how Ocelot had left me and that I was lost without him. I asked him for his help. He accepted graciously.

"I'll change his mind. I'll do that for you." He gazed solemnly into my grateful eyes. Then his old mischievous grin returned to his face. "Take me to your husband. I want to mess with his mind one last time before we start talking business."

"Business?" I asked.

"Now that I'm back with the living, I figure it's my civil duty to bring Teradom to justice. I've got to unload some info without leaking it to the wrong people. You and Ocelot are the only warriors I trust right now," he expressed.

"He'll report you, unless he tries to kill you first," I warned.

"He won't. I have just the information that'll hold him back. You'll see. As far as getting the two of you back together, that's an easy mission. He just needs to see us together. Jealousy will do the rest. I guarantee it."

"I hope you're right," I said.

"When have I ever let you down?" he joked sarcastically.

I thought hard about his question. A week ago I would have given a different answer, but today I had to say, "Never."

As we ambled back toward the Silver Zone, hand in hand, I advised him not to meet Ocelot at our house. Ocelot would only challenge Alaban as soon as he saw him. I remembered my husband's self-conscious attitude in public. I suggested a place for our meeting, although Ocelot would never agree to meet with the two of us. He would need to believe he was meeting with someone else.

582

I called Channol and explained the urgency of my request based on the fact that Ocelot had abandoned me and I desperately wanted to reconcile with him. I did not mention Alaban. He was surprised to hear of my physical condition. Ocelot had not spoken to him about it at all. He didn't even know Ocelot was quartered in Center housing. I asked him to lie to Ocelot, to tell him he would be meeting with him instead of me. I asked him to set up a meeting at the Lakeview Restaurant in Red Mesa at 0400. Channol agreed to help us. He even offered to appear at the restaurant entrance in person to direct him to me. I thanked him vehemently.

At 0345, I entered the place in plain view. Alaban cloaked until we cleared the reception foyer in case Channol was watching. We then convinced the manager to reserve all the tables in the south dining room section for us by phony orders of the Organization. This would help to keep us from being overheard directly, but would provide a visual audience, since the central dining room was open to the south section. We sat at a rounded booth overlooking the lake and its recreational boats at dock. Alaban ordered a round drinks for the three of us, although I doubted Ocelot would be willing to drink during this confrontation. Alaban clutched my hand in moral support. My abdominal pain was gone, but as the indicated hour approached, the dormant butterflies awoke to batter my stomach.

At 0401, Ocelot appeared by our table. He froze when he saw us. Hatred overtook his demeanor. He checked around him briefly and then slid into the empty space beside me. He spoke to me without taking his eyes off Alaban.

"What is this evil bastard doing here?"

Alaban was truly offended. "You want to talk about evil? How about a man who psychologically tortures his wife by telling her she killed her own child?"

Ocelot glanced at me for a second, but then returned his hateful gaze to Alaban's squared jaw.

Alaban scoffed. "How much of a man can this guy be? His name says it all. Ocelot. He's named after a big *pussy*cat."

Ocelot chagrined. He slid out from the edge of the rounded seat and stood facing Alaban. I nudged Alaban forcefully with an elbow to tell him to back down.

Ocelot spoke roughly to me. "If this is a challenge, I refuse to accept it. I don't know why the hell you lured me here to see this human piece of shit, but you can pitch him back into the sewer where he came from. If you're trying to make some final choice between the two of us, then take him. You're just as devious as he is. You'll make the perfect couple."

"No. That's not why we're here. Don't go, Ocelot. Alaban, please don't insult him, especially not his name. He won't stand for that."

Alaban behaved as if oblivious to Ocelot's seething anger. He coolly lifted his glass, took a moderate sip, and regarded Ocelot carefully. He turned to me.

"No offense, Sil, but I'd always assumed you'd choose a more intelligent mate. Obviously you wanted to be the smart one in your new family." He gestured towards Ocelot. "This one doesn't even seem to be aware of just how unworthy he is to look you in the eye, much less sire your child. I knew you were humble, but I didn't think you would belittle yourself. You're too good for this ape."

"Alaban, you're not helping. You said you would help. You're making things worse." I pleaded with him.

"You asked for help from him? Why would you ever trust him to help you? Every time he shows up, he screws up your life and leaves things worse than before. That's all he's ever done for you."

Alaban leapt up to stand centimeters away from Ocelot, resilient to him. Ocelot flexed his arms, preparing to fight if Alaban meant to attack him. Alaban held his hands out to his sides, palms up, limply expressing his unwillingness for physical contact.

He spoke satirically. "You're sure about that? That's all I've ever done for her? Let's see if you're right. Let's analyze the evidence to back that up."

"Let's see. What have I done for her?" Alaban bent down a finger for each example he counted. "I asked Wilbaht to be in the Public Valley to heal her when her airbus crashed. I risked my life and reputation by letting everyone think I was a traitor, just to keep her safe. I saved her life *and* yours on the space station by pretending you were dead."

Alaban stopped to sigh heavily, but then continued through clenched teeth. "I worked for the enemy to keep him away from her. I hid my spirit from her until I could be sure she was out of danger. I let her sleep with me without trying to mate with her. Oh, that was the toughest one."

He stopped to eye me with fond resentment. Then he turned to Ocelot once more. He became the aggressive clown once more. "Oh. I'm sorry. I lost count. Well, let's see what you've done." He counted to one, pausing jauntily. "You...attempted to keep her from joining the task force, but then you just stood by and got shot. That's it. All you had to do was stand by and get shot. And she chose you. Not me. You. Hey, if I'd known that was all it took, I would have shot myself a long time ago." He held out his hands as if to receive applause from his joke.

Ocelot's anger turned sullen. He let his arms relax to his sides as he shifted his weight in uncertainty, considering Alaban's point of view for the first time.

Alaban slid into the seat next to me. He grasped my hand in his. He dramatically kissed the top of it, gazing at me with that fake hypnotic stare he had used to make me smile so long ago. Now it was a horrible parody. My eyes begged him to stop. He turned halfway toward Ocelot, glancing at him from the corner of his eye.

"If you don't want her, just walk away," he said with a gleam in his eye.

He leaned back in the seat next to me and took up his drink again. He stared tauntingly at Ocelot. "If you leave her, I will pursue her longer, harder, and stronger than you ever did. Now you tell me who's the better man." He tossed back his drink, keeping his black eyes on his target.

I glanced with embarrassment at Ocelot. His jealousy forced him to sit again at my side. He squared his jaw. I put a hand on the tabletop near him, but he bristled. I withdrew the hand sadly. I clung to Alaban for support.

On a whim, Alaban continued his speech. This time he became bitterly serious.

"But you know something, I don't think she will ever have me. Ocelot. Brother. She's already had plenty of opportunities." He scanned Ocelot's face for a positive reaction, but found none. He played another frustrating card. "You know she slept with me the other night."

I gawked and almost lashed out at him, but he patted my hand to reassure me. Ocelot's nostrils flared as he glared at him even more viciously. Alaban leaned forward and held up three fingers to emphasize his point.

"That makes, what? Three? Four times total? Not once did she mate with me. I even tried different seduction methods back in the early days. She's the only woman who ever resisted my charms." He retracted the fingers into a tight fist.

"Do you know what her reason was? She said there was something 'missing' between us. The only thing I ever thought was missing between us was sex. Ah, but love is blind."

He relaxed his manner and reclined in the seat once more, wedging his shoulder next to mine almost playfully. "The funny thing is if you really had died, she would have married me out of pure loyalty. That's how good she is." He kissed the back of my hand again and then intertwined our fingers to rest the hands on the tabletop. "But she'd never be happy with me. She'd still believe in that missing piece. I guess you're it. Congratulations. Oh, wait. I forgot. You don't care about that. You already walked out on her. You lost one innocent life and you're ready to give up the battle."

Ocelot leaned in towards him. "It wasn't just an innocent life, you fucking imbecile. He was my son. He was a miracle and now he's dead." Ocelot gritted his teeth. He glared at me. "You destroyed our family for this jackass," he hissed. His anger welled up in a reddened scowl.

My heart shrank back in my chest to see him like this. I couldn't bear to look at him. I clenched my jaw tightly to keep my composure.

Alaban intervened. He held up a hand to deter Ocelot's fury, but the gesture stimulated an automatic reaction. I barely saw Ocelot's fist as it traveled at a disappearing velocity to contact with Alaban's face. His head immediately jolted backward, pressed deeply into the padded headrest, and then recoiled. I made a cry of surprise and grasped at him, but he blocked my hands gently. He grunted, but accepted the blow as punishment deserved. He showed Ocelot no opposition. He took a moment to compose himself, blinking and shaking his head. A discolored welt appeared at his left cheek. Ocelot poised defensively, but did not move or say a word.

Alaban plodded on with his speech despite his injury. Somehow, he still managed to speak evenly, this time without the asinine manner about him.

"It wasn't her fault. It was mine. I shouldn't have let the guard near her. I assumed he would do his job and follow orders only. Never put faith in the feeble-minded. I learned that a little too late." He paused to lick his gums beneath his wound. "If it were possible, I'd say I owe you a son. I guess some debts can't be repaid."

"Nothing either of you do or say can ever make up for what happened," Ocelot professed.

"You're right," Alaban admitted.

He paused to check the tension between the two of us. It was thick.

"But if Sil hadn't come to my rescue this time, let's just say it's better that you lost the baby now instead of later. He would have been born. You would have gotten attached to him. Then he would have died before his first birthday."

"What? How do you know that?" I asked him.

"We finally got the weapon without your help. That's part of the reason why I'm here right now." Alaban spoke sincerely.

All argument was suspended. He had our full attention.

"Let's continue this conversation somewhere a little more secluded," he suggested.

Chapter 56: A New Plan

Back at our house, Alaban scanned for unwanted recording devices and set up his interference pack even though he didn't find anything. I led him to the sunroom sofa to talk. Alaban stepped into the room and stopped. He turned around to observe it slowly.

"This is where it happened. I recognize this room. I saw it that night," he spoke.

I hung my head. Ocelot glanced between the two of us fitfully.

"I'm sorry, Sil," Alaban told me. Then he looked bravely to his former adversary. "I'm sorry, Ocelot. Please accept my sympathy for your loss." He bowed to him.

Ocelot didn't know what to say. The man he'd just called human shit now conducted himself with courtesy and honor.

I reached for Alaban's arm and pulled him gently to the sofa. "Tell us about the weapon," I encouraged.

He sat by me. "Remember in Trau's testimony how he said you'd be good bait? You were."

"What do you mean?" Ocelot asked.

"Ryker and I had to report to Teradom everything that happened with my 'concubine'. I had a lot of explaining to do about the guard. He got what he deserved, but if you were really who I said you were, I would have just beat the shit out of him but let him live. Teradom knew that. He's a smart blue bastard. He had you followed to the hospital. He found out who you are, where you live, etcetera. He confronted me with it the day after you left. He knows about our charade at the space station. He suspected all along, but never had sufficient proof."

"I'm surprised he didn't try to kill you right then," I mentioned.

"He gave me a choice. We all die, or I get the weapon out of the South Boldoy Research Bank and you live. My life was never negotiated. I'm still on his hit list."

"How did you get it?" I asked.

"We set up a phony deposit of some nuclear weapons components to get in. We posed as Organization soldiers. I broke from the group and got into the internal high security control room. Paleface ran interference with the guards, but she's not the best at covering her tracks. She left a trail of bodies. I had to move fast.

"I passed the box through a protective case to get it out. You taught me how when we read each other's minds the other night. I didn't realize how much strength it took until I tried it. I almost didn't make it out. At one point I was sure they'd catch me. I was standing right in the middle of a four-guard sentry. Have you ever projected a 360-degree cloak?"

"I never thought it was possible. You did that?" I asked in amazement.

"Necessity yields invention. I never knew I could do it until then. It drained me pretty badly. It doesn't matter if they caught me on camera, though. They could have concrete proof that I was there and they still couldn't touch me. I have the perfect alibi. Twenty-four generals from three planets will tell them I was bodyguarding for Teradom during a five-hour meeting in Boldoy at the same time I was in the security building. Even if Teradom wants me dead now, he'll never ask the generals to say otherwise. He can't have the theft linked to himself and his staff. Anyway, I made a bad decision when I got out of there. Paleface was about to shoot me, so I threw the box at her to distract her while I disappeared. I should have gone back for it, but I was pressed for time. No one expected me to go back to the castle, but I did. I had to get Willa. I barely had enough energy to get us out of there."

"At least you're not a wanted criminal," I mentioned.

"Yeah, that would make it even more difficult to get the stuff back," he said. Our eyes gleamed together in excitement.

"Count me in," I breathed.

"What is the weapon?" Ocelot asked with grating distrust.

"They call it Tetrasank. I don't know its makeup, but I know some of its components came from the spider we destroyed on Sor3. You wouldn't believe it if you saw what it does. It's a biological signal re-encoder. Attaches itself to parts of the brain as well as bone marrow and lymphoid tissues. On Vermilions and humans it screws up the blood. It causes a quantitative reversal in production of white and red blood cells, like a hyper-mutated leukemia. Instead of producing mostly red blood cells, the body produces mainly white blood cells. The white blood cells eventually outnumber the reds. Red blood cell production drops to almost nil. There's more to it than that, but that's the main effect. Symptoms are grim: all kinds of abnormal physical deterioration, dementia. Test subjects that didn't commit suicide went crazy and died with as much suffering as you can imagine. But it was slow. A lot slower than any common biological weapon. First affects on a healthy adult become noticeable within two to three weeks. Full-blown deterioration takes two to three months.

"They're planning on dispersing the drug through cloud seeding and natural rain in the southeastern quadrant. It will soak into the groundwater throughout most of the planet. People with heart problems, infants and the elderly will show symptoms and die first.

"They'll blame the outbreak on a cargo ship crash. It'll be carrying products from a planet-wide pharmaceutical company. The owners and stockholders oppose the commonwealth, so Teradom figured he'd bury them first. The public will do a lot of finger pointing. Jawlcheen medical scientists will go nuts trying to figure out the cause of the outbreak and how to control it. Prime Minister Lock will offer assistance but Jawlcheen will definitely refuse. The whole planet will be quarantined. All trade and travel will halt. Mass hysteria will take over.

"But the drug doesn't affect Fitmalos in the same way. It only causes flu-like symptoms. So when the death toll on Jawlcheen pushes the Vermilions to desperate measures, they'll finally allow Fitmalo scientists to step in. The Fitmalos will pretend to take a while to work with the Jawlcheen scientists' information and then 'together' they'll come up with a cure, which they already have."

"How do you know all this?" Ocelot interjected.

"There was a meeting at the castle in Hammerstead after you showed up. It was a silent meeting, top secret. A few hard-core Fitmalo Regimist generals were there, and some scientists. I couldn't identify all of them."

"What do you mean a silent meeting?" I asked.

"They all sat around with their computers and communicated on an independent short-range frequency. They only typed and sent messages to each other. They didn't speak to avoid recording. They didn't even use projection strings. They wore compufocal glasses. No staff or bodyguards were allowed near the meeting table, but you know me. It didn't matter if I was at the other end of the castle. I could still read most of their communications through meditation."

"What else do you know?" Ocelot pressed.

"They expect their campaign to unite Thrader will be accepted by most of the solar system after they pretend to rescue Jawlcheen from the Tetrasank. Jawlcheen will consider the Fitmalos their saviors. Then the Fitmalos will look like heroes to the whole galaxy. Everyone will support them; they'll buy more Fitmalo products, increase investments. Fitmalo's economy will hit an all-time high. Even the Fitmalo leftists will keep out of the current government's way. They'll be living high on the hog. Everybody will vote to have Lock reelected. They'll change their constitution to extend his stay in office. Lock's party will throw a huge celebration for the occasion. He'll display his military power with a parade of the army he's been training in the asteroid field.

"That's when the Regime's wheels start turning. They'll secretly support protestors in opposition to the military strength. Traditionalists and rebels will get louder. Teradom will demand an investigation of the source of the Jawlcheen outbreak and—oh, what a surprise—they prove Lock ordered to have it planted in the first place. The whole world rallies against him. Lock is out, along with anyone else Teradom doesn't like. We'll see a few public executions. The Regime takes over. They in turn use the army as a friendly scare tactic. Thrader is in their control."

"Do they have a backup plan in case the Tetrasank operation goes wrong?" I asked.

"They'll come up with something, but this is the best they've got," Alaban responded.

"Do you have a plan for getting the Tetrasank out?" I asked.

"Not exactly. I just know where it is and how to get it. Taking it out of the castle should be easier than getting it from the stronghold. The hive and the task force will be after us as soon as they know we're around, but we can handle them. The hard part will be keeping away from you-know-who and his connections long enough to destroy it and put it away for good," Alaban said.

"No. The hard part will be tracking down who now has any information about that formula so we can corrupt all their information without leaving a trail," Ocelot muttered.

"No one has it but the big boss and whoever invented the thing in the first place. I'm sure that team of scientists is long dead. Like I said, Teradom is smart. He knows not to allow anyone access to it," Alaban replied.

"Then why did he let you and this 'Paleface' get it for him? Didn't you say you're on his hit list?" Ocelot countered skeptically. I could see in Ocelot's face the dire urge to kill Alaban. I also saw in him confusion, self-doubt. He had lived with the deep-seated hatred of his rival for so long it now seemed incomprehensible to him that Alaban would not only relent me to him but that he appeared to be on his side. I saw him scrutinize Alaban with his sixth sense, searching for evidence of a lie.

"Yes, but I was the last one capable of getting it for him before he went with plan B. They were going to slowly take out existing guards and get their own men hired as replacements, but that would take too long. He knew I'd retrieve it for him in a day. I was blackmailed. He knew I'd come through for you." Alaban gazed at me.

"How did you get Willa out of the castle?" I asked him.

"The same way you got in, except I had a little help with the door. You know I like to blow things up." He gave me a wry smile. "Willa thinks I'm her hero now. At least she doesn't hate me anymore. She actually talked to me this morning before I sent her to Sor4."

I beamed at him reassuringly. I patted his knee. Finally content, he casually strung an arm around my shoulders.

Ocelot stepped towards us with an offended scowl. "Take your hand off my wife," he warned.

Alaban raised his eyebrows in mild surprise, but uttered an apology and did as he was told. Ocelot moved to sit between us to prevent the incident from happening again. Alaban and I leaned forward to speak to each other around him.

We discussed the location of the weapon within the castle and a few ideas of how to extract it. Eventually, the two of us became so excited about the prospect of adventure that we stood and paced together, passing each other in parallel paths, leaving Ocelot to sulk and ponder on the sofa alone.

Finally, Alaban coaxed Ocelot into adding a few ideas of his own. Miraculously, Alaban convinced him that he was the man to organize the strike. Despite his ongoing hatred for Alaban, Ocelot's sense of duty and his well-deserved hatred for Teradom's Regime offset his emotion long enough for him to focus on the proposed operation.

We formed a plan. We would not tell our contact general or anyone else at the Center. Even our trusted friends could undermine our actions by trying to get involved. With fewer people on our team, we had the freedom to act more quickly and without the risk of alerting any possible double agents to our plan.

Ocelot and I would run interference for Alaban at the castle while he re-stole the weapon and its information from Teradom's personal safe. Ocelot would break into Teradom's computers and files to botch the loaded information related to the Tetrasank. Next, depending on how well Ocelot could handle the formula itself, he could chemically alter it in a local lab, rendering it harmless, or take it to the nearest top-level security building, just north of Boldoy. If we brought it back to the Center, it might be returned to the Regime. In the stronghold, it would be safe from all outside hands at least for a while.

"Getting in is not so tough. Getting out, now that's where we need Sil's talent," Alaban mentioned.

"I'll need to combine power with both of you," I said.

"Just what I like," Alaban said.

He waltzed up to me, grasped my hands in his and danced me around as he hummed a recently popular tune. I went along with his rhythm. Alaban spun me around and dipped me towards the floor. He brought me back up to stand beside him. Then he spun me upward, levitating me into the air diagonally. He zipped me back to face him. We marched three steps together and snapped twice. We smiled and continued in an upbeat waltz. I mentally thanked him for bringing us hope again and for reminding me of the simple joy of life.

"Stop that," Ocelot complained. "It's not good enough. Even if we get out of the castle undetected, they'll be after us from the moment they discover it missing. Teradom will know it was us. Assuming we do get the thing to the fortress, they'll trace us there. With all the Organization agents they have on their side, they'll find us within minutes. Teradom's military forces will be after us as fast as they can fly. Even if Sil could hide us in the walls, they'd only need to wait us out."

"Hide in the walls," Alaban whispered excitedly. He let go of me. "That's brilliant," he called to Ocelot. "If Sil can move objects through each other, she can merge two objects around each other."

"And leave them there," I spoke in realization. "We can hide it in a wall someplace and no one will ever find it. We can lead them to the fortress. They'll think it's inside, but I could leave it anywhere."

Alaban and I glowed with the anticipation.

"What about our safety?" Ocelot asked, dampening our discovery. He stood from the sofa to pace where we had been. "Not just during the op, but right now. You said Teradom knows where we live. Now that you're out, he'll send someone looking for you here."

"Not yet. I let Paleface and Oso follow me to the interhelion express station here in Red Mesa. They intercepted me after I sent Willa to Sor4. Teradom wanted me escorted back alive so he could have the pleasure of killing me himself. I pretended to give up. They slapped the binders on me and loaded me on the first available flight. They made the call to him that I was in custody and on the airbus back to Boldoy. He told them to put me in cold storage for the night and that he'd see them in the morning. I know what he was talking about. There's a refrigeration company at one of our smuggling points. He's going to meet them there. Only they won't be there. I slipped out of the binders and tagged them both with a double sleeper. They'll be out until late tomorrow. They'll wake up on the other side of the planet. Unless Teradom calls them back to check on them tonight, we're safe here for at least another twelve hours.

"I'm sorry to put you out of your home, but you'll need to relocate to the Center for your own safety. Even if Ryker and Scythe come looking for us, you'll be fine inside the Center. They're good, but they're no match for hundreds of warriors. They're not looking forward to facing Sil, either. They've heard tall tales about your powers, courtesy of yours truly. When they do come looking for us, this place will be empty. We'll be in Hammerstead and they'll be out of luck. And if they're here, that means we'll have fewer problems to deal with at the castle."

Ocelot stared out the window into the late evening shadows of the garden. "I don't like this plan. There are too many variables."

Pensively, I moved to sit on the sofa. Alaban soon followed. We soon found ourselves again shoulder-to-shoulder, comfortable with our touch. As we thought of this dilemma, Alaban slipped an arm around me again. I leaned onto him. Ocelot did not warn him this time verbally. He only approached and stared down at us until I got the hint and moved over to allow him to sit between us.

Somewhat annoyed by Ocelot's jealousy after all he'd explained, and having regained his confidence, Alaban shrugged and rested his arm on the back of the sofa around Ocelot's shoulders instead. If I hadn't been wary of Ocelot's temper, I would have giggled. Ocelot gritted his teeth and flashed his eyes in distaste. Alaban pretended to ignore him. Ocelot leaned forward to avoid him.

We discussed the plan for another hour together, but the evening waned. So did our spirits. At a late hour, Ocelot regarded Alaban silently. Then he stood to show him out. "Let's evacuate this house as soon as possible. I'm walking you back to the Center. You still have a lot of explaining to do. Sil, get some things together. Clean out the information on the computers before you go to the Center." He turned to glare at Alaban. "Get this straight. I still don't trust you. I can barely stand the sight of you, but right now I don't have much choice but to go along with the plan. You're staying at the Center in a holding cell for the night."

Alaban protested. "If I stay at the Center, someone will alert my boss. Double agents are all over that Center. I know. I'd rather hide out in the suburbs at the Blue Zone overnight. Track me if you want. We can meet first thing in the morning. We should have twenty hours or so to get this done. Then he may move the stuff himself," Alaban spoke solemnly.

"Okay, but I don't want you anywhere near this zone or this house unless I'm with you. Got that?" Ocelot warned.

"Yes, sir. I understand," Alaban ceded, bowing solemnly to his superior.

The two men marched to the door. I followed, wondering what the two would discuss on their way.

"See you soon," Alaban told me with a wink. I waved to him warmly.

Ocelot said nothing. He didn't even look at me as he pulled the door closed. I stood sadly staring at the door before moving to my task of unloading the computers and compacting research data onto storage tapes.

After I finished with the den office computers, I sat in our room to look up the North Boldoy Research Deposit, the site we had proposed to break into. Of course no blueprints were available, only advertisements. The Deposit claimed to have the best security for backup research information on the planet. It mentioned a wide array of customers from government research offices to chemical and food companies.

I quickly turned off the lights. Someone approached the house—an assassin, then another—Ryker and Scythe. I rushed to collect a few vital items. I gathered all backup tape coils and set the self-destruct virus to run on the stationary computers. The men came closer. I filed a few personal items along with the tape coils into a sling back and strapped it on before throwing on full armor. They entered the front garden gate. I dashed up the stairs and out onto the roof patio. One of the assassins paused at the front entrance as he decoded and broke open the lock. The other sneaked around to the side of the house at the solar generator.

I sailed over the back garden past the dimly lit wall that divided our house and yard from the one behind it. I touched down on the neighbors' roof just long enough to gain my balance. I pranced across the bowed grid of walls, homes, and cobbled streets until I reached the river.

I had to make my way back around to the Center. I hoped these evil strangers had not intercepted Alaban and Ocelot on their way out. I jogged along the riverbank until it became too steep. Then I skimmed along the surface of the water to the next embankment.

I finally arrived at the Center near dawn, out of breath and drenched with sweat. I immediately requested Ocelot's room number. I found the room and pounded on the door. He opened it groggily. When he saw the state I was in, he forced himself awake. I explained my presence. I extracted his tape coils from my pack to return them to him. He accepted them greedily. He didn't invite me in, so I asked. He deliberated a moment before stepping aside.

The room was standard temporary quarters for one. A narrow cot lay open against one wall. A tiny open lavatory flanked the room. Ocelot's travel box rested beneath the cot. I stepped to the sink to rinse my face and neck and to drink a little water. He stored the tape coils in his box. I swiveled to face him. I asked to sit and talk to him for a while, but he said he was going upstairs to eat breakfast with Banjil.

"Banjil? He's still here? Why?" I asked.

"You knew about him?" He asked. He shook his head. "Someone sent him from Sor3. I'm hoping it was either Stennet or Jiao. I'd like to find out what I can before we have to leave. Alaban's meeting us at 0810 under the pedestrian bridge between the Blue Zone and the business sector. Why don't you stay in this room for now and get some sleep?"

He donned his over shirt and boots. His voice remained flat and unemotional. He washed his face and ran a comb through his hair before marching out. He behaved as if I were only a warrior, one he disliked. As the door closed behind him, I sighed.

594

I slept on his bunk with the menial comfort of his scent on the pillow. In my dreams, I began to put together the plan we had outlined. One uncertainty left holes in my prediction of success. Would we be able to work together peacefully to fulfill the plan? Would Ocelot give in to the temptation of throwing Alaban back to the enemy in order to escape? I prayed that his conscience would steel his integrity as a warrior and not allow a personal vendetta to interfere with the plan.

Ocelot's footsteps woke me upon his return from breakfast. I asked him about Banjil.

"He claims Jiao sent him. He may have been onto the ghosting program after all. I don't know if I trust Banjil, though. If it was really Stennet who sent him, that's exactly what he'd tell him to say. Banjil says Croso and his staff interrogated him. He says they kept him locked up for possible spying until yesterday. Then they exonerated him and let him go. He told me to check with Croso about it, but there's no time. He said he didn't contact Jiao about us yet. Jiao told him not to communicate with him until he was already on the ship back to Sor3. He said he paid him handsomely to do this." Ocelot sighed. "It had better be Jiao. If it is, this will be the first good thing that's happened this week."

"Ocelot, I'm..." I began.

"We still have an hour. I'm going to go ask Channol about something. You should eat breakfast. I'll meet you at the bridge," he spoke.

He jerked his travel box out from under the cot to extract his weapons packs. I gently rested a hand on his shoulder. He winced and stood quickly with his weapons. He kicked the box back to where it had been. He ambled away from me as he strapped the packs onto the uniform at his thighs. Determined to end this, I stayed after him. I grasped his hand just as he finished securing the last strap. He yanked the hand away from me.

"Don't," he warned. "Don't."

I stood crestfallen and angered as he escaped through the door.

At 0807, I bought a magazine card from a newsstand next to the pedestrian bridge. I walked slowly away with it, loading the information into my palm computer and reading through it. I stopped just beneath the shade of the bridge. I stepped into its concave niche, where I felt Alaban's presence. I leaned onto his chest and gave him a hug when I bumped into him. He squeezed me to him and caressed my head. As we released each other, I told him briefly of his former teammates' appearance at the house. He apologized for his miscalculation of time. I told him I didn't sense that they had followed us here. He agreed.

A moment later, Ocelot appeared at our side. He wasted no time, but started reviewing the plan.

"I broke into one of the Center's mainframes. I got blueprints and security data about the fortress. We'll need some basic supplies. Sil and I can get them from the Center. We can't bring electronic devices with us. The electronics monitors will pick up their signals. We'll have to depend on our sixth sense to get us through. The fortress is fully covered by multiple types of sensors, including olfactory in the interior chambers. We might be able to elude them by damaging the sensor outlets themselves. I just hope they're positioned where we can get to them. Most of the time, we'll be working in total darkness, but they'll have infrared on, too. We'll have to cloak at all times.

"If we want to make the break-in convincing, we'll have to get in pretty deep. Security personnel will be investigating once we're gone. We'll have to leave some evidence of timed interior room entry so they'll think we stored the weapon there.

"If we're detected, they'll have an army after us before we know it. Our odds of clean entry and exit are slim. We'll only consider the op a failure if we're caught before the package is in place. If and when we're caught, we'll escape by any means necessary. We'll stay around only long enough to help each other escape, and only if it's necessary. Then we'll split up and meet each other at a remote location in two days." Ocelot gave the latitude and longitude of the waterfall the two of us knew well.

Alaban agreed to meet there if separated.

"There's one other thing I found out about this place. The interior is a lot smaller than the exterior. The thick outer wall is actually a double exterior wall. The hollow between the two is filled with a circulating poison gas. We can't merge through the wall to get in. The roof is the same way. Underground, there's no gas flow, but the building is set into a natural rock basin. There are only two doorways. They're right next to each other. That's the other bad thing. They'll know where to wait us out."

"Good God, what do they keep in there that needs that much protection?" Alaban protested.

"I guess ours won't be the only weapon of mass destruction kept inside," I mused.

"No, but it's probably the slowest and most untraceable," Ocelot commented. "That's why it's their weapon of choice."

I thought of the picture I'd seen of the fortress before I'd been forced to evacuate the house. The doors were at the bottom of a steep slope from the entrance road. A person would have to be inside the compound and close to the building in order to actually see the doors. It could work to our advantage, but I had a bad feeling about it.

"We're short on time," Ocelot stated. "Let's finish preps and get out of here. Let's go get those supplies."

"I'll borrow a vehicle," Alaban said.

Ocelot stepped away as he spoke. "We'll meet you a block south of the Center in twenty minutes." He glanced at me. "Let's take different paths. I'll meet you in the supplies area."

I nodded. I moved to the curb and waited a moment as he crossed the street. Alaban called to me mentally. I turned to him.

"Don't let his attitude get to you. He'll be back with you when the op is over. Don't worry," he advised.

I watched Ocelot as he walked away from us.

"You've got to be at top strength to carry this out. Don't let him distract you. If you have to, focus on me. Okay?" He set an arm around my shoulders.

I regarded him thankfully.

He lifted one corner of his mouth. "Under the circumstances, I'd say he's taking it pretty well. He hasn't even considered killing me this time. That's a good sign."

We brought our hands together and clasped them tightly.

"We're on the job. Let's get tough, twin heart," he encouraged with a wink.

We gave our hands a firm squeeze in a warriors' handshake before exiting at opposite sides of the bridge.

Chapter 57: Theft

In the afternoon, we reached our first destination. Alaban parked the solar car behind a building on the opposite side of the canyon from the Regime castle. We collected our hover boards from the back of the vehicle and cleared the railing at the edge of the parking lot. We set the soles of our right boots into the hover board straps and switched the boards on. They pressed upward as if magnetized against the ground. We dove off the cliff into a brief freefall before crouching onto the hover boards. We whizzed through the mid-afternoon air, dodging outcroppings of rocks along the way. We cloaked in case one of the task force was scanning the canyon for intruders. The momentum of the fall cruised us to the castle's foundation. We hid the boards under some succulent bushes at the base of the canyon and began our invasion plan.

Instead of levitating all the way up the castle wall, we used common supplies to conserve our energy. Ocelot shot a pulley cord up to a midpoint where the tower met the foundation. The rope swished as we rose to the top of it. He shot a second cord up to the tenth floor of the tower. Carefully, we switched ropes to climb to a point at about the ninth floor. Alaban clicked his teeth to let us know he needed to get in here. We let go of the ropes and levitated horizontally to the nearest window. Alaban imploded the sensors around the window. I moved the glass apart to let us through.

We entered a foyer similar to the one I'd first entered at the top floor when I had come to rescue Alaban. He touched the nape of our necks to increase our psychic reception. He showed us flashing images, mapping out this floor. The rooms here included multiple guards' quarters, Teradom's own room and private office, a hidden safe room where the Tetrasank was stored, and a plethora of security monitors. I communicated back to him that the safest way for us to enter would be through the wall between the open living room and Teradom's office. The men nodded. We levitated through the foyer and into the living room area. The guards talked quietly just outside the door. We saw the shadow of one man in the doorway, but he did not approach the dark living room to find us.

We slid silently to the wall. I clutched the arms of my teammates for additional strength. The wall peeled open. Ocelot used the comfortable surge of power to shut down all sensors in the two adjacent rooms before letting go of me. Then he made for the computer. Alaban headed for the safe. I meditated in the doorway between the two to sense any danger.

Alaban saw the various numerical codes for breaking into the safe, but he needed Teradom's handprint to open the last door to it. He held my hand as I split open the safe and withdrew its contents. The objects piled onto the floor around us. We overlooked the money cards, keys, ownership document files, and jewelry. Alaban picked up some tape coils and a trapezoidal prism-shaped box. I sifted through some emergency weapons and information cards while he pocketed his find.

Alaban snapped his head towards the office and then sprinted to it. Ocelot had called him to help break a code. I stayed to check the information cards. Any information we could lift from the Regime would mean a better chance of defeating them. I slid the cards into my vest.

I stood again in the doorway between the safe and the office to meditate for their cover. They took several minutes to crack the computer, enter the program, and alter the files.

Ocelot was fascinated by the formula. He studied its three-dimensional structure and list of procedures before adding a few extra elements to it. He removed certain percentages of chemicals and living code buds from the parasitic strands as well, rendering the concoction nearly harmless. Later he assured us the worst that would happen to a person exposed to the newly altered formula would be a full-body rash; but it would go away in a few days. He exited and closed down the computer.

I helped Alaban return the unwanted objects to the safe. Then we planned to move out the way we had entered. Unfortunately, new guards escorted some hive members and a smuggling control contact to the living room area we'd just invaded. We stayed in Teradom's office, mentally observing the people on the other side of the wall from us.

The men in the living room waited impatiently for Teradom to return. Apparently Teradom had some business with the control contact. There was something uncannily familiar about him. I tugged at Alaban's sleeve. I asked him silently who the man was. He replied it was their drug and arms manager for the entire northern hemisphere. He was also a contact between the Soren helion and Santer. I clutched Ocelot's hand tightly.

"Is that who I think it is?" I asked him psychically.

"Piss on him. It's Klib," he answered.

I flashed some of our memories to Alaban. He squinted at the man. "If I'd known that, I would have taken him out while I still worked here."

I realized Alaban had never actually seen or met Klib when we were on Santer. But surely he'd seen pictures of the wanted man. Klib's image appeared in nearly every report following Wilbaht's announcement seven months ago. He must have had his face and prints changed. Even so, how could he have risen to this position of relative power in such a short time? A memory of the attempted rape glinted before me.

"I know my drugs. She'll be out for two or three hours tops. It won't kill her," Klib had said.

He knew his drugs. He wasn't speaking in jest. He was in the business. What about arms? What did he know about them? Suddenly, a piece of the puzzle fell into place. Klib had to have been a smuggler on Sor3, probably a middleman. This was his connection to Trau. He was probably running goods for General Zar, too. I wondered exactly what position he'd held in the Sor3 smuggling scheme. I had countered an insult to him once, saying I was surprised he'd gotten his pilot's license with the Organization at all. What if he was never an Organization pilot before his job on the Sonic Wake? He might have been a mere smugglers' pilot, the captain of an interstellar pirate ship. That would explain his personality perfectly. I communicated my thoughts to my men, who agreed with cynical enthusiasm.

Teradom's concierge entered the living room to speak to Klib and the other smugglers. "I'm sorry, sir. General Teradom is out for the evening. He's attending some urgent business in Boldoy. He invites you to stay as his houseguests for the night. He assures us that he will return to meet with you in the morning."

"Just remind him I work for his associate. If my boss calls me away, he'll have to wait until I get back from Fitmalo to meet again," Klib stated.

"Certainly, sir. If you'll follow me, I'll show you to your rooms." The concierge invited the men to lunch downstairs in the main dining hall and informed them of a larger meal to be served later in the evening.

The hive members grumbled, but Klib strode calmly after the Fitmalo man.

We focused on the path they took. The group was to be housed on a floor directly below Alaban's room.

"Before we get out of here we ought to pay this guy a visit," Alaban suggested.

"Do we have time?" I asked.

"We'll make time." Ocelot pulled my hand to let me know that we should go through the wall again.

We merged through and retraced our steps to the window. This time, Alaban stopped us at the window. He closed his eyes and held his hand out, I thought, to scatter its molecules. Instead, he grasped the handle of it and opened the window by conventional means. He thrust his head out and scanned the wall around us. Then he returned to us. He clutched our arms.

"Let's go to my room. He's a drug contact. I'll catch him when he's alone and ask him about some drugs. Then I'll get him to come upstairs. We can hide out in my room and scalp him."

"We've got to get as much information out of him as we can before he dies," Ocelot answered.

"Maybe we shouldn't kill him. He should be interrogated officially by the Organization," I said.

We paused a moment to consider it. Ocelot signaled us to move out. Alaban went first, skimming the wall to his small bathroom window. We followed. He smashed in the window, not worrying about noise within his room. I stretched the opening to let us through. I would need to rest before I could pull any more feats of psychokinesis.

Once inside, Alaban checked his room thoroughly for any alterations to his recording preventions. It appeared clean.

"We're safe for the time being. Take a nap if you want," he spoke aloud. "He'll be downstairs for at least half an hour. I'd offer to go next door and let you two have a conjugal visit, but sex drains the male's power, so it's probably not a good idea," he half-joked.

Ocelot flashed a glare at his indiscrete comment.

I tumbled onto the bed to nap. I forced myself to relax, hypnotizing myself into a fifteen-minute deep sleep while Ocelot and Alaban discussed what to do about Klib. I awoke to find Ocelot leaning in the bathroom doorway while Alaban reclined in his chair by the door. Both rested lightly with eyes closed. I smiled at the unlikelihood of the scene.

I perceived Klib downstairs. He had purloined a sandwich from the kitchen and was on his way to his room with it. If Alaban descended just one flight of stairs, he could intercept him and lure him to our snare without being noticed by the internal guards. Before I could notify Alaban of this, he opened his eyes and hopped up out of his chair.

"I'm reeling him in now," he announced.

Ocelot came alive at the doorway and motioned to me to join him in the bathroom to stay out of sight. If Klib saw either of us as he entered the room, he would run away or shout in panic.

A few moments later, Alaban opened his door and invited the vermin into his quarters. He spoke of some kind of drug he was interested in purchasing for himself. Klib expertly gave him some prices per kilo based on different drug sources.

"Is that a good sandwich?" Alaban asked Klib as he firmly shut the door.

"Yeah, it's pretty good," he admitted.

"Stop eating it," Alaban commanded.

I moved to exit the bathroom, but Ocelot caught me by the elbow. He shook his head. He made a motion for me to wait. He sidled past me to enter the room first.

I heard Klib protest. "Why? What's wrong with it?"

I moved nearer the doorway so I could see Alaban but not Klib. Alaban grabbed the sandwich away from him and sunk his teeth into it

"Nothing. It's good," he said with his mouth full. "Here, you want some?" Alaban tossed the meal over to Ocelot.

Ocelot caught the sandwich and took a bite. "Mmm. Too much meat."

"Sh..." Klib breathed. I imagined he felt ready to urinate himself.

"You always did eat more than your share of meat on the ship. Didn't he, Sil?" Ocelot intoned. He glared coldly at our victim.

I stepped out and behind Ocelot to appear next to him. "Yes, he did," I spoke in a sly voice.

As I'd suspected, Klib's face had been altered since the last time I'd seen him. His nose was smaller. He'd had a facelift to make him appear several years younger. But his salty beard still clung to his chin and his thinning grayish hair still lay closely cropped to his scalp. His chlorine-blue eyes were certainly original. They conveyed his utter, squirming fear.

"Shit," he swore.

Alaban cackled. He gripped Klib's shoulder like a vice. Klib tensed, but stayed rooted to the floor, knowing he had no chance of escape.

"Yes, that's exactly what I'd say if I were you. Well said. Hey, since we all know each other now, why don't you sit and talk to us a while? Tell us what you've been up to. We're dying to know—excuse me—I should say you're dying to tell us because that's exactly what you're going to do in a few minutes. You're going to die. You can even pick which one of us whacks you. It'll be a blast. Come on in. Have a seat." He dragged Klib confidently into the chair he had occupied before.

Klib stumbled awkwardly to sit at the edge of the cushion. His face flushed, showing red lines along the sides of his face and nose where the surgeon had sutured his skin. He looked like a frightened map.

"Are you going to finish that?" Alaban asked offhandedly to Ocelot.

Ocelot shook his head and passed the sandwich back to Alaban. He held it up to offer me some, but I held up my hand to pass. Alaban shrugged and munched another morsel. He nonchalantly flipped the lever at the bottom of the chair. The recliner bucked. Klib gripped the padded arms of the chair and nearly cried out as legs flung up to the reclined position.

"Comfy?" Alaban asked him. He jiggled his eyebrows at our ensnared foe.

Ocelot shuffled closer. "This is a soundproof room. All electronic signals are jammed. There's no calling for help. You're at our mercy. What he just said is true. You're practically dead already. You may as well bring the house of cards down with you," he informed him. "Let's start with your real identity. What's your name?"

602

Of the three of us, I sensed Klib feared Ocelot most. All the camaraderie he had pretended to share with Ocelot on the ship, in addition to the cowardly crimes he'd committed against Wilbaht and me, now made Klib a damnable tick to him and he knew it.

"You know my name: Klib Sarrow," he began.

I withdrew my laser cutter from its pouch. The laser sang between the black horns. Alaban grabbed him by the ankle.

"Should we play 'this little piggy went to hell'?" Alaban asked almost gleefully.

Klib gripped the arms of the chair and sat as straight as the chair's position would allow. "My real name is Klib Sarrow. I used another name on the smuggling side. They call me Hume."

Alaban released the ankle to lean on the wall next to him. "Let me guess. Your last name is Nescum. Trau sometimes called you 'human scum'. What a funny guy, that Trau. Always cracked me up." He finished some of the crumbs from the sandwich and licked his fingers.

I let go of the laser, but Klib did not relax.

"It's Nescu, no M at the end. What do you want to know?" Klib stammered.

"No M, huh? Boy, Trau was more creative than I gave him credit for. Well, then, Hume Nescu, a.k.a. Human Scum, tell us. Who did you work for first: Trau or General Zar?"

"I didn't work for either one of 'em. I worked around. I was an independent flyer," he replied.

"How long did you fly smuggling deliveries?" Alaban asked, now getting serious.

Anger pervaded Klib's fear. "I've been in and out of this job since you were in diapers, punk," he dared to say.

Alaban did not punish him for his disrespect but showed him a tightened fist.

"That's a long time," I said to the loathsome fiend. "Keep this in mind. We're only keeping you alive to ask you a few questions. The longer you hold our interest, the longer you live."

"You screw with us; we'll make this painful," Ocelot added.

Klib looked around at his controlling adversaries momentarily, hoping to figure out some way to con his way out of his situation, but then frowned bitterly.

"Entertain us," Alaban spoke, opening his fist in an inviting gesture.

"Why did General Zar order Trau's assassination on Sor3?" I asked.

Klib hesitated, but then decided to cooperate.

"Zar thought Trau ratted him out to the Regime," he admitted.

"But Trau didn't rat him out. It was you, wasn't it?" I pressed.

"Hell, no. I never ratted out anyone. I always kept my mouth shut. If you want to blame someone for Trau's death, look in the mirror. You two were the ones who got him arrested."

"Yes, we got him arrested, but that shouldn't have affected Zar. Trau didn't work with him. What did Zar have to hide from the Regime that Trau might have told them about?" I asked. "Was it a weapon?"

"I don't know about that. All I know is when Viga and Trau got rid of the old Vermilion gang and brought in their own people, Zar wanted in on the new business. He tried to skim a little on the side, buy some arms at a reduced price to build up his military rebel cache."

"And Trau agreed to help him?" Ocelot intoned.

"No," Klib said.

"So you offered to skim one of your shipments for him?" Alaban asked.

"No way. I couldn't afford lost cargo. I told Trau we could lose a few cases of arms from a couple of other ships, and then sell to Zar for a profit. Zar was all for it, but when I met with Trau about it, he got pissed off and told me to keep out of it or I'd wind up dead. Look who was talking," Klib scoffed.

"It was you he met that night," I said. I turned to Alaban, recalling the night of the bar tower incident. "I thought Trau was meeting with a Fitmalo Regimist about the weapon. That's why I reported him to the interrogation committee."

Now it made sense. Trau had left Alaban at the bar tower to meet with Klib about this proposal to scam weapons out of the Regime smuggling shipments, but Trau had turned him down. After we'd killed the spider, I had reported only what I knew against Trau: that he had left Alaban alone in order to meet with someone. Lam and Samson must have thought Trau was turning dirty deals behind their backs, so they took him in for questioning and tortured him. Zar and Klib thought Trau would tell on them about the scheme and that the Regimists would be after them as soon as they found out. But Trau had only mentioned Klib as "human scum" who had wanted an extra business deal. Trau had clearly stated to his interrogators that he had turned Klib down and that he had warned him, but that he hadn't made him pay, (with his life), because he was a "hand that fed". He was a supplier. Trau had covered for Klib. He hadn't ratted him out. Nor had he divulged anything about Zar. Zar had assassinated him for nothing.

After a few more questions, Klib told us what had happened from his perspective, during the time between Trau's arrested and the day we left Sor3.

"When I heard he'd been picked up, I went back to my ship to try and get out of there, but Viga's thugs were all over it. I figured Trau probably told on me to get out of interrogation. I almost went straight to Zar for asylum, but when I got on his frequency to call him, I heard his men talking about searching for me. I wasn't sure if he wanted me for a shipment or if he thought I was turning against him with Trau. So I went to a friend of his to get him to explain things to him so he wouldn't kill me, too, but he said Zar probably wouldn't believe me. He offered to help me out if I did him a big favor. I wasn't interested until I saw on the news how Zar had offed Trau. He didn't even wait 'til he was on the ground to get rid of him. He blew up a damned public airbus over a damned high-populated city.

"I knew I'd be dead within a week if I didn't find some way to leave the helion. So this friend of his made me a deal to get me off the planet if I'd pilot a ship for the Organization to keep tabs on you two. I didn't like it, but it saved my ass and the pay was good. He even got that computer whiz son of his to alter my files to show dual payroll status. He built a whole new ID on me and altered all my old pilot data so I wouldn't appear on the database twice."

"Zar's friend was Stennet, wasn't he?" Ocelot asked.

"Yeah. You were probably looking for me the whole time and I was right there in front of you. Some seers you are. You missed me every time. If I hadn't been here today, you'd still be looking."

Alaban ignored his comment. "When Stennet heard Sil and Ocelot were dead, he pulled the plug on your operation," he guessed.

"He paid me off at the space station and told me he didn't want to hear from me again," Klib admitted.

"If Stennet is a friend of Zar, he can't be a Regime supporter. So why was he at the space station at the same time we were? And why did he give you the saboteur program?" Ocelot pressed.

"I don't know why he was there, but he didn't give me the program. Swall Jade gave it to me. He's my boss. You want the house of cards, start with him and his daughter."

"Why did Swall Jade give you the program?" I asked.

"Your dark granddaddy knew too much," he spoke hatefully.

"How high is Swall Jade in the hierarchy?" I asked of Alaban more than of Klib.

Alaban gestured a thumb towards the ceiling. "He's like Teradom's twin. They're double evil. They're covering all sides of the law: Organizational, planetary, black market, the underground. Together they have complete economic and political control."

"If Swall is so high up in the Regime, how did you get close to him? Especially after abandoning your pilot's job on Sor3?" I asked.

"I worked my way back up when we were on Santer. Ran into Viga there. I told her the whole story. She let me back in conditionally. I had to get you to the space station and they'd give me my old job back. Then Swall Jade gave me the black box to get rid of Wilbaht."

"In exchange for what?" Ocelot chimed in.

"Big money. I run the line between Soren and Sant, with a main trading point here on Jawlcheen. Viga supervises arms and drugs to the five major trade helions. Some other guys control outer distribution, but they're small scale."

"And their Regime affiliates help keep it all legal," Alaban mused. "What business do you have with Teradom right now?"

"Arms from Sant for the new Thrader Defense military. Two hundred thousand pistols on order. They'll bring them in on general goods deliveries in cases of ten thousand each. I've got names and numbers in my room downstairs. If you'll let me go down to get…"

"Well, time's up," Alaban interrupted, kicking the lever of Klib's interrogation chair.

The foot of the recliner whopped to the ground. Klib nearly bowled out of the chair. He sat back into it as quickly as he could manage, pressing his body into the backrest, wishing for refuge from us, and hating us more with every approaching minute.

"Hold on," I said. "If you and the others you mentioned from Sor3 had nothing to do with the biological weapon, why did you send the microship to spy on the C.A.T.T. Center?"

"Trau hired me for a personal favor. He wanted footage of you and your exam as evidence. He said he was going to prove to his boss that the two of you would be perfect for grand theft. He said you could get into the Prime Minister's bedroom and steal his pillow out from under him and he would never know it. He had his eye on you a long time. He said he hoped you two would get it on so he would have an even better leverage to blackmail you."

He peered spitefully through his fear at Alaban. "I guess you two got busy after he was gone. Too bad Trau didn't live to see the porno shots. I could have gotten twice the price on shit like that."

He glanced between Alaban and me vindictively, now tired of the intimidation game.

"I guess she prefers dark meat. Never did let me in on it. I came close, though, didn't I, sweetheart?" He spoke menacingly, taking his last opportunity to insult me. "I had those pants unzipped and ready to go, didn't I, you little c…"

His last word was disrupted by Alaban's fist. Klib jerked to the side as blood spattered onto one arm of the chair and across the floor.

606

"You don't really want those to be your last words, do you, Mr. Scum?" Alaban spoke frankly. He jerked Klib back into a sitting position.

Klib's face twisted. He sat dazed and pained, holding a hand over his red, oozing mouth.

"Any more questions?" Alaban asked us.

"No. We're finished here." Ocelot spoke.

I nodded.

"Well, then. Here's the moment you've been waiting for. You get to choose your executioner. Who will it be?" Alaban presented the choices to him as if he were eager to make a sale. "I know who I'd choose. I'm the expert. You'll get it fast and clean if you go with me. Sil will probably kick you between the legs a few times before she does you in. I can't speak for Ocelot, but if he's using the sword, I'm sure you'll see your severed limbs on the floor before you die. And behind surprise door number four, I have a saber-toothed Metabrid in the meat room downstairs who would just *love* to have you for dinner. So who'll it be?"

"I don't give a damn. You can all roast in hell. Just do it," He muffled.

"Shall we draw straws?" Alaban suggested facetiously.

"I want him. He killed our commander," Ocelot stated, stepping in close to him. "And he tried to rape my wife."

"Your wife?" Klib asked in confusion. He glanced between us.

Realization gave way to insult. Through broken teeth and bleeding mouth, he pronounced, "You do get around, don't you, princess?"

In a flash, Ocelot dashed Klib's face to the floor. He then axe-kicked his lower ribs at his back. I stepped away to give him space. As Klib writhed from the blows, Alaban leaned down and twisted his wrist, heaved him up by the throat, and supported him in a chokehold. Klib staggered and gasped, groping at Alaban's arm. I grimaced at his distorted, discolored face while blood drained from his mouth and nose. Alaban supported Klib's body, straightening one leg to brace himself while Ocelot punched Klib three times in the stomach. The two jolted backward at each punch. Klib held his breath and then panted with agony and sharp pain. Alaban lifted his arm from Klib's neck and pulled his head back with it, exposing the jugular vein.

I was about to turn away to avoid having to watch the actual kill when Ocelot systematically struck him in three places about the thigh and neck to knock him out. Alaban released Klib's face to catch him under the arms. Klib's head lolled forward, dripping a strand of blood and saliva onto the floor.

"Let's go," Ocelot said.

Alaban dragged Klib to the window. He angled his body so that it would fit through. Then he dumped Klib outside. He poked one arm and his head out to watch the body and slow its landing to the ground. They hadn't meant to kill him after all.

Impressed by their unlikely cooperation, I hurried to join them at the window. While Alaban washed off the blood from his arms, I sensed a group of guards climbing the stairs to Alaban's room, probably to investigate the reverberating thud Klib's skull had caused when it hit the floor. We had to move fast. Once Ocelot cleared the window, I slipped through behind him. I lifted all the broken glass from the floor and refitted it to the window frame. I wasn't sure how long it would hold, but I hoped it would stay for at least a few minutes while we made our escape.

The bloodstains would alarm the guards. They would do a full search of the castle to find anything else unusual or anyone missing. When they discovered Hume was unaccounted for, they would call Teradom. I didn't sense Ryker or Scythe in the castle. I assumed they were on their way back to the castle with Teradom. They had been in Boldoy to meet with the other task force members. When Oso and Paleface hadn't shown up on time, and they'd found out Alaban was obviously not on ice at the refrigeration company, Teradom had probably thrown a royal fit.

After retrieving our ropes and pulleys, we zipped down to recover the hidden hover pads. Alaban took the burden of carrying Klib. As he hefted the cumbersome body onto his shoulder, I heard a faint tinkling of shattering glass from above. The windowpane had given way. We had to cloak and fly before the guards looked out the window.

We cruised on our boards to the opposite side of the canyon and exerted our powers to skim up the cliff. We strode to the parking area from the cliff's edge like a group of extreme sports athletes with our boards slung over our backs. Ocelot and Alaban each hung one of Klib's arms over their shoulders as they levitated his feet in time to walk him to the land vehicle, keeping a board in front of his red face. Several tourists grouped together a few meters away, but they paid no attention to us.

Alaban rode in back with Klib while I drove us around the canyon to the main bridge connecting Hammerstead to Boldoy. Ocelot poked around on his palm computer to find an Organization member in our vicinity. He found a pair of Arbormen stationed in North Boldoy at a hotel basement. He hailed them by phone. He explained we were fellow warriors in need of assistance on an arrest. He asked them to baby-sit a wanted criminal until a pickup team could retrieve him. They agreed.

We drove to the hotel, parked in its lower level, and met the pair by a service door. Alaban and Ocelot dragged Klib through the double doors while I waited. A few minutes later, they marched out. Alaban looked perturbed. He rubbed his cheek. Apparently, Klib had woken and punched him in an attempt to escape, but one of them had knocked him out again.

Once we resumed the trip, Ocelot messaged Croso about Klib's location. He did not explain how he knew Klib was there or where he was himself. I was sure Croso would send a pickup team and also an investigative team to find out how Klib got there and why we were in Boldoy. Croso would do everything in his power to locate us. Then we would have two opposing groups of people after us: our own Organization and the Regime.

Chapter 58: Penetrating the Research Deposit

Between the hotel and the North Boldoy Research Deposit, we reviewed our strategy for entry. Ocelot suggested we desert the vehicle and all electronic equipment in a public area and then walk to the hydro dam at the river close to our target site. The dam would provide light tourist traffic and would give us a partial view of the building. With the detectors around the perimeter of the building's compound, and the acid-filled outer walls, the safest way for us to get into the compound would actually be through the front gate.

We planned to enter with a guard or two, and then wait for them to pass through the front security chamber and hallway. Once they gave confirmation to the main security center that all was secure, we would knock them out. Then we would link powers to tunnel through the first floor and land in the basement main control room. Beneath the basement rested a coil system for earthquake damage prevention. The space for the coils had to be only a meter high or less. I planned on inserting the box of Tetrasank in the middle of one of the coils where it would be protected from the elements and where no one except Alaban or I could retrieve it.

While I buried the Tetrasank, Ocelot and Alaban planned to gain access to the security system control bank. If we were lucky, they might be able to code in and time down certain sections of sensors and security weapons, especially the olfactory sensors and laser screens. From there, we could remote-trip some of the internal security on purpose, drawing the attention of the guards to a deep, enclosed section, leaving evidence of a fake entry to the central parts of the Research Deposit without having to leave the control room at all. Then, when the building personnel began security sweeps, we could leave the way we'd entered: unseen, unsensed, and unharmed.

Unfortunately, we were aware that this plan had some major flaws. It was based on multiple assumptions, or simply on hopes. We hoped we'd be able to follow someone in. We hoped the front automated security didn't include a simple stratospheric sonar, which would detect our mass even though we couldn't be seen. We hoped the section of floor we meant to pass through could be parted unnoticed. We hoped the main control room sensors and automatic security did not contain chemical weapons or a laser grid. These and other factors came to mind as we strolled across the hydro dam.

Three-quarters of the way over the bridge, Ocelot told us to stop and sightsee. We leaned on the railing, barely touching elbows to communicate. We pretended to admire the water and the view of North Boldoy. We focused mentally on the target area. To our right and slightly removed from the river, we glimpsed the top of the Research Deposit. The building looked like a dome with its top chopped off. The dome sat three or four stories into a deep impression in the rock, as an upside-down bowl set into a larger bowl. The compound surrounding it contained rows of shade trees. Most people probably never noticed the building or knew its purpose. No guards patrolled the area surrounding it. Multi-sensor cameras took care of the outer security.

Alaban stood straight. He peered directly at the building. A vision flickered in his eyes. He clenched his jaw. He reached for my hand, but not to communicate. He pulled me away from the edge of the dam. He led me to walk with him. Ocelot caught up with us. We felt our enemies approach at a distance. They could be at our heels by sunset.

We made our way through winding sidewalks to pass the compound and to find a place to observe unnoticed. We found a school a block from the place with a few shops nearby catering to young students. We climbed to the top floor of one shop where we found an antiques dealer. He was a Kangaroo Lizard who didn't appear hopeful for a sale with us. He glanced at us briefly before returning to watch a dull comedy on his computer screen. Taking advantage of his indifference, we took the back stairs of the shop and ascended to the roof.

This building stood half a block away from the Research Deposit. Trees obscured our direct view of the building, but we were able to see the front gate clearly. However, merely seeing the place was no help. We needed to move in soon or drastically change our plans.

Feasibly, I could embed the box in the cornerstone of the very building where we stood, but Teradom and the task force would sense its whereabouts and would extract it easily. If I buried it in the ground, they would dig for it. If I wedged it into a section of the hydro dam, the water would be at risk of contamination. The Deposit was our best choice.

After nearly half an hour of waiting, Alaban and I did stretching exercises to stay alert. Ocelot remained statuesque, closed.

Finally, he said, "If we don't see some action soon, we're going to have to abandon the mission and start running. Teradom is getting close."

We knew he was right. Somehow he had been able to track us, possibly through connections to the Organization. He might have traced our land vehicle. That would have led him to the other side of the river. Our proximity to the Research Deposit gave away our location.

"There's someone pulling up to the gate," I noticed.

Alaban yanked me down and away from the roof's edge. "It's the task force, or at least some of them. Teradom is on his way."

We peered carefully over the ledge surrounding the roof. Ryker and Scythe stood impatiently at the gate's communication system. Ryker explained to someone on the inside that Teradom was on his way and that they'd better open the gates when he arrived. He probably made a few honest political threats to the personnel, like the fact that Teradom could have them shut down or that he knew many of the Deposit's customers personally and would openly express his disappointment to them if they didn't let him in to inspect the place. They waited impatiently for their boss and for a response from the Research Deposit personnel.

"The best way in is to play the parasite. We'll ride in on the backs of our hosts. Then we'll shed their blood when the time is right." Ocelot gazed at Alaban as if he were meant to be a victim as well. "You can hide your presence. When we link together this time, you'll hide all three of us."

"We'll expend too much power at once," I warned. "We still have to levitate and cloak. Plus I have to pass us through the floor. There had better be a safe place to rest for a while. Otherwise we'll all be completely drained before we can get out," I warned.

"He's right. It's the best way. We'll make it." Alaban assured me.

Ocelot motioned us to follow him. We each stepped off the roof in turn, sailing past the building to fall lightly into a narrow, treed garden below. We rounded the building to stand by an open space directly across from the gate. We hung back together just out of sight. I stood between my men. We gripped each other's hands as we cloaked both physically and spiritually. It was a strange feeling. Alaban took the lead in this power. I felt him draw energy from us. The energy flowed from Ocelot's being, through mine, and emptied into Alaban. At the same time, Alaban returned the flow of energy through a different channel so that our power moved in an infinite loop, like electricity.

As soon as our link was complete, Teradom's troupe of guards and remaining task force members arrived. Ryker and Scythe covered the mogul at the front. Paleface and Oso stepped out directly behind him. Although wary of a possible attack from us, they couldn't perceive our exact location. The group stopped at the gate to await permission for entry. We floated above the five principal evils like ghosts.

A lanky Torreon guard, an employee of the Deposit, strode towards us. He carried a decoder to open the gate. He bowed dutifully to the General, but did not speak. He gripped the center of the gate with the decoder and opened it slowly, stepping back to swing the gate inward. Teradom and his task force did not bow to him in return, but marched forward anxiously. We kept pace above them, dodging the limbs of trees as we flew. Then we followed them down the broad walkway, which dipped sharply for several meters before the fortress doors.

The Torreon excused himself to pass in front of them to open the door on the right. He stood aside for them as we all entered together. We passed through the disabled security scan room and into a holding area. The room presented an optical illusion. The ceiling mirrored the shiny white walls. The doorway directly in front of us was framed by a wide brown tile, causing the door to appear closer than it really was, since the room behind it was the same color.

The Torreon ushered the group through. They paused several times before entering skittishly. I hoped their apprehension would work to our advantage.

The brown room contained a desk at one end where a greenish blue Lizard sat, hands extended onto the desktop, visage sullen. Flanking the Lizard on either side of the desk were bubbled three-dimensional aquarium scenes of fish and crustaceans. The party approached her.

"Have there been any indications of a break in today?" Teradom asked pointedly.

"A break in?" the Lizard replied obliviously.

"Apparently not. Did anyone come in today to deposit or withdraw something?" Teradom continued.

As the Lizard told Teradom of some early morning visitors, we returned to the white room. We set ourselves down onto the floor, away from either doorway. We sensed carefully for a spot that was not strung with wires or sensors. I focused hard. Our cloak flickered. The floor surged up in a drifting wave of dark, sand-like particles. I clung tightly to the men for extra power, but they, too demanded more to keep up the cloak. I breathed hard. Ocelot slipped through below me first. I rested my knees on his shoulders. Then Alaban slid down above me. We landed, as planned, in the control room.

When Alaban had cleared the opening, I resealed the floor. I hoped it wouldn't appear too uneven from above, but my power waned. I could not waste more effort to perfect it. As Ocelot had predicted, the room we now inhabited was completely dark except for a few stray panel lights.

We rested a few moments, catching our breath before moving again. I took the Tetrasank box in my hands and knelt, waiting for my full power to return. The men observed our surroundings. They found a long systems control panel in the room for security as well as air circulation. Ocelot sensed no chemical weapons. Alaban warned us against pressure sensors on the computer panel, but no other weapons existed in the main control room itself. The door, however, was set with five different sensors. We were safe for the time being. We could even whisper to each other if we needed to.

"I don't think I'll have enough energy to go through the next floor to the coil level. What if I just insert the box in the support beam under this floor?" I suggested.

Alaban said it was a good idea.

I regretted the imperfection of the floor above us. Teradom would look for us here as soon as he saw it. If I failed to perfect the floor at this level, everyone would know where the Tetrasank was. Our purpose here would be moot.

I shone a tiny band light on the spot at the floor. To my dismay, it was covered with an elaborate diamond-shaped tile design.

"Oh, no. How am I going to put this back together?" I breathed.

"We'll help. We're not out of power yet." Alaban rubbed my back soothingly.

Ocelot ran a hand across the floor. "There's a thick steel beam under here. Let's try it."

Alaban held the band light in his teeth so I could focus easier. We faced the spot on all fours, overlapping our hands for energy flow. The Tetrasank rested before my knees. I spread the tiles, the concrete, and the insulation. Then I reached the steel beam. Its dense molecules were difficult to separate. I sweated. My breathing heightened. At last I made a hole large enough for the box. I fitted it into place, but I could not replace all the steel around it. I had to set some of it aside and replace the rest of the floor as it had been. I struggled to squeeze the materials back to their original state. Then I worked diligently to redesign the tiles despite nausea from the energy drain. Each blue tile had to align with the off-white tiles. Each green tile had to align with the dark brown tiles. I concentrated obsessively on perfecting the pattern. I had to pause for a few moments and rest before finishing. When the floor appeared smooth and correctly positioned, I lifted the pile of steel filings to form a sphere. I passed it to Ocelot.

"Maybe this will come in handy later," I panted.

He pocketed the sphere. "Drink some water. Replenish your energy. We'll need to get out of here fast. Let's take a look at that control panel."

I remained on the floor. I took a couple of swigs of water from my cylinder and then replaced it in my vest. I sat cross-legged, meditating to regain my strength as the two pored over the information.

"I'm reading some numbers here. We could code in and trip some of these internal sections if we had a pair of keys to unlock the pressure sensor on this thing." Alaban pointed to a few zones on the panel.

"It needs a pair of binary pulse keys. Maybe we can simulate some with this steel. Can you reshape it?" Ocelot asked.

"Only with help from my lighter side. Are you up to molding some metal?" he asked as he sat by me.

I moved to lean on his back. I extended an arm to cover his. I allowed him to direct our energies to adjust the steel, forming two five-pronged keys. When these were finished, I lolled over onto the floor, nearly losing consciousness. Alaban squeezed my arm with concern. Ocelot thrust a hand to my neck.

"She'll be okay. She just needs to rest a few minutes. Eat an energy bar and drink some more water. We still need you to cloak in a little while," Ocelot said, patting my face heavily to keep me awake.

"Here," Alaban offered.

He unwrapped a bar from inside his vest as I pushed myself up to lean against him. He held me to him while I ate. As soon as the first morsel hit my stomach, I felt my body absorb its nutrients frantically. I gulped water. I moved away from Alaban to sit on my own. I waved him away and nodded thankfully.

Alaban and Ocelot moved to insert the makeshift keys at opposite ends of the panel. Alaban quoted a series of twelve digits. They pulsed the code through the keys and into the panel. We all jumped from the loud buzz it made. Then we sighed, relieved that the buzz only meant the panel was now accessible. Ocelot exercised his talent. He programmed several doors to open throughout this side of the building. He also set certain motion-sensitive alarms to go off in three of the internal rooms sequentially on a countdown of five minutes. Next, the men pulsed a closure code to reset the pressure sensor.

As they removed the keys together, we felt Teradom and the task force above us. Teradom stopped to observe the floor. He demanded to be taken to this room. He warned the Lizard of our entry. As soon as they scrambled out of the white room, Alaban grabbed me by the shoulder.

"Let's go," he advised.

"There's no time. They'll be here before we can get through," Ocelot said. "When they open the door, we'll slide by them. If we're caught, you act as a decoy. We'll come back for you if you're trapped." He directed this order to Alaban.

Alaban did not hesitate, as I had hoped he would. "Yes, sir," he stated.

I feared that perhaps Ocelot really meant to leave Alaban here, but I could not argue with him. He was currently our interim commander, as Alaban had requested. Even though I disliked the prospect of leaving Alaban to fend for himself, I acknowledged the fact that Ocelot's decision was logical. We knew Teradom wanted revenge on Alaban most. He would be the perfect distraction.

We had no time to discuss secondary possibilities, as the party of six approached rapidly. We lined up against the wall near the door. The five sensor screens deactivated from the outside. We linked to cloak once more. The door shot open. Lights blazed on. Paleface was the first to charge through, brandishing a long-barreled laser pistol. I felt her searching the place with her sixth sense. Scythe was second through the door. He carried no weapons, but bared his sharp forearms before him. As Teradom entered, Paleface noticed the control panel. She mentioned it had been tampered with. The Lizard plodded through the crowd to observe. She was amazed that we had been able to accomplish this. We wanted to move through the door, but Ryker and Oso still barred our exit.

"It looks like they're making their way to the chemical section of the deposit," the Lizard opined.

"Go cut them off," Teradom said.

He retreated through the door, followed by Scythe and the Lizard. Paleface stayed to analyze the control board for another moment before following them. As she passed through, we whooshed up behind her. The Lizard attempted to shut the door, but it hit Alaban in the head and rose to full open again. The Lizard froze. Paleface whirled, pointing the gun right at Ocelot's face before he ducked. She fired at empty air. Ocelot nearly tipped her over as he sped past. We separated, sprinting in different directions.

"Bahn is here, sir. He just followed us out. He's cloaking. He's in here with us," Paleface shouted, aiming her gun from one side to the other with a twitch.

The five evils stopped to sense and observe the room, which was a dull, whitewashed concrete. I floated backwards away from them, hoping we could sustain individual power long enough to elude them. Oso's nostrils flared.

"I smell woman," he growled.

"So she's here, too. Lock down everything," Teradom ordered.

The Lizard rushed back into the control room. Instead of deactivating the pressure sensor, she merely touched it to set off the full alert and lock-down. The door to the control room slammed shut, sealing her in. She was no fool. She preferred to be alone in a locked underground room than in the line of possible fire among the task force.

The group ignored the resounding alarm. They scanned the space for our presence.

Ryker spoke confidently. "They're not in here. I'll bet they ducked back into the control room with that chicken Lizard."

Paleface rapped strongly on the door with the barrel of her gun. "Turn it off!"

The Lizard was unable to turn off the alarm without a second guard to turn the keys with her. Someone from outside the compound, someone with access to the building, would have to override the system to open the doors.

"There is a woman here in this room, not Paleface. Someone else. I know what I smell: human female blood," Oso insisted.

Silently, I cursed my physical state. He was right. Since my miscarriage, my bleeding had slowed, but had not yet stopped altogether.

Oso drew an electric sword and clicked it on. The others retracted to the wall near the control room door. Oso tread cautiously toward my end of the room. He swung around and slashed air with the sword, then beat the empty air around him with it.

Suddenly, Oso's sword smacked him on the throat, electrocuting him and causing a slow but steady blood leak on his neck. Paleface immediately shot at the space in front of him, but no one was there. Oso sat with a thump. He panted and grunted in frustration. Scythe leapt to a space in the air above Oso, slinging his arms about, but again, he hit nothing. Ryker pulled two guns from his belt. The bunch of bumbling ex-warriors felt about them, spun and swung at nothing.

Alaban suddenly touched my hand to let me know where he was. He indicated to me that we should meet at the top of the exit door. He would act as decoy, as Ocelot had indicated, while Ocelot and I merged through the thin titanium door. When I moved there, Alaban withdrew one of the makeshift keys from his pocket. He tossed it into the air. It landed amidst the task force members. Paleface and Ryker whisked around, aiming at each other. Then they retracted, aggravated by the joke.

Suddenly, Paleface's gun jutted forward and shot Ryker through the head. The butt of the gun came back and thwacked her in the mouth. Ryker's body crumpled. Paleface reeled.

"Put your weapons away!" Teradom shouted.

Ocelot and I met each other at the doorway. We held hands to power up together. Alaban shoved Oso's sword through his chest just as he was about to sheath the weapon. Hoping this distraction would cover us; I moved the door apart as fast as I could. We exited the space and landed safely on the other side, facing the Torreon guard. He arched an eyebrow at the strange metamorphosing door, but drew no weapon. Nor did he try to communicate the phenomenon to his coworkers. He merely blinked at it, perplexed.

We heard a clinking noise. We looked back momentarily to see Scythe's arm strung through the door. It jerked back and forth. He wasn't injured, only stuck. He had tried to follow us too late.

Finding no opposition from the Torreon, we scrambled to the next door. Our silent onlooker felt the wind we created as we passed him. He observed peacefully as the second door splayed open. He seemed to enjoy the privilege of watching this magic show.

The alarm stopped. As we rose to the top of this sloped gray corridor, all doors whooshed open. The Deposit guards' help had arrived. A shrill cry of agony resounded behind us. Scythe had lost his arm to the rising door. We continued to cloak on our way up the stairs to the brown room where we had first seen the Lizard. As we stepped through to the white room, a troop of security soldiers, heavily armed, filtered in. We waited until they passed by to exit.

Along the hill surrounding us, we encountered a disappointing sight. Fitmalo military soldiers—an entire squadron—lined the rounded crest, guns in hand. Some were armed with singe guns. Others had acid rifles. Two stood by a stationary weapon I'd only seen twice in my life.

It was a putty gun. I thought this was terribly old-fashioned, but I understood why Teradom would want to use it against warriors. It fired a liquid blob. The blob could be shot at, sliced in two, shielded, but it would keep coming. It attached itself to whatever it hit. The surface of the blob exposed to air would expand and harden first. As it hardened deeper, it would cook the body attached to it.

Ocelot pulled me to one side to levitate up the façade, over the heads of the soldiers, away from the building, and into the safety of one of the shade trees. We poised carefully on separate branches as we awaited some sign of Alaban. Now that the doors were opened, Teradom and his remaining two bodyguards moved out of the enclosed room. The Torreon who witnessed our escape reported to him what he'd seen. Teradom knew I'd gone outside instead of entering the unlocking the interior chambers of the Deposit.

Just then, two more land vehicles, filled with guards and Fitmalo military, emptied at the gate. The Fitmalos rushed to complete the semicircle around the others while the guards filed into the building. With so many new guards moving in, Alaban easily left the enemy to make his escape as well.

As the last pair of security officials entered the building, Alaban slipped out. He momentarily revealed his location to us. Unfortunately, we were not the only ones who perceived his presence. Teradom and Paleface darted out after him, followed by the wounded Scythe. Alaban dashed to one side of the outer doors. Paleface gave chase. Teradom retreated to the hilltop with his soldiers. He directed his troops to aim just in front of Paleface but not to shoot yet.

Alaban suddenly made a bad decision. He dodged his pursuer and backtracked around her. She felt the movement of air as he passed her by. She strafed to trip him. She then pounded his head with her gun. Alaban appeared momentarily, jarred by the blow. Teradom urged the men to hold their fire. Paleface kicked at Alaban, contacting with one of his legs, but missed him the second time. He flew up and behind her, but she now knew where he was. He only cloaked now to avoid blasts from the soldiers.

He attacked her from above, but she rolled to the ground and kicked upward as he descended upon her. Her power move flung him against the wall with a thud. The putty gunmen fired at the spot where they heard him impact. The dark, gelatinous blob hit an invisible object on the wall and then rebounded away from it. The gel touched the ground, rose half a meter, and then touched down again about two meters away from Paleface. It oozed onto the ground. This time it stayed there. Alaban was caught.

The putty melded with the ground, with Alaban's boot and the leg of his uniform. His cloak faded. Panicked, he tried to pull out of it, but this substance was too strong and sticky. The surface of the ooze foamed, puffing out to completely cover Alaban's calf. It expanded across the ground. Then its exterior began to crack and glow. Resiliently, Alaban stood straight to face his former puppeteer.

Teradom ordered his men to stand down, but remain ready.

"So. My best bodyguard is now a runaway and a thief. I'm not surprised, only disappointed. I'm not going to bother asking you where the merchandise is. We know it's here somewhere. We'll simply find it faster with your advice. Tell us and I'll be merciful. I'll give you a quick death. The longer you wait to cooperate, the more the flesh on your leg will deteriorate. I'll time you. Let's see just how valiant you really are, Bahn. How long will it take to break you? Keep your weapons ready, men. His lovely girlfriend may come to his rescue, unless of course she's inside the building, unable to hear his cries of pain. I am anxious to hear them."

Teradom sat on a box of spare ammunition overlooking the bowl where Alaban remained plastered. Scythe crouched by his master's side. Several other soldiers formed a protective wall around the General.

"I can get him out. We just need to get close enough," I whispered to Ocelot.

"That's what Teradom wants. He's baiting you," he replied.

"We can't leave Alaban there. I'm holding you to your promise. You said we'd go back for him," I pressed.

"We will, but not the way Teradom wants. Take out as many gunmen as you can before you reach Alaban. Teradom doesn't know I'm here. He'll concentrate on you. Distract him. They need one or both of you alive. They won't shoot to kill. I'll take them from the rear. Hit those five on the right, and take out that putty gun. Go," he told me.

I flew behind a tree to the far right and drew my sword. Its clatter attracted attention from the soldiers, but Teradom did nothing. I was sure he felt proud for correctly predicting my intervention. I swung up behind the pair of men at the putty gun. The onlookers shuddered as they watched their heads roll from their bodies. The other soldiers shifted about uneasily. A third soldier, and then a fourth went down. The fifth shot at my sword, since he saw the pattern of the spattering blood as it glazed me. However, this man, too, went down as several soldiers broke orders to hold back and opened fire on me. I burst into the air and then flipped to dive to Alaban's side.

Paleface intercepted me. We fought in the air around Alaban as Teradom shouted to his men to leave me alive. She kicked at me, dove towards my throat, and parried with her gun as if it were a sword. I fended her off. Her attack annoyed me. She was wasting my time.

Alaban intervened in our fight by shooting Paleface in the hip. She fell heavily. I rushed to Alaban's side. He already sweated profusely from the heat of the putty. It crackled and glowed like a ball of drying lava. Alaban touched my arm to give me what little power he had left.

"Hurry, before they try to hit you with a sleeper," he said. "I'll deflect what I can."

I pulled away some of the lava-like substance, but the more I peeled away, the faster it puffed and burned. Alaban cringed. Teradom sent his troops to surround us.

"Keep them alive. Knock out or capture only," Teradom advised.

I removed only about half the putty before I had to defend myself. I charged and swung wildly at the soldiers close by. Alaban shot and killed until his weapon depleted. He drew his sword, but he knew they wouldn't get close enough to use it against them. I cloaked and flew up above the scene, but the men shot at me. I dodged and defended with the sword. I feinted to the right. I threw my sword to Alaban's feet, confusing the soldiers as I withdrew my hand bow.

Alaban groaned and shook with pain. I felt heat crawl up my own leg as the putty burned into the flesh of his calf and ankle. I shot several plumes of acid at the growing crowd of Fitmalos as I jumped from side to side. The guards from the Deposit joined in the attack on us, although they didn't know of the order to shoot to disable only. Teradom and Paleface shouted at them to stand down, but they did not respond at first. Scythe joined in the attack despite his crippled state.

Some men rushed Alaban directly. He fended off two of them. I blasted a few more, to try and form a barrier between us. Still more arrived. I hit Scythe with an arrow, but the acid merely etched into his exoskeleton and frayed his uniform. He still wielded a flashgun. He managed to shoot me between the arm and ribs. The chemical pellet zipped past, only grazing the skin. I did not fall. Acid arrows nearly gone, I landed again with Alaban to retrieve my sword and to remove as much of the debilitating putty as I could.

I recalled my fantastical vision. Alaban was the bull dragon chained to the ground. We fought off our blue enemies, but they kept coming.

The more putty I lifted from his leg, the more Alaban suffered. My own left leg ached. I felt only a fraction of his pain, but it weakened me. I panted. I moved around him, shooting and cloaking, but the crippling sensation along with my significant power drain slowed me. I could no longer dart about as I had before.

Alaban bellowed to me in agony. "Sil, run! You can't save me. Get out of here!"

I attempted to obey him, but our pain left me without power to cloak. I tried to run away from him and fly out of the war zone, but soon found myself back at his feet. A blaze of pain blossomed at my stomach. I was hit, not with a sleeper, but with a laser blast. It left me writhing on the concrete beneath him. I lay on my side, curled up and panting. Alaban doubled over slightly from the shared stomach pain. The soldiers stayed back.

Paleface shuffled up to us, favoring her wounded hip and kicking a few bodies out of her way. She produced a laugh.

"You thought you were the best, but you, too, can be caught," she said to us. She looked over her shoulder. "She will live several hours, sir."

"Very good. Grab her and bring her inside with us. Hello, Sil, nice to see you again. You're going to show us where the box is. Then we'll let your man die quickly. His pain will end, you see. If you refuse, it will be easy to anchor him down with a second blast of putty. He'll lose both legs before falling unconscious from the pain. You don't want to see your loved one suffer. You'll be a good girl and show me where it is." Teradom stood from his viewing box.

Paleface leaned down to snatch my arm. She nearly lifted me off the ground, but instead released me. A repeated bang sounded. Some of the remaining soldiers fell and did not get up. Paleface jerked around, searching for the source of the noise. The others swiveled about to do the same. Alaban did not pay attention to it. His pain nearly consumed him. I fought to stay aware of the situation. Another repeated racket echoed through the scene. More soldiers fell.

"Where is it coming from?" many asked.

A third ripping clamor rattled close to us. I recognized the noise as the report of a repeating blade thrower. The lead discs it fired were only three centimeters in diameter, but could penetrate and exit an unprotected skull with enough momentum to slice through one skull and into the head of another victim two meters away. Ocelot took out nearly half the remaining troops this way.

I remembered how the lion had invaded the army of monkeys in my vision. Ocelot swept through, destroying the enemy in streaks. Then he disappeared again into the trees. I had never known him to display such power. He projected a complete cloak. He levitated. He flew swiftly. He defeated his enemy undetected. Then I recalled the owl. Wilbaht's spirit had returned here to help him. Our great leader had not left us. I faintly sensed his presence among us.

The soldiers closest to Teradom followed emergency procedures and rushed to cover him, but did not evacuate as they should have. They could not tell which was the safest direction. They huddled in a tight pack, some shouting requests for orders from the highest-ranking soldiers, two of whom instantly disagreed. One directed them to take shelter in the building. The other said the shots had come from the roof over the doorway and that they should stay under the trees. I barely caught Teradom's voice commanding the troops to hold position when again the blade thrower rang sharply, this time closer to us. Paleface staggered backward from a shot to the chest, but her flack vest absorbed most of the impact.

I had glimpsed this before, more than a year and a half ago, when I'd first seen Ocelot. The casualties and the wounded Fitmalos piled upon one another as the survivors backed away in panic. This was a battle from my crystalline shards of vision.

The next thing that happened, however, was unforeseen. A loud, humming fighter ship glided into the blue above us. Then two more arrived overhead. Croso had found us and had called in the military branch of the Organization to seize control of the war zone.

"This is U.G. Organization Military Law Enforcement. Throw down your arms now. Move back to the main gate immediately," someone called from one of the ships.

The Fitmalo soldiers let their guns fall, save the three officers at Teradom's side. They proposed to guard their leader against continued threat. Scythe also stood by him, still carrying a pistol. The others retreated toward the gate as ordered. Teradom demanded to stand his ground, unwilling to let us go. He spurted a few obscenities about the incoming U.G. military, saying they should come pull him out of here in person if they dared, verbally doubting that they had the gall to do so.

I did not see the fury in his wicked blue face, nor did I perceive any change in his temerity as his last Fitmalo comrades crumpled at his feet, but I could have sworn I heard a soft, fearful sound escape his throat just before his neck snapped. Peripherally, I saw his limp body fall to one side. I saw Scythe's shadow back away quickly, foregoing protection of his mentor in exchange for self-preservation. Ocelot appeared, standing over the former puppet master in victory. He dragged the body down the hill towards us, keeping a laser gun aimed at Scythe as he went. Scythe dumped his weapon. He held up his remaining arm and cowered back to the wall of the building.

Ocelot swiveled to aim at Paleface. She backed away with a limp.

"Put it down," Ocelot warned.

She gripped her long barrel even tighter. She bared her yellowed teeth at him. He shot her in the arm. The gun hit the ground. She growled at him in rage. He shot her again in the other arm for good measure. She fell backwards, defeated.

Ocelot ambled down to us with the body. He threw it to the ground before us and ripped open the General's jacket to reveal a variety of weapons. The jacket also held a flask of freeze fluid. Ocelot tore out the flask. He sprayed its contents generously around Alaban's clumped leg. The putty crusted, froze, and crumbled away with a few blows from his foot.

Alaban now panted hysterically. He fell over when the crystallized putty finally loosened completely. He lay on his back and covered his face with his arms. He groaned hysterically. The skin on the damaged part of the leg peeled and even flaked away with the putty to reveal a length of deeply pockmarked muscles. His boot disintegrated and fell away. His foot was not so badly damaged, but from his ankle to his knee, the sinews and bone were almost not enough to keep the leg together. If we didn't heal him, it would have to be amputated.

I lay as still as possible, but still shuddered from the dual injury. Ocelot pinned me on my back. He muttered something I did not understand. Then he shoved a finger into my wound. I jerked violently, but he pressed in until he'd touched the end of the laser hole. I shouted from the pain. Then the pain subsided as he slowly removed the finger. He rubbed the skin where the laser beam had entered. I gasped at him, but sat up as soon as the healing took full effect.

He snatched my tiny water bottle from my vest. He also extracted his own. As he did this, I hurled myself to Alaban. I was about to lay my hands on his bloody, deformed calf when Ocelot caught me by the arm and yanked me away.

"No. The acid will eat into your hands. Move away." Ocelot emptied the water onto Alaban's leg.

Alaban screamed and writhed. My own leg cramped sharply with his pain, but I fought it enough to control my actions. I lifted Alaban's water bottle from his vest as well. I handed the flask to Ocelot as he tossed the empty flasks aside. Again, he emptied the water over the bloody calf. Alaban yelled again. My leg stung.

I couldn't contain my urge to heal him any longer. I didn't care about my hands. I had to make him better. I nearly shoved Ocelot out of the way. I let my fingertips glide over the slick, oozing meat of his leg. I pulled out the injury with my fading strength. The water had deactivated the acid. My hands did not burn, but my healing wasn't working fast enough. Alaban bawled.

Ocelot wrenched me away from him. "I'll do it," he vowed.

I rolled away from them. Ocelot did not use a gentle touch. He clamped his hands around the bleeding sinews and squeezed brutally. Alaban gasped in shock before shouting this time. I jolted from the zap of pain. Ocelot chanted under his breath, as he pulled downward to the ankle. Alaban squirmed and nearly passed out. Our hearts palpitated ferociously. I feared cardiac arrest. Ocelot repeated the action three times. The muscles slowly regained their elasticity and smoothness. Alaban wiped tears and sweat from his face. He panted and moaned.

I moved to cradle his head and to hold his hand through his healing. My leg no longer cramped. It only burned a little. Alaban clenched his teeth. He determined not to yell anymore. His pain decreased with every passage of Ocelot's hands. Now the bottom layers of skin began to regrow. Alaban trembled. I caressed his face to calm him.

Alaban whispered shakily to Ocelot, "Bless you, brother."

A group of Organization military warriors interrupted the healing process. Two lifted Ocelot from his kneeling position. They whipped his blood-covered hands behind him and bound him with a pair of electrostatic binders. Alaban sat himself up and tried to stand. More warriors from the ships took us into custody as well. They separated us, escorting us each to a different ship. They told us all the same thing. We were under arrest for conspiracy, mass murder, breaking and entering, and other minor misdemeanors. We were to say nothing until our official interrogation. I trudged willingly away with them, only hoping now that our interrogators would be on our side.

Chapter 59: Separation

During the first two days of interrogation, I thought I might go deaf from the interrogators' shouts in my ears. Two Vermilion interrogators even shocked me with an electrical bar when I didn't give an answer they expected. They made preposterous insinuations about my involvement with Fitmalo rebel groups. One even came up with a tale about our imaginary role in the smuggling ring, saying that we had worked secretly with Klib during our year's journey through space. According to this man, we had organized arms shipments ourselves for various political entities and then framed Klib when he double-crossed us. I denied the ridiculous allegation with the same respectful tone I had used in explaining all other details to them. I understood why they approached me with such machinations. They had to follow every possible lead to the truth, just as I would need to do with a suspect. I was sorry to find myself in such a position, but I maintained faith. As long as the truly loyal warrior generals controlled the interrogation theater, I trusted that we would be exonerated from all charges.

Over and over, to at least three different interrogators each day, I recounted every detail I had lived through. I was careful not to give information that I had not witnessed first hand without saying so. Any incongruence between my statements could be used against me. I explained that I had hidden the Tetrasank somewhere in the North Boldoy Research Deposit, but I refused to indicate its exact location except in private to Yalat or Channol. The interrogators lied, saying they were not available. One even said they had left the planet. I told him point blank that I knew he was lying. He shocked me out of aggravation. I took the jolt silently.

At nights, I was thrown into solitary confinement, without running water and without my own clothing. I was given only a long shirt to wear. The rest of my clothing and belongings were taken from me. The long shirt was meant for use on multiple beings. It was cut to accommodate anything from a Furman to Vermilion, since it had four armholes and a large neckline. My only meal each day consisted of a bowl of thin soup. After the third day, I was given a lighted room with a sink and regular toilet, but no other amenities. On the fourth day, my soup contained a few leaves of cabbage. My conditions improved.

However, on the fifth day, my first two interrogators were Fitmalos, not warriors, but investigating agents from the Fitmalo government. They treated me badly. They left bruises on my face and upper body. They slapped me, pinched my nose and breasts, back-fisted my cheeks and jaw, and even pressed their sharp-nailed thumbs to my eyes. I yelled for mercy when the torture became too harsh, but did not cry, since I knew tears would bring more gleeful mistreatment from them.

They asked repeatedly what I knew about Swall Jade's relationship with Teradom, what had really happened on the space station and afterward, and what network information I knew about the smuggling rings. They asked me several questions for which I had no answer. This infuriated them even more. One man punched me in the ear, nearly breaking my eardrum. That night, they dumped me into solitary again.

The sixth day brought some relief. Yalat appeared in the interrogation room with me as an interrogator. She began with some of the same questions I'd answered already during the week. Then she asked me personal questions, like how I'd treated here and how my health was. I responded honestly. I ventured to ask her if she'd seen the men.

"You're not allowed to ask questions, only to answer them," she reminded me. However, she nodded to indicate that she had. "I'm sure your male friends are experiencing similar conditions."

She then passed me more information in the form of a question. "Have you sensed Alaban's successful healing process?"

"I only know I've not felt any more pain in my right leg," I answered.

She filled me in on a few things that were going on politically, like Teradom's funeral, a shift of power among generals, Klib's planned trial date, and Fitmalo's economic boom. She also surprised me with other news.

625

"Did Ocelot know that his uncle Stennet has been here on Jawlcheen for the last few months?" she asked.

"He never mentioned it. I didn't know he was here."

She nodded. "Jiao recently arrived as well. Did either of them contact you or Ocelot?"

"No, ma'am," I replied.

I wondered why they were here, but I could not ask. Now that we knew neither of them was involved with the Regime, I hoped Ocelot could renew his kinship with them.

"Did Channol mention anything about helping Ocelot before your trip to Hammerstead?" she asked.

"No, ma'am," I responded.

"Who did you think requested that Ocelot be released from solitary confinement ten days ago?" she asked.

"Ten days ago? He wasn't in solitary confinement ten days ago. We were arrested six days ago," I said.

"You mean to say you were unaware of his prior arrest?" Yalat asked.

I shook my head, perplexed.

"Where did you think he was?" she continued.

"After my miscarriage, he left me. He went to live at temporary housing at the Center. Channol never said anything about him being arrested," I told her.

"You mean no one told you he was arrested for inappropriate behavior to a general and assault on a secretarial staff member?" she asked informatively.

I blinked and knit my brow as I shook my head at her.

She narrowed her slick, black eyes at me. "After Ocelot left your house, he bullied his way into General Croso's office. He gave him a piece of his mind about your assignment to Hammerstead. Incidentally, I don't blame him. When the General's secretary tried to remove him, he punched her in the face. He knocked her out, apparently. If I didn't know better, I would say that he probably tried to strike the General as well, but that did not appear in the report against him. If it had, he would have been physically punished and fired. As it stands, he is on indefinite suspension without pay."

Sadly, I imagined Ocelot bursting into Croso's office, chastising him harshly for sending me to meet with Alaban. I saw in my mind his maddened eyes as the General's guards overpowered him. He'd spat at the General after he could no longer swing at him. He'd yelled insults and curses at him. Then the guards had thrown him into the dark solitary confinement room without removing the electrostatic binders from his wrists

626

and feet. How alone and defeated he must have felt. And betrayed. Guilt clung to me.

"You said during one of your interrogations here that you did not know Alaban was still working for the Organization until he told you himself at Hammerstead. Is this true?" she asked.

I said yes, it was true.

"I assume, then, that Ocelot did not inform you of my discovery the day we spoke so long at the Center. It was the day I believe the two of you became mates. I told him then that I had researched Alaban through a friend in payroll. We were able to prove within reasonable doubt that Alaban was still working for us. His pay was being banked in his name under fluid accounts. That's what the Organization does with payroll for missing or extreme covert warriors who cannot access their pay. It produces a higher earned interest for the Organization, you see. I specifically instructed your husband to tell you about it. He obviously neglected to do so. Why do you think that is?" Yalat clicked her nails, perturbed.

I thought back to that day when I had observed Ocelot from the window as he approached the house. He had appeared dejected, forlorn, but he also seemed to be considering something. I had assumed he was debating as to whether he should try to pursue me anymore. He could have been thinking of whether or not to tell me about Alaban.

"Maybe he thought if he told me about him, that I would contact Alaban right away. Maybe he thought I would volunteer to work with him after all," I guessed.

"Would you have?" she asked.

"No. I would have felt relieved. I would have believed that Alaban didn't need me to intervene. No wonder Ocelot was so adamantly against me contacting him. He thought I would find out and go with him."

"And leave him behind," Yalat finished. "Being a man who lost his parents at a young age, it is logical that he would fear that. Did you consider this before you accepted the job to go to Hammerstead?"

"Yes, but I still had to go. I had conflicting obligations. General Croso said he would distract Ocelot long enough so that he wouldn't have to find out. But things didn't turn out the way we planned." I hung my head.

"That, too, was an ill-gotten assignment. The block of information they gave Ocelot to decode was from a case nearly fifty years old. The information was so anachronistic that he realized he was being duped within a matter of hours. Croso's personnel delayed him, but he escaped and went straight away to look for you. I can only imagine the trauma he experienced, realizing his most dreaded fears had come true, and then having to witness the worst torture of all. My sympathies for the loss of your offspring." Yalat bowed to me politely, although her manner criticized me.

I thanked her sullenly, but said nothing else. She paused a long while.

"Your mate's strength is impressive. To endure such trauma and still persevere to lead your team...He is more powerful now than any of us, I'll wager. I wonder what will become of him."

Her last statement confused me, but I kept quiet, unable to question.

Yalat pondered a while longer. Then she came to me and smoothed my hair. She leaned the cool scales of her face against my cheek.

"No further questions," she said as she moved away from me. She lifted my chin a little with her claw. I saw the trace of a comforting smile on her face as she exited the room.

The next day, Croso himself came to see me. I felt embarrassment for having acted without his approval this time, but also I felt vindictive towards him. He had refused to see me after I'd risked my life and lost my child for a mission he had urgently sent me on.

"How many of you will it take to retrieve the Tetrasank from its hiding place?" he asked.

I sensed something odd in his voice. I feared for the lives of my men. "All three of us," I responded. "I need their concentrated energy to help extract it. It can't be anyone else, sir. We have the right combination of talents to do it."

Croso grunted. He eyed me suspiciously. "Where do you see yourself in three years' time, Warrior, professionally speaking?"

"I hope to continue on with the Organization to become a sub professor, sir," I replied.

"As I thought. Completely unaware. You cannot begin to aspire to a higher rank when you disgrace the rank you wear now. You and Ocelot abandoned your post to form a rogue unit on an unsolicited operation. That in itself is enough to have you fired. Do not presume that the Organization in any way supports your actions. My superiors do not care how much you *felt* you had to execute this plan. They do not give a worm's eyelash about your heroic intentions. The laws and regulations you broke compare to the ones broken by the galaxy's most wanted criminals. Your warrior's title is not a symbol of omnipotence. You did not have free license to break and enter, interrogate suspects, or kill other beings. If this had been an authorized assignment, the Organization would take responsibility for damages and casualties. It was not. *You* are accountable for it all. And unless you *are* omnipotent, you do not have the power or political weight to protect yourself from the law."

Realization struck me between the eyes. I flinched and then slouched, stupefied.

Croso rattled on. "Alaban's position was understandable. He was a deep covert agent on his own. He acted within his rights on his assignment. You and Ocelot, on the other hand, had direct contact with your superiors and an assigned, limited area of operation. You knew better than to try something like this without our approval. I cannot name two other warriors in our time who have been guilty of such blatant acts of stupidity! You are in more hot water than this Organization can hold. You swiped a level one biological weapon from a *Fitmalo general's bedroom*, for God's sake! *Then* you started your own war with the Fitmalo military!

"Even if we could protect you now, what Organization official would ever trust either of you again? You've proven yourselves beyond our control. You've completely defiled our hierarchy, thrown away all sense of respect.

"Press control is scrambling like crazy to patch this over with bogus stories to the public. Our image was almost shattered. You know what a precarious position we're in here in this helion. Our Centers are down on Fitmalo. We've only got a toehold here on Jawlcheen. Nitrogen1 is without representation. If we lose our Centers here, this solar system is on its own."

I bowed shamefully to him.

"Humph. It's too late to show reverence, Sil. Your attempt to save the planet nearly caused its demise."

I kept my head down still.

"Exceptionally talented, they called you. They should have added exceptionally foolhardy. Despicably foolish. What good is exceptional talent if it's commanded by a misguided mind? That haphazard rescue you tried left you completely vulnerable. Under normal directives, you should have left Alaban there and kept your own cover. You could have gotten out unseen. Instead you went back for him in the middle of a military ambush formation! Let me be the first to say that was idiocy! Whose idea was that?"

"Mine, sir," I said.

Croso's boots creaked as he leaned back against the wall and tightened his four fists angrily.

"Hundreds of millennia of evolution, careful education and training of our most intelligent and talented creatures alive, fantastic ability, and one *brainless* decision nearly renders it all worthless. I don't know if you're capable of understanding this after proving yourself so inept, but we had great plans for you. Your talent factor made you one of our most valuable warriors in your rank. You were once our secret pride. Now you've become a public disgrace."

"I had to do it, sir, no matter what. The planet's welfare was at stake. And I had to go back for Alaban. He and I..." I began.

"Yes, yes. The whole Organization knows of your 'connection'. It's downright embarrassing."

I kept my mouth shut.

Croso grumbled. He reminded me momentarily of Sangrol, the Metabrid. His shoes creaked again as he leaned forward slowly.

"I understand your motives for going back for Alaban. Now tell me why Ocelot went back for him."

"Ocelot is a good man. He had promised to go back for him. He kept his promise. He didn't want to see him suffer. He didn't want me to suffer with him. He healed us both. I don't know all his reasons for doing it, but we owe him our lives," I said.

He observed me with silvery green eyes. He rubbed his chin thoughtfully. I sensed his internal calm and wondered if perhaps the Organization's standpoint was not completely negative towards us after all. I considered that perhaps the purpose of his rash speech to me was actually to affect an impression on the officials who would witness this interrogation. Perhaps we would not be fired and thrown to the stoning public. I attempted to probe the General further, but he stood and walked towards the door.

"No further questions," he said.

I glanced up at him hesitantly, but then regained my irascibility. I risked punishment, but I had to speak. "Why didn't you meet with me as you had promised after the mission, sir?"

He regarded me with annoyance, but did not retort to me that I should not ask questions. Instead he answered.

"I was sorry to hear about your loss, but there was nothing to be done for it. You were alive. You were home. That's all I needed to know. You were in an emotional state. I prefer to see my warriors at their best whenever possible, and not their worst." He eyed my tattered attire. "Today, it was unavoidable. No further comments. End recording." Croso slipped out the door.

Later, I was taken to a lighted room with a full bath and a cot to sleep on. At the head of the cot was a thin pillow. At the foot of the cot rested a neat pile of my clothing. They had even returned my full weapons packs. I hoped this was not just a prelude to another series of mistreatments. I bathed gratefully. I even found a towel to dry myself. In the morning, a page delivered a box to me containing a small, round bread and a sliced fruit. I ate them with renewed hope. No soldiers came to my door to escort me to interrogations. I meditated calmly for several hours before an Arborman warrior arrived.

He led me out of the high-security area to a breezeway between the internal garden and temporary housing. Alaban and Ocelot appeared, also escorted by Arbormen. Alaban still hobbled, supported by a crutch. His injured leg was covered with a thin wrap of gauze. Ocelot displayed a slight gash on one eyebrow and the remnants of a black eye. His Fitmalo interrogators had obviously been more vindictive with him, since he had been the one who killed their general. We did not speak, but we all felt glad to see each other alive.

One of the Arbormen led us to a door at the ground floor overlooking the garden. We entered the dwelling. It was an unoccupied, but furnished, apartment. Croso stood by the kitchen bar. The guards led us in. One exited to stand outside the door. The other two flanked us as we stood facing our superior.

Croso spoke. "You are accused of collectively killing thirty-three Fitmalo soldiers by way of offensive, not defensive, attack. By normal regulations, you would all face immediate civil trial for mass murder. However, taking into account the magnanimity of your goals, we have decided to apply the law of temporary regulations suspension. By this law, you are allowed to break civil law only to prevent a much higher crime. You committed first-degree murder on thirty-two people. In exchange, you saved hundreds of thousands, perhaps millions of Jawlcheen citizens from the biological weapon. The Organization is protecting you for now. The bad news is you're not off the hook yet.

"Ocelot, you are on indefinite house arrest for your own protection. You are to remain here at the Center until we can clear up this problem with the Fitmalo government. They want you on high trial for Teradom's murder with immediate execution on interhelion broadcast."

I balked. "He can't be executed for killing a man who plotted genocide. What about the law you just cited?"

"That law only protects warriors and Organization employees under the umbrella of internal Organization law. It does not protect against the laws of individual planets. If their government chooses to file suit, the case goes to planetary trial. The Fitmalos want the head of the man who killed their high general and they want him bad. Even if they allowed evidence in Ocelot's defense, there's no physical proof of Teradom's plan," Croso reminded me.

"Yes, sir, there is, in Teradom's computer at the castle," Alaban said.

"The castle was emptied. Teradom's belongings are in Fitmalo hands." Croso spoke gravely.

"If we retrieve the Tetrasank and record the prints from the box, will that be proof enough?" I suggested.

Ocelot interrupted before the General could speak. "It doesn't matter. The Fitmalos want retribution. They'll find some loophole to hang me."

Alaban protested. "No. It's my fault you were there. I'll take your place. They'll be a lot happier with my head on a plate instead of yours, anyway. I volunteer, sir. If someone's got to take the fall for this, it should be me."

"Hey, I didn't just heal your leg so you could sacrifice yourself. You've got to use that leg to kick some more Fitmalo ass," Ocelot stated.

"Gentlemen, we're already working on it. I suggest you let me in on any ideas you have this time. We don't want another fiasco around here," Croso advised.

"Yes, sir," we said together. I immediately began scheming for Ocelot's safety.

Croso eyed my dark twin. "Alaban Jetscuro. When your former pilot told me what Ongeram did to get you in, I thought he had died for a lost cause. You were a wild card. It turns out you extracted more information in the last six months than we ever dreamed possible. You took calculated risks, smart steps. Ongeram was right about you after all. I congratulate you, son. You've made us proud. If your job were public, you'd receive a medal of honor. Since you're deep covert, we'll give you a different kind of reward. I'm adding three honorary years to your service record. You may apply for your next rank at your convenience." Croso grinned slightly.

"Thank you, sir!" Alaban sputtered.

"You deserve it," Croso informed him. "Now, your lives and the lives of every human and Vermilion on Jawlcheen will be in continuous danger until everyone in a position of power knows we've destroyed that formula and all its related research data. I'm sending the three of you back to the North Boldoy Research Deposit in the morning. Once you retrieve the weapon, we'll destroy it in the labs at the Deposit."

The door buzzed. Croso nodded to the nearest Arborman to open it. As the door swung open, the guard made way for Channol, who ducked the entranceway, reminding me of Wilbaht in his height. A humorous opposite trailed at his heels. Yalat's miniature, pudgy form waddled in, bright-eyed and alert. We were glad to see a third warrior enter as well. It was Jiao. He had not changed since I last saw him on Sor3. He wore the same expression on his face that I'd seen on him when he found me alive and well after the airbus crash. Ocelot's mood lightened when he saw his cousin.

"Professor Jiao will assist you in the chemical alteration of the formula," Croso told us.

"Yes, sir. I am honored to help." Jiao bowed to him.

"We'll all meet at the airfield ascension tower at 0600. Any questions?" Croso seemed satisfied with himself.

"Sir, are Alaban and I free to access regular quarters now?" I asked.

"Yes. You may go home if you wish, but take an escort vehicle and an extra pair of guards. Be on constant alert. Fitmalo intel may try a strike. We had a bomb squad comb your house. All bombs have been removed. Several warriors are still posted at your house," he said.

I nodded, only marginally surprised to hear about the bombs. "Thank you, sir."

The General dismissed our meeting. The Arborman nearest the door escorted him out. Jiao shook hands all around. The two cousins embraced each other tightly and slapped one another on the back a few times. Jiao expressed his gladness to see Ocelot alive again. Ocelot suggested they share an apartment while he was under house arrest. Jiao agreed, but gestured toward me and asked quietly if we were not staying together. Ocelot said no and that it would be better if we stayed apart as long as he was wanted by the Fitmalos. Jiao accepted this gladly. The two men made plans for the upcoming days at the Center.

My heart fell. Even after what we'd experienced together, he preferred to stay with his cousin instead of me. He didn't even confer with me about this decision. Feeling bitterly dejected once more, I turned to Alaban and Yalat. Yalat congratulated Alaban on his accomplishments. An Arborman held the door for him as he limped out into the breezeway. Yalat followed. I glanced again at the men before leaving the room. They chatted happily. I felt direly jealous for Ocelot's attention. I considered interrupting their conversation to confront him, but I knew Ocelot would react abrasively. I trudged after my old tutor and my best friend. Alaban noticed my sadness.

"Sil, why don't you come with me to medical? I have to change this bandage. You'll get to see how weird it looks. There's some scar tissue forming on one side that looks like a sand monkey. It dances when I flex the muscle. Do you want to see it?" he asked.

I forced a slight chuckle. I agreed to go with him. The three of us sustained light, yet uncomfortably tense, conversation until we reached a fork in the corridor. Yalat veered off to her hallway. She promised to see us in the morning.

"Why don't you stay with Yalat tonight? You don't want to be alone," Alaban suggested.

"You're alone," I mentioned.

"I'm supposed to be alone," he said.

"No you're not," I retorted.

"I didn't mean eternally. I only meant for right now. You didn't think I was being fatalistic, did you?" He peered at me with knowing eyes.

I opened my mouth to speak, but found no words. Alaban limped, but covered my shoulders with one arm.

"Give him a few days," he suggested.

At the med station, Alaban showed off his gnarled scab. I shook my head and laughed while he showed me how it could move. After leaving the med station, Alaban suggested we hang out at the game room for a while. He mentioned that we hadn't played Pings since we were in school together. He suggested we play a few rounds of the board game and discuss how to keep Ocelot out of the murder charge.

We followed his plan. Alaban won seven out of ten rounds of the game, since it was based on mathematical strategy, his strongest intellect. We soon abandoned the game to discuss Ocelot's predicament. Late in the evening, we arrived at many ideas, but our best plan was to fake an assassination on Ocelot in public. We weren't sure the administration would go along with it, and we certainly had learned not to follow through with our own plans without approval.

In Ocelot's absence, I was glad to have Alaban with me. The hour grew late, but I didn't care. We enjoyed each other's company more than ever. Alaban told me jokes, stories of when we were young, anything to take my mind off my worry. He was almost successful. I thanked him for being such a good friend. He said he owed it to me.

At about 0100 hours, we headed out to the ascension tower. We planned on sitting on one of the padded sofa benches and talking each other to sleep. The first person in our party to arrive would wake us. We'd take a quick splash of water to the face in the lavatory and be ready.

Sitting on the broad, flat, stiffly padded bench, we talked about all kinds of things I didn't even remember the next day. Eventually, Alaban lay on his side behind me. He placed his chin by my left hip and cradled my right elbow in his hand. We talked a while longer, but sleep beckoned. I turned to face his body. I rested my head in the crook of his waist. He lifted his head to rest his ear at my waist and then caressed the back of my head. I draped an arm around his head, feeling the rug-like stubble of his hair at the back of his neck. In this position, we seemed to form an ellipsis with our upper bodies, like a fluid form that completed our connection of energy. We felt whole this way, perfected, empowered and secure. Whoever passed by us must have thought the worst, but I defiantly denied that I cared. My wounded heart searched for comfort with my twin.

At 0550, I felt a stinging swat on my rear end. I jerked awake. I pushed myself up to kneel by Alaban's lounging body. Yalat stood akimbo beside us.

"What do you think you're doing here like this, girl? What's come over you? Sleeping on a public bench with a man who's not even your husband...are you daft?" Yalat yapped.

Alaban awoke groggily. "Oh, is it 0600 already?" he asked, rubbing his eyes.

Yalat swatted him on the head, causing him to wince awake and nearly tumble off the sofa. "What kind of friend are you? Are you trying to steal this woman from her mate? You ingrate!"

"Ow. No, ma'am," he said.

"Oh, shut up. Get yourselves cleaned up. You look like you've been nesting here for a week. What an embarrassment," she complained.

I didn't waste time trying to explain away what she'd seen. I couldn't think of any forgivable explanation for it anyway. I only rushed to the ladies' room, doused my face and wrinkled uniform with water, and then drank from the tap. I straightened my clothing as best I could.

Yalat marched into the bathroom with me. She smacked me hard on the hindquarters with her tail, nearly sending me to my knees with a yelp.

"What were you doing?" Her fury rose.

"We were only talking, Yalat. Then we fell asleep," I told her, regaining my feet.

"Tell that to your husband, or should I say ex-husband, when you see him. I tell you, I don't know you anymore, Sil. You've changed. You're reckless. You're imprudent. What person is this? You do foolish, foolish things! Do you love Ocelot or don't you? If I were fortunate enough to have a male in my life as honorable as yours, I would treat him with respect at the very least. How do you expect to flaunt this physical and emotional closeness to another man and expect your husband to be unaffected?" she said despicably.

"He saw us?" I asked.

"Everyone did! You should have seen Ocelot's face when he found you lying there with Alaban as if he were your mate. I'll tell you one thing. They may both love you, but their love will not allow them to forgive you forever. Don't lead them on. Once you make a choice, you should stand by it in every way. Don't leave us all disillusioned. If you are torn between two men, you'll soon find yourself without any."

I observed myself in the mirror as she presented her point of view. I knew she was right about the appearance of it. I felt guilty, yet indignant.

"Where is my right-minded student? You can't have killed her yet. You can at least bring back her integrity. You learned that credo long ago.

Have you forgotten it? 'I maintain my integrity by my own high expectations of myself.' Can you recite that honestly now? Think, young woman. Feel, yes, but think twice as much before acting. Think of what's right. Be the good warrior and the good woman you were meant to be, or prepare to suffer. If you become wayward, even by appearance, you'll become lost and alone. Far too many have fallen to that path. Think, girl. Do right by the ones who love you. That includes me."

Yalat glared at my reflection. She shook her head. Then she stomped out to the lobby, leaving my reflection and I to review one another reluctantly. When I left the restroom, Alaban met me. He had heard Yalat's scorn. He gathered me to him.

"I know where we stand. I'm not trying to take you away from him. I just want to spend time with you while I still can. I know we'll be separated again soon." He squeezed my hand. I smiled at him weakly.

When we boarded the ship to Boldoy, we both apologized to Ocelot. We bowed solemnly. We let him know that our appearance this morning did not reflect what had actually happened between us. We told him we had woken up as surprised as they were to find ourselves in such an awkward position. I saw the deep-seated criticism in the eyes of our mentors, but Ocelot attempted to appear indifferent.

With a low, subservient bow, Alaban said, "I respect your union with Sil. I do not mean to offend or challenge your position. We were not involved romantically in any way last night. I beg your pardon, sir. I was careless."

Ocelot accepted the apology simply and unemotionally. "Apology accepted, Alaban. Take a seat."

Alaban sat across from Ocelot and Jiao. I sat in the corner next to Channol and facing Yalat. I kept my head down humbly. Alaban proceeded to give a more lavish account of the night, at the end of which he laughingly explained away our appearance in the lobby. Then he mentioned some of the ideas we had come up with for Ocelot's exoneration. The mood of the group lightened somewhat. By the end of our ride to Boldoy, the others accepted his explanation and forgot about the incident, but Ocelot's heart was affected, just as Yalat had said. Alaban tried his best to bring him back to me. He retold the story of our entry to the Deposit, emphasizing Ocelot as the hero. He expressed his gratitude to Ocelot for healing his leg when he didn't have to. Again, Ocelot remained distant.

"You're a great warrior, sir. I can see why Sil likes you," Alaban said as I drifted off to sleep alone in the corner.

"Come on, sister. Let's move out," I heard him say next. I felt as though I had just closed my eyes, but we had been in the air for nearly twenty minutes.

I followed him out of the ship into the bright morning. The others stepped out behind me. Once inside the building, the Torreon and the Lizard we'd encountered the week before let us through to the control room. Alaban, Ocelot, and I stood over the spot in the floor where I'd hidden the box. They each held my hands to link for strength, but Ocelot resisted the link. I asked them to let go, saying I had absorbed enough power to extract the material myself.

I concentrated. The floor tiles lifted, expanded, swirled into pile of dust. Jiao said it was amazing. The others agreed. I delicately pulled the box out of the steel beam. I levitated it to Jiao. Then I replaced the molecules of the floor. The diamond pattern returned to its original order.

Channol, Jiao, and Ocelot were taken to the chemical lab by our hosts. They worked with the formula for more than an hour while the rest of us waited in the front foyer. I fixed the shiny white floor of the foyer, where I'd left a dull circle from our entry to the control room the first time. We leaned against the wall. We spoke little, knowing our words and actions were recorded.

When the hour was almost over, Alaban moved close to me. Yalat eyed him with disapproval. He nodded to her in a friendly manner. She frowned and turned to pace the length of the room. I held Alaban's hand at my shoulder and asked him psychically when he was leaving. He responded that he would leave tomorrow for Sor4 to meet Willa.

"I'll miss you," I whispered. I smiled a little in retrospect. "I know we'll always be together in spirit, though."

He stroked the side of my face fondly. He told me silently that he loved me as a kindred soul. I closed my eyes and returned the sentiment.

The three men from the chemical team returned. They left the newly altered Tetrasank in the Deposit along with a report of its new composition. The original was not recorded. The planet was safe from its poison.

As we walked out, I heard a clink on the concrete near the second door. It was one of the steel makeshift keys Ocelot and Alaban had used to unlock the control panel. I assumed Ocelot had tossed it away. I went to pick it up from in front of the second door out of curiosity. I hadn't seen Alaban's creation up close. As I stood holding it, Ocelot rushed up behind me. He grasped my shoulders.

"Don't move," he told me.

I looked at our reflection in the glass. Like our reflection in the pearled wall on the ship, Ocelot stood behind me with his face near my ear

637

to whisper to me. My eyes widened. As I had seen before, Alaban sailed into the reflection, sword drawn. He slashed madly. Blood splashed across our shoulders. I gasped and blinked in horror. Alaban landed next to us. Ocelot leaned forward, pushing me out of the way.

The blood around us wasn't red. It was dark ochre. The body of a Mantis lay twitching on the ground where we had stood. It was Scythe. I staggered to press my back to the wall, staring with shock at the body. We spread apart, searching the area for Paleface. If she was there, we did not find her. Cautiously, we all hurried back to the ship, leaving the body for the next group of warriors to attend to.

I glanced back in annoyance at the reflective door. Another misleading vision had been resolved. Yalat had been right. No vision was trustworthy. I decided at that moment that I would never again trust any vision. Nor would I base my fears on one.

When we landed again at the Center, Ocelot evaded me by marching right away to his temporary apartment under cover of his new bodyguards. Jiao paused as if he wanted to speak with me, but then excused himself to march away with his cousin, feeling perhaps that he would be disloyal to Ocelot if he spoke to me alone. I responded civilly. I apologized to Yalat for my behavior. She sullenly accepted. I also apologized to Alaban. I told him I needed to return home for the night. He understood. I slept in my own bed again that evening, although sleep was light.

Several times, I got out of bed to phone Ocelot. His phone buzzed, but he would not answer. I considered going to the Center to speak with him in person, but I couldn't ask Jiao to leave so that I could be with Ocelot. Ocelot wanted Jiao in the apartment to keep me from doing just that. I could only call to apologize to him and to beg his forgiveness.

On my last brave try, Jiao answered. "Hello, Sil. I'm sorry. This is Jiao. Ocelot says he prefers to speak with you in person. He asks that you go into hiding. He says you'll know where. He will meet you when his house arrest is finished. Goodnight, Sil. I wish you well."

I thanked him and was about to ask him to deliver a message to Ocelot for me as the connection clicked off.

The next morning, I met Alaban at the ascension tower. He was packed and ready. He no longer used a crutch to get around.

He embraced me. "I'm sorry for all the trouble I've caused. I'm going to try and pay you back for it all. You deserve a good life."

"So do you. You just take care of yourself," I told him.

He stared longingly into my face one last time. We understood each other's love. We blew each other a kiss and waved goodbye with proud smiles.

My smile faded as I watched his ship go, knowing I was now separated from my twin by distance and from my husband by resentment. I took my renewed burden of solitude in stride, determined to use this time to find a resolution, a happy ending to our plight, the kind Ocelot deserved more than any of us: a rewarded victory and peace.

Chapter 60: Dishonor

Wildlife vocalized loudly with the dawn. I lay awake in the balmy air inside my tent. Six days had passed and still no sign of resolution.

I had called to check on Ocelot's case several times, but Croso merely acknowledged the fact that nothing had been negotiated yet and that Ocelot should continue to stay at the Center under guard until further notice. Pessimistically, he informed me it could take a couple of months to play political card games with the Fitmalo government before any plans could be made and that he would let me know when something was decided.

I prayed for Ocelot's exoneration and his release so that we might reconcile and leave this planet for good. I prayed for his forgiveness, or at least some sign of his willingness to talk, but even through Jiao, he did would not answer my messages. Lonesome frustration stagnated in my heart. It clogged the flow of all other emotion.

I left my tent to wander up to the rock where Ocelot used to fish. Now exasperated, tired of my rancor, I pounced upon the edge of it, striking it with a scream. The outermost edge of the boulder crumbled and fell away into the water. The pond gulped the rock. Fish scattered from their hiding places below it. I growled as I levitated the pebbles at the shore and shook them about to let go of the frustration. I let them shower loudly to the ground. Birds screeched a warning to their kin and evacuated the surrounding woods.

I flopped onto the shore. I lay on my back, staring up at the swaying tops of the pines. I didn't care about the rocks and sand in my hair and on my uniform. I only scowled at the peaceful scenery, pondering the last few days' events and decisions, wondering if I could have prevented more of my errors if I'd only stopped to consider their consequences more seriously. No, I decided. Their effects were meant to be from the beginning. But to what end? My questions remained unanswered, my remorse unresolved.

Over the next two weeks, I accustomed myself to the camping routine by the water. My physical health returned to excellence. My emotions gradually settled into the depths of my mind. Life was calm, uneventful. I began to savor the peaceful surroundings. I trained hard. I held my breath underwater as long as I could. I ran several kilometers each day. I levitated, meditated, practiced. I regained my fortitude. Then my balance trembled once more.

As I jogged along the pebbled shoreline in the thick summer air, I sensed his presence nearby. I slowed my pace. I far saw to know his location. He positioned his tent among the trees, several meters away from mine. I wanted to read his emotions, but my own feelings stifled my perception. I turned around to jog back upstream, quickening my cadence.

When I arrived at the campsite, I stopped, leaning a hand on a tree trunk near his tent. I searched the landscape for him anxiously. He was taking up a pair of fish at the edge of the pond. He had levitated them out of the water this time instead of fishing for them. I was touched that he had followed my example. Next, he did something I had believed he couldn't do. Standing near the pile of kindling wood, he waved his hand and sparked them aflame. Had Wilbaht's power stayed with him? Had he absorbed power from Alaban and me?

I gathered a few sticks from around his tent to add to the fire. When I approached the campfire, however, he had disappeared, leaving the net of fish on the ground next to his boulder seat. I dumped my wood onto the flames and stepped back to look for him. I sensed him close by, but he cloaked from me. I retreated again to the forest for more wood. A branch cracked conspicuously from across the water. I traced the source of the sound. Ocelot cut a green branch and pruned it: a skewer for his fish. I watched in awe as he glided expertly into the air, crossing the stream with grace and silence. Was he showing off for me? I hoped. When I returned to the campfire, he sat facing it, preparing the fish to roast. I added my collection of sticks to the crackling pile.

Still staring into the fire, he spoke. "Jiao gave me your messages."

"Why didn't you answer any of them?" I asked gingerly.

"I didn't want to answer through Jiao," he contested. "Anyway, I was afraid there might be a tattler at the Center, someone checking on my correspondence and Jiao's. I didn't want you to be in danger if we had a Regime double-agent checking on us." He flopped a fish onto a flat board and scraped away its scales with a claw tool.

I understood his concern. I let the frustration subside, forgetting this worry altogether.

"Your power is greater than ever. I'm impressed." I stood near him, uncertain of his mood.

He replied in a dull voice. "Connecting with you and Alaban on the op was like an intense training session. Psychic abilities I'd struggled with for years finally made sense."

I felt his presence like an oasis in a season of drought. I wanted to rush to him, consume his life-restoring waters, and never leave him again. Yet he held me back with formality. I curtailed my selfish feelings. He needed to remain calm and talk sensibly, perhaps in grievance, before he could open himself to me again. I stepped to the boulder opposite him. I sat slowly, gazing into his face, golden from the firelight.

"Croso let you out yesterday?" I asked.

"Yes. Jiao is standing in for me at the house. Croso has warriors on guard around the clock just in case someone tries an assassination. The generals are still debating the possible case, but it would only be valid here in the Thrader helion. Croso wants me out of here permanently. He advised us to sell the house."

"Where is he sending you?" I asked.

"He doesn't care where I go, as long as I go. I thought of going to Jain, but there are too many bad memories there. I considered the Soren helion, but Alaban's headed that way. I'm not looking forward to running into him again any time soon." He set down his knife. He turned the fish to rake away leftover scales. His face remained solid, almost emotionless.

I stared down at the quivering fire. "I'd love to go back to Liricos. I haven't seen my family for a long time. You'd like them. They're easygoing people, very friendly."

"What will you tell your father when he asks about his grandson?" he asked. He set the fish aside. He held up the stick he had just cut and began to whittle it into a skewer.

"I'll tell him the truth. He's an understanding man. He won't lay blame on anybody," I explained, readily facing his discontent.

I gazed at him lovingly, hoping he would see the honesty in my eyes, but he did not look up at me. A strange, uncomfortable silence flickered between us with the fire. I couldn't take the physical distance between us any longer. I walked around the fire to stand by him. He stayed immobile, transfixed by the lapping flames.

"Forgive me, Ocelot. You know I wanted our baby as much as you did." I waited longingly at his side.

He set down the knife and skewer. "Did you?" he asked.

I grasped his body at the shoulders and pressed my face to his back. "Yes," I pleaded.

He sank his elbows into his thighs as he sighed. I felt his anger slowly boil within him. I retracted.

Suddenly he spouted, "He was a *miracle*. I had a vision of the evidence of his conception the first time I saw you. The fact that he was conceived at all was amazing. He grew in your womb for more than a trimester. He had a *name*." He tensed even more. "Why was he conceived if he was never meant to be born?"

I gripped my husband's shoulders with firm love. "I don't know. I'm sorry, Ocelot. Of all the abilities I have, I didn't foresee any danger to him until it was too late. I don't know why he had to go." I told him what I had realized many days ago. "But wherever his spirit is, he knows we wanted him. We both loved him. That's more than some children ever have."

He tried to calm himself to concentrate on stringing the fish onto the skewer, but then abandoned the task to rant once more.

"Was our union not meant to be? Was it *distorted* by your connection to Alaban? What? What was it? What went wrong? You know what everyone's thinking. They think I stole you from him. They think *I'm* the interloper and he's the cuckold, and that we didn't deserve to have a child because *he* should have been the father. Do you know what Channol said when he saw you two lying there? Without even thinking about it, he said, 'so the yin and the yang are together at last.' Do you have any idea how I felt? Maybe the rumors were true," he spat.

I shook my head. "No, they're not. It doesn't matter what people think. You know what rumors are worth. Don't pay attention to them. Listen to your heart. You know the truth."

He ignored me. "Alaban's power is complex, mathematically focused. Yours is elemental. It flows, like nature. Your abilities compliment each other to form a perfect warrior. How could I be of any use to you? When he named all those things he'd done for you, everything I had to offer couldn't measure up to half his list of accomplishments."

"No, that's not true," I insisted.

He continued acridly. "Then he had the audacity to tell me that I'd won, that he wanted you to be happy with *me*, as if he were playing the saint, giving his most prized possession to charity to make himself look good. I thought it was an act; that he was pretending to be selfless when his real goal was to impress you. You weren't pregnant anymore. You didn't have any children to tie you down to me. I was sure he was here to take you back. I almost wish that were true so I could relax and hate the man like I always did. Now I can't."

Ocelot ground his teeth and hunched over, fists jutting out over his knees. He stopped himself from losing his temper again. He breathed in deeply through his nose and exhaled from his mouth, controlling his emotion. I waited a few centimeters behind him, knowing not to touch him until he regained his stability.

Finally he pronounced clearly and evenly. "When the three of us linked together, a lot of things became clear to me. I learned things that I cannot adequately express in words. It was a revelation of spiritual and psychic energy. I learned control—control of power—through the two of you."

His expression of wonder and pride brought him a moment of declined ire. We remained still as the harbored wrath sweated from our skins to evaporate into the night.

The churning waters below the waterfall lulled. The wind bent the tops of the trees as they curved and swayed in a whispering dance. The fire lapped at the steaming fish. The beauty and calm of our surrounding should have covered over the rift between us, but Ocelot still contained turmoil, some disturbance he had not yet verbalized. I had to help him purge this unrest.

"I am as heart-broken as you are, Ocelot. Believe me. I want to make amends with you so we can move on. I am ashamed of what's happened between us."

I coaxed him. "Remember what Wilbaht said to us before he died. He said, 'Make the best of the time you have left together.' We never know how much time we have left. We may as well make the best of it."

Still, I received no response from him. He remained taciturn. I sat on a stone near him, waiting for him.

He went back to the preparations of our meal without speaking. When the fish was done, I accepted the plate from him with thanks. We picked the meat from the bones in strained silence while my mind wandered through possible reasons for his continued angst. I served us both a tea I had made earlier. He thanked me softly.

Sunset faded to dusk. We exchanged nervous glances over the firelight. After our meal, we washed up at opposite ends of the pond. Ocelot returned to the fireside with a bucket of water, but sat a moment to drink the last of the tea. I sat close to him. He seemed to want to speak several times, but did not. I tried to help him.

"You don't want to end our marriage. Otherwise you wouldn't be here. You'd still be at the Center with Jiao. Or did you come here to make peace and say goodbye?" I asked pointedly.

"No," he admitted.

"Then respond to me," I begged.

I hated to cry at this moment, but I became exasperated. What was he waiting for? I had to appease him with some kind of atonement, but I didn't know how. I struggled with myself for a few minutes before I threw off my worthless tears. I made one last attempt at beggary.

"Please, Ocelot." I heaved a breath and cleared my throat, searching for balance. I sniffed once more before gaining control.

His eyes remained hypnotized by the fire while he finally spoke.

"Why did you sleep with Alaban at Hammerstead? I'm not asking for an apology. I'm asking for an explanation. Explain it to me."

I searched the fire for memory. "We read each other's thoughts. We connected mentally. He realized he couldn't have me as a mate. I knew he wouldn't try anything. We only held hands. Then we fell asleep. We didn't lie close to each other. We didn't kiss. We didn't touch each other in a sexual way. We only slept," I explained.

"I know that," he growled. "Specifically, what were you thinking when you fell asleep with him?"

I grasped for an answer to appease him. "I was thinking of everything we'd been through. I thought of our plans. I thought we could all reconcile and get away from the Regime. I thought of our baby. I thought of you," I said.

He swiftly held up a hand to me. "You thought of me, but you didn't consider me. You thought of me enough to set him straight and keep him from mating with you, but you forgot to honor me. You slept with another man, Sil, both in his bed and in public!"

"I'm sorry, Ocelot, I..."

"You're sorry you did something to offend me, but you don't comprehend why it was wrong. That is what I cannot forgive! I know how you feel about him. I know you're bound to each other. But you are also bound to *me*. *We* are mates. *We* mate together. *We* sleep together. Do you know what it means to me just to sleep with you?" Ocelot gestured expressively. "To sleep with you...You satisfy every part of me. I have peace of mind to know that this beautiful sleeping woman is mine and no one else's. And you profaned that idea." He spoke to me in anguish. "You stole my peace of mind and gave it to him, as if you didn't care. You disrespected me. You disrespected our marriage, carelessly. Understand that, Sil. Know exactly what you did. Comprehend it."

I shrunk.

He glared into my eyes. The firelight danced about his contentious face. "I have abilities and power now that I only dreamed of before. Look."

Ocelot opened his palms before him. The fire charged up into the sky in a long, trunk-like formation, whirling its thin, licking flames. The charred wood below it creaked as he forced the energy out of it. I ogled the pillar of light, amazed. The crackling embers and flames spun out from the top of the trunk like branches and leaves that undulated into the night sky. The extremities of the tree of light popped like bubbles of amber, escaping into darkness. The trunk receded and then slowly relaxed back into a simple campfire.

"I can do what before was unthinkable." He closed a fist tightly before him. Suddenly the water from the pond seized up into a great sphere. Ocelot punched the tightened fist forward, towards the fire. The sphere jerked towards us, nearly reaching us where we sat. I gasped and scooted backwards in shock. The sphere changed its shape to become a clenched fist, threatening to pound the life out of the fire. Then Ocelot opened his fist and tossed his hand back. The water mimicked his movement, plunging back into the pond with a magnificent, frothing splash.

"But I have no peace of mind," Ocelot concluded. "You gave it away."

The squawking, screeching voices of frogs interrupted the thick tension between us. Their rantings seemed to criticize my conscience as he did. I called bravely to him over the din.

"How can I bring it back for you?"

His piercing eyes cut through the cacophony. "Swear to me, by God almighty, that you will never bed with another man as long as you live."

Humbled, belittled, I swore it.

"No other man should ever feel the confidence that comes from seeing you sleeping next to him. That glory should be mine and mine alone. I am your loyal husband! You are my wife! *Honor me!*" he shouted.

I immediately slumped to kneel before him. "I swear I will honor you. I will never rest with anyone but you." I breathed heavily with remorse and excitement. "I am your loyal wife. I understand now. Please forgive me." I set my forehead on his knee, raining tears onto his clothing, and swearing my unbending allegiance and love for him.

I felt his warm hands caress the back of my head. Then he leaned over me, rubbing my back, healing our wounds. His surging, dominant might rested. He touched his head to mine, nuzzled my weeping face, and whispered passionately to me.

"You mean the world to me, Sil. You're everything I have. I can't bear to lose you. I don't blame you for the baby. It wasn't your fault."

He lifted me gently to stand with him, caressing my humble body with forgiving hands.

He clutched my face to his in the dying light. "Do you love me? Do you forgive me?" He gazed at me with love and distress.

"Yes."

He held the back of my head as he leaned in to kiss me heavily. Then he drew my body to his tightly. I hugged him with relief as my tears ended.

"I understand now, Ocelot. I have learned your lesson. I have knelt at your feet. Please don't let me stay that way in your mind. Let me have my dignity with you. I cannot live peacefully knowing you think of me as a lesser being."

"No, I don't," he promised. "You are a powerful warrior."

"You're twice as powerful now," I told him. "Yalat said you must be the greatest of all of us."

"No, I'm not great. I'm just learning." He pulled away to face me. He apologized for all the cruel things he had said when I had lost the baby.

"We were both hurt," I explained with forgiveness. "Your dishonor is my dishonor. So is your peace of mind. We share it all. We're bound by will and promise. I promise to honor you in every way. I need the same honor from you. Please don't ever leave me again."

Faith shone in his eyes once more. He reassured me with an apology and a promise to never leave me. We moved to my tent, where we stripped away our remorse. We revisited each other's bodies with renewed wonder and appreciation.

At the end of the week, our marriage fully healed, we returned to the house, escorted by warrior guards. We packed what we could and sold the home back to the real estate company. We said goodbye to our neighbors, and to Jiao, Croso, Channol, and Yalat. We headed for Liricos on public express transportation under our assumed names of Kesserelle and Marchand.

Klib stood trial for multiple counts of illegal activities before his execution. His testimony led to the arrest of a few smugglers, but Viga and Swall Jade were not touched. They were protected by numerous alibis and friends in high places. In fact, Swall Jade left his thinly disguised position with the Organization to become a security general in Prime Minister Lock's cabinet. Some of Teradom's successor generals decided to make Teradom look bad to improve their own stations, so the charges against Ocelot were dropped before they were ever made public.

Jiao went to the Loam Center on Jawlcheen to work again with his father, who had been on suspension and temporary house arrest in another quadrant of Jawlcheen for supporting a Fitmalo military rebel group without consent from the Organization. Eventually, the father and son returned to Sor3. Yalat volunteered to sponsor Jiao's sister, Viel, for her last years of training.

Alaban and Willa lived together on Sor4, where Alaban was awarded his title of sub professor. He messaged us often at first, but after a while, his communications were delayed by covert ops work.

Ocelot and I traveled together on Liricos for several months before finally settling at my father's new school for exceptional children. My family accepted Ocelot warmly. Father talked us into giving a few lessons. I taught levitation. Ocelot taught swordsmanship. For the Organization, we worked in light espionage in the nearby town of Zescek, but always kept an eye on the political happenings of the Thrader helion.

Coincidentally, about three months after we left, a contagious rash became a major health concern on Jawlcheen. We laughed about it. Apparently, one of Teradom's cohorts had used the formula Ocelot had altered on Teradom's computer to follow through with the insidious plan. Just as we had predicted, due to prolonged economic success, the people of Fitmalo rallied to change their constitution and allowed Lock to serve a new term in office. Nearly a year after we'd left, Lock was blamed for the rash outbreak and for cyphening money out of the military fund for personal gain as well as assassination of two Jawlcheen officials who would not go along with him on commonwealth matters. Lock was ousted in a coup. Unfortunately, Swall Jade stepped up to become prime minister. We worried once more for the future of Jawlcheen and for the U.G.

Chapter 61: Life Anew

Soon after Swall Jade's appointment to the prime ministry, I had premonitions, dreams. I believed we would soon conceive another child. I hesitated to tell Ocelot about it, knowing it would be wrong to get his hopes up. I wasn't sure when I would conceive, but I was sure it would happen. I prayed for the health of the child, whenever it might come into being. I became disappointed at every monthly cycle, but I kept faith.

My dreams continued every night for several months. Most of the time, I did not remember them entirely. I only dreamt of a tiny life. Then one night, my dreams turned strange. I felt my child was in distress. He felt compressed, panicked. I saw Alaban come to his rescue. He held the baby to comfort him. I awoke deeply disturbed. I left Ocelot in our bed. I tiptoed out to our balcony, which was the rooftop of the classroom below us. I practiced all thirty personal defense forms. At dawn, Ocelot found me tumbling back into bed. Instead of starting his morning routine, he hugged me to him and slept in a little longer.

Many weeks passed. I ignored my dreams for a while. I had faith that if we were meant to have another baby, the time would come with or without my constant anticipation.

Then another haunting dream arrested my attention. I found myself in a room with a crib by a window. I walked to it. A baby cooed softly. He wore a simple blue suit with a clean diaper. He caught sight of me and smiled. He kicked and panted excitedly. I looked around the room, but no one was there. I reached down to the child's hand. He grasped my finger with a strong grip. I smiled at him. He observed me with wondrous, dark eyes as he gurgled.

"Whose baby are you?" I asked him tenderly.

He howled with laughter when I spoke. He pulled my finger back and forth. I laughed with him. I gently picked up the baby. I cradled him to me, staring into his sweet face. Natural instinct led him to turn his face to my breast to look for milk. I shifted him to try and deter his impulse, but his little hand clutched at my robe and pulled it away. I felt the strong pull from his mouth. An uncomfortable swelling expanded my breasts. I produced milk for this baby. I felt embarrassed, but at the same time amazed. The baby fed from me. I held his delicate body in my arms as he held my breast in his. A nurturing love swept over me. This was my baby. He looked up at me with the love and dependency of a helpless, hungry infant. I stared at him with joy. Was this my child's spirit communicating with me before he was even conceived?

He sighed with relief from his hunger. His little eyes grew sleepy with comfort. I nursed him until he drifted off to sleep. I lifted him carefully to my shoulder, patting him until he burped. I grinned and hugged the magical child to me, feeling his sleeping weight and smelling his unique scent. I replaced him carefully into his bed. I observed him with fascination. I awoke filled with a secret hope.

More months of recurring dreams went by, but each month, I dreamed a little less. Soon the dreams came only once a month, and then in longer intervals. I remained barren, but my nighttime child still haunted me. Half a year later, I dreamed the child crawled to me across the floor. We sat and played with a soft toy together. A year later, the toddler walked a few steps to me. Another year went by. He chattered to me about a pet turtle. I began to wonder if my dreams were only the product of a deranged obsession, but I could not, nor did I wish to stop dreaming of this child.

Nearly five years after we'd left Jawlcheen, I dreamed the boy and I sat at the pond by the waterfall. He asked me about everything he saw there. I showed him how to throw pebbles and make them splash in the water. We played with the rocks to see who could make the biggest splash. When he lost interest, we returned to his room at will. He got ready for bed. I tucked him in. He asked me to tell him a story. I told him a fairy tale my mother had told me as a child. I held his hand as he fell asleep. I stared down at him, hoping desperately, that someday he would be real.

One afternoon, my eldest niece, Kaycha, came to my door. She said there was someone here to see us from the Organization. She said he had lots of bright-colored squares on his shirt. I asked her to go and get Ocelot from the training field. No one had called us from the Center. I found it strange that one of our generals or sub generals would come to visit us unannounced.

I met Ocelot on our way to the entrance. I asked him if he knew about it. He was unaware as I was. As we rounded the corner of the administrative office, we saw a tall, dark human warrior in official gray uniform. I spoke his name as I rushed towards him.

"Jet Black is back," Alaban spoke to us proudly with outstretched arms.

We embraced each other. I noticed Kaycha was right. His shoulder shone with colored bars.

"Look at you! You're a professor sub general already?" I said excitedly.

"You may call me sir and wait on me as often as you like," he joked with a bow.

"Congratulations, sir," Ocelot chimed in. "They're still promoting the right people, I see."

My two favorite men shook hands gladly.

"Professor, it's good to see you."

"Come on up. We'll show you around," I said with delight. I tugged on his sleeve.

He resisted. He stood at attention. "Just a minute. I brought someone with me that I'd like you to meet."

We gazed at him with interest. He became very formal.

"Sil, Ocelot, I apologize for any shock that you're about to receive, but I've kept this from you for too long." He reached out to hold my hand. "It's someone I love dearly, who's lived with me for the last few years, someone I hope you'll accept."

I smiled joyfully at him. "Of course we will. I'm so happy for you, Alaban. Where is she?"

"Ah, no. Actually, he's male, not female."

I blinked. "I'm sorry. I thought…I thought you only liked girls," I said.

Alaban grinned again. "It's not what you think. All right. I'll show you." He turned to call behind him. "The coast is clear, son. You can come out now."

From behind the corner of the gated wall at the entrance to our school peeked half of a little face and a hand. My heart skipped a beat.

Alaban gestured to him to join us. The boy stepped away from the gate, but hesitated. I felt light-headed. His face—it was the same face I had seen. This was the baby, the little child of my dreams. He was real. We truly had met each other. So this was Alaban's son. Our spiritual connection had linked us even to our offspring. But this child was lighter skinned than Alaban. He had no noticeable facial features of his. His hair and eyes were brown. He looked more like Ocelot than Alaban. It couldn't be.

The child finally found the courage to climb the steps. As he approached us, Ocelot gripped my arm. He saw the uncanny resemblance as well. We all found ourselves sitting on the steps together. Alaban warned us not to scare him, but he wasn't scared. He approached us happily. He smiled as he bounced up the steps to us. The closer he came to us the bouncier he became. When he finally got to us, he headed straight for me. He ran to my arms. I hugged him to me gently. He wrapped his little arms around my neck, so sweet and innocent, like a bundle of pure love.

I giggled despite my overwhelming emotion. "Hi. I know you. Do you remember me?"

He pulled back from my embrace. He gave me a beautiful smile. "Yeah. We played with rocks. Remember?"

"Yes, we played with rocks. I remember," I told him. I laughed.

He grabbed my wrist and moved it around to see the hologram I still wore. "I like your bracelet. It's cool," he said in his tiny voice.

I was intrigued. He was amazing.

"Look, dad. It's a fresh water anemone," he said.

I was surprised at his knowledge and even more surprised that he could pronounce it.

"Wow. How did you know what it was called?" Alaban said to him, amazed at our connection.

"He told me," the boy said. He pointed to Ocelot.

I faced Ocelot with alarm. The child walked around our feet to stand in front of him.

"Right?" the dear creature spoke to him. He turned so that Ocelot could lift him onto his knee.

Ocelot regarded him with equal amazement. "That's right. We went to the imaginary waterfall together."

I set a hand to cover my mouth in awe.

"We caught lots of fish," the boy bragged to us. "There were like…this many." He stretched an arm up to show us how high the pile of fish was.

"Wow," Alaban breathed, impressed with the psychic communication between us, but the child assumed he was reacting to his fish story.

"Really. I'm not kidding. There were like a hundred and fifty-two. Wasn't there?" he looked to Ocelot to back him up.

"You're right. There were exactly that many." Ocelot examined the boy's face with excitement.

"When can we play that again? That was fun."

Ocelot was speechless.

Alaban stood abruptly. "Son, come here a minute."

He hopped off Ocelot's knee and marched up to Alaban. He stood at attention. Alaban had already begun training him.

"Yes, sir?" the fantastic child said.

"I want you to go play with those kids on the playground for a while," he told him.

"Aw, but I wanted to stay here and play with them," the boy complained.

"You can see them again in a few minutes. They're not going away. Don't worry. You can play with them again soon." Alaban pet the boy's shiny hair affectionately.

"Will you watch me?" he asked.

"Yes. I'll watch you from that bench over there. Okay?"

"Will you watch me, too?" he asked Ocelot and me.

"Yes, we'll watch you," Ocelot agreed breathlessly.

"Okay." He mounted the steps and ran off towards the play area with Tamia's kids.

The three of us walked spellbound to the benches that flanked the playground. Ocelot and I grasped for words, but couldn't find them. At last, Alaban spoke.

"I have to go to Karnesh for a pretty risky mission. I don't want to leave him with the nanny for that long. I was hoping you would take him in."

"Absolutely," Ocelot breathed.

"Actually, I brought him here to give him back to you."

We stared at Alaban with anticipation.

"I owed you a son. I'm sorry I kept him too long. I didn't want to let him go. I kept making the excuse that he was too small to take him on the interstellar trek over here. He's four now. He's growing up. He needs a good education. He needs to be with you. He's really your son. I guess you can see that."

"But how? How did you do this? It doesn't seem real," I said to him.

"Don't tell me you had access to the fetal tissue from Sil's miscarriage. You didn't clone our baby, did you?" Ocelot asked.

"Yes and no. That actually would have been easier, but no, he's not a clone. Anyway, clones don't have psychic abilities. Saul does," he said.

"What did you call him?" I asked in shock.

"Saul. His name is Saul."

Ocelot glanced at me. "Did you tell him?"

"No. I never told you we had already decided on a name for our baby, did I?"

"No. The name just came to me. I figured it was similar to your name, so that's the name I gave him." Alaban waved to him.

"If he's not a clone, then what is he?" Ocelot asked.

Alaban reacted defensively. "He's a human being like us. Okay. I had to do some genetic engineering to start. I stole a sample of the fetal tissues from your miscarriage from the hospital in Hammerstead and some DNA samples from both of you from Organization medical records."

We leaned in to hear his explanation.

"I didn't want to make a clone for you. Clones are too risky. They don't always turn out like they're meant to. The ones that look normal end up with some terminal disease early in life because they're genetically imperfect. Scientists will always claim they've finally found the right formula, but scientists are just people like the rest of us. What do they know about perfection? They couldn't make sure every aspect of the baby is formed just right physically and spiritually."

He shifted his view between the two of us uneasily. "I wasn't just planning a devious act of genetic engineering when I set out to do this. I did this for you because I owed it to you. It wasn't meant to be an act of selfishness. I never expected that I'd learn to love him as my own son."

He paused to clear his throat. "This is going to sound impossible, but I swear it's true. The boy is a true miracle. He is the boy you conceived the first time. His is that same spirit you brought to life five and a half years ago. It's the same powerful soul. His body may be slightly different, but I wouldn't be surprised if that's the same, too."

"How?" I whispered.

"Clones and test tube babies lack a vital element in their being. Their genetic makeup is imperfect, but it's more than that. It's as if they were missing something; almost in the same way that you always said there was something missing between the two of us, Sil."

He took a moment to collect his thoughts. "Let me start a different way. When people create new people, they usually do it naturally. But people don't always find the right mate for themselves. They're not always compatible. Couples who feel true love and physical attraction for one another have the most compatible elements for the creation of offspring. The two of you, for example. It's not just a physiological coincidence. There's a spiritual side to it as well.

"Why do we mate? We mate because we have this instinct, this desire to do it, but its real purpose is procreation. We know that. But what if there is a spiritual importance to the mating ritual as well? I believe the male and female elements must join together naturally to form a physically and spiritually complete offspring. That's why the clones are incomplete. They're created without passion, without sexual contact between parents. In most cases, the biological parents never even meet."

Ocelot shook his head. "Where are you going with this? I don't understand."

"I know. It sounds convoluted. Do you remember Willa, my concubine?" Alaban asked me.

I nodded.

"Her blood was compatible. She supplied the host egg. She was the surrogate mother. She did it willingly. I didn't force her. She volunteered. I didn't tell her it was your child. I just told her I wanted to create a baby."

"She's a Vermilion. How could you create a human zygote with two different species?" I asked.

"I genetically altered the egg in vitro using your elements I just mentioned. Latest technology. The Vermilion egg was converted into a human egg. That's the technical side. It shouldn't have worked, except I did something no scientist would ever dare to try. I could have fertilized the egg synthetically, but then he would have been just another test tube baby with few chances for survival. Or if he did survive, who knows what he would have turned out to be? I knew the possibilities were trillions to one that it would work. So why waste my effort on something I knew was pointless anyway? It would either work the right way or not at all."

He held his hands, palms up, before him. He seemed to meditate a few seconds before continuing. "I had a mortal debt to pay. I had taken so many lives. I destroyed a miracle that was your baby. I had to give it back somehow. I knew that genetically altered egg was unholy, devoid of natural life. Only God can make holy that which is unholy."

He paused again, exhaling slowly before continuing. "I said the longest, most sincere prayer I've ever said in my life. I begged our creator to allow me to perform an act of atonement for what I'd done. I asked him to bring the spirit of your child into my body so that it would pass through me to fertilize that egg. I made love to Willa as if she were the only woman in existence. I concentrated all my power from every aspect of my entire being into bringing life into her womb. And it worked," he spoke almost in a whisper.

We all turned to gaze at Saul. He played contentedly in the sand with another child.

"He is a true miracle. He is a godsend, literally. He was meant to live," Alaban said. "I'm sorry I never mentioned him to you before, but I was sure you wouldn't believe it until you could see him for yourselves."

We stared at Saul as if in a trance. We hung there in shock for several minutes.

Alaban reached for my hand. He broke the enchantment momentarily. "I always wanted to be the father of your child." He smiled and turned to Ocelot. "I just never expected to be the father of yours."

Ocelot stood. He glanced at him inquisitively. "You did this for us?"

Alaban nodded at him. Ocelot gripped Alaban's free hand and shook it ferociously. Alaban stood. They hugged each other like long lost brothers. When they finally moved apart, Ocelot gripped his arm.

Ocelot vowed, "I take back every bad thing I ever said about you. What can we ever do to thank you?"

"Don't thank me. He is a gift from God. I'm just the courier. Like I said, I kept him too long. I should have brought him to you before," Alaban said humbly.

"There's just one problem. He thinks I am his father. I didn't explain to him what I just told you. He wouldn't understand any of it yet. It would scare him. He throws some pretty incredible temper tantrums when he's scared. His power is impressive."

"We'll think of something. It doesn't matter as long as he's alive. Alaban, thank you." I embraced him tightly, and then held onto the arms of both men shakily.

Alaban attempted to calm us. "I guess you've been visiting each other in dreams. That's great. He came here thinking we were going to visit you for a while. I didn't tell him he's going to stay. We'll have to decide what to tell him."

"What about his surrogate mother? Does he think she's his real mother?" I asked.

Alaban looked down sadly. "Willa committed suicide three years ago. She wasn't good with the baby after all. During her pregnancy, she started showing signs of psychic abilities, even levitative power. Those things came from Saul. When he was born, she lost all that. She was jealous. She mistreated him sometimes. Once she tried to scald him with hot bath water. She might have meant to kill him. I don't know. He knew something was wrong. Even though he was so little, he had the psychic sense and the strength to turn the little bathtub upside down. When I went in to see what had happened, Saul was crying like crazy. He was levitating at the ceiling. Willa was screaming at him.

"I couldn't let her have another chance with him. I gave her her freedom, even though she didn't want it. I sent her out. She hanged herself right in front of our house at our gate just to spite me. I don't know who she hated more: herself or me."

"I'm so sorry," I told him.

"I'm just glad Saul doesn't remember her. His early memory is excellent, but the traumatic experience must have made him blot out that memory. He doesn't know who his mother is. We moved to Organization housing where I hired a nanny for him. She's an elderly Grey, a retired warrior. She's good with him. Sweet old lady. I was sorry to let her go, but I see he'll be in good hands here. I hope you'll let me come and see him often. I don't want to lose contact with him."

"No. Of course you can see him as often as you like." I held his hand tightly.

Just then, Saul came running up to us excitedly. "Hey, dad! Look! I found some cool rocks. Look. This one's a laser crystal. We can make cool weapons with it. And this one's really sharp. Look. You can cut sticks with it. And this one just looks pretty. It's got spots on it, like a birdie's egg. See? Can I keep them?"

655

We all sat again to observe our miraculous boy.

Alaban became wistful. He hugged the child to him.

"Sure you can, son." He kissed the boy on the top of his head.

As he released the tender creature, Saul asked, "Can you hold them for me? I'm going to go find some more." He emptied the pebbles into Alaban's hand. "Dad, when are we going to eat? I'm hungry."

I interrupted. "We're going to have dinner in a few minutes. Would you like to join us? We have a big table. There's plenty of room for everybody. We'll have soup and bread and some other things. Would you like that?"

"Yes, ma'am," the dear thing replied. "Are you my Aunt Sil?"

I looked for support from Ocelot and Alaban. They waited for my decision.

"Why do you say that?" I asked Saul.

"My dad says you're 'celepsial' twins. So that means you're the sister and he's the brother. That makes you my aunt, right?"

I couldn't deny such flawless logic from him. "Yes, that's right."

I glanced at Ocelot for approval. He nodded. There was no way we could explain the amazing story to him in a way he could understand. We hardly comprehended it ourselves.

"We're glad you came to visit us." Ocelot reached out to pat Saul's back.

"Me too. I like it here. Dad, can we stay here for a while?" he asked.

"Yes, Saul. You'll be staying here a long time." Alaban cradled Saul's rock treasures in his palm.

"Just me? You have to go away *again*? I don't want you to go away. Why can't you stay here with me?" The poor tyke whined.

"I don't want to go away, either, Saul. You know I'd rather be with you than anyone else in the world. But dad has to work for some big generals who told me to go far away for a while. Sil and Ocelot will be here with you."

"What about Nanny Nim?" Saul whined.

"She had to stay on Sor4, son. Remember?"

Saul cried loudly. "No! I don't want you to go! I don't want you to go!"

He jumped into Alaban's arms and held his neck in a vice-like grip. Alaban patted him on the back several times. He looked weary. He apologized to the boy and tried to calm him.

Ocelot and I exchanged looks of realization. Our son did not know us yet, nor did we know him. This would be the toughest assignment we'd ever encountered: to learn to be parents to a son we'd only dreamed of. It would take patience and endurance, but we rejoiced at the challenge. Here at last was our son, our miracle returned, our gift from God and Alaban.

Chapter 62: Nurturing

After dinner, we helped Alaban and Saul settle into a spare bedroom for the night. Saul went to sleep early. We stood over him, breathlessly observing his beautiful face. His genetic makeup showed the best qualities of both of us. Alaban's physical features didn't show on him at all. He was right. This was Saul, our original Saul. We took turns kissing his perfect forehead before leaving him to sleep soundly.

Alaban walked with us to the courtyard, where the late summer sunset painted the sky. Alaban assured us that Saul wouldn't be frightened if he woke up alone in the room, since he always sensed where he was. As we strolled, he filled us in on Saul's likes and dislikes, his training thus far, and his temperament. Saul had a tendency to levitate things and throw tantrums when frightened or angered. Alaban was heavy of heart knowing he'd have to leave him for so long. Soon we found ourselves near the steps where we had first met our miraculous boy. I felt as if this afternoon had been a dream, one I never wished to leave.

Just then our serene conversation was interrupted by shouts from beyond the gate. My sister, Grace, had arrived home early from a date gone bad. They had gone to eat at an upper middle class restaurant. She was dressed in the low cut mini dress I had advised her not to wear. Her suitor followed her up the first few steps, trying to sway her opinion, but she turned on him.

"No!" she spat.

"Okay, but I thought..."

"You can stop right there. You thought? You did not think. If you had actually thought about it, you would have realized that first of all, I didn't give you permission to do anything with me but eat dinner. Secondly,

I have a job. People depend on me to be here on time and ready to deal with fifteen little kids the whole day."

"Okay, but…"

She held up a hand to him. "No, it is not okay. You can just get back in your cab, rent a concubine, and forget about me, because you know something? I don't ever want to see you again." She whirled away from him and wiggled her way up the stairs.

The man was about to follow her, but Ocelot stepped down with clenched fists and gave him a warning look. The man swore all the way back down to the cab.

Grace pointed violently at Ocelot. "And I do not need you to lecture me tonight, thank you."

He shook his head at her.

She cleared the steps and came to me with open arms.

She embraced me momentarily, speaking as quickly as she could in one breath. "You would think an astrophysicist would know how to communicate better. He is definitely educated beyond his intellect. He's such a slime ball. Right after dinner, he said he had some kind of surprise for me. I was expecting something nice like going dancing or to the nebula theater or even something intellectual, but no. He took me to this sleazy hotel. He is so shallow! This man studied at the university for ten years and he is an idiot."

"You can't judge a man by his résumé. You have to like his personality first," I told her. I shook my head at her with sympathy.

"You should take your sister's advice." Alaban stepped a little closer to us. "If I had listened to her the first time around, we'd all be a lot healthier."

Grace suddenly noticed him.

"Oh, I'm sorry. I didn't realize we had company," she said in a small voice. Then she looked at his title pin. She gasped. "You're Alaban. I didn't recognize you. You probably don't recognize me. It's been so long. I was only twelve when you left our old school. I remember you when you were a teenager. I'm Grace." She stopped to catch her breath. "Sil told me everything about what happened."

Alaban took her hand. He held it a long while. She wasn't willing to let go either. I watched the sparks of attraction move between them. I was overjoyed. I raised my eyebrows at Ocelot. He observed with interest.

"You've grown into your name, Grace. You're very graceful." Alaban turned on his mesmerizing charm. It was well received.

She smiled brightly and asked if Alaban was here to visit or if he would stay a while. Their manner dampened as he told her he had come to

658

enroll his son in our school. When he told her Saul's age, she informed him with a more formal smile that she would be his teacher.

Alaban smiled affably, stating it was good to know he would be leaving Saul in such good, and lovely, hands.

I leaned to Grace's ear and whispered, "He's single."

She tried to pinch my arm, but I caught her by the wrist and smiled, offering to organize a going away party for Alaban to ease the difficulty of saying goodbye. Alaban supported the idea gratefully.

The four of us walked back toward his guest room patio. Alaban and Ocelot shook hands again. They thanked each other once more. Then Alaban lifted me into his arms.

"I still love you, Sil." He set me down again.

"I still love you, too, my old friend. I always will." We kissed each other on the cheek. He brushed my face with his hand.

He turned to Grace. He took her hand once more. Alaban leaned forward to kiss her cheek, but lingered near her face a moment longer. She was enticed by him. He stood slowly, keeping his eyes on her. Then he said goodnight. He waved to us as he stepped into the room and closed the door.

We all stood outside, staring in joyous confusion at each other before going back to our dwellings. Ocelot and I could not sleep almost the whole night. We compared stories of our dreams of Saul. We thought of hundreds of questions to ask Alaban about him. We nervously planned activities to do with him. Our minds swam. We said prayers of thanks, rejoicing at his life.

The next day, after morning exercises, Alaban and Saul helped us set up and decorate for our party. I tested Saul's levitative abilities while he helped hang streamers. His strength and distance were excellent. He only needed direction on finite control. I complimented him.

Ocelot and Alaban played with Saul before lunch. They sword-fought with foam swords from Ocelot's class. Saul directed the two while he acted. Alaban was the evil dragon and Saul was the warrior hero. Ocelot was the hero's sidekick. The men hopped around the short stairway slicing at each other.

Alaban pretended to spear Ocelot through the ribs. Ocelot groaned in imaginary agony as he draped himself over the stairs, with one eye on Saul during his performance, hoping for his approval.

"Ha, ha! The mighty dragon wins again!" Alaban professed.

Ocelot called for Saul. "Help me, hero warrior! You've got to save the planet. Strike him under the arm!" Ocelot reached up for Saul's hand and tagged him.

"I'm going in!" the boy shouted as he bounded towards his foe.

Our acrobatic child leapt up to Alaban, swinging his sword. Alaban blocked his attack. The boy caught his arm and hung onto it as if it were a tree branch, and kicked him repeatedly anywhere he could get a hit. Alaban retreated, suppressing laughter.

Finally, the boy followed Ocelot's advice. He let go of the arm and squished the foam sword into Alaban's ribs before leaping away from him.

"Ooh, good hit. I mean; I'm done for! He's pierced my evil heart. Aaah!" Alaban lay on the ground while Saul held up his sword in victory.

"I claim this victory in the name of the United Galaxy! Freedom!" Saul yelled. He stamped a foot atop Alaban's chest.

Alaban recoiled, sitting up and clutching Saul around the waist. "Now I've rejuvenated! Ha, ha!"

Saul squealed. "Help me, friend, help me!" he called to Ocelot.

He sprang back to his aid.

I observed this hilarious act with glee. I laughed until I felt a twinge of pain in my side.

In the early evening, after all our regular students went home, our ten boarding students stayed behind, as did Kaycha and Nima, (Tamia's girls), and of course, Saul. Tamia and Jem arrived ready to dance and eat. My next oldest sister, Chena, and my father joined us, as did Grace and some of the other teachers. Alaban greeted my father with honor. He encouraged Saul to do the same. Father shook Saul's hand and welcomed him to the school. As Kaycha guided Saul off to the food line with the other children, the three of us explained to Father whom Saul really was. His bewilderment matched our own. By the end of our explanation, he was a proud grandfather all over again; glad to have a grandson to offset his two granddaughters. He said this was truly a day for celebration.

The children finished their food first. They ran around the open dance floor in the dimly lit courtyard, playing tag and caterpillar. Saul enjoyed being with the other children. We watched him lovingly from our table. Ocelot and Alaban finally spoke to each other as if they were lifelong friends.

"When you first saw us yesterday you called yourself Jet Black. Is that your pseudonym now?" Ocelot asked him.

"It's my last name, Jetscuro. That's what it means. Only my closest associates know me by that nickname. It's just satire. You know how it is."

"It sounds sinister. Are you sure you're not trying to cover yourself in the world of cutthroats with a name instead of a costume now? Who would want to battle Jet Black, the heartless?" I suggested.

"They know I'm not heartless. I haven't had to do an assassination since I was a Sub Professor. Some people think the nickname doesn't match my character, but I think it does.

"See, my theory is this: people think of goodness and light as similes. I disagree. If you go by ancient theology, which I do, then you assume that this universe and all others together form the body of God. There's a lot more darkness in a universe than there is light. I think we rely on light too much. I mean...I know it's important—energy sources, heat, sight, physical life springing from solar influence—but there's so much more. All the darkness and supposed emptiness of space is also important. It's not evil. It's only poorly perceived. So to answer your question: no. Just because I'm Jet Black doesn't mean I'm sinister. It just means I'm misunderstood." He took a bite of his food as we considered his profound viewpoint. "Besides, black is cool. Just ask Saul."

We smiled at each other, but he soon looked away to the boy. Parental worry showed on his face.

"You only allow exceptional children here?" he asked.

"Yes, they're tested for the ten intelligences before they're accepted," Ocelot explained. "From what I can tell, Saul will fit in perfectly."

We observed as Saul and a couple of Lizard children took turns jumping and levitating to touch the branches of a fruit tree.

"The wonders of evolution," Alaban mused, gesturing after them. "Not too many centuries ago, almost nobody knew how to levitate. Now there are millions of us. If our ancestors were advanced enough to produce just the right elements in us, and if we, the exceptionally gifted, produce successful offspring, imagine what they'll be able to do." He indicated the kids. "Maybe someday a human being will reach the first intelligence. Maybe Saul will see his grandchildren reach that level."

We observed Saul dreamily.

"Let's just hope they inherit the common sense to use their abilities for the right reasons," he added.

"What is your job these days?" Ocelot asked him.

"I was tracking Hume's old band. Recently, I've been on Viga's work. Mainly, I do invisible trailing. I follow a group of smugglers through their entire delivery run on one of the Soren planets without detection. Then I report back to the boss and I go home to be with Saul. Easy living. Now that I've just been promoted, they're putting me back into aggressive espionage.

"Karnesh and Godel are almost completely on contract with the Thrader helion. They're trying to convince Jain to follow suit. Not that Jain has anything the Regime really wants, except a place to spend their money while they're on vacation, but they don't want Jain to stand in the way of some of the deals they're setting up with the other two planets. I think the Lapas helion is the safest planet in the U.G. right now."

"You know if you need any backup info you can't ask your superiors for, you can always count on us," Ocelot added.

Alaban thanked him just as Grace approached. She looked very attractive in a modest Tambuo outfit. She invited us all to form two lines on either side of the courtyard to play the trapper dance with the children.

We held hands in the line facing the other adults as the children skipped between our lines. They sang a simple rhyme about the trapper. At the end of each stanza, the adult lines moved in closer together. Eventually, the children scooted by over our feet. Finally, we trapped as many kids as we could between us. The whole party enjoyed the event. The children who escaped were given the privilege of riding on the shoulders of the adult of their choice and making him do the horse dance.

Saul was one of the escapees. He chose Alaban as his steed. Three other kids rode on the shoulders of Jem, Ocelot, and Father. They marched around the courtyard in a circle and then rushed each other, jostling the children into peels of laughter. While this silly dance took place, my sisters cornered me by my table and demanded to know what was going on. I gave them only the basic details.

I grasped Tamia's hands as I spoke to her excitedly. "His name is Saul. He's my baby, Tamia. Alaban brought him back. He's alive."

My three sisters gaped and stared at the child and at Alaban.

"This is the man you turned down? I would have taken him in a heartbeat," Chena spoke in hushed tones. "He is hot."

"How long will he be gone? He's not just leaving Saul here and never coming back, is he?" Grace asked with genuine concern.

"He'll be gone a year at the least. I'm sure he'll message Saul nearly every day. He's like a father to him." I refrained from giving more information.

Grace wouldn't let me avoid the subject. "Saul's enrollment form says his last name is Jetscuro, not Quoren. What does that mean?"

"Alaban had to register him under his own name on Sor4 to be able to travel with him. He's listed as his father," I explained.

"Then who's listed as his mother?" she asked. "He left that information blank on the enrollment form."

This I didn't know. I assured her we'd work something out later and that I trusted Alaban's decisions on Saul's documentation. Anyway, no matter what his information said on his birth and travel registration, Ocelot would be able to break into official archives and change them as needed. My sisters regarded me insecurely. Then Tamia hugged me around the neck. Chena hugged us both. Grace hugged the lot of us and gave me a quick kiss on the forehead.

The horse song ended with a cacophony of glee from the children. They were ushered off the dance area for the spring dance. Most of the adults and some of the older children returned to dance together. At the end of the spring dance, males and females partnered off. All the people who did not choose a partner sat again with the kids. Chena danced with Alaban. Grace danced with Father. At the summer dance, however, Alaban bowed to Chena and immediately asked permission to trade partners. We eyed Grace and Alaban as they talked solemnly during the dance. I expected Grace was grilling him for information about Saul.

When I came close enough to hear their conversation, Alaban asked Grace about her choice of profession.

"Sil tells me you graduated at the top of your class in aerospace studies. Why would an aerospace scientist want to work as a teacher at a boarding school?" he asked with a kind smile.

"I had to help my father after my mother's death. This school is his dream. I couldn't leave the planet knowing he was so close to achieving his goal. I'll go back to school as soon as we find a reliable replacement," she answered sincerely.

Alaban slowed his step. He leaned close to us. "Please don't let anyone replace her this year. She's the perfect mentor for Saul. Besides, every boy should have a crush on his first teacher. I would hate to see her replaced by some large male Furman."

Ocelot replied loudly. "I never had a crush on my first teacher. He *was* a male Furman."

We all laughed heartily. Grace forgot her skepticism for the moment to laugh with us. Throughout the autumn and winter dances, the dance participants dwindled. The children screamed and chased each other happily among the potted trees that lined the terrace. We clung to each other lovingly, fulfilled by the serendipitous knowledge that our son was alive and well.

When the music finished, Chena suggested one more lively dance to end the party. She played music for the Harvest Wheel. In this dance, the men turned slowly on one heel to follow the movements of the women. It was one of the women's hip-shaking dances that some people made fun of, but we enjoyed it. The music consisted of varied percussion interrupted by short pauses, in which we clapped once, then twice. At the end of the dance, the men knelt on one knee as we spun one last time. We landed kneeling, facing them, our knees touching theirs. We clasped hands. Finally, we helped each other to stand with the applause of the finished party. Alaban complimented Grace on her dancing before saying goodbye.

Saul convinced Alaban to take him with him as far as the ascension tower of the nearby Center. Ocelot and I accompanied them. Saul sat on Alaban's lap in the van. They talked about the party, the school, where Alaban would be traveling, and how they would keep in touch. At the ascension tower, Saul asked if he could go on the ship with him, but Alaban explained it was against regulations. He said his superiors were afraid Saul would stow away on the ship and then they would have to turn around and come back to leave him, delaying Alaban's trip, thereby delaying the time it would take for him to come back. Saul seemed embarrassed as well as disappointed, having apparently planned to do just that. After a hearty round of hugs and kisses, Alaban gave Saul a pep talk and reassurance.

"You'll always know where I am. I'll always know where you are. Be brave. Obey Sil and Ocelot and Master Blen. They love you as much as I do," he advised.

The two embraced each other again. Saul patted his back. Alaban waved to us once more before ducking into the cargo hold of his new ship from Sor4. We stayed to watch the ship depart. Saul whimpered as it left. Ocelot picked him up. Saul immediately hugged Ocelot's neck and whined all the way back to the school. They looked so much alike. I watched them mistily. Ocelot was proud to hold the boy during his sorrow. He began to feel like a true father.

Chapter 63: Home

At the end of the scholastic year, after Saul's fifth birthday, many political changes shook the U.G. The Jain planet struggled to keep its autonomy from the movement to form a Keres commonwealth, much like the Commonwealth of Thrader. (Jawlcheen had allowed itself to become absorbed in its helion's conglomeration after all). Croso and Channol still worked on Jawlcheen, determined to somehow maintain the integrity of the Organization there. However, their efforts went unnoticed.

Then a disturbing announcement was made from our neighboring helion of Gold Wind. Rybalazar and Xiantalix made a pledge of association with the interstellar policing begun by Fitmalo. Now Thrader Defense Space Station One was only one of hundreds of similar entities floating in space, supposedly regulating trade and travel between helions. Being a long-time enemy of Liricos, Rybalazar's pledge worried those of us who understood the undermining ramifications of such an allegiance. Ocelot and I kept abreast of the situation through personal contacts more than official Organization intelligence, since we suspected disloyalty at every level and rank, both civil and military.

Alaban's communications came to us less and less. I perceived that he felt he might not make it out of Keres. Grace worried for him as well. She had communicated with him over the year as much as anyone else. Finally, a year and two months after his departure, he began his journey back to us again. He messaged us daily on his return trip. His notes to us all became more personable and humorous by the week. Once he reached the Soren helion, he sent Saul a video message in which he told a child's version of his adventures, punctuated by sound effects and illustrated with makeshift puppets. Saul proudly displayed it to his friends.

A few days before Alaban's scheduled arrival, Saul woke us with a heart-wrenching scream. He cried. He wet his bed. He levitated objects all over the house and then let them clatter into each other. After several minutes of wailing, he became somewhat coherent.

"I don't want my daddy to die! I don't want daddy to die!" he cried.

"Saul, sweetheart, what did you see?" I asked him patiently.

"Spaceship blows up!" he sobbed.

Ocelot and I traded faces of discouragement. I hadn't foreseen any danger to Alaban. I felt he was fine. I didn't have any premonition of death or harm to him.

We abandoned Saul's wet bed. I gave him some clean clothes and tucked him in bed between us. I explained to him that sometimes we imagine things that don't really come true just because we're afraid of what might happen. I promised him in the morning we would hail Alaban on real time messaging so he could see and talk to him and tell him about his bad dream.

As promised, we obtained a successful connection with Alaban on board the ship. Saul told him in detail what he had seen. He dreamed that Alaban was alone in a large fighter ship that ran into a bigger ship and blew up. Alaban explained to him that right now he wasn't in a fighter ship. It was a research cruiser. He didn't plan on being in a smaller ship or a fighter anytime soon. He urged Saul not to worry about it as we had. He was sure we'd see each other again by the end of the week. He showed him a wrapped package of something he'd bought for him on Jain. He said it was a kind of a toy and that he'd play with it with him the day he saw him again. Saul's spirits lifted. By the end of the week, he was excited and bouncy again.

Alaban surprised us all by arriving at Saul's classroom at the end of reading time. Grace told us that Saul jumped once, and then flew to his arms from across the room. He hugged him and then hopped up and down, asking for his present. Alaban apologized to the class for his interruption, but Grace was so overwhelmed by his arrival that she gave the class the rest of the time period as a recess.

The toy turned out to be a twist ball, which changed its trajectory, sometimes in midair, making it a real challenge to catch. The two immediately began to play, following the ball all the way out to the practice field where Ocelot and his students were doing fencing practice. Ocelot gave his students the rest of the day off as well.

At dinner that night, Father mentioned Alaban in his prayer. "We are glad to have Alaban back with us again. We hope he will feel at home with us and that he will stay as long as he likes. We thank you, Lord, for his presence among us. We also thank you for Sil's quick recovery. We thank you for this chance to be together as a family. Amen."

After we repeated his amen, Alaban asked about my surgery.

"It was your right side, wasn't it? On the lower part of your lung," Alaban asked. "I've felt a twinge there recently."

"Yes. She still had a piece of shrapnel there from the airbus accident years ago. Her body had developed a small growth around it," Ocelot interrupted. "She's fine now. We're keeping an eye on it just in case."

Alaban regarded me silently until Saul drew his attention to his food.

Later, Saul asked to share a room with Alaban on the ground floor where they had stayed the first time they had come to us. We prepared the extra beds together as Saul chattered to Alaban about all the things he'd missed while he was away. Alaban told him of a few things he'd seen in the Keres helion, like acid spiders and other strange animals. At a late hour, Alaban convinced him it was time to sleep and that they'd talk more tomorrow. He promised to stay with him for at least three weeks before he'd be obligated to check in at the Center, but even then he expected to be allowed to live here with us for several months. Saul relaxed from his hyper state when he heard this.

Alaban sat on Saul's bed by his feet as he told him a story of a plains otter that had successfully evaded an acid spider. Ocelot went upstairs to get some extra clothes for Saul. I leaned to kiss our son goodnight. As I stood, Alaban pulled me to sit beside him at the foot of the bed. Saul nestled into his pillow with eyes closed at last.

Alaban gripped my hand tightly. He stared longingly into my eyes. "You're not dying on me are you?" he asked me silently.

"No, not yet," I answered. "Twin heart."

We loosely hugged each other as we pressed our foreheads together.

"Why are you hugging like that?" Saul asked us. He shifted in his bed to see us better.

We retracted slowly. I replied, "We missed each other. We love each other very much."

Saul gazed at me. "Are you really my mom?" he asked innocently.

I quickly knelt by his side. I hesitated, but decided it was time. "Yes, Saul. I am. How did you know?" I asked, holding his small hand in mine.

"I remember I used to be inside you, and then a scary man kicked you really hard and dad beat him up. I got scared, but a nice lady came to get me. She said she's my grandmother. She said I had to wait before I could see you again. Then I came back." Saul lay tensely on his back.

I observed him with amazement. I smoothed his hair as I replied. "Saul, that's right. Why didn't you tell us before?"

Saul shrugged. "I don't know. Why'd you say you're my aunt? You're not really brother and sister, are you?"

"No, not genetically. What I mean is..." I stammered.

"We didn't lie to you about being twins, Saul. We're celestial twins. That means we're brother and sister in our spirit and in our hearts, but we don't have the same parents," Alaban interjected.

"So Uncle Ocelot is really my step dad?" he asked.

"No, Saul. He's your real dad," Alaban said with difficulty.

"Huh?" Saul made a face of exaggerated confusion.

Just then, Ocelot returned with Saul's clothing. Saul sat up straight in bed. Ocelot brought the clothing to the table next to him. Saul bolted to stand in the middle of the bed. He pointed at him angrily, determined to get to the bottom of this.

"Are you my real dad?" he demanded loudly.

Ocelot was taken aback, but then became delighted. He had already worked up a short speech to explain things to him. He approached him and set a hand on his shoulder.

"Yes, Saul. I'm your real father. Sil is your mother. We lost you a long time ago. Alaban found you and took care of you for us until he could bring us back together." Ocelot glanced at us uneasily, but continued his explanation. "He did such a good job of taking care of you that we decided to let him be your dad still. We didn't want to tell you before. We were afraid you were too little to understand. Now you're big."

Saul looked from one parent to the next and the next. His mouth pouted in dismay. "I don't understand," he whined. He headed for Alaban, ready to cry large tears. Alaban held the child. "You have to be my dad. You were there when I was born. You held me first."

Alaban became tough with him. "Saul, be brave. There's nothing wrong. We'll explain things to you, but you have to calm down. You know we all love you very much. That's the important thing. Now will you listen to me?"

Saul responded well. He nodded. A genuine curiosity overtook him.

"You look at yourself in the mirror every day, don't you, son?" Alaban asked.

Saul nodded. "When I brush my teeth."

"Look at Ocelot. Look at yourself. Look at me. Which two match?" Alaban insisted.

Saul dutifully pointed to himself and then Ocelot.

Alaban nodded. "He wanted to be there when you were born, but he couldn't be. Neither could your mom. You remember the bad man who hurt her. He's the one who made them lose you. There were a lot of strange things that happened between then and when I 'found you'." He glanced at Ocelot, assuring him that he would go along with his explanation. "I guess you could say you were taken from one mother and put into another one so you could finish growing. I supervised your birth. I'm the one who was there for you because they didn't know where you were."

"I have another mom, too?" he asked in a small voice.

"No, son. She was just a lady who helped me keep you alive until you were born. She wasn't really a mother to you. She's what we call a surrogate mother. She carried a baby that wasn't hers. She's not part of your family." Alaban spoke frankly to him.

"How come she never came to visit us?" he asked.

668

"She died when you were a baby, Saul," Alaban said.

"Because of me?" Saul asked.

"No, son. She died several months after you were born. She wasn't really a mother to you. She didn't love you like we do. She didn't take care of you. Nanny Nim and I took care of you most," Alaban said honestly.

Saul observed his family with more wisdom than before.

"We all love you, Saul. I missed you so much, sweetheart. When your dad brought you back to us, it was the happiest day of my life," I told him.

"Mine, too," Ocelot said tenderly.

I reached out cautiously to pat him on the back. He rushed to hug me. He then said what I'd waited so many years to hear.

"Mommy," his tiny voice spoke happily.

An influx of joy uplifted me. I grinned victoriously. "Oh, that's the best thing you could ever say to me, Saul. Thank you, baby. I love you."

"I love you, too, Mommy," he said.

Ocelot strung an arm around us. Saul moved away from me.

"Will I get in trouble if I still call you Dad?" Saul asked Alaban, who glanced up at Ocelot.

Ocelot smiled understandingly. "No, of course not, son."

"What do I call you?" Saul asked Ocelot.

"Call me whatever you like. We know who we are," Ocelot stated.

"Just don't call him mom," Alaban joked.

"Dad, this is not a time to be funny," Saul corrected him.

"You're right, Saul. I apologize," Alaban admitted with a grin.

"I'll call you Dad," he said, pointing to Alaban. He turned to Ocelot. "And I'll call you Daddy, okay?" Saul informed them decidedly.

Both men agreed warmly. We went through another series of hugs and kisses before bed. Saul said goodnight to each of us by our new names. He fell asleep with a hint of a smile on his face, as did the rest of us.

At the end of the three weeks, Alaban moved to temporary housing at the Sprague Center in Zeseck, but returned nearly every evening to spend time with us. During the new school year, Grace traded jobs with another teacher, moving up a level to be with Saul. He felt close to her, and this gave her more reason to communicate with Alaban, although she kept a professional distance. They did not date, but only spoke to each other frequently. I could tell they were both avoiding romantic attachment. I once asked them separately if Alaban's past with me was getting in their way of approaching each other, but they both denied it. Neither of them seemed to know what held them back, except fear of rejection. They each cared a great deal about the other's opinion of their roles with Saul and his education. Neither wanted to seem too forward.

As Saul's sixth birthday neared, relations between Gold Wind and Lapas began to break down. All of Gold Wind's planets had aligned with the commonwealth idea. Lapas was unkindly encouraged to play along. Our normal trade with Jawlcheen was rerouted through a checkpoint between the Gold Wind and the Thrader helions. This mandatory stop was taxed to our commerce committee, leaving us with an economic problem in the sale price of exported goods. Liricos and Tambuo looked for help from the U.G. about it, but officials from all planets in question had agreed upon this particular commerce situation. If we wanted to change the route, we needed first to go through these men of power.

The next frightening event put us all on edge. One sixth of Thrader's air force was sent to Gold Wind for outpost training. Everyone talked of Rybalazar's uncanny connection with Fitmalo, and of its growing power. Even though its leaders cited lesser attempts at peace and unity with our helion, we knew cooperative economy with our ancient enemies would bring the downfall of our society. Negotiations rendered little change in the next few months. Lapas formed a coalition to strengthen the solar system as an independent economic unit, finding ways around interhelion trade as a means of income and boycotting certain imports that imposed high taxes on us. The Jain planet had attempted the same type of resistance against the Keres commonwealth and had failed, but we took courage in the fact that our helion was not yet broken up by opposing allegiances. In fact, the planets of Lapas supported each other now more than ever. We prayed that our peaceful strike would allow us to hold out under interstellar political pressure.

At home, Saul grew strong. His extended family nurtured him through learning, misbehavior, achievement, and every aspect of his precious life. My strength, however, began to fluctuate almost as it had when I had penetrated the castle at Hammerstead the first time, only without the surges. I experienced weakness, which snapped back into normality. Then my power slumped again. I knew why. Ocelot knew but was not ready to admit it. Alaban felt remnants of what I suffered, but refused to give up on me.

Both encouraged my visits to the regional hospital, where I underwent modernized gene therapy and was given implants of errant cell growth tracers, counter-encoders and nano-cybernetic polyp eradicators. All of these were uncomfortable procedures, none of which eliminated the symptoms I suffered for very long. Alaban asked permission to heal me. I wouldn't let him. I tried to convince him that I preferred conventional means this time. During a few nighttime massages, Ocelot pulled the illness from me in secret. He denied that this was a true healing, but I knew his intentions. Still, the cancer returned. Like my mother before me, I had inherited the errant gene. This time, the disease was more aggressive, vindictive. I had drained temporary life and power from others. Now the temporary healing had finished its stay in my body. I imagined this weakness was what Wilbaht had experienced in his last few weeks with us.

Wilbaht had once said that I had lowered my life expectancy by at least twenty years when I cured Ocelot. The other artificial healings I'd received contributed to my fate. Wilbaht and his brothers had healed me at the Public Valley. Alaban had healed me at the space station. Ocelot had healed my laser blast wound at the Research Deposit. The timetable for my inevitable plague was stepped up, possibly by more than thirty years.

I treasured everything about my life now. I gathered my courage as I made preparations for Saul's inheritance. I collected information about our families, organized accounts of our training and experiences over the last few years so that Saul and his descendents might use the information one day. I made a list of advice and references for our son, believing I would not be with him much longer.

My pessimism about my health relented, however, when Ocelot arrived one day with encouraging news. He had gone to visit a chemical and genetic research lab in a different quadrant. There he had obtained an experimental serum that was sure to improve my health and would induce remission of the errant cell growth. He explained the whole makeup and active function of the drug to me. I willingly tried it. Apart from a side effect of nausea and headache at first, the medicine worked. Within a week, my power had returned to normal. My strength and stamina flourished.

Chapter 64: Final Decision

"The Daughter is here, campaigning for a new route for smuggling."

"Viga is here on Liricos?" I balked.

Alaban stood akimbo. "Not Liricos. The old plastic bag is on my home planet. She figured Gird only needed her to show up to convince them. Lapas needs a new way out of the exportation problem. She's selling an idea."

The three of us convened in our main living area. Saul had gone to visit his cousins with Grace at Alaban's request. He wanted a serious team for brainstorming without distractions.

"She's offering them a first rate smuggler's deal, I'll bet." Ocelot crossed his arms.

"Only the best for her customers. Bring out your buckets. You'll be sick when you hear what General Darpon assigned me to do with her. He wants me to clear a path for her, stave off the opposition. He wants her to begin a smuggling plan. I'm actually supposed to help put it into operation," Alaban said with aggravation.

"What? Why?" I replied in shock.

"They want to catch the smuggling operation in full swing so they can flaunt the evidence to the world once they expose her." Alaban scowled.

"I've heard that before," Ocelot intoned.

"So have I. Her connections will turn the tables on anyone against her and then we'll end up in the same problem as Jain. That's why I agreed to take on the project, but I'm not willing to see it through. I've got a better idea."

Alaban outlined briefly the mission proposed to him by our superior. Then he informed us of his plan to twist the chain of events to our advantage. He proposed a double-cross. His men would set up the mission as designated. Then at a crucial point of the business agreement, he planned to ambush Viga and her representatives in a mass killing. Not only would this put an end to the smugglers' ambitions. It would also send a message to the Regime that the Lapas helion would not be tricked into an alliance.

"I'll make it look like an outside job, but of course somebody is going to point to me. If I'm found out, I'll take full credit for it. I wanted you to know just in case things go wrong. Saul should know my real intentions just in case I'm made to look like a criminal. I also was hoping you'd help me with some computer records." Alaban tapped his foot lightly as he waited for our response.

"Where's the meeting? How many men are you talking about bringing down at once?" I asked.

` "It's at the Lighthouse Assembly Center. Main targets are Viga, her two clones, five direct bodyguards, personal assistant, and three advisors. One advisor I especially want done is also an overseer hired by Swall Jade to check up on his little girl. He makes sure she doesn't agree to anything daddy wouldn't like." Alaban paused to scoff. "Ha. Little girl—she's probably forty-eight now, but she's had so many surgeries you can't tell how old she is."

"That's a lot of scattered targets to control, not to mention Organization reps and building security, plus any trade officials she'll be dealing with. How do you plan to do it?" Ocelot asked.

"I have four good men. I'll prep them to defend the Fitmalos, but I'll also give them a coup scenario. I'll tell them if one of her bodyguards makes a signal to turn on us at any time during the meeting, they should shoot to kill. When I set them off, they'll take down at least four of the bodyguards. I'm going for Viga right away, then the assistant. The advisors should be easy prey once the mayhem starts, even with extra warriors scrambling to cover them." Alaban narrowed his eyes as he spoke.

Ocelot interjected. "Bad plan. The first explanation your men will give is that you told them to fire. General Darpon will have you expulsed from the Organization for treason. This time your traitor label will stick. Let's think of a different approach."

I bit a thumbnail, but then stepped forward with an idea. "What if your men fire in self defense? Remember when we were at the Research Deposit on Jawlcheen. When we were trapped in the room with Teradom and the task force, Alaban cloaked completely. He made Paleface shoot Ryker. From what we could see, it looked like she did it on her own. All you would need to do is start the pendulum. Make it look like one of Viga's own men means to fire on her, then have another shoot at an Organization warrior. Then your men will kill the bodyguards, and maybe even the advisors, too. Any other loose ends will be easier to finish in the confusion," I spoke.

Alaban smiled mischievously as he had years ago. "I love the way you think, sister."

Ocelot suggested we stay close by for secondary backup outside the building. He offered to help Alaban power up before going in.

Alaban was touched by his offer. "I appreciate it, but I've learned a few tricks about that. I can drain power from anyone who stands still long enough. I only need direct skin contact."

"How much power?" I asked warily.

"Enough to put the host to sleep for a few hours. Enough to cloak and fly twice as long as usual," he explained. "But I wouldn't advise it. It's sort of like a reverse healing."

"You'll have to show us how some time," Ocelot said.

Alaban promised he would.

On the decided date, after leaving Saul in Grace's care for the evening, Ocelot and I flew to Gird. We met on the rooftop across the street from the Lighthouse to oversee Alaban's work. We cloaked to keep from becoming security sniper targets. If at any moment I felt Alaban needed our help, we would enter through one of the top windows and rush to his aid.

Two teams of Organization security deterred traffic around the place. A long, black vehicle escorted by two personal security trucks pulled up to the back entrance of the building. Viga's younger clone stepped out of the first luxury vehicle, escorted by two low-level bodyguards. From another luxury vehicle behind it stepped Viga, the original, and her bodyguards. From a third vehicle stepped her second clone. Each woman dressed alike, in a silver and black tailored suit with a four-pointed hat that looked like an abstract beetle. We knew immediately who the real vixen was from the way she carried herself. Although the other two imitated their sister's air of snobbery, they were unable to capture her subtle intelligence and her utter disdain for the people around her. After these vehicles pulled away, a fourth approached to deliver the rest of her entourage along with additional security.

Alaban's crew waited alongside the entrance and inside. I visualized the scenario. The three Vigas waited in a guarded room for the advisors and her personal assistant. Then the real Daughter was escorted to the meeting room, where several desperate, yet powerful, men and women stood to greet her. As soon as all the desired targets entered the room, Alaban made his move. Shots were fired. Viga and her assistant hit the ground, seeking protection from her closest bodyguards. The guards fell around them, leaving the path open for their assassination. We sensed Alaban and his men played their parts well.

Soon local authorities and security of every kind filled the street around the Lighthouse. Alaban would play innocent along with his own men. He would use his acting skills to feign anger with all those involved. He would regrettably report to his superiors that Viga was ambushed by her own men and that he felt personally responsible for the failure of his team to adequately defend her from them. It would work. He did not need our help after all. I was proud of my twin, although I understood he had broken his pacifistic vow to do it.

Later in the week, Ocelot and I watched the news report about the assassination. Of course the Organization fed the press a lie to cover the real occurrence. According to the news, an unknown sniper had killed Viga as she exited her limousine to the Lighthouse, where she was about to view a private theater production. Her father, being prime minister of a commonwealth planet, offered a reward for any information that might lead to the identification of anyone involved in the assassination. Knowing the Organization would never throw one of its own to the enemy in public, we relaxed.

However, a month later, the worst possible effect occurred. Swall Jade used situational evidence to point to betrayal from the Organization itself. He claimed the Organization in the Lapas helion had become corrupt. He challenged the planetary governments to prove him otherwise. Gird sided immediately with Swall, much to Alaban's dismay. Liricos supported the Organization. Tambuo remained undecided. The planet of Lapa had such a low population that their opinion had little influence, but they, too, remained undecided. As a token of good faith to the Commonwealth of Thrader, the government of the planet Gird made a horrible decision. They allowed Swall Jade and his troops to inspect the Organization on their planet as a show of good will. All Fitmalo ships, military or otherwise, would be welcomed on the planet.

"Damn it. They're going to plant a Fitmalo training facility right there on Gird!" Ocelot roared. He snatched up his sword and made for the practice field to destroy several log targets.

Saul jiggled objects in the room with levitation as he gripped my hand. "Why is Daddy angry?" he asked with fearful eyes.

I sat the tot in my lap and leaned him to me. I explained as best I could that some bad men were going to put soldiers on a planet close to ours. Daddy didn't like them because they were mean and might try to keep us out of our jobs if they ever came to Liricos. They didn't want our Organization warriors spying on them so they could do bad things without anyone knowing about it. We hoped they didn't come here. Saul pried for more information, but much of it he couldn't understand.

Saul's sixth birthday was spent in half-hearted celebration. Alaban was unable to attend due to the scramble to appeal to the Fitmalo and Gird officials. The Fitmalos did as Ocelot predicted. Despite overwhelming protest, Gird allowed a Fitmalo military outpost on its least prosperous quadrant in what was formerly an Organization center. From there, the Fitmalo investigators made even more of a nuisance of themselves.

When Alaban did return, he confided more bad news to us. "I'm doing what I can with this Fitmalo infiltration, but everywhere I turn, there's another Organization general on the take with them. I suggest you start making plans to move out. This is not the safest place to be anymore. The Organization itself is starting to crumble."

"I'm not interested in running," Ocelot answered. "If there's a standoff, I want to be active against the Fitmalos. This is home. They don't have the right to change it. The people here will stand by that."

"What about Saul?" Alaban asked.

"I'm not moving him until I have proof that he'll be in danger." Ocelot stood fast by his decision.

"If it comes to that, let me take him to Sor3 with me," Alaban insisted. "I have a bad feeling about this planet right now."

"Everyone has," Ocelot admitted. "If our lives are in danger, you know we'll work together to move Saul and the others to safety."

Alaban excused himself to go find Saul.

Ocelot and I decided to walk off our frustration and to brainstorm for ideas. We traipsed past the school buildings, trying our best to maintain optimism in the face of our political problems. Saul dashed past us to his classroom. We whirled to follow him. He didn't usually avoid us like this, nor would he normally run into an empty classroom by himself. We followed him in and asked him what was going on.

"I'm playing hide and seek with Aunt Grace and Dad. Quick, hide! Don't let them see us." Saul dragged us in past the support pillar to a row of cubbied toys. "Hurry. Cloak me," he ordered.

He didn't know how to cloak yet. I was sure he'd be a terrible mischief-maker once he learned, but for the time being we decided to go along with him. We held him between us to complete the cloak. Ocelot hid our presence. We stayed very still.

Alaban marched straight to the classroom. He had sensed Saul's path. Grace followed. Alaban strode halfway through the room before announcing, "I know he's in here somewhere. I can smell him. He smells like dirty socks. Phew!" He waited a moment. Saul cringed with excitement, suppressing a giggle.

Alaban turned his back to us. "Well, I guess he doesn't want to come out from hiding. Too bad. Aunt Tamia brought everyone's favorite ice cream. She's just about to serve it. I guess only the girls will eat desert today."

Saul gave up. He burst from our grip and ran up behind him. Grace widened her eyes to see him appear out of thin air. I squeezed Ocelot's hand to let him know we should wait, invisible, for a few minutes. I was curious to see the interaction among the three of them.

Alaban grabbed at Saul, but Saul dove into his class seat. Alaban pretended to be surprised to see him. He asked him what he'd been studying all by himself there. Saul replied he'd been working on math.

"Saul really takes after you in math class," Grace spoke proudly.

676

Alaban regarded Saul with feigned anger. "Saul! What have I told you about biting your toenails in class?"

Saul giggled with glee. Grace smirked.

"Dad! I don't do that," Saul laughed with a dazzling grin.

"I thought you said he takes after me in math class. That's what I used to do in math class," Alaban joked.

"No you didn't," Saul laughed.

"How do you know? You weren't there. My teacher used to send bad reports home for doing that," he said between Saul's chuckles. "Well if you don't take after me about the toenails, then you must be playing castles and dragons."

Saul made a funny, but guilty face.

"What are castles and dragons?" Grace asked.

"You build up a wall of numbers. Each layer of numbers has one more digit than the one before it. Your opponent does the same thing on the other side with different numbers. Then you find a number dragon that can burn down the walls by division. You can only choose two double- or triple-digit dragons. The winner is the person with the best wall at the end," Alaban explained.

"But you can't use prime numbers. That's cheating," Saul intoned.

Grace stared at Saul with wide eyes. "How often do you play this game, Saul?" Grace asked him.

"I only play it when I'm finished with my work. Sometimes I play different games, but I like dragons and castles because I can win most of the time." Saul gazed up at her with pride.

"He even beat me once, three out of five," Alaban bragged, tousling the boy's hair.

Grace tried to keep her composure as much as possible. "Saul, that's great, but promise you will only play after finishing your regular assignments."

"Yes, ma'am. I promise." Saul swung his legs under his chair happily.

"Saul, why don't you go out to the playground with your Aunt Tamia for a while? Go get your ice cream, okay?" Alaban suggested.

"Yes, sir. Hey, Dad?" Saul called.

"What, son?" Alaban bent close to him.

Saul hugged him around the neck. "I'm glad you're my dad."

"Me, too, son." Alaban smiled as he patted the boy on the back.

As Saul ran out the door, Grace stared at Alaban in amazement.

Alaban approached her slowly. "Maybe you should give him some higher-level problems to challenge him."

"I guess I'll have to," she said, still unable to believe it.

Alaban stepped closer. "How is he doing?"

"He's doing well with every subject. He's brilliant. I love him." She smiled complacently. She leaned on the support beam by the door.

Alaban stood less than a meter from her. "How are you?"

Grace was flustered, not prepared to talk about herself. "I'm fine. I'm worried about the future like everyone else, but I'll manage."

"You have a right to worry. We'll face a difficult time soon." He searched her face.

"I know." Grace looked up at him bravely. They stared at each other for a long moment. "I'm not like Sil. She feels she can make a difference with these political changes. I don't. I'm just a girl who left her university career to teach preschool. I'm not a tough warrior. I'm not like her. We may look a lot alike and we both dance Tambuo, but that's where the similarities end."

"You think I'm interested in you because Sil is taken and you're the next best thing," he challenged her.

She fixed her eyes on his bravely. "Yes."

Alaban stood fast. "I used to be in love with Sil, but not anymore. I've known better for years now. I thought we were supposed to be mates at one time. There were so many indicators that led me to believe we were meant to be. Even her name: Sil. It's so common here on Liricos now that people have forgotten its meaning. It's an acronym, you know? S.I.L. She Is Light. Of course, I'm the exact opposite. I thought we were divinely matched as mates, but there was so much I didn't understand at the time. All I knew was that our elements had to come together to create a child. At the time, I only knew of one way to do that. But my ideas were naïve compared to the real plan. Sil's elements and mine together were not enough. We only formed one spirit. Offspring are brought about by the union of two complete beings. Sil and I together were incomplete. Sil and Ocelot together were nearly complete. They were only missing my half of Sil's spirit. Saul needed us all. And that's all I needed: to help my twin bring her offspring into existence. It was a special plan of steps we were meant to take so that Saul could live. As obsessed as I was with Sil all those years, I think I was more driven to see Saul alive. I'm glad he's here. I love him like a son."

Grace tilted her head and gazed up at him, intrigued.

Alaban continued explaining. "I love Sil in a unique way. We're linked by a spiritual aberration. She's not my mate and shouldn't be. I'm glad she never accepted me. Any children of ours would have turned out…wrong, spiritually inbred. She knew that before I did. She knew from the start that there was something missing between the two of us. Then she found her missing piece."

He reached out to slide his hand around her waist. "And now I believe I've found mine."

Grace gazed at him with true admiration, but did not lose her nerve. She nearly spoke to him, but he interrupted.

"I don't want you to be like Sil. I'm glad you're not." He smiled slightly. "You're the only woman I've ever met who understood my jokes about integral astrophysics."

She returned the smile.

"You're a brilliant. You're beautiful. You love Saul. And you're the first woman I've been close to who hasn't tried to hit me."

They both smiled fully, but then he became serious. "You have not dated anyone since we met here." He touched the tip of his nose to hers. "Neither have I."

She held an enamored trance before him. Then he whispered to her some things I could not hear. She caught him by the sides of his face.

"I would love to be your mate. When can we start?" she asked him softly.

They kissed passionately right there in the empty classroom. I fought the urge to applaud. Grace invited Alaban to her apartment. They rushed out the door and up the stairs.

Ocelot and I released our cloak, but still held hands tightly. I kissed his knuckles excitedly. All remnants of old jealousy towards Alaban escaped Ocelot's eyes. We chuckled to each other before hurrying out onto the playground with Saul. We entertained him at our house for the rest of the evening. Before his bedtime, he asked why his dad was sleeping with Aunt Grace instead of in his room downstairs. I told him he should ask his dad about that tomorrow, probably after lunch.

The next evening at dinner, after speaking with Saul and Father separately, Alaban and Grace announced their marriage. The family received them with shouts and applause. A party was arranged for them for the following evening. At the summer dance, we wrapped the hugging couple in the long gauze and paraded around them as they kissed. Even Saul laughed and enjoyed the festivities. He was not jealous of his father's attention. He had more family attention than most people ever wanted. He even understood when the pair went on vacation for a few days.

However, Grace returned to us three days later alone.

She hurried to me. "Sil, something's wrong. The General called him early this morning. He had to go right away. He couldn't tell me what was going on. He just sent me home and told me to be ready to pack to go to Sor3. He said he'd either call or come home in two days. I can't contact him."

I held her hands in mine. "Don't worry." I closed my eyes a moment to far see. "He's fine. He'll be fine. He's in no danger, but he's working with dangerous people. He'll come home to you in a couple of days. I wonder what's going on."

Grace rebuilt her fortitude. She went to her apartment to organize her things. I communicated with Ocelot about it. We both tried to research recent happenings in at the Center, but met only dead ends.

Two days later, Alaban appeared, not at his bride's doorstep, but at ours. His terrible seriousness unnerved us.

He spoke in a deathly tone. "At 0600 hours tomorrow our time, every Organization Center on Gird will shut down by demand of the Regime, and by recommendation from the U.G. board itself. In three days, Liricos Organization Centers will give over control to investigators from Fitmalo. In seven days, Tambuo will do the same. The U.G. claims this is a deterrent to war. They say it's a temporary shut down as a sign of good faith to the collective commonwealth. They claim no takeover. They only want proof that no one will try to organize an assassination attempt on Swall Jade while he's here. It's all an inside job. We're done for in this solar system. In less than a month, we'll have an aerial parade of power from the Regime with Swall Jade himself at the helm. He'll be overseeing his new territory."

"The warriors will never stand for that. There has to be at least some secret Organization plan to prevent this." Ocelot contained his anger to plot tensely.

"There is. The only problem is we can't all trust each other. There are about eighty warriors of your rank or higher who met here on Liricos yesterday. They couldn't agree on any plan of attack. They're disorganized. They can't meet in safety again. The best idea they had was to send out a campaign of anti-Regime propaganda based on information we've collected on the Regime and the smugglers—Teradom, Hume, Viga, and especially Swall Jade himself—for the last twenty years. We'll organize the broadcasting of the information in pieces to every planet and every mainframe computer in the U.G. as simultaneously as we can manage. We're taking all top-secret files related to the Regime off the shelf and showing them to the world. No more of this divided Organization with generals taking bribes from the smuggling rings. If we're to stay alive, we have to stay together. I refuse to give my loyalty to a general who's willing to sell us out or to a sub general that goes along with the others because he's afraid to oppose his superiors and stand up for what's right." Alaban's speech became animated.

"I've collected plenty of information to bring the whole pyramid down. When's the broadcast date?" Ocelot agreed.

"Fifteen days from today," Alaban said. "But there's more. Swall Jade and his military leaders are not willing to go down without a fight. They'll be here on Liricos when it happens. They'll make an excuse and attack this planet just for spite. They'll probably parade over a major city and start dropping bombs. The Organization is at a freeze. They won't retaliate until it's too late. I won't let that happen. I'm planning on boarding one of their ships and taking out the whole parade."

"That's a suicide mission," I said.

"It could be," Alaban responded. He stared at me with definite purpose.

I shook my head at him. "Let us see the details. Maybe we can find another way."

Alaban showed us a sketch of the triangular pattern that the Fitmalo military normally used. He expected they would begin formation as they pretended to leave peaceably. He pointed to the two small escort fighter ships at either end of the triangle as possible targets for takeover. These two- and four- passenger ships would be easy to take. The center ship was the command center. The ship directly below it was the bomber. He planned to fly along with the fleet until they passed over a desert area with low population. Then he'd break formation, fly directly between the bomber and the command ship, and fire all weapons to the hover pad of the ship above him, causing it to collapse onto the bomber. Both ships would explode. Depending on the level of weapons contained in the bomber, all ships in the formation could be destroyed in the explosion.

"How are you going to fly and fire all weapons at the same time in a ship you're not even familiar with?" I chastised. "This is a two-person job at least. Who's going with you? Who's running interference for you on the ground?"

"I'll get a couple of my regular men to stand with me," he explained.

"What, the ones you set up at the Lighthouse? Why would they be willing to stand with you this time?" I complained.

Ocelot intervened. "Never mind that. This attack plan only has a fifty percent chance of working. Look. You're taking a ship at the end of the formation. It's about half a kilometer between your flight pattern and the central command ship. If you don't know how to fire something or set boosters properly on your run, the side ships will shoot you down before you even get close to the leader. You'll lose your life for nothing," Ocelot added. "There's got to be a better way."

"How many people are on the leader's flank ships?" I asked.

"Ten to twelve. There's no way I could overpower that many before someone alerts the boss," Alaban answered.

681

"A team of three could," I told him. They tried to interrupt me with protests, but I explained anyway. "We could infiltrate the ship just before they take off. We take out the troops and leave two men to fly and carry out the operation. There has to be someone else willing to take this on. Who can we trust to do it? We need men on the ground as well as in the air. What if we get enough people with us to fly both the flanking ships? Then our plan would work with less probability of casualties. You don't have to go, Alaban."

"The problem is: first, getting someone to believe this, and second, to depend on him to go through with it. This is not an authorized Organization directive. I can't ask someone to do this unless I know he's dedicated enough to risk it." Alaban drummed his fingers on the table. "I'm not asking you to help except with the information broadcast. If all of us go to this mission, it's likely we won't come back. Saul would go from having three parents to having none. I can't allow that. I'll see what I can do about getting warrior support. In the mean time, get ready to send your data."

Ocelot nodded. "I'll contact Jiao on Sor3. He'll be ready with his side of the story as well. Channol and Croso probably won't go along with it. They're in a bad position on Jawlcheen."

"Don't make any definite plans until the broadcast, Alaban. Let us know what you decide to do," I warned him.

He agreed.

As he left our house, I grasped Ocelot's hand. I kissed him goodbye before he left for his class. I walked out onto our balcony and watched him descend to the practice field where his students already lined up to greet him. I surveyed the valley surrounded by rolling hills. Our peaceful land had to remain free. I couldn't bear to allow the Regime to taint our lives anymore. I pressed a hand to my right side, suppressing pain and nausea. I made my final decision.

Chapter 65: Post Mortem

The entire U.G. was in an uproar about the underhanded deeds of the Regime members and their associates. Swall Jade's military force he'd brought with him stayed on constant alert. The majority of local protesters demanded his head. The diplomats asked simply that he leave the helion to return to Thrader for trials there. The Organization was not allowed to reopen its centers in the Lapas helion until after the man left, for fear of retaliation. He did not contest the accusations or the evidence against him. He stayed away from all press and even turned away government officials. Alaban reported to us as planned.

"The plan is on. I have a few men who are willing to do ground work, but I don't have anyone on board with me after takeoff. We have two days to set up. I know the risk. I probably won't come back. But I have to do this."

"No, you don't," I told him firmly. "You're staying here. I'm taking your place."

The men regarded me with alarm.

"I'm dying anyway. My errant cell count is up again. The serum's not working anymore. I'd rather go out like this than have my family watch me suffer for months," I told him.

They stared at me incredulously.

"Check the cell count yourself. I just took it this morning." I held up the med reader so Ocelot could see it. He grabbed it from me. As he read through the numbers, I described the preparations I'd made for Saul and for the school.

"You're not dying, Sil. We'll get the best Torreon team in to heal you. You're not going anywhere." Alaban held my arms adamantly.

Ocelot sat awkwardly into the chair behind him and wove his fingers into his hair. He flung the med reader onto the table, its numbers indicating forty percent increase since last reading.

"This body has begged for healing energy too many times. It's my time to go. This mission was meant for me. Let me do it. I know ship's weapons. I can do this," I explained.

"You're not a pilot, Sil. You'll be found out the minute you try to get into formation," Ocelot argued.

"He's right," Alaban added.

Ocelot stood brusquely. "I'm going with you. I can pilot the ship." I began to disagree with him, but he stopped me. "You've made me suffer enough in this life. Don't make me suffer the years without you. I swore I'd never leave you. I didn't mean that figuratively." He intermeshed his fingers with mine as we sometimes did to remind each other of our bond. Silently, I conceded.

"Forget it. This is my plan. You're supposed to stay here with Saul. That's why I brought him to you in the first place," Alaban protested. "Ocelot, you stay here." He regarded me bravely. "I'll go with Sil."

I answered. "No, Alaban. The choice is clear. If you and I go together, Saul will be left with a broken home. He'll have one father in mourning and no mother to care for him. You're his father, too. Grace is good with him. She'll be an excellent stepmother. You have a future together. You'll both live to see Saul grow up. He needs you. He lived without us the first four years of his life. He can live without us again. You brought him back to this world. Stay here to guide him through it."

Alaban's face showed his indecision. Then he turned to pace the floor, grumbling derisively.

Ocelot drew me close to him. "You saw this coming since we met," he realized.

I nodded, and then presented a tough front. "Wilbaht told us to go save the world. Let's not disappoint him. Let's get this plan right so Liricos won't suffer for one man's madness."

"I'll take care of the ground work," Alaban professed fiercely. "You take the air. Damn it. This had better work."

"It'll work. I'm sure of it," I said.

"I'm healing you tonight. I won't need any extra life energy if this is the end. You'll need top strength to do this assignment," Ocelot told me.

I did not answer, but simply caressed my husband's hand with loving fingertips and observed him with sad appreciation.

Alaban separated us with a stern visage. His frown deepened. He stared at me a few moments, shaking his chin. I returned the stare unwaveringly. He gently enclosed me in his arms.

"If our spirits are linked, what will happen to us once your body is destroyed?" he asked sincerely.

I understood his fear. I worried for him. "I don't know. All we can do is have faith," I told him.

"Will your spirit stay in limbo until I die? Will you be absorbed into me? Will God take you away completely? Will I be an incomplete being until I die?" he asked psychically.

I could only reply that I didn't know. He squeezed me to him until we both jerked away from each other, affected by a sharp twist of pain. Ocelot intervened. He held onto my elbow with one hand and placed a palm to my right side. He extracted the pain quickly, trading it for his own strength. Alaban held his side momentarily, comprehending the finality of this decision. We hung back from one another, realizing that death would soon exercise its right over me, and that its power was infinitely greater than our own. Our desires for life were of no importance to the cycle of life and death. We accepted the hard truth of mortality, no longer asking why.

The next day, we moved Saul into Grace's spare room at her apartment so our death would not cause him to be displaced and confused. We explained to him that we were trading him to live with Alaban and Grace for a while. We'd had our turn with him. Now it was their turn. We explained that we were not moving him out because we didn't want him anymore, but because Alaban and Grace wanted a chance to be with him, too, and that we trusted them enough to share our favorite boy with them. He thought the idea was strange, but went along with it.

Saul helped me polish the handle of the sword that Ocelot had made so long ago. We set it in a treasure box. Ocelot told him it would be his sword some day, but it was only to be used on very special occasions, like whenever he presented his final examination at the end of his training. I took off the anemone bracelet, cleaned it, and set it in a metal box along with a brief story about it. I gave the box to Grace. I told her if Saul ever had a daughter that it would be for her.

Grace responded tearfully. We explained to her all we could. Later in the evening, she reluctantly produced a sketch of our mission flight, showing which would be the best path to take around the other ships in the formation for gravitational and air-stream reasons and to keep us alive as long as possible. Through solemn tears, she promised to be a good stepmother to Saul. I thanked her with a warm embrace.

During the week, Ocelot and I went through all our belongings, discarding some and marking others for different people in our families. We set all our financial and legal affairs in order. We sent a copy of Wilbaht's unofficial ship's log to Jiao with a note asking him to please share it with his sister, Viel. We left the second copy with Alaban, asking him to pass it along to Saul when he was old enough.

The night before the mission, I observed my husband more gratefully than ever. I told him how much I appreciated everything about him. He returned my compliments, detailing physical features, kindnesses, and our best memories. Nostalgia and fear shuddered within me as tears streamed down. Self-doubt brought me to the basin of humility. We prayed and supported each other through weakness before finding our balance once more. We caressed and kissed each other for hours as we made love for the last time.

Before we slept, Ocelot sang the old lullaby to me in a sleepy, peaceful voice. *"How long will I stay by your side?"*

"*Forever and ever, my love,*" I answered him.

We clung together all night and into the early morning, not willing to let go. We hardly slept under the weight of the impending mission.

At the determined hour, Alaban met us in full armor at the gateway to our school. Saul and Grace stood by. Grace held back tears as best she could. We each said goodbye to them bravely. I knelt to speak with our son.

"We won't be home tonight, Saul, but I promise you we'll see you in your dreams as often as you like," I whispered to him. "Your dad will be home with you soon, though."

"Are you going on a dangerous mission?" Saul asked us.

"Yes, son, we are. You'll say a prayer for us?" Ocelot asked him.

"Yes, sir. Be careful," Saul said to us.

We stroked his shiny brown hair, told him we loved him, and then kissed his forehead with a blessing one last time before heading out. Ocelot and I held hands tightly on the way to the vehicle, but once inside we steeled ourselves against our emotions to concentrate on the mission.

We abandoned the vehicle in a public area, walked to the edge of the building's roof, and flew under full cloak several meters over trees and optical security fences to arrive at the Center. We entered the airfield cautiously. Alaban directed his men, who posed as airfield maintenance workers. Ocelot had retro-altered their ID's so they would not be stopped or questioned. Still cloaking, Ocelot and I advanced to our target ship.

Swall Jade and his men boarded the ships. Alaban's men took care of last-minute external ship checks. One made sure the main door on our target ship did not seal completely so that they could help fix the seal while allowing us inside. Once the seal cleared, the crew of ten Fitmalo men went about standard takeoff procedure.

As the ship lifted into the air, we drained the Fitmalos' power one by one, just as Alaban had taught us. To their crewmates, it looked as though they relaxed onto the backs of their chairs. To us, it felt like a delicious rush of energy. I felt like a vampire extracting the life from these fiendish victims. When we had finished with eight of the ten, the first two at the helm became concerned about them, since they asked twice to confirm readouts without response. These last two men we killed quickly, breaking their necks as we whipped them out of their harnesses. We took over their controls.

Ocelot analyzed the ship's flight panel, and then gripped the steering mechanism. I perused the weapons panel, finding multiple nuclear and plasma defense devices. I unlocked all of them. When the lead commander from the top ship ordered all ships on formation, Ocelot waited to hear the confirmation from the other ships in the fleet before replying, disguising his voice as best he could to imitate the previous pilot.

We moved into position with the other Fitmalo ships. Our pyramid showed on one screen on the side panel. We were perfectly hidden among the enemy. We passed over several mid-population cities. These were of no interest to Swall. He set course for Lira, the highest populated city on the planet. After clearing a desert tundra and an icy fjord, Swall planned to fire on the wintering city just as the sun climbed to its highest peak. But we would not allow him to leave the fjord.

Swall Jade himself broadcast a message to his soldiers, confirming his intentions. "All Fitmalo forces to full alert. Five minutes to drop explosive. Fitmalo fleet prepare to pull up."

As the tundra fell away below us into the sharp, glistening crags of the fjord, Ocelot yanked the controls to turn us. I fired two nuclear micro warheads at the hover pad of the command ship above us. Panic echoed on the communicator. The lead ship's hover pad blinked out with the nuclear impact. The ship below it popped loudly. I felt relief, knowing we had completed our mission. Then our ship was tossed violently to the west from the repercussion of the blast. Unable to steer us away, Ocelot sideswiped another ship at the side of the pyramid, sending alert signals flaring everywhere. Ocelot attempted to pull us up, but our sister ship fired on us just as it, too became engulfed by the speeding mass of fire. Our ship burned at the tail as we sailed towards an outcropping of rock.

Ocelot let go of the controls and gripped my hand. "I love you, Sil!" he shouted, although I could not hear him from the bang of our exploding fuel drum.

"I l…" is all I managed to say to him. These were the last physical words I pronounced, ground apart by the crags of rock that invaded the helm of the ship.

The ship disintegrated into shards of metal and flaming gas. They blasted around us, through us. The hulking explosion from all five ships crumbled the glacial ice and metamorphic rock around us. Its reverberating shock was so great that the land, ice, and debris of the vessels leapt skyward. The whole ballistic mass roared upon us as a wave—a tidal wave upon the snow. Its orange and black volume charged forward, falling harshly on a land unaware of its meaning. Shards of metal zipped through the air. As the searing pieces of debris mixed with billows of smoke that curled above the fjord, I realized our destiny.

The shards of glass and metal, the chunks of rock and ice from the fjord, were the same shards I'd seen years ago in my dreams and visions. The shards withered away to the melting snow, shimmering with images of our lives. They glittered and whirled, bearing down on us like a mouth filled with vapor and fangs, swallowing us into its fiery wake.

We felt no pain. The momentum of the explosion did not move us forward. We hung suspended, apart from physical laws. We no longer needed to obey them. We searched for and found each other. We saw each other by will.

"I love you," I finished.

We embraced among the whirling atoms. We understood the heat from the obliterated ships, but we remained unaffected. We were past physical life. We were living spirits. We kissed each other.

"We can kiss?" Ocelot spoke to my soul.

"What else can we do?" I smiled to him.

"Anything we want," he realized. "Look at this." He moved across the vast tundra in one motion. I stayed where I was, and yet we were still together. Space was a negligible commodity.

"Let's go visit Saul," I suggested.

Before he even agreed with me verbally, we appeared at the boy's side. He looked up at us, only mildly surprised.

"Hi. I thought you said you wouldn't be back tonight," he spoke. He saw us. We were overjoyed.

Grace sat straight, watching and listening to Saul's side of the conversation. She scanned the empty air with a chill.

"We're here, Saul, but I don't think your Aunt Grace can see us, only you," I told him.

"Are you cloaking?" he asked.

"Sort of," Ocelot told him.

Grace sat straight, watching and listening to Saul's side of the conversation. She scanned the empty air with a chill.

"Tell Grace we'll be here to visit you every now and then and it's nothing to be afraid of," I said to him.

"Okay, Mommy. Will you still visit me tonight?" he asked.

"Yes, son. Anytime you want. You just call us, okay? We have to go see your dad now. We'll be back later." I blew him a kiss.

We rolled through time and space back to the instant when our bodies had been destroyed. We found Alaban in a short-range ship on his way home. One of his men drove. Alaban gripped the arms of his seat. His face filled with sorrow. He closed his eyes and whispered my name.

"I'm here, twin heart. How do you feel?" I asked him, even though I already knew.

He opened his eyes for a moment, but seeing nothing apart from the interior of the ship, he closed them again. He thought clearly to me.

688

"I'm whole. The part of my life that was yours is with me now. I can never thank you both enough for everything. I'll never let Saul forget you."

"You have our blessing," Ocelot generously told him.

"Thank you, sir," Alaban said quietly. He squared his jaw as he sat straight, his heart full.

We said our goodbyes and then flipped through the leaves of time as if they were scattered pieces on a forest floor. We returned to the hills to witness our memorial service. The family had bought a statue in our honor: a life-size image of each of us facing one another, one hand clasped between our hearts, one hand reaching up to touch the other's face. The statue's base bore the same message as the statue of Ocelot's parents: "Love transcends life". We understood now how true this message was.

We listened gladly to the kind words our loved ones mentioned about us. I understood my family's need to grieve, but I tried to bring them hope. We gathered a flock of small parrots from the forest, compelling them to fly together to the memorial site. The crowd buzzed with amazement as the whole flock perched around the statue. The children of the family were amused. Alaban grinned and held out an arm to them. Several birds flew to him and sat on the extended arm, which he lowered for Saul to see. Saul beamed with wonder. He lifted a hand to one bird. It hopped onto his finger. Saul held the parrot close to his face and petted him. The parrot followed my orders to give Saul a kiss on the nose. Saul giggled with glee. The other people cautiously approached the birds as well. The family's tears mixed with joyous laughter. Then I released the birds, which squawked loudly with confusion, retreating all at once. Saul immediately turned to Alaban and asked for a pet parrot. Alaban lifted the boy into his arms and promised to buy not one, but two for him that same day. Grace agreed.

We peeked in on them at a different time of their life. Alaban and Grace had taken our apartment for its space, as we had asked. A much bigger, twelve-year-old Saul raced from his room with a tent pack over his shoulders. He said goodbye to Alaban and then Grace as fast as he could before sailing out the door. They called goodbye after him.

Alaban sat at the table finishing a plate of food. "Be sure to bring home plenty of frogs to scare your cousins with!" he shouted after him. Then he eyed his wife. "Are you sure he isn't coming back for anything?"

Grace moved to stand behind him. She caressed his shoulders. "I double-checked his list. He packed everything. Tamia promised to have them all back by sundown tomorrow."

She leaned next to him. "Did you like it?" She kissed the side of his face gently. She stood next to his chair.

Alaban wiped his mouth on a napkin before answering. "Delicious."

He looked at her slyly and swiveled to face her. "Almost as good as..." He whispered something into her ear.

She smiled and returned the sly glance. "Would you like a taste of it right now?"

Alaban ran his hands along her hips. "Mmm. I would love to. Is it ready?"

Grace gave him a sultry look. Alaban wet his lips with his tongue and wiggled his eyebrows. Grace held his chin in her fingers and spoke to him in a soft, yet commanding voice.

"Yes. It's moist and warm and ready for you." She winked at him and then strutted to the kitchen.

He watched her go with a smile. A few moments later she returned with a plate of her best tangerine cake. She set the plate before him. He smelled its warm aroma before tasting it.

"Oh, this is good. Mmm!" he managed through chewing jaws.

His mouth full of cake, he leaned back in the seat and gazed up at her. She kissed him quickly on the mouth. She smiled as he ate. He put an arm around her and rubbed her backside.

"I have something else ready for you, too," she said in her sexiest voice. She clutched his hand as it glided along her curved body. Then she moved away from him. She stepped behind him and then made for the bedroom. "But you'd better come and get it while it's hot."

He looked back and forth between his plate and his wife. Grace disappeared through the doorway.

"Can I bring my cake?" he called to her.

"Yes!" she called back.

"Oh, baby! Grace, you are my kind of woman!" he shouted with enthusiasm. He scooped up his plate and fork as he hurried to meet her.

We smiled at the scene and moved ahead a few months more. Grace was happily pregnant. Saul grew tall and lanky. They watched the news with the family on a new holographic viewer at Father's house. Alaban and Father led a round of applause as they viewed the appointment ceremony for the new prime minister of Fitmalo. We were glad to hear his name: Hallon. This was the Fitmalo I had spared on Santer so many years before. I knew he would lead his people to regain their honor in the U.G.

We sifted again through the leaves of time to Sor3 at Saul's testing time. He was given the same room I had used when I tested there. Saul observed the place, impressed by its size. His stature was near that of his dark father's, but his face and build were almost identical to Ocelot's. We felt parental pride from his success. Alaban, Grace, and Saul's little sister,

690

Lirica, descended the steps to the main gallery with him. Saul and Alaban played a while with the levitation stones, passing them back and forth like juggling tools. Alaban proudly wore the title of sub general. Grace carried a palm computer, whose cover brandished her name and title. She was now head aerospace engineer for the Lapas Helion Transit Committee. Lirica, now seven years old, skipped across the floor to see the mural of history.

"Hey, everybody, come look! It's important!" she called to them.

They put away the stones and sauntered towards her. She drew their attention to the last square of the mural.

"Look. There's the Fitmalo fleet on Liricos and a picture of two warriors. It says, 'Sil Rayfenix and Jainocelot Quoren, the warrior heroes of Liricos." Lirica beamed at her family.

Saul blinked at it anxiously. "That's my mom and dad."

Alaban clapped him on the shoulder. He and the others observed the mural square. My spirit heart sang with joy. Ocelot held my hand within his spirit chest to let me know he felt the same.

Soon we heard voices calling us. We reunited with my mother, with Ocelot's parents, with Wilbaht and his wife. We celebrated in our celestial home. In time, we welcomed our extended family to us as well.

We understood so much now, and yet we still had much to learn. Throughout our eternity, many words of wisdom passed among us. One phrase of truth I always admired came from Alaban.

He gave a talk to our son after he received his title. He told him, "Every choice we make affects us and those around us in ways we cannot foresee. Benevolence, cruelty, reproduction, science, industry, attempts, successes, failures, everything we decide and put into motion creates this teeming ocean of life, both seen and unseen. Do the best you can with the life you have in this world. You are an incredible, exceptional human being. But no matter how intelligent or talented a person may be, he is still just a person. He still makes mistakes. Even a man with superhuman power falls short of perfection. Even a person who sees the future cannot fathom the repercussions of every action or nonaction in this universe. So when you make a decision in your life, make sure you can stand by it in every way. Taking that stand requires steadfast strength of willpower, and it's rarely painless, but the reward is a victorious life. I challenge you to live that life."

Saul took the words to heart. His life was filled with trials and adventures that rivaled our own. Our son did make foolish mistakes, just as we had, but in the end, we welcomed him to us with pride. May he do the same for his children. May you do the same for yours.

About the Author

This multitalented author is an avid student of Tae Kwon Do and a teacher of Spanish. After earning a double Bachelor's degree in foreign language and fine art, she spent six years in Mexico where she became a wife, mother, and English teacher. She returned to the U.S. at the turn of the millennium, thanks to support from friends and family in both countries, and unyielding perseverance and hard work. She and her husband have recently achieved their goals of suburban success in Central Florida, where she now teaches high school Spanish and continues her life-long hobby of creative expression.

Printed in the United States
17566LVS00002B/22-147